MW00905058

Too Many Promises

pondbank

published by c.c.pondbank publishing
a division of C.C.Companies, Inc.
2104 Roosevelt, Suite E., Dalworthington Gardens
Arlington, Texas 76013

ISBN: 0-9652168-0-2

Printed in the United States of America
by Royal Book Manufacturing, Inc.
24 Stott Avenue, Norwich, Connecticut 06360

First Edition

First printing: June 1996

10 9 8 7 6 5 4 3 2 1

Too Many Promises

A NOVEL

by

ccpost

To Susan + Dennis,
With love and best
wishes always,
ccpost

𝒳
pondbank

This book is dedicated with all my love
to my husband and my best friend,
BUZ POST,
who has made all my dreams come true
and
who has loved me unconditionally
since nineteen-seventy-four.

AUTHOR'S NOTE

In 1988, I began writing this novel in longhand on the bow of the magnificent sailing vessel, *Wind Spirit*, while cruising the French Riviera. If I had known then what I know now, it's possible that I would have spent a lot more time sunbathing and sightseeing instead of writing. When I was young, my mother used to tell me how she picked cotton in scorching fields by summer and walked five miles to school through snow in winter—Oh, and just to set the record straight for mothers everywhere: not one kid has ever bought that guilt-trip as a means of getting cooperation—well, anyway, after what I have been through in writing this book, she no longer gets any sympathy from me, not that she ever really did. (Sorry, Mother, but be proud, at least I bought the honesty thing.)

Writing a book takes discipline and dedication and a passion for people, words and places. And even though I possessed all of those qualities, plus a strong desire to entertain others with my unique vision, creativity and talent for story telling, I wasn't sure if I had what it takes to see a project of this magnitude through to the last page. And now I know I do because it has been eight long years since I last saw Princess Grace's "Pink Palace" high up in the hills over-looking Monaco and the deep blue-green waters of the Mediterranean. I must admit that, even though I didn't think so at times, all the sleepless nights, the sunny days spent indoors, and the endless drafts, rewrites and more drafts were worth the end results.

My eclectic cast of characters, although they are strictly a total figment of my somewhat warped, colorful and extremely vivid imagination, came to life; they became real people that visit real and exciting places. In all parts of the world, they love, they lust, they laugh, they hurt, they cry, they fight and fight back, they play, and they even pray, and, in turn, the reader loves and hates and laughs and cries in all the right places. This story has a shock-value that centers on the soul as a means of holding the readers' attention, both physically and emotionally, stirring every emotion known to mankind until the end. This is a truly romantic adventure that I am proud to share with you. I invite you now to join Nealy James on her trip of a lifetime where she learns that, in life, promises mean very little and timing is everything...

My sincerest best wishes for
your reading pleasure,

ACKNOWLEDGMENTS

First, I must thank Buz Post of Buz Post Pontiac, Isuzu, GMC, and David Moritz of Moritz Cadillac for giving my construction and interior design company enough projects to financially support this expensive endeavor. Thank you both for believing in me as a writer.

Thanks to my mother, Mildred Burns Camfield, for giving me life and for marrying my daddy, the late Billie Camfield, who provided us with a sense of stability and all the worldly goods that children think they need and come to expect.

Thanks to my brother, James Kerry Camfield, and my sister, Sherry Camfield Ross, who shared my childhood and refreshed my memory about places, people and events. Our love goes deep, possibly because we shared so much, but perhaps it's because we shared some common enemies.

A special thanks to the many people out there—too many to name names, but you know who you are—who have touched my life in one way or another and inspired me to create characters and events that grew into stories worth repeating. It's ironic that as a child, people paid me to shut-up, and as an adult, people pay to talk and weave tales. Of course, I didn't have to go to Ireland and kiss the Blarney Stone to receive "the gift of gab," I inherited it from my mother and my grandmother. But I must say that my ability to meet and get to know people has brought me together with people all over the world, which I found fascinating enough to listen to and turn and twist and embellish the stories of their lives into fabulous tales of make believe.

Not having children of my own, I want to thank my nieces and nephews for making me feel as important as a parent. A part of this book is dedicated to the memory of Jeremy Post, my fourteen-year-old nephew who died in a freak accident a year ago. His love made me feel special and he will live on in my writing forever.

Thanks to all my family and Buz's family who have supported me and who are eagerly awaiting to see this book in print. Thanks for being patient and allowing me to share my overwhelming enthusiasm for my characters and the stories that they have to tell.

Thanks to my lifelong friends, the Tinker Twins—Sheila and Susan—who have been there for me since the third grade. We are more than friends, we are family. We have been through so much together, and since this book epitomizes special friendships, I dedicate that portion of my book to them. I also want to thank my longtime friend, Fran Carson Thompson, for the friendship and the laughter.

Thanks to my friends of many years who have assisted in making my life easier or with my research: the Laulands, the Hiltons, Pam and Anthony Amato, the Potters, the Stones, and Randy Helgason who has been there for me during my many computer crises.

Thanks to my readers from the bottom of my heart. Without your love for the characters and this story and your excitement to read more and all of your encouragement, I could not have continued. I want to say thanks to Penny Cloud and Evelyn Kuhns, my first readers, who gave me all the inspiration that I needed to persevere. To Dr. John Pickel, my physician and my friend, who edited the medical situations that occurred and advised me so that I could accurately portray the diagnoses and procedures, as well as inform and educate women in similar circumstances. John, thanks for being a good sport about editing a work of fiction that was written primarily for women about a villainess doctor whose shocking behavior will surprise people all across America.

Thanks to the remaining members of my reading committee:
Sharon Yeary and Susan Elenbaaf, my travel consultants with Carlson Travel Network. Kristi Underwood, my assistant at Buz Post Pontiac, whose body language expressed the degree in which my book touched her life. Also, I need to thank Kristi for assuming my personal and financial responsibilities which allowed me more time to write. The one and only, Dr. Fran Johnson, who researched Paris with me by day and edited my manuscript by night. Jennifer Dodson, my niece, who edited Too Many Promises and helped me do research in Ireland for Sweet Hearts of Steel and who navigated us through the subways in Paris and London so that I could pay attention to the crowds in order to show my readers how the "real people" live in those places. My mother-in-law, June Post, and my adorable and enthusiastic friend, Stacy Daniell, who took on the task of reading the final draft in search of inaccuracies or flaws.

Thanks to all of those who have helped me learn the publishing business and held my hand in times of need:
Reba Blevens, Rob Hendrickson, and the staff at Access Creative, Tom Moore and the staff at Southern Publishers Group, and Patti Thunberg of Royal Book Manufacturing, Inc.

A heartfelt thanks to my artist, Dennis Farris, who tolerated my perfectionist personality while trying to paint my visions for the covers of my books. His talent, in my books, cannot be matched.

A simple "thank you" cannot express my debt of gratitude to Cindy Peabody who, even in her time of grief, kept a smile on her face while she slaved over the layout of my book. With a first novel, that is always a grueling task, therefore, I will always be grateful. Also, I want to thank the South Arlington Kinko's Computer Services for affording her the time to meet my deadline, and her co-workers, Todd Ramsey and Mark Osborne, who came to our rescue in our hour of need.

A special thanks to the owners and staff at the Homestead Inn in Greenwich, CT, who allowed me to visit the inn and portray the romantic ambiance which was essential to my story. In my mind, I had visualized the cover for years and it turned out to be the Homestead Inn.

An enormous thanks to Tom Iwanski, all of our managers and their families, and the entire staff at Buz Post Pontiac, Isuzu, GMC. Your hard work and dedication keep us going. We love you all.

And last, but certainly not least, my editorial assistant, Lisa Reedy, without whom, even in the event of a miracle, I could not have gotten this book to the printer on time. I cannot express my gratitude for the grueling task of trying to decipher all my scribbling on draft after draft. I sincerely appreciate your hard work and undeniable dedication.

My sincere appreciation and thanks
to American Isuzu, Pontiac Motor Division,
and General Motors Corporation
for giving me the opportunity to
travel around the world
and
visit all of the wonderful
places that I share
with my readers.
But, even more importantly, I want to
thank my sales managers and our
incredible sales force who
made all of those trips possible.
Also, I would like to thank Incentive Associates,
Wayne Wright and his staff,
for working so hard to take me deeply into
the places around the world and introducing
me to the people, the cultures, and the landscapes.

Too Many Promises

CHAPTER ONE

Galveston, Texas
October, 1976

NEALY'S FACE turned bright red as she tugged desperately at the zipper on her fourth and final suitcase. "I need to call my mother right now and yell at her!" she screamed. "I inherited the problem of overpacking and running late from her. My daddy always said 'she'll be late for her own funeral.' "

Standing in the doorway nearby, Kendall shook his head and replied chauvinistically, "Nealy, you can't help it. *All* women have this problem."

"Oh, really," she snapped sarcastically. Exhausted from the battle of *woman vs. suitcase*, she rolled her big green eyes up to glare at him from the floor where her long legs were crossed Indian-style. "You mean a *problem* like the one men have? You know, the one that causes them to incessantly flip the remote control."

"Why are you getting so upset? You do this every time you go somewhere. Just accept it. You're not going to change."

"Thanks for the vote of confidence, *Dr. Psychology*. I guess this is the same lecture you give a horse that keeps jumping the fence and cutting its leg on the barbed wire."

"No, as a matter of fact it isn't. Horses are just dumb animals that don't know any better. You're an intelligent woman who knows what she's doing wrong: You're taking too many damn clothes."

"*Oh, please*...spare me this sermon. I'm in a hurry, and I'm getting your opinion on how women should pack."

"Okay," he said, making a T-sign with his hands, "time out. How can I help?"

"Well, instead of lecturing me, you could take a couple of my bags out to the car. God must have had some purpose in mind when he created man," she chuckled, exposing her large, pearly white teeth and the deep dimple that creased her left cheek.

"Carry 'em yourself." Angrily, he turned and headed for the backdoor. But suddenly he stopped and turned around, just in time to see her stick her thumbs in her ears and make a face.

Kendall stared at her in disbelief. "You're goofy as hell. It's impossible, dammit," he exclaimed, trying not to smile, "for me to stay angry with you. You *always* manage to make me laugh."

"Good, then let's go. I'm gonna be late. And of course, if I am, it'll naturally be your fault," she said, smiling and moving quickly past him.

"That's it!" he snapped, rushing past her and pushing the screen door so hard that it slammed against the outside wall. Nealy stood there in shock, since Kendall rarely lost his temper. Obviously, he wasn't in the mood for teasing.

"Wait!" she screamed. "Kendall, I'm just kidding. I promise I won't say or do anything else," she pleaded, running after him. She grabbed his hand and dropped to her knees in her most dramatic performance. "Please, my lord, I beg of you."

"Nealy James," he said, reaching down to pull her up, "you make me crazy. But in spite of it, I'm in love with you."

Nealy leaned her head back, taking Kendall's face sweetly between her hands. "Kendall, I'll be back soon. Please don't be upset. It's just a vacation."

"I know," he whispered. Nervously, he pushed the strands of reddish-blonde hair across the top of her eyebrows. Then, to avoid staring into her eyes, he fidgeted with the long strands of hair that draped across her shoulders. Finally, his eyes returned to meet hers, while his hands smoothed her silky hair down her back. Kendall let go of her hair, allowing his arms to relax around her waist. Then suddenly, he stiffened. "Let's get your luggage. If we don't get going, you *will* miss your plane." He gently pulled away from her, giving her a quick smile before he turned and walked back towards her house. Nealy followed in his footsteps, at least until he stopped abruptly, causing her to crash into him. He cut his eyes around and gave her a no-nonsense look that got her attention.

As they drove out of town, the arched incandescent body that appeared to be rising out of the Gulf of Mexico, created a lavish display that reflected across the still waters like spun gold, stretched and polished to perfection, beneath the bluish haze. What a beautiful day the *Lord* hath made, Nealy thought, as she admired her surroundings. The crisp, dry air had been a welcomed change from the hot, humid summer. When they crossed Strand and Mechanic, the smell of fish saturated the morning fog that hung close to the ground along Galveston Bay, tracing a path to the early rising fisherman who were preparing their boats for a long day at sea. Hundreds of seagulls, who appeared out of nowhere in every direction, squawked annoyingly as they dived aggressively for discarded bait from the shrimp nets; they loomed over the boats in anticipation! Two small boats were being maneuvered across the deep waters of the port toward Seawolf Park on Pelican Island. As a child, Nealy had often played on that island while her parents fished. Her memories were long when it came to Galveston. After all, she had been born there almost twenty-eight years ago.

At the top of the causeway, connecting Galveston Island to the mainland, a parade of ships and tankers were leaving the docks in Texas City where they had been loaded with oil and gas; some of them were being pulled by tug boats along the five mile stretch of the Texas City dike out to the deeper waters in the ship channel. At the bottom of the causeway, Nealy exhaled aloud and Kendall reacted with a puzzled stare.

Catching his stare out of the corner of her eye, she turned to look at him. "I guess you're wondering why I did that," she said, smiling. "Well, believe it or not, there is a perfectly logical explanation. When we were kids, my brothers, my sister, and I, played a game in the car: Whoever held their breath the longest while crossing a bridge, won. That's all. So now, every time I cross a bridge, I hold my breath. Actually," she said, scratching her chin, "it was my parents' idea. I think they started it for a little peace and quiet, and it worked so well that it became a game." Nealy cocked her head, raised her eyebrows, and shrugged her shoulders. "You probably thinks it's dumb, huh? Kidstuff? Well, at heart, you see, I'm just a big kid," she giggled quietly.

Kendall didn't respond, except for a half-hearted smile. In fact, he had said or done very little—a whispered "yeah" or a slight nod here or there—since pulling out of her driveway en route for Houston's Intercontinental Airport. From his silence, Nealy knew that they were probably thinking the same thing, wondering if this would be their last good-bye.

Walking down the long corridor in the airport, Nealy looked back to wave. Kendall appeared comatose, still standing by the security station. Nealy waved wildly trying to attract his attention, but he didn't respond. Haunted by feelings of guilt, she waited until he turned and walked out of sight before she proceeded towards the gate. Why did she still feel so guilty? After all, he chose to stay at home, telling her to go, insisting that she go, but he looked so sad. It had become very obvious during the past six months how much he wanted to get married and have children. Knowing her as well as he did, he probably planned this to make her feel absolutely rotten for going without him; men do that sometimes. They say, "No problem. Go. Have fun. Be independent." But they really don't mean it. He probably thought she'd feel so guilty and, with absence making the heart grow fonder, she would be counting the days, hours, and minutes until she could get home, fall into his arms, pledge her undying love, and marry him; therefore, becoming barefoot and pregnant every time he hung his pants on the doorknob. Well, his mind game isn't going to work. Not only was she going, but she planned on having a great time. But if that's the case, why did she feel like a first class creep? Walking slowly, avoiding the people that rushed around her, she tried desperately to ease her conscience by recalling every last word of their conversation the evening before:

"Kendall, I feel terrible going on this cruise without you. We had planned to take this trip together. I could cancel—"

"No," he interrupted, glaring at her.

"Maybe," she paused, waiting to see if he would interrupt her again. Instead, he just stared so she continued, "If we tell them that you're a doctor, the cruise line would consider giving us some of our money back, or perhaps, they would let us take another cruise at a later date—"

"Nealy, I said, 'No!' " he shouted.

But she ignored him, talking faster. "We wouldn't have to mention that most of your patients have four legs." She smiled at him, forcing him to smile back.

"No, Nealy, I want you to go." He pushed the clothes aside that she had laid out on the bed and sat down, pulling her down beside him. "It'll be fun for you. A change in scenery could be just what the doctor ordered." Kendall smiled at her, feeling very clever with his choice of words.

"Okay, Dr. Cross. I give up. But it won't be the same. Would you at least take me to the airport?"

"Sure. What time's your flight?"

"Eight-fifteen. But I want you to pick me up at six."

"Six," he mirrored. "Are we talking about six a.m.?"

"Is that a problem for you?" she asked, annoyed at his sarcastic tone.

"Not for me. But you...you'll never make it."

"I beg your pardon," she snapped.

"Nealy, let's face it. You're not exactly a ball of fire in the morning."

"Maybe not. But I can be when it's necessary. Especially when I'm going to France."

"We'll see. I'll be here at six." Kendall leaned down, kissing her lightly on the lips.

"Kendall, before you go, could we talk for a minute? Seriously?"

"Nealy, don't look so guilty. I'm okay. Honest." He took her small, delicate hand in his and stroked her slender fingers.

"But, I wanted us to spend some quality time together. Just the two of us. I know that you've been upset with me during the last six months because I keep avoiding the subject of marriage. Maybe being together, like we were in the beginning, might help me resolve my feelings."

"Nealy, that isn't the reason I'm not going. But, since you brought it up, I do think it's time that we make a commitment if that's where we're headed."

"Kendall, please come to France with me."

"Nealy, I really feel that the time apart may help you come to terms with the doubts and insecurities that you have about marriage, about me. Besides, you know how I am about vacations. The thought of spending two weeks aboard a ship...well, truthfully, I'd feel like a hostage." Nealy giggled at his pitiful attempt to humorously excuse himself, but truer words had never been spoken.

"But, Kendall—"

"Nealy, go. It's okay. I promise."

Nealy searched his smiling face for a moment. "Well, okay, but you're passing up the trip of a lifetime."

The smile on his face turned very serious. "I'll tell you what. If you decide to marry me while you're gone, I'll gladly take two weeks off and take you wherever you would like to go."

"In that case, Dr. Cross, I'll do a lot of soul searching while I'm being held hostage on that ship!" They both laughed, but Nealy could see the sadness in his face which he tried to camouflage with an obviously faked smile.

Kendall reached out and pulled Nealy into his arms, hugging her almost desperately for a moment. Quickly he pulled away, realizing that he needed to leave now, that is, if he intended to leave at all. It had become important to him to find out if Nealy wanted him as much as he wanted her. "Come on. Walk me to my truck. You need to get busy if you're going to be ready by six." He put his arm around her shoulders and they walked, without a word being exchanged between them, outside to where he had parked his truck. After kissing her good-night, he climbed into his truck and started the engine, but he didn't leave, he just sat there staring at her. Then, finally, he slowly drove away.

Nealy watched him as he turned the corner, wishing that she could say yes to his proposal, but something kept holding her back. The last year had been filled with good times, bad times, and lately, sad times. Nealy had looked forward to this trip for a long time and deserved to get away from the fast paced life of a woman who managed two successful businesses more than two thousand miles apart. Traveling alone to a foreign country and touring the Mediterranean for two full weeks would be the ultimate challenge for most young women, but for Nealy Samantha James it would be the trip of a lifetime.

CHAPTER TWO

SETTLING INTO her seat and preparing for a very long flight across the ocean, Nealy's attention focused on a young woman with four small children. The oldest boy appeared to be about three; the little blonde girl, two; and the toddlers, who were obviously identical twin boys, were maybe a year. Now that, Nealy thought to herself, is the ultimate challenge. Feeling a little sad about not having children, Nealy observed them closely. After all, most of her friends and her brothers and sister had children. So, if she had accepted Kendall's proposal only a month after they'd met, maybe things would be different now; she might be expecting a child instead of going on a trip to France alone.

During the past six months, Kendall had brought up the subject of marriage and family many times, but Nealy still had too many doubts to make that commitment. She had only been in love twice in her life: the first time with her high school sweetheart, Jerrod Jones, and the second time with Dr. Phillip Pepper. The first time had been built on habit and familiarity and teenage lust, but her second had been built on love and trust and friendship. As long as she lived, she would never forget Phillip, nor would she ever stop loving him. He became her best friend and she missed him every day of her life. And even though it had been more than a year since she had seen him, she could still feel how deeply, almost desperately, one person could love another; she didn't want to settle for anything less. In many ways she loved Kendall, but there had been something missing from the beginning, which she still contributed to being on the rebound from Phillip. But because Kendall had so many good qualities, she thought that maybe she would fall in love with him in time; after all, it's not impossible to grow to love a special person. Unfortunately, she felt less in love with him now than ever before. So, out of fairness to Kendall, as well as to herself, she needed to make a decision about their future.

Kendall worked many hours. He had been totally devoted to his veterinary practice since nineteen-seventy when he first hung out his shingle. In fact, his mother had told Nealy that even before Kendall was old enough to talk clearly—pronouncing *v*'s as *b*'s—he used to say, "When I grow up, I want to be a *beterinarian*." Nealy knew from the beginning that his practice came first in his life. Kendall, a very independent person, really didn't have the time or the interest to be involved in Nealy's work. And unlike most men, he didn't require a lot of attention.

Nealy began dating him after spending hours at his clinic when her golden retriever, Chance, was recovering from surgery after being hit by a car. Nealy sat outside his cage, hand-feeding him through the small door, tears streaming down her face. "Dr. Cross, you probably think that I'm a real idiot for behaving this way, but Chance is all I have now. He's the only good thing that came from my divorce."

Slowly, he reached down to help her up. Feeling helpless, he hugged her. "Don't cry. He'll be just fine," he said sweetly.

"But, you don't know—"

"Oh, but I do know exactly how you feel. I got custody of my dog in my divorce, too."

Amusingly shocked by his confession, Nealy's puffy red eyes grew wide, and they both laughed. As their love affair blossomed, they often referred to their first meeting as: *Love at first laughter.*

Nealy, a beautiful, sophisticated young woman, who spent much of her time involved in the world of glitz and glamour as the owner of a successful dance and acting studio and a theatrical placement agency, had not fit into the world of farming and ranching very well. In the beginning of their relationship, things were new and different. Just being with Kendall had been wonderful. They grew closer in many ways, and yet, they grew further apart, not having many things in common. Her idea of a night out included dinner at a nice restaurant and a good comedy or love story at the movies; his, vaccinating the neighbor's horse.

During her three years in business, Nealy had trained many dancers and aspiring actors, and it became very frustrating when she couldn't find an agent that would handle them. Most of the talent agents in New York that Nealy had contacted didn't want to handle beginners, maintaining that it took too much time and effort to find a producer or director that would give a novice a chance. Determined and unafraid of hard work, Nealy decided to open a small talent agency in New York City, even though it meant commuting between New York and Texas.

The talent agency, Fame with Nealy James, Inc., quickly gained recognition and financial success. During the first year, Nealy commuted between New York and Galveston almost every week, soliciting auditions for her clients. Becoming so busy with her career, she had less and less time left to spend with Kendall, which put a strain on their relationship.

When Nealy wasn't in New York, she was in her studio teaching students who dreamed of becoming actors and dancers, bringing back fond memories of the career she had given up to marry her childhood sweetheart.

CHAPTER THREE

July, 1960

WHEN NEALY was just thirteen, Miss Janik, her dance teacher, encouraged her to enter a talent contest that was being held in the nearby town of Texas City at the Showboat Theater. That was the beginning of a dream which became a strong driving force in her life. For the next ten years, she devoted her time to lessons in singing, dancing and acting. Immediately following college, Nealy fled to New York to pursue a career in the entertainment business. As a means of support, she developed a portfolio from modeling part-time during college, which she used to land photo shoots and assignments. It was hard for her to believe that she had finally made it to New York since it seemed like only yesterday when Miss Janik pushed her onto that stage.

"Nealy, are you ready?" Miss Janik asked, standing next to her just inside the curtain. Miss Janik could see the stage fright in Nealy's face, so she nudged her slightly.

"But, Miss Janik, what if I forget the words? Or my routine? What if they hate me?"

"They'll love you," she said, prying her hands from the plush velvet curtain that she clung to for dear life. Miss Janik's voice grew firm and serious, "They're waiting for you, Nealy—"

"Okay, I'm going...I'm going." She took a deep breath and then skipped out onto the stage. Instinctively, she began to sing and dance.

"Tan shoes and pink shoe laces,
a polka dot vest, and man, oh man..."
Nealy tapped and strutted to the music.
"and a big panama with a purple hat band!"

The piano player continued to play after Nealy completed her act and ran off the stage. Miss Janik motioned for her to go back out and take a bow. Quickly, she turned, bouncing back out onto the stage and bowing several times as the crowd cheered and whistled. The excitement overwhelmed her as she ran backstage into the arms of Miss Janik.

"I did it, Miss Janik. They like me. I'm going to be a star. I can feel it!"

"Nealy, I knew you would knock 'em dead! This is just the beginning. All you have to do is reach for that star, not stopping until you get there, and you will be a *big* star!" Nealy beamed as Miss Janik praised and encouraged her.

Ten years had passed since that day on the stage at the Showboat Theater.

Nealy's pretty face lit-up as she stood on the corner, looking up to the top of the Empire State Building. It seemed as far away as that star Miss Janik had told her to reach for so long ago. Since Miss Janik had once been a dancer for the New York City Ballet Company and a successful drama coach, she gave Nealy a list of agents to contact when she settled in New York. Nealy called every agent on the list, but none of them seemed to be interested in someone without any singing or acting credits to her name. Later that evening, Nealy received a call from an agent who had been referred to her by one of Miss Janik's agent friends. Now Nealy understood what people meant when they said, "It's not what you know, but who you know." Thank God for Miss Janik. The agent, Tony Rose, invited Nealy to his office the next day for an interview.

Up early, Nealy dressed and caught a cab. Normally she would have walked, but today she wanted to look her best; the dampness would friz her hair and cause her make-up to run. Entering the old building, she took the stairs up to the third floor. Quietly, she opened the door and walked over to the receptionist's desk. "Hi, I'm Nealy James," she said with confidence. "I think...uh, I'm here...uh, Mr. Rose is expecting me," she finally said sharply, her knees shaking and her confidence definitely wavering.

The woman looked up over her half-glasses until Nealy finished stuttering, and then she spoke. "Yeah, shu-ah," she slurred in a thick Brooklyn accent, sounding like she had three pieces of Bazooka bubble gum stuck in the roof of her mouth. "Sit ov-ah there," she said without smiling, while pointing to the couch.

Nealy, feeling like a blubbering idiot, wandered over to the brown naugahyde sofa where the less-than-receptive receptionist had motioned for her to sit. The pictures on the wall were some of Hollywood's greatest stars— Clark Gable, Carole Lombard, W.C. Fields, Marlon Brando, Rita Hayworth, Helen Hayes, and Juliet Prowse. Nealy expected Tony Rose to be older than he had sounded on the phone since his selection of photographs were at least a generation older than herself.

A few minutes later the office door opened, and a man appeared. "Nealy, I'm Tony Rose," he announced, walking across the room and extending his hand.

"Hi, Mr. Rose." Nealy nervously jumped up from the couch to shake his hand. "Thank you so much for giving me the opportunity to talk to you."

"It's my pleasure. But, please, call me Tony. Come on in. Let's see if we can find you some work." Tony led Nealy into his office, but before he closed the door, he glanced at Mary, his receptionist, giving her the *Gracho Marx* sign of approval by repeatedly raising his eyebrows. Tony definitely liked what he saw and hoped she had the talent to match.

Tony turned out to be as young as Nealy had conceived him to be when they had spoken on the telephone. Maybe the photographs were a collection given to him by his father or an uncle. They were certainly some of the biggest stars. Tony, although he was only five-nine or so, carried himself tall, like many short men tend to do—chin up, shoulders high, chest out. What he lacked in height, he made up for in other areas. He had a well-developed body, a handsome face, and a warm smile. From the neck up, he looked enough like Nealy to be related because of his reddish hair—more red than Nealy's—and the same blue-green eyes, big, warm smile with straight, white teeth, and deep dimples in both cheeks. But, unlike Nealy, Tony had a million freckles from head to toe—well, at least the parts that were visible. Nealy liked him immediately, and it was obvious that he liked her, too.

Having all the right credentials, Tony appeared to be reputable, but he admitted that he hadn't represented anyone really famous yet. Of course that didn't matter to her because he was all she had and they seemed to have a lot in common. So, after the contractual legalities were taken care of, Tony immediately lined-up her first audition the next morning where she landed a small part in an off-off-Broadway satirical production of "The Music Man." It wasn't much, but it was a beginning, and she knew all of the music since she had played the part of Marian, the librarian, when her thespian club performed the play in high school. The lead understudy, Kate, who had just landed the part the day Nealy arrived, asked if she would help her learn her lines. The two of them spent most of their time together singing the words to the songs over and over again. During the breaks, the cast gathered to listen as they sang.

"There were bells…on the hill,
but I never heard them ringing,
No, I never heard them at all
Till there was you."

The cast loved to be around Nealy. As well as being pretty, she was so full of life, talented, and witty. When her friends asked her to do her imitation of the trombones, the cornets, and the one and only bass, she strutted around the stage and sang.

"And I oom-pahed, oom-pahed, oom-pah-pahed,
Oom-pahed up and down the square."

As she marched, Nealy pretended to switch instruments, singing the words and imitating the sounds. The cast had a great time watching her, but by the time she finished, she had pulled everyone into her production. Nealy enjoyed choreographing and teaching and directing; they simply came naturally to her.

Still in search of more work for Nealy, Tony sent the owner of a nightclub in Greenwich Village one of Nealy's demo tapes. He must have been impressed because Tony received a phone call from him the next day instructing him to have his singer at the club around eleven-thirty that night to perform a number for him. Tony called Nealy and arranged to pick her up.

Tony arrived at Nealy's flat at ten-thirty. When she answered the door, he cheerfully asked, "So, are you ready?"

"Tony, I'm ready, but I'm a little skeptical about this place. That neighborhood is not very safe."

"Nealy, it'll be fine. Besides, this is *New York*; no place is safe."

"Tony, I'm serious."

"Nealy, you've got to trust me on this. I got you that part on Broadway, didn't I? And that turned out okay. Trust me on this one. After all, I *am* your agent."

"I know. That's what worries me," she teased. "Anyway, it's *not* on Broadway. It's barely off-off-Broadway. It's a cheap attempt to bring the play back to New York. I think I'd call it off-off-the-bowery. Let's go, before I change my mind."

"That's my girl. You'll thank me when you're a big star," he bragged, helping her with her coat.

They drove over to the Village and found a parking place a couple of blocks away from the nightclub. After parking, they walked down the street until they reached the neon sign flashing *"Freddy's."*

Following the entrance signs, they walked down the stairs one level below the main street into this dreary nightclub. Tony told the bartender that he and Nealy were there to see the owner Freddy. A few minutes later, a short, fat man, smoking a cigar greeted them.

"You Tony Rose?" he asked gruffly.

"Yes, sir. And you must be Freddy Finkle?" Tony asked, looking at Nealy and praying that they could keep from laughing at the very sight of this man. That name really fits this guy, Tony thought to himself, mentally depicting him with a playful rhyme. *Fat Freddy Finkle, sat on some periwinkles, and crushed them into perfume!* Becoming so distracted by his own silly thoughts and the loud music, Tony didn't hear Freddy speaking to him.

"Hey, Rose," he mumbled loudly. "This your singer?" He nodded his head towards Nealy, looking her up and down.

"Yes, sir, but she's all yours now," Tony replied, grinning, observing the delight in the eyes as he puffed rapidly on a huge cigar.

"She ain't mine 'til I hear 'er sing."

"We're ready, if you are," Tony snapped.

"Gimme a minute. I'll be right back," Freddy said, motioning for them to stay put.

Nealy had kept quiet while the two men talked, staring in amazement at this man who, God forbid, might become her boss. When Freddy Finkle walked away, Nealy looked at Tony, thinking for sure that he had lost his mind. "Tony, you must be kidding. I can't work for this man. He looks like a psychopath. Did you see him looking at me? It gave me the creeps."

"Nealy, sweetie—"

"Tony, no, you can't sweet talk me into this. I don't—"

"Quiet, here he comes. Look excited. And smile. Where do you think Streisand started?"

"O.K., Doll," Freddy called, motioning for her and Tony to come over near the bar. "My girl here—he nodded at the young woman standing next to him—will take you backstage. You're on in three minutes." He winked at Nealy with one of his small, seedy looking eyes, giving her a slightly crooked grin.

"Thank you, Mr. Finkle," she said politely, before turning to follow the girl backstage.

"Dear *God*, what have I gotten myself into this time?" Nealy mumbled, pulling Tony along behind her by his sleeve.

The curtain that surrounded the small stage opened, and Nealy stood by the piano holding a microphone. The accompanist began to play the music that Nealy had requested, and on cue she started to sing.

"*People, people who need people,*
are the luck-i-est people in the world."

Nealy tried to concentrate on her song and not the heavy smoke that hovered over the room, which separated her from her audience. After the first few bars of the song, she finally relaxed, capturing the attention of the entire crowd with her sweet soprano voice and whispered words.

"*They're the luck-i-est, peo-ple, in…the…world.*"

The audience clapped and cheered as Nealy took a quick bow, smiled graciously, thanked her audience, and headed backstage.

Tony looked over to the side of the stage where Freddy Finkle stood with his cigar hanging listlessly between his pencil thin lips. When their eyes met, Freddy nodded his head, squashing his multiple chins together. Then he smiled, giving Tony the thumbs-up sign.

"All right!" Tony exclaimed, dashing backstage to give her the good news.

"Nealy, you got the job! Freddy Finkle loved you."

"Oh, that's great, Tony," she remarked, trying not to sound too ungrateful and even somewhat excited. "I felt like Edith Piaf singing in some sleazy bar on the back streets of Paris. The only thing missing was a cigarette sticking out of a long cigarette holder, held between two fingers in that same sultry way in which she used to hold them. Spare me. I couldn't see anyone in the audience. Tony…I…I don't know if I can do this."

"You'll be fine. I'll admit, it's not the Twenty-One Club, but it's a start. It's a real neighborhood-type club. You know, with lots of regulars. It'll be fun. At least, it'll work until something better comes along. It's experience. Come on, Nealy. Say you'll do it. Pretty please…we need this job—"

"Okay, okay, I'll do it. God knows, I do need the work. And I did love the applause. You're right, Tony, thanks. I'll make you proud," she said, hugging him. "Tony, I'm glad you're my agent…and my wonderful friend."

"That's my girl. Now, let's get out of here."

Nealy and Tony chatted, smiling at each other as they walked down the stairs from the stage area into the hall.

"Tony, you have to admit, Freddy is pret-ty strange, but I guess I can handle him," she said. They stopped to let a drunk stagger past them. Their eyes followed him, and when he disappeared into the ladies' room, they looked at each other and burst out laughing.

CHAPTER FOUR

June, 1971

ELEVEN MONTHS in New York felt more like eleven years. Nealy's schedule was exhausting, rushing out every morning at five-thirty to get to the Village by six for play rehearsals. Nealy had been given a few more lines, two extra dance numbers, and even a few solo lines in a couple of songs. The acting classes that she took on her evenings off lasted some nights until midnight, especially when the group had trouble getting into character. The fast-paced life in New York had certainly been a rude awakening for a girl from Galveston, Texas. The flat that Nealy and her two roommates had rented was not what she had imagined, but it was all that they could afford. It had two small rooms: a kitchen to back in and out of and a bedroom that had three small beds with drawers underneath for clothes and four tiny closets. Nealy could live with the cramped conditions, but the community bathroom shared by everyone on her floor, now *that* still bothered her. Needless to say, they had managed, but it certainly had not been the comforts of the middle-class homes that the girls had been accustomed to.

Nealy's roommates, Denise and Alexandra, were both from Lufkin, Texas, a small town in East Texas. Both of them had been brought up in nice families—upper middle class—and lived in brick homes and had nice clothes. In East Texas, a young girl's popularity is determined by where she lives, what size her family's place is, how she dresses, and what her daddy does for a living. According to the townsfolk, big city, store-bought dresses are worn by the rich; local, store-bought dresses are usually worn by the middle class; and homemade dresses that were made from tacky feedsack-looking calico prints are more often worn by the poor or less fortunate.

Denise Pratt grew up the daughter of the town's only judge. By trade, he had been an attorney but became the judge when the town judge died after forty years on the bench. Denise had been very popular, mostly due to her outgoing personality. But, her crystal clear blue eyes and head full of dark black hair attracted people to her as well. She had been blessed with beauty and brains and wanted desperately to become an actress. As a child, she acted out the part of her father's witnesses when he was trying a case. So, when she went away to college, she majored in fine arts.

Alexandra Lawson, on the other hand, had long blonde hair and extremely fair skin. Alex came to New York to be a dancer, and because of some connections—the aunt of a friend—she auditioned for the Rockettes and made the line; the very end of the line because of her average height of five-foot-four. Alex's parents owned a large local grocery store that had been in the family for years. Most of the townspeople traded there, and therefore, everyone knew Alex. This made her very popular at school, or so some said, but being a sweet, pretty and kind person, she would have been popular anyway. Alex's family lived in what the town called "the Murdock Mansion." It had been the old homeplace of Alex's mother's family. Even before it had been passed on legally to Alex's mother after the death of her grandmother, her family had always lived there. The house was massive, and even the smallest room in the house was larger than the flat that the girls shared in New York. But, in spite of the close quarters, the girls seemed to be perfectly happy and enjoyed one another's company. Denise and Alexandra realized that Nealy had still not adjusted to the bathroom situation and ragged her constantly about her modesty and inhibitions.

"Nealy, for god's sake, the shower stall has a curtain," Denise shouted at her, watching as she stepped into the shower wearing her swimsuit, a habit she had maintained for almost a year.

"I can't help it! I didn't grow up parading around in my birthday suit. In my family, we dressed in our rooms," she said defensively.

"Well, I'm certainly glad that you didn't have aspirations of becoming a strip tease artist. This modesty *thing* would definitely be a handicap," Alex shouted loudly in order to be heard over the running water.

"Gimme a break, guys. I've always been a very modest person, a virtue that you people are obviously not familiar with!"

"Nealy, I haven't noticed one single person hanging around the shower to get a glimpse of your big knockers," Denise shouted back at her.

"I've been here!" shouted a familiar male voice from the shower stall next to Nealy's.

"Well, shit!" Nealy screamed. "Now I'm never coming out of here." They all started laughing at her.

"Hey, Marty, is that you?" Denise asked.

"Yeah, it's me," he answered, shouting back. "Nealy, don't worry about it. The walls in our apartment are so thin that I feel practically like family anyway. What I haven't seen, I've heard enough about to paint a pretty damn good picture!"

"Marty, if taking a shower in your bathing suit isn't weird enough, you should see her—she dresses in her damn closet. We've been roomies for a year, and I've never seen her undressed."

"Denise!" Nealy yelled. "For your information, I dress in my closet because our room is freezing most of the time!"

"Yeah, right, Nealy. Face it. You're never going to change. I wonder what it'll be like when you get married. I bet you'll still dress in your closet," Alex chuckled smugly. Everyone laughed at her. And although Nealy took the constant abuse well, it didn't change her modest habits.

The girls dressed, then hurried off to their jobs. This day marked their first year in New York together, and they had a big evening planned to celebrate.

Freddy Finkle, who treated them like daughters, had given them a bottle of wine—Chateau Moncontour Vouvray-1966—to celebrate their first year. It was Denise's Sunday to cook, and she wanted to serve something special. She stopped by the market on her way home from the Village where she had just finished performing in the Sunday afternoon matinee at the Sullivan Street Playhouse. Of course, they were still on a limited budget, but they all chipped in to splurge for the occasion. Denise loved to cook, in spite of their kitchen that had obviously been designed for "little people" because anyone over five-nine had to duck. So, at five-ten, Denise had nearly knocked herself out several times, which made the others laugh. Even at three in the morning when they were sound asleep, it struck them funny to hear this loud "thud" followed by a whole string of filthy swear words.

Coming in the door, Nealy took a big whiff. "Oh, God, Denise, that smells wonderful. What is it?"

"Lobster bisque."

"I've never even heard of it. Where did you learn to cook that?" Nealy questioned, raising her eyebrows in total disbelief.

"You remember when we first got to New York, and my cousin Jessie, who worked at *Tavern On The Green*, helped me get a job there in the kitchen until I could find something else. Well, this happens to be one of their specialties. I paid attention when the chef prepared it. It's really easy," Denise said smiling, delighted that Nealy seemed pleased.

"It smells delicious. And I'm so hungry my stomach thinks my throat's been cut. What else are we having?"

"Spinach salad with raspberry vinaigrette, lamb chops with mushroom sauce, french bread, and the wine that Freddy gave us."

"Damn, you're good. I'm glad it's your night to cook. When do we eat?"

"Hi, guys," Alex said, coming through the door. The smell of food filled her nostrils. "Geezus, what's cooking?"

"Our celebration dinner. Are you ready to eat?" Denise asked.

"I sure am. I'll be over in a minute!" Marty shouted, overhearing their conversation through the walls. "Anything that smells that good definitely deserves to be eaten by someone who appreciates good food."

"Marty, you nut," Denise shouted back. "Come on over and join us. It's our first anniversary. We're celebrating. So please, come join us."

A few minutes later, Marty knocked and stuck his head in the door to their apartment. "It's only me. Thanks for the invite. It smells yummy, but I got a date."

"Oh, okay. We'll give you a rain-check," Denise said.

"That'll work. Enjoy your celebration."

"Thanks. See you later, Marty," Alex smiled, watching as he closed the door.

A second later, he opened it again, but just long enough to make a teasing remark. "Hey, Nealy, I'll see you in the shower tomorrow. Maybe I'll get lucky."

"Marty!" she screamed. "See what y'all started? Nothing is sacred."

After decorating the tiny table with candles, the three of them sat down to eat. "Cheers. Here's to another year and bigger parts," Nealy exclaimed, lifting her glass. Denise and Alex copied. "It's been good, but next year will be our *lucky* year. In my crystal ball, I see great parts, great pay, and stardom."

"Here, here!" Alex shouted.

"This has been the most wonderful, but most tiring year of my life. Thanks guys for all your support. Let's toast!" Denise cheered. After gently clanging their glasses together, they took a sip of wine. "Now, let's eat, drink, and be merry, for tomorrow we'll be back on cheerios, tuna, and peanut butter." They laughed and helped themselves to large portions.

"Denise, you did good," Nealy praised, after stuffing herself until she couldn't eat another bite. "Thanks for cooking."

"Denise, I ate so much it's sinful, but it was wonderful," Alex groaned delightfully. "Thanks for going to so much trouble for us."

"You're both very welcome," Denise accepted the compliments graciously, giving them a big grin and a little curtsy.

After doing the dishes, the three of them were too full to do anything other than retire to their beds to watch television. And by nine o'clock they were being lulled to sleep by the raindrops hitting against the tin roof on their building. Then the phone rang. Startled, and half-asleep, they all grabbed for it—praying as always—that their agents had found them a bigger and better job.

"Hello," Alex said.

"Is Nealy there?"

"Sure, hold on," she said, handing the phone to Nealy. "I think it's Kati Sue."

"Thanks," she said, excited at the prospect of hearing from one of her best friends back home. "Kati Sue, is that you?"

"Hi, Nealy. How've you been?"

"I've been great. Gosh, it's good to hear from you," she said, fluffing her pillow up behind her back. "How've you been?"

"Real good. You haven't forgotten about the reunion, have you? It's next week-end."

"Oh, Kati Sue, I'm so glad you called. I have been so busy that I'd forgotten about that darn thing."

"Nealy, you gotta come. It's five classes— '64, '65, our class, '66, of course, '67, and '68. We—the planning committee, that is—thought it would be more fun because a lot of us dated outside our class, like me, for one. Also, it will ensure a really big party at the Galvez Hotel. Everyone is dying to see you. They can't wait to hear all about New York."

"It sounds like a blast. I'll have to work some things out here, but, yeah, I'll be there. I'm dying to see everyone, too. How's Betty Lou?"

"She's doing real good. She had planned on calling you, but I told her I'd call, and I quote, 'Tell her to get her butt down here.' As you can see, she hasn't changed." Nealy and Kati Sue laughed about Betty Lou's directness.

"Yep, that sounds just like her. Gosh, it's really great to hear from you. I'll call you back in a couple days to confirm my plans. So listen, take care and tell Betty Lou 'Hello' for me."

"I will. It'll be just like old times. Nealy, plan on staying through Sunday. We have a great picnic planned."

"Oh, that sounds great. Give everyone my love. Bye, Kati Sue."

"Okay, bye, Nealy."

The *jolly-good-girls*—a pet name given to the twins in grade school—had been best friends with Nealy since they were all in the third grade. They had grown up on the same street and lived there until they all went away to college. Betty Lou and Kati Sue were identical twins who had always been very popular. They were both outgoing, but they had different personalities. Betty Lou had been known as the bossy, yet adorable one; her mouth opened and God knows what came out. Whereas, Kati Sue had always been more reserved, but equally as sweet, thoughtful and very cute. Both of them had a great sense of humor. Their bright blue eyes danced, and when they smiled they revealed a set of large white teeth; perfect for the *Doublemint Gum* commercials. Nealy's mother could never tell them apart because they dressed alike, wore their hair in the same shoulder length flip, and they both had the same high-pitched voice. So, she would stop them to look for the beauty mark that Betty Lou had above her lip in order to know who was who. The girls were cheerleaders for as long as everyone could remember, and, although they were twins, they saw things very differently which led to harmless bickering. Nealy always seemed to be between them, and, most of the time, she refereed. And, with a last name like England and cheerful phrases such as "Jolly good" and "Simply splendid," which they borrowed from the Beatles, coupled with the fact that they were good girls, it seemed only appropriate to call them the *jolly-good-girls*. The name fit them perfectly, making life fun and interesting.

In order for Nealy to go home for the reunion, she would have to get a stand-in to do her solos, that is if the choreographer approved, but that shouldn't be a problem since she hadn't missed any rehearsals or performances; and Freddy would understand. Being too busy during the past year, Nealy hadn't gone home, so she looked forward to seeing her family and friends again. But Nealy knew exactly what to expect: her mother would drag her around to the stores where her friends worked, bragging to them about *her daughter, the actress*, from New York City. Of course, Nealy would be embarrassed, but it would be okay; everyone knew and loved Gracie.

Grace James, who stood only five feet tall, had short strawberry-blonde hair and blue-green eyes that grew very wide as she spoke, and she had tremendous energy, constantly moving, laughing and talking. Nealy was certainly her mother's child, inheriting her personality, mannerisms and physical appearance, all except for her height and her stubbornness, which she had undeniably inherited from her father.

To prove that opposites attract, Grace married a tall, dark, handsome young man named Neal Samuel James, III, when she was only eighteen; he was twenty-four. Neal James was a man of few words, but highly intelligent. And, following graduation from college with a degree in engineering, he went to work full time in the family business in Galveston. Being very conservative, Nealy knew that her Daddy thought she had wasted her education by going off to New York in pursuit of an acting career. He very much considered it to be a frivolous lifestyle and had very little to say when she talked about her nights at Freddy's, the play, and her life in New York. Nealy could remember how he looked at her when she told him that she wanted to go to New York. Neal James glared at her with his dark brown eyes, never saying a word. Nealy felt like crawling under a table. Of course, Gracie went to bat for Nealy and argued that she should be allowed to follow her dream. Finally, he gave her his blessing, even though his expression never changed.

During her return trip home for the reunion, Nealy anticipated spending most of her time with her childhood friends, the ones that would be her friends forever, no matter where she went or what she became. And Jerrod Jones, her high school sweetheart, would probably be there. Nealy had not seen him since breaking their engagement the night before she left for New York. But they had talked by telephone a couple of times; Jerrod called her in New York just to say "Hi." It made her nervous to think about seeing him again, but deep down she wanted to. Nealy had loved Jerrod for such a long time, and even though she wouldn't admit it, she had missed him terribly at times. But, in spite of her love for him, Nealy had to pursue her career as an actress because she had always loved to sing, dance and act. During her teens, she became obsessed with going to New York. Therefore, she had to go; she had to find out if this was the life that she really wanted for herself. And who knows, once she tried it, she might have a change of heart, and, if so, she would probably be ready to settle down and get married.

During college, she and Jerrod had been pinned—going *steady* was a high school thing. Then, at Christmas during her last year of college and Jerrod's second year of medical school, he proposed. Reluctantly, she agreed to marry him the following September. He convinced her that being his wife would be enough to make her happy, but the week following graduation, she had a change of heart. Nealy realized that she *had* to go to New York. When she told Jerrod, he refused to accept it and became furious every time she mentioned it. Nealy wanted to do this more than anything that she had ever wanted. She tried to make him understand and told him that if things didn't work out she would come home. Then, if they still felt the same way, they could get married as planned. Nealy felt that they should call off the engagement, at least for the time being; it wouldn't be fair for him to wait until she decided which she loved more: her career or him. Jerrod, accustomed to always getting his way, did not take her final decision well at all. Therefore, the last evening that Nealy and Jerrod spent together had been extremely unpleasant. But, in spite of the terrible fight and the many hateful things that he had said to her, Nealy still wanted to see him again. A part of her wanted him to be fat or bald—or both—or married, engaged, or something that would keep her from losing sight of her goals. Nealy had always had a strong physical attraction to him, but who wouldn't. Jerrod Jones was the best looking guy in school, and the girls drooled all over themselves whenever he passed them in the hall. Nealy didn't drool, but she admitted that her heart pitter-pattered every time he looked at her for the first six months.

Nealy discovered that dating the most eligible boy in school had its advantages, but it also had many disadvantages. During Nealy's first year of high school, the senior girls didn't like her one little bit, frowning heavily upon sophomores dating their guys. Oh, how she suffered at *Initiation*. In fact, they pulled her out of bed before five o'clock on three different occasions for more initiation parties. But, she had to be a good sport about it or it could have been even worse. And because Nealy had no intentions of turning Jerrod away, she had to pay the price. For the most part, Jerrod had been worth it, but, at times, he revealed another side that caused him to be inconsiderate, spoiled, selfish, vain, hateful and rude. There was only one problem: Nealy had fallen head over heels in love with him, accepting his behavior on all levels, like most smitten teenage girls do. And Nealy had a naive nature, which is another pitfall of a young girl—and some older girls, too. But as Nealy grew older, Jerrod showed only his good side because Nealy had blossomed into a desirable young woman.

CHAPTER FIVE

The Reunion: Galveston, Texas
July 2, 1971

THE PLANE LANDED in Houston. As soon as Nealy walked through the doors that led into the airport, the entire James family descended upon her—Neal, Gracie, Lucy, Jim, Jess, Patrick, Retisha, Jessica, and Jeremy. Seeing the family again was great, and Nealy had to fill them in on every last detail starting with the day that she had left for NYC. Even Neal, Nealy's father, showed signs of interest in her activities. They had written, but somehow hearing it just seemed more exciting. When they arrived in Galveston, she barely had time to throw her things in the house before her mother had loaded her up for the stores, just as Nealy had expected.

The family had a great visit on Thursday night. On Friday morning her mother received a phone call from her aunt who lived in East Texas. Aunt Ella had fallen and had to be put in the hospital with a broken hip. Nealy's parents were going to have to go to East Texas to take care of her and her place for a few days. They felt bad about leaving after only spending a short time with Nealy, but it couldn't be helped since Aunt Ella didn't have any other family. But maybe, if all went well, they could be home before Nealy left on Sunday. At least now Nealy wouldn't feel torn between spending time with her family and her friends.

Nealy helped them pack, kissed and hugged everyone, and waved good-bye to them about five o'clock. That gave Nealy just enough time to get ready, drive over to Betty Lou's, and ride with her to the dance that started at seven-thirty in the high school gym. It would be just like the old days: A sock hop.

When Nealy drove into Betty Lou's driveway, everyone came running out to greet her—Betty Lou, Kati Sue, Gayleen, and Rhoada. Following a quick visit, they all loaded into the car and continued laughing and talking all the way to the gym. On the way, they passed Mayor Raley's home, and Nealy teased Kati Sue, who at fourteen, had fallen madly in love with a senior boy, the class president, no less. Kati Sue and Nealy had gone to the movies, but they left the theater in the middle of the show. They walked two miles and hid in a ditch across the street from the boy's house where they remained for at least an hour before he came home. As he climbed out of his bright red Chevy 409, they took his picture. Kati Sue's heart throbbed so loudly that Nealy swore she heard it. With the pictures, Kati Sue designed a poster for her wall entirely *dedicated to the one she loved*, Don Raley. They reminisced about boys, parents, college, and the so-called sluts from their high school days. These were the girls who were pretty wild and went all the way with the boys, some more sleazy than others. Nealy's group may have been naughty, but, if they were, no one ever knew about it. They were the so-called, nice girls. They even chanted:

"We don't smoke and we don't chew and we don't associate with those who do!"

Yes, those were the good old days. Life had been so simple then. Now that Nealy had been on her own, she had realized just how easy her life really had been during the days of her youth. The little things that had seemed so life shattering back then, seemed so silly now.

The gym looked great. Some of the graduates from all five classes, including all of Nealy's closest friends, had been at the gym all day decorating. Nealy wanted to help, but she had decided to spend what time she could with her parents since she would be spending most of the weekend with her friends. They had even rounded up a jukebox to play some of the greatest hits from the sixties during the band's intermissions. Everyone ran around kissing and hugging old friends, telling one another how fabulous they looked. Several of the guys that had been such nerds in high school had blossomed into fine looking young men, and some of the jocks that had been *really fine* had changed for the worst in only five years. A circle of old friends gathered around Nealy, talking and laughing about their lives after high school. The lights were dimmed, the music played, and the band sang an old Elvis favorite *"Can't Help Fallin' In Love."* In the middle of the conversation, Nealy completely lost her train of thought when she looked across the crowded room and there stood Jerrod Jones.

At the same moment, Jerrod saw her and immediately made his way across the room. He wanted to hug her, but he wasn't sure at this point just how receptive she would be. "Could I have this dance?" he asked instead, putting his hand out.

"Sure," she smiled, taking his hand and following him onto the dance floor.

Jerrod tried to talk above the music, but he felt as if he were shouting. "I'm glad you came. I was afraid you wouldn't since you live so far away. You do still live in New York?"

"Yeah, but Kati Sue said that everyone was expecting me, so here I am," Nealy responded, leaning closer to him to allow him to hear her over the band. "How is medical school going?"

"Good. In September I'll start my cardiology rotation, and I'm really looking forward to it. Right now, I'm working in Obstetrics and Gynecology. I'd give up medicine if that was my only choice," he said, making a face that made Nealy laugh. "Neal—short for Nealy—you can't imagine the patients that I have to treat. With the medical school being part of John Sealy Hospital, we get all kinds. Last week I had a patient that weighed at least three hundred pounds. This woman was so fat that she didn't even realize she was pregnant.

I'll be glad when this service ends."

The song ended, but Nealy and Jerrod were still dancing and laughing. "Jerrod, you never did have any patience, and you won't if you don't change your attitude," she teased. "I think we need to work on your bedside manner before you take the Hippocratic Oath."

"I can't help it, Nealy, it's the truth. If I never see another pregnant woman again, it'll be too—"

"Forgive me for interrupting, but people are staring at us." Giggling, Nealy looked at her classmates and gestured that she and Jerrod were crazy by pointing her finger at her brain and making a circle. "Come on. I want you to say hello to the gang."

"Do we have to?"

"Oh, come on," she insisted. "Hi, guys, look who I found," Nealy said, pulling Jerrod over to where her friends were talking.

Betty Lou tugged on Rhoada's arm, pulling her close enough to whisper in her ear. "Oh, great, Dr. Jekyll." Not to hurt Nealy's feelings, Betty Lou smiled and addressed Jerrod, trying not to sound too sarcastic. "Well, well, if it isn't J.J. himself. Our one and only, *Mr. Ball High School*. Or is it Dr. Jones now?" she said, smiling.

"Not yet. I've got another year of medical school," he answered, but he didn't smile. There had never been any love lost between Jerrod and Nealy's friends, but because they all loved Nealy, they at least tried to be civil to one another.

Betty Lou leaned over to Rhoada again and whispered, "No, it's Mr. Hyde," and then she looked at him and smiled a very forced smile.

Nealy gave them her humorous account of Jerrod's service in ob/gyn, which made them laugh. It felt good to be back with the old gang. She and Jerrod spent the rest of the evening together, dancing the way they had in high school. A former jock, Jerrod danced like a gorilla: shoulders and knees raising up and going down at the same time. The more beer he drank, the lower his knees got to the floor. Regardless of the song, except for the slow songs, that was the way he danced, while everyone else, except the other jocks, did the swim, the twist, the monkey, the watusi, the hop, the bump, and the hulley-gulley the right way. Nealy avoided looking at him because it hurt his feelings when she laughed. There were prizes for various categories, and Nealy won the prize for traveling the longest distance and most likely to succeed. Her old classmates teased her about becoming a big star, and later saying, "Galveston? Where's that?" The lights in the gym came on, which meant what it had always meant: the dance was over.

All of the girls in Nealy's crowd had planned on a slumber party at the Jack Tar Hotel. They had spent *Senior Night* there five years before, and they looked forward to staying awake until four or five o'clock in the morning reminiscing, much the same as they had back then. The girls huddled in front of the gym to decide who would ride with whom to the hotel. After breaking up, Nealy looked for Jerrod to tell him good-bye. Of course, he had waited nearby, so she didn't have far to look.

"I'm riding to the hotel with Betty Lou. Are you going out with the guys?"

"Yeah, I think we're going to shoot some pool. We'll probably drink a few beers, bullshit a little, and then go home. The same old stuff we used to do. Can I call you tomorrow?" he asked, his voice soft, almost pleading with her. "Would you be my date for the party tomorrow night?"

"Jerrod...maybe we shouldn't," she said. But when she saw the disappointment in his face, she smiled. "But, what the hell. Maybe we should for old time's sake."

"Yeah," he smiled, "for old time's sake.... Neal, you *do* remember the good times, don't you?"

"Sure, I do, silly. We were together for a long time, and I remember lots of good times...and some not so good. But, Jerrod, that was kids' stuff. Teenagers thrive on the pain and suffering and heartbreak. It's all part of growing up. A little fighting here and there keeps things interesting. I hope that we've grown up enough to put those times behind us."

"Neal, it'll be good to be alone with you again. Just to talk like we used to do." Their eyes met, and he wanted to kiss her, but he didn't dare. Jerrod knew her too well to push her.

"Jerrod, as I recall, we did a lot of things when we were alone, but talking wasn't one of them," she blushed. "I need to go. So, come on. Walk me to the car."

Outside the car, Nealy kissed him sweetly on the cheek. "See you tomorrow." Then she slid into the front seat.

Betty Lou peeled out of the parking lot, honking the horn in their secret code: *beep....beep, beep, beep, beep, beep...beep, beep!* The girls screamed and hollered, just as they had done after the dances and the football games. In the hotel room, Kati Sue popped the cork on the bottle of champagne to celebrate being together again. Slipping into something more comfortable, they emptied their overnight bags, and within minutes the room looked like a disaster area. Clothes, curlers—spongy pink ones and bristled ones in all sizes—shoes, nylons, make-up, and more girl stuff was scattered from one end of the room to the other. Settled into comfortable positions throughout the room, they laughed and talked about the people they had seen at the dance. They were amazed at how some had changed for the good, while others looked far beyond their years already. Thoughts of boys they had kissed or made out with made them screech with remorse. "Gag me," they screamed. They reminisced about some of the slumber parties that they had during high school. Once at the England's house, Nealy put on Grandma England's dress, which had to be a size twenty-something, and she stuffed the enormous bust with clothes, towels and pillows to fill them out. Then, she strutted around the room like *Gypsy Rose Lee*, singing, "*da, dun, dunt, dah…dah, dunt, dun, da, Let me entertain you, let me make you mine.*" As she sang, she yanked the stuffing from her bosom, hurling each piece around the room. So, when Nealy decided to go to New York, none of her friends were the least bit surprised. Her energy was endless, and entertaining meant everything to her.

The girls cleared the middle of the hotel room so that they could imitate the guys dancing. It was getting pretty silly, but it was fun doing stupid things again, acting as if they had found a way to recapture their innocence. Not all of them had attended the same college, so Betty Lou insisted on Nealy sharing the story about the time Jerrod invited her to his college fraternity party, and the pride of their fraternity, the newly chosen sweetheart, passed out, falling face first onto a floor that was covered in beer, wine and everything else wet and gross.

"Well, let me tell you, it wasn't a pretty sight," Nealy grimaced. "When those guys lifted her up by her armpits and placed that crown on her head while booze dripped from her hair and face and the band played 'She Is So Beautiful,' I was appalled. And Jerrod—what a guy—he joined in with the rest of those assholes who screamed and shouted insulting remarks. I was embarrassed for her and for myself for witnessing such inhumanity. I asked Jerrod to take me home. He refused. So, I left. I tried to call Betty Lou at her dorm, but no one answered. Then I called a cab to take me to the bus station, and I returned to Nacogdoches alone."

"But that's not the best part," Betty Lou said, eager to finish the story. "Jerrod called me the next morning at six o'clock. Let me tell you, he was extremely pissed off, demanding to talk to Nealy. Now that scared me. But then Kati Sue told me that she had gone back to Nacogdoches. Anyway, when he found out she wasn't there, he went berserk, shouting, 'Your precious friend is an immature, naive bitch. She made a fool out of me in front of all my fraternity brothers for the last time. Her disappearing days are over! But, I'm glad she left. Her holier-than-thou attitude makes her a real party pooper. So, in case she's interested in knowing what I did about it, you can tell her that I went home with two other girls that really knew how to party. They covered my body with whipped cream and licked it off. Just tell her that it turned me on far more than she ever did.' "

The girls screamed with laughter. "He said that?" one asked.

"But, wait, there's more. I said, 'Oh, you poor, poor thing, J.J.' Then I said icily, '*You fucking idiot*, Nealy's not into whipped cream. The last guy she told me about covered himself in hershey bars. He got so hot the chocolate melted all over his body. And you know how much Nealy *loves* chocolate.' At that point, he called me a few choice names and hung up on me. I loved it!" Betty Lou's dramatic accounting—slowly licking her lips—made the girls scream and roar wildly; even Nealy. But, of course, he later claimed that he'd made up the whole story because he had gotten so angry with her for leaving. And, as always, naive Nealy believed him. Unfortunately, she and her friends were all too good for their own good most of the time. So, in an effort to tarnish their reputation, they would chant *"damn, hell, shit… plop…plop!"* Who knows where the *"plop"* came from, but it became a well-known word around school. So, they made it mysterious and, maybe naughty; they hated being called *Miss Goody Two Shoes*.

For the most part, the night had been pretty wild and crazy, but the girls did spend some time talking seriously, too, about their husbands and their children —everyone except Nealy.

CHAPTER SIX

THE SUN SHINED through the half-drawn drapes, not at all disturbing the lifeless bodies stretched out on beds, chairs, and every inch of the floor. The telephone rang. Lauryn, the only one who heard it, searched through the debris for its whereabouts. Half-asleep, she managed a weak "Hello." Then in a response to the voice on the other end, she tossed the phone toward Nealy who slept on the floor nearby with her head buried under a pillow.

"Nealy," Lauryn said, barely above a whisper. "It's for you." Gayleen heard Lauryn and nudged Nealy with her foot a couple of times before Nealy raised her head out from under the pillow. Slowly, she reached for the phone.

"Hello," she said, trying to sound awake, as people usually do when they answer the phone out of a dead sleep.

"Good morning, Sunshine," Jerrod said pleasantly.

"Hi. What time is it?"

"It's almost ten."

"Oh, my God, I can't believe it's that late." Nealy spoke quietly, trying not to wake the others.

"How about lunch or a late breakfast?"

"I'm too tired to eat, but okay. Pick me up at noon at my parents' house."

"Now promise me that you won't go back to sleep."

"I promise."

"See you at noon," he said softly. Jerrod had been awake since six thinking about her. He wanted to call her earlier, but he knew what she and her friends did when they got together: talk, talk, talk all night long. So, he dosed on and off, giving her a little more time to sleep. And besides, he wanted to be rested, too, for the long day ahead. He had stayed out until three o'clock swapping stories with his buddies. Naturally, they had all bragged and lied about all of the gorgeous women who couldn't keep their hands off them in college or about their collection of worldly goods, like the brand new nineteen-seventy-one Chevy Corvette which they had left at home so it wouldn't get banged up in the parking lot.

Jerrod drove into Nealy's driveway. When he glanced up at her bedroom window, it made him think about the nights when he went out with the guys, got drunk, and proceeded over to her house to throw rocks at her window.

Nealy would sneak downstairs and quietly open the front door. "Have you been drinking?" she asked, whispering.

"No," he whispered back. But his amorous attitude and the smell of beer always gave him away. Jerrod pleaded with her to let him stay. "Please, Neal, just for a little while," he would say.

And Nealy, too in love to turn him down, would give in. "Okay, but only for a few minutes." They'd fool-around until things got too close for comfort and fear brought her to her senses. At that point, and in spite of his pleas, she had to send him home; motherhood was not on her immediate agenda.

But Jerrod never gave up easily. "Oh, Neal, please, ten more minutes," he whined. "Okay, five...two." Well, he always lost the battle, but he didn't lose the war; he didn't go home, at least not directly. His aroused and drunken condition found him seeking the affections of other girls. So, he would cruise the various hangouts about town and pick up one of the *faster girls*; guys who got turned down in their peak of passion by their prudish little girlfriends were always on the make. The memories made him smile, but now he felt guilty for deceiving her. Maybe he *had* grown up.

Standing at the front door in anticipation, he rang the doorbell. When Nealy opened it, she looked prettier than ever. The kelly-green skirt and blouse that she had on made her eyes even more green. And everything else matched perfectly, from her hair clips down to her shoes. "Am I green or what? I believe you call me *Miss Coordination*," she giggled sweetly.

"No, I call you *Sunshine*, remember?" he smiled. Her beautiful face and her bright cheery smile could light up the earth.

"Oh, that's right. How quickly one forgets," she teased, inviting him inside. "So, have a seat. I need to change my purse and I'll be ready." Jerrod had been there so many times over the years that he made himself at home while Nealy went back upstairs. But, with less than a minute on the couch, he decided to *really* make himself at home.

Appearing in her doorway, she smiled at him. "And just what are you doing up here?"

"I'm lonely down there by myself." He walked toward the closet where Nealy stood. When she turned around to hang up her robe, he pressed himself against her back and slowly moved his arms around her waist. "Do you realize that this is the first time that I've ever been in your bedroom?"

"That's right. My daddy had rules that made the bedrooms off limits to the opposite sex. It's probably a good thing. Knowing you, not only would you have been in my bedroom, you'd have been in my bed."

"I would have done my best," he quickly responded, pulling her closer.

"Jerrod, you haven't changed—"

Jerrod spun her around, pressing his lips tightly against hers to silence her. Between kisses, he whispered softly, "I've missed you."

Nealy wanted him, too, but feeling uncomfortable, she pulled away from him. "Jerrod, maybe we need to think about things before we get romantically involved again. We put this behind us once already. It's too painful," she said softly. Looking at his handsome face made it so difficult to resist him. Nealy had always had a strong physical attraction to him and obviously still did. He had a head full of thick, silky black hair and long dark lashes that surrounded his deep blue eyes. His stare held her gaze like a magnet. Just looking at him made her tingle.

"Nealy, I can't help it. I'm still in love with you. I dated a lot of girls after you left, but I kept comparing them to you. I tried to forget you, but I couldn't," he said, pulling her closer to him and kissing her again.

Again, she pulled away from him and cried out, "Jerrod, we can't do this yet. I need some time."

"But, Neal, please—"

"Jerrod," she said, her voice shaking. "I don't want us to get hurt again."

"Okay," he said, smiling, "I won't push you," he promised, taking her hands in his. "Would you like to go to Gaido's? You always loved their crab salad."

"I'd like that." Relieved, Nealy smiled at him. She didn't want to fall so quickly, but she didn't know how long she could deny her feelings.

Gaido's served them a wonderful lunch while they talked about their lives. Proud and interested, Nealy asked him about his life as a medical student. She even insisted on the gory details, quietly, of course, not to offend the other patrons. Their conversation wasn't really appropriate for lunch, but it excited him so that she had to let him talk. Jerrod's eyes danced as he discussed his seventy-two year old Mexican-American male, his assigned cadaver in lab, that he used in tracing the circulatory system. Nealy found the details rather morbid, but she enjoyed seeing him so happy.

When Nealy's turn came around, Jerrod never took his eyes off her. He appeared happy for her and fascinated by the busy life that she had in New York, even though he felt jealous because he could see how much she liked it. Holding hands across the table, their hearts pounded from the memories of times gone by. Future plans of both were discussed, but nothing personal was said until Jerrod finally broke down and asked her if she had ever regretted breaking their engagement. Nealy looked at him, but she didn't say anything.

"Uh, not that I'm trying to rush you two lovebirds or anything, but can I get you anything else?" the waitress asked for the third time. "I can see that you're enjoying each other's company, but maybe you'd like some ice cream or coffee or something?"

Nealy felt her face flush. "I don't, thanks," she said, smiling up at the waitress who had a mass of ratted curls piled up on top of her head. "Jerrod, do you want anything?"

"No, I'm full, thanks. So, Neal, we better go." After more than two hours, they left the restaurant. Jerrod insisted on taking her over to his house, which, of course, was his way of telling her that he wanted to spend some time alone with her. Jerrod gave her the grand tour of his small apartment that definitely needed a woman's touch. The furniture, a brown couch and chair, a table with two chairs, two bar stools, a bed, a desk, and a chest for clothes, had zero personality. There were no pictures, except for a wall that had been mirrored with marbled-mirror squares, no plants, one lamp on his desk, and very few dishes. Nealy wondered why his mother hadn't helped him decorate. But, knowing Jerrod, he probably hadn't told her where he lived, he insisted on his privacy. The darkness, his choice for sure, created a cozy atmosphere for sleeping and making love.

Jerrod sat down on the couch. Luringly, he looked up at Nealy. While staring deeply into her eyes, he slowly pulled her into his lap. As always she couldn't resist. Her heart pounded. He kissed her passionately over and over again. Mindlessly involved, Nealy didn't notice Jerrod unbuttoning her blouse and lifting her bra up over her breasts; the soft moistness of his mouth against hers had her undivided attention. When he pushed her long, silky hair away from her face and neck, she took a deep breath. Her chest grew full with feeling. Slowly, she rolled her head back, giving him permission to caress her soft, porcelain skin. Jerrod knew just how to touch her, to excite her to a point of no return. He wanted complete control of her emotions. And he knew exactly what to do and how to do it. As they made love, the world ceased around them.

"I love you," he whispered, snuggling her against his body.

"I love you, too." Tears rolled down her cheeks, which she quickly wiped away. Nealy didn't want him to notice her tears for fear that he would mistake them for tears of sadness instead of contentment; it had been so long for her. Wanting to cuddle, she curled up in his lap and wrapped her arms tightly around his neck. "Neal, what will become of us?"

"I don't know," she responded quietly, trying to hold back the tears. The thought of not being with him made her sad.

Wanting to put what she felt into proper perspective, Nealy quickly sat up. "We need to get ready for the party."

"Oh, not yet. Please, Neal, I don't want to go. I don't want to share you right now. Please, stay with me," he begged, pulling her close to him. Softly, he kissed her neck, his warm breath reeling her back into his arms.

"I'd love to, but Jerrod, we really have to go to the party. I promised I'd be there. We'll be together," she assured him, trying desperately to resist the temptation of making love again. But, it felt good. Nealy wished that she could capture this moment and make it last for the rest of her life. New York wouldn't matter; in fact, nothing would matter. Many nights during the past year, she had thought about Jerrod and the many things they'd shared. They grew up together. She had given her virginity to him. And when they went off to college, they had written to each other every day. They never dated anyone else, or, at least, she hadn't, not in an intimate way. The thought of spending her life with someone else had never entered her mind, and that had not changed. Nealy wanted so much to tell him how she felt, but she couldn't because her goals were still important to her. But how important were they? More important than being with Jerrod? Being with him now, after being in New York, might make her change her mind, but she needed to be sure. It wouldn't be fair to give him false hope. But, it frightened her to think about leaving for New York and possibly not ever seeing him again. Being near him, feeling his heart beat, and sensing his strong desires for her made her want to say to him, "To hell with New York, I want to be with you!" but she couldn't. She had to control herself. Somehow, she had to be strong. Nealy pulled away from him, attempting to adjust her clothes. "I really need to go."

Firmly, he pulled her back. Softly, he spoke, his lips barely touching hers. "I need you, Neal. Don't leave me. Make love to me again," he pleaded, sliding her blouse off her shoulders. When the tightness snapped from around her chest, and the soft cotton brushed across her bare skin, her heart beat faster. Nealy could no longer resist him or her desires. At that point, her movements were second nature.

Tugging at her arched body, he shuddered when her hair stroked his exposed thighs like a feather. His chest tightened as she dug her fingers into his hard skin. He closed his eyes to increase his sensuality. Tightly, he squeezed her buttocks, pulling her closer. His mind raced wildly. He lusted after every part of her body; he couldn't get enough; he wanted more and more and more.

After several deep breaths, they stretched out on the couch and fell asleep in each others arms.

When Nealy awoke, she gathered up her things. Kneeling down beside the couch, she shook him gently, "It's time to get up."

Opening his eyes, he smiled at her. "I've been up twice. Can't you get enough?"

Turning red, she shrieked, "Jerrod—"

"Hey, it's okay. I'm not complaining. I like the new sex crazed Nealy," he said, pushing her hand down to cup his most prized possessions.

"Jerrod, you're the sex maniac," she giggled shyly, jerking her hand away. "It's just been a long time, that's all. But for now, I gotta go," she said, patting him lightly on the chest.

"And just *how* are you going?"

"I'm taking your car," she sassed, blowing him a kiss from across the room. "I'll be back at seven."

"Do we have to go?"

"Yes, but, if you're a good boy, we can leave early," she giggled, rolling her eyes and shaking her head.

"Yes, *mommy-dearest.*"

CHAPTER SEVEN

THE BALLROOM at the *Hotel Galvez* had been chosen as the perfect setting for the greatly anticipated main event. The hotel, known to the native Galvestonians as The Grand Old Lady of the Seawall, had been built in nineteen-eleven and faced her first major storm in *nineteen-fifteen*. The violent storm brought death and paralyzing destruction with her brutal forces of one hundred and twenty mile-an-hour winds, driving rains, and massive flooding that received national attention as a devastating disaster. But the Galvez proved to be as strong as a fort, yet graceful and statuesque in all her high and mighty refinement. Without a doubt, every graduate of Ball High School felt at home nestled in the bosom of her beauty and elegance.

The night air was salty and damp, and the moon was full, supplying the romantic mood for the occasion. The people gathered inside, selecting their favorite foods from the buffet table. The smell of the sea had been brought indoors with platters filled with shrimp, lobsters, oysters, crab, gumbo, and several seafood dishes created by the chef. The band, playing from the stage area at one end of the room, sang their version of Herman's Hermits' tune *"There's A Kind Of Hush."* Memories stirred. Some people had gathered out on the terrace to feel the breeze off the ocean, in spite of the warm, humid air from the mid-summer heat. The walls were decorated with memorabilia—pictures of students, teachers, and places; pompons, posters for the Tors to stomp the Stings; go Tors; pep rally: three o'clock in the gym; bonfire tonight at six-thirty before the game. Balloons, painted with the letters, BHS, floated above the table tops that were decorated with streamers of purple and gold. The noise level increased with the shrieks of one lost friend spotting another across the room. Some guests danced, while others just listened to the music. As the band finished playing *"Sweet Little Sheila,"* the 1966 Class President, Walter Hare, who had coordinated the reunion, made his way up to the stage to make some announcements.

"Ladies and Gentlemen, may I have your attention," he shouted to be heard over the noisy crowd. "It's wonderful to have so many distinguished guests from Ball High School—Classes of Sixty-four, Sixty-five, Sixty-six, Sixty-seven, and Sixty-eight." The crowd cheered loudly. In an effort to regain control, he put his hands up. "Okay, okay. And for those of you who missed the party last night, we had a great turn out, with lots of laughs, and, from the way my body felt today, a lot of booze," he said, making a face and holding his stomach. The crowd roared with laughter and made comments to one another about Walter being the same funny guy that he'd been in high school. "Last night we gave out some awards, which, by the way, are posted on the back wall for those of you who couldn't make it. One of the award recipients took home two of the awards: one for coming the longest distance and the other for most likely to succeed. And that honored guest, who I'm proud to say is with us again this evening, is none other than Miss Nealy James, Class of Sixty-Six!" he shouted, clapping his hands, encouraging the crowd as they clapped and cheered. Not being able to recapture the crowd's attention, he placed his two index fingers between his lips and whistled into the microphone. The sound almost deafened everyone. "Okay, but what I wanted to say before you guys went into orbit is that Nealy came all the way from New York City where she is singing and acting on Broadway. Wait!" he shouted, holding up his hands again. "We would like to ask her to sing once again the song that she sang for us on graduation night, *Over the Rainbow*. That song had such a special meaning to us because we were all leaving high school in pursuit of our dreams. Nealy, please...come sing for us." Walter put his hand on his brow to follow the spotlight that searched for her in the crowd.

"Come on, Nealy Samantha," Betty Lou said, taking her arm and pulling her towards the stage. Nealy begged Betty Lou to tell them that she had laryngitis, but she refused and led her up to the stage. Nealy gave Walter a *go-to-hell* look as he flew off of the stage to join the others.

Nealy picked up the microphone and seriously vowed, "Walter, it's lucky for you that I matured during the last five years, because back then I would have called you an asshole." The crowd lost it, laughing uncontrollably until Nealy put her two little fingers in her mouth and whistled. "Well, since Walter left me no alternative, I'll sing, even though I'm no Judy Garland, but first I need to clarify something—damn, I wish I wasn't so honest!" she exclaimed, causing everyone to roar with laughter once again. "Hey, guys. Let's get a grip here. I'm a singer, not a comedian. It's true that I'm performing in a play, *The Music Man*, but it's not the play you know it to be and it's not Broadway. In fact, it's more like off-off-Broadway. That means twice removed from Broadway, and our audiences are mostly wine-os, hookers, thieves, welfare recipients, and anyone else who can't afford to buy a ticket on Broadway." The crowd roared. "But hey, I shouldn't complain, it's getting better. Why, last week *only* three people were raped, mugged, or killed after the show. So, I hope that if any of you are ever in New York, and if you don't mind risking your life, you'll come see the play," she teased, giggling with the crowd. "No, seriously, guys, it's not that bad, but just don't expect it to be Broadway. I'm having a wonderful time. And I'd love to have you come if you ever get a chance. Now, I'll sing." Nealy turned to face the band and gave them the cue—a smile and a quick nod—to start playing. Her classmates were still laughing and mumbling, but as soon as the music started, a hush fell over the room.

"Somewhere, over the rainbow, way up high..."

The crowd listened with pride as Nealy's crystal clear voice sang the words that Judy Garland had made so famous.

"and the dreams that you dare to dream really do come true."

Jerrod watched intently. How could he ever ask her to give up something that she obviously had been born to do? He couldn't help thinking about how pretty she looked upon the stage and how funny she could be, so natural, so instinctive. Her lovely voice projected, but so softly, barely above a whisper, as she sang the last few words to the song.

"If happy little blue-birds fly beyond the rain-bow,
why...oh why...can't...I?"

Nealy bowed, blushing, her faced turned a brighter red than her hair, but she managed a big smile and blew them a kiss. She was deeply touched to receive such a tremendous applause from her peers. Once again she graciously bowed, then turned and headed down the steps from the stage. These were the people that mattered most to her. Judy Garland's Dorothy was right, "There's just no place like home."

Jerrod was waiting for her. "Baby, you were great. I'm so proud of you." He barely had time to give her a hug before he was being pushed and mashed by the people that were gathering around them, so he decided to move out of the crowd. A million questions were being screamed at her: How did you get your start? Where are you singing? Do you like New York? Some of them even asked for her autograph, which embarrassed her, but they claimed that they wanted to tell their friends that they knew her when. So, from a distance, Jerrod watched her, feeling happy because she was so good, but also feeling afraid that he could never have her.

When Nealy realized that Jerrod was gone, she desperately searched the room for him. She prayed that he could cope with her new popularity. And when she spotted him talking with some of his old football buddies, she felt much better. During school, he had been horribly jealous, but surely he had matured enough to realize that her celebrity status would end with the evening.

The clock struck midnight. The band played their final song, "Yesterday," paying tribute to the Beatles. Couples snuggled on the dance floor for the last dance. When the song ended, they all looked at each and smiled instead of giggling as they had in school. The kids had grown up.

"Neal, you ready?" Jerrod asked.

"Gotta go, guys. See you at the picnic tomorrow," Nealy said, hugging everybody. Jerrod tugged at her arm, and finally they succeeded at making their way out to the car.

"Did you have fun?" she asked Jerrod as they drove out of the parking lot.

"Surprisingly enough, I did. But that's because I was with you. I enjoyed your singing. And from everybody's reaction, you were a pretty big hit. Are you that popular in New York?"

"No, not hardly. In the theater, I'm just one of many with a little part, but at least it's a start," she answered positively. "And at Freddy's, well, I do the midnight show, so I'm mostly singing to drunks. Even if I were horrible, they'd be impressed. It's sort of like the women in the bar, you know, with each drink they get better looking. Well, it's the same principle, I just sound better."

Jerrod laughed, putting his arm around her and pulling her closer to him. "You are coming back to my apartment with me, aren't you?"

"Jerrod, maybe—"

"Neal, you're only going to be here one more day. I just want to hold you. Please, baby."

Nealy sat quietly for a moment, wanting to, but frightened of her own feelings. She had already started to feel sad about going back to New York and leaving Jerrod. "Oh, Jerrod, I'm not sure. We may be moving a little too fast. Maybe I should just go home tonight. We can go to the picnic together tomorrow."

"I know, let's go down to the beach like we used to and talk for a while. We'll take a walk. Want to?" he asked, turning the car around and heading back toward the boulevard.

When they were in school, everyone parked on the West end of the island; the deserted narrow gravel roads leading down to the ocean offered plenty of privacy. Jerrod slowly pulled into their favorite spot and stopped the car. The sound of the ocean roared when he opened the door. Before getting out, they took off their shoes, and Nealy took off her garter belt and stockings, letting the sand sift between her toes. Sand always soothes tired, sore feet, especially after being cramped-up in dress shoes for hours. Jerrod took off his jacket, pitching it into the back seat. Then he removed his bow tie and his cummerbund; he had been smothering in that "monkey suit." The night air felt damp, but the warm breeze blowing out of the South across the ocean made it comfortable. The skies were perfectly clear, and the moon sat high in the sky, surrounded by a milky shadow. The stars, that were never as visible in town because of all the street lights, twinkled by the thousands. The waves rolled and broke as the waters beneath the white cascading swirls were being sucked out to sea by the strong current of the tides going out. Jerrod and Nealy waded along the beach, jumping each wave as it made its final break and raced ashore. They held hands as they walked and talked, stopping frequently to kiss under the full moon; a romantic setting that couldn't help but stir up old feelings.

When they returned to the car, Jerrod directed Nealy into the backseat. As she bent forward, he lifted her skirt to her waist and attempted to remove her panties. "Jerrod, stop it," she scolded, sliding into the seat.

"Come on, Neal, take your clothes off."

"Jerrod, don't spoil the romance."

"I'm sorry. I just want—"

"I know what you want. I want it, too, but first I want to enjoy the mood," she smiled, kissing him lightly on the cheek. The brightness from the moon created streaks of light and shadows across their faces. They stared at each other, exchanging little soft kisses, savoring every moment. "I love you, Neal," he whispered.

"I love you, too," she said, kissing him and wrapping her arms around his neck.

"Baby, raise up," he encouraged, pulling her forward and unzipping her dress.

"Jerrod, please don't rush things."

"I'm not. I just want to make you more comfortable, that's all." He released the hooks on her strapless bra, rubbing her back for a moment where the hooks-and-eyes had left impressions in her soft skin. "Now, doesn't that feel better?"

"Uh-huh," she whispered breathlessly and closed her eyes. Surrendering herself, she yearned for his touch.

"That's my girl," he praised sweetly, baring her chest. As a reflex, she reached up to cover herself, but Jerrod stopped her. Sliding his hand under the fullness of her breast, he entertained the reddish-brown peak until it reached the precise tautness, before moving on.

Controlling her destiny, he single-handedly unbuttoned his shirt and maneuvered it off his broad shoulders. With passion building, he held her face tightly between his hands and covered her mouth with his, pressing hungrily.

Unable to control his emotions, Jerrod tugged at his pants, fighting the restraints of the back seat. His breathing became shallow, almost panicked. Struggling to pull her dress down, and then up, he grew so frustrated that he bunched it around her waist. And then, clumsily, he fumbled with her panties, but time grew even more critical. With seconds to spare, he forced her further down into the seat, pushing wildly against her body in search of warmth. She curled towards him. He cried out. She drew short, shallow breaths. He shuddered. She trembled. He relaxed. She cuddled.

Weak and tired, he slid back and rested his cheek on Nealy's chest. She stroked his hair and softly scratched his back with her long fingernails, sending chills up his spine. The windows had fogged up and the air felt sultry, but nothing stirred them as they lay silent, exhilarated, and contented.

"Jerrod," she said, pushing him up. "I hate to spoil this moment, but there's something stabbing me in the back."

When she raised up, he lifted up his coat. "Oh, sorry. It's the pin from my boutonniere."

"I thought I felt something sticking me—"

"Well, I should hope so," he said, smiling naughtily.

"Jerrod," she gasped, embarrassed by his obviously erotic innuendo. She lay back down, putting his coat over her bare chest.

"Neal, you know we belong together, don't you?" he asked. "We're so comfortable with each other." Jerrod pressed his head against her chest and curled a strand of her hair around his finger. "Neal, do you remember the first time that we *did it* in the back seat of my old Chevy? Remember? I told you that I wanted to marry you someday?"

"I remember. But you also said that you wanted a house with a bed because the car was too uncomfortable. Marriage just made that possible. Or so you thought at the time," she said smugly.

"I'm being serious. I still want to marry you, Neal. I love you."

Nealy sat up. "I love you, too. And someday I want us to be married. I do. But I'm just not sure when."

"Neal, don't go back to New York. I need you. Please—"

"Jerrod, I have to. I have commitments there right now." Nealy turned to face him, adjusting her clothes. She slid onto his lap and wrapped her arms around his neck. And then, kissing opposite cheeks and speaking softly, almost seductively, she said, "But, when the time comes...and we do get married...I want you to promise me that we will always come here and make love in the car."

"Why? We'll have a big house. We can make love in every room. Why come way out here?"

"Well, for one thing, it's our place. It's romantic...it's promiscuous...and it feels great when you get stuck!" she said, grinning at him devilishly.

CHAPTER EIGHT

July 4th, 1971

THE SUN SHINED brightly above everyone who had gathered together for the picnic on the West end of the island at the beach house of Walter Hare, the Class President. Good old Walter. Big mouth Walter. *Mouth of the South*—the nickname that he so readily deserved. But, still, everyone loved him. The smell of hamburgers and hotdogs and pickles and onions filled the air. Eating at the beach had to preserve every organ in the body; with each bite, a person consumed at least a teaspoon of salt, or so it seemed. The food tasted like grit—good grit. But, it's just part of being at the beach, like running into the waves, splashing, building sand castles, playing volleyball, surfing, flying kites, and lying face up and face down to cook the skin a lovely shade of red. The gang took advantage of all the activities. The next reunion, which was already scheduled for nineteen-seventy-six, seemed a long way off, so everyone held on to the last bit of sun before bidding farewell to one another.

The reunion had succeeded. The fact that no one had drowned or experienced any other major catastrophe excited Walter. He just knew that some damn kid would disappear into a wave never to be seen again, or that at least one person would get sun poisoning and end up in the hospital, or that someone would be stung by a jelly fish. Thank God Walter's worst fears were spared.

Nealy and Jerrod had bid everyone good-bye and settled back down on their beach towels. Galveston had been unusually crowded because of the July 4th holiday, so they wanted to relax and enjoy the solitude before heading home. The beach was peaceful. The sound of the ocean had a way of soothing the soul; it pulled it in and out with each wave, reaching deep inside a person to stir every emotion—a lonely person becomes lonelier, a person in love becomes more in love, a happy person becomes happier, and an angry person mellows into place where all that's wrong in the world seems right.

The sun set in the West, tinting the sky gold. Bordered by magnificent shades of pink and red, the dark skies pushed their way down to the water. Night falls. The wind whipped the sand on the deserted beach. The tide rolled ashore, and restlessly the ocean will continue to toss and turn until a new dawn appears.

Nealy and Jerrod arrived back at her parents' house, but no one was home. Nealy removed and read a piece of paper hung on the door. "It doesn't look like my parents are coming back today," she remarked sadly, putting her key in the door to open it.

"Why? What's the problem?" he asked, following her inside and turning on the light.

"This note's from Gloria Pierce. You remember her." He looked puzzled. "Oh, you know, my mother's friend forever. The one that lives next door."

He thought for a second. "Oh, sure. Short, pygmy looking person—"

"Jerrod," she snapped.

"I'm just teasing. She's a real nice lady."

Nealy gave him a disgusted look, and then continued. "Well, it looks like Aunt Ella's hip had to be operated on this morning. I'd better give them a call. I'll have to call Betty Lou to see if she can drive me to the airport tomorrow. Make yourself comfortable. I'll just be a minute. Hungry? If you are, help yourself," she said, heading upstairs to put her things down and make her calls.

Jerrod turned on the television, then sprawled out on the couch to relax. It had been a very busy, exhausting weekend. Nealy joined him a few minutes later, snuggling up next to him. They talked a little, but within minutes, both of them were asleep.

Nealy woke up at ten-thirty and shook him. "Jerrod, it's late. You better go."

"Nealy, come on. I'm too tired. Let's just sleep here."

"I can't let you stay here. What would the neighbors think?"

"Nealy, you're not a teenager. You're a grown women."

"I know, but this is my parents' house. I wouldn't feel right letting you spend the night. I don't want the neighbors calling me a 'hussy.' But surely they know that there isn't any such thing as a twenty-three-year-old virgin anymore," she said, smiling at him.

Jerrod laughed. "Are you kidding? There are very few virgins over thirteen anymore."

"Jerrod, that's terrible...but, it's probably true. Sad, but true. Come on. I feel worse now. You need to go," Nealy said, pulling Jerrod to his feet.

"I'm not going unless you're going with me," he said, folding his arms in front of his chest.

"Jerrod, I have to leave tomorrow. I need to get my suitcase packed. Betty Lou is coming to pick me up early tomorrow morning. I really should stay here."

"Then I'm staying with you. It's that simple. It's your last night here, and I don't even know when I'll see you again," he put his arms around her, pulling her pelvis together with his. "And beside, we have to *do it* at least one more time—"

"Jerrod, I don't believe you said that. I'm being serious."

"Sex *is* serious."

"I'm not *doing it* in my parents' house."

"Then get your things. I'll drop you off in the morning on my way to the hospital."

"Why do I put up with you?"

"Because you can't resist having sex with me."

"Honestly, Jerrod, I think you live for sex."

"So do you. You're just too proper to admit it."

"Proper? Oh, I give up. Let's go."

As usual, Jerrod got his way; they made love more than once during the night, and since he had to be at the hospital at six-thirty the next morning, five o'clock came real early. Jerrod dropped Nealy off at her house at six-o'clock, just in time for her to wave to Gloria who was outside collecting her morning paper.

"Well, hell," Nealy whined. "Isn't that great. Now I feel like a sleazy slut sneaking around while my parents are away."

"Well, you're not a slut. A little sleazy, but that's good," he teased.

"I'm not sleazy, am I?" she frowned, burying her head in his chest.

He lifted her chin and kissed her lips. "No, baby, but you've certainly got potential."

"What's that mean?"

"I'll explain it to you someday. But for now, I have to get to the hospital. Come on, I'll get your things," he said, getting out of the car to take her suitcase out of his trunk. He walked Nealy up to the front door. "I wish you'd change your mind and stay."

"I can't, Jerrod. You know I can't."

"If you say so. But, Neal, I'm here waiting for you whenever you're ready. I'll call you."

"Okay," she said, trying to fight back the tears. "Jerrod, I do love you," she managed to say as he stepped off the porch.

He turned around to look at her for the last time. "Don't just tell me, Neal, show me by coming back," he said, looking very serious. Jerrod stared at her for a long moment.

Nealy could feel the tears coming, and she didn't want to cry. "Jerrod, go. You'll be late. And since I'm looking forward to being a doctor's wife, I don't want them kicking you out before you take that oath." She smiled, trying desperately to hold back the tears. Nealy motioned for him to go, waving as he drove out of the driveway. As soon as he turned the corner, she walked inside and burst into tears.

Nealy showered, letting the hot water spray against her face, soothing her red puffy eyes. It seemed stupid to cry. After all, he wanted to marry her. She's the one who kept saying no. Confused, she continued to waver between her career and Jerrod. It seemed impossible to choose. Time would tell. But for now, she had to get ready to go back to New York.

Betty Lou arrived with her baby, Kimberly, and they quickly gathered up Nealy's things and left for the airport in Houston. The clouds hung low over the Houston skyline, and the morning fog seem to be burning off slowly. Nealy felt miserable, and the dreary day only made her feel worse. Betty Lou sensed her misery and broke the silence, calling Nealy by her nickname. "Hey, Sam, well?"

With a long face, Nealy looked at her. "Well, what?"

"It's me, your best friend since third grade. I know something's bothering you. Is it Jerrod?"

"He wants me to marry him."

"Is that bad?"

"I don't know. I love him. And I know he loves me, but Betty Lou, I'm really confused."

"Neal, is he worth giving up your dream?"

"I don't know. But I miss him already. Sometimes I feel certain that he's the one, that my career doesn't matter. Then, other times, I'm just not sure. We've had some great times, but we've had some pretty s-h-i-t-t-y times, too." She spelled the word because of the baby.

"I know what you mean, Sam. I do. And one day, you'll know, too. Something will happen, and you'll know," Betty Lou said, pulling into the airport.

Nealy hugged Betty Lou and the baby. "I'll write."

"We love you, Sam. Take care of yourself."

"I will. I love you, too. Thanks for the ride," she said, giving them one last big hug.

"Call me if you need me to pick you up at the airport next month," Betty Lou teased, but the tone in her voice insinuated that she would be seeing Nealy soon. Betty Lou kept her thoughts to herself, but she really felt that Nealy would be making a terrible mistake if she gave up her career to marry Jerrod. Maybe, just maybe, he had finally sown his wild oats. Jerrod had always had plenty of women who would die to have him. Betty Lou, a dietician, worked at the medical center where Jerrod went to medical school. Rumors flew about him constantly, referring to him as *Mr. Swim Club*. Betty Lou didn't understand the phrase, but she was sure that it had plenty to do with women and sex.

At the hospital, Betty Lou constantly overheard nurses talking about Jerrod. They talked about him as if he were a god. But, who wouldn't, except for Nealy's close friends who really knew him as a snob and a liar. In high school, the guy had everything—great looks (gorgeous eyes, huge dimples, super body, thick dark hair), athletic prowess, money, (super wealthy parents), intelligence, popularity, expensive clothes, sports cars, charm, and the prettiest girl in school. Even though he obviously loved Nealy in his own way, he always wanted to have his cake and eat it, too. No one ever told Nealy that J.J.—nicknamed by her friends—didn't stand for Jerrod Jones; it stood for *Jackoff Jones*.

CHAPTER NINE

THE RAIN beat hard against the streets of New York as Nealy flagged a cab. After leaving Houston at ten o'clock in the morning and not arriving back on Manhattan Island until almost midnight, she felt completely exhausted. And with the hectic events of the day and the pouring rain, she could easily be mistaken for a homeless person; her clothes were a wrinkled mess and she was wet from head to toe, but even so, she tried to help the cab driver load her suitcases into his trunk that had at least two hundred cans in it.

"I see you collect cans," she said, watching him crush them with her bags. But when the trunk refused to close, he pulled out her bags and then leaped up onto the bumper and stomped the cans to make more room. Nealy flinched at what sounded like an aluminum explosion, and the words *You idiot* almost escaped her lips. Still dumbfounded by the fact that a cab driver had a trunk full of junk, she didn't realize that he had opened the back door for her.

He cleared his throat loudly. "Uh, miss."

"Oh, thanks," she said, amazed that she had traded in a perfectly normal existence for a cerebral-awareness education in a city where sane people dare to roam; what made these people tick would always be a mystery to her.

"Where to, miss?" the cab driver asked.

"On the corner of Eighty-sixth Street and Lexington. Please, God, grant this man thirty minutes of sanity," she mumbled.

"What's that?" he asked over his shoulder.

"Nothing, I'm talking to myself." But she prayed that he wouldn't drive like a maniac in the rain. Of course, that would be too much to pray for since most of the cab drivers in New York only know one way of driving: *out-of-control*. No sooner had the thought crossed her mind when a truck pulled out in front of them. The driver slammed on his brakes, throwing Nealy forward into the front seat.

"Are you okay?" he asked.

"Are you crazy?" she screamed. Her body doubled across the frontseat and her head hung towards the floorboard. "Of course, I'm not okay. I nearly went through the windshield."

"Can I help you?" Nervously, he attempted to help her up.

"No! Don't touch me!" she cried. She slid back over the seat and tried to compose herself. "Okay," she mumbled, taking a deep breath and raising her head up to look at the driver. "We can go now." The driver looked back, staring at her. "Don't look so worried. I'm okay. Really, I'm fine. Shook up, but fine. Just get me home in one piece, please. This has truly been a day from *hell*."

"I'm sorry, miss, but you saw it. That truck pulled out in front of me," he apologized in self-defense.

"I know. It wasn't your fault. I'm sorry I yelled at you. Can we *just* go now? I really want to get home." Nealy smiled at him, trying to hold back the tears that had been building up again.

"Sure," he replied, turning around and slowly pulling out into the traffic. Needless to say, the poor guy, who appeared to be almost as shaken-up as Nealy, cautiously proceeded toward Nealy's apartment. They didn't exchange many words. And Nealy felt bad about screaming at him; after all, it really wasn't his fault.

Pulling up in front of what he believed to be the address that she gave him, the driver asked, "Is this the building?"

"Yes. Thank you , God," she said, opening her door, getting out, and looking up to make the sign of the cross on her chest. Not being a Catholic, she always had trouble remembering which direction went first. But regardless of which way she did it, she felt sure that *God* got the message and graciously accepted.

The rain had stopped, and the cabby jumped out to help her get her luggage, even offering to carry them up the stairs. Normally, a New York cab driver slams on the brakes in front of the house, announces the fare without an ounce of expression, and offers no sign of ever considering any assistance. The fact that they had almost been killed must have moved his conscience. At least one good thing had come from her near-death experience.

"Thanks," she said, taking her bag from the cabby. "Oh, the fare. How much is it?" she asked.

"It's on me, miss," he replied, smiling.

"No, I can't let you do that. But thanks for trying. How much?"

"Sixteen-fifty."

"Is that all? Are you sure? I felt sure you'd charge me double for the excitement," she teased. Even exhausted, her compassion and sense of humor remained true. The cabby laughed, and Nealy stuck a twenty dollar bill in his pocket.

"Thanks, miss. I hope tomorrow is a better day for you."

"Thanks."

Inside, she quietly opened the door, trying not to disturb her roommates in the middle of the night.

"Nealy, is that you?" Denise asked, raising up in her bed.

"Yes, it's me. I'm sorry to be so late, but it's a long story."

"Call Jerrod. He's called at least five times tonight."

"I'm sorry," Nealy said apologetically. "I guess he's worried. I should have been home this afternoon, but…I'm lucky to be here at all. Go back to sleep. I'll tell you all about it tomorrow."

"Okay, but make sure you call him. I told him I'd have you call the minute you got home," Denise said, rolling over. Nealy started toward the telephone when it rang again. "Sorry, guys," she quietly apologized, grabbing the phone.

"He's got it bad," Denise mumbled, pulling the covers over her face.

"Hello," Nealy whispered.

"Nealy, thank *God*. When did you get in?" Jerrod asked. "I was really worried."

"I'm sorry. I just walked in the door. It's been a long day, but I finally made it."

"Are you alright?" he asked.

"Well, to make a long story short, my flight out of Houston was canceled because of mechanical problems, so they put us on a flight that left three hours later. And then *that* plane had some sort of electrical problem—the lights flickered and bells dinged for two hours, so we had to land in Atlanta. And after waiting there for two or so hours, we were finally put on another plane. And due to the inclement weather, we had to circle over New York for almost an hour before we landed at JFK. And then, if that wasn't enough, a truck almost hit the cab that I took from the airport and I landed in the front seat. Other than that, I'm fine. So, how are you?" she exhaled, out of breath from spitting out her tale of woe.

"I'm better now that you're home," he sighed. "Neal, I can't take this. I miss you already."

"I miss you, too. But I'll be home for Thanksgiving."

"Well you can't miss me too much, that's five months away."

"I know, but it'll pass—"

"You mean to tell me that we spent all weekend fucking our brains out and you want to wait five months before we see each other again! I'm sorry, Nealy, but I don't get it. You said 'you loved me.' Isn't that what you said?"

"I do, but I'm not sure—"

"Not sure about what, Neal?"

"About marriage. Us. Your career—"

"Neal, baby, don't do this to me, to us. We love each other. I need you."

"Jerrod, please give me some time. I'm…so tired—"

"I'm sorry, Nealy, please don't cry. I know you're tired. Get some sleep. I'll call you tomorrow. We can talk then, okay, baby," he said softly, sorry that he had upset her.

"Okay—"

"Neal, I love you. Do you love me?"

"Yes."

"It's going to be alright, baby. We'll work something out, okay?"

"Okay."

"Now get some sleep. I love you."

"Good-night." Nealy clutched the phone with both hands, holding it tightly to her chest for a moment before slowly hanging it up.

Alex lifted her pillow and exposed her face. "Nealy you're crying. What's that asshole done now?"

"Geez. I can't believe it. She slept through hours of thunder and lightning, and now she wakes up," Denise complained. "But since we're all awake, what did the asshole do?"

"It's nothing. I'm just tired. Y'all go back to sleep. I'll explain it tomorrow."

Over the next month, things returned to normal. But Jerrod called Nealy every night, even when she didn't get home until three a.m. And sometimes they talked for an hour. Nealy told Denise and Alex that she didn't plan on going home, but they knew she missed him. Nealy talked about the reunion, filling them in on all the details, even the most intimate ones, without, of course, getting down to the bare facts about the time she'd spent with Jerrod. They were like sisters and shared everything. Nealy even told them that she loved Jerrod, but that she wasn't ready to make any decisions about her life yet. She felt confused and torn between wanting to go home and wanting to stay in New York.

Unable to hide her feelings, Nealy knew that her friends at the theater could sense her confusion, especially Claudia Biaugus, one of the dancers in the play who had become good friends with Nealy. Claudia was a beautiful twenty-five year old half-Black, half-French woman, with soft, black curls, one blue eye and one brown eye, and light olive-colored skin. Growing up in Biloxi, Mississippi, was not the safest place to live for black folks, but Claudia escaped the heat –*literally*—from the Klan followers because they were not exactly sure about her nationality. With aspirations of becoming an actress, Claudia moved to New York the day after graduating from high school. But because of her accent, a strong Southern drawl combined with Black jive-talk, she hadn't had much success with acting; however, being an incredible dancer, she made lead dancer in the play. Since Claudia and Nealy were both from the South, they looked out for one another, and lately, Claudia had noticed a change in Nealy that concerned her.

"Honey-child, are you okay?"

"I'm fine, Claudia. Why?" Nealy asked, hoping that she wouldn't force her to pour out her heart about things she wasn't sure about.

"You've lost that spark."

"I have not," Nealy snapped. "I may be a little tired, but I haven't *lost* anything, Claudia."

"Yeah, you have, honey-child. I've seen that look. You're in love with Jerrod." She put her arm around Nealy's shoulder.

"Okay, I do, but I love my work, too. Claudia, I've wanted to be an entertainer all my life. I'm really confused...but it'll pass. I wish I hadn't gone home for that damn reunion. I wouldn't be in this mess," she whined.

"Nealy, if a girl loves her man so much it hurts, she ought to be with him. I ain't tellin' you what to do, but that kind of love doesn't come along too often."

"I know, but I need to be sure. That's why I came back. I don't want to make a mistake. My heart says one thing and my brain says another. I keep thinking that one day I'll just know what to do, that something will happen to give me a sign."

"Well, honey-child, if I wuz you, I'd be between them sheets with *my man*. I'd be snugglin' up close and keepin' him warm on cold nights. Nealy, he's gonna be a doctor, for crissake. He can give you ever' thin' you want. Let's face it, honey-child, this business has its moments, but it's a tough way to make a livin'. Why would you want to follow a dream that's so hard to follow when you could have ever' girl's dream. Nealy, this isn't some bum. He's a fine man. A man who loves you. You gotta give your heart a chance. Who ever heard of brains warmin' up the bed on cold nights," she said, smiling at Nealy and giving her a big hug.

"Thanks, Claudia, but it's just so hard to give up your dream, even for another one. You're a great friend," she said, hugging her back. "I'll think about what you said. I promise."

On Friday, August the fifth, Nealy rushed backstage to remove her headdress, curl her hair, and get dressed in order to get to Freddy's on time. She had just climbed under her dressing table to unplug her curlers when she heard Claudia screaming for her.

"Nealy! Where the hell are you?"

"I'm under here."

Claudia raced towards the back of the room and pulled Nealy up from the floor. "What's your man look like, honey-child?"

"What man?"

"Jerrod. You dumb shit. What's he look like!" Claudia screamed, shaking Nealy.

"Well, he's about six-two, dark hair, and big blue eyes. Why? What's going on?" Nealy questioned, her face quickly turning a lighter shade of pale.

"Someone asked for you. A beautiful man. He's waitin' outside the stage door. I got so flustered when he asked where he could find you that I forgot to ask his name. Geezus, Nealy, if that's him, you're a damn fool, *girl*, lettin' him get away."

"Oh, God, Claudia, it couldn't be him. Why would he be here? How do I look?" she asked, looking in the mirror. "I'm so nervous. Come with me, Claudia," she said, pulling Claudia by the arm. "Now this is stupid. Why am I so nervous? If it's Jerrod—but, Claudia, what if it isn't? Then who is it?"

"Nealy, come on. Let's go see. I'm right behind you." Claudia walked behind her like a mime until they got to the door. Nealy opened it and slowly stepped outside, closing the door behind her. Claudia waited until she couldn't stand the suspense any longer, and then, she opened the door and peeked out. Nealy must have recognized him because Claudia had never seen kissing like that between strangers. After Nealy had kissed and hugged him for what seemed like five minutes, she noticed Claudia's head sticking out the door and her mouth hanging open. Nealy turned and motioned for her to come out.

"Jerrod, this is Claudia Biaugus. Claudia's the lead dancer and one of my very special friends."

"It's nice to meet you, Claudia," he said, shaking her hand.

"If *she* won't marry you, I will," Claudia blurted out. "Excuse us a moment, Jerrod. We'll be right back," Claudia said, pulling Nealy aside and whispering to her. "Honey-child, this is what I call a hunk. The answer is 'Uh-huh, honey.' Got it," she scolded. "Come on. Let's give that man what he wants."

"Nealy, it's obvious that Claudia knows what's best for you. And I happen to agree with her," Jerrod said, walking over to Nealy who stood quietly next to Claudia. Jerrod took Nealy's hand, knelt down on one knee, reached into his pocket, pulled out an engagement ring, and carefully placed it on Nealy's finger. "Nealy, will you marry me?"

Nealy stood there, speechless, staring at her finger. When her eyes met Jerrod's, her face lit-up. *That moment* had finally come and she knew *exactly* what she wanted to do.

"Jerrod, I can't believe this," she cried, and then she smiled at him.

Jerrod stood up. "Well, is that a yes?"

"Yes! I'll marry you," she cried, throwing her arms around his neck and kissing him. When they finally heard the cheering of the crowd that had gathered around them, they froze, and then slowly turned around.

"You can't back out of this now, Nealy. I have a number of witnesses that heard you accept my proposal," Jerrod said smugly. The crowd laughed and cheered again. They were too excited to consider how sad they would be when Nealy left the play and returned to Texas to become Mrs. Jerrod Timothy Jones, III—'til death do us part.

CHAPTER TEN

NEALY AND JERROD rushed from the theater to Freddy's, grabbing some popcorn and beer to snack on while they watched Jillie finish up her set. Jillie came to New York to be a singer and a stand-up comedian, and, like Nealy, she had also come from Texas and ended up at Freddy's. Jillie had grown up in the very southern part of Texas in a small town bordering Louisiana. Everyone teased her about being a "Texan sprinkled with Cajun spices," which explained her real spicy humor and stage persona. Being of Bohemian descent, she talked about her *colorful* family and referred to them in her comedy routine as *"that damn bunch of bohunks,"* lovingly, of course. Nealy would come in early some nights and finish Jillie's set with her. They were quite the contrast: Nealy had fair skin and light reddish hair, whereas Jillie had brown hair, brown eyes, and to-die-for olive skin that gave her a year-around-tan.

"I really hate you, Jillie," Nealy would say in jest during their playful little word-fights. "Just look at me. Next to you I look like a damned-by-the-devil unearthly-albino. That's *soooo* unfair. Did y'all get it?" she would ask seriously. "You know, like, I'm a ghost...and she's...un-fair." She shook her head and made a ticking sound with her tongue against her teeth. "How sad. You people have no sense of humor," she'd say, but then she'd burst out giggling, which made everyone laugh along with her.

For an even further contrast, Nealy had perfect curves and long legs, and towered above Jillie who was "cute as a button" and petite; she stopped growing before she reached five feet. They called themselves the "Towering Texas Albino and the Stubby Cajun Starlet." The crowd had a great time when Nealy and Jillie teamed together and sang such songs as *"Deep In the Heart of Texas"* and *"The Battle of New Orleans."* Together, they had the audience laughing, singing, clapping, and dancing in the aisles. Crowds came in just to see them, and, naturally, "Papa-Freddy" loved it.

"Nealy, toots, is that you?" Jillie asked, spotting Nealy in the audience—her hand held over her brow to reflect the bright lights. "Who's that gorgeous creature sitting next to you? I hope he's single and likes short Bohemian women with great personalities." The crowd roared with laughter, all except for Jerrod. Nealy hadn't had time to prepare him for Jillie, yet. Everyone in the club began screaming for Nealy to join Jillie, but Jerrod tried to persuade her not to leave him. Finally, she insisted that she had to go and she quickly joined Jillie on stage.

Jerrod was terribly jealous of the life Nealy had made for herself, but he could manage to act like he was enjoying himself now that they were officially engaged and since she would be coming home soon. Even with that, he couldn't wait for her show to end so that he could be alone with her. After all, that's what he came to New York for, not to sit in some sleazy nightclub and watch Nealy make a fool out of herself. Of course, he had to keep his opinions to himself, at least, until they got married; then he could keep her at home where she belonged.

After her set, Jillie decided to join Jerrod for a while. If she spent some time with him, she could decide whether or not he was good enough to marry her friend. "Listen toots," she said, pulling out the chair and taking a seat next to him, "you got any brothers? What about cousins? Since Texas genes are real strong, they can still carry good looks down that far."

"No, sorry. I'm an only child," he answered sharply.

Jillie sat up straight in her seat, put her hand on her hips, and began to lecture. "Now, toots, don't your folks know that it's sinful to stop producing after only *one* kid? Especially one who looks like you. Seriously, toots, it's folks like yours who have caused many a young girl to settle for some ugly guy, completely destroying all chances for a world of beautiful people!" Jillie waited patiently for a response.

Coldly, he replied, "I'll be sure to tell them."

"Tell 'em! Hell! Forget 'em. You and Nealy can start tonight. Produce in masses, that would provide some redemption!"

Smugly, he smiled at her. "Well, Millie—"

"It's Jillie, toots," she quickly corrected him.

Jerrod looked up at her as if she were nuts and said, "Well, whatever. Anyway, that's the best idea I've heard all night. The thought of it gives me a hard-on. Come on, lets go find Nealy. I'm ready to get started." Jerrod pulled her up by the arm, delighted in the fact that his brashness had embarrassed her, even though she was doing her best to appear cool. They found Nealy, who had just finished her set, listening to a joke that Frank the bartender had been waiting to tell her all night. Of course, Nealy didn't really appreciate jokes, but she loved Frank, and it always made him feel good when she listened enthusiastically. So, after everyone stopped laughing, Nealy introduced Jerrod to her friends.

Jillie turned to Nealy and tried to whisper, but she whispered like a cheerleader. "Toots, I'm certainly not above throw-backs, if you get my drift," she said, looking up at Nealy and rolling her eyes up toward Jerrod. "But *that one* will definitely take some work. He has a nasty and somewhat annoying attitude problem," she nodded, turning to give him the once over. "But, he's damn good lookin'. And besides...I like a good challenge." For a moment, she stared at Jerrod coldly, then winked at Nealy and strutted off.

Jerrod wrapped his arms around Nealy's waist and snuggled up to whisper in her ear. "She's nuts. And I'm nuts about you. Can we go now?" Jerrod pulled her closer and nuzzled her ear lobe.

Nealy looked up at him and kissed him softly. "Okay, let's get out of here." Nealy pulled him through the crowd, up the stairs, and out onto the street to catch a cab.

"Where to?" the cabby asked.

"The Waldorf-Astoria," Jerrod answered, putting his arm around Nealy and pulling her closer to him.

"The Waldorf!" she exclaimed. "Jerrod, that's so expensive."

"This is special. It's not everyday that the most beautiful woman in the world agrees to marry me. I want to take you to the best place in town," he said, placing his hand gently on the side of her face and lifting her chin up with his thumb to kiss her. "I love you, Neal."

"I love you, too...Oh, Jerrod, I'm so happy. Will we be this happy forever? God, I can't believe it. We're finally going to get married. Just think. No more getting up at four a.m. No more showers in my bathing suit. No more cab drivers," she rambled. "Jerrod, I know it's right. It has to be right. We've waited so—"

"Nealy," he said, putting his finger on her lips to silence her. "Shut up and kiss me. I mean *really* kiss me." Nealy didn't argue; she kissed him passionately until she realized that they were getting a little out of control in front of God...and a very interested observer in the front seat.

"Jerrod," she cried out as quietly as possible, trying to free herself from his clutches. "Jerrod...the cab driver...he's watching us in his mirror."

"It's okay. I've missed you," he said, trying to keep her attention by kissing her neck.

"Jerrod," she said, pushing him up. Without realizing it, they had slid down in the seat of the cab.

"How far are we from the hotel?" he moaned.

"Not far. Come on. Sit up. Tell me about school."

"Nealy, I don't want to talk. I want to make love to you," he said, trying to kiss her again.

"Jerrod, we're in a cab on Fifth Avenue. You're such an animal."

"That's true. And when animals mate, they don't care who's watching," he said, pushing her back down into the seat.

"Jerrod, stop," she cried. But, it was no use. He didn't stop trying to seduce her until they got to the hotel.

They checked into the hotel and spent what was left of the night in each other's arms making love over and over again to satisfy Jerrod's unrelenting sex drive.

The next morning Nealy and Jerrod had a late breakfast in one of the restaurants in the hotel, talking over their wedding plans while eating the most delicious Eggs Benedict that she had ever eaten. Nealy "oohed and aahed" so much that people began to stare. She felt like *Elly May Clampett*.

"Nealy," Jerrod whispered across the table, "I think I arrived just in time to save you from this life of deprivation. From what I'm observing, this pilgrimage almost cost you your dignity."

"Oh, Jerrod, I'm just enjoying myself. Lighten up."

"Well, it's obvious that you were living on a tight budget."

"A *very* tight budget. In fact, I don't think I'll ever be able to eat another bowl of cherrios or another banana in my life."

"Oh, you can't give up bananas. They're great for honing your skills to perform fellatio—"

"Jerrod!" she cried indignantly, almost choking on her food, "that's so sick, *not to mention* crude and somewhat stilted."

"Stilted, as in stiff, is very good in this case," he said with an air of pompousness. "And it is certainly not vulgar, if that's what you're implying. In fact, it's perfectly natural, *not to mention,*" he mirrored her words, "exceedingly pleasurable. For a novice, such as yourself, it may be a bit awkward at first, but practice makes perfect. So, therefore, my future bride, the bananas stay."

Since Nealy couldn't wipe the look of disbelief off her face, she wiped her mouth with her napkin, and then she used it to cover her face until the three women sitting next to them stopped staring. "You talk about me," she whispered across the table. "People are really staring at you. We need to set a date for this wedding before I change my mind."

"The date's set," he snapped. "I want to get married on my birthday."

"September twenty-third?"

His lip curled up displaying an obvious sneer. "Nealy, I happen to know when I was born."

"Jerrod, that gives us less than two months."

"I can't help it. That's the date," he said, determined to get his way. "I want you for my birthday. I'll bring the bananas."

"Oh, Jerrod, stop. Be serious. How can we do that?" If they got married that soon, it meant that they had a month and a half to plan a wedding. Knowing so many people and not wanting to offend anyone, they knew the wedding would have to be a large one. Nealy couldn't be in New York and in Galveston at the same time, and she had so much to do. The more they discussed it, the more impossible a large wedding seemed.

"If we can't do it, then let's elope tonight."

"Jerrod, we can't do that. You're an only child. Your mother has looked forward to your wedding day since the day you were born."

"To hell with my mother. We're the ones getting married. And we both agree that it will be too difficult to make all the plans by the twenty-third of September. So, I vote for eloping."

"Okay, you win. If it's the twenty-third you want, the twenty-third you'll get. If we keep it simple, we can do it," she said, smiling at him and patting his hand. He looked just like a young boy who couldn't get his way. Jerrod, a very spoiled only child, had mastered the technique of pouting.

"Okay, but I want us to get married on *that* day, regardless of what anyone else says," he relented reluctantly.

"I'll manage everything with the help of our friends and family. You just show up at the church at six o'clock. I'll be the one in white," she teased, leaning across the table to pinch his deeply-dimpled cheek. Jerrod reached up, took her hand, and kissed it softly. He could be so charming, in spite of his arrogance and spoiled-brat ways, even to the point of being very irresistible, especially for Nealy.

"Are you ready?" he asked.

"Yes. I'm stuffed, but it was *so hummm-good*."

"Now don't start that slurping shit again." Nealy stuck her tongue out at him. "Oh, and that's real ladylike." She giggled her high-pitched giggle as he held her hand and led her through the restaurant. In spite of his less than enthusiastic attitude about sightseeing, she insisted on showing him her town.

They caught a cab to Battery Park to take the ferry over to visit the Statue of Liberty. Lady Liberty stood so prominent in the harbor. Jerrod didn't seem to be too impressed, even though as always, it gave her goose bumps. As always, she tried to get a positive reaction out of him. "Wouldn't it be great if we had Kate Smith with us so she could sing 'God Bless America?' Wouldn't that be the ultimate in patriotism?"

Jerrod cut his eyes towards her. "Thrilling. Can we go now?"

"Jerrod, how can you be so unaffected by all this? This is your roots."

"It's interesting, okay. But I've seen enough."

They took the ferry over to Ellis Island, totally against his wishes. But Nealy didn't care, he needed to see these things and she knew she'd never get him back to New York again. He was born on the *Rock—Galveston Island*—and he would die on the *Rock*. As they wandered around the grounds reading about the millions of immigrants that came seeking personal freedom, Nealy visualized her great-grandparents arriving there in the late eighteen-seventies from their native countries of Germany and Scotland.

As the ferry passed the Statue of Liberty on the way back, Nealy took one last long look. "Jerrod, isn't she incredible? I can't get enough of her; she is truly an awesome structure."

Jerrod closed in behind her, his hands slowly following the curves of her body. "I'm holding the only awesome structure that I'm interested in right now. And I can't get enough either."

Stepping down from the bench, Nealy seemed annoyed. "I guess you've never heard of Emma Lazarus, the poet who wrote, '*Send these, the homeless, tempest-tossed to me: I lift my lamp beside the golden door!*' She was referring to our ancestors."

"Neal, I never thought of you as being so literary. I'm impressed," he said glibly, as he put his arms around her and pulled her close.

"Why am I marrying you?" she asked apathetically.

"Because you love me. And because I'm offering you exile from this life of exhaustion and poverty—'*Give me your tired, your poor, your huddled masses yearning to breathe free, send these, the homeless, tempest tossed to me: I lift my lamp beside the golden door!*' "

"You have read Emma Lazarus," Nealy said happily. "Now, Dr. Jones, I'm the one that's impressed."

Nealy took Jerrod to 20 Broad Street, off Wall Street. This he had to enjoy because he had a certain affinity for the finer things in life, which, naturally, took a lot of money. Nealy knew for certain that there were two things that Jerrod Jones never intended to do without: Money and Sex—and not necessarily in that order. Money had always spelled success in Jerrod's family, and they had plenty of both. Nealy led Jerrod through the busy Stock Exchange that had been founded in Seventeen-ninety-two by twenty-four brokers who had grown tired of trading on the street corners. The rooms were massive, filled with people frantically buying and selling securities. The walls were filled with television screens that flashed information in vivid colors. Jerrod finally got a pulse; he actually showed signs of something resembling enthusiasm as he watched the nation's system at work.

Nealy wanted to take the subway back to the hotel so that he could see what it was really like to live in New York. Millions of people road the subway to and from work everyday, and it had become a new way of life for her. And although she hated to admit it, she would actually miss it.

They caught the Lexington Express to Fiftieth St., which was quite an experience for Jerrod. Then they walked over to Park Avenue and back to the hotel. But before going inside, Jerrod pulled Nealy aside, pinning her against the wall. "Miss James, soon to be Mrs. Jones, I'm going to make you the happiest woman on the face of the earth. I'll worship the ground you walk on," he whispered, holding her face between his hands. Jerrod kissed his future bride, and she kissed him back. Love was in the air as they stood pressed together as one on a sidewalk in New York.

They made love until Nealy left for rehearsal. And later that evening Jerrod attended the play again since it would be the last time that he'd ever see Nealy perform—other than the duties of a wife and a mother someday.

When they got to Freddy's, Nealy left Jerrod at the table and joined Jillie on stage. When Freddy noticed Jerrod sitting alone, he made his way through the crowded room. Since he had come to love Nealy like a daughter, he wanted only the best for her, so he wanted to make sure that Jerrod's intentions were honorable and long-lasting. But, after spending an hour with him, Freddy had some reservations. For once, he had to keep his opinions to himself because he could never spoil Nealy's happiness.

After the show, Nealy joined them, telling Freddy all about their past and about their plans for the future. Neither Freddy nor Jerrod mentioned the "father and son talk," and reluctantly, Freddy gave them his blessing. Deep down, Freddy could see that Jerrod loved Nealy, but he also felt as though the "pretty boy" loved himself equally as well, if not more.

"Let me warn you, young man," Freddy said. "If ever you hurt my little Nealy, I'll send one a my boys to break your legs." Not that Freddy had any boys, but he wanted to put the fear of *God* in Jerrod, just in case he got a little too rich and good-lookin'.

From the look on Jerrod's face, Freddy knew that he had gotten the message. He could see that this rich-kid didn't relish the thought of having the crap kicked out of him in a dark alley. Freddy knew just how to bluff this one, or, at least, he thought he did. But, he'd been fooled before, so, who knows, this guy may be dumber than he looked. Maybe that's why Nealy felt the need to protect him.

"Oh, Freddy, don't. You'll scare him half to death," she said, putting her arm around his shoulders and giving him a kiss on the cheek. "Jerrod, don't listen to him. He's kidding. We call him 'Papa Freddy.' He's an over-protective, self-appointed father figure. Really. He's teasing. Freddy, tell him."

"Nealy," Freddy said, staring at Jerrod, "there will always be a place *here* for you." Freddy turned to Nealy, reached over and squeezed her hand. Then he picked up one of the five glasses of wine and toasted the future bride and groom.

As they waited for the cab outside of her apartment, Jerrod hugged Nealy tightly. Although they didn't look forward to this brief separation, they accepted it, because very soon they would be together forever. Nealy referred to her impending position as a *"sadie,"* meaning married lady in Yiddish. Jerrod's cab pulled up to the curb. And after giving Nealy one last kiss, he climbed inside. Sadly, she turned and walked about five steps, and then, with a burst of energy, she spun around to bid him farewell with a little song and dance.

"Sadie, sadie, married lady, that's me!"

Nealy took her bow. As the cab rounded the corner, she blew him a kiss, and he disappeared in a yellow flash.

A couple of people standing nearby clapped, so she curtsied once more. Nealy never failed to take time out to be gracious to an audience, but, for now, she needed to get going. There was so much to do and so little time, that is, if she didn't back out.

CHAPTER ELEVEN

ALL OF NEALY'S friends were thrilled for her in spite of how much they would miss her energy, her wit, and her smile. They had grown to love her and respect her talent; in time she could become a big star—only now that could never happen. Denise and Alex threw a bridal shower for her in the hall outside their apartment. Every tenant on the floor had no choice but to attend because the doors to their rooms had been blocked off with chairs and streamers. Laughter filled the large hallway each time Nealy opened another embarrassing gift such as bright red edible underwear, a large dildo shaped like a man's erect penis with spikes on it, black crotchless panties, and a large book with explicit illustrations for sexual positions. Nealy blushed and said, "Oh, Jerrod will love these gifts, especially this sex manual. I know he'll insist on trying out every position."

The director cast another actress in Nealy's place at the theater, and the large cast and crew had a going-away party for her after her last performance, showering her with more pleasure seeking apparatus and articles of clothing. And even though it's the thought that counts, Nealy didn't share her friend's enthusiasm for such items, nor did she anticipate using them.

Nealy found it hard to say good-bye to the many people that she had come to know over the past year. It made her sad. "Stay in touch," the production manager said, hugging her. "Nealy, you have a lot of potential. I wish you'd reconsider." Before rushing away to take care of some details for the next performance, he gave Nealy one last pleading look. "Oh," he turned and shouted, "I'm just a phone call away if you ever change your mind."

"I'll remember that, Oliver. Thanks." For the first time since Jerrod asked her to marry him, Nealy had doubts. A queasiness crept over her, and she wanted to cry. Did she really want to do this? Nealy leaned against the wall. Why did she feel so empty and so afraid and so lost?

"Honey-child...Nealy!" Claudia shouted. "You look like you're a million miles away. I'm so envious of you. Marrying a gorgeous doctor...and gettin' the hell out of this rat race."

"Claudia, are you sure I'm doing the right thing?"

"Absolutely. Anything beats comin' to this damn theater at five-thirty every morning, rain or shine. Hon, it's nuts, what we do," she snapped. "Nealy, you do love him, don't you?"

"I do, Claudia, but I'm giving up my life long dream."

"Oh, honey-child, everybody gets cold feet when it comes to marriage. That's a *big* commitment, but you two kids are in love. It's obvious. You'll be fine," Claudia said, hugging her.

"Thanks, Claudia. I'm really going to miss you. You *will* come to see us in Texas, won't you?"

"Honey-child, you know I will. I want you to find me one of those rich, drop-dead-gorgeous doctors like yours."

Nealy giggled loudly. "Wait a while, I may give you mine."

Even though Nealy was laughing, she felt afraid and uneasy. She had a definite case of cold feet. Desperately, she needed to be cheered up, so she took the subway home with her friends from the theater. What had normally been a subway car full of tired, worn out dancers became a lively party. They passed around a bottle of cheap brandy disguised in a brown paper bag. They were loud, singing and cutting up and making the most out of their last ride together. Once Nealy became Jerrod's wife, the wife of a doctor, she would have to act more dignified. Her past would seem rather juvenile, but she would certainly never forget the friends that she had made and the many wonderful hours that they had spent together. Her dream, well, she had traveled far seeking stardom, and, to some extent, she had found a little part of it. Now she had another dream, however, at the moment her insides were tossing and turning as if she were trapped in the middle of a nightmare and couldn't wake-up.

The next day, Nealy got up early to take care of a few things before she met Tony Rose for lunch at the *Top of the Six's* on Fifth Avenue. She arrived early and asked the hostess if she could admire the view from the windows since it would be her last time, except for occasional visits later on. It was a beautiful summer day, and the sun glistened brightly over the city. The panoramic view from the restaurant was breathtaking. New York came to life as Nealy spotted the Statue of Liberty, the Plaza Hotel across from Central Park, the NBC Building, the Hudson River, St. Patrick's Cathedral, and the Empire State Building. Before Nealy could complete the roll call of the splendid places that brought her such joy, knots formed in the pit of her stomach and tears filled her eyes.

"Boo!" Tony said, tapping her on the shoulder.

Quickly, she turned around and put her arms around his neck to avoid eye contact. She didn't want him to see the tears that she couldn't stop from rolling down her cheeks.

"Hey, Nealy, are you okay?"

"I'm okay. Just a little sad, I guess."

"Does this mean that you might stay?"

"No. It's just hard, that's all," she said, pulling away and digging through her purse to find a tissue. Tony handed her his handkerchief.

"Thanks. I'm sorry, Tony, for being such a baby."

"You're not a baby. Like Shakespeare says, '*Parting is such sweet sorrow.*' And, anyway, I know why you're sad. You're going to miss *moi*," he said, pointing to himself and smiling.

"Oh, Tony, I'm *really* going to miss you. I'm going to miss all my friends. The play. Freddy's. And even Freddy, too."

"Sir," the maitre d' said, "your table is ready."

"Oh, thanks. Nealy, you ready?" Tony asked her sweetly.

"Ready as I'll ever be," she smiled. They weaved their way through the restaurant to be seated next to the window.

Seconds later, the waitress appeared. Nealy didn't acknowledge her, so she turned to Tony. "Something to drink, sir?"

"Two glasses of your house wine, please," Tony ordered, while Nealy gazed out the window. The waitress handed Tony two menus and walked away. Tony tapped Nealy on the shoulder with the menu to get her attention.

Nealy took it. "Thanks," she whispered, and then she began to stare blankly at the menu.

Perusing the menu, Tony glanced up occasionally to look at Nealy. When the waitress returned for their order, Tony cleared his throat, but Nealy continued to stare. "Nealy, yoo-hoo, Nealy, this lady is waiting to take your order," he said, leaning forward and addressing Nealy in a soft, but insistent tone. The waitress stood with her hand on her hip and her lips pursed to one side of her face, staring coldly.

"Oh, I'm sorry...uh...I'll...have...the clam chowder and a small salad," Nealy said, handing the waitress her menu. "Oh, and can I get the dressing on the side?...uh...red-vinaigrette, please. Thanks."

"I'll have the same thing," he said, absent-mindedly handing her his menu. "Nealy, are you sure you're alright?" Tony asked.

"I'm sure," she smiled.

"I've never seen you so distracted."

"I have a lot on my mind, that's all." The waitress brought the two glasses of wine and placed them on the table. "Wine? What's the occasion?"

"A toast to the future that I think, you think, you want," he replied rather sarcastically. Tony didn't understand her decision at all. They talked about her future as an actress because he hated to see her quit at this point in her career. Even though Nealy had some doubts about her decision, she had to convince Tony that she had made the right choice, and she owed it to him to listen to whatever he had to say on the subject. They had become very good friends; they hung out and jogged together several afternoons a week. While they ran, Tony shared stories about the stars he'd helped during his short career and the rewards of the business. Because of Tony, Nealy had come to appreciate what she had chosen to do with her life. But it had been much harder than she ever imagined. The truth is simple: Nealy Samantha James had never liked to fight. As a kid, she gave her sister the jacks and the jump rope, simply because she didn't want to fight. And, even as badly as she wanted this for herself, she lacked the drive to fight for it, and it takes that fight to make it in New York. The hardest part, the part that makes her want to tuck her tail and run home is that, even for someone with exceptional talent, the great, the gifted, the *Helen Hayes' of the world*, it takes a lifetime to make it on Broadway.

"Tony—"

"Nealy, please, just give it more time," he interrupted, pleading with her. "Think about what you're giving up. I wouldn't say this if you had *just* average talents. It's true, it takes years for some. New York is full of people roaming the streets, dreaming about becoming a star. But, Nealy, they don't have it, goddammit it, you do!" he said, embarrassed that he seemed to be losing his cool. "Sorry, I'm just frustrated. But I know you can do this. It's just a shame to see you throw it all away."

"Tony, thanks for believing in me. I love what I do. And, at times, I even think I'm pretty good. But the truth is that I either love Jerrod more, or this is not my real passion. Or maybe it's timing, and I'm just not mature enough to make this type of commitment. But all I know is that I have desperately wanted two things in my life: to come to New York and to marry Jerrod. I've tried this and loved it, but now I want to be with him. Tony, I've loved him since I was only fifteen years old. Please try to understand. You've been a wonderful friend, and I can't tell you how much I appreciate everything that you've done for me. When I get home, I'm going to help Miss Janik. I'll take some young dreamers under my wing, and when they're ready, I'll send them to you. That's what Miss Janik did for me, and I was fortunate enough to find you. You helped me fulfill my dream, Tony, but now I need to fulfill Jerrod's dream. I promised him. I owe it to him, Tony. Because, you see, a year ago, I chose this life over him. And even though I'm dying on the inside for some unknown reason—God only knows what that is, I guess—I have to keep my promise. Who knows. God's probably scratching his head," she giggled slightly, giving him a goofy, cross-eyed look. "Tony, I have to go home. But what if I'm doing this for all the wrong reasons? Oh, Tony...it's just so hard for me to say good-bye to you, to this life," her bottom lip quivered. "But," she took a deep breath, "okay, on a lighter note...it's coming. Just give me a minute. Thank God, it's here," she exhaled, sighing heavily. "Because I'm going to miss 'moi' over there," she pointed to him, "you know I'll be back, at least for a visit." Nealy placed her hand over his, and even though she had tears trickling down her cheeks, she managed to smile at him.

"Sweetie, I understand. I do, but you're just *so* good. I just hate to see you give it up, especially now when you're just starting to get some recognition—"

"Tony, please. Trust me on this one. I could be making the biggest mistake of my life, but I don't think so. It's something that I have to do. I *want* to do it."

"I trust you, Nealy, but I just want so much for you."

"I know, and I love you for it."

As Tony and Nealy ate their lunch, they discussed the projects that he had been working on for his other clients. Nealy felt somewhat uncomfortable giving him all the details of her wedding, but she did anyway, wanting to share them with him. She even invited him to the wedding, but she let him know that she would understand if he couldn't make it.

Tony didn't get to meet Jerrod when he came to New York to ask Nealy to marry him, and he really wasn't sure that he wanted to. Tony had been sweet on Nealy ever since he laid eyes on her, but he wouldn't allow himself to pursue his feelings because of their agent-client relationship. But, if he had ever felt that maybe she wanted something more, he would have said, *"Forget this agent-client, non-fraternizing bullshit"* and thrown himself at her feet. He would have appeared foolish, but she would be worth it. Unfortunately, that had never happened and now it certainly never would since she was about to marry someone else. He almost wished now that he had wined and dined her a little more, that he had let her know how he felt, but he hadn't, so it's all *"water over the bridge"* or however that saying goes. Well, at least, he knew that she thought of him as a very special friend, and he always wanted her friendship. Special people like Nealy James didn't come along too often.

The lunch had been special, and it gave him the opportunity to sit across from this beautiful creature, to have her all to himself, to talk with, to laugh with, and to just enjoy her company for what could be the last time. He hoped not, but if she were married to him, he wouldn't let her out of his sight. And that's probably going to be Jerrod's sentiments exactly.

After they finished lunch, they headed south on Fifth Avenue towards Tony's office. Nealy had to sign some papers releasing her from her contract, against Tony's better judgment.

"You know I'm here if you change your mind," he said seriously.

"I'll remember that you said that," she said, smiling on the outside, her heart pounding on the inside. It was as if she were saying good-bye to one of her best friends and not knowing when she would see him again. People sometimes just go away. Nealy hugged him tightly, but she quickly pulled away, not wanting to cry. This was the final curtain call on her dream. "I'd better go, Tony. I'm going to miss you, but I'll be back. I promise. If you can come for the wedding, I'd love to have you." She gave him one last quick hug. "Bye, Tony, I love you for everything."

"Bye, Nealy, I love you, too...and more than you'll ever know," he said under his breath as she walked towards the door. He wanted to say so much more, but he just couldn't. She had tried so hard not to fall apart. So why make matters worse for both of them. No, he had to let her go. After all, it's her life. If things didn't work out, maybe she'd be back.

Nealy stepped into the hall, but, before she closed the door, she looked back, waved and smiled at him and his gum chewing receptionist, Brenda. She just kept telling herself that she'd made the right choice. Her teeth had practically locked from trying to stifle her tears, and she could barely breathe. The second she stepped outside, she threw herself up against the brick wall and burst into tears. But then, in the middle of her outburst, she felt someone tap her on the shoulder. Too embarrassed to look, but curious to know who would actually show signs of concern for her in a city where people rarely stopped to help someone being mugged, she turned around and came face to face with two little old ladies.

"Miss, are you alright?" one of them asked sweetly.

"Yes, I'm fine. But thanks for asking," she answered, tears still rolling down her cheeks. Nealy took another kleenex out of her purse and wiped her eyes. She smiled at them, and they turned away from her slowly, whispering to one another.

As they walked away, Nealy overheard them saying. "I'll bet the poor little thing's pregnant—"

"And that son-of-a-bitch won't marry her!" Looking back again, they nodded to each other in complete agreement.

Shocked at their perception, as well as their language, Nealy stood there with her mouth open, but nothing came out. As they disappeared into the crowd, Nealy actually giggled. How had they arrived at that conclusion? Did a public outburst constitute unwed motherhood? Amazing, although terribly amusing. Nealy couldn't stop giggling because of their incensed expressions that spelled Evil; only a man *spawned by the devil* could jilt a young woman carrying his child. They probably couldn't wait to tell their friends: a bunch of gossiping old biddies who went to Bunco parties and played canasta, bridge and scrabble. But, thanks to them, Nealy had regained control of herself and blended back into the crowd.

The bright orange sun had moved behind the gigantic buildings and created strange shadows where it peeked through. Even though she didn't need her sunglasses, she put them on to cover up her face after seeing her reflection in a store window; *Mama is u-g-l-y.* Then she looked at her watch. It was only four o'clock, but it seemed much later. On her last night in New York, Denise and Alex were taking her to the Majestic Theater to see *Fiddler On The Roof,* and then to Toot Shor's for a farewell dinner. On her way to catch the subway at Forty-Second and Park, she stopped for the light on the corner of Thirty-Fourth and Fifth Avenue. Suddenly, she heard someone scream, "Look how far away it is!" Nealy saw a young boy pointing up towards the cloudless skies. Instinctively, she glanced upward. And once again, her eyes filled with tears as she gazed up at the Empire State Building. Forever, she would remembered what the first time on this corner had meant to her, and now, until the end of time, she would remember her last.

Adding some comfort to Nealy's decision, the play featured a man and a woman who had been matched by their parents to wed. In spite of the fact that they had married without a courtship, they had learned to love each other and lived happily-ever-after. So her marriage should be that much and more; she and Jerrod had the advantage of years of getting to know each other and sharing a mutual respect, as well as being very much in love.

After dinner at Toot Shor's, Denise talked Nealy and Alex into having just one more drink in the bar. The only seats available were at the bar, so the three of them climbed upon the stools and ordered another drink. When the bartender placed their drinks down in front of them, Denise insisted on a toast. This would make her fifth toast—one with each margarita. "To love and marriage and Nealy pushing a baby carriage."

"Well, love and marriage, but I'm not too sure about this baby carriage thing yet," Nealy replied, lifting her glass and toasting. "I want kids someday, sure, but I want to wait a few years. I can't see myself as a mother just yet."

"You'll be a great mother," Alex said. "You love children."

"I know, but I want to spend time with Jerrod first. We've been apart for a year. We need to make up for lost time."

"Well, you know what I think?" Denise said, spilling her drink on Nealy's arm. "Oops, sorry. I think—"

"I think you've had enough to drink," Nealy replied.

"Don't patronize me, Sammmm," she slurred, taking a drink. "Now let me tell you what I think. Not what you think."

Nealy winked at Alex. "When she calls me Sam, it's usually not good," she shook her head. "Okay, Denise, what do you think?"

"I think that Jerrod is a *horny little devil* who'll make up a year in the first seventy-two hours!" she burst out laughing.

"And I think it's time to leave," Nealy said, tugging at Denise's arm.

Pulling away, she gulped-down the rest of her drink. "I'll have another one, please."

"Denise, I think you've had enough already."

"Hey, bartender, what's your name?"

"Brian."

"Okay, *Brian*, ignore her, please, and give me another drink."

Nealy winked at him. "He thinks you've had enough, too, don't you, Brian?"

Denise raised-up on the barstool and pulled the bartender's head down next to hers. Cheek to cheek, she attempted to whisper in his ear. "One of my best friends is going back home to Texas to marry the biggest asshole in the world—and I do mean the *biggest*. So, see, I need a drink."

Seeking approval, he addressed the man sitting at the bar next to Denise who had unavoidably overheard her loudly-whispered plea. "What do you think, Doc?"

The well-dressed man had a cute baby face, dark blonde curly hair, fair skin, and incredible blue-gray eyes. When he smiled, his eyes sparkled brilliantly. Leaning forward, he peered past Denise to intentionally make eye contact with Nealy. "I think your friend probably knows you a lot better than I do.

And...anyone that pretty wouldn't be unfairly judgmental about a good friend. Is she the 'best friend' that you were referring to?" he nodded at Nealy.

"That's her," Denise acknowledged, glancing around. Suddenly, she detected this mutual-admiration-type-thing happening between Nealy and the good doctor. "Hey, wait a minute. She's taken. But me, I'm free as a bird," she shouted, jumping up and flapping her arms in the air.

They all laughed loudly for a minute before Nealy got up, trying to avoid the attractive man who continued to stare at her. "Well, I think this proves my point, Denise. So, it's definitely *bye-bye-birdie* for us now." Still giggling, Nealy forbid herself to exchange one last glance with the very cute *Dr. Somebody*— why hadn't she introduced herself? Now she would be forever trying to match a name with that sweet face. Pushing her friend towards the door, she vowed not to look back...but then, flirtatiously she turned and smiled.

The next morning, Nealy got up and dressed. Alex cooked a going-away breakfast, while Denise nursed her hangover with a handful of aspirins and a hot water bottle. After they ate, Nealy called the cab. "I want you both to be in my wedding. Promise me you'll come."

"We promise. You know we wouldn't miss it," Denise replied painfully.

"I'm going to miss you both so much. Y'all will let me know what's happening with your careers?"

"You'll be the first to know if anything big comes along," Alex promised.

"I know you're both going to become big stars." Afraid that she would start the water works again, she tried not to drag out her good-bye-scene this time. They embraced, huddling together until they heard the cab's horn.

"Nealy, it won't be the same around here," Alex said, her eyes filling with tears.

"Oh, now, don't do that, Alex, you'll make me cry. And contrary to popular belief, *I'm not pregnant*," Nealy said in jest. She had shared her story about the two little old ladies with them at dinner the evening before, so they all laughed. Arm in arm, they walked Nealy downstairs to her cab. "Well, this is it, guys, but I'm not going to cry." Nealy gave both of them one last hug and ran down the sidewalk to the cab. To keep her wits about herself, she just kept mumbling "I'm definitely not going to cry. I'm not...I'm not...I'm not going to cry."

The girls waved wildly as the cab driver pulled away and Nealy rolled down the window to wave back one last time.

"See you in a month!" Denise screamed, then she grabbed her poor aching head. The cab turned the corner and Nealy was gone.

"I hope she's doing the right thing," Alex said, shaking her head and frowning.

"Me, too. She deserves so much," Denise sighed. "I had to get drunk to bear the thought of her marrying that snobbish, lying, cheating, perverted, no good son-of-a-bitch. Oh, hell, my head is throbbing."

"See what happens when you say bad words," Alex snickered.

"Alex...shut-up. You hate him as much as I do."

"No...I hate him worse!"

Denise laughed. "Alex, don't make me laugh. It hurts."

They laughed, but they were both sad and depressed. Even though Nealy seemed convinced that Jerrod was ready to settle down and be the perfect husband, they were still having trouble accepting it. As hard as they tried to put the past behind them, they couldn't forget their college days and what a love-'em-'n'- leave-'em ladies' man he had been.

Denise and Alex had both gone to the University of Texas for two years, the same school Jerrod attended. Jerrod had been a big shot on campus, and girls went totally *gaga* over him. They threw themselves at his feet, and he certainly hadn't been known for ignoring their advances. Several reliable sources shared their intimate stories about their nights of rapture with the very accommodating "campus stud." Both Denise and Alex watched and listened as some of the girls on their floor hung on the telephone in the hall of the dormitory for hours, calling him, crying, and begging him to see them. The ones that confided in Denise or Alex had no idea that he had a girlfriend, and since they didn't know the arrangements between Nealy and Jerrod in regards to dating, it wasn't their place to tell them.

For any football or fraternity function, Nealy had always come to Austin to go with him. In fact, that's how Denise and Alex met Nealy. Denise and Alex roomed next door to Betty Lou and Kati Sue England. Whenever Nealy came to see Jerrod, she always stayed in the dorm with Betty and Kati. Returning to the dorm after curfew, the five of them stayed up until all hours talking. Nealy never said too much, but it was obvious that she loved him. Neither Denise nor Alex knew her well enough to get personal, but they knew that Betty didn't care much for him, in fact, she couldn't stand the "two-timing-son-of-bitch." She said many times how she prayed that Nealy would meet someone at Stephen F. Austin and fall madly in love with him so she could personally tell Jerrod to drop dead or worse. Of course, they noticed how Betty kept her opinions to herself whenever Nealy came to visit. Nealy never questioned Jerrod's extra-curricular activities, or maybe she was afraid to ask. People fussed over him all the time, even in front of Nealy. His popularity was obvious, but that isn't unusual for a rich, good-looking jock. Nealy didn't seem to be the insecure type, but even if she were, Jerrod, *king of the smooth-talkers*, could have convinced her that everyone called him *St. Jerrod* because of his undying loyalty to his high school sweetheart. Most people believed everything he said, regardless of how absurd it sounded. He definitely had charisma. Around Nealy, Jerrod acted like a perfect angel, but if the truth were known, he was really a fuckin' wolf in sheep's clothing who had been known to follow many a *little-red-riding-hood* home through the forest to expose every *big* thing about himself.

Over the two years, Alex and Denise became good friends with Nealy, mostly because they all aspirations of going to New York. So, after completing their sophomore year at the University of Texas, Nealy persuaded them to transfer to Stephen F. Austin because of its excellent Fine Arts Department. After moving into her dorm, it didn't take long for them to realize that Nealy had been totally true-blue to the "campus stud," but they didn't have the heart to tell her about his reputation.

During the last two years, Nealy went home almost every week-end, except when she was in a play, at Jerrod's insistence. He had started medical school, and he needed her to be by his side while he studied. It was actually nauseating, but Nealy normally did what he asked her to do. So, if he screwed around during that time, he had to do it during the week, which was exactly what he had done during college. Also, during her last year of college, he asked her to marry him. At the time, everyone assumed that her dream of going to New York had been replaced by impending wedlock.

Denise couldn't believe it when Nealy told her that she had changed her mind and planned to go to New York with them. Of course, they were thrilled and figured that she had finally seen Jerrod's true colors or caught him fooling around, but if she did, she never admitted it.

In New York, she mentioned him occasionally. She said she still loved him, but she wanted her career more. When he called, she always got a little depressed for a few days, but she bounced back. Denise wanted to tell him to leave her alone, or better yet, to "fuck off." Nealy had a lot of talent, and they wanted her to make it to the *big-time*. With the latest development, well, he seemed madly in love with her, so maybe he'd grown up. After all, he was only a few months away from becoming Dr. Jones, and he had come all the way to New York, got down on one knee, and asked Nealy to marry him. Hopefully, for Nealy's sake, the guy had sown his wild oats, because he had certainly left more than his share of broken hearts behind.

CHAPTER TWELVE

NEALY ARRIVED at the airport an hour before her plane would leave for Texas, so, after checking in, she made a few phone calls; life had been so hectic during the past three weeks that she hadn't even had time to call Betty Lou and Kati Sue to give them the news.

"Hello," said a sweet female voice.

"Would you like to wear a peach dress?" Nealy asked.

Betty Lou screamed into the telephone. "You're getting married! Oh, Sam, I'm so happy for you. When?"

"September Twenty-third."

"Next month?"

"Exactly twenty-nine days from today."

"Nealy, how can you do that?"

"With the help of my matron-of-honor, that is, if she accepts. You will, won't you?"

"I'm your best friend. I'd better be!" she exclaimed. "Oh, Nealy, I can't believe it. You're coming home. Thank *God!* I really need you."

"Is something wrong?"

"Oh, no, I've just missed having you to talk to."

"I've missed you, too. And just think, we'll be able to see each other all the time. I'm glad I called, Betty Lou. I was getting cold feet, but I feel much better now. Just wait until you see this ring. You'll die!"

"When did you get that?"

"Jerrod surprised me. About a month ago, he came to the theater, got down on one knee, and proposed."

"You're shittin' me? Jerrod Jones did that? The J.J. that I know?"

"I couldn't believe it either. Listen, I'd better go. They're calling for me to board. I'll tell you all about it when I get home."

"I can't wait to hear the whole story. Call me when you get here. Bye, Nealy," Betty Lou said, excited, but crazy with curiosity. How did he talk Nealy into leaving New York? Well, that was an easy enough question. Of course it had to be his undeniable charisma. That guy could sell ice water to freezing, friggin' Eskimos! That's how he did it. With his charm and an oscar winning performance for his cause, he could get his way with just about anything or anybody. "That J.J. What a guy," she mumbled sarcastically to herself.

Nealy's sister, Lucy, picked her up at the airport and asked her a million questions on the way home. She couldn't believe that Nealy had given up her career to get married.

When they arrived home, the rest of the family was waiting for Nealy, and once again she told the whole story. She immediately asked for volunteers to help her get ready for the ceremony. Her brother, Jim, who had graduated with Jerrod, didn't seem particularly thrilled since he had never been a real Jerrod fan. But Nealy had to do what made her happy, so if that meant having Jerrod for a brother-in-law, he would have to accept it. Nealy's Mother insisted on the whole family being present when she called Jerrod to congratulate him.

Jerrod had been waiting to hear from Nealy, but he hadn't expected to talk to the entire family. On call at the hospital, he didn't have too much to say, and besides, he had always been jealous of Nealy's family. Of course, Gracie went on and on, thanking him for bringing her back home again. Before they hung up, Jerrod asked if they could help Nealy with the wedding since he would be tied up at the hospital until September twenty-first. If he intended to take a honeymoon, which he did indeed, he had to finish his rotation in ob-gyn.

Nealy delegated as much as she could to his three aunts. His Aunt Janey would take care of their honeymoon because she had offered them her cottage in Bermuda. The cottage had been part of her divorce settlement from Dr. Roland J. Randall, the head of Cardiology at the Medical Center in Galveston. When Janey returned home from a trip abroad a few days early, she caught him in their bed with *his* nurse. She successfully cleaned his clock by taking almost *all* of their worldly possessions.

Aunt Ruth offered her enormous Victorian-style home on Offat's Bayou, and her services for the reception, an offer that thrilled Nealy's mother. With the two of them throwing the party, Nealy knew that it would be wonderful. The backyard was larger than a football field and had many different trees, including palm, cedar, weeping willow, oleander—all perfectly arranged to create a park effect. Flowering masses of jasmine, bougainvillea, and hibiscus lined the fence for beauty and fragrance. (Should more flowers be needed, Aunt Sarah Beth, who owned a floral shop, had offered to supply them.) The trails leading down to the bayou were furnished with tables and park benches, and after dark, large, three-globe pole lamps lit the pathway to create a romantic atmosphere. No place could be more perfect for a reception, and Aunt Ruth would spare no expense for her precious nephew.

Nealy's friends and family helped her pick out her dress, and the dresses for the attendants, Betty Lou, Kati Sue, Gayleen, Rhoada, Lucy, her sister, Denise, and Alex.

Nealy's brother, Jim, decided on the attire for the groomsmen since Jerrod had asked him, of all people, to be his best man.

Jerrod's parents took care of the rehearsal dinner and furnished the list of their family and friends who were to be invited to the wedding. Jerrod's mother offered to help Nealy select and address the invitations, and Nealy accepted since Nadine Wexler (one of the richest families in Galveston) Jones had grown up in the pillar of society, knowing all the *do's* and *don'ts* for wedding etiquette. And also, Jerrod's father delegated to his secretary, as well as his mistress for the past fifteen years, Christine Criswell, the tedious task of addressing the envelopes. Christine had beautiful penmanship, and as a participant in the wedding preparations, it would give Jerrod Jones, Junior, a legitimate excuse for inviting her to the wedding. Most people had known about their affair for years. It had merely been accepted because he had never flaunted his affections for Christine in public. He treated her like his secretary—bring me this, get me that, do this, do that, you're a doll, what would I ever do without you. Christine was a beautiful blonde, ditsy, but likeable, friendly and fun. She had *all* the curves in all the right places, and because she was twenty years younger than Nadine, gravity had not yet taken its toll. Most likely she had stroked his ego and created a more interesting sex life for him, and according to Jerrod, Nadine had no interest in sex at all. In fact, one night during a conversation between Jerrod and Nealy about—what else—sex, he took a stand in regards to his father's infidelities.

"Nealy, it's not my Dad's fault. A man needs to *get some* now and then, even at my Dad's age. We talked about it. He said, and I quote, 'I love your mother, but she's pretty stingy with her puss—' "

"Your father said that?" she cut him off, appalled that a man in his position would be so crude, especially with his own son. "Well, at least I know where you got that mouth."

"Oh, Nealy, guys always talk like that. You girls do, too. You just carry on like a goddamn pious princess most of the time."

"I hardly think so, Jerrod. Ladies, except on occasion, try not to be unrefined and offensive."

"Shut-up and offense this," he said, pulling her into his lap.

"Jerrod!" she screamed in that same revolting-tone that really never mattered. Jerrod went right on. Nealy couldn't win against him. How had Nadine lived with these two men all those years?

Nadine, the good-little-girl, having been reared in a proper Southern Baptist family, probably thought that sex, even with her husband, was a bit uncouth, except for the conceptional act of creating a child, of course. And once that took place, well, it should be kept to a minimum, if at all. That was most likely the reason that the Jones' had not produced any more children. Well, obviously, Jerrod had taken after his father who came from a good Catholic family, and he didn't believe in abstinence under any circumstances.

Jerrod's father agreed to work with Nealy's mother on the foods for the reception since he owned and operated a chain of seafood restaurants along the gulf coast. Also, he insisted on making the accommodation and assuming the financial responsibility for all the out-of-town guests. All room arrangements were delegated to Christine. That way he could stand over her, slip his hands down inside her blouse, and fondle her voluptuous breasts while she asked him which hotel would be most suitable for which guests.

Nealy and her entourage of close friends had gone together to select her china, stoneware, linens, stemware, and all the other amenities necessary to set up housekeeping. Eibands, the most expensive store in town, registered her gift list. The girls had a great time shopping for all of the things which they needed to make Nealy's wedding an elegant affair: lace, ribbons, bows, satin, chiffon. They hunted for something old, something new, something borrowed, and something blue. Checking out the sexy lingerie made them giggle and blush as they whispered childishly to one another and held the garments up to their respective parts. Nealy showed them the red nighty, similar to the one that Mrs. Jones had opened one Christmas in front of the entire Jones-Wexler clan, the nighty Mr. Jones had bought for Christine. When Mrs. Jones pulled out the tiny laced top and matching panties, a hush fell over the room. Her face turned as red as the garment, and so did his, but not from embarrassment, from anger. Nealy found it rather amusing, but she dared not laugh; Jerrod enjoyed it immensely, encouraging his mother to model it for everyone, or at least for his father. He urged, "Come on, Mommy, give the man a thrill." Of course, she found it to be in very bad taste.

Jerrod and Nealy had been meeting with the priest twice a week. In order for them to be married in the Catholic Church, Nealy had to undergo classes in Catholicism even though she did not have to convert unless she later chose to do so. The church actually preferred more time for an engagement, but since they had gone together for so many years and attended St. Mary's together, the priest made an exception. Nealy did agree, without reservations, to rear her children Catholic; it wasn't her faith, but it didn't upset her, and it made Jerrod happy. She had been reared with the understanding that as long as a person believed in *God*, denomination didn't matter.

Two weeks before the wedding, the invitations were finally mailed. They read:

Mr. and Mrs. Neal Samuel James
request the honor of your presence
at the marriage of their daughter
Nealy Samantha
to
Jerrod Timothy Jones, III
On Sunday, the twenty-third day of September
at six o'clock in the evening
at St. Mary's Cathedral
Galveston, Texas

The week before the wedding, Jerrod insisted on a dinner for the wedding party and their guests at his father's restaurant, The Jones House on Sixty-first and Seawall Boulevard. The dinner honored his future bride. The menu had been carefully selected for the special occasion. Seafood lovers had filet of trout with sauteed crabmeat and mushrooms in wine sauce; the beef lovers had filet mignon topped with garlic and wine sauce.

Following dessert, a scrumptious Baked Alaska, Jerrod rose, offering a toast to his bride-to-be with a glass of one of the finest champagnes, Dom Perignon, vintage nineteen-sixty.

"Nealy, my darling, I will love you with all my heart. And I will cherish you beyond the beliefs of the most romantic son-of-a-bitch in America!" he said, holding his glass in Nealy's direction and waiting for her reaction. It was obvious that Jerrod had been served several glasses of wine at the pre-dinner reception, as well as during dinner. He looked around the room, chuckling at his choice of words.

Nealy shook her head, "Please, don't laugh. We shouldn't encourage him."

But Jerrod was determined to continue his toast. "I promise to make you happy. And I'm very proud that you chose to marry me. I know that you made the ultimate sacrifice in giving up your career for me, and for that, my darling, I owe you a wonderful life." Jerrod reached down, took Nealy's hand and pulled her up to face him. The room fell silent, with all eyes on Jerrod and Nealy. "I want to make a toast to the most wonderful girl in the world—he held his other hand up to quiet the crowd—not to mention, the smartest, the most beautiful, and a lady in all respects of the word. Let's toast. To Nealy, with all my love." Jerrod leaned down and kissed her sweetly on the cheek. Then he carefully tapped his glass together with hers first, and then turned to continue the toast. The toast carried throughout the dining room, and everyone stood to applause. "Oh, and one last thing. Everyone, please, take your seats." Jerrod looked down to where Nealy had returned to her chair. "Neal, do you think that there may be a chance that we might see even a little bit of cleavage—he gestured with his thumb and forefinger and a squinted eye—in your selection of wedding gowns?" he chuckled, raising his eyebrows wishfully. The crowd roared with laughter, enjoying his playfulness. Nealy blushed, rolling her eyes up at him.

"Well, Jerrod, there *is* a possibility that you may get a free shot of my bare bosoms. So, I guess you'll just have to show up to find out," she said coyly, smiling up at him. "You know, Jerrod, you're a bit fickle." Nealy's face turned red at the thought of her parents being present, but she continued anyway. "Why, just last week during one of our intimate conversations, you told me, and I quote, 'these babies are for my eyes only!' Now, Jerrod, I'm very confused. Do I make them public or keep them private?" Nealy blushed. Jerrod even blushed. The crowd lost control; the women clapped and cheered, screaming, *"That's our girl!"* The men chanted *"Public, public, public!"*

"Wait," Jerrod shouted, whistling an ear piercing whistle above the roar of the group. "Wait! Okay, maybe I did say that, but this is one of those exceptions. I must think of my friends, the guys," he motioned at the men seated around the table. "It's not often that they get a chance to see someone as beautiful as you dressed all in white and looking like a vision of purity and femininity."

"Oh, spare me," Nealy cried. "Jerrod, you're drunk. And you're a big chauvinist." The younger women booed and hissed, while the older crowd laughed, finding the two of them sweet and playful.

"Okay," he shouted. "Maybe, that's only partially true. The real reason is that I want every man in the church to be green with envy of me on my wedding night!" The younger men cheered.

"Jerrod, you're sick. I can't believe I'm marrying you. But, because I've known you so long, I know that this is your sick way of paying me a compliment," she smiled and giggled. Then she stood up and gave him a sweet kiss on the cheek. "You're a big jerk, you know that. But you're my big jerk." The wedding party clapped, oohed and aahed.

But for the most part, it was true. The men *were* jealous and so were the women. Wanting what they have is only natural. The two of them complemented each other in every way. Jerrod and Nealy were both extremely attractive, smart, and talented. Jerrod had plenty of money, a great future as a doctor, and Nealy would be everything that a doctor's wife should be: gracious, charming, beautiful, and a great mother for his children. They were *perfectly suited*—or so it seemed. The strong love between them had become apparent, creating swooning sounds from most the guests as they watched the love birds touching and teasing each other. When Jerrod declined a bachelor party, opting for this dinner instead, he had definitely surprised Nealy's friends. But when he said that he didn't want to be involved in any activities where his future bride could not be present, they found it hard to believe that this was the same guy from years past. When would the real Jerrod Jones, III, come out of the closet?

CHAPTER THIRTEEN

September 23, 1971

THE DAY of the wedding had become total chaos. Everyone ran around frantically attending to the last minute details. The fellows decorated Jerrod's car; he let them do whatever after he cheated them out of a bachelor party. The ladies dressed in the church parlor, and as time grew near, they grew more and more stressed.

"Where are my damn shoes!" Nealy cried, crawling around on the floor to look under the furniture.

"Calm down," Betty Lou pleaded. "They're here *somewhere*. We'll find 'em."

Nealy was starting to panic as she dug through the piles of clothes scattered around the room. "I'm going to look *real cute* walking down the isle in my thongs."

"Are these the ones?" Gayleen screamed.

"Nice try, but I'm the bride, remember? I'm in white. You're in peach." They all laughed, even though they knew that Gayleen was only trying to distract her. Nealy had become a nervous wreck, which was totally out of character for her.

"Oh, shit! Forgive me Lord—addressing the crucifixion hanging on the wall—for swearing, but people can't help it in a crisis. Jerrod took my shoes by the shoe shop to have some pearls sewn on back of them. I guess he forgot to pick them up. Shit! Now what?"

"Nealy, calm down. I know, you can wear mine," Betty Lou said, pulling off her shoes. Her shoes were white because the bottom of her dress had peach and white lace sewn together; the white ones had looked better. "My dress is so long that my feet won't even show. Besides, those damn things were killing me. I guess my feet are swelled. So, for now, I'll just be barefoot and pregnant." Betty Lou looked sorrowfully at Nealy, and then at Kati Sue.

"What?" screamed Nealy and Kati in unison. Then all the girls screamed and gathered around her.

"Why didn't you tell us?" Nealy asked.

"This is your wedding day. I didn't want to steal any of your thunder. And besides, I just found out yesterday."

"Well, you bitch!" Kati shouted. "I'm your twin sister and you didn't even tell me."

"I'm sorry, Kati Sue, but I just wasn't ready to talk about it. Can we drop it for now? There will be plenty of time to talk about it after we get through with this wedding."

"Well, can you at least tell us when it's due?" she asked, annoyed.

Betty Lou hesitated for a minutes. "February Fourteenth."

"Oh, Betty Lou, that's so sweet. Just think. Your very own Valentine's Day sweetheart," Nealy said joyfully. "I'm so happy for you and Beaux."

"At least somebody's happy about it," Betty Lou said ruefully.

"Nealy, it's time," Neal James said, knocking on the door. The girls looked at each other and froze. "Nealy—"

"Okay, Daddy, we'll be right there." The butterflies flew recklessly in the pit of her stomach as she turned to look at herself in the mirror one last time. "Oh, y'all, this is it. I'm so nervous. Maybe I shouldn't do this."

"It'll be fine. We better go," Denise smiled.

Studying Nealy's reflection in the mirror, they all became teary-eyed. Wispy bangs framed her face beneath a crown of delicate flowers, babies breath, and hearts of pearls. The back of her hair had been pulled up into a bunch of loose curls that rested on top of a veil made of long layers of soft, sheer mesh. Her satin gown fit each curve perfectly, as if it had been sewn together with her in it. The sweetheart bodice could have shown some cleavage as Jerrod had requested, but an inset of sheer mesh, stitched with delicate lace flowers and hearts of pearls, brought the neckline up to rest slightly beneath the elegant pearl necklace that Jerrod had given to her. The pouffed satin shoulders gracefully tapered down her arms to form a heart of pearls on the back of her hand.

"Nealy, you look stunning! You look like a fuckin' picture on a bride's magazine!" Betty Lou exclaimed. The girls cracked-up.

"Betty Lou, you're in church!" Kati Sue admonished.

"Kati, don't be so damned sanctimonious," Betty Lou snapped, her eyes tearing. "Just look how gorgeous she looks, and I'm fixin' to swell up like the goddamn *Good-Year Blimp!*"

"Listen to her," Kati Sue said. "A house of ill-repute or a church, it doesn't matter to her."

"Oh, Kati Sue, it's okay. She's upset. Anyway, Jerrod acts the same in both of those places, so she can too. Grandmother James always said that 'God accepts us for what we are. That includes our ignorance and our stupidity. Thank goodness and Amen.'" The girls giggled, and Nealy handed Betty Lou another tissue. "Now Belle, you know there's nothing more beautiful than a pregnant woman," she said, putting her arms around her. Nealy couldn't put her finger on it, but something had to be wrong. Betty Lou had loved being pregnant the first time, glowing the entire nine months.

"Nealy, you're the prettiest bride that I've ever seen. And that's saying something 'cause I looked pretty damn good," Betty Lou said. The girls burst out laughing at her. "Come on. Let's go. I can't wait to see the look on Jerrod's face."

"I guess it's now or never," Nealy said under her breath.

The girls straightened her fifteen foot train of satin and lace and followed her into the foyer of the church.

Here Comes the Bride...........

The organ music filled St. Mary's Cathedral. The stained glass windows had ornate designs that reflected brilliant colors of red, blue, green, and yellow. The walls and ceilings had Gothic Revival detailing. The church marveled in historical affluence, depicting its age. The damp, musty smell resulted from the rock and stucco material that had held the structure together for many decades. The organist played, "Sunrise, Sunset," Nealy's favorite song from "Fiddler On the Roof." Alex Lawson, one of Nealy's former roommates from New York, sang, and her lovely voice echoed throughout the cathedral. Nealy selected this song for her mother and Jerrod's mother. The lyrics expressed the thoughts and feelings of a mother as she witnesses the marriage between her daughter and her daughter's childhood sweetheart. She remembers them as children, comparing them to seedlings that blossomed overnight. And now, they stand before God to be joined as one. How swiftly the years had passed.

The bridesmaids looked just like Scarlett O'Hara on the set of *Gone With the Wind*. The elegance and graciousness so steeped in tradition lived on as these Southern beauties made their way down the aisle. Their peach gowns gathered across their shoulders, cinching the waist to accentuate the hugh tiers of chiffon that flowed femininely over their hoops. The large brim hats in soft peach gave their faces a peachy glow. They carried large bouquets of peach roses and yellow daisies. White candles, surrounded by ferns and chrysanthemums lined the aisle, and the smell permeated the air. Nealy's niece and nephew, Jessica and Jeremy, tossed rose petals to mark the path to the altar.

The trumpet sounded to acknowledge the presence of the bride. The crowd rose. On the arm of her father, Nealy entered the cathedral and walked slowly down to greet her handsome groom. The crowd made soft sounds as Nealy passed. Her eyes sparkled like flawless emeralds when she smiled at her groom who waited patiently at the altar. The sound of sniffles echoed throughout the church. Nealy's fairy tale had come true. Jerrod looked more handsome in his white tuxedo than any storybook prince; more like a god that had been articulately sculptured in Rodin's Paris garden.

As they approached the altar, Nealy's father lifted her veil, kissed her cheek, and placed her hand in Jerrod's. A camera flashed, creating a clicking sound, meriting an expression of disapproval from the Priest.

"Please kneel before the altar for prayer," he said softly.

Afterwards, they rose to repeat their vows. Nealy and Jerrod had requested a less than traditional Catholic wedding ceremony, creating their own simple vows. And since Jerrod's father contributed large sums of money to the church, all of their requests had been granted by the Priest without the aggravation of bureaucratic red tape.

"Dearly beloved: We are gathered here in the sight of God, to join together in holy matrimony, Jerrod and Nealy."

Nealy's heart pounded and her palms sweated as she recited her vows. On her final word, Jerrod raised her left hand and slipped the ring onto her finger. Then slowly, he brought her hand up to his lips, gently kissing her fingers.

"Jerrod Timothy Jones, please recite the vows that you have written."

"I Jerrod, ask my precious Nealy, to be my lawfully wedded wife. I will walk hand in hand with you, sharing every day of our lives together to the fullest. I will love you completely in sickness and in health. For always, my faithfulness will be as strong as my faith in God. I promise to love, honor, and cherish you until death do us part. I will hold sacred in my heart our faith, our hope, and God's greatest gift, our love." Nealy lifted his left hand and placed a gold band on his finger. Holding right hands, they placed their left hands over their right. And together they completed their vows.

"These rings signify a circle of love that will never be broken, and our hands signify the shelter that will protect that love throughout eternity." They turned to the Priest, tears forming in Nealy's eyes. Jerrod removed his initialed handkerchief from his pocket and blotted Nealy's tears.

"Now, what God has joined together as one, let no man put asunder. Before God and this congregation, I now pronounce you, husband and wife. You may kiss your bride."

The organ and the trumpet played. Mr. and Mrs. Jerrod Timothy Jones, III, turned and hurried down the aisle, smiling and waving to their guests as they passed. They couldn't wait to get outside and smother each other with the feelings that had built up inside of them during the ceremony. As they passed through the doors, Jerrod lifted up her into his arms and kissed her passionately. He didn't care who watched, after all, they were married.

After the pictures, they climbed into the limousine to go to Aunt Ruth's for the reception.

"Nealy, you looked so beautiful coming down the aisle that I wanted to make love to you right there in front of everyone."

"Now that would have been a first for Father McKaye. The church bulletin next week would read like a tabloid:

*'ANXIOUS GROOM CONSUMMATES MARRIAGE
IN PLACE OF VOWS—
PRIEST FAINTS AT BIZARRE SACRAMENT!'* "

"Nealy, you're nuts," he said, pulling her legs across his lap. "Where did you get those shoes?—Oh, no, I forgot yours. Sorry."

"That's alright. I wore Betty Lou's. Oh, Jerrod, speaking of Betty Lou. She's pregnant!"

"I wish you were pregnant."

"Jerrod," she exclaimed, shocked by such a statement, "we *just* got married."

"I want us to have lots of kids. I can't wait to rub my hand on your naked stomach and feel our baby kick," he said, running his hand up under her dress to touch her stomach.

"Jerrod, you're embarrassing me," she cried, attempting to pull his hand out from under her gown.

"Oh, no you don't, Mrs. Jones. I have a license that says I can legally and morally touch you anywhere, anyplace, and anytime I feel like it. You're my wife, and," he said, tugging at her underwear, "I want to make love right now."

"Jerrod, the driver," she whispered, noticing the driver smiling at them in his rearview mirror.

"So...we're married. Please, baby...we have time. That reception will last too long, and I can't wait."

"Jerrod, I said, 'No!' Now remove your hand, please," she said, struggling to detach his hand from her thigh. "And I thought you were bad before I married you," she giggled, kissing him.

The limousine proceeded down Seawall Boulevard so that everyone could enjoy the sunset—gorgeous pink and gold skies—but Nealy missed most of it because of Jerrod's unmanageable behavior and his one track mind. "Okay, I'll wait, but let's get this reception over with quick," he said. "Cover your eyes."

"Why?"

"Don't ask why. Just cover your eyes."

"It's not that kinky sex stuff?"

"Oh, for Christ's sake, Nealy, you're so paranoid. I have a surprise for you. Now, cover your eyes."

At the corner of Sixty-first Street, the driver pulled in next to a horse-drawn carriage that Jerrod had hired to escort them to the reception. After the car stopped, the driver got out and opened the door for them. "Can I open them now?"

Jerrod hopped out. "Okay. You can open them."

"Oh, my God, how romantic. I can't believe it. Where did you find a horse and buggy?"

"With money, Neal, you can find anything. Come on. Let me help you." She gathered up her train and climbed out of the limousine.

The wedding party, separated into in *his* and *hers* limousines, complete with champagne, followed the bride and groom. Jerrod had told no one, except his family, about the horse-drawn carriage, and the bridal attendants marveled at this romantic side to J.J.

"Can y'all believe this?" Betty Lou said, watching Nealy climb into the carriage. "Is this the same J.J. that we went to school with? That asshole turned out to be a fuckin' prince!"

"Betty Lou! You're terrible. Is your vocabulary so limited that you have to talk like that?" Kati Sue screamed, cocking one eyebrow in disapproval. Solemnly, she drew a deep breath. "But, it is a fuckin' miracle!" The girls squealed and made tacky toasts to the *new* J.J.

The carriage pulled up in front of the thirty room columned mansion that had been built in the late eighteen hundreds. The smell of fresh paint lingered in the salty breeze. The grounds were immaculately manicured. Red carpet had been placed on the sidewalk between the circle drive and the front door for the bride's entrance.

"Jerrod, you're spoiling me," Nealy said, placing her hand in his. Stepping down, she knew exactly how cinderella must have felt.

Most of the guests had arrived and were out on the terrace—the patio to ordinary people—eating elaborate hors d'oeuvres of all shapes and sizes. Huge trays of food were displayed throughout the area. Food to compliment individual taste had been provided—shrimp, lobster, crab claws, beef kabob, chicken fingers, steak fingers, egg rolls, oysters, seafood gumbo, finger sandwiches of assorted meats, and even peanut butter and jelly for the kids.

"What are those?" asked Nealy's little nephew, Jeremy.

"Fried frog legs. Try them. They'll make you tough," said the caterer, laughing at Jeremy's horrible expression. To a child, the thought of *Kermit the Frog* having his legs torn off and dunked in a pan of hot grease would be very troubling.

"Yuk! Gross!" he screamed, running off.

A huge fountain flowed with champagne and a smaller fountain flowed with punch for the Baptist side of Nealy and Nadine's family and friends. The dessert trays were scattered around for those who did not want to wait until the cake had been cut.

"What happened to all the brownies?" asked Jerrod, looking annoyed.

"They disappeared through the mouths of babes," Aunt Ruth replied, smiling at the children that had been plucking from the brownie tray all evening. She winked at little Jessica who looked like the cat who had just eaten the canary —big eyes and a full mouth.

"Why did all these people bring their little rug rats anyway?" Jerrod teased, cocking his head and squinting his eyes as he glared at all the kids standing nearby. "*I* didn't get *one* single brownie!" he complained, playfully picking up Jessica and Jeremy and swinging them around in the air. Aunt Ruth laughed at his frolicking with the children. Being an only child, and the only boy in the family, she had always felt sorry for him during his childhood; at the family gatherings, he had never had anyone to play with. Nealy walked up beside Jerrod and put her arm around his waist. "Are you okay?"

"I'm fine...but did we really invite all of these people?"

"We sent out two-hundred and fifty invitations, so I guess we did."

"I didn't know we knew that many. I sure hope they leave soon. I'm hot in this monkey suit. And I'm hot for you," he said, pulling her close and kissing her soft, pouty-shaped lips.

Night had fallen on the reception. The small orchestra played music and some of the guests danced on the terrace that had been cleared for dancing. Nealy and Jerrod couldn't believe that Aunt Ruth had hired a *band*; she referred to the group of musicians as an orchestra.

"Nothin' but the best for 'My Precious,' " Nealy teased, making light of Aunt Ruth's adoration for him. " 'Precious did this,' and 'Precious did that,' " Nealy mocked.

"You're just jealous," he said smugly, leaning down to kiss her neck. "Come on, baby, let's get out of here. I'm horny."

"Shuu, Jerrod, people can hear you." Nealy turned to see if anyone had overhead him. "Maybe you should slow down on the champagne. You know how it always puts you to sleep. Wouldn't you like to stay up tonight? After all, it is our wedding night, and I'm horny, too," she said seductively.

"Mrs. Jones," he said, shocked, "I can't believe that came out of your prim and proper little mouth. I'd have married you a long time ago if I'd known it would loosen you up this much."

"Let's go cut the cake. Then I'll change clothes, and we can get out of here," she said patiently. "Will that make you happy?"

"Yes, if you don't drag out that cake-cutting shit. In the meantime, I'll fantasize about your being buck naked, blindfolded and tied to a pole."

Nealy looked horrified at first, but then she giggled loudly.

"Now, that *is* a fantasy. But I've got to hand it to you, J.J, you've got a real vivid imagination."

Nealy had him escort her over to the cut the cake where everyone had gathered. To make him happy, she cut a tiny piece and handed him half. Quickly, they fed it to each other.

Moving right along, Nealy threw her bouquet, and, of all people, Betty Lou caught it.

"That's not fair!" Denise screamed. "She's got a husband!" Betty Lou was shocked since she wasn't even in line for the bouquet.

Betty Lou looked over at her husband, Beaux, who stood a few people away from her. He turned and walked away. Betty Lou's face went blank. Nealy had been watching them all evening, noticing how distant they seemed, not even talking to each other. But, how could that be? They were expecting another child. Could that be the problem? Betty Lou worked full time, and Beaux had gone back to school to get his master's degree. She remembered Betty Lou telling her that they had agreed not to have anymore children until after Beaux finished school. Nealy knew that she needed to talk to her as soon as she and Jerrod returned from their honeymoon. Hopefully, it had just been a shock and they'd work through it.

The guys cheered for Jerrod to throw the garter. He sat Nealy down in a nearby chair, and raised her tight fitting gown up to her thigh to expose the garter. He looked straight into her eyes, moving his hand slowly up under her dress and circling her inner thigh before returning to the garter. Nealy blushed. The crowd hushed, becoming dead-still, as though they had been frozen in place for a moment.

Nealy leaned down close to his face. "Take it off," she whispered.

"The dress?"

"No, dear," she said, whispering nicely, "the goddamn garter."

Knowing that Nealy didn't use such language loosely, he immediately pulled off the garter and tossed it into the crowd of prodding males.

"Thank you," she sighed. The time had come to get him out of there and soon. It had become embarrassingly obvious to almost everyone that the groom had consumed a little too much champagne, which wasn't unusual. But this night had to be perfect; it was *definitely* time to go.

Before Nealy left to change, the photographer asked if she wanted to take some pictures with her family. When she agreed, Jerrod became upset, but Christine quickly came to her rescue. "I'll take care of him, Nealy."

"Oh, thanks, Christine," Nealy said. "Get him some black coffee."

"I'll do better than that," she said, smiling and pulling him towards the house. "Come with me, my pet. Christine will take care of you."

Nealy's family gathered around and the photographer spent at least thirty minutes getting everyone positioned in front of a hugh umbrella-shaped tree before snapping several shots.

After the pictures, Nealy looked for Jerrod, but no one had seen him for awhile. Finally, Christine appeared.

"He's *much* better now, Nealy. I took real good care of him. You'll find him in the kitchen with a pot of black coffee."

"Oh, good, thanks, Christine. I'm really glad you came."

"Oh, I always do," she laughed, sounding as if she were sneezing a bunch of little sneezes.

"What's so funny?" Nealy asked, thinking mostly about how much she hated this woman's laugh.

"I always do," she repeated.

Nealy looked puzzled. "Uh...never mind," Nealy said politely, shaking her head. Christine had a reputation for being a pure dingbat; a sexy, hotblooded dingbat.

Nealy, in searching for Jerrod, wandered into the kitchen where she found him sitting on a stool with a cup of coffee in his hand. "Hi, I've been looking for you. Did Christine take care of you?"

"Yeah. I'd rather have you, but she's good for a quicky."

"Jerrod, honestly," she said, getting frustrated with his behavior. "Drink your coffee while I change." She brushed past him and headed upstairs to change.

Nealy took her clothes out of the bedroom closet of the and removed her veil. Minutes later, the door opened and Jerrod walked across the room and hugged her. "I'm sorry, Neal."

"It's okay, Jerrod. I can understand you drinking too much. This has been extremely stressful for both of us. But it's over now, thank goodness. I thought you were supposed to be sobering up."

"I am sobered up. I missed you. I thought I'd help you," he said, turning her around to unbutton the tiny buttons on her gown.

"What if someone sees you in here?"

"Relax. We're married, remember? We said 'I do,' and now we can."

"I know, but it still makes me uncomfortable to have you undressing me with all those people downstairs waiting for us."

"Nealy, we've *got* to work on this hang-up that you have about sex and nudity. I'm your *husband*. So I'm allowed to see you naked," he said, struggling with the tiny little buttons.

"Jerrod, I don't have a problem. In fact, I like sex as much as you do. I just think that there's a time and place for everything. And *p,d,a* —public display of affection—makes me uncomfortable. Some things should be private."

"Cool your jets. I didn't say you had a problem. You're just a little inhibited. But I can help you with that. It's a good thing I'm here. These buttons are nasty little boogers."

"It takes one to know one."

"Okay, I'll admit it. I'm a little perverted. And before it's all over and done, you'll be perverted too...and you'll love it. There. I'm done. See what a useful husband I am already," he said, sliding his hands inside of her gown and cupping her breasts. "God, I love these—"

"That's it!" she cried. "Out!" Nealy pushed him out the door and put her face into her hands. "Dear *Lord*, I've married a nymphomaniac."

Hurry!" he screamed back at her.

Nealy walked to the top of the stairs, looking down at the people that had gathered to see her in her going-away outfit. She had on a emerald-green, two-piece suit, with a shawl collar that criss-crossed across the bodice, fastening with two large round gold buttons on each side. Knowing that she would be wearing her favorite color, Jerrod had left a gift on the dresser containing a magnificent pair of emerald earrings. The card said:

"To my wife with love, Jerrod."

From the bottom of the stairs, the emeralds sparkled almost as much as Nealy. The guests gasped, whispering amongst themselves. Making her way through the crowd, she hugged and kissed everyone, thanking them for coming, telling them just how much it meant to both of them.

When they walked out, the car looked like a big ball of graffiti: "She'll be his tonight," "He'll get her tonight," "Horny groom on the loose," "He's on top/no she's on top," "No clothes allowed," "Legal sex." Everyone laughed hysterically, shouting as they read the words. Jerrod and Nealy ran towards the car, dodging the rice.

As they drove away, they noticed an enormous brassiere hanging from the radio antenna.

"Look at the size of that sucker!" Jerrod exclaimed.

"It's at least a forty-four *double F*," Nealy said in amazement.

"If that's yours, Mrs. Jones, you've been holding out on me."

Jerrod and Nealy planned to spend the night at the Galvez and leave for Bermuda the following morning. And, after dropping their bags on the floor of their room, it took Jerrod less than a minute to strip her down to sexy green panties and matching bra.

"By, God," he shouted, looking at her chest. "They are a double F!" They fell back on the bed, laughing about what people would say when they saw that mammoth thing hanging on his car. "Baby, I'll tell you one thing for sure," he said, rolling over on top of her, "when they see that thing, they'll *know* I didn't marry you for your money."

"Jerrod Jones, you're incorrigible! You couldn't get any worse."

"Don't count on it, *Mrs. Jones*."

CHAPTER FOURTEEN

JERROD WHISPERED in her ear, "Good-morning, Mrs. Jones, it's time to get up."

"It can't be six o'clock yet," Nealy moaned.

"We need to get up and get ready. I told Aunt Janey that we'd be there by seven-fifteen."

"I need to rest just five more minutes...please," she pleaded, turning away from him and pulling her legs up into a fetal position.

"Okay. Five more minutes. But if you don't get up then, I can't be responsible for what happens," he said, snuggling up to her warm, naked body.

The rising sun cast a little light into the room through the sheer drapes, and a strong wind blowing in off the ocean created a slight roaring sound in the stillness of the morning. Jerrod's mind drifted back over the wedding and just how beautiful Nealy had looked walking down the aisle. The vision moved him to raise up on his side, staring at the woman he'd married just twelve hours before. He brushed her long, beautiful hair away from her face and quietly watched her sleep. She looked so peaceful. Jerrod could feel the passion swelling up inside of him. Between his strong physical attraction and his over-active hormones, he could not resist the urge to make love to her. He softly kissed her pretty little ear, tracing the curve of it with his finger. The fresh smell of her hair and the sweet fragrance that she had worn to bed excited him even more. He nuzzled her neck, her most sensitive area, gently biting it to arouse her. He knew her body would respond to his tender touch, even from a deep sleep.

Nealy began to move closer to him, moving her head to pull her hair off her neck, encouraging him to continue. Excited by her quiet moaning noises, he slid his hand over her firm stomach, pulling her compliant body into the crescent of his own warmth.

"Jerrod, what about getting up?" she whispered.

"You took care of that. I'm up," he said, pulling her closer and kneading himself against her to make his point.

"You're terrible," she said, wiggling away from him.

"No, you just turn me on," he replied, gently massaging the smooth skin on her stomach and her inner thighs.

"Oh," she managed to whisper, moving freely as he held her hips close to his body, and rolling her over onto her knees. Amorously, she stretched her arms out above her head and gripped the edge of the bed. As he thrust himself against her, again and again, her body responded spontaneously, and pleasurably they came together for one last hard push.

Moments later, contented and breathing deeply, he rolled back onto his side and pulled her with him.

"I love *doing it* with you, Neal. I want us to *do it* at least three times a day for the rest of our lives."

"In that case, we'll be dead by the time we're forty," she giggled. Suddenly, she opened her eyes to look at the clock across the room. "Jerrod!" she screamed, rising up to get a closer look at the clock. "It's six-thirty. We're going to be late."

"Isn't that just like a woman," he said, sitting up in the bed. "Now that you've had your way with me, you're ready to jump up and run off."

"Like I've said before, you're a very sick person," she teased, pushing him back onto the bed and putting her pillow over his face to smother him. Then she jumped out of bed and screamed, "Last one in the shower is a rotten egg!"

"You're on!"

After her shower, Nealy, feeling as if she hadn't eaten in days because of all of the excitement, called room service to bring them some bacon, eggs, and, most of all, some coffee for a much needed boost of energy.

"Are you ready?" he asked. "Of course, Aunt Janey will understand why we're late. After all, she had a honeymoon once. And from what I hear about Roland Randall's kinky sexual behavior, he probably caused them to be late quite often. It's easy to lose track of time when you're into blindfolds and bondage."

"Is sex all you think about?"

"No, but that could be interesting. Maybe we should try it sometimes," he said, expecting a reaction.

"You can forget it," she retorted coldly.

"I'm just kidding. I know you'd never be interested in experimenting with a little deviation. But, like they say...'Don't knock it 'til you try it.'"

"And I guess you'd really like to try it?"

"Why not...it might be *very* exciting."

"I knew you'd say that. But so far, I find our sex life exciting enough."

"Well, I do, too. But now that we're married, we'll be doing it more often. We could get bored doing the same old stuff. So, at least try to keep an open mind when the time comes."

"Jerrod, you *just* never stop."

"I know. I think that's why you love me. That and my big—"

"Don't you dare," she cut him off, meaning that she had heard quite enough for one day. Sometimes, he really made her crazy.

They took the elevator down to the lobby. While Jerrod checked them out of the hotel, Nealy walked over to the nearest picture-framed window. Staring

out at the ocean, she marveled [...]es as they broke, creating a fine mist
that rose fifteen feet or so into [...]

Across the parking lot, the w[...]rd against their faces. The car was
pathetic. Bethel, the boulder-hol[...]ne that Jerrod had given the double
F, still remained on the antenna, [...] the breeze.

"Well, it doesn't look as if an[...]e to reclaim Bethel," Nealy said,
chuckling. "I suggest that we drive [...]wn in search of the lost boulders
that Bethel binds."

Jerrod laughed loudly, "And you [...] sick."

"You are sick. If that thing had a[...]t me, you'd have married me a
long time ago, with no questions aske[...]

"You're right. The minute you grew [...]t triple D, we'd be on our way
to Vegas and the Honeymoon Hotel." [...]

"Exactly my point. You're strictly a b[...]an."

"Not true. I'm just as crazy about your [...]tle ass," he said, grabbing her
butt.

"Jerrod," she cried, "keep your hands to[...]elf out here. Now, let's get
back to Bethel. I definitely think we shou[...]ng her inside for the ride
downtown."

"Okay, I'll get it," he said, opening the sa[...]in that secured the strap,
"but I'm holding on to Bethel. Who knows[...] Jones, this may fit you
someday." Jerrod smiled and held the garment [...] Nealy's chest.

"I doubt that."

"Now don't be so insulted. If I remember cor[...]y, your grandmother had
a pretty healthy set of knockers. In fact, Bethel c[...] have some sentimental
value to you," he teased, dangling the large brass [...] in the air. He laughed
when the wind caught the cups and filled them ou[...] their enormous size.

Nealy grabbed the bra. "Excuse me, but my gran[...]ther's clothing had no
particular sizing. They were designed especially for [...]by Omar."

"Who the hell is Omar?"

"Omar the Tent Maker!" she said, giggling.

Most of the writing on the car had turned to streaks [...]m the salty dampness
in the air, but some of the words were still legible. As p[...]ple passed them, they
gawked and snickered.

When Aunt Janey opened the door, Jerrod apologiz[...], kissing her on the
cheek. "Sorry we're late."

"Oh, honey, I didn't really expect you to be on time. Marriage does that to
you," she replied. Jerrod elbowed Nealy and raised his eyebrows. As far as he
was concerned, Janey had just confirmed the rumors about his ex-uncle's sexual
habits. And after being married to that man for twenty-five years, she had to
be a reliable source.

Janey drove them to Houston's Intercontinental airport to catch the plane
to Bermuda. On the way, she filled them in on the sights to see, the food to eat,

places to dance, and the cottage. Janey ha... ...ot of time there following
her divorce from her husband because th... ...atmosphere and the beauty
of the island seemed to give her comfor... ...he got out and opened the
When Janey stopped at the depar... ...It's perfect for a honeymoon.
trunk. "Okay, my darlings, have a wond... ...ol with eight other cottages. I
The cottage is very private, but you sh... ...o special. I only wish now that
remember my honeymoon in Bermud... ...cover-up how much it still hurt
I'd taken a different man," she said, l...ed Jerrod very seriously. "Jerrod,
her to think about the past. Then sh... ...but if you *ever* do to Nealy what
you're my *only* nephew, and I love y...de. Now go and have a wonderful
Roland did to me, I will not be o...ging each of them.
time. Tell Judy hello for me," she ..." Jerrod said.
"Thanks, Aunt Janey, for eve... good-bye.
"Thanks, Janey," Nealy said...ealy sat in the seat next to the window
After changing planes in M...uda. It seemed as if they had flown over
eagerly awaiting their arrival in...t finally in the distance, the sprawling
hundreds of miles of open oc...eared that the plane had flown slightly
Bermuda Islands were visible...their approach into Bermuda. The pilot
west of the islands, turning B...over the islands, while speaking over the
flew close to the ground, di...t the sights below. It was like a free air tour,
cabin intercom system to po...ed cottages and the beautiful beaches were
and the views of the whit...ne hundred and fifty islands and islets linked
spectacular. There were aln...enty square-mile area. It had to be the most
and clustered together in...e that Nealy had ever seen. The seven major
wonderful setting of any...lges and causeways, were like one lush body of
islands, all connected by...picturesque islets and reefs. The vegetation was
land attended by throng...rs of green. The beaches were white with a pink
thick and variegated in...ns and millions of coral shells that washed ashore.
tint provided by the mi...d never seen anything quite so beautiful. And to
Nealy was in awe; she...would spend the first five days of their married life
think that she and Jerr...cal paradise. The excitement overwhelmed her. What
together in this truly tr...and she couldn't wait another minute to wake Jerrod
a treat they had in sto...Garden of Eden.
and show him their o...

"Hey, sleepy head," she said, shaking him gently. "Guess where we are?"

Slowly, he opened his eyes and sleepily asked, "Where?"

"Bermuda, silly," she said, smiling at him. "Oh, Jerrod, you have got to see this." She leaned back so he could look out the window.

"Yeah, it's beautiful," he said. He rested his head on her chest and wrapped his arm around her waist to snuggle up closer to her. "I'm so tired."

"Jerrod," she whispered, "you can't be that tired. You've slept most of the way."

"Trust me, I'm that tired. But I should be. You kept me up most the night attacking my body." He nuzzled his head against her bosom.

"Jerrod Jones," she whispered. "I should be the one that's tired! Now sit up and enjoy the view. We can sleep on the beach later."

"I prefer resting right here," he mumbled, biting her breast.

"Jerrod stop it."

"Only if we can go skinny dippin' as soon as we get there."

"Jerrod, I'm not skinny dipping in the ocean." Nealy glanced at him and gave him a no-way look.

"Sure you can," he said, talking quietly. "I read about the private beaches here where people do that all the time. It'll be great."

"Remember when we were kids and the National Geographic seemed most pornographic to us," she said. They leaned their heads together to talk privately. "Remember how the boys used to smuggle them out of the library to look at the native women's bare chests, and then they would show them to the girls who sat next to them in class. I remember getting so embarrassed because the native men wore just those little drawstring looking things to cover themselves. You know Jerrod, as much as you like being naked, I bet you were probably an African in a former life. If we went far enough back in some old issues, we'd probably spot you posing," she teased.

"I know you think you're real funny, but you seem to remember a lot about those magazines for someone who was such a prude."

"I'll admit it. I looked at them. But it was purely in the interest of education," she vowed sternly.

"I don't believe that for a minute. I think they turned you on. So maybe we should pretend we're Natives for the next five days and run around naked. We'll take some pictures and start our own National Geographic," Jerrod raised his eyebrows and nodded his head in favor of the idea.

"Jerrod, you are starting to annoy me. Let's get out of here."

Not affected by Nealy's annoyance, Jerrod continued to make quiet conversation. "You know, Neal, if I'd been born female, I'd either be a high class hooker or a classy porn queen."

"Jerrod, I don't doubt that for a minute. Thank God you turned out to be a man. Somehow, I can't imagine myself married to a porn queen."

After checking their bags through customs, Nealy looked for Judy Chapman, the woman that Aunt Janey had asked to pick them up. Judy owned one of the cottages in the same village as Janey, and they had been friends ever since the two couples had bought their cottages years before. And from what Janey said, they both spent quite a bit of time together in Bermuda after divorcing their husbands for similar reasons. Janey described Judy as a petite woman in her fifties with *decided-blonde* hair—one day she just *decided* to become a blonde—and a great tan.

"There she is," Nealy said, giggling.

Jerrod searched the crowd. "Where?"

"Well, I don't actually see her, but read that sign," she said, pointing towards a sign being held above the crowd.

"*Oh my God,*" Jerrod sneered, reading the sign out loud:

"*Jerrod and Nealy fell in love and said, I do.*
Now your love cottage is waiting for you!
My hair is blonde, my eyes are blue.
In case you don't see me, this sign's for you."

As they approached her, Nealy smiled. "Hi, Judy. I'm Nealy Jones. And this is my husband, Jerrod."

"Hi," he said, wanting to tell her what an idiot he thought she was for telling the whole world who they were and what they would be doing during their stay in Bermuda. It's his place to tell the world that he came there to screw five days away, not this ugly pig-bitch. Just looking at her pissed him off.

"It's really nice of you to pick us up, Judy."

"Oh, no problem. It gave me something to do besides lie in the sun. Sorry about the sign, but I couldn't resist," she said, smiling at both of them. "Janey described you both, but we have so many people coming here that I was afraid I might miss you."

"I found the sign to be creative and cute," Nealy said sweetly.

"Oh, yeah, it's cute alright," Jerrod said sarcastically. Nealy didn't want him to hurt her feelings, so she discreetly elbowed him and cleared her throat.

"Where are you parked?" Nealy asked.

"In the parking lot. It's not too far. Let me help you with that bag," Judy said, taking Nealy's small bag from her hand.

When they got out to her car, Jerrod glanced at Nealy, and then at the Mercedes, a very small Mercedes. Jerrod climbed into the back seat with difficulty. Because of the limited space, and his size, he had to ride with a rather large suitcase in his lap.

"Jerrod, I'm sorry about the suitcase," Judy said, apologizing for her small car.

"I'm sure you are," he replied, rolling his eyes. He hated this bitch. No wonder her husband dumped her, he thought, glaring at her.

"Well, how was the wedding, dears?"

"It was wonderful," Nealy responded. "We've really been looking forward to coming here. It's so gorgeous."

"I'm glad you decided on Bermuda. It's a wonderful place for a honeymoon," she said, smiling at Nealy and glancing back at Jerrod who sat pinned between the front and back seats.

"Gosh, I love these houses so much. In all my life, I never thought I'd like a pastel—pink, blue, green, turquoise—colored house. And everything is so neat and clean." Nealy raved at all the sights as they made their way through town.

"Well, here it is. Your love cottage," she said, grinning at them as she stepped out of the car to unlock the trunk. Jerrod looked at Nealy as if he wanted to say something, but he didn't. "If you need anything, just call me. My number's by the phone. Have a wonderful honeymoon, dears. I'll see you Friday," she said, waving and sliding behind the wheel of her car.

"Thanks again for picking us up," Nealy said, waving her away.

"You mean we're going to let that woman take us back to the airport?" Jerrod growled.

"Well, she offered."

"Forget it. I'd rather take a cab."

"Jerrod, you're so ungrateful."

"That's easy for you to say. You weren't sandwiched between the seat and your suitcase in that toy car."

"You'll live," she said with little sympathy. "Isn't this cottage wonderful? It's so cheery. And Jerrod, look out here. Look at the view of the ocean." She opened the sliding glass door that led out to the terrace and walked over by the rail that wrapped around the patio. Jerrod walked out behind her and wrapped his arms tightly around her waist. "It's so beautiful. Let's put our things away, and go down to the beach."

"Maybe later, Mrs. Jones, but I have something much more exciting in mind." He picked her up, carried her back inside, and put her down on the bed. Then slowly, he lay down on top of her. They made love until the sun had almost disappeared.

Getting hungry, Nealy talked him into getting up. She wanted to try one of the restaurants that Janey had suggested. And being that it was just a short distance from the cottage, she wanted to walk and enjoy the crisp night air.

So, after showering, she slipped into a sundress and sat down at the dressing table to put on some make-up. Jerrod walked up behind her admiringly. "I love that dress, but I'm a little surprised to see you in something so revealing. Most of your dresses are very matronly."

"Thanks. I thought you'd like it. If you look closely, you might even see a little cleavage," she said, smiling at him in the mirror.

"Neal, you should always wear this type of dress. You have the most beautiful shoulders." Staring at her in the mirror, he bent down and kissed her shoulder and the nape of her neck.

"I'm really glad you approve. You'll be happy to know that I brought several sundresses very much like this one."

"Well, that's a start in the right direction. We're going to work on some of your inhibitions while we're here. It'll be a *coming-out* experience for my pretty wife," he said softly, sliding the thin strap off her shoulder and running his hand slowly down the front of her dress.

"Jerrod," she said, leaning forward and pulling the strap back up onto her shoulder. "If you're referring to skinny dipping, the answer is still no. I love you, but our sex life is something that I intend to keep private."

"We'll see."

As soon as she finished, they left the cottage and walked on a park-like trail that took them past the other cottages. The breeze off the ocean seemed cool, but not damp like Galveston. Bermuda didn't have the pollution, so the air smelled fresh and clean. In the distance, the restaurant lights appeared.

The Cove By the Sea had a very romantic atmosphere with dim lighting and a small dance floor. Jerrod ordered the Bermuda Red Snapper with asparagus a la Hollandaise; he always liked to sample the local fish. Nealy had the Dover Sole with down-home peas'n'rice. For a vegetable, both of them tried a less familiar dish the waiter had recommended, Bermuda Pawpaw. It was a papaya that had been baked and mashed, even though it looked like a creamy cheese casserole. The waiter also recommended the house specialty drink, Rum Swizzle. Watching them eat, an observer would assume that they hadn't eaten in weeks. Nealy even ordered a piece of sponge cake drowned in sherry and laden with strawberries, bananas, chopped nuts, custard, and whipped cream for dessert. It was sinfully delicious, and she wanted to ooh and aah, but she didn't dare. Jerrod might chastise her again as he had in New York, perceiving such behavior to be undignified.

Following dinner, Jerrod was in such a good mood after having three Rum Swizzles, that he actually asked Nealy to dance. He held his new wife close, laughing and talking for more than an hour. By ten o'clock, they were both extremely tired, so they returned to the cottage.

The sun came up, and Nealy left Jerrod sound asleep to take a quick dip in the ocean. The water felt wonderful, and she could see the bottom for a long way off shore. She swam and played in the water and floated on her back so that she could look up at the light blue sky full of fluffy, fat clouds which created patches of dark blue water below.

"You left me," Jerrod said, grabbing her arm.

"God, Jerrod, you scared me," she screamed, putting her arms around his neck and kissing him good-morning.

"Why didn't you wake me?"

"You looked so peaceful. I wanted to let you sleep a little longer. I knew you'd know where to find me. Isn't this paradise?" Nealy pulled away and swam freely around him.

"No skinny dipping, huh?"

"Don't you ever give up?"

"No," he answered, swimming towards her.

"Race you back to shore," she yelled, swimming away from him.

"No contest!"

Nealy and Jerrod raced up to the cottage. After dressing, they went into Hamilton to rent mopeds for a day of sightseeing. In town, they passed the Birdcage, where a policeman directed traffic from a cage in the middle of the main junction. The mopeds were great fun as they rode down Queen Street on the harbor. There were many historical buildings and museums. All of the buildings had white limestone roofs which enabled the Bermudians to catch the rainwater for drinking. The Bermuda Cathedral, built in nineteen-eleven, caught their attention because it perpetuated the Early English style. Front Street had some neat stores where they did a little window shopping and grabbed a tuna sandwich for lunch.

After lunch, they headed for Ft. Hamilton to see the spectacular views of the city and the harbor. Nealy loved the skirline ceremony with Scottish dancers in their kilts, playing the bagpipes. Jerrod led the way over the Sommerset Bridge, the smallest drawbridge in the world, and then took them on a tour of the Maritime Museum on Ireland Island.

Later, they rode over to St. George's Town, which had been founded in sixteen-twelve as the original capital of Bermuda.

"Jerrod, doesn't it look like Easter here? The houses remind me of candy easter eggs. I've never seen pink, blue, and cinnamon colored houses in my life."

"Let's check out this dunking stool? I think these people had the right idea. Over three hundred years ago, this was a punishment bestowed upon promiscuous women or women who were chronic gossips. They were tied to that stool and dunked until they repented. Maybe we should try that on our women."

"Today's women are too damned tired to be promiscuous or to waste time gossiping. They have so much work to do taking care of the home, the family, and all of the many chores that they are expected to do. It's like having in-bred obligations."

"What kind of shit-talk is that? Next thing I know you'll be joining some women's group."

"I'm not a feminist, Jerrod."

"It sure sounds like it. But anyway, we were discussing busy-bodies and fooling-around here and there."

"I know what we were discussing. And like I said, women don't have time for such crap."

"Nealy, you are so naive. Everybody, and that includes women, fools around at some point—"

"Are you trying to prepare me for something?" Nealy stopped and stared at him angrily.

"No, just drop it, okay. I'm sorry I said anything."

On the way back to the cottage, they stopped at a local market to pick-up some wine and cheese and some fruit to snack on.

After a light dinner, Jerrod suggested that they take a walk on the beach. The moon shined so brightly that it lit the trail down to the beach.

"This is so wonderful," Nealy said, sitting down on the sand to watch the tide being pulled out to sea. The waves made an incredible splashing sound as they broke on top of the water.

Jerrod sat down beside her. "This is nice, Neal," he said, putting his arm around her.

"It's hard to believe we're really here. That we're really married. We talked about it for so long, and now, here we are."

"I know. But I'm so glad that we finally did it. It's a dream come true for me, Neal," he whispered, pushing her down on the sand and rolling half-way on top of her.

"Jerrod, we just showered. Now we'll have sand all over us."

"We'll just have to shower again together," he said softly. He kissed her, staring deeply into her eyes in a darkness brightened only by the moonlight. "I want to make love to you."

Nealy kissed him back. "Let's go back to the cottage."

When she attempted to get up, he pushed her back.

"I want to make love here, under the moonlight. We can listen to the ocean and feel the wind against our bare skin."

"Jerrod, it's not that late. People will be walking on the beach."

"There isn't anyone out here," he said, kissing her again.

Withdrawing, she cried out softly, "No, Jerrod, let's go inside. I'm not comfortable out here."

"Baby, please. Come on. I'll stop if someone comes," he begged. He held her arms above her head and pressed himself against her.

A part of her wanted to, but she couldn't, so she pleaded with him to stop. "No...please...I can't do this here."

Finally, he relented. "Shuu...it's okay, Neal. We'll go in." Jerrod got up slowly and pulled her to her feet. Then he hugged her sweetly for a few minutes to comfort her.

After brushing the sand off, he held her hand and led her back up the trail. At the door, Jerrod picked her up to carry her across the threshold, which was really the terrace door. He laid her down on the bed, turned off the lights, and then lay down beside her to cuddle her. "I'm sorry, Neal, I didn't mean to upset you," he said, brushing her cheek gently with the back of his hand.

"I'm sorry, too. I just can't do that. I want our sex life to be sacred."

"I know. I understand," he whispered, lightly kissing each cheek and then her mouth. Once she showed signs of arousal, he slid the thin straps off her shoulders and down her slender arms, pulling her top down far enough to expose the flesh between her neck and her nipples. As her mood softened, he moved the palm of his hand slowly from shoulder to shoulder across her chest, massaging away the tightness with his finger tips. She loved his touch; it took her breath, allowing her to breathe very deeply and to relax again. Within minutes, they were making love.

Bright and early the next morning, Jerrod and Nealy headed for the beach to do some snorkeling. The incredibly clear water had visibility up to two hundred feet ahead of them as they searched just below the surface of the water for sea creatures. Hearing about an old ship in a cove close by that had wrecked more than fifty years before and feeling very adventurous, they decided to try and find it.

Locating the old ship, they were fascinated at the sea life that had built homes aboard the old vessel. As the time passed, they swam further, discovering other ships that had sunk off the shores of Bermuda.

On Thursday, they slept until ten o'clock, but remained in bed for a long time snuggling together and watching the waves break across the water and dissipate into thin air. The cool breeze coming through the open windows felt wonderful, as well as the fact that they didn't have to rush; they had no commitments, no pressures. Just peace and tranquility, feelings which most people never afford themselves.

That afternoon, they took in the sights at the Botanical Garden, with flowers galore in every color imaginable, and then they treated themselves to a ride on a glass bottom boat. They epitomized newlyweds with their constant touching and holding hands as they walked slowly, enjoying every minute of being together.

Nealy suggested that they cook burgers on the grill since the weather was perfect for eating outside. She whipped up a salad and baked some potatoes, while Jerrod cooked the burgers on the grill. The moon hung high in the sky, surrounded by stars, and Nealy provided a little more light to their table with a centerpiece of candles that flickered in the breeze.

After dinner, Nealy straightened up the kitchen while Jerrod followed her around in a constant effort to distract her with his sexual advances. The cottage had been so neat when they arrived that she hated to mess it up. The small kitchen had bright yellow cabinets that were trimmed in bright white. Aunt Janey had good taste when it came to decorating, and the cottage was typical of her style—tailored furniture, bright colors, flowered pillows everywhere, crisp, starched-looking curtains and draperies, and pictures that had bright, pastel colors with tall plants standing besides latticed screens and high-backed chairs. There were no signs of clutter, not even a stack of out-dated magazines. Her phone book had a dainty cover and looked as if it had never been opened. Nealy turned off the light in the kitchen, and Jerrod suggested that they take a walk on the beach.

The sand felt great slipping through their toes, and their feet left prints in the wet sand as they walked near the edge of the water. When they reached the end of their cove, Nealy climbed up onto a rock wedged between a cluster of rocks that created a pier that led out into the water.

"Here's a nice flat rock. Let's sit for a while," she said, patting the rock for Jerrod to sit down beside her.

Lowering himself down next to her, he said happily, "I'd be happy to join you, Mrs. Jones."

"Isn't it beautiful out here? It's just *soooo* romantic."

"It really is. The moon's so bright. No wonder marriages back in the olden days lasted for a lifetime. The moon and candles were all the light that they had to talk, eat, and make love by. That had to be a romantic period. And I, for one, have really enjoyed our little bit of the past. We've used very little electricity, except for the physical kind, of course—"

"Jerrod," she said, cutting him off, "the way you see things. I'm always amazed," she said, smiling at him as she lay back to gaze up at the moon and the stars.

Jerrod lay back beside her and took her hand and brought it to his mouth. Softly, he kissed her fingers and slipped them between his lips, allowing his tongue to slowly slide across the tips of each finger. "Neal, I'm so in love with you that I can't keep my hands off you. You know that, don't you?"

"I love you, too," she said, ignoring the question. "Isn't it wonderful gazing up at the stars? It's so ironic, but out here, even this rock's comfortable."

Jerrod rolled over on his side and pulled her to face him so that they could cuddle together for a while. Holding her tightly as a form of foreplay, his male urges grew more aggressive, and he preferred to do more than just snuggle. "Are you about ready to head back?" he asked, moving his hand up and down her arm slowly, weaving his fingers between hers.

"I guess so," she whispered, raising up and stretching her arms above her head to catch the breeze with her hands.

Jerrod stood up and pulled her to her feet. "It's such a nice night, maybe we should go for a swim in the pool."

"Yeah, that'd feel great."

Back at the cottage, they slipped into their suits. Jerrod finished getting ready and cried out, "I'm going down."

"Okay. I'll be there in a minute." She debated between her one piece green suit or the yellow two-piece, finally deciding on the two piece in order to save the one piece for daytime swimming at the pool. Two piece suits in public places always made her feel a little self-conscience. Wearing them on the beach didn't bother her too much because people were usually preoccupied and didn't really notice what others were wearing like they did around a pool. After looking in the mirror at herself and whining, as most women do about being too fat, she grabbed her terry cloth robe and headed down to the pool to join Jerrod.

When she got down there, Jerrod was already swimming laps. He had always loved the water and always placed first on the swim team during school. Nealy loved watching him swim, and he looked great in his swimming trunks because of his nice little tush. Jerrod wanted her to love the water as much as he did, but she hated the fact that swimming was not conducive to good looks on a girl, leaving her with no make-up and wet hair. It was great at the beach with just Jerrod, but she preferred to lie by the pool or splash around in the shallow end when there was a crowd.

"Hi," he called out. "Come on in. The water's great."

Nealy dropped her robe on a nearby chair and walked over to the steps, sticking her toes in the water to check out the temperature. "Oh, it's warm," she said, stepping down into the pool and catching her breath as her stomach reached the top of the water. After submerging herself, she swan only a couple of laps before Jerrod caught her leg and pulled her over to the side where he had stopped to rest.

"Jerrod," she screamed, coughing. "My nostrils weren't designed for swimming backwards."

"I'm sorry, but I missed you. Come here," he said, pulling her close to him and kissing her neck. "Isn't it wonderful out here."

"It really is," she said, looking up at the moon. "Thanks for bringing me here. I love it."

"And I love you," he whispered, holding her face between his hands and kissing her. Sliding further down into the water, he pulled her legs around his waist. Kissing passionately, Jerrod unhooked the back of her suit and pitched it out of the pool.

Nealy realized what he had done and tried to pull away from him, but he held her tighter.

"Jerrod, no, someone could see us," she resisted. "Please—"

"Neal, I'm covering you, and besides it's just us out here," he said softly, kissing her deeper and deeper until she was overcome with desire and kissing him back. He pulled her legs tighter around his waist, drawing her into his body and pressing himself against her as hard as he could. When he felt her heart racing, he pulled off his suit and set it free. Holding her tightly with one hand and kissing her harder, he pulled her legs from around his waist to remove her bottoms.

When Nealy felt the water against her bare bottom, she panicked and pushed hard against his chest in an effort to stop him. "No, Jerrod, we have to stop. I can't...I just can't!" she cried out.

Jerrod yanked her back into his arms. "Nealy, stop it! I know you want me," he shouted, shaking her and then forcing her mouth to his.

Breaking away again, she screamed, "No!...Don't!...Jerrod, now stop it! This isn't funny."

Even though she fought him, Jerrod became more determined to get his way. Forcibly, he pulled her bottoms off and pulled her legs around him.

"Nealy, you're being childish," he shouted angrily, trying to hold her.

"Jerrod, dammit, let go of me!" she yelled, getting so angry that she finally freed herself from his clutches. She jumped up onto the side of the pool, grabbed her robe and her top and ran up the stairs to the cottage.

"Nealy, get back here," he screamed. He stood in the water, angry and frustrated, not really wanting to understand her feelings. Why couldn't she make love to him? What was the big deal? He put on his suit and climbed out of the pool. Too furious to follow her, he went down to the beach where he swam and walked for at least two hours before he returned to the cottage and crashed on the couch.

At daybreak, Jerrod got up and got ready to go on a deep sea fishing trip which had already been arranged. At least, being gone all day, it would give him some time before he had to deal with her and her sexual hang-ups. He eased around the bedroom, not wanting to wake her. But, after crying all night, a bomb couldn't have brought out of the exhausted state of deep sleep that she had finally fallen into.

This had been their first fight since they had been back together, but she had principles, and making love in a public pool was against all of them. Why would Jerrod want to take a chance on someone watching them make love. Nealy thought about the time as a teenager when she went fishing with her parents. She remembered observing the porpoises during mating season. It embarrassed her just to think about it now, and it had certainly embarrassed her then. Nothing embarrassed Jerrod; not even people viewing his private life. In fact, due to his actions and the things that he said, it seemed as though he might find it exciting to have an audience. Somehow, even though she brought herself to consider such a ludicrous idea, Nealy found it hard to accept.

"Jerrod," she called out, still half-asleep. When she realized that he hadn't come to bed, she jumped up, grabbed her robe, and walked into the living room. "Jerrod," she said, walking toward the other bedroom. Where could he be? Then she spotted the note hanging on the refrigerator. *"Gone fishing."* Removing the note, she started to cry, but then she got angry. It's their honeymoon, he should have at least said good-bye. Regardless of what happened, he owed her that much. Did he not hurt like she did? Obviously not. He didn't even wake her to talk about it. To hell with him. She'd shop. If games is what he wants, then games he'll get. But then, she started to cry again. "No," she said out loud to herself, "you just get a grip on yourself. There isn't anything that you can do about it until he gets back. So just get dressed. He isn't worth getting yourself all crazy...but you are crazy. You're talking to yourself."

Nealy showered, and then dressed quickly, not allowing herself any time for pity. Feeling the need to bury her frustrations, though, she walked from the cottage to Front Street in Hamilton, which turned out to be a long walk. But she enjoyed it. In fact, she felt much better by the time she got to town. She browsed in most of the shops, and bought herself a beautiful crystal picture frame. When she saw it, she immediately thought about how perfect it would be for their wedding picture. But, since the jerk didn't even bother to say good-bye, she imagined her favorite picture of her parents in it instead.

Since she didn't eat breakfast, she was famished by noon, so she walked down the street to a little sidewalk cafe that she had passed on her shopping spree. It was an absolutely gorgeous day; perfect for eating outside. Her heart sank when she spotted a young couple holding hand and kissing across the table. How could she deal with this? Then she heard someone call out her name.

"Nealy. Hi!" Judy screamed, heading up the street towards the cafe. "Where's Jerrod?"

"Hi, Judy. He's fishing."

"Oh, so you're doing a little shopping while he's gone?"

"Yes. It's really fun to shop here. I bought myself a crystal picture frame. I'm having them ship it home so it won't get broken. Want to join me for lunch?"

"Sure. Pick a table." They ordered seafood salads that were piled high with shrimp and crab on top of a head of lettuce. Nealy played in hers, not having much of an appetite. Every time Judy mentioned Jerrod's name, a sharp pain went right through her heart. She felt sick, but she couldn't let it show, even though, it must have.

"Nealy, are you alright?" Judy asked. "You're not eating your lunch."

"I'm fine. I'm just not real hungry."

"Oh, silly me. I forgot. You're a newlywed. No wonder you're upset. Your honey's not here. I remember how much I missed Herald when we first got married. I would have gone to work with him if he would have let me. I couldn't stand to be away from him, and I couldn't wait for him to get home everyday. In the first six months, I bet we didn't eat supper more than twice. The minute he got home from work, we headed for the bedroom. Gosh. What wild days those were. We must have worn each other out. Maybe that's why we barely touched each other during the last twenty years of our marriage. It's sad to think about how that passion fizzles out," Judy said, shaking her head and looking terribly sad.

"I'm sorry, Judy," Nealy said, smiling at her. "I don't mean to be pry, but have you been divorced long?"

"A year today," she said, her eyes tearing.

"Oh, I'm sorry, Judy. I shouldn't have asked."

"It's okay, darling. It's my fault. I quit trying. Herald wanted to work it out. I just couldn't. I was too tired. I reared five children, and, to be truthful, I didn't have much time for him. So, when I couldn't tend to his needs, he found someone that could. It's all water under the bridge now. But let me give you a little advice from one who knows. Take care of your man. If you don't, you'll lose him. Sometimes it's tough, but make time, and do what he wants as long as he wants you," she said, patting Nealy's hand. Nealy wondered if that meant making love in a public pool. After all, that is what Jerrod wants to do. Judy seemed so sad, it almost convinced her to try it. She loved Jerrod, and she never wanted to have this conversation in regards to herself. "Can I give you a lift home, dear?"

"Uh...yeah, that'd be great, thanks," Nealy said, as if she had been a million miles away.

Judy stopped in front of the cottage to let her out.

"Have fun dear. Catch a few rays. He'll be home soon," Judy said, winking at her.

"I will. Thanks again," she said, waving. Nealy slipped into her suit, gathered up a few things to eat, put them into a picnic basket, and then headed down to the beach. She decided to walk down the beach a ways to a more secluded beach that she and Jerrod had found earlier in the week. It was in a cove away from the mainstream of beach sun seekers. It made a perfect u-shape and was not visible from the ocean. It seemed private, and she needed privacy to think about things. She spread out her towel, covered herself in lotion, and stretched out face down to get some sun and take a little nap. When she closed her eyes, she had an instant replay of the night before, and she could still hear Jerrod screaming at her. Why was she so uncomfortable with these things? Did others feel the same way or was it just her? Could she ever feel differently about the things that Jerrod wanted her to do? Maybe he was right. Maybe she just needed to relax, and give it a chance. But *doing it* in front of *God* and everyone seemed so exploitative. Perhaps she should try it as Jerrod said. It was just like *doing it* in the back seat of a car at the drive-in. Well, sort of, but just a little more risky. She thought about the worst case scenario: Sunday morning. Under the clear skies, she and Jerrod were naked on the beach. She was on top, rocking with pleasure. And then, right in the middle of the act, a nice little old lady taps her on the shoulder, "Sorry to interrupt...." Then she asked for directions. Now would that be so bad? After all, they *were* married. But Nealy got embarrassed just thinking about it. Her parents had reared her to be a *good girl*. Even the fact that she and Jerrod had sex before they were married made her feel guilty and ashamed. And now, even though they were married, she still felt guilty. Her modesty went way back. Even in school, she never showered with the rest of the girls. She would wait until they were dressing and take a quick shower and dress in the stall. Letting it all hang out had always been too immodest. But Jerrod was her husband, and his feelings had to count for something. If only she could understand why he would want to take a chance on exposing her physically. Maybe she was making a big deal out of this. Guys liked the excitement of taking a chance, riding on the edge, almost getting caught. It kept things interesting for them. Nealy had to talk to him and she knew they would work things out because they loved each other. It would take sacrificing some of her principles, or at least altering them somewhat. It would be just one step further than *doing it* on the beach under a large blanket, which she hated to admit that she had done several times in the past.

Her eyes felt very heavy as she listened to the birds singing and the sounds of the ocean off in the distance. All of the thoughts that rushed through her head made her too tired. She couldn't think anymore for now. The time had come to relax and enjoy the sunshine that brought warmth to her backside. Feeling a bit daring and just about asleep, she reached behind her back and unfastened her top so she wouldn't have a tan line. Could she be changing already? And with that thought, she slept.

"Hi, sleeping beauty."

Nealy slowly raised up, blinking her eyes and trying to focus on the person standing above her. Once she woke up enough to recognize him, she muttered a sleepy "Hi."

Jerrod sat down beside her, but he didn't speak for a minute. Then sheepishly, he asked, "How was your day?"

"Good."

"How was yours?"

"Oh, I caught a marlin, but it was too small, so I threw it back. I thought he might have a beautiful wife waiting for him at the bottom of the sea. I'd feel terrible separating them," he said, looking like a sad little boy.

Nealy raised up higher on her elbows, pulling her towel up to cover herself since she had unhooked her suit. She smiled at him. "Jerrod, I'm sorry for what happened—"

"No, Neal, I'm the one that's sorry," he said, stretching out beside her. "Sometimes I just get carried away, and I do stupid things."

"Jerrod, I thought about a lot of things today. We need to talk about things more. I never want us to go to bed angry again. I love you. And contrary to popular belief, I want to please you. If you help me, I know I can work out my inhibitions."

"I'll help you, baby. I won't pressure you again. I promise," he said, putting his arm around her shoulders and kissing her sweetly.

"Promise me something else," she said, still touching his lips with hers. "Never leave without saying good-bye. That hurt me."

"I promise," he said. "I just want to share everything with you, Neal. I want us to experiment with life and all it has to offer. I want to consummate our love in every possible place, in every room of our house, and even in our yard, that is, when we get one. I love you so much, and I want everyone to know it. Maybe that's why I don't care who sees us. It could be a subconscious thing. I don't know. But I won't hurt you ever again. I promise, cross my heart and hope to die."

"Jerrod, I was so miserable. I'll make you happy, no matter what that takes," she said.

He smiled and handed her a brown bag. "I brought us some wine and some cheese and crackers, just in case I found you."

"Is this a peace offering?" she retorted, smiling.

"Well, I hope I don't need it now."

"You don't. I didn't eat much lunch," she said, feeling relieved that they had settled their differences. Nealy sat up, still holding the towel up to her chest, and dug through the bag.

"Isn't unhooking your top a little bit out-of-character for you?" he asked, his dimples making deep creases in his face.

"Oh, you noticed. Well, I didn't want a line across my back, so what the hell, I undid it. Could be subconscious," she said boldly. "It's part of my *coming-out*, I guess." They smiled at each other.

"Here, let me fix it. I don't want to take a chance on you dropping the towel. It'd probably cause me to break a perfectly good promise," he said, reaching behind her to hook her top.

"There, you're a respectable woman again."

"Thanks...but, actually, it felt better unhooked."

"Well, in that case," he grabbed at the back of her suit.

"I'm just kidding," she screamed, giggling.

"Mrs. Jones, never say or do anything that you don't mean. I always take you very seriously, especially when it comes to seeing you naked." Jerrod leaned over and sweetly kissed her. "Now, feed me before I get carried away."

"Go ahead. Get carried away," she whispered seductively.

"Okay," he said, pulling her into his lap.

"I'm teasing!" she screamed, giggling wildly.

Holding her tightly in his lap, he stared deep into her eyes and smiled mischievously as he said, "Make up your mind, Mrs. Jones, are you going to feed me or fuck me?"

"Feed you!" she screamed, covering her face with her hands.

Jerrod put his hands around her waist, pushed her up onto her feet and then stood up to face her. "Man: hunts for firewood. Woman: cooks," he teased, mimicking Tarzan by pounding on his chest. Nealy giggled and pulled the food out of the bag. She put it on the towel that she had spread out while Jerrod headed into the trees that divided the cove from the ocean.

Shortly, he returned with enough branches to build a fire. After he expertly built a fire, he opened the bottle of wine, poured each of them a glass, and then buried the bottom in the sand so that it wouldn't spill.

Night fell and the fire flickered in the light breeze. Jerrod sitting across from Nealy, held his wine glass up for a toast.

"Here's to the most wonderful four days of my life."

"Mine, too." They tapped their glasses together.

During the next half hour, they fed each other and consumed the entire bottle of wine. Not accustomed to indulging in alcohol, Nealy was in a giddy mood after four glasses of wine. She rambled on and became very touchy. Jerrod rested on his side, listening. Her eyes sparkled when she laughed. And her face was flushed from the sun and the glow of the fire, as well as the wine, that had obviously gone to her head.

Slowly sliding onto her knees, Nealy reached behind her back and unhooked her top, which she tossed towards her beach bag. For a minute, she just sat there motionless, staring at him. Her behavior left Jerrod in shock; he had never seen her behave quite so indiscriminately before. She stood up slowly, and he followed her with his eyes only, watching closely as she removed the bottoms to her suit.

Jerrod raised up, not sure how to react. He felt as though he should stop her, but he was enjoying it too much to even speak. She looked like a goddess standing before him, something much too precious to even touch. "Neal...baby...uh," he mumbled, not knowing what to say or do.

"Shall we go for a swim?" she asked, reaching out to him.

"Mrs. Jones, I'm not sure what's happening here, but I'm not about to question it." When he reached for her hand, she turned and ran towards the water. Quickly, he stepped out of his suit and ran after her. Chasing her out into the water, he caught up with her, but she disappeared out of sight. When she didn't surface after a long moment, he panicked and screamed out for her. "Nealy!" Fearful, he looked around and searched the surface of the water for her. The moon shined brightly, which provided some light, but his heart raced when he couldn't see even a trace of her in the dark waters. Nealy had always been a good swimmer, but because she had been drinking, it frightened him. "Nealy, dammit, this isn't funny," he screamed. "Where are you?" Then, when he heard splashing behind him, he turned to see her surface. Racing toward her, he grabbed her and pulled her into his arms. "Don't ever do that again," he scolded, hugging her tightly.

"Oh, Jerrod, I'm sorry. I was only playing with you."

"You scared me. I couldn't find you."

"I didn't mean to scare you—"

"I just love you so much," he said, pulling her face to his and kissing her desperately. Madly, she kissed him back and tightly wrapped her legs around his waist, just below the surface of the water. As he kissed her neck, and then her breasts, she dropped her head backwards. Totally uninhibited, she stretched her arms above her head and floated freely. Jerrod traced her parted lips with his salty finger and traced a line with water from her chin down through the middle of her body, over and over again. When she arched her back and squeezed her thighs against him, he reached under the water and cupped her bottom. As he pulled her hips towards him, he entered her again and again until they both quivered.

Jerrod eased his arms under Nealy's back, pulled her up into his arms and held her trembling body. "Oh, baby, now, that's more like it," he whispered, rubbing her back.

Nealy giggled quietly, snuggling against him. "I know. I'm dizzy."

"See Nealy, this wasn't so bad."

"You know what's so ironic," she said, still giggling like a little child. "All these years I've worried about those poor porpoises having to make love in front of God and everybody. And now I find out that they couldn't have cared less."

"Neal, I can assure you, if they were having as good a time as we were, they wouldn't have cared if the Pope himself had been watching with binoculars," he said so matter-of-factly. "Come on. Let's *do it* again. I think you're really getting the hang of this. A couple more times and you'll be ready for the *Swim Club.*"

"The *what?*" she asked, splashing water in his face playfully.

"Oh, nothing. Come here, you sea goddess."

"No," she screamed, swimming away from him.

After seducing her into another *roll-in-the-water*, he picked her up and carried her to shore, where he gently placed her on the towel by the fire. Because the fire had dwindled down to hot coals, he added a few branches to rekindle the flame before he settled in beside her and covered her with his towel.

Feeling light headed and emotional, she snuggled her back against his chest and softly said, "Hold me."

"I've got you, baby," he said, resting on his elbow. He wrapped his arm around her waist and pulled her closer. "Neal, I love you for doing this. I know how difficult it is for you. But, damn, baby, you're good...you're a natural."

"Jerrod," she whined modestly and elbowed him lightly. They lay there, staring at the fire for a while before making love again to satisfy Jerrod's insatiable appetite. Afterwards, Nealy fell fast asleep.

Jerrod eased away from her, gathered up their things, and then poured water on the fire. He couldn't get over how Nealy had asserted herself; he got excited just thinking about it. Not that their lovemaking over the years had been bad, but it had become very predictable. This time, she seductively initiated it, which really turned him on like a strong aphrodisiac. They had experienced a new sexual freedom, a perversion of sorts. Jerrod would use it as a stepping stone for the aberrant sexual heights that he planned to explore with her; he certainly didn't intend on letting her slip back into her pathetically prudish existence. If drinking four glasses of wine opened her up that much, he'd build her a winery. "Neal, it's late," he said, shaking her very gently. "Raise up." Slowly, she got up and stood before him totally naked. Slipping her arms into his cover-up, he buttoned it down the front and enjoyed the contact that his hands made with her beautiful breasts. This night had made all the difference in the world in their relationship. Now he could see a bright future filled with excitement in the truest sense of the word. They walked hand in hand back to the cottage.

The next morning, they woke-up early to prepare for their trip home. It was a beautiful morning, so they walked up to the cafe for breakfast. Nealy needed some food, which she hoped would take care of her headache and all else that ailed her. But, unfortunately, the papaya, which she loved, was about all that she could manage after the night she'd had. It hadn't bothered Jerrod, so he filled up on banana pancakes covered with fresh coconut syrup and macadamia nuts.

After breakfast, they took one last walk on the beach, breathing the fresh air and admiring the absolutely beautiful blue-green water and absorbing the glorious sunshine. They climbed up on *their* rock and looked out over the ocean. "You know, Neal, your eyes are the same color as this water. So from now on, whenever I look into your eyes, I'll think about our honeymoon."

"Oh, Jerrod, that's really sweet."

"But right now, with all those red streaks, I'm reminded of that wildly promiscuous creature that I encountered last night."

"I knew you'd bring that up."

"Trust me, I'm not complaining. Oh, no, not at all. In fact, I can't wait to meet up with her again." Standing behind her, he rotated his hips, pressing hard against her.

"Jerrod, we can't start this now. We have to leave soon."

"I'm not doing anything," he argued, reaching up to cup and massage her breasts.

"Dammit, Jerrod," she screamed and jumped off of the rock. "I'm a person, not a fucking sex-machine!" Angrily, she walked back towards the cottage.

Jerrod ran after her and held her. "Neal, baby, I'm sorry. Please don't be mad," he pleaded.

"Jerrod, you're wearing me out."

"I know, but I can't help it. Please don't be mad at me. I love you."

"I love you, too, but we can't even touch without it leading to something sexual."

"I know, Neal, I'll work on that. After all, you're working on overcoming your inhibitions, so I'll work on my horny nature. Okay?" he smiled.

"Okay," she said, smiling back at him. "I'm just so tired today."

"Well, in that case, I'll carry you." Jerrod picked her up and carried her back up to the cottage. He certainly didn't want to get her angry, especially since they were making progress. If he had patience and didn't force her, she would eventually open up to his erotic explorations.

Jerrod decided to call a taxi, sparing himself the torment of fighting with their luggage in the backseat of Judy's car. Nealy called and said good-bye to her, explaining that they wanted to do a little sightseeing on the way to the airport. It wasn't a complete lie since they wanted to stop at St. David's Lighthouse for a quick tour.

The taxi dropped them at the harbor in Hamilton, and a small ship took them back to St. David's Island where they took another taxi over to St. David's Lighthouse, the most popular lighthouse in Bermuda. It had a tidy pink cottage alongside the tower, surrounded by a six-acre park. The view from the lighthouse was wonderful, but not nearly as incredible as the view from Gibb's Lighthouse that had a three hundred and sixty degree panoramic view of the islands. Nealy and Jerrod stood close together, enjoying the view and making the most of the remaining moments of their honeymoon.

"I love this lighthouse. It's so romantic," she said gazing out at the water.

Resting his chin on her head, he held her, rocking slightly from side to side.

"Neal, you're right. It's really romantic. Maybe, we should take advantage of this cozy little place. After all, we have it all to ourselves," he said, pulling up the back of her dress.

Nealy refused to get upset and calmly looked up at him. "Jerrod, I hate to be the bearer of bad news, but mating season for porpoises ended last night."

"But what about my little mermaid? I watched her thrust about in the water. I heard her cry out, 'Grab my tail!' "

"Jerrod Jones! I did not," she screamed, giving him the exact reaction that he enjoyed the most: resistance.

CHAPTER FIFTEEN

"JERROD, THERE'S AUNT JANEY," Nealy said, waving high above her head to get Janey's attention. They could barely see her walking towards them in the crowded airport corridor.

"Hi, darlings," she said, hugging each of them. "How was your trip?"

"We had a great time," Jerrod answered, putting his arm around Nealy's shoulders, "Didn't we, Neal?"

"We really did. We can't thank you enough for letting us use your cottage. We didn't want to come home."

"After last night, I could have stayed there permanently," Jerrod said, winking at Nealy and puckering his lips to imitate a kiss.

"What happened last night?" Janey asked curiously.

"Ignore him, Janey. He's just being Jerrod," Nealy said, giving him the evil eye and fighting off feelings of guilt that gripped her stomach.

"Did Judy get you picked up alright?"

"Yes. She's really nice," Nealy replied. "She's still a little sad about her divorce. We had lunch one day, and she told me that she had been divorced a year to the day. I felt bad."

"Well, don't. From what I understand, that husband of hers was sleeping with everyone in town. She's much too nice, and *no one* deserves that sort of treatment," Janey said disgustedly.

Acting a little uncomfortable, Jerrod offered to get their luggage and meet them out front by the loading area. Janey went to get the car out of the parking lot, and Nealy stepped into the ladies' room.

When she came out, she mistakenly turned the wrong direction and ended up walking back towards the baggage claim area. After realizing what she had done, she turned around. As she made her way through the crowd, she spotted Jerrod on the opposite side of the baggage area with his arms around a young woman who was obviously crying. He appeared to be comforting her, or at least, trying to. Nealy stood there for a minute just watching them, not knowing exactly what to do. She didn't recognize the young woman, and therefore, she felt uncomfortable with the thought of approaching them. Her heart pounded. What should she do? It seemed so strange to see Jerrod holding another person. Obviously, it had to be someone that he knew fairly well since he seemed so concerned. Nealy watched as Jerrod removed his handkerchief from his back pocket and handed it to the girl.

Nealy followed them, feeling like a spy. Jerrod escorted her as far as the security station. Obviously, she intended on catching a plane, and Nealy hoped that it would be a one way ticket to some far away place—preferably Bum Fucked, Egypt. Now who's the trash mouth? she silently asked herself. She's becoming more like Jerrod everyday. God forbid that should happen! But who is this person? And why did Jerrod look so concerned? She had to be the wife or girlfriend of a good friend of his or something very innocent like that, and because of her emotional state, he felt obligated to console her. Sure, that's probably it. For whatever reason, Nealy still felt threatened, but she didn't want to overreact. Jerrod would have a perfectly good explanation, which she felt sure he'd share with her on the way home. But, for now, she needed to get out of there so that he wouldn't catch her spying.

Nealy hurried outside to where Janey had told her to come. Several cars were lined up, but Nealy, still in semi-shock, couldn't even remember what Janey's car looked like.

"Nealy," Janey called out, motioning. "Where's Jerrod?"

"He's coming," she replied. A huge knot formed in her stomach. Nealy felt frightened, but she tried to keep calm and act as if nothing had happened. Anyway, she trusted Jerrod. They had always had a very open and honest relationship, or so she thought, and he had always seemed so devoted to her, so true blue.

Jerrod walked through the double doors with a cart filled with suitcases, which he loaded into Janey's trunk. Thank goodness it wasn't another Mercedes. Jerrod offered to drive, and Janey let him, putting Nealy in the middle.

It had been thirty-minutes since they had left the airport and Jerrod couldn't get over how quiet Nealy had been. She came from a long line of talkers, and she loved to talk, so it wasn't like her not to enter into the conversation. "Neal, are you okay?"

"I'm just a little tired," she said softly, glancing at him and offering only a slight smile. The fact that he hadn't even mentioned that girl or woman had upset her. And to make matters worse, he acted as if he hadn't seen anyone at all.

Back in Galveston, Jerrod drove straight to the hospital. He pulled up in front and stopped the car. "I need to check my schedule for tomorrow. I have to find out where my group rotation will be meeting. I won't be long. I'll walk home," he said nonchalantly. "Aunt Janey, why don't you drop Nealy off at the apartment. When I get home, we can drive Nealy's car over to your house to pick-up the luggage. Maybe, if we're lucky, Neal, Aunt Janey may even offer to feed us since our cupboards are bare."

"Jerrod, she's done enough. We can't impose anymore."

"That's fine, darling," she said, patting Nealy's hand, and then she got out of the car.

Jerrod slid out from behind the wheel and waited by the car for his aunt to walk around to the driver's side. He gave her a big hug and kissed her on the cheek as he always did.

He closed the door and leaned down. "Neal, I'll see you at home soon," he said, smiling at her.

Nealy gave him a half-hearted smile. "Whenever." Then they drove away.

"Nealy," Janey said, pulling up in front of the apartment, "give Arlene a quick call and tell her I'm bringing some people home for dinner. Tell her it's nothing special. So don't fuss. After twenty-five years as my housekeeper, she's used to surprise meals. Oh, and call your new in-laws. Tell them you're home and invite them for dinner. They'll be glad to see y'all. See you soon, darling."

"Thanks for everything. It was wonderful, Janey." Nealy faked a smile and waved good-bye as she drove away. The vision of Jerrod with his arms enveloping that person wouldn't go away. It made her crazy to think that her husband of less than a week had been in the arms of another woman and hadn't offered any explanation.

At the door of their apartment, where Jerrod had lived for three years, Nealy found a note taped next to the door handle, which she removed before walking inside. It had Jerrod's name on it, so she laid it on the table for him, unopened. Then she picked up the phone to call Arlene.

After hanging up, she sat there staring at the envelope. Something told her to read it. After all, they were married, and so anything written to Jerrod should be her business as well. That sounded right, but since she had never been married before, she wasn't totally sure if opening your husband's mail would be considered an invasion of privacy. To hell with privacy, she thought. It smelled of perfume, and his name had been written in long hand—pretty and feminine—so obviously it had been written by a female, and, therefore, that made it her business. Slowly, she opened it, her heart beating like a drum. Her hands shook as she read it:

Dear Jerrod,

By the time you read this, I'll be on my way to my new life. I got the nursing job at the hospital in Los Angeles that I told you about. I'm excited, but I'm really scared to be moving all the way to California alone. I'm real happy for you, and I wish you well. I will miss everyone at the hospital, and I will especially miss the "Swim Club." We had a great time together during the last two years. If you ever need me for anything, and I mean anything at all, Cheryl or Jan will have my address and telephone number. I hope that you get to see them sometimes; we were all so close. This is a hard letter for me to write since I had hoped that someday I could have meant more to you than just one of the group. Although at times, I did feel that I was more special than the others, but I guess not. Take care, and I hope that I get to see you again someday. You will always be in my heart, and I loved you more than I could ever tell you.

My love to you always, Kris

Nealy sat there for a few minutes reading and re-reading each line. Who's Kris? A very close friend who obviously wanted more than friendship. Swim Club? What the hell is that? Did the fraternity have a swim team? If they did, he never mentioned it to her. Could Kris have been the person at the airport? Could she have known their flight schedule and arranged to be there at that exact time? If so, why would she leave him a letter? Why not just tell him in person? It must have been a coincidence. But that girl didn't look like a Kris. A Babs or Barbie maybe, but not a *Kris*. She looked so young, so petite, and so unsophisticated. It had to be someone else that he knew, just happened to be upset for some tragic reason. As soon as Jerrod came home, she would ask him about the girl and give him the envelope, not telling him that she read it. Of course, he would open it immediately and explain everything.

Carefully, Nealy put the letter back into the envelope and laid it on the table. Running out of time, she had to shower and get ready to go over to Aunt Janey's for dinner.

"Neal," Jerrod called out, "I'm home." When he didn't get an answer, he walked towards the bedroom and heard the shower running. He quickly pulled off his clothes and stepped into the shower behind her.

Nealy let out a loud scream, and whirled around, when Jerrod put his arms around her waist. "Oh God, Jerrod, you scared the hell out of me."

"I'm sorry, but I couldn't resist taking a shower with you."

Pulling away from him, she turned around to wash the shampoo out of her hair. "Next time resist. Or at least call out before you get in. After seeing *Psycho*, I'm a little paranoid in the shower." Nealy closed her eyes tightly as the water forced the shampoo from her hair.

Jerrod leaned down and covered one breast with his mouth and rubbed his hand between her legs.

Jerking her head out from under the shower, she pushed him away angrily, "Jerrod, don't start. I need to hurry."

"Don't you like the element of surprise? Wouldn't you like to be blind folded and wait for something exciting or unexpected to happen to you? It keeps life interesting, Neal," he said, taking the soap from the soapdish. "You've lived such a sheltered life, always knowing from one minute to the next what's going to happen. I need to teach you how to relax. You're so tense. I could feel it when I touched you."

"I'm not tense from living a sheltered life, Jerrod. I'm tense from seeing you at the airport in the arms of another woman," she said, staring coldly at him for a minute and then stepping out of the shower.

Without a word, he stepped forward and let the water hit him in the face. Nealy dried off and put on her robe. When he stepped out of the shower, she was putting moisturizer on her face and staring at him in the mirror. "What time are we supposed to be at Janey's?"

"Jerrod, don't change the subject. Who was she?"

"Neal, she's nobody. Just a friend. A nurse that swam over at the fraternity house a few times. She's moving to California and it upset her to be going so far away from home, that's all. When I saw her at the airport, I felt sorry for her. Okay? Don't make a big deal out of this. It isn't like you," he said, sounding annoyed.

"Is her name Kris?" she asked, turning to face him as he tucked the end of the towel, securing it around his waist.

"How did you know her name?"

"She wrote you a letter. It's on the table. I think she felt more than friendship for you." Nealy walked out of the bathroom and came back with the letter, which she handed to him.

He stared at it for a moment and then walked into the bedroom and laid it on the dresser next to the bed.

Nealy followed him. "Aren't you going to read it?"

"Why? I don't care what it says. It's not important. We were friends, I said. That's all. If she cared more for me...well, that's her problem." Nealy stared at him, and he put his arms around her. "I happen to love my wife. I'm married to you now, and anything that happened before is history. It's not important. Nealy, I wasn't a hermit last year while you were in New York. I had friends. I went out occasionally, but I never loved anyone other than you. I missed you everyday. I asked you to marry me before you left, but you turned me down. What was I supposed to do? Sit home alone and pine for you? Since this is upsetting you so much I wished I had, but I didn't. I never want you to mistrust me. You mean more to me than anything else in the world. I happen to love you. Do you understand that? I love *you* and only you, forever," he said very adamantly, speaking very softly.

"I'm so relieved," she said, her eyes watering. She put her arms around his neck and buried her face in his bare chest for a moment. When she turned around and started to walk away, he caught her and reached around her waist to untie her robe, which he eased off her shoulders and dropped to the floor. "Jerrod, we'd better get dressed. Aunt Janey's expecting us at seven-thirty."

From behind, he lightly bit her neck and her ear. "This won't take long," he said softly, removing his towel and bending her forward on the edge of the bed.

From that moment on, Kris, nor anyone else with whom Jerrod had fraternized with during their separation ever came up in conversation. Jerrod made sure of that. Life goes on, and the past was simply that, the past. Jerrod was right. It's done, it's over, it's history, and everyone knows that history can't be altered, but it has been known to repeat itself.

The following Monday, Jerrod called Nealy and asked her to meet him at a house about a mile away from the hospital. It was a small rock house on a corner lot with a white picket-fenced yard filled with trees and beautifully arranged flower beds. When Nealy arrived, Jerrod was waiting with the real estate agent, who he immediately introduced. He told her that he had wanted to surprise her with the house, but he wanted her to see it first.

"Well, what do you think?" he asked anxiously, obviously wanting her to say that she loved it.

"It's precious, but Jerrod we haven't even talked about a home yet," Nealy answered, looking rather confused.

"I know, baby, but that apartment is so small. I want you to have a home to decorate. And besides, my folks are buying it for us. My dad tried to give me a house after my second year of medical school, but I wanted to wait," he said, taking her by the hand and leading her through the hall to the bedroom. He motioned for the agent to give him a minute. "Just think, Nealy, you can fix it up however you want to. It'll be all ours. If it'll make you feel any better, I'll pay my dad back as soon as I get my medical practice off the ground."

"But Jerrod that's a long time away. You have a four year residency ahead of you," she said, uncertain about the idea of buying a house so soon.

"Nealy, I'm...no, we're not poor. My grandfather left me a lot of money when he died. And I can take it out of my trust whenever I need it. I want you to have this house. It's perfect for us, and it even has room for a nursery when the time comes," he said, smiling and rubbing Nealy's stomach as if she were pregnant already.

"Jerrod, that's a long, long time off."

"I know, but it can be used as a guest room until that time comes. Suppose your roommates from New York want to come for a visit. Or that crazy Millie. Or your dancer friend—"

"Claudia. And it's Jillie, not Millie."

"Oh, yeah, that's right. Anyway, they said they'd be coming for a visit. Where would we put them? That apartment has only one small bedroom," he talked fast, pleading his case.

"Well, I guess you're right. That place is pretty small. And I'll admit, I'd like living here much better." Nealy slowly turned around. The house had a certain romantic ambience that made her feel happy. It had an arched doorway leading into the bath and two swing-arm lamps with soft blue shades that accented the darker shade of blue on the walls. The lamps were situated on the walls so that a double bed would fit perfectly in between them. The lights even had a dimmer switch that she turned on and then slowly rolled back the dial.

"Won't that be perfect for those cozy evenings when we spend the whole night making mad, passionate love to each other," he said, walking up to her and curling himself up to her backside while she played with the light switch.

"We'll see," she sighed, sweetly glancing at him on her way out of the room. She walked into the other bedroom, which Jerrod had referred to as the future nursery. He followed her. Minutes later she turned around and smiled at him.

"Neal, please."

"Yes!" she screamed, jumping into his arms and hugging his neck tightly. He hugged her back and twirled her around in the empty bedroom. "I'll work and do the decorating myself," she excitedly proclaimed. Their own home. A love nest. It was a far cry from that tiny flat that she had shared in New York. Jerrod was truly her prince. It was like a dream come true—the fairy tale wedding, complete with horse and carriage, and now, an adorable little ginger-bread house with a white picket fence. Nealy James Jones had married a prince alright, whose only thoughts were of her happiness and making sure that she lived happily ever after.

They signed the papers and moved in the following week-end. Nealy painted the other rooms, leaving their bedroom the blue that perfectly matched his eyes. She'd always told him that he had *bedroom eyes* and *bedroom mentality* to match. It seemed as if he had a one-track mind for nothing other than sex, sex, and more sex. He lived to be a doctor and to *do it*, but not necessarily in that order.

Even though babies were something so far in the future that Nealy refused to talk about it, she painted the second bedroom, the room Jerrod referred to as "the baby's room," a soft sea green. It would be aesthetically pleasing to their guests, which was a major concern when she selected the color. The color reminded her of the blue-green seas surrounding Bermuda; it always made her feel happy and serene. The kitchen became a bright, sunny yellow color, with white floors, counters and cabinets. Nealy had a cabinet maker switch the doors on the top cabinets to glass so that she could admire the beautiful dishes that they had been given as wedding gifts. The dining room, positioned between the kitchen and the living room and separated by large archways, needed a special touch, so she wallpapered it with an elegant pastel floral print and covered their living room furniture with the matching fabric. She sanded down the hardwood floors in the living and dining rooms herself and refinished them. The remodeling had been a true labor of love, even though it had turned out to be a bigger project than she had originally anticipated. But, being their first home, she wanted to give it her own special touches with her own two hands.

Nealy and Jerrod spent his rare evenings away from the hospital, snuggling in front of their cozy fireplace on a large, white, fluffy rug, while they supposedly watched television. Jerrod, of course, preferred to spend his evenings in the bedroom, but he knew how much she enjoyed the romance, and he enjoyed the foreplay, so it worked out. Some evenings, she had even coaxed him out onto the front porch after dinner to sit with her in a large swing that she had hung with the help of a friend. They were the perfect couple: in love and in lust.

One evening, Jerrod appeared at the backdoor with a basket that had a huge red bow tied to the top of it.

"What's that?" she asked curiously.

"Your Christmas present," he said, handing her the basket.

When she lifted the lid, she squealed, "A puppy! Oh, Jerrod, he's so cute. Thank you." Nealy picked up the tiny puppy and cuddled him in the nape of her neck.

"I took a chance on getting you a golden retriever, but I know how much you love dogs, so I figured breed wasn't that important."

"Oh, I love him. Is it a him or a her?" she asked shyly. And being Nealy, she would never verify gender, even in front of her own husband.

"It's a him," he said, smiling at her naivete.

"What shall we name him?"

"How about Stud?"

"I don't think so. Stud just doesn't fit this precious little face." But, they both laughed when she put him on the floor and Jerrod called out, "Here Stud," and the little pup looked up at them so innocently and made a huge puddle on the floor. Immediately, Nealy grabbed him under his tummy and front legs to take him outside for his first lesson in potty training. Jerrod followed to judge her technique.

"What about Chance?" she asked, watching the puppy as he snooped around in the grass. "That's perfect since you took a *chance* that I'd like him."

"I guess Stud is out, huh?"

"You saw his reaction to Stud. Anyway, he's going to have enough problems with you as a father-figure. So, please, don't encourage him. Chance, come," she commanded. When he came running, she grabbed him up into her arms. "See, he loves it. And I love him, and you," she exclaimed, forming a huddle of people hugs and puppy kisses.

CHAPTER SIXTEEN

TWO WEEKS AFTER Nealy and Jerrod had returned home from their honeymoon, Nealy had gone back to teaching at Miss Janik's dance studio. Dancing had always been a major part of Nealy's life and she never planned to give it up, even if all she could ever do, *now* that she had married Jerrod, is teach part-time for Miss Janik. At least, it gave her something to do, and the money helped out with the decorating expenses for the house. The studio specialized in theatrical dancing and stage performance and had been in existence for twenty years under the direction of Lelia Janik. Over the years, she had built a successful business with a good reputation. Miss Janik had become well-known for grooming professional dancers and actors for the stage, and, of course, she had been a *major* influence on Nealy's career. Nealy had taken lessons from Miss Janik since the age of three, and started teaching part-time when she turned fifteen. When she came home from college in the summers and on holidays, she spent most of her time at the studio teaching and observing Miss Janik.

Once Nealy had completed decorating the house, she added more dance classes to her schedule at Miss Janik's request. Not sure of her ability to coach drama, she reluctantly agreed to teach five classes a week to high school students who had ambitions similar to those of her youth: To become working actors. The fact that they all wanted so badly to become stars, just as much as she had, gave her the confidence to accept the challenge. And of course, Miss Janik, who had nothing but encouraging words, made her feel much better when she shared with her the story of how she became a drama coach many years before.

Miss Janik had never been an actress, even though, when she first moved to New York, she did have a small part as a dancer in a play, with a line or two of dialogue. But that certainly didn't qualify her to coach drama. It all started when a young man that she met at an audition asked her to help him with some lines and the emotions of a character that he had been cast to play in an off-off-Broadway production. His character was a washed up dancer, trying to pull his life back together. Since Lelia was a dancer, he thought that she could help him with the emotions and read the dialogue with him. Of course, it also gave him the chance to spend time with her, which was really at the root of his intentions.

Not long after their meeting, she was hired by the New York City Ballet Company. When she was not rehearsing, he was always at her apartment rehearsing and talking in general about life and his ambitions as an actor. He never asked her out, and he made jokes about being a starving actor, so she just accepted that as the reason. Eventually, one thing led to another, and they fell in love. They would make love into the early hours of the morning, even though he never once spent the entire night. In those days, a nice girl would never allow a man to live with her without the benefit of matrimony. Their romance continued out of her apartment for the next year, with only an occasional trip out for a quick meal at a dirty little Chinese restaurant not too far away. But she loved him so much that she was happy spending the time alone with him.

Finally, Gene got a break and landed the lead in an off-Broadway production. Lelia, during every spare minute, rehearsed with him and coached him with every line. At times he would take a kissing scene far from where the script left off, maintaining that it made the character more real to him. On stage he would imagine Lelia in his arms instead of the actress and let his mind take him to far greater pleasures, which he knew would be felt by the audience. And sure enough, it finally paid off.

On opening night, Gene's performance was so brilliant that he became an overnight success. The following morning, anxious to read the reviews, Lelia opened the *New York Times* to the entertainment section, and there was Gene standing center stage, with a long article about him and the play next to the picture. As she read, her finger followed the print, and within minutes the paper became smudged to the point of not being legible. Lelia had discovered that Gene not only had a wife, but he had a child, a six year old daughter. How could that be? They had been together for five years, seeing each other almost every day. She also discovered that he had been using a stage name because he came from a wealthy family and wanted to achieve success on his own merits. It didn't seem possible. It simply wasn't true. She practically had to pry her finger from the paper. Too shocked to cry, she sat there glaring at the picture, thinking that it had to be a misprint. Maybe they had confused him with another actor. Surely he would have slipped at least once in five years, saying something about his daughter or his wife, but he had never even mentioned another woman, much less a wife. They even talked about marriage, but he told her that he needed to wait until he could give her all the finer things in life. She believed him with all her heart and loved him with all her soul.

A few minutes later there was a knock at the door. It was only eight o'clock on Sunday morning, and no one, except Gene, ever came to see her that early. By now he had seen the paper, and he knew that she had seen it, too. When she didn't answer, he let himself in with the key that she had given to him. She couldn't look at him. She sat there staring desperately at the newspaper, praying that it had all been a big mistake and that it would go away.

"Lelia, my darling, please listen to me," he said, walking slowly towards the table where she sat. "I wanted to tell you, but I didn't know how. I had only been married for two years, and my daughter was just a baby when I met you. She had been born with Down's Syndrome. Do you know what that means?" he asked, but she didn't answer. "It's a genetic disease where a baby is born with one extra chromosome. She was born mentally retarded, but it's worse than that," he explained, leaning down beside her. "Because of her birth defects, she developed some respiratory problems. They cautioned us not to take her out much from fear of exposing her to other illnesses which, under the circumstances, could lead to life threatening infections. Therefore, my wife never left the house; she just stayed at home caring for the child. Our marriage was bad from the beginning. I didn't love her, but I had to marry her because she was pregnant. We hadn't known each other long, and I felt so trapped. Then, after Lindsey was born and we found out about all of her problems, I felt guilty for not wanting her. Then, I tried to make the marriage work. I wasn't a good husband, but I knew I had to take care of them. My family bought us a nice apartment on the Central Park West, and I've kept them there ever since. You see Lelia, I've loved you from the minute I saw you. You were the most beautiful woman that I'd ever seen. I wanted to touch the porcelain skin on your face and run my hands through your long, silky, black hair. To me, you were the prima ballerina of my dreams. I had to have you. I thought that once Lindsey got a little older and her health improved, that Liz would want a life of her own, and then I would be free to marry you. Oh, Lelia, I love you," he cried, laying his head in her lap. "Please don't leave me. You're the only thing that kept me going. Please don't leave me."

"Gene, my poor darling," she said, holding him as he wept. "I won't leave you. Not now. Not ever."

"Lelia, Lelia, my beautiful Lelia, we'll get married someday soon, I promise," he cried, kissing and hugging her.

Three years went by and Gene remained married, still supporting the wife and child, even though he hardly ever saw them. He had moved into an apartment close to Lelia's since she still refused to live with him until he divorced his wife and married her, but they spent many nights together, either at his place or hers. They often fought about the fact that he hadn't even talked to his wife about a divorce, but he always had some excuse why the time wasn't right. If Lelia threatened to leave him, he would fall apart and beg her not to go.

Since she had never met any of his family, she asked to join him for a family dinner party at his parents' home. When he refused, she decided to call it quits. So, that night when he returned, she had locked him out and left a note on the door, telling him to go away. But, after making a scene outside her door, she finally let him in, and he promised to take her to meet his family the following week.

After that, she often read about them in the society columns of the newspapers where they were giving money to one charity or the another. And once she even read where his wife Liz had attended some charity function with him, but when she asked him about it, he said it wasn't true and that the media had mistaken his sister, Lizza, for his wife. Several times during the year, he would visit his parents at their country home in Connecticut, but he never once took her as he had promised. He would always say, "Soon, my darling, soon. This isn't the right time. Please, just be patient."

Gene's career was in full bloom. Lelia still coached him with every role even though she was always kept in the closet as far as their personal life was concerned. They were just friends who had a professional relationship.

At Gene's insistence, she opened up a dance studio in the building where he lived, teaching more than fifty students a year. They both had solid careers and seemed happy, but Lelia still longed for the band of gold and a new last name. None of Lelia's friends or family ever knew his last name and she never mentioned it—that bit of information will go to her grave with her. She only referred to him as *"my Gene"* or *"that man,"* depending on her mood.

After a nine year career, Gene finally won a Tony Award and he gave credit where credit was due, contributing his success to Lelia Janik, his acting coach. Even at that point, after standing by him for nine years, he couldn't share anything but the stage with her. That night finally opened her eyes and she vowed, "I will never get romantically involved with another man until he takes me home to meet the family." The talk about marriage had all been a big lie to keep her from throwing him out of her life. There was a lot more to the story about his wife and family that she didn't know, and what she did know had probably been lies. If *only* she had listened to her mother who, every week when she called home, told her the same thing: "No man's gonna buy the cow if he gets the milk for free."

Lelia Janik finally told *that man* to drop dead. Of course, he cried, begged, promised, and did everything that he could to try and convince her that, "This time it'll be different," but this time she didn't buy all the lies. As far as she was concerned, the final curtain had fallen.

Being a smart woman and not wanting to burn any bridges, she talked with all of her clients and turned her business affairs over to a lawyer. Before the month had ended, Lelia Janik had moved home to Galveston, Texas. Feeling sorry for herself, she grieved for months until one day she realized that no man's worth such agony. And that was the day she opened up "Miss Janik's Studio for Performing Arts," teaching everything from ballet to tap to toe to modeling to theatrical dancing and acting. And the rest, well, here again, it's history.

Now, two decades later, a woman who had practically become an institution in the entertainment industry, even operating more than two thousand miles from the hub of it all, had to turn-in her ballet slippers.

Two months after Nealy started teaching full-time, Miss Janik asked her to stay after her last class because she had to discuss something very important with her. Nealy turned off the lights in the studio and tapped on Miss Janik's office door.

"Miss Janik, sorry to interrupt you."

"Oh, that's fine, darling. Please, come in. I'm just going over some paperwork which I'll gladly push aside. I'm thankful to the *Good Lord above* that he gave me some creative ability because my mathematics are pathetic," she laughed.

"I know what you mean," Nealy commented, giggling out loud.

"Have a seat, darling. We might be here a while. Nealy, my doctor has insisted that I retire—"

"Oh, no. Are you ill?"

"Well, yes, and no. I have a disease called, Osteoarthritis, a degenerative joint disease caused by wear and tear on the joints. Because of the knee injury that I suffered as a dancer, and because I have stood on pointed toes for many years, I have developed a serious problem in my knees and feet. It's not a life threatening situation, but the symptoms are becoming more frequent and more painful, in fact, there are some mornings when I get up at four to stretch and walk so that I can teach by nine. I think it's time, Nealy. As much as I love what I do, I'm tired. I'd like to travel, to see places that I've never had to time to see. This business will really tie you down, but it's worth it. The rewards are great," she said, speaking to Nealy more seriously than she ever had before.

"Miss Janik, I'm so sorry. Is there anything that I can do to help?"

"Yes, honey, I think there is," she said, getting a little teary eyed. "Nealy, I've worked very hard building this studio, and I started with nothing in a town where culture was something that you read about. Now, people count on me to teach their children what the arts are all about and how to become a part of them. There is so much more to it than just teaching them to step-ball-change. I want my work to continue and I think that you could do that for me. Many of the mothers of my students have raved to me about the outstanding job that you are doing with their children. One mother told me the other day that, with your help, she felt sure that *her Bethany* would be the next *Shirley Temple*. Now that, my dear, is a compliment. Especially since that child could not sing, act, or dance her way out of a paper bag the first day she stepped foot into my studio. You're good, Nealy. Really good. And you're smart, too. That's why I'm willing to sell the studio to you at a very reasonable price, allowing you to buy it out over the next several years. I've made my money out of the studio with a profit; it's fixed me well enough that I can live my life very comfortably. Now, all I want to do is leave it in good hands. I trust you. You're a winner. You'd have become a great actress had you not chosen to get married, but you probably made the right choice. Show business is tough, and with Jerrod being a doctor, you'll have a good life. I wasn't too sure about him being the right one, but I trust your judgment. You know him much better than I do, and I wish you all the best. You certainly deserve it. I don't want you to give me an answer right now. I want you to go home and discuss it with Jerrod. It will require long hours, but you know that. It's work. I won't lie to you, but you've known me long enough to know that too. That's why I want you to talk to Jerrod. In a few years when he becomes a heart surgeon, you won't need to work. He will make more money than either of you could spend in a lifetime, if he doesn't have it already. After all, Jerrod comes from a very wealthy family. He may not want you to have your own career. I remember that being an issue before you went off to New York. But I want you to think about it for yourself as well. I didn't have much experience with men, but what I did have told me a lot about them. They are, for the most part, self-centered, self-indulgent, sons-of-bitches. Pardon my frankness, dear, but that's why I never married. Now, don't get me wrong. There are some fine men out there—your father is one of them—and I hope you found one to equal him, but trust me, they are far and few between. Just in case, and I'm not insinuating anything by this, the day comes that you would have to become self-sufficient, this would be just the right thing for you. You could set yourself up for life. Nealy, please don't think that I'm being a bit negative about marriage, but better men than Jerrod have left their wives, or died for that matter, leaving their wives without a life of their own. Not that you would ever have that situation arise, but I'm a firm believer in not putting all your eggs in one basket. I know you, Nealy, well enough to know that you want to be your own person. And without your identity, you won't be happy. All I'm saying, dear, is to consider everything before you make a decision. It's my belief that no one, not even the wife of a rich man, should ever be in a position to *have to depend* on someone else for happiness or livelihood. It's just not healthy. A mother with children, maybe, but that's not even good anymore. It's a cruel world, Nealy, and a girl has to do what a girl has to do. I can say this to you because you're like my own. If I'd had children, I'd have wanted a girl just like you. So please, think about what I've said. Consider it girl talk," she lectured, in a caring sort of way. Miss Janik stood up, taking a tissue from the box behind her. Then the tears that Nealy had struggled to hold back, burst free. "I'm sorry dear, I didn't mean to make you cry."

"That's okay. Could you please pass me a tissue."

"Certainly, dear."

Nealy blotted the tears and smiled very kindly at Miss Janik for a moment. "You know you've been like a second mother to me, and the thought of not having you here in this studio everyday is hard for me to accept, but I'm also concerned about your health. I'm flattered that you would offer me something that is as important to you as this studio. It's been your life. I also appreciate your confidence in me, and I'll give this a lot of consideration, with and without Jerrod's opinion and/or approval. He *is* my husband, and I know him. He'll want what I want, even though it'll be difficult for him to accept my wanting more than just being his wife. Let's face it. Most men have large egos. But, I can deal with that delicately. I'll see you in the morning," she said, rising from her chair and smiling at Miss Janik. Her pretty green eyes had become red and puffy, and her jaws ached from stifling her need to cry. Like a child, she wanted to be held to ease the pain, so she gave Miss Janik a big hug, which she returned tenderly.

"Okay, dear," she said softly, flashing her stage smile, but without the use of her fingers. If the pupils at Miss Janik's studio didn't learn anything else, they at least learned how to smile in front of an audience. Nealy could always count on Miss Janik to give her *the smile:* index fingers forcing the cheeks upward towards the cheekbones, and a big toothy grin. Whenever she was on stage, that gesture alone somehow calmed her down and got her through.

Nealy cried all the way home. How could she carry on without Miss Janik? This would be like losing one of her parents, and she couldn't bare to think about that. And, even if she bought the studio, how could she make that transition? Teaching was one thing, but running a business was another. She had never even considered something so permanent. Singing, dancing and acting came naturally, but managing money and taxes seemed totally foreign. In college, Nealy had earned a degree in the Arts; she knew about the world of make believe. But business, now *that's the real world.*

CHAPTER SEVENTEEN

NEALY STOPPED at the grocery store to pick up a few things for dinner. Preparing Jerrod's favorite meal—steak and potatoes—might make things go a little smoother when she broke the news. Looking in her rearview mirror, she put on some lipstick and a little powder to cover up the fact that she'd been crying. It never failed; whenever she looked her worst, she always ran into a student or one of their mothers.

When she got home, it was already seven. Jerrod wasn't on call, so he had planned on being home for dinner. He had been working long hours, and they hadn't spent much time together, at least not the way they had in the early days of their marriage. Life as an intern is pretty hectic, but Jerrod loved being a doctor. And in August, he would start his residency in Cardiology; it took twenty-one years of school to achieve his life long dream. Nealy spent most of her extra time at the studio getting ready for recitals, but whenever Jerrod had a night off, she gave him her undivided attention. Since she had screened in the back porch, she thought it would be fun to grill the steaks and eat out there; it was a beautiful night, especially for June. Nealy set a pretty table and had dinner ready by eight-thirty, just as Jerrod pulled into the driveway.

"Hi, Neal, something sure smells good."

"I fixed steaks. How was your day?" she said, putting her arms around his neck and giving him a big kiss.

"Good. How about yours?" he said, patting her on the bottom.

"Interesting. I'll tell you about it after dinner," she said, hurrying about to get dinner on the table.

"Why not tell me now?"

"It's a long story. Wash up, and let's eat. Steaks aren't good cold."

They ate and talked about some of the things that Jerrod had been doing at the hospital; he loved talking about his patients, especially the children at the Burn Institute. The children were special to him, but the thought of children being burned beyond recognition broke her heart, always bringing tears to her eyes. As a doctor, Jerrod forgot how upsetting such tragedies could be to a sensitive, non-medical person, so he would change the subject if he saw her tearing up. It was hard to believe that they had been married for almost two years, and that he would be hearing soon about whether or not he would be accepted for residency at John Sealy; But, they were reasonably sure that he would get it since his father was on the board. Money makes a big difference, even in the medical profession.

Jerrod helped clean up and fed the dog. On his nights off he liked to spend as much time as possible playing catch up. So to get her in the mood he would give her a kiss on the neck or rub up against her occasionally as they worked.

When things were done, Nealy decided that it was now or never if she intended on telling him about the offer to buy the studio.

"Jerrod, sit down, I need to talk to you about something," she said, sitting down at the table and pulling out his chair.

"Baby, can't it wait 'til tomorrow? I'm tired and it's late. And besides, I've got an early call tomorrow."

"Please, I really need to talk to you now. It won't take long," she pleaded.

"What is it?" he relented. He sighed heavily, obviously annoyed.

"Miss Janik wants to sell me the studio," she said, getting right to the point.

"What?" he blurted out in shock.

"She has some health problems, so the doctors recommended that she retire and relax. Selling is the only way to get her out of there. And she wants me to have it. It would mean so much to her to know that it's in good hands. It's her life long work. I want to do it, Jerrod. I love that studio as much as she does. I've been going there for more than twenty years—"

"No!" he shouted. "That's out of the question. You don't need to get yourself tied down to that place. You're there too damn much as it is."

"What? I'm always here when you are. I've never once slighted you because of my work."

"And you're not going to either. We don't need the money. I've told you that a million times."

"It's not about money, Jerrod," she said, trying not to let him upset her, which she knew would lead to a big argument.

He paced the kitchen floor. "Nealy, no, this won't work. Just be happy that I haven't made you quit—"

"Excuse me. What do you mean, *'made me quit'?*"

"Just what I said. I'm ready for a family. I'm starting my residency, so it's a good time to start our family. I've been patient with you about waiting. I've wanted to start a family ever since we got married, but you insisted that we wait. But I'm not waiting any longer, and I want you at home. I'm not going to allow my children to be reared by some stranger while you're out teaching everybody else's kids to curtsy. Who gives a flyin' fuck about bowing anyway?"

"Jerrod, that's unnecessary—"

"Well, I think it *is* necessary, because obviously you aren't taking me seriously about this. The answer is not 'No!' but *'Hell no!'* I won't help you out financially and that's that."

"I don't need your money," she said calmly, fighting back the tears; she wasn't about to cry, and she wasn't about to give up. She had every right to her own life.

"Of course you need money unless she's giving it to you, and that's highly unlikely," he said sarcastically.

"No, she isn't giving it to me," she said, just as sarcastically. "I'll pay her what she wants for the business out of profits. She doesn't need the money, and she's willing to let me pay it out over the next five years."

"Well, isn't that nice of her. The answer's still No!"

"Jerrod, I'm going to do it," she said adamantly.

"No you're not, Nealy. I said, 'No!'" he shouted again. "I told you that I want a family now, and I want you home taking care of our children. You can't own a business and take care of a family, too."

"Jerrod, women do it all the time. I can handle this, and besides, I want to do it. I have a life too, you know. I'm a big girl, and I gave up my career—"

"I knew you'd throw that up to me. I knew it was coming," he shouted. "Listen, you wanted to marry me. I didn't hold a gun to your head. You could have said no, and I'd of left your broke ass in New York in that sleazy, cramped boarding house!"

"I wanted to marry you, dammit," she cried, tears escaping down her cheeks. "I love you. And I want to be with you. But I'm entitled to my own life doing what I love, just like you have!" she shouted back at him.

"No! Nealy, enough—"

"Jerrod, don't tell me what to do. I'm not your child. I'm your wife. I thought you'd want success for me. I want that for you. In a year or so I'll have the business going, and then I'll have a child. I'll take the baby to the studio with me," she said, trying to reason with him.

Jerrod stormed out of the room. Nealy sat there not sure whether to let him go to bed or finish the argument. But then, out of curiosity, she got up and went into the bedroom when she heard the medicine cabinet door slam.

"Jerrod, what are you doing?" In disbelief, she watched as he stood over the toilet with her birth control pills, punching out the plastic tabs and letting the pills fall into the toilet. "Jerrod, stop that!" she screamed, grabbing for her package of pills.

He flushed the toilet. "No, you stop it!" he yelled. He grabbed her arm and pulled her into the bedroom, pushing her down on the bed. "I've had enough of this, Nealy. We're going to have a baby. I married a woman that wanted to give me kids, and I intend to make her live up to that. Do you understand me?" he said, pulling off his clothes.

Nealy rolled over and cried into her pillow. Suddenly, she felt him leaning over her and untying the bows on each shoulder that held up her sunsuit. Before she knew what was happening, he had pulled her clothes down and over her feet, pitching them onto the floor. Shocked by his actions, she turned over and began screaming and fighting him.

"Jerrod, what are you doing?" she shouted, struggling against his strong grip.

"What's it look like? It's baby making time. That'll stop you," he yelled, holding her wrists out to each side of her head and straddling her. "If you're my wife, then act like it." He leaned down, forcing his mouth on hers.

"Stop it!" she cried. "Get off me!" she screamed louder, fighting to free her arms. "Jerrod, don't—"

"No, *you* stop it!" he yelled, leaning over her. He pushed one of his legs in between hers.

"Jerrod! You're hurting me...please don't do this!" she pleaded with him, becoming almost hysterical.

Suddenly he let go of her, "Neal, it's okay," he said, sitting on the side of the bed and pulling her into his arms. "I'm sorry. Oh, baby, please don't cry. I'm sorry. I'd never hurt you. Shuu," he whispered, rocking her like a baby as she sobbed sobs that jolted her upper body.

"Jerrod, how could you—"

"Hush now. It's over. I'm sorry," he whispered, holding her tighter and rocking her harder, kissing the tears away as they rolled down her cheeks. "Oh, God, Nealy, I'm so sorry. I just got so upset. I'm so afraid of losing you. If you get too independent, I could lose you. I know. I almost lost you once. Please don't cry," he pleaded, tears rolling down his cheeks. Jerrod had never cried in front of her. When they fought, he would shout, but he had never, in all the years that she had known him, cried.

"Jerrod," she said, raising up to face him. "Don't cry. It's okay."

"Nealy, please don't ever leave me. I couldn't stand it," he cried, putting his head on her chest and crying like a baby.

"I'm never going to leave you," she said, rocking him, soothing him as if he were her child. Feeling his pain made her forget about her own. "I'm your wife, remember? Until death do us part and all that good stuff." She held him, kissing his head and rubbing his face, while tears rolled down her own cheeks.

"I love you too much, Neal," he spoke softly. "I'm sorry."

"It's okay. I love you, too," she said, reaching over and turning off the light above the bed so it wouldn't shine in his eyes. They lay in each others' arms and fell asleep to sounds of sniffles and deep sighs. It had been a terrible ordeal, but thankfully it had ended before it went too far.

The next morning Nealy slipped out of bed and made coffee. It was only five o'clock, but she couldn't sleep. She and Jerrod had only had one other fight like that where he became physical, but she didn't hang around to finish it. That was the night she left for New York. Did he cry then, she wondered. If he had, she wouldn't have left. Nothing had ever disturbed her as much as it had to see Jerrod cry. Girls cry all the time. It makes them feel vulnerable and releases tension, and when it's over, well, life goes on. But to see a guy cry...it's hard. He had lost it. She had never seen him so angry and out of control; he became abusive. Would he have really raped her? Of course not. Husbands don't rape their wives. Jerrod was just upset, it even scared him when he realized what he was doing. She could tell. He had never forced her to make love to him if she didn't really want to. Although sometimes, when she wasn't in the mood, he would play around by holding her down and kissing her aggressively until she responded, but he never continued if she said no. Jerrod liked a little fight—the me-*Tarzan-you-Jane* type ego trip—and she knew it. The resistance excited him; the take intoxicated him. Nealy had been so shy when he first met her that he made fooling around like a little game: teasing, touching, more teasing, more touching, and then bingo, "I got ya." Of course, she was young, just barely fifteen. They had three dates before she let him kiss her on the mouth; it took three more dates to get his tongue inside. It took a long time and plenty of patience before he actually touched her breasts, and he had almost given up when she allowed him to unhook her bra. Getting between her legs was almost impossible; he practically had to pry them apart, deciding that maybe they didn't part above the knees. And they fought constantly about *going all the way*. After exhausting all of his patience, he finally said, "Nealy, the time has come. We are going to *do it*, or I'm history." So, on the night that she graduated from high school, they *did it* on the beach under a blanket. Afterwards, he held her while she cried, and then he explained about the semen. She lost her virginity, but she gained invaluable information about the birds and the bees.

Nealy slipped into the bedroom at five-thirty to wake Jerrod since he had to be at the hospital at six-thirty. He looked like an angel, so sweet, all curled up under the comforter that he had pulled over them in the night. She still felt a little unnerved from their horrible fight, but she would try to forget it and not mention it unless he brought it up.

"Jerrod, it's five-thirty. Time to get up," she whispered.

"Alright," he mumbled, turning away from her.

"Come on. You'll be late. I brought you some coffee. Sit up," she said, pulling a pillow up to prop against the headboard for him.

"Okay," he whispered, sitting up. She kissed him on the forehead and headed for the bathroom to take a shower and get ready for work. As she stepped out of the shower, Jerrod stepped in without saying a word, so she didn't say anything either. Maybe he just needed some time to think about things, or he was too embarrassed about what had happened to talk to her yet. For whatever reason, he obviously wasn't speaking to her, so she would just wait.

After she dressed, she made the bed and went into the kitchen to take care of Chance, who must have slept on the backporch. He wasn't accustomed to screaming, and he always took cover at the first sight of violence.

When she called out to him, he came inside. "Chancey boy, I'm sorry if we upset you. You're such a good doggy. Here's a treat as a peace offering," she said, petting him on the head. He took his treat and out he went to either eat his treat or bury it.

A few minutes later, Jerrod walked briskly through the kitchen towards the back door. He stopped before he opened it and looked back at Nealy who stood motionless in front of the sink. "I'm sorry for what happened, but my answer is still no. Work there for now if that makes you happy, but you're not a buyer. Tell your precious Miss Janik to find herself another player." He opened the door and started to walk out, but then he stopped. "And one more thing. Stay off the pill," he said, glaring at her for a minute. He left angrily, slamming the door to confirm his stance.

Nealy couldn't believe what she had just heard. Her blood boiled, she wasn't sure whether to laugh, cry or shout. "The nerve of that guy," she said, looking down at Chance. "Who does he think he is? He tries to rape *me*, and then he has the audacity to act as if he had been attacked. I don't think so," she said to herself. Nealy stormed out the door. She would never give him the satisfaction of making her cry over this. It was her life and she was not about to let him tell her how to live it. Marriage is a union, not a prison.

At the studio, Nealy marched into Miss Janik's office and proudly told her that she would love the opportunity to take over the studio whenever the time came.

Miss Janik hugged Nealy, and said, "That's wonderful, dear. So, Jerrod agreed?"

"He didn't have to agree, Miss Janik. I told him that I wanted to do this more than anything. It's my choice, like the one he made to become a doctor," Nealy snapped, smiling.

"Well, I guess I underestimated Jerrod. I fully expected him to contest your decision," she replied, smiling back at Nealy, proud that she had considered her own needs.

Nealy didn't look at her. She couldn't because she felt like a liar, but she wasn't, she had only avoided all the ugly details. "My class is waiting. Let me know what we need to do. I'm ready when you are," she said, grinning on the outside and jittery on the inside. It was done; the decision had been made. And once Nealy made a decision, she lived with it, come hell or high water. Any other decisions would be Jerrod's to make. Of course, the thought of that terrified her, but after what he had done, she felt angry enough to accept the consequences. Nealy danced her heart out all morning, keeping busy.

At lunch, she and Miss Janik discussed all the details, while they snacked on popcorn and jelly beans. It wasn't much of a lunch, but she didn't feel like eating; she was too depressed, too excited, too afraid, and just too everything.

At five o'clock, the phone rang, just as Nealy had dismissed her class. One of the students answered it and called Nealy to the phone. With her heart beating against her chest, she took the phone and held it against her hand for a minute. She had waited all day for Jerrod to call, flinching every time she heard the phone ring. Oh, please let it be him, she thought. Please make him change his mind. Make him say he's sorry. Make him tell me how much he loves me. Finally, she lifted the phone up to her ear and moved into the office to hear over all the noisy little voices. "Hello," she said bubbly, depending on her ability to deceive.

"What's for dinner?" Jerrod asked, his voice cold.

"I didn't plan dinner. It's Friday. You're never *home* on Friday nights," she answered stiffly.

"Well, I'm coming home tonight. I expect dinner at seven."

"I won't be there."

"What?" he snapped back.

"You heard me. I said 'I won't be there,'" she enunciated each word.

"Well, if you don't mind my asking, just where in the hell will you be?"

"I have a meeting with Miss Janik."

"About what?" he asked, his voice excelerating.

"I prefer not to insult your intelligence, or question your memory."

"Nealy—"

"I've accepted the offer, Jerrod. It's done," she said coldly.

"No, it's not," he whispered as loud as he could, obviously at the hospital with someone standing close by. "I made myself clear this morning."

"I'm sorry, Jerrod, but I don't take orders from you. I'm your wife, not your puppet. I don't jump every time you try to pull my strings."

"I'll see you at seven. You'd better be there," he said bitterly before hanging up on her.

To save face, Nealy said good-bye and gently returned the phone to its receiver. A pain, sharper than any knife, shot through her heart. It had become a nightmare, but she didn't intend to back down. He would have to accept it sooner or later. What was he going to do, divorce her? That would be taking it a little too far, much too far for a good little Catholic boy. This would open his eyes to the fact that she had needs too and that she intended to stand by them. She would not be bullied, especially not by her husband who supposedly loved her. What happened to the, "I want you to have everything that you ever want out of life. I owe that to you for sacrificing your career to marry me," vows that he had made? Not one time did he say he wanted to boss or abuse her into his way of thinking. Not one time did she agree to be bossed or abused, and that would not change.

Nealy and Miss Janik met with a lawyer friend of Miss Janik's who also happened to be a friend of Nealy's parents. It was just merely a formality in case of Miss Janik's death. After the clock struck seven, Nealy became very uncomfortable, praying that Jerrod wouldn't show up and make a scene. Surely, he wouldn't do that; at least, she hoped not. But the way he had been acting lately, she didn't know what to expect. If anyone had ever told her that Jerrod could act the way he had the evening before, she would have *never* believed it.

By eight-thirty, everyone had left but Nealy, and she wanted to straighten up a little before she went home. Anything to buy her a little time before she went home to face a possible firing squad. The thought of that made her laugh out loud, but she also felt very frightened at how close it might be to the truth. And since she didn't want to take the Buy/Sell Agreement home just yet, she decided to read it there, making sure that she clearly understood everything. She didn't want Jerrod to ever be able to accuse her of being an idiot for signing something that was not in her best interest, not that Miss Janik would do anything like that. At Nealy's insistence, Miss Janik had agreed to put the business in Nealy's name as the sole owner. Since Texas is a community property state, it didn't really matter. Half of what she had would belong to him and vice-versa. The lawyer told her that it might not fly like that, but that he would at least leave it that way for now.

At ten o'clock, Nealy was sitting in the office reading over the document when she heard someone pounding on the front door. It frightened her, but when she heard Jerrod's voice, she quickly put the papers away and went to the door.

When she opened it, he grabbed her and pushed her back down the hall towards the office. "I told you to be home at seven!" he screamed, his face filled with anger.

"Jerrod, you're hurting my arm."

"Nealy, goddamn you, I'm tired of talking about this. You have pushed me too far this time—"

"*This time?* What are you talking about?"

"Shut-up!" he yelled. "Don't play dumb with me...but, with the way you're behaving, maybe you are just a dumb fuck."

"Don't you ever call me that again."

"I call 'em like I see 'em. Maybe that's why you're doing this. Maybe you don't realize what this means," he shouted, shaking her as if to shake some sense into her.

"Jerrod, I'm buying a business. A good business. It's what I want. I'm a grown woman. A college graduate. Not some bimbo off the street," she shouted back at him.

"Well, you're acting like one!" he shouted right in her face.

Nealy slapped him. It shocked her, but it shocked Jerrod even more. All her life she had been a completely non-violent person who wouldn't hurt a fly, but he had pushed her to the limit. Quite frankly, she had heard enough, and when he questioned her integrity, well, that did it. The time had come to fight back. "Now, get out of here," she screamed. "Leave me alone!"

"Leave you alone. I'm your husband. I don't have to leave you alone. We're getting out of here," he said, dragging her down the hall towards the door.

"Jerrod, let go of me!"

Angrily, he wheeled around. "Stop screaming," he shouted and slapped her right across the face, knocking her to the floor. "Now, how did that feel? It hurts, doesn't it? I know because you did it to me." He pulled her up from the floor, and started to drag her towards the door again.

Before reaching the door, it flew open, and Randy Richfield, a doctor that they both knew, stood in the doorway. "What's going on here?" he asked, his voice elevating.

"This is none of your business, Richfield. It's between me and my wife," he said, lowering his voice, but still shouting. "Did you hear that? My wife. Now get the hell out of here."

"You're right. She is your wife, not one of those whores—"

"You'd like to tell—"

"I'm not telling anybody anything," he interrupted. "You're drunk, Jerrod! Or is it pills? Maybe it's both this time."

"You don't know what you're talking about, Richfield!"

"You can't fool me. I saw you at the fraternity house. Jerrod, stop...before you do something you'll regret," Randy pleaded.

"I'm not drunk. And this is none of your fuckin' business. I'm having a discussion with my wife. And we were just about to leave when you showed up. What a noble man you are for coming to rescue a damsel-in-distress."

"Jerrod, I think you need to leave—"

"And let you take my wife home. Not on your life, Richfield. I know how you feel about her. Everybody does," Jerrod interrupted, snapping sarcastically at him. "Nealy, stop that blubbering," he said, walking over to the chair where she sat with her face in her hands, crying uncontrollably.

"Jerrod, I'm warning you. Get out, or I'll call the police."

Jerrod leaned down next to Nealy and pulled her face up out of her hands, gripping her jaw between his thumb and fingers.

"Neal, tell him to leave, so we can go home—"

"No, you leave! I can't stand anymore of this," she cried, jumping up from the chair and running down the hall into the office.

"Thanks, Richfield. You got what you wanted. Not that I'm trying to knock her off that pedestal all you assholes have her on, but she isn't the perfect little angel that you think she is. Ask her who hit who first," Jerrod said, storming past him.

"Go home, Jerrod, I think you've done enough for one night," Randy said sharply.

"Fuck you, man."

"No, fuck you," Randy shouted reflexively. Then, realizing that he had allowed himself to stoop to Jerrod's level, he felt ashamed. He waited until Jerrod peeled out down the street before shutting the door and turning the bolt and locking it. Randy didn't give a damn about Jerrod Jones, in fact, he loathed the guy. But he did care about Nealy and her well being, which had him upset because she had blood all over her face and her clothes.

Randy rushed down the hall to find her. "Nealy, what happened?" Randy asked her, entering the office where she sat with her elbows on the desk and her hands covering her face. "Are you alright?"

Nealy tried to answer him, but she just kept crying. "I...I don't—"

"It's okay," he said, kneeling down beside her and pulling her face around to him. He wanted to find out if she was hurt and where the blood was coming from. "Nealy, let me look at you. You're bleeding. Here look at me," he said softly. "Wait here. I'll be right back."

"Randy, don't leave me," she cried out.

"I'm not. I'm just going to get a towel," he said, smiling to reassure her. Randy would have rather been going after that sorry son-of-a-bitch that hit her. He found it hard to believe that anyone could do such a terrible thing to her because Nealy was one of the sweetest people that he'd ever known. And Jerrod was right, he did care about her, but he also respected the fact that she was Jerrod's wife, even though, he certainly didn't deserve her. Randy had become friends with Nealy over the past two years because she taught dancing to his six year old daughter, Alicia. He also knew her through the fraternity that he and Jerrod had belonged to during medical school, and he still saw her from time to time at the *frat* house for an alumni function of sorts and they would talk idly about Alicia. And he felt especially grateful to Nealy for giving Alicia special attention since her mother, Alice, had died during childbirth. The fact that he cared so much about Nealy kept him from telling her the truth about Jerrod. But knowing Jerrod, he'd just deny it, which would cost him his friendship with Nealy. For now, he had to keep his mouth shut, but eventually Jerrod would screw up and do himself in. He just hoped that Nealy could deal with it when the time came, and he wanted to be there for her, at least, as her friend. Nealy was every man's dream: pretty, bright, sweet, smart, witty, and most of all, genuine.

"Nealy, look at me," he said, pulling her face around to wipe away the blood. "Your lip is cut inside and out. That's where all the blood is coming from."

"I know, I can taste it," she said, searching the inside of her mouth with her tongue.

"I don't see anymore lacerations to the head, face or scalp, but you have some large contusions on your upper arms, some small ones on your forearms and left wrist, and a couple on your face and neck. You'll probably have more by tomorrow."

"Randy, you sound so serious. You sound as if you found somebody brutally battered and left for dead in some dumpster," she said, managing a smile.

"I'm glad you find this amusing...at least it's taking your mind off the real problem here." He pulled a chair over next to her and sat down.

"But as sad as it sounds, I feel battered, especially after the last two nights," she said, putting the towel over her face and wiping her eyes.

"Nealy, I'm not trying to pry, but what happened?"

"Oh, Randy, it's a long story."

"I've got time. Tell me. What happened? It had to be pretty serious. Jerrod's a jerk, but this was even beyond what I thought he was capable of," he said, staring at her.

"Where's Alicia?" she asked, concerned that she may be in the car waiting for him.

"She's spending the night with her little friend. Now tell me what happened."

"Why did you come here at this hour? It's after ten."

"This is the last question that I'm answering until you tell me what happened," he replied, wiping her face with a clean towel. "Alicia left her book satchel here. When I called to talk to her this afternoon, she asked me to pick it up after I left the hospital. Of course, I was so late that I knew no one would be here, but when I passed by on my way home, I saw Jerrod's car outside. I knew it was his since he's the only person in town that drives a red porsche with J.J. III on his ego—I mean—license plates. When I saw all the lights on, I decided to come in. But when I reached the porch, I heard shouting. I didn't want to intrude on a domestic squabble, but I didn't like what I heard, so here I am. What did he call me...a nobleman? Of course, I've been called worse," he grinned. "Now, what happened? I want the whole story, friend to friend."

Nealy took a deep breath and sighed, "Oh, Randy, it's such a mess."

"I can see that. So, tell me," he said, patting her hand.

"It all started last night when I told Jerrod that I wanted to buy this studio because Miss Janik wants me take over. She just found out that she has some health problems and she has to retire. He said that I couldn't buy it. In fact, he *forbade* me to buy it. Then he became very angry and told me that I had put off having a baby long enough. He even threw out my birth control pills, telling me that I couldn't run a business and be a mother at the same time. I had never seen him so outraged. Randy, he...he...I can't," she said, tears rolling down her cheeks.

"Nealy, it's alright," he said, squeezing her hand. "Go ahead. I'm listening."

"He tried to force me to have sex so I'd get pregnant. He was talking crazy," she said. Her voice shook and her hands trembled. "It was so awful. He'd never done anything like that. I shouldn't be telling you all this. I'm sorry." She put her head down on the desk. Randy stroked her long, silky, amber hair that had fallen out of the bun she'd had it twisted into during the day.

"No, Nealy, you need to talk about it. That's what friends are for. Then what happened?"

"I became hysterical, so he stopped. He even cried. Then I felt sorry for him, but this morning he told me to forget this crazy idea. It's all so nuts...I just want to dance. I want children, but I'm not ready yet. I want my own life. Is that so bad?" she asked, tears streaming down her face. "I didn't mean to hurt him. I just want this *one thing* for me. Jerrod's a doctor. His life's complete." Nealy put her arms around Randy's neck and her head on his shoulder. Her heart was breaking, and his broke for her. How could he help, other than listen? How could Jerrod do this to her? Why didn't he want her to have her own business, her own freedom to find happiness doing what she loved and what she did so well? There was more to this; he could feel it, especially since he tried to force himself on her. What would raping her accomplish? Now that's really going too far. Thank God, for Nealy's sake, he didn't go through with it. If he had, Randy would make Nealy face the truth about him, that is, if he could. Now he wondered what else he had done other than attempted rape, knocking her around, and trying to destroy her emotionally. What a guy.

"Nealy, is that what made him show up here tonight?"

"I guess so. He called me at five and told me to be home at seven and when I told him that I couldn't, he asked why. I told him that I'd made the decision to buy the studio; I had accepted the offer. Then he became very angry. He seemed more upset than usual, as if he'd been drinking, but it was only five o'clock and he's never through at the hospital by then. When he got here, he began screaming and shouting and grabbing and shaking me, and then he called me a 'dumb fuck'—I'm sorry for using such terrible language. I hate that word, but that's what he called me—and then he called me a 'bimbo,' so I slapped him. I just lost it, and I slapped him. I've never hit anyone in my life."

"Is that what made him hit you?"

"No, he hit me later when he tried to drag me out of here, and I screamed. That happened just before you got here. It was...I—"

"Oh, Nealy, I'm so sorry about this. I wish I could help you, but I can't. He'll get over this. Men like Jerrod have very large egos and he wants to keep you all for himself. He's afraid you won't need him," he said so softly, so kind. He hugged her. "Sweet, sweet, Nealy. Don't cry. It'll all work out."

He tried to calm her down. He knew that it had been a very trying two days for her, both physically and emotionally. If she didn't get it together, she would make herself sick. That would probably suit Jerrod just fine; then she would be forced to stay home. Why was he so insistent about children? With his extra-curricular schedule, he didn't have time for fatherhood. Randy smelled a rat, a very dirty, perfidious little rat.

"I'm sorry, I'm being a blubbering cry baby," she said, sitting up and trying to pull herself together. "God, I must look awful." Nealy put the towel over her face.

"Complaining about the way you look is the first sign of recovery. I think you're going to be alright," he said, lifting up the towel and smiling at her.

"Randy, thank you. You're a great friend," she said, standing up.

Randy stood up, and she hugged him tightly. That hug made the whole night worth it. He hated Jerrod for hurting her, but he thanked him for giving him the opportunity to be with her, even under such adverse conditions. "Nealy, I don't think you should go home. Jerrod's been drinking. After I left the hospital, I stopped by the frat house to get some notes, and Jerrod was out by the pool drinking with the guys. That explains his behavior, although it doesn't excuse it by any means. But, it might not be good for you to go home, just in case he decides to add insult to injury."

"I'll be alright. I really need to get home, but thanks for caring. Will you wait with me while I lock up?"

"Wild horses—or wild husbands—couldn't run me off," he said, smiling at her. He was so glad to see the old Nealy again, and he knew that she would bounce back quickly; she's a fighter. Seeing her so upset, though, had been pretty hard to take. As she ran around turning off the lights and the air conditioners, he watched closely. He had never known anyone could do *so much* for a yard of material. Even though she had wrapped a long skirt around her waist, he could still see how great she looked in her leotard. That was one of the reasons that he managed to get free from the hospital by six on Tuesday evenings. Of course, he loved watching his little girl, and the fact that the teacher had long red hair, a beautiful face, long, shapely legs, a tiny waist, and perfect breasts to compliment her perfect hips just made it more enjoyable.

"Ready?" she asked, stepping out the back door. He followed her into the dark area where she had parked her car behind the building. "Randy, I know I was rather hysterical tonight, but I heard you say something to Jerrod about *whores*. What was that all about?"

"Oh, I was just upset. I said something about not treating you like a whore. I'm sorry, I shouldn't have said that. I was angry," he replied, not looking at her. He had hoped that she had missed that slip, but Nealy was quick; she didn't miss much, if anything.

"Oh, that's okay. I can't thank you enough. I don't know what would have happened if you hadn't shown up," she said, giving him a kiss on the cheek and a quick hug.

"My pleasure, sweet lady. Nealy, here's my number at home. If something should happen, please, call me. I won't mind, in fact, I'll be upset if you don't," he said, holding her hands and smiling at her. "You need to rest tomorrow. You've had a pretty eventful time here lately."

"I will. I get through with my classes at noon tomorrow. I think I'll go down to the Jones' beach house and spend the night. It's always so peaceful down there, and no one ever goes down there. I need some time to think and a couple of days away from Jerrod."

"That sounds perfect. The key word here is *rest*, not swimming or running. Doctor's orders."

"You doctors...you people are always full of orders," she said, giggling.

"You're too kind. Most people claim that we're full of shit!" They broke out laughing, and it felt good.

Randy followed her home to make sure that J.J.III wasn't there, but he didn't expect him to be. Almost every Friday night, like clockwork, Jerrod could be found in the pool at the frat house, fraternizing with a friend or two or three or four.

CHAPTER EIGHTEEN

NEALY WOKE UP with the bright sunshine spilling in through her bedroom window. Quickly, she turned over to Jerrod's side of the bed which hadn't been slept in. Where was he? Where had he spent the night? Her heart sank, but then she thought about what he had done. Why did all of this have to happen? Buying the studio should have been one of the most wonderful times of her life, like her engagement and the day she got married. She and Jerrod had shared so many good times. Why couldn't they share this, too? Her dream turned into a nightmare. She lay there staring at Jerrod's pillow, while tears filled her eyes, stinging them before they gently rolled down her cheeks. Well, here the waterworks come again. No, she was tired of crying. At this point and time, he just wasn't worth anymore tears.

Chance jumped upon the bed and started kissing her face. Dogs always know when their masters are upset. They're real sensitive, especially when things change so drastically and overnight as this situation had. Nealy hugged him and talked to him like she would a person, but he seemed to be all she had at the moment.

Out of necessity, she forced her tired, sore body to stand up and move slowly towards the bathroom.

"Oh, God," she said, looking into the mirror. How would she explain the bruises on her face or her swollen lip? Well, she'd just have to lie, that's all. She couldn't tell anybody, other than Randy, who knew it all already. Telling the truth would be too painful, not to mention, humiliating. But what would she say when people asked her what happened? Being the actress, she could say, "Oh my God, am I bruised and swollen? How did this happen? Did I fall? Geezus, look at me." Or she could tell a twisted version of the truth: "Well, when I told my husband about buying the studio, he got so excited that he attacked me—see the bruises on my thighs, wrists, and breasts—good news really turns him on and he gets kinky, you know, a little S&M(sadism and masochism)." Or maybe she could just say that they liked to get physical when they argued. It's good to let it out. And this slight difference of opinion looks much worse than it really was. Or she could pretend to be a politician and do a little side stepping: "I'm sorry, but I don't understand the question;" "I acted only in self-defense;" "If your character was in question, what would you do?"

Nealy wandered back into the bedroom, wondering if she were more depressed about the way she looked, her fight with Jerrod and the fact that he didn't come home all night, or what she would tell Miss Janik—"Oh, thank goodness," she whispered, suddenly remembering that Miss Janik had gone to Houston. Nealy couldn't bear Miss Janik knowing how badly Jerrod had reacted; it made her feel like such a fool.

With Miss Janik gone, she would need to call Francine. She couldn't tell her the truth because it would be too embarrassing, but she couldn't lie to her either. Nealy had known Francine Cruiser, for more than seventeen years, both as her dance teacher and her friend. And Nealy had encouraged Francine to go to Bennington College in Vermont to pursue a degree in Modern Dance. Then, when Francine returned home after only two years, Nealy was the one that encouraged her to commute to Houston to finish her degree at the university and assist Miss Janik in the studio whenever she could; she was very qualified and wanted to own a studio someday. And now that she was graduating, the timing was perfect for her to become Nealy's assistant. Francine was bright beyond her twenty-two years, energetic enough for two people, yet she moved with grace and style, and the students loved her. Nealy had watched her grow from a lanky, awkward little girl into a beautiful young woman with a long torso, slender arms and legs, and long dark hair; the vision of a professional ballerina. Since Francine had never cared much for Jerrod, which was obvious to Nealy even though she tried not to show it, she couldn't tell her the truth because it would only make her think less of him. Therefore, she had to call and simply say that she wouldn't be able to make it to the studio today and ask her to take over her classes. Francine wouldn't mind because Nealy had taught classes for her on several occasions over the past year while she completed her degree. They worked well together, and that is why Nealy looked forward to having her as an assistant; she felt sure Francine would accept.

Nealy felt relieved when Francine agreed to take over her classes for the day without any hesitation or suspicions. Naturally she had mixed emotions when Nealy told her that Miss Janik would be retiring, but of course Nealy understood because she had felt the same way. However, when Nealy told her that she would be working for "Nealy J's Dance and Theatrical Studio," she became ecstatic, and even more ecstatic when Nealy asked her to be her assistant. So everyone was getting what they wanted except for Jerrod, who, under the circumstances, didn't deserve anything as far as Nealy was concerned.

Nealy hung up the telephone and quickly gathered up her things for the beach; she wanted to get away before Jerrod came home. But who knew when that would be, if ever. He had been pretty angry, and most likely that hadn't changed. Maybe if she turned up missing without a trace, he would miss her and realize how much he loved her, business and all. Was she playing games? Happily married people don't play games, but "happily" was in question here.

Nealy had locked the door and taken only a few steps away from the back door when she heard the telephone ringing. She stopped, but she couldn't decide whether she should answer it or not. But after the fifth ring she decided to answer it just in case Francine needed her. If it were Jerrod, she'd just tell him that she needed to get away and that she would see him Monday night.

Panicked, from fighting with the lock, Nealy ran for the telephone and grabbed it for fear that the caller would hang up before she got there. Nervously, she fumbled the phone, and by the time she got it up to her mouth to speak, someone was already talking: a distraught young woman who Nealy assumed had the wrong number.

CHAPTER NINETEEN

THE DRIVE DOWN to the west end of the island took her about forty-five minutes since she had decided to brave the week-end traffic and take the boulevard. "People watching" would take her mind off her troubles. She watched all the young people in their convertibles, sitting on the top of the back seat and screaming at people in other cars. Their radios blared, and they sang along. The reckless days of youth blinded them from feeling like complete imbeciles. Chance hung his head out the window letting his mouth catch the wind, causing his tongue to flap up and down. As a retriever, he loved the beach, and Nealy always took him with her. He was the perfect companion: loyal, loving and unconditional in every way.

Nealy opened up the house and let the air circulate. Then she began to clean up the mess that someone had left, which confused her. His parents had been out of town for the past month, not together of course, and she had never known them to let anyone other than the family use the place. And Jerrod didn't like to go there because he said the walls were too thin, and he envisioned his parents with a glass up to the bedroom wall listening for moans and cries of ecstacy. Nealy found that contradictory for someone who found it exciting to *have sex* in public. But, because of his paranoia, she and Jerrod had only gone there a couple of times during the past two years. Nealy loved it, but Jerrod never wanted her to go down there alone; he claimed that it was too dangerous. The house was small and cozy with a kitchen and living area combined and two bedrooms. Even though the house was separate, it had been built in a small, but spacious community environment that shared a pool with a deck and large gazebo-style clubhouse for parties, and a separate bathhouse complete with a whirlpool and sauna. Ironically, Jerrod had talked his parents into buying it because the fraternity alumni had bought the one next door to use for entertaining. That's the way with boys and their toys: It's not getting what they want, it's wanting it after they get it. How quickly the thrill dies.

Nealy put her food away and changed for the beach. Chance couldn't wait to romp up and down the beach, diving for the frisbee. The sun sat straight-up in the sky, marking it high noon. The sun's rays were warm and wonderful, but Nealy put up her umbrella to prevent too much sun too soon; her fair skin burned easily, causing her to freckle even more. She stretched out, relaxing to the sound of the ocean and listening to the seagulls singing off key, impersonating a squeaky tenor and a gravelly baritone. Chance had settled in next to her for his afternoon nap. The beach, for the most part, was deserted. The ten houses in the beach community took up almost a mile of beach front, making the area almost private. Nealy tried to fight off the demons that wanted to disturb her peaceful surroundings by reminding her of Jerrod and what a pompous ass he had been. The day was much too beautiful to be tarnished. The temperature rose high into the eighties by two o'clock, but the cool breeze off the water kept her comfortable, even when she chose to ease out from under her umbrella to catch a few rays. Every so often a fat cloud would drift over her, giving her a break from the extreme brightness of the sun. If only she could sleep, but she couldn't because she just kept thinking about her life and wondering why things happen the way they do. Suddenly, Chance jumped up and took off down the beach. Nealy raised up and lifted her dark sunglasses to see what attracted his attention. She noticed a man and a small girl walking towards her; the man had a basket in his hand and a bundle of towels under his arm. Then she saw Chance in the edge of the water in front of her playing with another dog about his size. The child came running towards her.

"Miss Nealy, hi."

"Oh, hi, Alicia," Nealy said, sitting up. "Where did you come from?" she asked, watching as Randy approached them. He had an athletic build, but, because of his busy schedule, take out and greasy hospital food, he had put on a few extra pounds around the middle. But he still qualified as a nice looking guy and he had a good-hearted disposition and he was always the perfect gentleman.

"My daddy didn't have to go to the hospital today, so he brought me to the beach," she said happily and full of life.

"Well, that's wonderful. I'm glad you're here."

"I'm glad, too," she said, giving her a big toothless smile. "My daddy will be glad, too. He thinks you're real nice, and pretty too." Smiling, the little matchmaker scooted off towards the water.

"Hi," Nealy said to Randy when he walked up next to where she remained seated. His dark hair blew forward in the wind, framing his kind face that sported a grin from ear to ear.

"Hi, Nealy. I hope you don't mind if we intrude. I got the day off, and Alicia threw a fit to come down here. And to be perfectly honest, I was a little concerned about you."

"That's really sweet. Please, sit down," she smiled, patting the ground beside her. "Actually, I'm glad to see you both. I felt a little lonely."

He spread out his towel and sat down. "I'm sorry if you were lonely, but I'm glad you took the day off."

"Well, since Jerrod hates to come here, I knew he wouldn't show up. It seemed like the perfect place to hide, as well as to rest and relax. Isn't that what you ordered me to do, Doctor?" she giggled.

"I did, and I'm glad to see that you actually followed my orders. Jerrod doesn't like it here, huh?" he asked, looking rather puzzled. That seemed very strange since Randy ran into him there quite often. Poor Nealy, Jerrod had her so snowed about his devotion that she just accepted whatever he told her as the truth. One thing for sure, if ever a contest came up for the World's Greatest Liar, Jerrod would take first place; but one of these days he'd stump his toe, tell one lie too many, and the wall will come tumbling down. Unfortunately, Nealy would be the one to suffer, which didn't seem fair, but life's not always fair, not even to the nicest people.

"Randy," Nealy said softly. "Thanks again for last night. And I apologize for being such a baby."

"I think you reacted better than most, but that doesn't surprise me. You're a fighter, remember that," he said, patting her on the back.

"Ouch," she said, pulling away from him.

"Oh, Nealy, I'm sorry. Does your back hurt, too?"

"Yeah, I guess I landed pretty hard when Jerrod hit me."

"I'm really sorry. I—"

"It's okay. Just call me Rocky," she chuckled. Randy laughed too. Nealy didn't really feel like company, but Randy had been so nice to her that she needed to at least make him feel welcome. He had turned out to be a great friend. Since marrying Jerrod, she hadn't had time to see too many of her friends, and besides, they were all married and had children. So having Randy as her friend had been nice. At times, she sensed that he could feel more than friendship if she weren't married, and that made her a little uncomfortable. But accusing men of wanting more from a female friend than a purely platonic relationship seemed unfair and a bit conceited; she had always had men friends and sincerely enjoyed their company. For one thing, they were kind and polite and respectful. Never once had a guy ever gotten out of line with her. But, in Nealy's case, everyone knew how much she loved Jerrod. Most people thought that her devotion to him was totally unappreciated, but it really wasn't any of their business; their concerns maybe, but not their business.

"How about a quick swim?"

"Okay," Nealy answered, using his hand as a pulley. The five of them, which included the two dogs, played in and out of the water for more than an hour. The salt water had even taken some of the soreness out of her body. What had seemed like an intrusion on her privacy, now felt like a blessing, brightening her day as they laughed and played as if they were a family spending the day together.

Hungry from all the activity, Nealy and Randy headed back to the umbrella for lunch.

"How about a peanut butter and jelly sandwich?" Randy asked her, digging through the basket that he had prepared.

"Alicia's favorite, I presume?"

"Of course, but it's mine, too," he chuckled. "The body grows up, but the little boy always remains when it comes to *a good p,b and j.*"

"Has it been tough rearing Alicia on your own?"

"Well, yes, and no," he answered. "Because Alice died when Alicia was born, I never knew any other way. I had to take care of her myself since I was in college and I couldn't afford much help. But I managed. Some days were more difficult than others. One thing for sure, I developed a great respect for mothers."

"You've done a very good job. She's a very special little girl, but that's because she has a very special daddy," Nealy smiled sincerely.

"Thanks. I'll take that as a compliment," he said proudly, although somewhat surprised that she had opened up so much.

"Please do." Nealy mirrored his smile. Thoroughly enjoying themselves, the two of them watched Alicia build a sand castle. Occasionally, she would scold the dogs for messing up her creation.

"Nealy, have you ever regretted giving up your dream to become an entertainer? I know that's not a fair question, especially now that you're angry with Jerrod, but I know that must have been a difficult decision." He watched her very carefully as she thought about the question. His dark brown eyes centered on her face, searching for a sign of remorse.

"At times I wonder if I did the right thing, but then I look at Jerrod, and I know I did. Randy, I know that you don't really like him, but he's been very good to me. Until now, we've never had any problems. Jerrod has always been sweet and thoughtful, giving me everything that I could possibly want. He's spoiled, I know, but he's never acted spoiled with me. And I don't really understand it. This is the person who never stopped telling me how he wanted me to have it all, but now, when I want something for myself, he's acting very selfish. It's as if I have no say in what happens in my life now. As I watch Alicia, I think having children would be so special, but I'm really not ready for that kind of sacrifice. Is that being selfish?"

"No, it's being honest. Nealy, you're smart to wait, even if Jerrod pushes you. After you have children, your life is not your own anymore. Your life belongs to them. I'm not saying it's not worth it. It is. It's the most wonderful thing that can happen to a person. But, it's such a responsibility, one that consumes your life for at least twenty years."

"I guess that's why I'm not ready. I need to feel that I accomplished something really important. I want to be a good role model for my children. And to me, that's what being a parent is all about," she said, nervously drawing a happy face in the sand with her finger.

"You're right. When the time is right, you'll be happy about it, Nealy," he said, drawing a happy face next to hers in the sand.

"I just hope I can convince Jerrod of that," she sighed.

The afternoon passed quickly, and the sun slowly sank into the ocean just West of them. The sky resembled a giant abstract painting with splashes of bright pink and orange paint across a blue background. Randy started a fire and straightened out the ends of coat hangers for roasting marshmallows. The fire flickered from the wind, and Alicia screamed frantically when her marshmallow caught fire; Randy blew it out. Nealy imagined herself back on the beach in Bermuda were she and Jerrod snuggled together by the fire after making love under the full moon. The thoughts of those times made her sad and distracted, but she tried to keep her mind on the friends that had rescued her from an emotional hell.

"Girls, I say we call it a night." Randy announced. "I hate to end such a perfect day, but I've got to be at the hospital at six." He pulled his watch out of his pants pocket to check the time. "It's almost eight."

"Oh, Daddy, do we have to?" Alicia whined.

"I'm afraid so, honey. Besides, Ms. Nealy came down here to rest. But we didn't let her rest much, did we?"

"We'll do it again soon, Alicia," Nealy said, pulling Alicia close to her and giving her a big hug.

"Okay, Ms. Nealy, if you promise."

"I promise, dance teacher's honor," she said, putting her first two fingers up in the air. Nealy got up and slipped her cover up over her head. "Ouch, I guess I burned myself today," she admitted, holding her top away from her back.

"Well, now you can be black and blue and red all over," Randy said, chuckling softly.

"Very funny, Dr. Richfield," Nealy said, cutting her eyes to give him a disapproving look, but then she bursted into a loud giggle.

"Huh? I don't get it," Alicia said, looking up at them.

"It's nothing, honey. Your father thinks he's funny. Ha, ha, ha," Nealy said.

"Yeah, Daddy, ha, ha, ha," Alicia said, taking sides.

"That's right honey. Us girls have to stick together." Nealy gave her another hug. "Now, let's get this show on the road. It's getting late. The three of them gathered up the things that they had scattered around and shook the towels, leaving the sand at the beach.

Nealy walked out to their car with them. Randy loaded up their belongings, while Alicia climbed in the front seat. Before he got into the car, he quietly said, "I hope you aren't angry for what I said, but I couldn't resist."

"No, it was funny...and true...but sad...but still funny," she giggled. "It's always best if you can find humor in something tragic."

"Thanks for being so good with Alicia. I feel I've cheated her out of a mother, but I just haven't met the right person yet. It's going to take a special person to fill those shoes. And I'm not trying to flatter you, Nealy, honest, but

I want whoever it is to possess the same wonderful qualities that you have. I've watched you with her in class and her whole face lights up whenever you hug her. Right now I feel like smiling. You got any hugs left for her old man?"

"As a matter of fact, I just happen to have one left," she giggled softly, giving him a little hug.

Randy got in the car and started the engine. "'Bye, Alicia. I'll see you in class next week."

"Okay, 'bye, Ms. Nealy." She and Randy both waved as they drove away, and Nealy waved back.

Later that night, Nealy showered and curled up on the couch with a book. Reading a romance novel might take her away to some glorious place where women like to go when their own life is on the brink of disaster. By midnight, she was fast asleep.

At ten o'clock the next morning the telephone rang. Nealy jumped up feeling a little disoriented from coming out of a deep sleep and facing unfamiliar surroundings, she turned in several directions before answering the phone.

"Hello."

"Good-morning," Randy said cheerfully.

"Good-morning," she said, looking at the clock.

"I woke you. I'm sorry."

"That's okay. I can't believe I slept so late."

"You needed the rest. Anyway, it's a perfect day to sleep since it's pouring down rain."

"You're kidding," she frowned, looking out the window. "I was so tired I didn't even hear it. Well, that took care of my day in the sun. But I'm pretty red, so it's just as well."

"Are you staying down there another night?"

"I think so. I don't feel too forgiving yet."

"I don't blame you. Well, I just called to check on you. I'll see you Tuesday afternoon at Alicia's class. Go rest some more, and call if you need anything."

"I will, Randy, thanks. See you Tuesday." Nealy hung up the phone and offered Chance the opportunity to face the torrential rains for his morning business, but he declined and curled back up on his rug. After staring out at the water being pushed and battered by the wind, she decided to sleep a little more if she could. She loved the sound of the rain beating hard against the roof; it was her favorite time to sleep, but it could also be sad and lonely and somewhat depressing. Depressed already, her mind ignored her orders to go back to sleep, so she finally got up and took a shower. Needing some positive reinforcement, she decided to visit her parents and tell them about her new studio; they would be thrilled for her because, unlike Jerrod, they truly cared about her dreams and her happiness.

While dressing, the urge to call Jerrod finally got the best of her, but she hung up after the second ring. What would she say? I'm sorry. No way. Even though she wanted to talk to him, she just couldn't do it right now. He had hurt her deeply, so he had to make the first move. After all, he had the problem, not her.

Nealy arrived at her parents' house around one in hopes of getting a good meal. Every Sunday after church, her mother always cooked enough for any and all of her children that might stop by for food and fellowship. Nealy ate a little pot roast and mash potatoes, but, for the most part, she played in it, scooting her peas and corn around the plate clockwise.

"Nealy, stop playing in your food," Gracie James scolded. "You're so thin, honey, you need to put some meat on those bones."

"I'm fine, Mother," Nealy retorted softly. "What if I got big and fat and jumped around *my studio* in a pink ruffled tutu looking like Hildegard the Hippo. Would you want your child taking lessons from me?" she giggled, waiting for a reaction from her father who rarely missed anything.

"Oh, Nealy, you are such a clown. I don't—"

Neal James interrupted his wife. " 'My *studio*.' Could you explain that, please," he said, listening intently.

"Miss Janik has to retire. She has some health problems—"

"Not serious, I hope," her mother fretted.

"Well, serious, but not life threatening." Nealy continued to fill them in on all the details, but she avoided talking about Jerrod all together. But, it didn't work.

"How does Jerrod feel about this?" her father asked sternly.

"Well, of course, he's delighted—"

"Gracie, I asked Nealy," he scolded politely, obviously wanting to hear it from the horse's mouth, so to speak.

Unable to lie to her parents, Nealy carefully chose her words. "Uh...he would rather start a family, but...he'll get over it. He knows this is something I want. It's a dream-come-true—"

"I don't mean to interrupt, Nealy, but I'm not clear about Jerrod and the *family thing*," her father gestured.

"Well, it's not like my biological clock is ticking out of time. I'm only twenty-five."

"But twenty-six is just around the corner," her sister, Lucy, quickly volunteered.

"Thanks for sharing that, Lucy. I can always count on you," Nealy said, cutting her eyes towards her sister and her two other siblings and their wives.

"Why are you giving me that evil-eyed look, Nealy? It's true. Thirty is closer than you think, sis. Maybe Jerrod's right."

Nealy could always count on her big brother. "She's got plenty of time to have babies. This is a golden opportunity—I'm sorry about Miss Janik—but things like this don't come along everyday, you know."

"Thanks for your never-failing support, Jim," Nealy said kindly.

"Well, honey, you *have* been married for a while. What's the problem?"

"Gracie, I can't believe it," her father said in an annoying tone. "That's none of your business."

"Oh, Daddy, I don't mind this *obvious invasion of my privacy*," she sneered dramatically, but she couldn't get angry with them, they were all too close, so she giggled, causing a rippling effect of laughter.

"You're right, honey, he'll come around," her mother reassured her. "Most men prefer their wives to stay at home. This women's liberation thing is still a little mind-boggling for them. They simply weren't brought up that way."

"Your mother's right, Nealy, Jerrod wants to be the bread winner—"

"It's ego, pure and simple," Lucy blurted out.

"Like I was saying," her father said, glaring at Lucy, "he wants to take care of you. He'll accept this in time."

"But, honey, you and Jerrod will make beautiful babies, and just think about all that fun you'll have trying."

"Mother!" Nealy squealed, shocked beyond words.

"Gracie, I don't believe you said that. You're *amazing*."

"I know, dear, you said that during *our* baby-making days," she grinned

All the way home, Nealy prayed that Jerrod wouldn't call her parents' house. If he did, no telling what he might say.

When she opened the door, Chance ran past her and headed for the beach, so she followed him. The rain had past leaving the air thick and salty. Nealy loved the fresh, clean smell after a rain, but she hated the dampness. Since hair and humidity didn't mix, she had often been accused of trying to impersonate Orphan Annie; she had serious frizzies.

With each step, her feet made deep impressions in the sand that quickly filled with dirty water from the rough, turbulent seas. Nealy called out to Chance when the sun, barely peeking through the lingering clouds, prepared for it's nightly ritual of dropping off into the ocean; she wanted to get back to the house before dark. The large rainbow, which she had been admiring, had faded to only a hint of pink and green and yellow. Oh, how she loved rainbows; she felt safe because she could still hear her grandmother's voice saying, "Nealy, see the rainbow. That's God way of sending his love."

Almost home, Nealy saw two perfectly formed sand dollars face up and side by side in the sand. When she bent down to pick them up, she became engulfed by a cool breeze that felt as if tiny tentacles were softly stroking her face. A rush of soothing serenity enveloped her and that face appeared; that adorable face of *Dr. Somebody*. Over the past two years, he had interrupted her thoughts on many occasions and every time she immediately smiled. Isn't it funny how a person can touch someone for such a brief moment and then return from time to time as a reminder of what *life* is all about. Life has a heart and a soul that together create feelings. Feelings that are good, bad, sad, silly happy, angry, indifferent, loving, lasting, kind, evil, and true. Feelings that come and feelings that go. One minute the feeling is there, and poof, just like that, it's gone. But Nealy had held on to that happy feeling; the one that had moved her when she and *Dr. Somebody* exchanged one last smile on her last night in New York. And even though she had gone on with her life and she knew that she would never see him again, she wanted to hold on to that feeling in hopes that it would be there in her times of need. It didn't make sense, but it didn't matter, she liked the feeling, even if it only lasted for a few seconds. Nealy carefully picked up the sand dollars and held them in the palms of her hands. Like life, they were so fragile. And without tender, loving care, their edges could chip away slowly until there was nothing left but the broken pieces of shell that once brought joy to the eyes of the beholder. Nealy carefully wrapped them in a tissue that she pulled from her pocket.

And suddenly like a raging storm, disturbing her inner peace and tranquility, Jerrod rushed back into her mind, a place where she had forbid him to go. Chance danced on his hind legs, barking to get her attention that had wandered off into the depths of the ocean. "What is it fella? Is it dinner time?" she asked, smiling when he took off up the trail.

Later that night, Nealy called Francine to talk shop. And after a long chat, she turned-in; the stress and lack of sleep had taken its toll, and she wanted to be at the studio early on Monday.

But the darkness and the silence brought back the sadness and the loneliness. Nealy missed Jerrod. She missed the warmth of his body next to hers. But she couldn't call him. She couldn't go home. And even if she could, she wouldn't, for fear that he might not be there. Her stomach tied in knots. She tossed. She turned. Every hour she looked at the clock, praying for morning. Misery deserved company, but Chance slept like a baby on the rug next to her bed. And finally, at twenty to five, she got up, made coffee, took a shower, and then dressed for work. Her mind raced with thoughts of what the day would bring. Two days had passed since she left home. Had Jerrod tried to find her? Did he even care that she had disappeared without a trace? Obviously not, or she would have heard from someone.

Leaving the beach house at six, she drove along the boulevard to watch the sun come up. But heavy clouds and thick ground fog made it difficult to see, so she drove slowly, pulling into her driveway at six-thirty. The light in the kitchen shined dimly, and when she put Chance in the yard, she wanted desperately to go inside, but she didn't.

Her heart ruled her head and she slammed the car door wanting to be heard in the stillness of the morning. But nothing happened. No one appeared at the door. No one peeked out the window. She started her car and waited. Was he there? Maybe he had already gone to the hospital; he left lights on all the time. Her heart ached. Tears filled her eyes. Had she found her dream...but lost her love?

CHAPTER TWENTY

THE STUDIO still felt damp from the rain so Nealy turned the air conditioning units on to dry the air. Then she turned on some music to occupy her mind. She pulled out the papers regarding the sale of the studio and read over them again, getting excited again. If only Jerrod could be excited too, she thought. At seven-thirty, Miss Janik and Francine walked inside talking and laughing about one of the little guys in the six year old ballet class that Francine had taught on Saturday. He had cried all during the class saying over and over "I'm not a sissy," which his friends had been calling him for wearing a leotard.

"Poor little fellow," Nealy said, "but he'd better get used to it; it'll only get worse as he grows older if he continues to take lessons. Maybe his mother should reconsider and let him play baseball. I'd hate to be responsible for giving the kid a lifetime of emotional problems." They chuckled, but it was sad for little Tad, who had been nicknamed "Tadpole" by the other children in the class, which made matters even worse.

"Well, Nealy, are you ready to sign the papers?" Miss Janik asked her. "Fred Fredricks called me last night, and he's ready if we are."

"Sure," she answered. "But, Miss Janik, are you sure about this? I could run the studio for you, and that way you wouldn't be giving it up completely. I wouldn't mind. In fact, I can't imagine this place without you."

"No, Nealy, I'm sure, but I appreciate the offer. I want to travel. Do you know I've never been to Europe?"

"Are you telling me that I'll never get to go to France, my fantasy since childhood, if I buy this studio?"

"No," Miss Janik said, chuckling, "but it'll be a while, so don't pack your bags yet."

That afternoon Fred came by with the papers in final form for Miss Janik and Nealy to sign their lives away. The terms were simple, so all went smooth. They hugged and cried, and even Francine got in on the action by officially becoming Nealy's one and only assistant. Nealy felt numb and excited and happy and scared, all at the same time. So much had happened that she hadn't given much thought to her problems with Jerrod, but she would have plenty of time to settle up with him later, unless...no, she had to think positive. Things would work out.

By four o'clock the studio came to life and children were everywhere screaming and shouting at one another. The door opened, and a young man carrying a vase of red roses walked in and asked for Nealy Jones. Nealy had just started the music in an attempt to get her class going. Francine stuck her head in the studio and motioned for her to come out for a minute. When she saw the flowers, her eyes watered, and she knew that Jerrod had finally realized how selfish he had been.

"Oh, they're so beautiful," Nealy cried.

"Well, open the card," Francine scolded, even though she knew full well who had sent them. At least one Saturday a month, Nealy received some sort of gift from Jerrod, most likely Francine thought, to ease his guilty conscience. Francine took an adult class from Nealy on Monday nights. Some of her classmates, who were nursing students at the University of Texas Medical Branch, the branch where Jerrod interned, were not aware of the relationship between Francine and Nealy, and therefore, they talked pretty freely around her when Nealy wasn't in the room. One night, Francine overheard them talking about Dr. Jones and his friendship with some of the nursing students, as well as some nurses that had graduated the year before. They never said Jerrod, but Francine put two and two together. Why else would they shut up when Nealy came into the room? Of course, Francine had never mentioned it to Nealy because she really wasn't sure what type of relationship he had with these people, so it would merely be gossip. Why hurt Nealy if she really didn't have the facts? Maybe they were jealous and it had only been a doctor and nurse thing: hand me this, get me that, or even a little pat on the butt here or there. It could be basically harmless, or even wishful thinking on their part. Anyway, Francine found the tales about Jerrod so hard to believe because he seemed head-over-heels in love with Nealy. Francine watched Nealy's face brighten as she read the card. "Well, what does it say?"

> *"Congratulations to the new owner of Nealy J's Studio. I'm very proud of you. We're having a celebration party in your honor at Aunt Ruth's tonight at eight o'clock.*
> *I love you, J.J."*

"Well, once again, I underestimated Jerrod," Miss Janik admitted, surprised that he had taken it so well. She had always put him in the same category with *that man, My Gene.*

Francine smiled at Nealy, happy that she seemed more ecstatic than usual, and Nealy smiled back, grinning enormously. Now she could relax and enjoy it all: her dream and her love.

Miss Janik took over Nealy's class so that she could go home early and get ready for the party. At seven the phone rang. Nealy grabbed it.

"Hello," she said nervously.

"Neal, I'm sorry I behaved so badly. Please forgive me," Jerrod said remorsefully. Nealy didn't say anything. "Neal...I...I can't lose you, so please, please forgive me," he pleaded.

"Jerrod, I'm trying. I want to understand, but you make it so difficult sometimes—"

"I know," he interrupted, "but, Nealy, I'll never do anything like that again. I promise. I'll never, ever hurt you again. Please, baby, give me another chance. Come to the party, please," he begged softly. Nealy didn't let on about how excited that she'd been when the flowers came. She wanted to keep him feeling unsure of her for just a little longer. He needed to know that she could not forgive such an attack against her so easily. Maybe it would be better for both of them if she played hard-to-get-back.

"Okay, I'll be over about eight," she said, still sounding distant.

"Nealy, one other thing," he said, "there's a white limousine in front of the house waiting for you. See you at eight. I love you, baby."

Nealy ran into the living room and looked out the window. "Oh My God." She couldn't believe it. The neighbors probably thought someone had died. They might even think that she had become the victim, especially if they had heard all of the shouting that had been going on in their house over the last few days. It seemed crazy, but she didn't know what to do now. Did she go out to them or would they come to the door and ring the bell at seven-thirty or so? Well, she'd wait, and if they didn't come for her, she'd go out and knock on the window. That didn't seem too classy, but what else could she do? Nealy had never been in a limo in her life.

At seven-forty, the doorbell rang. That took care of that dilemma, even though she felt rather strange being escorted to the car by the chauffeur. But, if the neighbors were watching, which they probably were since limousines rarely came into their neighborhood, at least they knew she was alive and obviously well.

The gang awaited her arrival, cheering when she drove up. It seemed very exciting, but at the same time it made her feel self-conscious and a little embarrassed that Jerrod had made such a big deal out of it by getting the entire family and their friends involved. Graciously, Nealy hugged everyone. As usual, Aunt Ruth had thought of everything. The tables were covered with chicken, brisket, ribs, and hamburgers smothered in barbecue sauce that lingered in the air. People manhandled their ribs and some even licked their fingers. Nealy looked up, and the stars were everywhere, thick and bright. "Hi," a voice said from behind her. She turned around, not really recognizing it.

"Hi," she said, without expression. For some reason, even with the party and all, she had not totally forgiven him. "You look tired."

"I am. I haven't slept much. I really screwed up, didn't I?" he asked reluctantly.

"Jerrod, you're right. You did screw up, but you're my husband," she said, staring at him, her heart pounding like a drum.

"Does that mean I'm forgiven?"

"Not exactly, but yes, this time," she said cautiously.

"Oh, Neal—"

"Not so fast, buster," she said, pushing him away as he went to put his arms around her. "I need time, Jerrod. I'm not a real forgiving soul. I need to come to terms with my own anger first before I can totally forgive you."

"I understand. But don't take too long, baby. I missed you and I'm dying to take you in my arms," he said, his eyes begging her.

"Jerrod, please—"

"Okay, I'll give you time, but I'll be close by when you're ready." He walked away slowly and her heart told her to grab him, but thank goodness, she didn't. She watched him carefully as he passed the beer keg. Looking back, he gestured that he had not had one single drop of any intoxicating beverage the entire evening. It almost caused her to laugh, but she maintained her composure. If nothing else, Nealy had proved her ability to be a good actress. No one even suspected that she and Jerrod had not seen each other since Friday night and that they had experienced one of the worst arguments that anyone could imagine. They still seemed like the perfect couple, except more mature, not nearly as lovey-dovey as they had appeared on their wedding night, but that's expected.

The party began to break up by nine-thirty because most of the guests had been there since seven waiting for Nealy to make her entrance. Jerrod appeared very gracious and thanked people for coming to help him share in Nealy's success. He put his arm around her, but kept in mind her request for space. Jerrod wasn't stupid; quite the contrary, he was extremely smart and always charming. He could feel her tremble when he touched her, but he didn't dare pursue it. Nealy's physical attraction for him had always been strong, and Jerrod was well aware of it. He knew how to stir her emotions, leaving her extremely vulnerable. But for now, he had to back off because she had a stubborn streak, and he knew only too well not to push his luck. She would come around soon if he took a step closer and closer, but at a very slow pace.

With only a few people left, Jerrod encouraged Nealy to leave. Since she had come in the limousine, she would be riding home with him. She stared out the window, trying desperately to hang on to her anger, but she could feel the urge to be next to him taking over. When they got home, he pulled the car into the garage and quickly ran around to help her out. When they reached the backdoor, he unlocked it and pushed it open. Before she could resist, he had lifted her up and carried her, once again, over the threshold to a new life. He walked through the kitchen and into the bedroom, gently laying her down on the bed, and then lying down beside her. "Don't say anything, just let me hold you for a minute," he said softly. He nervously played with her fingers, swept the hair from her face, and softly kissed her forehead. When he felt a tear on her face, he quickly kissed it away and then softly brushed his lips over hers.

"Jerrod—"

"Nealy, please forgive me. And please don't cry. I never want to make you cry again. I'm so sorry, baby," he said, kissing her face and her fingers that he held tightly against his lips. "I love you so much."

"I love you, too," she whispered, putting her hand behind his head and guiding his lips to meet hers. Nealy let her emotions take over, which led her back into the arms of the man she married for better or worse. They held each other, kissing and cuddling like newlyweds in the darkness of the room, with only their blind passion and their emotions to guide them. Nealy unbuttoned his shirt slowly, touching and feeling her way very seductively.

Jerrod caressed every part of her body tenderly, slowly stimulating and arousing each area of known sensitivity. Their hearts were filled with unleashed affection, and the night stood still to allow what appeared to be the purest form of love making, where one loves and feels loved. As their warm flesh touched, soft sounds of excitement echoed in the silence, enticing the other to open up to greater pleasures. Jerrod talked softly, insisting that she savor each moment, so he could take her beyond euphoria. Their love deepened, growing more indestructible as their hands passed across the softness of a breast or the stiffness of a nipple. Mindless and crazy with desire, Nealy didn't sense Jerrod's chest moving against her breasts, or her hands pulling him closer and drawing him into her, and she never knew the moment that separated them.

A few hours later, Nealy awoke feeling fulfilled as she lay snuggled up to Jerrod's warm naked body. The thought of ever being separated from him again frightened her. But a few minutes later, driven by another desire, she slipped out of bed and found herself standing in front of her opened refrigerator in search of something to eat. Chance sat at her feet, looking up at her with his adoring puppy dog eyes, begging. Both she and Jerrod had the same effect on her, and she had trouble saying no to whatever they wanted. After pouring herself a big glass of milk, she pulled out some turkey and made a sandwich, and then practically split it with Chance. Trying to be as quiet as possible, she tip-toed through the bedroom and into the bathroom, pushing the door almost closed and then switching on the light. Since Jerrod hadn't given her a chance to wash off her make-up, her face felt terrible and she needed to brush her teeth. The mirror had fogged up from the hot water, but she could still see the door opening very slowly behind her. It scared her at first, but then she figured it was Chance coming to pay her a visit. She watched as Jerrod pushed his way inside and snuggled up to her.

"Come back to bed, baby, I need you," he whispered.

"I think this is the real Jerrod," she teased, looking at him in the mirror, his chin resting on her shoulder and his eyes shut. "Yes, I do believe this is the one with the very active libido, so if I come back to bed as you have requested, I must warn you of something first," she softly said, drying her face with a towel. "I spent the most wonderful hour of my life being made love to by your angelic counterpart, so your performance will be judged." His eyes didn't open, but she felt his desires growing stronger as he rubbed himself against her. All of her life, Nealy had heard that men had several erections during the night and even woke up with a hard-on, which made them ready and raring to go. And now, the fact that Jerrod stood behind her physically aroused, but existing in a state somewhere between sleep and wake, she knew that it was not just a myth. The longer Nealy stood there, the more she realized that what lay ahead would not be fit for comparison because this time it would be the sex that she usually experienced with Jerrod: strictly physical.

"Baby, come on, I'm horny" he said, pulling at her and untying her robe, even though he hadn't yet opened his eyes.

"Let's go, loverboy," she said, turning him around and heading towards the bed. "It's time to tame the tiger so that we can get some sleep."

CHAPTER TWENTY-ONE

MONTHS PASSED and Nealy spent most of her time at the studio doing what she did best. Her classes grew larger, and she had Francine working with her everyday in order to keep up the pace. As a promise to herself, she took a night off every two or three weeks to spend time with her friends. Friendship is important, and, like any other relationship, it needs to be nurtured. Nealy's best friend, Betty Lou, had suffered so much with a difficult pregnancy and an unhappy marriage that Nealy needed to spend time with her. One of the happiest moments in Nealy's life was the night she helped Betty Lou bring her baby, Erica, into the world; birth is such a miracle. The fact that Betty Lou didn't want Beaux to go through natural childbirth classes with her made Nealy terribly sad, but she had loved sharing that experience with her best friend, even though it didn't change her mind about motherhood; however, it did affect Jerrod. Who hinted about becoming a father many times afterwards. But Nealy still had reservations about starting a family. She saw the problems in Betty Lou's marriage, and even though she and Jerrod rarely had disagreements, she had not forgotten the two most horrible nights of her life and how deeply they had affected her. Although she had to admit that Jerrod became a better husband after that, so maybe a little conflict, not physical violence, every now and then can keep a guy on his toes. To Nealy's surprise, he encouraged her to help Betty Lou by offering to babysit her two little girls, and then the four of them would go to the circus or do other things that children liked to do. He rarely spent Friday nights away anymore, in fact, Friday had become their night to be together, even if it meant having dinner in the doctor's lounge at the hospital. Nealy would fill a picnic basket with goodies and spend two or three hours hanging out with him, eating between patient calls and visiting with some of his special patients. At times, it seemed like the blissful days of courtship, which many marriages tend to lose touch with as the years pass.

On their third anniversary, Jerrod sent Nealy a dozen beautiful red roses to the studio. The card read:

Mrs. Jones,
   Thank you for three of the most wonderful years of my entire life. I would be honored if you would join me for dinner at Gaido's this evening at seven o'clock.
                                                          I love you, J.J.

Of course, Nealy cried and left early for a date with her husband. It took her a long time to decide what to wear because she wanted to look especially beautiful. Finally, she picked a pretty yellow sundress that had a deep scoop neck, which she hadn't worn since their honeymoon. It had been one of Jerrod's favorites, so she knew he would like to see her in it again. When he walked in the door, Nealy walked out of the bedroom.

"How do I look?"

"You look beautiful," he said, walking over and giving her a sweet kiss. "You wore that dress in Bermuda. It's my favorite."

Nealy put one arm in the little bolero jacket that matched her dress, but before she could get her other arms in, Jerrod had taken it off her arm. "Jerrod, what are you doing?"

"I like it better without the jacket. Please, for me."

"Jerrod, I'll be cold."

"I'll warm you up," he said, pulling her close to kiss her.

"Okay," she said, laying the jacket on the chair.

"That's my girl."

The sun had hidden behind some heavy clouds, but it hadn't rained. The air was damp but warm, so Nealy didn't mind leaving her jacket even though she still felt a little uncomfortable wearing a low cut dress out in public that only had two little spaghetti straps holding it up. It always made her self-conscious, but Jerrod loved her half-naked, and she wanted to please him. He had been so good not to harass her about spending so much time at the studio, and at times he even seemed very interested and pleased with her success. Jerrod had asked for a special table in the corner next to the window, which he knew was Nealy's favorite. She said that watching the ocean made her feel warm inside, and since he had something along that line that he wanted to talk to her about, he needed all the help that he could get. The waiter took their order and left them alone with their glasses of wine.

"To my bride of three years," he said, holding up his glass.

Nealy lifted up her glass and touched his carefully. "Three years," she said softly, smiling at him.

"Are you happy, Neal?" he asked, taking her hand in his.

"Yes, of course I am. What made you asked that?"

"Well, I guess I just take it for granted that you are. So, I just needed a little reassurance."

"Jerrod, you've never been insecure."

"When it comes to you, I am at times. I really love you, Neal. I never want to be without you. Everyday, I find myself wanting more and more of you."

"That's so sweet, Jerrod. Is my work the problem?"

"Oh, no, Neal, your work's fine. In fact, I'm really happy that you have it. I'm gone so much now that I'm glad you have the studio to keep you busy. It keeps me from feeling guilty."

"Here's your dinner, sir," the waiter said, setting a nice plate of fried shrimp and hush puppies down in front of both of them. "Can I get you anything else?"

"Another carafe of your house wine, please," Jerrod said.

"Yes, sir," he answered, hurrying away, and returning within minutes to refill their glasses. Nealy and Jerrod ate and talked casually throughout dinner. The darkness came down on the ocean like a curtain, allowing only the white caps to be visible from the window. Far off the shore, the lights from an oil rig could be seen. Nealy stared out the window in silence.

"Jerrod, see the lights on that rig. Doesn't it look like a giant Christmas tree?" she commented perceptively.

He smiled at her as he reached across the table and touched her hand. "It does. Don't you love to watch children at Christmas, Neal? They are so much fun."

"Yes, Christmas is definitely for kids."

The moon didn't appear, but it reflected through the heavy cloud, bringing some light to shine upon the dark waters.

As they left the restaurant, Jerrod suggested that they take a walk out on the Sixty-first Street Pier since they hadn't been out there in a long time. Nealy loved the idea because of her romantic nature and her love for the ocean. Even though the night was warm, the wind was cool. Jerrod offered Nealy his jacket and held her hand as they walked out onto the pier.

"Let's sit down for a minute," Jerrod said, sitting on a bench near the end.

"Okay," she replied. "This is nice, Jerrod." Nealy leaned her head on his shoulder and gazed out at the dark ocean.

"Neal, I want us to have a baby."

"What?" Now she put two and two together: the circus, the comment about babies, children this and children that.

"I think it's time. Don't you?"

"Jerrod, I thought that we had decided to wait for a while."

"We did, but Neal, that was a year ago. I told you that I want more of you, and a child would give me that. I want this, Neal, more than I've ever wanted anything," he said, turning her to face him. "Please," he whispered.

"But, Jerrod, I'm so busy right now."

"Neal, I don't want to wait any longer. You've got Francine, and if you need more dance teachers, hire them."

"But, then I'd need time to teach them. I don't know, Jer."

"Neal, please don't put me off any longer. I've tried to be patient, but I want you to have my baby. You'll be such a great mother. I've seen you with Betty Lou's children. They love you and you love them. And Neal, we'd have great looking kids. I want a son, and then I want a little girl that looks just like you. Please, baby, please do this for me," he said, hugging her tightly and begging with soft pleading whispers.

Nealy pulled away, stood up and walked over to the edge of the rocky pier. She stared out at the ocean as if it would send her a signal. "Me, a mother? Gosh...I...I—"

Jerrod walked up behind her and wrapped his arms around her. "Neal, please, I want to put this warm feeling in your stomach that will grow inside of you."

"Are you sure we're ready?"

"I'm ready to be a father," he said, rubbing her stomach as if she could get pregnant through osmosis.

"Jerrod, you're gone so much. There's more to being a father than just planting the seed."

"I know, Neal, but I'm a doctor. I'm always going to have a responsibility to my patients. I'll be there as much as I can, and when I'm not, you can give our kids enough love and guidance for both of us." Afraid that she might refuse, he decided to use the power of persuasion that he knew always worked on her: the power of touch. Pulling up the front of her dress, he slipped his hand into her panties and rubbed his hand against the soft flesh of her stomach. "I want to hold my hand right here," he said, gently pressing his hand on her abdomen in a non-sexual way, "and feel the movement of our child and his heartbeat as he gets stronger."

Nealy closed her eyes as she leaned back against him trying to imagine this little creature growing inside of her. She relaxed, allowing the warmth of Jerrod's hand against her stomach to flow through her body.

After standing there very quietly for a moment, she reached under her skirt and placed her hand on top of his as if she could actually feel a life being nurtured by her body. "I want this baby, too," she whispered.

"You do? You really do?"

Nealy removed his hand and turned to face him. "Yes," she said, smiling at him.

"Oh, Neal!" he shouted. "Yes! Oh, thank you!" he shouted out to the ocean, hugging her and twirling her around in the wind. "Want to *do it* right here. Maybe you'll get pregnant."

"Jerrod, I have to stop taking the pill first. It'll at least take a few months.

"No, we'll hit the first month. I'm real potent."

"Oh, do we have proof of that out there somewhere?"

"No," he said indignantly, "but I did run a test on my sperm count last week. And, baby, I got lots of those little fellows just waiting for the green light."

"You knew I'd agree, didn't you?"

"No, but I wanted to be prepared just in case."

"I guess now you'll be wanting me to take my temperature and run home for a quicky here and there."

"Absolutely. You're officially on call. I'll do whatever it takes to get our kid in the cooker as soon as possible. I'm going to bring home one of those basal thermometers tomorrow, and when I hear, 'Come to mama,' I'll rush home with my best sperm pumped and ready for the race," he said, giggly as a child.

"You're something else," she said, smiling at him. "I think our sex life is going to be more like the early days of our marriage."

"Hey, what can I say, practice makes perfect. So, let's practice," he said, pulling up her dress.

"Jerrod!" she shouted, pushing her dress back down.

"Oh, Neal, don't panic. I'm just playing around, but not for long. So, come on, let's go home. I've got seeds to plant."

CHAPTER TWENTY-TWO

THREE MONTHS LATER, Nealy checked into the hospital for tests, at Jerrod's insistence, since she hadn't become pregnant. Jerrod wanted a son and he had become totally obsessed with the process. Every morning he woke her up and took her temperature, and then, he marked her chart so that they knew exactly when she ovulated. Each month during the two days before and two days after her ovulation, he would call her at different times during the day and insist that she turn her class over to Francine and meet him at home. One afternoon, when he couldn't get away from the hospital, he convinced Nealy to come to the hospital with a crazy notion that they could use a hospital room for the five minutes that it took. After he asked a nurse to stand guard outside the door, it took him fifteen minutes to get Nealy settled down enough to make love. As they walked out of the room, Nealy almost died of embarrassment when the nurse flashed a gloating smile at them and said, "You're a lucky woman, Mrs. Jones. I never had a quicky that lasted sixteen minutes and thirty-nine seconds. I bet the rabbit dies."

"I hope your right, Nettie," Jerrod said, smiling back at her like a super stud. Jerrod had become so obsessed that he had started to doubt his own sperm count, so he ejaculated into a test tube when they made love one morning and rushed it to the hospital under his arm pit. Nealy knew how desperately he wanted a baby, but she had become exhausted from all the clinical love making sessions; she felt like a fool standing on her head afterwards.

After the tests, the doctor told them that everything looked great, and that they needed to relax and just let things happen. Jerrod didn't buy that, so he asked another doctor to look at the tests and examine both of them again. Nealy felt responsible for his actions because she couldn't conceive, but she didn't know what else to do. She had done everything that he'd asked her to do, and most of it against her own wishes. Maybe, the problem was the fact that she didn't want to do it at two o'clock in the afternoon when she wasn't in the mood or at ten o'clock in the morning. She hated leaving her class to have Jerrod hump her from behind, and then force her to keep her head down and her butt up in the air for another twenty minutes. Nealy felt guilty about not wanting to make love anymore; she hated what it had become. For the most part, their marriage had existed on their strong physical attraction, and the fact the they had always been able to fulfill their sexual needs and then some.

All of their problems were resolved by kissing, touching, and fondling, which always led to *doing it*. When that stopped, they didn't have much to do with each other. Nealy tried to talk to Jerrod and tell him how she felt, but he always got irate.

"It's all that dancing!" he screamed. "I want you to stop. Let Francine teach those fuckin' little brats to curtsy. Better yet, sell that goddamn place to her!"

"Jerrod, watch your language. I hate those words."

"Don't change the subject."

"I'm not. The doctor said that the exercise would be good for me throughout the pregnancy. And it's certainly not preventing me from conceiving."

"What's he know. You're not pregnant, and it's been almost four months since you stop the pills...you did stop taking them didn't you?" he asked attackingly.

"Don't be ridiculous," she answered angrily. "You need to relax and stop treating me like a machine. We don't make love anymore—"

"That's all we do!" he yelled.

"No, what we're doing is *not* making love. It's purely mechanical with one thing in mind," she screamed. "I never even bother undressing from the waist up. We don't kiss—"

"We agreed on this, and we're going to do what we have to do to get you pregnant, regardless of how mechanical you think it is. I made you an appointment with another specialist on Friday. He's supposed to be the best—"

"No!" she snapped, cutting him off. "I'm not going to anymore doctors right now. I've seen three, and that's enough. Nothing is wrong with us except for the fact that you're obsessed."

"You don't want to get pregnant, do you, Nealy?"

"Of course, I do. But I'm tired of this nonsense!"

"I really hate your fuckin' attitude about this. All I want is for us to have a child, and then our lives will be set. And all you can do is bitch, moan, groan, and complain about my not kissing you anymore, which, by the way, isn't true. I expect you to see this doctor. Here's his name. He's in Houston."

"Houston...you're kidding."

"I've never been so serious," he said, putting the paper in her hand and squeezing her fingers tightly around the paper.

"Ouch," she cried, pulling her hand away and glaring at him. "Okay, fine. I'll go. But this is the last one." Nealy's face turned beet red. Her temples throbbed. Her heart pounded, rushing the blood to her brain. The words *"Go see him yourself and then you can go straight to hell"* lingered on the tip of her tongue.

As he opened the backdoor, he turned to get the last word in and condescendingly said, "You can stop seeing doctors when you get pregnant. So maybe you'll try a little harder. And do me a favor...try working on your fucking attitude."

"Go to hell," she screamed and stormed out of the kitchen. She'd lost the battle, but she'd win the war, which, as far as she was concerned, had just been declared.

In two days, Nealy would face the humiliation of spreading her legs to be felt, mashed, poked and pricked by another doctor, a thought which absolutely made her cringe. And, like the others, he would tell her that physically she was perfect, but that she and Jerrod needed to relax. But the word *relax* wasn't in his dictionary. In fact, he had become a complete basket case and couldn't think of anything else. They never talked about anything else and now *that* subject had become unpleasant. The actual baby had not been mentioned at all, and when she asked him about names in an effort to make conversation after their so called love making sessions, he would say that he had to get back to the hospital. All he wanted to hear were the words "I'm pregnant." Nothing else interested him or mattered, and they had no life outside of trying to make a baby.

Nealy went to the studio on Wednesday and Thursday and didn't see Jerrod until Thursday night at eleven when he came home from the hospital. He had been on call Wednesday night, which had been just as well, but he did call to ask his usual question, "Heard from your friend Richfield lately?" Ever since their terrible disagreement about the studio, he had been just as obsessed about her relationship with Randy. On Tuesday nights, he would even pop in the studio to see if Randy had picked up Alicia and left, or stayed to talk to Nealy. In all of the years that she had known Jerrod, she had never seen him act so obsessed about things. Of course, Nealy and Randy had remained friends, but only to speak or visit a minute or two when he came for Alicia. Nealy didn't want to upset Jerrod anymore than she already had, especially since he and Randy had to see each other at the hospital. Many times on Tuesday night, Nealy would have Francine teach her class, which she hated to do because she missed her friendship with Randy, but it worked out better for everyone concerned.

When Jerrod came home on Thursday night, he walked straight to the nightstand and pulled out the ovulation chart. But after looking at it, he quickly dropped it back into the drawer without saying a word. Nealy knew that she wouldn't ovulate for another week, so Jerrod would have no interest in *doing it* until the time came. Wanting so much to be near him, her heart ached as she watched him get ready for bed without even acknowledging her existence. And when his head hit the pillow, he was out like a light. Feeling so alone and sad, she would sit there, pretending to read. Something inside had begun to die and continued to die a little more each day. This beautiful man that she had wanted to marry for most of her life seemed so distant; she didn't know this person. What had happened? Tears rolled down her cheeks as she watched him sleep. He looked like an angel, but lately he only acted like the devil himself, with no feelings at all, just cold and uncaring. Nealy wanted, just as desperately as he did, to become pregnant so things could settle down again. She wanted the old Jerrod back, or she didn't want him at all. How sad. In the night, she would try to snuggle up to him, but he would move away from her if she wasn't ovulating; Jerrod had to save his sperm for the peak performance. It seemed as though he held everything back, fought every urge to touch her, except when the time came to have intercourse for the sole purpose of conceiving. One of the doctors that Nealy and Jerrod had consulted with found Jerrod's behavior very unusual. He even told Nealy horror stories about women who drove their husband's crazy trying to conceive, but this had been his first case of role reversal. It didn't make sense to anyone, except Jerrod, and he refused to talk about it.

Nealy had made arrangements for Francine to take over her classes on Friday that so she could make the trip to Houston to see the specialist. She gathered up all of the test results that Jerrod had given her to take along and started out the door, patting Chance on the head, when the telephone rang. Being in a hurry, she almost didn't answer it, but being in business, one never knows what might be important.

"Hello," she said in a rushed voice.

"Nealy, I need you! Can you come over?" Betty Lou screamed, crying hysterically.

"Belle, what's the matter?"

"Please come! Beaux may come back."

"I'll be right there," Nealy said, hanging up and rushing out the door. The terror and urgency in Belle's voice was alarming.

As she opened the car door, her hands trembled and she fumbled nervously, trying to put the key in the ignition. What had Beaux done to make her cry and scream like that? It was obvious that they had some sort of argument. But, geezus, she had never, in eighteen years, heard her voice shake and crack with sobs and screams like that. Well, whatever had happened, Belle needed her and they had always been there for each other, especially in a crisis. Nealy drove as fast as she could, trying to remain calm, praying that things weren't too bad and that the children were alright.

Nealy pulled up into the driveway and jumped out of the car and ran as quickly as she could up to the door.

"Belle, it's me. Open the door," she cried out, banging on the front door. Finally Betty Lou opened it.

"Oh God, Neal—"

"What happened?" Nealy asked, holding Betty Lou in her arms.

"Where are the girls?"

"In their rooms. It was so awful," she cried.

"What? What was so awful?" Nealy tried to understand her, but Betty Lou was crying so hard that she could barely make out her words.

"Come on. Sit down," she said, walking her over to the couch. "Try to calm down."

"Beaux tried to rape me again. I fought him off, but he hit me, again and again. Then, when I got away from him, he chased me and when he caught me, he threw me up against the wall. It hurt my back so bad, but I kneed him, and he fell down to the floor holding himself. Then I ran and got the girls and pushed them into the bathroom. I locked the door. A few minutes later, I heard him leave," she said, still sobbing.

"Maybe I should get you to a doctor?"

"No," she screamed. "We need to get out of here."

"Okay, come on. We'll get away from here. Then we'll decide whether or not you need a doctor," Nealy said, heading to the bedroom. She gathered up some things for the children in case they were gone a few days. Belle gathered up her clothes, but Nealy had to keep encouraging her. "Come on, Belle, we need to go before he comes back. He will you know. I'll take you to my house."

"No, Neal, he'll go to your house," she cried, frightened for their safety.

"Okay. Just calm down. We'll stop and call Kati Sue. I'll drive y'all up to Houston. I was headed that way anyway," she said, hustling everyone towards the car. Nealy could handle Beaux, but she wanted him to have time to calm down first. Besides, she needed to find out exactly what had caused them to have such a problem. But, she knew from past experiences that it didn't take much to anger some people.

A few miles from the house, Nealy pulled into the seven-eleven. "Kati Sue, this is Nealy. I'm on my way to Houston. I have Betty Lou and the girls with me. Beaux did something, I'm not sure exactly what, but, anyway I'm bringing them to your house."

"Nealy, what happened?"

"I'm not sure. We'll get it out of her when we get there."

"Okay," Kati replied reluctantly.

On the way, Nealy didn't ask Betty Lou too many details in front of the children, but they talked about some things using more clinical language. Jolynn, who was almost five, and Joyce Ann, who had been the surprise pregnancy that slipped out at Nealy's wedding, was two and a half. They were beautiful little girls, with really sweet dispositions, but both of them seemed upset by the fighting that had been going on for some time. They cried most of the way, but finally fell asleep just before they arrived at Kati's house. Nealy and Betty Lou carried them inside and put them to bed in Kati's room. Then Betty Lou told Nealy and Kati Sue the whole ugly story.

It seemed that Betty Lou and Beaux had been having a lot of problems ever since she had become pregnant with Joyce Ann. Nealy remembered Betty Lou telling them at the wedding that she did not want another baby until after she had finished school. Nealy thought that Betty Lou might even terminate the pregnancy because she seemed so upset by it. When Beaux and Betty Lou got married, they were just juniors in college, so Betty Lou dropped out to help put Beaux through school with the agreement that she would go back as soon as he graduated and found a job. Then, right before he graduated, she got pregnant with Jolynn and did not go back to school until she was six months old. But, at the same time, Beaux decided to get his master's degree which meant that she would go to school full time, take care of the house and the baby without any help from him, except financially. Beaux didn't see any reason for her to go back to school because he had a good job, and when he got his master's degree, they wouldn't need her help financially. And besides, he thought that she should stay home and be a good little wife and mother. But Betty Lou wanted to get her degree, and since that had been their original agreement, she went right on. But, with school, the baby and taking care of the house, she didn't have much time or energy left over for Beaux. They often fought about it, but she told him that he should have waited until after she finished school to go back, and then he could have helped her with the house and the baby. One thing led to another, and then one night he stopped off at a bar on his way home from school and didn't make it home until three a.m. When he tried to make love to Betty Lou, she pushed him away and he became irate, forcing himself on her. The second pregnancy came as a result of what Betty Lou termed as "rape" because they failed to use extra protection, and the pills weren't a sure prevention for Betty Lou. Therefore, she blamed him. Their sex life had become almost non-existent over the last couple of years, which didn't leave them with much of a marriage. Most of the time they fought, and now things had finally reached the boiling point. Now it seemed as if things had gone too far.

"Belle, do you want me to talk to Beaux when I get home tonight?" Nealy asked, wanting to help in any way that she could.

"No," she snapped. "I'm not ready to talk to him."

"Okay, but you know he'll call me."

"Just tell him that you don't know where I am."

"Of course, you know this is the next place he'll look, Betty Lou," Kati Sue said, sitting next to her twin sister with her arm around her shoulders, comforting her.

"Betty Lou, I think I can talk to him. But if not, I'll tell him that you're getting a restraining order against him," Nealy said.

"Will that work?" she asked in a shaky, frightened voice.

"I think so. But you just stay here until I call you." They visited for a while longer, and Kati prepared them some sandwiches, since no one had eaten.

Nealy left about three o'clock to avoid some of the Houston traffic and to get back home before dark. With all the excitement, she hadn't even taken the time to call the doctor and make her apologies; she would call and reschedule on Monday. Now, all she could think about was Beaux and Betty Lou. Beaux and Nealy went way back because their families had been friends for years, and she knew that she could talk to him once he realized what he had done.

As Nealy drove by the same Seven-Eleven that she had called Kati Sue from, she decided to go back and call Beaux before he did something stupid. When he answered, Nealy talked to him and asked if she could come by for a while. Of course, he agreed, knowing that she knew where Betty Lou and the girls had gone.

When she arrived at their house, Beaux greeted her at the door. He appeared shaken and remorseful, and they talked for at least two hours. Beaux agreed to give Betty Lou some time to sort things out, and then he put his head on Nealy's shoulder and cried, which made her cry, too. Why did these things happen to people who obviously loved each other? They had to love each other because the pain was there: the crying, the trembling hands, the anger, the frustration. So, with that, she suggested that they get some professional help with their problems. And Nealy insisted that he call Betty Lou and let her know that he had calmed down and that he didn't intend to cause any more trouble. Nealy called with Beaux standing at her side, and Betty Lou finally agreed to talk to him. Thank goodness, things seemed to be working out, but only time would tell whether or not the marriage would survive. Nealy understood completely because there were times when she wondered whether or not her marriage could sustain the test of time.

"Oh, Beaux, I've got to go. It's almost seven. Jerrod will be wondering where I am. But, please be patient...it'll all work out. All marriages have their problems, but most of them are worth saving, or at least, trying to save," she said, hugging him. In her arms, she could feel his body shaking. It brought tears to her eyes, but she still felt angry at him for behaving so violently towards her best friend.

Nealy left feeling sorry for him even though she knew that he deserved no sympathy. The fact that he had forced himself on Betty Lou was inexcusable and possibly unforgivable. When a man brings harm to a woman, whether it be physical or emotional or both, it's just not something that is easily forgotten and, in many cases, does not merit forgiveness.

CHAPTER TWENTY-THREE

NEALY DROVE her car into the garage. When she got to the gate, she could see Jerrod pacing back and forth across the kitchen. Chance met her, jumping up and down, excited to see her, but he chose to stay outside when she opened the door and invited him in. Obviously, he knew that the *shit was fixin' to hit the fan*. "Uh-oh, Chancey, I think I'm in trouble," she whispered, leaning down to pet him. Slowly, she stood up and took a deep breath. "Well, here goes nothing," she sighed, opening the door and stepping directly into the line of fire.

"Where the hell have you been?"

"I'm sorry, but I didn't think you'd be home yet, or I would have called," she answered, laying her purse down on the cabinet.

"I'm always home by seven on Fridays!"

"Oh, Jerrod, you're not either."

"What did the doctor say?"

"I didn't go—"

"What!"

"If you'll calm down, I'll explain."

"This better be good," he said, glaring at her.

"Betty Lou called me at seven o'clock this morning. She was hysterical because she and Beaux had a terrible fight. So, I went over there to see about her. Then after I got there, I ended up driving them to Houston to Kati Sue's."

"Wait a minute. You mean to tell me that you went to Houston, but you didn't go to the doctor?"

"Jerrod, didn't you hear what I just said? Betty—"

"I heard that. But why didn't you go on to the doctor?"

"Because it was too late. I'll call Monday and reschedule."

"Oh, that's just great! Listen, you need to decide what's more important, making me happy or baby-sitting your fuckin' friends."

"Don't use that language. This is my best friend. And that's not fair—"

"I can't believe that you deliberately missed your appointment. I need to face it, Nealy. You don't really want to have a baby."

"Well with the way you've been acting lately, I'd be an idiot to bring a child into this marriage anyway," she cried, totally exasperated. "Men. What's wrong with you people? You're either forcing us to have sex or forcing us to have children."

"You fuckin' bitch!"

"Don't you ever call me that again!"

"I'll call you anything I want to. See. I knew it. You don't want to get pregnant. Well, thanks for telling me!"

"Jerrod, what's wrong with you? You've become obsessed with the idea of having a baby, but you don't even act as if you love me anymore."

"If we don't have a *kid* soon, this marriage won't work!"

"Why won't it work? It used to work, and we didn't have children," she screamed angrily.

"It just won't, so I guess we might as well call it quits now!" He stormed out the back door, slamming it behind him.

Nealy stood there staring out the kitchen windows, watching as he pulled out of the garage and peeled out down the street. Then she walked out the back door and sat down on the steps. Chancey practically crawled over to her with his tail between his legs. "Oh, Chancey, what's wrong with him? I don't understand this," she cried, tears spilling out of her eyes and landing on the dog's head. Carefully, she wiped them away with a finger-painting stroke. How could they go on like this? Maybe they weren't going to if Jerrod had meant what he said. Surely, he would come to his senses soon. He had just taken the fact that she couldn't get pregnant very hard. Maybe he blamed himself. When he cooled off he would come home as he always did, and she could promise to go to the specialist on Monday. And she also needed to practice what she preached; maybe she and her friends could get together and get a discount with a marriage counselor, a group rate. Seriously, the time had come for her and Jerrod to get some professional help; maybe they should have done that much sooner and spared themselves the anguish.

After watching the ten o'clock news, Nealy paced from window to window watching desperately for his car. Where had he gone? Didn't he want to make up? She hated the fussing and fighting and the tons of emotional baggage that she really didn't know how to cope with. Her parents had always gotten along famously. Maybe once a year, they would shout at one another for a couple of minutes, but then the air cleared and the dust settled and the dispute seemed to be resolved, never being brought up again, at least not in the presence of their children. And never once had her parents engaged in a physical tiff, but there again, not in the presence of their offspring. Who knows, maybe they stored their anger and had a real knock-down-drag-out when the children were out and about. Now Nealy wished that she had paid better attention when her parents did argue because they always settled their differences before things got out of control, something she and Jerrod couldn't seem to do. Why couldn't they just get along? But through all of this, she had learned something about herself, something that she had never realized before: she would stand up for what she believed in. But, even so, she hated to quarrel, and it upset her. Like an old dog, everyone wants to be loved; nobody wants to be kicked around.

By midnight, Jerrod still had not come home. Nealy kept dozing off in front of the television, but she kept waking up to look at the clock. They needed to talk before things went any further and totally destroyed their marriage.

When the clock struck on the next half hour, she jumped up and grabbed her yellow sundress out of the closet, which she knew he loved. It seemed a little enticing, like a temptress, but if it helped his mood when he saw her in it, it'd be worth it. He had probably gone back to the hospital, so she would just go there and try to settle this matter once and for all. Nervously, she buckled the strap on her sandals, then grabbed her car keys without picking up her purse.

Nealy drove into the parking lot near the emergency room because she felt safer getting out of the car there. She hurried up to the cardiac ward and searched up and down the halls, looking quietly in each room. The halls were dark and quiet and smelled medicinal. Finally, she stopped at the nurse's station and asked the nurse, whom she had seen several times, if she had seen Jerrod. Before the nurse could answer, Randy Richfield walked around the corner.

"Nealy, what are you doing here? It's almost one."

"Have you seen Jerrod?" Nealy asked, playing with her car keys. "We had an argument. I thought maybe he came back here."

"Come with me," he said, pulling her gently by the arm.

"Where are we going?"

He took her into the doctor's lounge. "Nealy, Jerrod isn't here. Why don't you go back home. He'll cool off and come home," he said, unable to look at her.

"Randy, you've seen him, haven't you? Where is he?"

"Nealy, please, just go home," he pleaded, still avoiding eye contact with her.

"Randy, where is he? The fraternity house?" The look on his face gave it away. But why had he gone there? He told her that the study group didn't meet there anymore. So what would he be doing there at this hour?

"Nealy, go home, please. I'll make Jerrod explain all of this tomorrow. It's time," he said, relieved that he'd finally broken the silence. But when he looked up at her, he felt terrible because she looked so frightened, so pale.

"Randy, what is it? You're scaring me. What's he doing at the frat house? Is he studying?"

"Is that what he told you he did over there?"

"Yes...why?"

"Nealy, let me take you home. Wait here a minute. I need to check out with the nurses. They can page me if they need me," he said, walking out of the lounge and heading down the hall.

Before he could finish, Nealy ran past the nurse's station and got on the elevator. By the time he reached the elevators, the doors closed in his face, so he took the stairs. When he got outside, he saw her running across the street. He ran faster, but she had gone inside long before he could catch up with her. He hoped that Jerrod had gone already, but he felt sure that he hadn't. His nights in the pool at the frat house and down at the west-end beach house usually lasted until the early morning hours. And Randy knew he had been there earlier because he had seen him when he picked up a book from the medical library on the second floor. Maybe if Jerrod had seen him, he would have left for fear that he might tell Nealy if she called looking for him. All he could do was pray that she didn't find him there.

Nealy walked in the front door of the fraternity house and walked down the hall towards the stairs where she could check out the library. Before she started up the stairs, she heard voices belonging to both males and females, coming from the pool area. When she reached the door, she heard Jerrod's voice. She froze. Her heart pounded. She felt queasy. Reaching for the doorknob, she turned it slowly and opened the door. For a minute, she just stood there quietly, observing the ten or so people who were laughing and talking in the swimming pool. As she stepped out onto the patio, she could clearly see that some of them were females.

"You bastard!" she screamed. All of them turned around to stare at her. Enraged, she screamed again. "You fucking bastard!"

Jerrod panicked. "Nealy, baby, I can explain."

"No!" she yelled, her voice quivering. "Let me guess. Gynecology, right? The female anatomy? The study of how the vagina expands under water when exposed to a hardened mass of male tissue."

"Nealy, please." He climbed out of the pool.

"Oh dear *God*, you're naked," she said, covering her face with her hands and rubbing her eyes as if they were playing tricks on her. Slowly, she lowered her hands down her face until her finger tips pressed hard against her lips. Coldly, she starred at Jerrod. Then finally, in a horrified voice, she asked, "Were you *doing it* with all of them?" This had to be a bad dream. Nealy appeared to be praying, with her hands held together in front of her mouth, trembling so much that her speech vibrated when she spoke.

With all her attention focused on Jerrod and his playmates, Nealy hadn't noticed Randy walking up behind her. "Nealy, let's get out of here," Randy whispered softly, touching her arm with a gentle nudge.

"Richfield, take your goddamn hands off my wife!"

Nealy screamed viciously, "You're acting like a perverted porpoise humping a school of sluts in the middle of mating season, and you're telling Randy to let go of me. You've got some nerve," she cried angrily, her eyes fixed on him.

Not moving a muscle, he shouted back in his own defense, "This isn't all my fault. You should have been more exciting. You're such a frigid bitch."

"What did you want me to do? Join your water nymphettes?"

"See, there's that holier-than-thou attitude of yours. If you'll let me explain," he shouted, starting towards her.

Putting her hands out in front of her, she backed up and bumped into Randy. "Don't come near me," she ordered. "If this is what you wanted, then why were you driving me crazy about having a baby? Why for godsakes?"

"Why don't you ask your friend behind you," he yelled.

"Nealy, please, this needs to be discussed in private," Randy pleaded. "Come on, let's go."

"No! I need to know this now," she snapped, pulling her arm away from him. "I want you to tell me, Jerrod."

"He's been blackmailing me. I got these letters that said 'If I didn't tell you, he would.' I knew they were from him because he's been dying to tell you—"

"You're nuts, man. I'd never stoop to blackmail. I've had plenty of opportunity to tell her if I'd wanted to."

"Then who else would do that? From the beginning, you thought she was too good for me. And you've known about this since before we got marr —"

"You've been screwing with them all along?" Nealy interrupted, shouting.

"No! I've only done it a few times since we got married. And I wouldn't be here tonight if you'd gone to that goddamn doctor."

"Oh my *God*, I can't believe this," she said, growing so weak that she could hardly stand up.

"Don't you understand? Nealy, I love you so much, and I was afraid you'd find out."

"You *love me*? This is how you love me?"

"Yes, goddammit! I love you. If you'd gotten pregnant, this would have never happened. I didn't intend to ever do it again. If we had a child I knew you'd never leave me, even if you had found out about me doing it in the past. I know you. You'd never take a child away from its father, no matter what."

"You worthless bastard! I *never* want to see you again," she tried to shout, but her words came out barely above a whisper.

"Nealy, please, give me a chance," he begged, walking towards her.

"Jerrod, stay away from me. Don't you ever come near me again," she cried, gaining enough strength to turn around. "Randy, I feel sick. I gotta get out of here."

"Come on," he said, leading her through the door.

"Nealy, get back here! You son-of-a-bitch, Richfield. I hope you're happy. First, you blackmailed me. Now you've set me up!"

When they reached the door, Nealy stopped and leaned over.

"Nealy, are you alright?" Randy asked. At first he thought that she was hyperventilating, but then he realized that something else was wrong, seriously wrong. Randy held her up, but before he took another step, she collapsed, grabbing her stomach. "Nealy!" he cried out. He picked her up in his arms and ran as carefully and as quickly as he could across the street to the hospital. By the time he reached the emergency room, he could feel the wet warmth that he knew had to be blood on his arm. And by then, she was unconscious. "I'm Dr. Richfield from Cardiology. I need a doctor in here stat. Where can I put her?"

"In here, doctor," the nurse said, quickly leading him into the only private room available.

"Stay with me," Randy ordered.

"What happened to her?" the nurse asked.

"I'm not sure. She grabbed her abdomen. She's hemorrhaging. There's a lot of blood. Obviously, she's aborting. Go call Dr. Morris in Obstetrics. He's here. I saw him earlier. Get an I.V. started. And get her on the monitor. Come on, let's go. She's shocky," he shouted.

Within minutes, Rob Morris raced into the room. "Randy, what's the problem?"

"My guess would be a ruptured ectopic pregnancy. She's lost a lot of blood, and her vitals aren't good."

Dr. Morris lifted up the sheet to palpate her abdomen first. Then he pulled the stool beneath him to perform a pelvic examination. Probing, he talked softly to Randy who stood beside him. "We've got a large boggy mass on the left side of the uterus, and I think we have blood in the cul-de-sac because the posterior fornix of the vagina is bulging."

"Sounds like we need to get her up to surgery," Randy said anxiously.

"You're right," Dr. Morris replied, looking up at Randy and the nurse. "Let's get her upstairs. Order an ultrasound scan. Let's go ahead and get her prepped for surgery," he said, motioning for immediate response. They moved Nealy over onto the gurney and wheeled her out of the room.

In the operating room, the doctors and nurses rushed around hooking up monitors and preparing Nealy for surgery. Randy stood next to her, looking down at her pretty face that had grown so pale. The longer he stood there, the angrier he became at Jerrod. How could he have done this to her? She's so pretty and so special. Being back in an operating room, watching her fight for her life, brought back all the memories of his wife; she had lost her fight. Nealy couldn't die. She had to fight, but right now, after going through what she'd just been through, would she still want to fight? How could he make her know that Jerrod wasn't worth it, that life would go on for her. He stroked her face and squeezed her delicate hand. It broke his heart to see her so fragile. "Nealy," he whispered, "you're going to be fine, but you've got to fight. Please fight. Alicia would never forgive me if I let something happen to you." He squeezed her hand one last time, and then moved out of the way for her doctor to start the operating procedures. He hung around until he was called back to Cardiology, but Dr. Morris promised to call him when he finished.

Two hours later, the nurse called Randy and told him that Nealy had been taken to recovery, so immediately he headed downstairs to talk with Rob.

When he walked into recovery, he found Rob washing up. "Rob, hey. How is she?"

"Well, it was ectopic alright. She was about five weeks along. I removed the embryo, placenta and the surrounding tissue and repaired some torn blood vessels. She had a severe loss of blood, so I gave her a blood transfusion to replace what she'd lost. Her tube was damaged somewhat, but I don't think it'll be a problem. Her chances of conceiving may be slightly reduced, but that's about all. I need to tell her that ectopic pregnancies can recur, so she'll need to have tests and check-ups frequently if she's considering getting pregnant again. I want to keep her here for the next few days because she suffered hypovolemic shock. I want to keep her on a heart monitor and watch her blood pressure. The fact that you got her here so quickly made a big difference. I'm sure she'll be grateful. Nealy's a nice lady. I ran some tests on her a couple a months ago. I didn't find anything, but because she wasn't pregnant the first month after she stopped the pill, Jerrod insisted that something had to be wrong. Does this guy have some sort of problem?"

"Not when it comes to being a doctor, but otherwise, the guy's an idiot. In fact, Nealy caught him over at the frat house partying with the *wild women* from that so called *Swim Club*."

"Oh no. I guess that put the icing on the cake. The fetus had already started to abort, and then the trauma of that brought things along a little sooner. Clinton Wallace, our infertility specialist, had seen Nealy and Jerrod a while back and he mentioned something to me about Jerrod's little swim group, but I just blew it off as rumor. I guess it isn't rumor, huh?"

"No, not hardly."

"Poor Nealy, what's going to happen now? Think she'll divorce that bastard?"

"I think so. She's a good sport, but I think he went a *little* too far this time. I'm concerned about her getting the rest that she needs to get over this. He's so stuck on himself that her health isn't a major concern to him."

"I'll keep an eye on her. Let me know if you want me to talk to Jerrod. See ya, Randy," Rob Morris said, firmly patting him on the back as he left the room.

"Nealy," Randy whispered. "Hey, sleepy head. You'll do anything to get out of teaching my little girl to shuffle-ball-change, or whatever you call it." He picked up her hand and held it between his. He had enjoyed removing her jewelry, especially her wedding rings. In fact, he would like to throw them as far as he could into the Gulf of Mexico. Hopefully, she'd be smart enough not to ever put them on again. It would serve that spoiled little prick right. No one like him deserved someone like her. Nealy had been so loyal and devoted to him, and look what she had gotten in return. Not that Randy liked to see any marriage breakup, but when it's so one sided, it just can't last. When his beeper went off, he put her hand back down on the bed and eased out of the room. "Evelyn, keep a close eye on her. Call me when she wakes up. I'll be upstairs," he said to the nurse as he left recovery.

CHAPTER TWENTY-FOUR

NEALY OPENED HER EYES only to see white walls, white floors, white sheets, and people running around her in white clothes. She felt strange: lifeless and numb. Could this be heaven? But then she felt as if she were coming out of one of those dreams where one tries to wake up but can't, and things get more and more bazaar. She tried to move her arms and legs, but they wouldn't move, and then she tried to raise up. It couldn't be heaven, she had pain. "Oh God," she whispered, slowly moving her hand over onto her stomach. At least she could move her arm now, she thought. Her eyes blinked over and over, and her mouth felt very dry. Nealy tried to figure out where she was and why. She just kept trying to focus, but nothing looked familiar.

Walking over to her bed, Rob Morris softly spoke to her. "Hi, Nealy, how are you feeling?"

She tried to focus, but things were blurry. She raised her hand. Rob took her hand in his. "Where am I?" she asked, barely whispering.

"You're at John Sealy," he replied, smiling at her. "It's Rob Morris. You had a little problem last night. I had to do surgery. But you're going to be fine."

"Surgery? What happened?"

"You had a ectopic pregnancy. It's what occurs when the egg doesn't make its way through the fallopian tube," he explained.

"I was pregnant?"

"Yes, but just barely, about five weeks. The pregnancy had already started to abort. That's why you've been bleeding during the last week or so, which you most likely believed to be your period."

"Did I do something to cause it?"

"No, Nealy, it wasn't your fault. It was inevitable. Try to rest," he said, patting her hand. "You're still pretty groggy from the anesthetic. I'll be back a little later. We can talk then. If you need anything, just ask one of the nurses. Randy will be down in a minute. He brought you in here this morning. Now, just relax and try to rest."

"Randy?" she whispered, trying to remember. Why did Randy bring her there?

"You rang?" Randy said, walking into the room just in time to hear his name. "How's our beautiful patient doing this morning?"

"I...I had a miscarriage."

"That's right. But you're going to be fine. You can still have children, Nealy. It's just one of those freak things," he said, pushing her hair back from her forehead.

Nealy started to cry. "It's my fault. I didn't really want to have a baby right now. I'm being punished."

"Oh, no, Nealy. You couldn't help this. Women have tubal pregnancies everyday. The main thing is that you're alright. Please don't cry," he begged. "You're much too pretty to cry."

"But Randy—"

"No but's. You didn't do one thing to cause this. The pregnancy was bad from the beginning. Rob will go into all of this later. Right now you need to rest so that you can get over this sooner. You were pretty sick."

"Randy, I need to call my studio...and my dog needs to be fed."

"Nealy, that's all been taken care of. I called the studio early this morning and talked to Francine. She's taking care of things there until you get better. And I took Chance over to my house. He and Rags will have a great time together. So, you have nothing to worry about. You can concentrate on getting well."

"Oh, thank God. What would I do without you," she said, still fighting the urge to sleep.

"Nealy, get some rest. You're going to need your strength," he said, staring down at her, rubbing the soft hollow between her eyes. He remembered how he used to do that to Alicia when she was a baby; it put her right to sleep every time. Nealy looked pale. Her emerald-colored eyes showed sign of strain; they were a pale gold color. So far she hadn't recollected the turn of events that preceded this incident, and, for now, he felt relieved, he was grateful. Once she recalled that nightmare, she most likely wouldn't be able to sleep at all, at least, not until she came to terms with what had happened and what she planned on doing about it. Time would tell.

Later that morning, Nealy woke up feeling weak and tired, but at least she could see, hear, think, and feel. And the memories from the *midnight from hell* were all coming back. Jerrod's face and his nakedness kept flashing through her mind; she couldn't stop that vision. She wanted to cry into her pillow, but the tubes that the nurses had going into her hands prevented her from moving much at all. Nealy closed her eyes tightly, hoping to stop the tears, but they came anyway. The irony of it all: "If only you had gotten pregnant, I wouldn't be here." How could he have done such a horrible thing? How could she have been so naive? He had been right about one thing, she is a naive bitch; she believed all his lies. What an idiot. A fool. A blind fool. Deaf, dumb and ignorant. Everyone must have known, except for her, but the wife is always the last to know. Randy knew, but he never told her. How could he have kept that from her? They were friends, and he deliberately let her go on being deceived and become the world's biggest buffoon! But if Randy had told her, and she in turn confronted Jerrod, he would have lied. And she would have believed him because she is the world's biggest idiot. No, stupid idiot. Oh, God, how could she have been so blind! Randy did the only thing that he could do by letting Jerrod hang himself, which he knew he would eventually do. And because of it, there is no way that he can lie his way out of this one. Nealy saw it. Heard it. So she had to believe it. But Jerrod had made one wrong assumption: Nealy would have left him when and if she found out the truth, baby or no baby. Ironically the last, horrible year had been in vain.

The doctor ordered Nealy to be taken to her room about noon, and she drifted in and out of sleep for the rest of the day. A large bouquet of flowers came from the studio with a sweet card wishing her well. So far, they were the only ones that knew where she was but sooner or later everyone else would have to know. Right now, she just wanted to be left alone to grieve.

"Well, how's our girl?" Rob Morris asked, waltzing into the room acting very chipper.

"You tell me," she whined.

"I think you're terrific," he said, laying his hand on her arm and smiling.

"I'm glad you think so. I feel like I've been run over by a herd of stampeding buffalo's," she mumbled. "And I look worse."

"Nealy, your worst is most people's best," he chuckled, winking at her.

"Thanks, but I know you're just trying to be kind," she complained, managing a little smile.

"We need to talk," he said, pulling up a chair and sitting down beside her.

"What about?"

"I didn't call Jerrod this morning before I did your surgery, but under the circumstances, I...well, I just didn't. But now I think he needs to know."

"No," she cried, "please don't call him Rob. I'm not ready to face him yet. Please don't call him," she begged, fighting the urge to cry.

"Nealy, he *is* your husband."

"Not for long," she said, turning to stare out the window.

"I know what he did. And I don't blame you for being so angry, but Nealy he'll find out sooner or later."

"What difference is it going to make? I lost the baby. It's over for us. Rob, I can't see him now. If I did, what would I say, 'Oh, Jerrod, been swimming lately?' I don't think so, Rob. I don't mean to sound bitter, but I can't help it."

"Okay, I see your point. Do you want anyone else to know, like your parents, sister, brother, or maybe a friend? I'll call them and explain things as delicately as I can without going into detail," he said, feeling sorry for her.

"Rob, I *would* like you to call someone for me. Jerrod's aunt. Her name is Janey Randall. She used to be married to Roland Randall."

"I know her. She'll definitely sympathize. Everyone at the hospital heard about Roland's dalliances. But, Nealy, she *is* Jerrod's aunt. Are you sure you want to call her? Won't she call Jerrod?"

"No, not if I ask her not to, and especially after she hears what he did."

"Okay, I'll call her. Do you need anything?"

"No, I'm okay. But I'll probably need a good shrink before all of this is over." Nealy actually giggled softly. She didn't know how she had the courage to laugh, being the biggest laughing stock on *The Rock*—a nickname for Galveston Island. Just *what* were people calling her? How could Jerrod sleep around or swim around or whatever the hell he did for three years and she not suspect a thing? What an idiot! Her only regret was that she didn't slap him harder when she had her one and only chance. That lying, conniving bastard; he made Roland Randall look like a Saint.

"Can I come in?" Randy asked, sticking his head inside the door.

"Sure."

"I won't ask you how you are. I know the answer to that. Is there anything you need? A friend maybe?" he asked, taking a seat in the chair by the bed.

"A really good friend will work," she smiled.

"Nealy, I'm really sorry about this mess. I wanted to tell you, but I just couldn't. It wasn't my place and besides—"

"Randy, I understand. I wouldn't have believed you. You know me better than I know myself. I *had* to see this to believe it. It hurts...it really hurts, but I'll get over it. Thanks for being here. And thanks for saving my life." she blinked back the tears.

"You're welcome. But, I wish I could say something that would make it hurt less. It just takes time, I know, I've been there,"

"I know you have. And I guess in a way Alice betrayed you, too, even though she really didn't." Nealy took his hand. Randy placed his other hand over hers.

"Yes, I was angry with her for dying and leaving me...and even more so for denying our baby the love that only a mother can give. But Nealy, you'll heal when you deal with the anger and forgive him. To be able to forgive him will be the hardest thing that you ever do, but until you do, you won't be able to move on. You're a wonderful person. You're sweet, kind, loyal, honest, and, more than anything trusting."

"Yeah, I'm a regular girl scout alright," she said cynically, catching the tears that rolled down her cheek.

"Nealy, I am *so* sorry that he hurt you," he said, pulling her arms around his neck, allowing her to cry on his shoulder. After a few minutes, she raised up and he handed her a tissue.

"Aren't you tired of me blubbering all over you? You have to be," she cried, "because I'm sick of doing it." Nealy wiped her eyes and blew her nose. Then she reached for the box of tissue. "Just give me the whole damn box. I can tell

I'm going to need it."

"You can blubber on me anytime," he said, smiling. "You're going to get through this. You're a tough lady. If you ever need to talk, I'm here. But you know that. Francine said she'd be up later."

"Did you tell her not to say anything to Jerrod?"

"Yes, but she wouldn't. She hates him."

"Did you tell her everything?"

"No, but I really didn't have to."

"You mean, she knew about him?"

"Well, not really, but she had her suspicions."

"Oh, Dear God, I'm such an idiot," she said, burying her face in her hands. Pushing her hair back away from her face, she looked serious. "When can I leave here? I need to get away."

"Two or three days. Where will you go? To your folks?"

"No, most of my family have gone out of town to a family thing in East Texas, thank goodness. I'm not ready to tell them about this yet. I don't know where I'll go, but I need to go away by myself for a couple of weeks. Randy, please talk to Rob and ask him to release me tomorrow."

"Nealy, tomorrow's too soon, but I'll ask him. I gotta run. Call me if you need me," he said, leaning down and kissing her on the forehead.

"Thanks, for being my friend. And for taking care of me."

"I'm just glad that I was there for you." He smiled, waving good bye.

Nealy lay there, staring out into the darkness. The night looked so peaceful, but it couldn't be; nothing could be peaceful in all her pain. At least some of the pain in her stomach had stopped, but she still felt weak. Of course, all of her fits of crying hadn't helped. She had to get up and go to the bathroom. What could she possibly look like after this ordeal? It would be very bad, but maybe that would encourage her to snap out of it. There's nothing worse than puffy red eyes and a shiny nose brighter than Rudolph's. And poor Rudolph wasn't happy either. No one is happy when people are laughing and calling them names. Even when they deserve it.

"My God, Nealy, 'Naive bitch!' You do look like hell," she grumbled out loud as she stared at herself in the mirror. "The humiliation you've suffered because of Jerrod's secret love spa is bad enough that bastard but you're making it worse by looking like death warmed over. You need to get a grip...and *stop* talking to yourself." She leaned down, holding her sore stomach, and washed her face with cold water. A shower would be much better, but she had to wait one more day; doctor's orders. Make-up would help, but she didn't have any. Maybe Francine would have some when she got to the hospital. Where was Janey? She should have been here by now. Perhaps she wouldn't come once she heard how her precious nephew got caught with his pants, not only down, but off. Yes, that's right, naked as the day he was born; his birth being unfortunate for her. That slimy little sneak had a damn harem of water maidens. And that little sleazy slut Kris at the airport had been one of them. How could anyone be so naive? Buying the house right off the bat finally made sense; he did that to keep his girlfriends from leaving anymore notes or calling or coming over for a little *coffee, tea, or best of all, me.* That slimeball. It's positively amazing that a woman with reasonable intelligence could be so gullible. But women are often blinded by love, and unfortunately, more often than not.

"Nealy, honey, are you in there?" Janey asked, knocking softly on the bathroom door.

"Yes. I'll be right out."

"Oh, Nealy, are you alright?" Janey looked terrified by Nealy's paleness.

"I'm fine. I just look awful. Hospitals do that to you," she said, smiling, reassuring Janey that she didn't intend to die.

"The doctor told me what happened. I'm so sorry, darling."

"What all did he tell you?" Nealy asked.

"Well, he told me about the pregnancy and that you lost the baby. He also said something about you and Jerrod having a terrible argument and that you didn't want me to say anything to him until I talked to you."

"All that's true. But it wasn't a terrible argument. It was more like a Dr. Jekyll and Mr. Hyde or a Dr. Jones doing as Dr. Randall did, except he preferred six crotched mermaids in six feet of water. I'm sorry, Janey. Forget all that gibberish. I need to just start from the day you picked us up at the airport. You might as well sit down, it's a very long story," she said, pointing to the chair and slowly climbing back upon the bed. Nealy proceeded to tell Janey everything, including the fights and how it all came together. Jerrod had just gotten himself in too deep the perfect cliche and he didn't know how to get out. These needs that he had for sexual perversion outside of the confinements of his home and for the sharing of multiple partners had the same effect on him as alcohol or drugs. But would he ever admit to a problem and consider a cure? Or would he prefer to live his life by those standards?

Appalled and devastated, Janey insisted that Nealy go to New York and stay in her Central Park West apartment for a couple of weeks. The time away would do her good, help her see things more clearly. After what she had been through, she needed the time away. Nealy accepted because it sounded like the perfect place to pull herself back together and make some important decisions. When Janey got ready to leave, she and Nealy hugged and cried on each other's frail shoulders. Together they were sisters on the front line fighting for their freedom, desperately trying to free themselves from the clutches of the men who battled against them.

"Get well, darling," Janey said, hugging her.

"Thanks for coming."

"I'll see you tomorrow. And in the meantime, I'll make arrangements for my neighbor to meet you at the airport. In your condition, I don't want you taking a cab from Kennedy Airport." Janey smiled and disappeared into the hallway. If by some chance, she ran into Jerrod, Janey would most likely ring his neck. Her heart broke for Nealy because she knew exactly how difficult this would be for her. How could Jerrod do this? He had everything, including the perfect wife. If Janey lived to be a hundred, she would never understand men. But she knew that she had to forgive Jerrod because he had been her pride and joy since the day he was born. He made a terrible mistake, and she prayed that Nealy would find it in her heart to forgive him, but she couldn't blame her if she didn't. Infidelity cuts deeper into the soul of a woman than almost anything else a man can ever do, and forgiveness is almost impossible, because forgiving means forgetting.

Nealy felt better after telling Janey, even though it bothered her to be a tattletale. Under normal conditions, she wouldn't dream of ratting on Jerrod to his own aunt, but she desperately needed to talk to someone that would truly understand. Nealy listened to the chatter in the halls and the clanging of what had to be the stainless steel covers on the meal trays or bedpans. It had been quite some time since a nurse had been in to check on her, but she certainly didn't mind. In eight hours she had been poked and prodded and stuck with enough needles to last her a lifetime. If only she could go home, but that meant facing Jerrod; she couldn't do that yet. But what if someone had recognized her and told him where he could find her. What would she do? Scream for him to *get out* or talk to him? Definitely no talking. She would scream and probably try to claw his eyeballs out. Thinking about eyeballs reminded her of how tired hers were. They open and closed slowly several times. Then she dozed off until a familiar voice woke her up.

"Hi, Nealy," Francine whispered.

"Oh, hi," Nealy said, forcing her eyes open.

"I'm sorry to wake you, but Randy told me that you would be upset if I didn't."

"That's true. How are things at the studio?"

"They're just fine. I taught both of our classes today and told everyone that you had an emergency that you had to take care of. That wasn't exactly a lie, but I didn't really want to answer a lot of questions."

"That's perfect. Francine, this is such a mess. I guess Randy told you everything?"

"Well, sort of, but he mostly told me about your miscarriage."

"I'll tell you all about it when I get home from New York."

"You're going to New York?"

"Jerrod's Aunt Janey offered to let me stay in her apartment for a couple of weeks. I need to rest and I have to decide what I'm going to do."

"Will you be well enough to travel?"

"Randy said that Dr. Morris would release me on Monday, if all goes well."

"That sounds good. And Nealy, don't worry about the studio. I can handle things while you're away, and Miss Janik offered to help if I need her."

"Is she back from Europe?"

"Yes, she got home yesterday. She's rested and would love to teach a class or two for old time's sake."

"That's wonderful. And her timing's always been perfect," Nealy giggled, remembering Miss Janik:

"Girls! Girls! Let's go. We don't have all day. Take it from 6,7,8, tap,tap,tap,tap, shuffle...."

"What about Jerrod? Have you talked to him?"

"No, and I don't want to until I get back. If he calls, tell him I'm out of town."

"Nealy, I'm sorry he hurt you. I know you love him, but sometimes things work out for the best. Remember last year when Tom and I broke up? I thought I was going to die when I caught him in bed with my roommate. Can you imagine? I heard through the grapevine that he's living in California with some woman old enough to be his mother, who, by the way, is supporting him. The guy's a gigolo. And I thought he was *wonderful!* Boy, am I lucky I didn't marry him. You don't pay me enough to support him," she laughed, trying to cheer Nealy up a little. Nealy giggled, grabbing her stomach.

"Francine, don't make me laugh. It hurts."

"Sorry. Of course, I'm just teasing about the salary. But, Nealy, I know that someday I'll meet *Mr. Right,* then I can bury the past forever."

"You will, Francine. Some smart and wonderful guy will come along and sweep you off your feet. If, by some chance, he happens to be a doctor, make sure you ask Randy Richfield to tell you all about him before things get serious."

"Why Randy?"

"Francine, everyone knew about him, except me. Randy wanted to tell me, but he couldn't. But I understand why. I feel like such a fool. I shouldn't have married Jerrod after being away in New York for a year. I didn't even ask him about other women. I guess I didn't really want to know. So, just ask questions and put two and two together. Use your heart, but also use your brain. And make sure that there's more to your relationship than sex. A good marriage starts when you get out of bed, not when you get in," Nealy said, profoundly. Tears rolled down her cheeks again.

"Nealy, you're making me cry," Francine had never liked Jerrod; now she hated him. He had hurt Nealy far more than she could have ever imagined. Nealy had always seemed so together, so strong, so perfect. Seeing her vulnerable side seemed strange, but it made her even more beautiful, more feminine, and more human. Not that she wanted Nealy to be hurt—she loved her like a sister—but now she could be there for her instead of the other way around. Jerrod would live to regret his actions. Nealy had to see him for what he really is.

At three o'clock in the morning some orderlies came in with Dr. Morris and quickly moved her to a different room. Nealy had been sedated and barely knew what happened, but when she woke up, she knew she wasn't in the same room. The bells chimed at Sacred Heart's Catholic Church, which told her that Sunday had arrived; but they also reminded her of Jerrod on their wedding day. He had certainly taken those vows lightly. All those promises were nothing short of lies.

As she lay there listening, consumed with a mountain of self-pity, Dr. Morris came in.

"Hi."

"How did I get in here?"

"Jerrod's looking for you."

"Oh, no, I knew it."

"It's okay. He won't look for you here. This is *high-rent* district." In fact, President Roosevelt and Marilyn Monroe slept in that very bed," he said, attempting to cheer her up.

"Is that a fact. Come to think of it, Marilyn and I have a lot in common. Big boobs, and stupidity when it comes to men." She shrugged.

"I think you're being too hard on yourself." Rob Morris was very fond of Nealy. She had been a good friend to his wife and taught ballet and tap to his two little girls who both adored her. Right now his only concerns were for his patient and his friend, and even though ethically, he should talk to Jerrod, he didn't intend to. In his book, Jerrod's actions had taken away any rights for consultation in this case. Maybe later, he would sit him down and give him the facts, but, for now, Jerrod needed to keep his distance.

Randy checked on her several times during the day and into the night. They were desperately trying to keep her whereabouts hush-hush, especially since Nealy had been so adamant about not seeing Jerrod until she returned. Jerrod knew that Nealy had been taken to the hospital, but he thought that she had gotten so hysterical that she collapsed. When he approached Randy in the hall on the third floor, Randy admitted that he had brought her into emergency because she had become so distressed. Evidently, his aunt had talked to him and told him to leave her alone for awhile. Jerrod angrily told Randy that he had no intentions of upsetting her again, but he wanted to know where and how she was. Randy refused to offer any information and walked away. Jerrod made some sarcastic remark which Randy didn't acknowledge.

In an effort to organize a plan, Randy asked for Francine's help in packing some comfortable things for Nealy to take to New York. Francine had been terrified in Nealy's house for fear that Jerrod would come home and catch her.

Even though Randy had assured her that he was on call, it still made her nervous. Francine had made arrangements to meet Randy at the studio on Sunday night to pick up her things; his get-a-way plan had to be perfect.

By nine o'clock, the hospital had grown very quiet, but Nealy couldn't sleep. She had become very restless and couldn't wait to leave Galveston, to get away, far away from everything that reminded her of Jerrod.

She walked over to the window and looked out into the darkness. It had rained all day; the streets were wet and glossy. Why did he do it? Why? Why? She kept asking herself, over and over again in her mind. If anyone should have been unhappy, it should have been her. Sex with him mostly left her sad, lonely and empty. Was she not a good wife? Had she been a terrible lover? Did she not satisfy him? Hell, who could. He couldn't *get* enough. Jerrod had never seemed discontented, but he usually fell asleep within minutes. He had never talked afterwards, except, of course, when he wanted something. Why did he want her to marry her? He had the *mermaids*. A "naive bitch," is what he had called her. Did he really want her to become an exhibitionist, kinky and perverted? She had asked herself a thousand questions, exhausting her brain. She couldn't think anymore, she had to sleep.

Still dark outside, the nurse quietly slipped into Nealy's room and gently shook her, whispering, "Mrs. Jones, you need to wake up now."

Nealy barely opened her eyes. "What time is it?"

"It's five a.m. Dr. Richfield will be here to get you in an hour. I'll get you some juice."

"Okay, thanks." Nealy got up and took a shower. The hot water felt good beating against her head and back, both sore from bed rest.

After Nealy showered, she put on a blue shirt-waist dress that Francine had brought for her to wear. Digging through her cosmetic bag, she searched for the ivory-based make-up and powder, peach blush, green eye-shadow, and black mascara; Francine had dumped the entire drawer into her bag.

By the time she finished dressing, her appearance had improved one hundred percent, she felt like a new person. The nurse had put a tray of scrambled eggs, bacon, toast, and half of a grapefruit in front of her, strongly suggesting that she try to eat at least some of it before she left. Unfortunately, she didn't feel like eating.

"Randy, where are you?" she muttered anxiously.

"Hi, sweet lady. Your ride's here," Randy pushed a wheelchair through the door.

"A wheelchair. I'm not an invalid."

"No, but it's hospital regulations. So please, have a seat, my dear."

After sitting down, she cut a reluctant smile up at him.

"Nothing personal, but this hospital thing has truly been an experience. One I can assure you that I won't forget for a very long time. So, do me a favor," she growled, "before you put me in the slammer again, at least ask me."

"No problem. So, let's get out of the *slammer*."

Randy pushed her out into the hall and onto the open elevator that the nurse had waiting. When the door opened on the cardiac floor, both Randy and Nealy saw Jerrod at the same time and froze. He and another doctor were walking towards the elevator, obviously discussing a patient because he had a chart in his hand and appeared to be reading it.

A lady got on the elevator, and just before the door shut, Jerrod spotted her at the elevator, "Nealy, wait, I need to talk to you." The door shut in his face.

Nealy covered her face with her hands and slumped over in the chair. She wept, trying hard not to make a scene. The people on the elevator felt for her, not knowing why, but their hearts went out to her. Randy gently rested his hands on her shoulders.

When the elevator opened on the first floor, he rushed her outside to the car that he had parked at the side entrance. If possible, he wanted to get her away from there before Jerrod got downstairs. He opened the door and helped her inside without a word. Randy threw her bags in the car, got in, and took off. In his rearview mirror, he saw Jerrod run out of the sliding double doors, screaming for them to stop, but he just kept going. Randy felt so sorry for her that he almost stopped, but he knew that she was much too vulnerable and that Jerrod would take advantage of her weakened state of mind. So, he drove several blocks before he stopped to comfort her. "Nealy, are you okay?"

"Yes," she managed to say, taking the handkerchief that he held out for her. "Dammit!" she screamed. "Why am I letting him get to me? I hate him so much."

"Nealy, you've been through a lot. That's why I didn't stop. If you made a decision right now, you'd regret it. Once you get a little stronger, you'll be able to see things more clearly, and you'll get over all the hurt and the anger." Randy took her hand and held it for a minute.

"I know you're right...because one minute I love him, and then moments later, I hate him. I'm so confused about all of this. How can I love him if I really hate him? And I do hate him, Randy. I have to hate him after what he did."

"Nealy, please, just relax and give yourself some time. Now, take a deep breath. Come on, doctor's orders," he smiled at her. "Okay, once more....Now, one more time. That's my girl," he said, squeezing her hand. "You okay?"

"Much better."

"Good. Just think about New York. It'll be so nice there." Randy reached behind the seat and grabbed her overnight case so that she could touch-up her face; he knew that would bother her.

For the next twenty minutes, Nealy didn't say too much, but every so often she would dab her eyes with Randy's handkerchief. Finally, Nealy broke her silence. "Where's Chance? See, I told you I'd be a horrible mother. I've deserted him."

"He's fine. Alicia's babysitter took Alicia and the dogs down to the beach."

"Oh, good. Please take good care of him."

"I promise, scout's honor," he pledged.

"How long did it take you to get over Alice?"

"That's a hard question. Remember that day at the beach when I told you that I hated her for dying? I did just what you're doing. One minute I cried because I loved her, and the next I yelled because I hated her. The thing that I regret most is that I didn't even realize how much I loved her until she died."

"What?"

"Well, she was three month's pregnant when I married her. I didn't love her. And I certainly didn't want to marry her. I had to finish college. And I wanted to be a doctor more than anything. I resented everything about our relationship. I didn't do anything mean to her, but I didn't do anything nice for her either. I rarely saw her. I worked and went to school full time, and so did she. And then, during the last month of her pregnancy, she became ill. I took care of her, as I would any patient. When I got to know her, it amazed me how much we had in common. There were times when we talked all night. Alice had some very special qualities, and I had never taken the time to notice. The whole thing was so ironic. I wasted six months hating a person that I liked from the first day I met her. Then, when I fell in love with her and wanted so much to be with her and share a life and our child, she died."

Tears rolled down Nealy's cheeks. "Oh, Randy, I'm so sorry. I had no idea."

"Nealy, it's okay. It took me a long time to forgive myself. That's why I know how much Jerrod will regret what he's done to you. Special people are hard to find, and I didn't know that until I lost one. I tried to make it up to Alice by being a good father, and I think she has forgiven me. At least I'd like to think so. Anyway, I learned a very valuable lesson. So, next time I find what I want, I'll treat her like a queen. I won't waste one precious minute." Randy smiled sadly. He turned off I-45 onto Jetero Blvd and headed East to Houston's Intercontinental Airport.

The parking lot didn't have many vacant spaces close by, so Nealy insisted that Randy drop her off. He pulled up in front of American Airlines and stopped the car. Then he opened the trunk and handed her suitcase to the attendant.

"Thanks for everything, Randy, especially your friendship."

"As always, it's my pleasure. And Nealy, I *am* your friend, so if you need anything, I'm here." He hugged her.

"I'd better go, or I'll cry again."

"Okay, but remember three words. Rest, rest and rest."

"I will, I will and I will. Will you look out for Francine for me?"

"That'll be my pleasure, too," he said, his eyebrows dancing.

"Silly," she said, giving him a I-think-I-get-the-message look.

"Oh, and don't forget to check my mail."

"Why? Is there something coming that I'll need to mail to you?"

"No. It's just that I've been expecting to receive notification that I've been inducted into the "Idiots Hall of Fame.""

Randy cracked up. "I can see that, in spite of all this madness, you're going to be fine," he smiled happily, still laughing.

"I'm glad *you* can see it because, unfortunately, it's not that clear to me yet. Anyway, can you go see Chance and Alicia and take care of Francine. No...go see Francine—Oh, hell. Well, you know what I mean," she giggled.

As he drove away, she waved and smiled. "Hmm," she said under her breath. "Now that could be a match made in *Heaven*."

CHAPTER TWENTY-FIVE

LESS THAN AN HOUR LATER, Nealy's plane had reached its cruising altitude of thirty-eight thousand feet. Staring out the window, she focused on the airless movement of the masses of billowy cumulus clouds that separated the earth from the heavens. Nealy didn't really care for flying, but it's one of those necessary evils, so she wore God out praying until her feet were planted safely back on the ground; at least it kept her occupied.

Far across the clouds, she noticed a large area that appeared smooth as glass. The outline reminded her of Sam Rayburn Lake where her grandparents went fishing when she was a child. Nealy didn't like to fish any better than she liked to fly, but she wanted to be with them. Nealy watched in horror as they took those slimy little fish off their hooks; those poor, defenseless creatures gasping for their last breath. It seemed rather cruel. But, let's face it, fish aren't the brightest of God's creatures. They are attracted to limp, lifeless worms that are dangled before them to tease and torture. Now wait a minute. Isn't that exactly how she reacted? Jerrod dangled his bait, set the hook, and then slowly reeled her in, hook, line and sinker. A sick mental picture made her laugh out loud and she muttered under her breath, "Yes, Nealy, you're a not-so-bright little minnow alright."

"Oh...look, a rainbow," she whispered to herself. God had sent her another sign. But, if he loved her, why had he allowed her to marry a lying, philandering worm that wiggled his way back into her life. The truth is that she did it to herself. It must have been God who sent her away to follow her dreams, leaving Jerrod behind. And then, when he reappeared like Lucifer disguised as Prince Charming, cleverly luring her back into his clutches, she created her own destiny. Why didn't she listen? Something kept telling her that he wasn't the one, but *nooooo*, she didn't listen. "You dummy."

"Were you talking to me?" the man sitting next to Nealy asked.

"Oh, no, sorry. I was just thinking out loud, I guess," she said, shrugging her shoulders. Poor guy. He thought she called *him* a dummy. Oops. This whole thing with Jerrod had made her crazy. Lord knows what she'd do next. Nealy quickly turned back towards the window because she didn't feel like visiting and because she didn't want to encourage this man in case he did.

"Would you care for something to drink?" the flight attendant asked.

"Excuse me," the man said, tapping Nealy on the shoulder. "Would you like something to drink?"

"Oh, uh...yes," she said to him, and then she looked up at the flight attendant. "Apple juice, please." Why did she say yes when she really didn't want anything. Maybe her body needed fluids since she had been crying for days. Did tears come from bodily fluids? What an interesting question. Exactly where do tears flow from when the mind calls them up? Everyone knows that they exit through the tear ducts, but where did they form? Well now, this is nuts. Nealy you've finally lost it, she thought to herself. Then she laughed out loud again. In an effort to think about anything other than that jackass, she had lost control of her mind. Anyone who became mentally involved in the body's ability to produce mass tears and their place of origination had to be teetering on the edge of insanity. On *The Bob Newhart Show* Bob's patients always talked about twisted or mind-boggling subjects. Nealy couldn't shut her mind off, vacillating from sad to silly to ridiculous. Shouldn't she just be angry? After all, she had spent the past three years and four months being tormented by that low-life, worm-dangling water womanizer. Nealy laughed out loud again.

"What's so funny?" the man next to her asked.

"Oh, sometimes I just amuse the hell out of myself. But, actually, I'm dizzy from watching the clouds go by so fast," she said, giggling. My god, did she sound crazy or what?

"I wish I could do that," he said, shaking his head. "I'm on my way back to New York to give my ex-old-lady a piece of my mind and a huge piece of my paycheck. You see, we got a couple of kids, and when I lost my job, I got behind on my child support. And the minute I found another job, that greedy bitch expected me to pay all the back child support in one lump sum. I tried to tell her that I couldn't, but she just couldn't let it rest. The next thing I know, I'm face to face with this sheriff who hands me some papers. I hope the bitch is satisfied, she almost cost me my new job!" The man's face turned bright red. Nealy didn't know what to say.

"Well, maybe she needed the money for braces or dance lessons or something," Nealy replied making conversation.

"Who told you? That's exactly what she said. You women use the same line just to make us poor guys suffer! I'm going to find me another seat. Maybe if I sit by a man, I can get a little sympathy," he shouted, storming out of his seat and down the aisle.

"And I thought I'd lost it," Nealy said, turning to look at the people in the seat across from her. They laughed, and then she did too. It hurt her stomach, so she held it tightly. A couple of the people who had caught only part of the conversation, scooted over into his empty seat to find out what had tripped his trigger. Nealy didn't seem to be the only one wallowing in self-pity these days. In fact, Jerrod probably had someone cornered at this very moment to pour out his heart about this bitch who left him *just because* he took a midnight swim or two with a few friends.

When the plane landed, Nealy smiled at the man on her way out. He gave her a slight smile, but Nealy didn't expect much. He probably wore a baseball cap that said, *"Why not, everyone else does."*

As Nealy walked out of the jetway into the terminal, she heard a woman shouting. "Hey," the woman said, looking straight at Nealy. "Are you Nealy Jones?"

"Yes. How did you know?"

"I'm Sharon Smart. Janey described you perfectly."

"Did she tell you to look for the dummy with red, puffy eyes?"

"Oh, honey, our work's cut out for us. That guy must have really done a number on you." Sharon took Nealy's arm and led her down to the baggage claim area. Afterward, they headed into the city in Sharon's car: a shiny, red Mercedes. All of Janey's friends were divorced, and they all drove Mercedes. Divorce certainly had *some* benefits.

Sharon Smart had to be in her mid to late fifties and still very attractive for her age. She had short, dark brown hair and fair skin and a very funny, but mischievous personality. Her dark eyes squinted when she talked about that "no good, rotten rat's ass that dumped her for that sneaky bag-of-bones bitch who set her up with bad advice so that she could steal her husband. They'll get you every time, those goddamn shrinks," she said. Sharon gave Nealy a descriptive play-by-play account of her own marital woes. It made Nealy giggle, but Sharon didn't mind. It had been several years since she and her husband divorced, so Sharon laughed, too. But Nealy had the distinct feeling that Sharon could hold her own in a battle. In fact, the poor guy had probably been lucky if he got the clothes on his back when that divorce had all been said and done. The only thing that saved him from losing everything was his status as a prominent New York attorney. But regardless who he was, Sharon got what she wanted: she had hired Marvin Michelson.

When it came time for Nealy to share, she told her a milder version of what had really happened. It just seemed too bizarre to be true, so she spared her the details about Jerrod's harem of Polly Porpoises. Of course, Sharon had plenty of good advice for Nealy that went right to the heart of the matter, or maybe to a more specific part of the anatomy.

"Honey, my advice to you is to do just what I did. I stripped that no good rotten rat's ass down to his birthday suit. I wanted it all. And since I had a death grip on his privates, let me tell you, honey, *I got it all*. He'll think twice before he ever gets caught, literally, with his pants down again, if you know what I mean," she boasted, displaying pride in her vengeance.

"Did you ever regret it. I mean...did you ever wish that you'd forgiven him?"

"Well, after I got over the bitterness, the humiliation and the hurt, we tried to get back together again, but it didn't work. I just couldn't trust that little shit again, no matter how much I wanted to. And besides, something had died inside of me," Sharon said, hoping that Nealy wouldn't let that cheating husband of hers come back too easily, if at all.

"Was it hard starting over again?" Nealy asked.

"Oh, at first. I'll admit, I got lonely from time to time. And that's really why I agreed to try it again, but going back for the wrong reason never works. The problems that caused him to cheat on me in the first place were still there. I didn't make him happy, and he didn't make me happy. We didn't have anything in common except sex, which had more or less died somewhere along the way. We both needed something that we couldn't give each other, no matter how hard we tried. Going back to a blah relationship rarely works, but I tried it. But...if I had that choice again, I wouldn't do it. I'd have to grieve all over again. One thing that I did learn, though, is that I deserved half the credit for the failure of the marriage. So, I don't hate him anymore. Sugar, it takes two to tango," Sharon said, winking at Nealy.

"Do you date now?"

"Oh, honey, do I date. I got me a honey that fits me like a spoon. We laugh about our divorces, and he says, 'You can't strip me down to my privates 'cause I sport a pair of five-star-generals.' And honey, you see this smile on my face? Well, he ain't lyin'." Nealy giggled almost hysterically, it nearly killed her stomach. But it felt good to laugh.

After Nealy stopped laughing, she smiled at Sharon. "Thanks. I feel better already. But you've given me a lot to think about."

"Well, I'm glad. And I know it's hard, but just give yourself some time. It hurts too much to make the same mistake over and over again. Try to figure out what went wrong. Once you know that, then you can decide whether or not the marriage is salvageable. Believe me, Nealy, there's nothing better than having the right man in your life. And when he comes along, you'll know it. It'll be the best sex you've ever had, and you won't even have to get undressed to do it." Sharon laughed, but she meant every word.

Sharon drove up in front of the posh apartment building across from Central Park, with a green jeweled-toned awning that extended out to the street. The doorman promptly opened the door.

"Jigs, I want you to meet Nealy Jones. She'll be staying in Janey Randall's apartment for a while."

"Nice to have you, Mrs. Jones," he said, nodding his head.

"Thanks. But please, call me Nealy."

"As you wish. I'll get Ms. Randall's key and take your bags up." He seemed puzzled when he pulled Nealy's bag out of Sharon's trunk; women in New York rarely travel that light.

"Thanks. Oh, I love being back in New York," Nealy said, whirling around to take in all the sights: the park, the traffic, all the people quickly moving about. "There has always been something about this city that intrigued and fascinated me."

"I love it too," Sharon said. "Listen, sugar, I gotta go let my dogs out. Call if you need anything."

"Okay. Thanks Sharon." Nealy stood on the sidewalk enjoying the perfect day. The sun shined brightly, but it was a bit chilly. Nealy felt better already, just being out of Galveston. That terrible tightness in her chest had already lifted somewhat, allowing her to breathe much better.

"Are you ready, Ms. Nealy?" the doorman asked.

"Oh, sorry. I'm just so thrilled to be back here." Nealy met Sharon, who was wearing a fluffy, calf-length, white fur coat, coming out of the elevator. She had her two French poodles with her, Jo-Jo and Mr. French. Sharon seemed like the poodle type. Nealy could picture her zig-zagging down the street behind the two dogs. And when she stopped to pick up their tiny dropping, she would do it with such grace and style.

"See you later!" she said, singing the last two syllables. "My babies just love their afternoon walk."

Nealy took the elevator up with Jigs to the ninth floor. He assisted her with the door and sat her luggage inside. Nealy tipped him.

"Thanks, Jigs."

"Thank *you*. If you need anything, just call downstairs."

"Thanks." Nealy closed the door. Janey's exquisite taste flourished. Nealy took off her shoes. Her feet sank down into two inches of eighty-ounce light blue carpet; ooh, cushy. This apartment had class. Even the French Provincial furniture, that Nealy didn't particularly care for, looked wonderful. She eased around the apartment, checking things out since this would be her monastery for the next two weeks. The living room had an enormous bay window with a great view of Central Park. It's amazing how many wealthy people there are in the world, and half of them have an apartment overlooking Central Park. The master bedroom had a gorgeous Queen Anne bedroom suite in Cherrywood, and the accessories were right out of Eighteenth century France. The bed sat up so high that its occupants would need oxygen. A thick comforter, made of blush-pink satin with a tapestry border that edged the top of the bed in brilliant colors, fans, and flowers, covered the mattress. The rugs and pillows scattered around the room matched the tapestry border in the comforter, so apparently Janey had not bought this stuff at a garage sale.

Moving right along, Nealy wandered into the guest room, which would become her room for the time being. All she could see were ruffles, ribbons and bows that covered the canopy bed, creating the perfect quarters for the pitiful princess who had married the pathetic prince. The tiny light blue and white flowers devoured the dark blue cotton fabric on the bed, dressing table, and chair. The entire room felt like spring—light and bright and airy—and it even smelled like flowers. If this place didn't improve her mood and her attitude, nothing would. Nealy walked from room to room admiring the tiny Limoges boxes, elegant porcelain Lladros, and the ornate Dresden figurines. The apartment had old-world charm; elegance personified.

Nealy sat down in a big, over-stuffed chair by the bay window and watched the children playing in the park. When the sun sank behind the tall buildings to the west, the people disappeared. She unpacked and decided upon a hot bubble bath to improve her bewildered state.

Nealy filled the tub to the top and sank down into hot, steamy water, causing bubbles to rise all around her. Leaning back, she relaxed until thoughts of Jerrod brought back uncontrollable tears. Even when she tried to stop sobbing, she couldn't. It hurt so much to think about what he had done, and she couldn't forget that scene at the fraternity house. There would be an indelible picture in her mind forever! The things he said to her had not stopped ringing out in her mind, and she wondered if they ever would. "Did he want to get caught?" she asked herself. Well, he must have, because he did it right there where everyone knew him. Or was he just so sure that no one would say anything? Well, if that were it, he was right, because it had been going on for more than three years, and no one had said a word. Not *one* word. It seemed as if the tears had been flowing like faucets forever, but finally they stopped and she became so angry that she wanted to kill him. Not really, but castration would be good. Just cut it *right* off. One clean whack with an axe on a chopping block. The thought made her feel vindicated, but doing it would even be better. That guy loved to *do it* more than anyone else in the world. It took balls to do what he did, so thank goodness he got his share. A normal person couldn't have kept up the pace: a wife and a pool full of horny mermaids lusting after him. That was too incredible for words. Did he do it to all of them in one night and then come home and *do it* to her, too? Geezus, that's really incredible. "Nealy stop this," she cried out, grabbing her towel and getting out of the tub. This had become too overwhelming, so she had to do something to get her mind off this. She started singing and didn't stop until she got her pajamas on. Quickly, she wrapped a towel, turban-style, around her head and went into the living room to watch television. Flipping from channel to channel, she finally settled on a re-run of "I Love Lucy," which she knew would make her laugh. All night, she lay there, watching and dozing, trying to forget about all of the sadness around her. Dr. Morris had given her some sleeping pills, but she didn't want to take drugs. Drugs numb the pain only temporarily; they couldn't take it away, so it would be better to deal with the problems. Like Sharon said, "Find out what went wrong, and then you'll know if the marriage can be salvaged." That's what she had to figure out. And no pills were going to help her do that.

The doorbell rang, and Nealy got up from the couch where she had evidently spent the night. A bright ray of sunlight beamed through the picture window.

"Who is it?"

"It's me, Sharon."

"I'll be right there," Nealy said, glancing at the large mirror on the wall. "Oh my God." She tried to fluff her hair, but it didn't help. So, with no place to run and no place to hide, she opened the door. "I know. I look like hell."

"You sure do, sugar," she laughed. "But that's part of the recovery process. Let me guess. Last night you sat in the chair, staring out the window until it got dark. Then you took a hot bath and cried for hours. You tossed and turned and prayed for morning."

"How'd you know?"

"I've been there. And I've had lots of friends go through the same thing. Janey sat in that very same chair and cried herself sick, but she lived through it. And contrary to popular belief, you will too."

"What time is it?"

"Almost ten. I did a little shopping for you. The week following my break-up, I wouldn't have eaten at all if one of my friends hadn't brought food to me." Sharon pulled several things out of a big bag. "I went down to the deli where I buy all my meals. I got you some ham, turkey, three kinds of cheese, pasta salad, two kinds of bread, milk, and some soup. Hope you like sandwiches and broccoli-cheese soup. Also, I picked-up some eggs. The protein will give you energy. Oh, and I got you some fruit, and some real gooey chocolate stuff guaranteed to perk you up."

"Sharon, this is so nice, thanks. Let me find my purse so I can pay you for all of this," Nealy said, walking towards the bedroom.

"No, no, sugar, someone did it for me, and someday you'll do it for somebody else. We're a large group: *The Gullible Girls Club*. With each bite, you'll get stronger and angrier guaranteed."

"This is so sweet, thank you. Maybe, before I go, I can buy your dinner."

"That'd be nice. But, for now, my man waits. I'm going to Vermont for a few days for lots of *sex*—"

"Sharon," Nealy said, blushing.

"To blush like that, you must know what I'm talking about," she smiled mischievously. "No, seriously, Nealy, remember what I told you. You only have two weeks before you have to go home and face him. And when you do, for godsakes, have yourself pulled together. Search your soul for some answers. They're there, you just need to find them. Eat and enjoy. Here's my number in case you need to get in touch with me, but don't be surprised if I'm really out of breath."

"Sharon, you're terrible," Nealy said, giggling at her.

"No, I'm just in love with the right man. You'll know exactly how I feel someday. Take care, sugar," she said, hugging Nealy and darting out the door.

Laughing at her, Nealy closed the door. "What a nut she is," she whispered, "but she's sweet, wonderful and very funny." Nealy walked into the bathroom and took a good look at herself in the mirror. "Ah, man, you really look like shit—pardon my language—you poor miserable slob." She just stood there staring at her puffy eyes, dark circles, and her flat, matted hair. "But, frankly, my dear, I don't give a damn." Nealy laughed at her lousy Clark Gable impression. In the kitchen, she put away her food and ate an apple, even though the thought of food made her feel ill. Not having much energy, she slowly walked back over to the couch and lay down again. The time had come to start thinking about what had happened. Unfortunately, she only had two weeks and she didn't know where to start. Should she start back in junior high school, or college, or when she left for NYC, or last week? Maybe she should start with their break-up after college when she went to New York. That had been hard. But, at the time, going to New York had been the most important thing to her, even more important than Jerrod. In fact, he said, "If you go, we're through for good. And I mean it!" But she went, never once looking back. Then why, a year later, did she look back? Was he a way out of a situation that had been harder than she ever imagined, or did she really love him? New York's tough. Show business is a cut throat business. Did the cushy life of a doctor's wife, a very rich and handsome doctor's wife, make it very tempting?

The phone rang. Nealy sat up and stared at the phone, as if it were a rattle snake. The thought that it might be Jerrod terrified her. She didn't want to talk to him yet. But, it might be Janey or Francine. On the fourth ring, she answered it.

"Hello."

"Nealy, how are you?"

"Oh, Randy, thank God it's you."

"Are you okay?" he asked.

"Oh, yeah, I'm fine. I thought it might be Jerrod, and I'm just not ready for that. How are you?"

"I'm great. I just wanted to check-up on you. See if you're resting."

"Yes and no. Sometimes and sometimes not, but I'm better. Janey's friend and next door neighbor, Sharon, has been great. The only thing wrong with her is that she makes me laugh too much. It hurts my stomach."

"Speaking of that. How is it?"

"Good. A little sore, but not too bad. How's Chance?"

"He's great. Alicia has become quite the doting sitter."

"She's such a little doll. Will you thank her for me, please. And be sure to give her a hug tell her that I miss her."

"I'll do that."

"How's Francine doing at the studio, or have you had time to call?"

"As a matter of fact, I talked to her last night and this morning, and everything's fine. I'll see her tonight when I pick-up Alicia after ballet class."

"Be sure and thank her again for me, too. She's a sweetheart."

"I couldn't agree more. And I'll even give her a big hug, from you of course."

"You do that, *from me of course*," Nealy laughed. Well, she thought, sometimes things do happen for a reason. "Hmm."

"Hmm, what?" Randy mimicked.

"I'm just thinking out loud. In fact, lately I've been doing too much out loud." Nealy laughed when she told him about the poor guy on the plane and about Sharon, but, of course, she didn't tell him everything Sharon said. It would make her uncomfortable.

"Nealy, it's so good to hear you laugh again, but I knew you'd bounce back. Listen, I'm gonna run. You still need to take it easy for a few more days, so keep that in mind. I gave Rob Morris your number there. He wanted to call and check on you, too."

"Oh, okay. Randy, thanks for calling. I still have my moments, but it'll all work out. Tell Francine hi and make sure you give her that hug for me."

"If you insist," he chuckled.

"I do insist."

"Now you take care of yourself. See ya soon." Randy smiled when he hung up. He felt so much better because she sounded more like her old self. He knew all along that she'd be fine, but she had been through so much, and she seemed very upset. He half way expected her to turn around and come back to Jerrod. She's the type that makes a promise and keeps it, especially the solemn promise of "until death do us part." Thank goodness Nealy's intelligent enough to know that Jerrod will never change; his vows had meant nothing. And because of that, her pride will not allow her to tolerate his lifestyle. Beside she has too much class for a jerk like that. Speaking of class, Francine had class *and great legs*. She wasn't quite as pretty as Nealy, or built as well, but she had the same look, that back-to-the-basics look with pretty skin and silky hair. Maybe he *should* give her that hug. Just thinking about it made him blush and feel as if he'd be cheating on Nealy because of the terrible crush he had on her. But, in his heart, he knew that their relationship would always be platonic. Nealy didn't love him like that—as a friend, sure—but it didn't take a rocket scientist to see that she wasn't "in love" with him or could she ever be. So, maybe the time had come for him to move on, but no matter what happened, he always wanted to be Nealy's friend.

For the rest of the day, Nealy wandered around the apartment aimlessly, always returning to the overstuffed chair by the window in the living room so that she could watch the people in the park. By six o'clock, night had fallen and she moved to the couch to try and read for a while. At six-thirty, the phone rang, and she froze again. On the third ring, she answered it.

"Hello," she said softly in case she had to disguise her voice.

"Nealy, it's Rob. How are you?"

"Oh, Rob, hi," she sighed with relief. "How am I? Mentally or physically?"

"Let's start with physically. Is the soreness subsiding?"

"Yes, it's better, but it still hurts when I laugh."

"You've been laughing, huh," he said, pleasantly surprised. Nealy told him about Sharon and some of the other amusing moments that she'd had since she left the hospital, all of which pleased him. He had been so afraid that she would sit around and feel sorry for herself.

"Should I do some walking or something? I'm feeling a little stiff."

"Have you had any bleeding or discharge or cramping?"

"Is this something we really need to discuss?"

He chuckled. "Yes, I'm afraid so."

"Okay, well, I had a little discharge and bleeding yesterday. And every so often I feel a little cramping, but it doesn't last long."

"Well, that's normal. I still want you to rest until Friday, and then you can take a walk. But don't overdo it. Okay. Next category. How are you emotionally?"

"I'm not sure. I wander around feeling numb, and then out of the blue, I burst into tears. Perhaps, I've lost it."

"Nealy, this is normal. It'll all come together in time. But please, rest as much as you can, and if you need anything, you have my number. Oh, I...I talked to Jerrod today. I kept debating on whether or not I should mention it, but I guess I should go ahead and tell you. He asked me what happened. He said he'd heard all kinds of rumors around the hospital. So I told him about the pregnancy. At first, he got very angry, but then he calmed down and started blaming himself."

"I guess I should have told him, uh?"

"No, I think it's much better that he heard it from me. I told him that you had gone away to rest and that you would talk to him when you returned. Nealy don't cry. It's alright. This is very difficult for both of you, but, Nealy, he brought this all on himself. You can't forget what he did just because you feel sorry for him."

"I know," she cried. "But it's not about him. I feel guilty about the baby. I didn't really want a baby so I may have—"

"Nealy, it couldn't be helped. I told you that. You *didn't* cause this. So, for now, please just try to rest."

"Okay, I'll try," she said, choking back the tears.

"I'll call you later. Take care of yourself, and call if you need me."

"Thanks, Rob." Nealy put the phone back on the receiver. And she dropped down into the chair beside the phone. The tears just kept coming and coming.

For the next two days, Nealy hung around the apartment and thought about her life, her marriage, and her future. Remembering special times with

Jerrod made her cry at times. The baby or the loss of the baby made her cry. But finally, with each passing day she started to come to terms with herself and her situation; she slept more and cried less. Growing tired of warm milk sprinkled with cinnamon had to be a sign that she was getting stronger. Her life started to make sense again. At times, she thought she'd figured out what went wrong, but then at other times, she wasn't sure. On Thursday night, Nealy decided to call her parents and tell them that she was in New York on business. After all, divorce is a *very messy business*. It wasn't exactly the truth, but it wasn't exactly a lie either. Nealy didn't want to worry them before it became absolutely necessary. And she wanted to be emotionally strong and sure of her plans.

At nine o'clock, she gathered up enough courage to put on her happy face and made the call. Her mother answered, and when Nealy told her that she was in New York, she became so excited that Jerrod didn't even enter into the conversation. Nealy's mother had always been star and stage struck, so all she wanted to hear about were the plays and whether or not Nealy would be able to see one during her visit. Knowing her mother well, Nealy had done her homework and called to see what plays were on Broadway. When she told her that she might try to see Maggie Smith in Tom Stoppard's *Night and Day* at the Virginia Theater, her mother said how much she wished that she could join her. Nealy's heart almost stopped.

When Nealy first moved to New York, the second week as matter of fact, she, Denise and Alex had gotten tickets to see Elizabeth Ashley and Keir Dullea in *Cat On A Hot Tin Roof*. As perfect timing would have it, Nealy's mother called the night before they were to go, only to discover that Alex had taken ill and couldn't go. Immediately, Gracie volunteered to take her place and caught a plane the next morning. Even though she had been great fun, this would not be a good time for one of her mother's spur-of-the-moment decisions, so she had to think fast and come up with something good.

"Oh, Nealy, Maggie Smith is one of my favorites."

Think fast Nealy, think, she thought, racking her brain. "Well, I'm pretty tired, so I may just rest, ya know. And besides, it's really tough to get tickets this time of year. I may just wait until closer to the holiday. Maybe you could come back with me."

"Oh, honey, that would be marvelous."

"Great! We'll do it. Tell everyone hello. And give Daddy my love."

"I will, honey. Take care and watch out for muggers. Crime is *so high* in that city."

"I will, Mother. I Love You." Nealy loved her mother dearly. And right now, more than any other time in her life, she wanted her mother and her daddy's shoulders to cry on. But she couldn't tell them about the mess that she had made of her life. Disappointing herself was one thing, disappointing them was another. Besides, they wouldn't understand because their marriage had been rock-solid for forty years, and Jerrod's behavior would be something right out of a movie, a very bad, low budget film, filled with sex, violence, drugs, and a Parental Guidance Advisory: Not suitable for children under eighteen.

Nealy hung up and went to bed to read a book that Sharon had given to her by Dr. Leo Buscaglia, proclaiming to be a God-sent for betrayed women. "The man is a miracle worker. He's fabulous. So read, read, read!" Sharon had said, handing her the book that morning when she dropped off the food. Of course, that was the day that Nealy had looked like death warmed over, so no wonder she insisted that she read about *life after loving*.

CHAPTER TWENTY-SIX

THE NEXT MORNING, Nealy woke up a little after seven and wandered into the kitchen to make coffee. So, while waiting on the coffee to perk, she flipped on *Good Morning America* in an attempt to catch up on the news. As the aroma of fresh brewed coffee filled her nostrils, she took a deep breath; she really liked the smell better than the taste. But, like most people in America today, she needed the caffeine to get herself going. On her refrigerator at home, she had a magnet on it with a frazzled looking woman on it that said, "People who act happy before 10 A.M. should be institutionalized."

Minutes later, the beep forced her up from the couch, and she ambled into the kitchen for her liquid rush. Just as she pressed the cup against her lips for her first sip, the telephone rang. She jumped, spilling hot coffee all down the front of her gown. "Shit," she screamed, grabbing a paper towel and then running around the bar to grab the phone. "Hello."

"Nealy, good-morning, it's Rob."

"Hi, Rob," she said, dragging the phone cord back around the bar to blot-up her mess.

"How are you?"

"Well, other than the fact that I just scalded myself with hot coffee—"

"Did you burn yourself?" he asked, too concerned to let her finish.

"Oh, no, I'm okay. I'm just a little jumpy these days."

"Afraid that Jerrod will call?"

"That's part of it."

"How's the tummy? Still sore?"

"No, not too much. I still have a slight pain here or there if I bend or get up out of bed a certain way. But I feel good," she said, sounding almost good as new.

"Good, I'm glad. But you still need to take it easy for a while longer. You're not completely healed on the inside yet."

"I will, but so far all I've done is rest. I haven't left the apartment all week."

"Well, I think it's about time you do. In fact, that's one of the reasons I called. A good friend of mine practices in New York City. We went to med-school together. He had a ob-gyn practice for a couple of years and then went into psychiatry. I told him that you were there, and he offered to keep an eye on you. So he's going to pick you up at eight o'clock and take you out for a good meal. I'm sure that you haven't had one."

"Rob, I appreciate what you're trying to do, but I don't need a psychiatrist," she resisted.

"I didn't say you did. But during times like this it helps to have a good listener, and Phillip is a great listener. And besides, a little company will be refreshing. I remember how you took time out to visit my wife when she was ill and this is just a little payback. It'll do you good to get out. He's a good friend and you'll enjoy yourself. So I won't take *no* for an answer because I want to hear from someone else that you're doing alright. I'll call you next week," he said and hung up.

"Grrreat! Just what I need...a date," she grumbled. Nealy stood there stunned. While pouring herself another cup of coffee, she complained to herself, and then she walked over and sat down in her favorite spot to gaze out at Central Park. How could he do that? Set her up with some guy, a psychiatrist of all people. He probably wanted him to check out her arms and see if she had tried to slit her wrists. After all, the last time Rob saw her she had been an emotional wreck. It embarrassed her to think about how pathetic she had acted—all that blubbering and carrying on. Oh, *dear Lord,* what a fool she had made of herself. Well, maybe by going to dinner with this guy, she could prove to everyone that she hadn't tried to harm herself or attempted to jump out the window of the ninth floor. But,if he planned on her spilling her guts, he had another thing coming; she'd never dream of telling this horrid story to someone that she'd never seen before in her life.

At eight o'clock sharp, the grandfather clock chimed at the same time the phone rang.

"Hello," she said, nervously.

"Ms. Nealy, you have a guest here to see you, a doctor."

"Thanks, Jigs. If he insists, tell him to come up."

Nealy couldn't believe that he had arrived on time. Doctors aren't punctual. They always keep their patients waiting. It makes them appear important and makes way for their condescending attitude; they love to patronize their patients to prevent them from asking too many needless questions. But, a psychiatrist, he's different. He ask questions and then he gets paid to listen. And at this rate, people complain a lot less or talk a lot faster. Speaking of psychiatrists...ready or not, she had to answer the door.

"Nealy, hi, I'm Phillip Pepper."

"Hi, Phillip, listen—"

"Nealy," he politely interrupted, "Rob told me that you'd try to send me away, but I have orders that I'm not to leave here without you."

"I see. Then in that case, why don't you come in." Nealy stood there looking at him because she really didn't know what to do. She smiled, and he smiled as he swayed back and forth with his hands in his pocket. The guy seemed harmless. He had dark-blonde curly hair, fair skin, and a nice smile that fit his cute baby face, making him look younger than his mid-thirty years. Only slightly taller than Nealy, he carried himself well and obviously worked out because he had a muscular build with nicely defined chest and arms. Crying on those broad shoulders could be very comforting, she thought, a little shocked at where her mind had dared to roam in regards to a *man* that she just met. Nealy hadn't been physically attracted to another man since the night she sat in front of Jerrod and his buddy at a basketball game in the tenth grade. His eyes were an incredible blue-gray—God he looked familiar—that curved down to the corners like a puppy dogs, which made him look sweet, angelic and highly trustworthy; a godsend for a man in his position. And for a blind date, she had to admit, he wasn't bad. But, cute or not, she wasn't ready to date. "Uh...would you like to sit down?" she asked politely.

"Actually, I think we should be going. I made dinner reservations for eight-thirty," he said, trying to place where he had seen her. But, if he had he'd remember. No man ever forgets a face like this one and damn sure doesn't forget a body...Well, it's really time to go. Wow! Rob you did real good. I owe ya, man, he thought trying not to stare at her.

"Oh, okay. You'll have to forgive me, I'm a little out-of-it these days. Now what did you say your last name was?"

"Pepper," he said proudly.

"As in Dr. Pepper?" she questioned.

"Exactly," he smiled.

"No wonder Rob sent you. He thought I needed a real pepper-upper," she giggled, and he laughed. "I'm sorry, but I'm sure you get teased all the time."

"Yes, I'm used to it. Are you ready?"

"Ready," she said, picking up her purse. "I guess if you were a sergeant, you'd be taking me to a *Lonely Hearts Club* meeting since I'm sure you know my entire life story."

"Well, as a matter of fact, I intended to invite you to my therapy group next Monday, which, by the way, *is* called *The Lonely Hearts*. I wasn't sure if you needed it, but now that I've met you, I'd like you to come anyway, just in case," he said, following her into the elevator.

"Thanks, but I'll probably pass this time," she said, grinning. Her eyes still felt swollen and red, and the clothes that Francine had packed for her were not exactly what she would have chosen to wear out to dinner in New York, especially with a cute doctor.

"Ms. Nealy, how nice it is to see you going out," Jigs, the doorman, said.

"It's nice to be going out," she said, smiling a big toothy smile, revealing the large dimple in her left cheek.

"Enjoy your evening Ms. Nealy, and you too, Doctor," he said, glancing enviously at Phillip Pepper who smiled back proudly. It had been a long time since he'd been out with a beautiful woman. In talking with Rob he had classified her as a "head turner." And that she is. In fact, she had to be one of the prettiest women that he'd ever seen. As Bogart would say, "A *real classy dame.*"

Phillip and Nealy walked up the street, and she came to a dead stop when he walked over to a huge Dr. Pepper truck sitting by the curb and reached out as if to unlock the door.

"I don't think so," she said, stopping dead in her tracks.

"Oh, I'm sorry, Nealy, I should have told you that I drive a truck. Is that a problem?" he asked sincerely.

"Uh...yeah...well, sort of. Phillip, please don't think I'm a snob, but I don't think I'm up to bouncing around in that big thing," she said, grimacing and backing up.

"Oh, don't worry. I'll drive slow. I hold my meetings in here. People really tend to open up on the road," he urged.

"You're kidding. People pay you thousands of dollars to ride around in a Dr. Pepper truck?"

"Oh, absolutely. I shake them up real good, and it's incredible how they open up. It's like an explosion." Then finally, when he couldn't hold back any longer, and he burst out laughing.

"That's not really your truck," she said, feeling as if she'd been had.

"I'm sorry," he said, laughing out loud and walking towards her. "When I saw it, I couldn't resist. It became the perfect prop to test your sense of humor. And your reaction was beautiful!"

"Phillip, I can't believe you did that," she cried. "I imagined myself riding up and down Park Avenue in that monstrosity—forgive me if I sound snobbish— bouncing around, sharing my problems with a shrink named *Pepper*. I'm crazy, *Doctor*, but not that crazy."

"That couldn't of been more perfect if I'd planned it. I got cha good!" he laughed, getting more and more tickled.

"Yeah, right. Ha, ha, ha. And look at you. You're so proud of yourself. You know, a friend of mine, who is also a psychiatrist, told me that a good psychiatrist had to be a little nuts in order to fully understand his patients. Well, Dr. Pepper, I think you just validated his theory," she said, shaking her head. Then suddenly she giggled wildly, not at his prank, but at him.

They were still laughing as he took her hand and led her a little farther up the street. "Here, is this better?" he said, pointing to a black porsche.

"If I say yes, I'm admitting I'm a snob...but go ahead, call me a snob," she said, smiling at him. When they both cracked up, he hugged her, which clearly broke the ice on what Nealy had expected to be an awkward evening; now she actually looked forward to it.

Phillip took Nealy to a quaint restaurant on Pier 17 at South Street Seaport for a clam dinner. The night air was too cool to sit outside, but he requested a table by the window so that she could enjoy the passing parade of ships, boats, or barges that might cruise in or out of the East River. Caroline's seemed to appeal to the yuppie crowd. So Phillip thought that the vivid tropical colors might brighten Nealy's mood, especially after what Rob had told him about her life during the past year.

The lights created a rainbow of colors across the water, which made Nealy smile. "This is really nice," she said sincerely. "Thanks for bringing me here."

"You're welcome. Do you like clams?"

"I don't know. I've never had any."

"You grew up on the coast and you've never eaten clams?"

"Never. We didn't net clams, so we mostly ate fish, shrimp, and oysters— well, I didn't eat oysters. They're disgusting," she said, making an ugly face.

"Nealy, you've missed out. There's nothing better than having a slimy little creature slide down the back of your tongue."

"Oh, Phillip, please. That's so nauseating." He enjoyed teasing her and watching her quick and expressive reactions. Her large, round eyes danced when she smiled.

"Nealy, please forgive me for staring, but I keep thinking that we've met somewhere, but maybe you just remind me of someone. I keep staring at you trying to figure out who you remind me of, and I finally figured it out."

"Oh, no, this ought to be good coming from a psychiatrist. It's not Rita Hayworth is it?"

"No, but I can see that resemblance, too, especially the body."

"Phillip," she said, embarrassed at his candor.

"Nealy, you have to know that you have a great body. When we walked through the crowd, every guy in here turned to stare, drooling like starving dogs."

"Phillip!" she screamed, "you hardly know me and listen to you."

"Nealy, this discussion has nothing to do with how well I know you. It's just how it is. You have great curves which no one could deny. And everyone, with the exception of a blind person, would notice, whether they knew you or not. You're what guys refer to as a *head-turner*."

"I guess that's a compliment. Thank you."

"You're welcome. Now where was I...oh,yeah. The way you look has nothing to do with the person that you remind me of. It's the mannerisms. The expressions and personality, and even more so, the laugh."

"Well, who is it?"

"Goldie Hawn. You know, the actress on *Laugh-In*."

"Goldie's a blonde and real zany," Nealy informed him.

"Well, you're hair's blondish—and red—and you're real zany, too. You have big, round eyes like hers, the same big grin, and that same high pitched giggle that people can't get enough of. And, to be honest, she's one of the cutest actresses on television. Someday she'll be a big star; she has that wide-eyed innocence, plus a great deal of talent."

"I take it you like her?"

"She's one of my favorites. I like happy people and I like happy people to be happy. You're a happy person, but are you happy?"

"Now I get it. My session begins, right Doctor?"

"This is strictly social. I'm getting to know you, that's all. So, Nealy, are you happy?"

"No. Is that the answer you're looking for?"

"If that's the way you feel. What would make you happy again?" He watched her carefully as she looked out the window, searching for an answer. Phillip could see the heartbreak that she had experienced, even though she worked very hard at trying to cover-up her true feelings.

"I don't really know, but I wish I did. I'm struggling with myself to find out what I want to do with my life. Where do I go from here? So, Doctor, how much do you know about me?"

"Well, I know you've been married a few years to a doctor and that you recently found out that he'd been unfaithful for some time. I also know about your miscarriage, but that's about all." Phillip stared directly into her eyes for a moment, and then she looked down, fidgeting with her utensils.

Suddenly, they were interrupted by a young woman who walked up to their table. "Hi, my name is Brandy, and I'll be your waitress tonight," the petite young woman said, looking from Nealy to Phillip and back to Nealy. "We have three clam dishes as specials tonight. Or you can have the All-You-Can-Eat special that includes clam chowder, salad and fried clams. Are you ready to order, or shall I get your drinks?"

"Nealy, do you know what you want?" he asked.

"Hmm... to keep it simple, I'll have the All-You-Can-Eat special and ice tea please," she smiled.

"Me, too," he said, smiling at the waitress as she walked away. "I know how painful it is to talk about your marriage, but I think it will help if you do." He reached across the table, allowing his hand to gently touch hers.

"I know, but I feel like such a idiot. Jerrod came back into my life at a time when his proposal seemed to be the best and the smartest thing to do. My career had gotten off the ground, but that was about all. And I had seen how hard and how long it takes to really make it in show business. I think I allowed myself to take the path of least resistance. I loved him, too. I'm not saying that I did it just for security, but the life he offered me made more sense than the one I had. There were so many times when I wished I hadn't given up...but then I looked at the life I had, and I felt comfortable, protected." Nealy stared out the window, not wanting him to see the tears in her eyes.

"Nealy, it's okay. I know how hard this is for you. My wife left me three years ago and married her gynecologist."

Stunned at his unsolicited confession, Nealy whirled around, her eyes locking with his for a long moment.

"Are you serious?"

"Very serious," he said, shaking his head up and down.

"You know, I'd always heard that women fall in love with their obstetricians or their gynecologists, which ever the case may be. And you know, it's perfectly understandable. This is a person that knows you better than anyone and who has seen every conceivable part of your body, professionally, of course. It's been said that women spend more time primping before they go to visit their gynecologist than they do when they go out to dinner with their husbands. In my case, I know that to be a fact. I always gave myself a pedicure, which I hate to do. And I shaved my legs everyday for three days before I had my appointment," she stated matter-of-factly.

"I never noticed," he said, unaware of such concerns.

"And, even more, women discuss their deepest, most intimate secrets with their doctors. You know things that they would be much too embarrassed to discuss with their best friends. In fact, my gynecologist is the only person on earth that I would feel comfortable discussing hemorrhoids with," she blurted out, but tried to whisper to avoid sharing the conversation with the people at the table across from them. Then Nealy turned red, but she giggled out loud, amused at herself for being so brutally honest.

Phillip laughed, a little surprised that she had opened-up enough to discuss something so private. "Nealy, my patients were never that open with me, but I guess my wife shared that, and much more, with hers."

"Oh, Phillip, I'm sorry. That was very insensitive of me. And I certainly didn't mean to make any connection between your wife and her—"

"It's okay, Nealy, I know what you meant. But, in this case, I take full responsibility for my marriage failing. And you're probably right, he listened to her when she had a problem. I never did. I had my patients to think about, and I just never thought to ask her how she felt or what she needed," he sadly said, "but, if I ever get married again, I will do things differently." Phillip stared at her as he moved back away from the table so the waitress could put his food down in front of him. Without taking his eyes off of Nealy, he politely said, "Thanks." He couldn't imagine ever cheating on someone like Nealy. What could this guy have been thinking? Nealy had everything that any man could ever want: beauty, brains, sensitivity, and a terrific sense of humor.

For the next fifteen minutes, Nealy didn't say too much, except to brag on the food occasionally, and neither did Phillip. The food tasted great, but any hot meal would have been good to her since she had been subjected to only hospital food and light, snacking stuff lately. Phillip had a way of making her feel comfortable; she didn't feel as though she had to make idle chatter. As he ate, he glanced at her from time to time and flashed a reassuring smile.

"Good?" he asked, wiping his mouth with his napkin.

"Yes, delicious, thanks. I'll order clams again."

"Well, truthfully, not all clams are this good. They have a reputation for being tough."

"What do you have a reputation for being, Doctor?"

"In what respect? Personally or professionally?"

"Professionally, I guess. Do you treat neurotic housewives or the real nut cases?"

"Mostly, I treat actors, and people involved in the entertainment field. Some of them are neurotic and some are just lonely or scared."

"You mean, like big stars—Liza Minelli, Marilyn Monroe, Marlon Brando —or the less famous?"

"None of those, but I do treat some pretty big stars and some little ones, too. But people are all the same. Big or small, they have all the same problems."

"Well, in that case, I consider myself lucky to have the opportunity to *bleed all over your couch,*" she giggled. Rob didn't tell her that his friend was a shrink to the stars. Her problems probably seemed rather insignificant and trivial to him; in fact, she hoped he wouldn't ask her anything else because she sounded so common, trite, and unsophisticated.

"Nealy, I know you well enough already to know that you're too guarded and much too proud to tell me anything that you don't want me to know. In a way, you're a shrink's nightmare because you won't open up. But, on the other hand, you're very refreshing because you'll lead me inside your mind with humor."

"You're good, Dr. Pepper," she said, smiling at his ability to see right through her. "But, tell me this. Why does a rooster want to *get-it-on* with every hen in the henhouse, and a whale, who could have any fish in the sea, only have one mate for life? And don't say it's because a whale is a mammal. Men are mammals, too, and some of them prefer the henhouse."

"Maybe the rooster hasn't found that *one hen,* the one that can make him crow and strut like the cocky and vain creature that he has been bred to be," he said quite seriously. "Do you know that a rooster will fight to protect his territory and his hens? And it's been proven that a rooster who has been put in a cage with a single hen will eventually kill that hen if he can't get out to service other hens. They must like variety." Phillip waited in anticipation for her response.

"You know I never cared much for roosters. And cockfighting is absurd, even though I hear it's become very lucrative in some parts of the country," she said, totally absorbed in the revelation of his plot.

"Nealy, I can't imagine your liking any kind of violence. In fact, I'd bet money that you've never hit anyone in your life."

"And you'd lose."

"Who'd you hit?"

"Jerrod...but he made me do it. He had been drinking and called me some very unflattering names, so I slapped him. I'll have to admit, I shocked myself. Until that time, I'd been a totally non-violent person. I just lost it."

"You'd never done that before?"

"No, but now I'm glad I did. I think Little Red Riding Hood should have asserted herself and slapped the big bad wolf long before she did. Maybe she would have been better prepared for the worst."

"Any dessert for the two of you?" Brandy asked, removing their plates.

"Nealy, dessert?"

"We have a great New York cheesecake," Brandy tempted.

"Okay, you twisted my arm. But don't feel bad, it's happened before," Nealy giggled softly.

"Excuse me," the waitress asked.

"Oh, ignore me. I'm just being *zany*," she smiled at Phillip.

"Make that two, please."

"Two zany people or two cheesecakes?" Nealy asked.

"One zany person and two cheesecakes."

"Am I missing something here?" the waitress asked, squinting.

"I'm sorry. It's been a tough week," Nealy admitted, feeling bad about confusing her. "We want two cheesecakes and coffee for me and—"

"Me, too," Phillip said. Nealy transferred her eyes up to the waitress briefly, and then right back at Phillip.

"Got that?" Nealy asked kindly.

"Two cheesecakes and two coffees."

"Brandy, you've been great. Please ignore us." Nealy leaned closer to talk to the waitress. "The truth is, this guy picked me up at a Lonely Hearts Club meeting and we're swapping stories to see which one of us got dumped on the most. And so far, I'm ahead three to one. In fact, I'm in line for '*Yahoo of the Year.*' " Nealy never could keep a straight face for long. When she burst out laughing, so did Phillip and Brandy.

Brandy smiled at Nealy. "Where are you from?" she asked.

"I'm from Texas."

"I knew it had to be somewhere in the South. I like your accent. It's cute. And it matches your personality. I'll be right back with your desserts."

"Thanks," Nealy said in unison with Phillip.

"See there. She thinks you're cute and zany, too," he said, nodding at the waitress before she hurried away. He had never seen anyone with such an enchanting ability to capture the attention of others so innocently. She didn't have one pretentious bone in her body; her beauty came not only from the outside, but the inside as well. Refreshing was the perfect way to describe her. Nealy was purely a breath of fresh air: so sweet, so pure, so intoxicating. If he allowed himself, he could fall madly in love with her, but he knew that it would be a very long time before Nealy would be ready for another relationship. He certainly intended to do everything possible to speed her recovery, as a friend and a therapist, of course.

"Phillip, I hope I didn't embarrass you. Sometimes I do strange things before I even realize I'm doing them," she grimaced, hoping he hadn't been offended.

"No, Nealy, you didn't embarrass me at all, in fact, that would be impossible. You're a nut. But I'd see you as a beautiful and funny nut regardless of what you did."

"Thanks...I think." Nealy looked at him strangely, but even though he had called her a nut, she knew that he meant it as a form of flattery.

The waitress brought them their dessert, and they talked and chatted, enjoying the delicious cheesecake. Phillip asked a few more questions about her family, her marriage, and her career. He shared more about himself and his personal life to avoid sounding so therapeutic. They talked about his friendship with Rob Morris during medical school and about their continued friendship over the years. It had been a very pleasant evening, and Nealy had appreciated his interest in her, even if he had been told to take her out. But, she could tell that he had enjoyed himself, so she didn't feel quite so guilty. Obviously, Phillip didn't have a special person in his life, but it had been only a year. Because of the circumstances surrounding his divorce, he planned to take his time before getting too seriously involved in another relationship; betrayal cuts deep.

An hour later, at almost midnight, they drove up in front of Janey's apartment building. Nealy couldn't believe that they had spent almost three hours in the restaurant, but she had really relaxed and enjoyed the evening immensely.

"Did you enjoy yourselves?" Jigs asked before pushing the button to the ninth floor.

"Wonderful," Nealy smiled. "Goodnight, Jigs."

"Phillip, I had a really nice time. Thanks for giving up your evening."

"Nealy, sitting across the table from you for three hours ranks in the top ten most pleasant experiences of my life," he said, sliding his hands down into his pockets and swaying side to side. Phillip appeared nervous, and rightfully so because Nealy had been the best thing that had happened to him since his divorce. At this point, he didn't want to do or say anything that might make her the least bit uncomfortable, but he really wanted to see her again. Even though she was technically a married woman, he knew that a divorce would be inevitable because she shared his values when it came to trust; she couldn't live with someone who had been unfaithful, at least, not forever.

When they got off the elevator and walked across the hall, Nealy kissed him on the cheek and smiled. "Well, Dr. Pepper, I had a great time. Thanks for not taking no for an answer."

"I hope that I'm not out of line, Nealy, but maybe we could get together again before you leave town."

"I'd like that, Phillip. I feel better after only one session with you. Just think how good I'll feel after two," she giggled.

"You have a great laugh," he said softly. "It really turns me on, but it's late, so I'll control myself." At that moment he hated the word control because he would give anything to take her in his arms and kiss her, and the fact that she smelled so good made it harder to move away from her. "I'll call you. Maybe you'd like to catch a play?"

"'Blow in my ear and I'll follow you anywhere,'" she said, and then she giggled out loud.

"You do watch *Laugh-In*," he said, surprised that she took the time to watch television.

"It's one of my favorite shows."

"Mine, too. We have so much in common, Nealy. We're going to be great friends."

"I think so, too. Good-night."

"Nealy...never mind. Good-night." He walked across the hall to push the button on the elevator. When the elevator came for him, almost within seconds, he smiled at her as she stood watching him from the doorway. Even though she was smiling, he didn't want to get too excited because he knew that she had a long way to go before she would consider anyone more than a friend, but *he really and truly liked her.* The thought frightened him, but he didn't care. Besides, time with her would be worth the risk.

CHAPTER TWENTY-SEVEN

THE FOLLOWING DAY, she got up early and decided to take a nice brisk walk in the park, and maybe even do a little shopping. On Saturday the city would be packed, but she needed to find something very special for her next outing with the bright and adorably funny Dr. Phillip Pepper. Of course, they were just friends, but she still wanted to look her best. What a fun guy. She smiled just thinking about him and that Dr. Pepper truck.

The fresh, very brisk air, felt wonderful as Nealy walked along the path through Central Park. For a week, she had watched the walkers and joggers, wanting to feel well enough again to join them, and finally she did. In fact, she felt great, smiling and speaking to the people that she passed along the path. The shrill, high-pitched screams and the laughter of children playing was music to her ears: sweet, innocent, and carefree. The leafless trees were stiff and solemn. And, along the walkway, there were mounds of frozen dirt and debris from previous snowfalls with only a little snow scattered around on the North side of the park. So far, the winter had been unseasonably mild, with little snow, but, with months left before spring, New York would surely see a lot more of *Old Man Winter.*

Nealy walked for almost an hour and then returned to the apartment to shower and get ready to *shop until she dropped;* a hand full of credit cards seemed to ring out the sweet smell of revenge. During her year in New York, Nealy would walk through Sak's Fifth Avenue dreaming of the day when she could afford to buy one of the fabulous Oleg Cassini Originals. The closest she came was sewing a Sak's label, that she had found on the floor while dreamingly walking through the store, into one of her own dresses. But, it wasn't the same. Now she could buy several. As they say, "Those who play, must pay." Oh, and pay he will.

Nealy spent the day trying on dresses, shoes, hats, coats, sportswear, make-up, and even jewelry. By five o'clock, she had become exhausted, but the day had been very successful from a shopper's standpoint. Nealy had bought so much stuff that she couldn't carry it all. The stores agreed to deliver the rest. Amazingly, her frame of mind had improved drastically, although she had to admit that even after all he had done, she felt a little guilty about spending so much money.

When she stepped out of the taxi cab, Jigs came to her rescue and grabbed some of her packages. "Hi, Ms. Nealy."

"Oh, hi, Jigs."

"You must have had a good day, Ms. Nealy."

"I had a glorious day, Jigs. Absolutely perfect. In fact, I can't remember when I had such a good time shopping." She handed the cab driver his fare and picked up as many of her bags as she could carry.

"Well, I'm glad," he smiled back, picking up the remaining bags. "You must have shopped all the stores."

"I sure did," she said, laughing victoriously. "I tried my best to buy out Macy's, and so I controlled myself a little more in Sak's, Bloomie's, Bergdorf's, and Bonwit's, even though it doesn't look like it."

With boxes stacked up over her head, Nealy walked onto the elevator. Jigs had to catch the phone, so he told her that he would bring the rest of her things up shortly. When she reached to punch the button for the ninth floor, her packages came tumbling down. "Oh, my gosh," she mumbled, bending down to pick them up.

"Here, madame, allow me to help you."

"Thanks." Nealy sensed the man staring at her. When she lifted her head, she came face to face with the best looking man that she had ever seen in her life. For a moment, she stared directly into his huge, brown-velvet eyes. Then, she felt her face turning red, her scalp perspiring, her heart beating like a scared rabbit, and a wildly, strange feeling in her stomach. For the first time in her life, the mere presence of another human being had made her blush far beyond her control.

Finally, she regained her composure and stood up with half of the boxes and bags stacked in her arms, permitting him to carry the remaining packages. "Nice day in the shops, I see," he said charmingly, with a heavy French accent.

"I...uh...yes," she stuttered.

The elevator door opened,and with his eyes only, he motioned for her to get off.

"Uh...I'm in nine-eleven," she said walking across the hall.

"Excuse me, but this is the eleventh floor. It's my fault, I should have asked you for your floor," he said.

"I feel terrible that you're having to act like my personal valet, riding up and down the elevator."

"Is the job available?" he asked softly, his eyes deep with feeling.

Nealy blushed again. "Excuse me?" she asked shyly.

The elevator door buzzed. "This is your floor."

"Oh, right," she giggled out loud. "You must think I'm some kind of dimwit." Embarrassed, she quickly rushed out of the elevator.

"I'm sorry, but I don't know that word."

"Oh...it's someone who is mentally challenged," she giggled nervously.

"I could never believe such an outrageous thing about such a beautiful woman," he said, staring at her while she dug through her purse for her key.

"Here it is." Nealy nervously put the key in the door and opened it. When she reached to take the packages, her hand touched his, and she blushed again. Why was she behaving like a schoolgirl? After all, she had been called beautiful by men before, even though she didn't really see it. But, she had never been swept off her feet by a gorgeous Frenchman. After putting the packages on the couch, she returned to the door for the rest. Once again her hand touched his, and at that very moment, when her eyes met his, a mystical feeling overpowered her; her emotions raced unbridled and free. Never in her life had she ever encountered anything quite so magical, nor did she ever expect to again. "I really appreciate your help," she said, "I'd probably have packages scattered all over this building if you hadn't been there." Nealy put her hand out. "I'm Nealy James. I can't thank you enough."

He reached for her hand and slowly raised it to his mouth, kissing the back of it very softly. "You are most welcome, Nealy James. I'm Michael Coupair," he said in a deep masculine voice and that marvelous accent. His hands were strong and slightly rough. She could still feel the sensation of his soft lips against her hand. His eyes were a magnetic force field; she couldn't disconnect. "It's been a pleasure meeting you. Until we meet again." He smiled, and his perfect teeth were bright white against his naturally colored lips. His dark hair matched the color of his eyes, and his smooth, olive skin featured him as a model for a suntan product. A George Hamilton look-a-like, but more handsome.

"You people really do that," she said, surprised, even though his expression never changed. "I thought that was only in the movies...you know, the hand kissing thing." Nealy giggled, her heart palpitating, skipping beats like crazy.

"Ah, yes, the movies and beautiful American women."

Her mouth fell open. She couldn't speak.

Slowly, he backed towards the elevator. "Maybe I'll see you again Ms. James." His eyes searched every inch of her before he stepped into the elevator, not even acknowledging Sharon as she stepped out. Nealy's stare clung to his, holding on for every precious moment until the door closed.

"Well, you didn't waste any time," Sharon said to Nealy, who stood gawking at the elevator.

"What?"

"That man. The one who just left. Where'd he come from?"

"The elevator..."

"Nealy, snap out of it!"

"Oh, I met him on the elevator...well, I actually met him here formally about one minute ago."

"Damn, now that's one good looking man. Look out Omar! Oh, and close your mouth, hon! Your tongue's hanging out."

"Sharon, it's not either," Nealy cried, embarrassed.

"Well, it's okay to look and drool, but I know that kind. They make great lovers, but that's about all. European men are, for the most part, crazy in-love with themselves. Those good looking ones especially. And they have about as much respect for women as they do a rattle snake. Let me put it to you like this: In their country whistling and hissing mean the same thing. So be careful, hon. See you later." Sharon disappeared into her apartment.

Slowly Nealy walked into the apartment and closed the door. She leaned back against the door and stood there, staring off into space. Why did she tell him her name was Nealy James instead of Nealy Jones? Her mouth had opened and James just popped out. Nealy, you heard what Sharon said, snap out of it. But mentally, she couldn't let go. You'll never see that man again. And anyway, Sharon's right about those guys, and besides, you're still married to one of those gorgeous kinds. And where did that get you?

A knock at the door brought her back to reality. "Oh, hi, Jigs," she said, still blushing.

"Hello, Ms. Nealy. Where do you want your things?"

"Put them on the couch. Thanks."

"You're welcome." Jigs quickly rushed out and closed the door. Nealy had wanted to ask him about the tall, dark stranger, but she didn't have the nerve. He'd probably think that she had the hots for him or something just as ridiculous. So, she just forgot it and went on about her business. The day of shopping had exhausted her, so she decided to take a nice, hot bubble bath and relax. First, she hung up her new clothes and put the rest of her things away, admiring each thing as she recalled how happy it had made her each time she charged something to Jerrod.

Right before she stepped into the tub, the phone rang. "Well, hell, I knew that would happen." She grabbed her robe and quickly ran into the bedroom to answer it.

"Hello."

"Nealy..."

She didn't answer; his voice sent chills up and down her spine.

"I won't keep you, but I just wanted to call and make sure you're alright...and to say, I'm sorry. I know that's not enough, Neal, but I am."

Heavily, she sighed, "I know. But I don't want to talk about any of this yet. I'm just not ready. We'll talk when I get home."

"When are you coming home?"

"Next Sunday."

"Who's picking you up at the airport. It better not be that asshole, Richfield."

"Jerrod, don't start. It's only going to make things worse."

"What can be much worse? I know you're going to divorce me, so what do I really have to lose?"

"Jerrod, please."

"Please what, Nealy? Please let you divorce me without an argument. Am I supposed to say, 'Okay, fine?' I can't do that, Nealy, I happen to love you."

"If that's the case, just what in the hell were you doing in that swimming pool with all those naked people?" she shouted.

"Fuckin' their brains out! Now, are you satisfied? I admitted it. I'm a no-good bastard. I'll admit that, too. But I'm a no-good bastard who loves his wife."

"Jerrod, you're sick. I don't want to talk about this. I can't. I'm not. We'll talk when I get home. And *not* until then. So don't, and I mean *do not* call me again. I'll call you when I get home."

"What do you mean? 'You'll call me.' We happen to live in the same house as I remember."

"I've got to go. Good-bye, Jerrod." Nealy hung-up the phone and walked back into the bathroom and quickly climbed into the tub. Then, she quickly climbed back out, grabbed her towel again and walked back into the bedroom and took the phone off the hook. When she climbed back into the tub, her eyes watered, but she didn't really feel like crying. At this point, she only felt pity and anger. The bastard, as he called himself, had admitted to his own guilt, but he said he was sorry. Well, he's right, sorry isn't good enough. A person doesn't intentionally live life with a no-good bastard. Nealy lay back and soaked for a half hour. Tears rolled very gently down her cheeks, but the tears she shed tonight were different from before because she realized that something had died inside of her.

When she crawled into bed, she picked up her book to read, but her mind switched between Phillip's pretty blue-gray eyes and those deep, brown velvet ones. They were a nice alternative to the things that had occupied her thoughts lately. Once again, she laughed about the Dr. Pepper truck, and then she blushed at the kiss from the handsome stranger. She slowly drifted off into a peaceful sleep and her dreams reflected her thoughts: Phillip rolled on the floor with her, tickling her so that he could be enlightened by her laughter. Then she sensed someone watching her, and by some mysterious power that she couldn't identify, her eyes were drawn up to see the handsome stranger standing high above her like a Greek god.

At seven-thirty, she lay awake. The sun had come up, bringing life to the city and its people, and the church bells rang out, announcing the Sabbath.

Nealy dressed and put on comfortable shoes so that she could walk over to Fifth Avenue and Fiftieth for the eleven o'clock mass at St. Patrick's Cathedral. Even though she wasn't Catholic, she enjoyed visiting the older cathedrals because of the presence of a Higher Being, the feeling of love for one another, the vivid colors of the Saints and Disciples of God adorning the stained glass windows, and the period architecture; the ambience overwhelmed her, strengthening her convictions.

On the way back, she stopped off at a little sidewalk pizza place for a take-out lunch picnic in central park. She found a bench in a nice sunny spot and relaxed for a couple of hours while she ate and people watched. Afterwards, she took a walk and returned to the apartment about five o'clock.

Tired, she took another bath; she had developed web-like wrinkles on her hands and feet from living in the tub, but it relaxed her. By eight o'clock, she had curled up on the couch with her romance novel in which the heroine had been caught in a triangle, torn between two men who were fighting for her affections. Eager to find out who won her heart, she read until two o'clock in the morning. When the hero—good over evil—that Nealy had been pulling for got the girl of his dreams, she smiled, gushing aloud. "Oooh, how sweet...I loved this book. Will I ever find what they found?" Even though the story stopped there, Nealy knew that they lived happily ever after. When it's meant to be, there is no obstacle too big to cross, no mountain too high to climb, no burden too heavy to bear; destiny always prevails.

After her late night, Nealy slept in until ten, and then got up and dressed for her walk. The air had a distinct chill, but the sun would soon warm it up. First, she made a couple of laps around the park, and then she decided to head east on Broadway and end up at Time Square. It would be quite a journey, but she felt better and invigorated.

While she walked, she did a little window shopping and even spotted a few more things that she wanted to pick up before she went home; shopping had become an addictive pastime.

When she reached the corner of Park Avenue and Fifty-third Street on her way back to the apartment, she heard someone call out her name. They had to be talking to her because she had never met another "Nealy" in all of her twenty-six years. Shocked and pleasantly surprised, she saw Phillip walking towards her.

"Hi," she cried out over the bustling crowd.

After making his way around the lunch seekers, he gave her a quick hug. "What are you doing over here? I thought you jogged in the park?"

"I felt adventurous, so I walked all the way up to Madison Square Park. And now I'm going home—or Janey's home that is."

"Oh, I thought maybe you came to pay me a little surprise visit. My office is in that building right there," he pointed to a huge building on the corner.

"Well, I would have if I'd known where to find you," she smiled.

"How about seeing a play with me tonight?"

"Sure. I'd love to."

"Anything in particular that you'd like to see?"

"Well, I'd like to see Tom Stoppard's *Night and Day*. But we can see anything. I love them all."

"Let me see if I can get tickets to *Night and Day*. Are you on your way back?"

"Yes, as fast as my little feet will take me."

"Good. I'll call you before five to let you know where we're going. Be ready by six. I'll buy your dinner," he winked and waved as he rushed back towards his office building.

Nealy had to hurry since it was almost three o'clock, and she still had a twenty-minute walk ahead of her. In order to be ready on time, she picked up the pace a little.

At five Phillip called to confirm their plans, and then, at six o'clock sharp the phone rang.

"Ms. Nealy, this is Jigs. There is a *Dr. Pepper* here to *pick you up*," he said, sounding as if he thought it was a joke.

Nealy giggled. "Thanks Jigs. Send *Dr. Pepper* up."

When the doorbell rang, Nealy quickly sprayed her long layered hair for the last time and rushed to the door.

"Hi. Come in."

"Wow! You look great," he exclaimed, walking all the way around her for a good look.

"Do you like my new dress? I bought it on my shopping spree yesterday." The dark jade green satin dress had a sweetheart neckline and hugged her body all the way down to her mid-thighs. The cummerbund-belt cinched her tiny waist and had a perfect bow that rested on her backside, bustling below her waist.

"I love that dress. And green is definitely your color," he commented, pursing his lips and whistling sharply. "I made reservations at the Rainbow Room."

"The Rainbow Room! I've always wanted to go there. I looked in once when I lived here, but I couldn't afford to go in. Has anyone told you how wonderful you are?"

"Of course," he laughed, kissing his finger tips and then patting his face affectionately.

"You're too much," she laughed, giggling wildly.

"Come on. I'm ready to show off that new dress," he smiled.

When the elevator door opened, Nealy's heart stopped and all the blood in her body rushed to her face. Once again, she found herself staring into the *brown-velvet eyes* of Michael Coupair.

"Good-evening, Ms. James. We meet again," he said.

"Hi," she managed to say, trying to pull herself away from his stare.

Michael Coupair spoke to Phillip, without actually speaking *to him*. "Have a nice evening Ms. James," he wished without sentiment, looking her up and down before he walked out into the lobby.

"Thanks. You, too," Phillip snapped jealously. Nealy couldn't bring herself to speak. She just watched him nod to Jigs and walk out through the double doors ahead of them.

Phillip guided Nealy passed Jigs. "Good-night, Jigs."

"Enjoy your evening, Ms. Nealy. Good-night, Doctor."

"Good-night, Jigs." When they got outside, Phillip knew that he had no right to feel jealous, but he did. "Do you know that guy?"

"Who, Jigs?" she said, avoiding the real issue.

"No, the man in the elevator?"

"Not really. He helped me with my packages yesterday when I dropped them all over the elevator."

"Well, I've never witnessed 'open foreplay' before. He devoured you inch by inch. Hey stand there and let me try that," he said gently holding her arm.

"Phillip," she exclaimed. "Open foreplay?"

"Well, he did, but I really can't blame the guy. You look positively gorgeous."

"Phillip, that's sweet."

"I'm also a little jealous. But, I'm the lucky son-of-a-gun that gets to spend the night—"

"Night?"

"Well, I *meant* evening. Wishful thinking put words in my mouth."

Nealy cut her eyes at him. "Phillip—"

"I'm teasing. Well, sort of," he quickly interjected, opening the car door for her. "Why did that guy call you Ms. James? Isn't your name Jones?"

"When I met him, I opened my mouth and James came out. So, you tell me, Dr. Pepper. Why did I do that?" she asked sharply.

"You're in denial. You feel that you made a mistake, but you can't figure out how to gracefully put it behind you and move on. But that's normal, Nealy, people hate to admit to failure, which is how they perceive a marriage that took a dive."

"Was that word of choice, or just coincidence?"

They burst out laughing, although it really wasn't funny.

When they entered the NBC building, they took the special elevator up to the *Rainbow Room* on the sixty-fifth floor. Phillip gave the maitre d' his name, while Nealy walked over to a nearby window to look out at the view. The sun was setting. The dusky view of the city and all its grandeur made Nealy feel proud to have lived there, even if it were for only a year.

"Our table's ready," Phillip said, walking up behind her.

"Okay. Isn't this view spectacular?"

"It really is. There's no place like New York. Come on," he urged. The hostess led them to their table right on the dance floor.

"Oh, Phillip, thank you for bringing me here. I love this place."

"I thought you would. It's like eating in the theater or in the middle of a grand musical. Look at the cigarette girl," he said, pointing to a beautiful girl wiggling her way around the room. "Nice pair of gams," he added.

"You men, honestly," Nealy said, shaking her head. Nealy watched Phillip as his eyes followed the pretty blonde wearing a costume from the forties. Nealy had to admit that she looked pretty good wearing that hot-pink satin teddy, displaying plenty of cleavage and a twenty inch waist that had obviously been cinched by a very tight corset. Her long, shapely legs, or gams as only a man would call them, extended from beneath a bustled bottom, which she prissily swung from side to side as she walked. Nealy thought about how men were attracted to particular areas of the female anatomy such as the breasts, the buttocks, or the legs, and they didn't mind making their preference known in their actions or in words. They will stare, drool, and some, even touch. Women often have the same preferences in respect to the male anatomy, but at least they try to be more discreet. "A leg man, I presume." Nealy said, watching Phillip as he stared at the legs of the cigarette girl who was bent over talking to someone at the table next to them.

"I'm sorry, Nealy, did you say something?" he asked, quickly taking his eyes off of the girl's lower anatomy and turning towards Nealy.

"Never mind, I think I know the answer," she smiled and giggled at the boyish expression on his face.

"What's so funny?"

"You're a leg man, aren't you?"

"A leg man. Well, not really. I like it all. In fact, I was thinking about how good you'd look in one of those little outfits, but I couldn't be held responsible for my actions," he sighed and shook his head as if trying to shake the thought.

"Phillip," she gasped.

"Hey, I'm just being honest. And you're the one that said 'honesty is the basis of a good relationship.' " A busboy spooned ice from a gleaming silver bowl into their water goblets placed next to white shiny china plates trimmed in gold. The tablecloth was made of silver lamé fabric and sparkled under the soft lights. Everything looked so elegant and romantic. Soon the waiter appeared, wearing two-toned cutaways, and gave them each a menu and announced the specials. Both of them decided on the special of shrimp and crab simmered in lemon, butter and herbs.

Nealy took several bites of her dinner before she began to make her usual soft, savoring sounds. "Hmm, this is the best shrimp I've ever eaten. And I grew up on shrimp."

He chuckled softly, staring at her.

"What's the matter?" she asked self consciously.

"You're so cute."

"Why? Because I make funny noises when I eat? I can't help it. I take a bite, it taste good, and then those sounds just come out," she giggled.

"I love your funny noises," he confessed, reaching across the table to touch her hand. "But you're cute because simple things make you happy."

"Phillip, this place is not what I would call simple," she looked around the room in awe, bobbing her head as if it were on a spring.

"No, but I didn't have to bring you to a place as fancy as this to make you happy, although I'm glad you like it." Since the entertainment didn't start until nine o'clock, and they had to be at the theater before eight, Phillip had made special arrangements for them to return later for dessert and dancing.

Later that evening, they returned to the *Rainbow Room* and to the same table. Phillip ordered the baked Alaska and they watched intensely when the waiter lit the culinary flame.

"That's wonderful, but doesn't that scorch the meringue?" she asked the waiter preparing the dessert.

"Yes, it does, but it's supposed to. That's what makes it so good," he smiled, watching her watch him. When the flame died away, he served Nealy first. Then he fidgeted for a moment, waiting to witness her reaction when she tasted the dessert.

"Oh my God. Now *this* is sinful," she said expressively, "and loaded with calories. But, it's worth every one though."

The waiter chuckled, artfully placing a large slice on Phillip's plate. "I'm glad you like it, madame."

"It's soooo wonderful," she said, smiling at the waiter and then at Phillip.

After they finished dessert, Nealy leaned across the table to talk to Phillip because it was already past eleven o'clock. "I'm glad we came back here, but I'm worried about you having to get up early tomorrow."

Phillip smiled. "I'm fine. I moved my patients around. I don't see anyone until ten. I wanted you to enjoy yourself."

"Are you always so thoughtful?"

"No, I'm sorry to say," he admitted, softly tapping her hand. "Would you like to dance?"

"I'd love to, Dr. Pepper." Nealy held his hand while he led her out onto the thirty-two foot revolving dance floor. She put her arm around his neck and followed his lead as the band played soft tunes, mostly motion picture theme songs.

"Having a good time?" he whispered. She smiled and nodded. He pulled her closer, and they danced cheek to cheek. Just holding her made his heart beat faster than normal. She was the *closet thing to heaven* that he had ever experienced— feminine and soft, just like a girl is suppose to be. When the music stopped, he reluctantly released her and clapped for the band.

Back at the table, he ordered them a cappuccino to enjoy while they shared stories about their childhoods and their friends back home. Back on the dance floor, they snuggled closer with each slow song until midnight signaled an end to their evening at the *Rainbow Room*.

At the apartment, Nealy invited Phillip inside to keep them from standing in the hall and talking; they seem to have so much to say to each other. Still wound up from all of the excitement, she made them a cup of hot cocoa and they relaxed on the couch.

"Nealy, I know this is really none of my business, but have you made any decisions yet?"

"You mean about my marriage?"

"Isn't that why you're here?" he asked seriously.

"For the most part, yes. And I think that you know what I've decided. You've been inside my head since the moment we met. But, that's your job, isn't it?" she smiled.

"Yes, but you're a tough one. You hide things better than most people, and you know how to dance with the one that brought you." He put his arm on the back of the couch behind her where she sat sideways, facing him.

"Are you calling me an actress?"

"Yes, but you're also a very sweet and sincere person. You only act to protect yourself."

"You're very perceptive, Doctor. And I may be jumping to conclusions, but I bet you've worked hard piecing together my entire life story haven't you?"

"Most of it. I know that you married your childhood sweetheart because you felt lonesome and frightened by the big, scary world of show business and that you doubted your own ability to hang in there. Even though you weren't that happy, you tried to make the best of it by becoming the perfect little doctor's wife, but found out that it wasn't enough and that you wanted more. But when you tried to go after your share of the world, he fought you, literally. You fought back, literally. Threatened by your need for freedom and his need for constant physical gratification, he sought the security of the people who could satisfy his needs and stroke him. It caught up with him. You found out. You left. And now you're free to pursue the independence that you fought to preserve. You grew up, Nealy. It's that simple."

"I'm amazed. But I shouldn't be. People pay you plenty of money to sort out their lives," she said, shaking her head that he had recapped her entire life, but carefully avoided any of the nasty, negative details that she had, for some unknown reason, shared with him. Phillip could definitely read between the lines.

"But, going home to face him will test your strength. You know he won't let go easily."

"I know. He called me the other night."

"I know. Saturday night, right?"

"How did you know?"

"Well, I called you from eight o'clock until about ten-thirty, and your line was busy. I figured he called to try and mend some fences, and when you didn't accept his apologies, he got angry, causing you to become angry. To prevent any further communications, you took the phone off the hook."

"You're psychic, Doctor." Nealy looked at him in disbelief, but at that moment she realized just how good he was at his profession. He knew exactly what made his patients tick and how to put them back together again when they stopped ticking.

But, more importantly, he knew how to push all the right buttons, that would even help his patients find their own answers. Nealy sat there with her mouth slightly open, staring at him.

He leaned forward, slid his arm around her back and kissed her open mouth. Not prepared to object, she kissed him back. When he moved away from her, she didn't move. "Sorry, but your lips were in the perfect kissing position," he said softly. "I've got to go." He got up and pulled her to her feet. She followed him to the door, even though she didn't really want him to go.

"I had a wonderful time," she said sweetly.

"Me, too."

"You really know how to make a girl fizzle, Dr. Pepper," she said, giggling quietly.

He laughed and opened the door. "Good-night, Nealy."

"Good-night, Phillip."

CHAPTER TWENTY-EIGHT

NEALY CLIMBED into bed, picked up her book and planned to re-read the last chapter which she felt sure would program her mind for sweet dreams. She opened her book, but instead of reading, which is usually better than any sedative for falling asleep, she rested the book on her chest, crossed her hands over it and clutched the edges. In her thoughts, she recalled the story in the book and its characters. Why had the heroine been drawn to the man who obviously was not good for her? But then, in the end, she realized that all along she had loved the right one, but she didn't know it. Why didn't she just tell that jerk to kiss her keister in the beginning and marry the good guy? If Nealy could answer that question, she could spare herself, as well as many other females, any further grief in their lives. And why, for crissake, was she wasting good sleep time on something that no one has or will ever figure out? Throughout history women have been making the mistake of falling into the clutches of rotten men. So why not just go to sleep? Well, for one thing, sleep didn't come easily these days. But, by trying to save the world's population of women from committing emotional suicide, she had managed, for the first time in weeks, to escape reality, which included Jerrod, the mermaids, the miscarriage, the decision to forgive and go on, or end it and go on, and now, her relationship with the cute and clever doctor, Phillip Pepper. Nealy couldn't deny that something seemed to be happening between them, yet both of them knew that she wasn't ready for any type of romantic involvement. But she smiled when she thought about him; they had fun together and laughed a lot. He had such a gentleness about him that made her feel safe and secure, and his sweet, soft kiss made her feel special.

When she met Jerrod in the tenth grade, she tingled from head to toe, and that turned out to be undeniable eroticism; after the first time they *did it*, years later of course, she couldn't say no to his frequent and persistent requests. In fact, *fooling around* took precedence over any other activity if Jerrod got his way, which he usually did. And, unfortunately, Nealy's strong physical attraction to him still existed, even after all he had done. Over the years, everything good or bad, had always been settled with a good *roll in the hay*, exploding with sexual pleasure but totally lacking in communication. When she tried to talk to Jerrod about things, he said that talk was cheap and actions spoke louder than words, so he would drag her into the bedroom for the *superpleasure* of sexual experiences. Initiating sex had always been Jerrod's way of avoiding needless talk about family, finances, his work or hers. And of course, after his tantalizing tactics and multiple orgasms, she had no idea, nor did she care, what it was that she had wanted to discuss with him. So many times afterwards, she wondered why she had let him substitute sex for conversation, but any woman would find it hard to resist a handsome man who made it a point to satisfy her until she felt as weak as a kitten; the sexual fantasy of every woman. The physical sex had been fantastic at times, but the emotional part didn't exist. If she mentioned anything about the lack of snuggling together afterwards, he took that to mean that she hadn't gotten enough. So he gladly engaged in enough foreplay to get her attention, as a means of turning idle chatter into cooing sounds. So, she stopped bringing it up and just accepted the physical act as the most that he could give, but she suffered silently, longing for the tenderness and the talk. It would have been much more meaningful if she had been able to talk quietly, make love, and laugh softly about funny things as she lay snuggled in her man's arms until the stillness of the night and the feeling of being loved relaxed her enough to ease her into a peaceful sleep. Nealy's eyes blinked slowly. The thoughts in her mind faded away. And she slept.

The sun peeked through the window, and Nealy turned over to look at the clock. She had slept until ten o'clock without waking up once; her first night of real peace since arriving in New York. Rising, she stretched every muscle. Her long walk the day before had made her a little sore and stiff, but it had been good to push herself. After allowing herself one cup of coffee, she slipped into her jogging suit and left for her morning workout. Unfortunately, winter had arrived in a big way: A thick blanket of snow covered the ground, while large snowflakes continued to fall from the sky. Not dressed for the weather, she returned to the apartment and changed into warmer clothing—thanks to Jerrod's unbeknownst generosity—and set out once again.

As she walked through the park, she felt uncomfortable because she didn't see many people. The crime in New York had gotten much worse, and she wasn't used to paying attention to what went on around her at every moment. After once around the park, she decided to walk into the city. It seemed crazy to walk in such adverse conditions, but, Texas born and bred, she didn't get to enjoy the snow very often. In fact, it was kind of exciting.

When she reached Lexington Avenue and Fifty-eighth Street, she decided to take the subway out to her old flat on Eighty-sixth Street. She had wanted to call Denise and Alex since the day she had arrived in New York, but she just hated the thought of telling them about her problems. And besides, they would probably say "I told you so" because now she knew that everyone, except for her knew about his cheating. What a fool she had been.

The subway stopped and she got off. Nealy took the stairs up to the street where she encountered blizzard-like conditions. When she reached her building, the thought of going in made her nervous, but she gathered up enough courage to proceed. The three girls had been so close for such a long time, and it saddened her to think about how little they had spoken since her marriage, but their busy schedules left little time to stay in touch. However, when people are close there is a spiritual bond that keeps them close even when they are apart. The excitement of seeing them again made her heart pound, although she tried not to get too excited in case they weren't home. Both of them were in plays Off-Broadway, or at least they had been eight or nine months earlier. Nealy remembered them calling to tell her about getting their parts: She had only been married for six months, and her days in New York were finally starting to fade into fond memories. And when they told her, she was thrilled, but she felt a little jealous too. After hanging up, she cried for hours. Jerrod had been at the hospital for two days, and she felt so alone and so depressed. It took her days to get over it, and that was the first time that Nealy questioned whether or not she had made the right choice.

The building seemed quiet, dark and dismal. Nealy walked up the three flights of stairs and down the hallway where the girls had given her wedding shower. She knocked on the door, but she didn't hear any sounds of life coming from the apartment. So she knocked again, but finally decided that they weren't home. Disappointed, she slowly turned towards the stairs. Then suddenly she heard a door open, so she turned around, but the hall was so dark that she couldn't see very well.

A very sleepy sounding voice muttered, "Who are you looking for?"

"Denise, is that you?" Nealy questioned, not recognizing the voice. Slowly, she walked back towards the open door.

"Oh my God, Nealy, it's you," she screamed, running out into the hall in her pajamas. They hugged and danced around in a circle, acting like children. "What are you doing here?"

"Well, it's a long story."

"Uh oh, Nealy, I think you'd better come in."

"I thought y'all would both be at rehearsal, but the mood struck me to come, so here I am," she said, closing the door.

"Come. Sit down." Denise jumped back into bed, covered her legs, then patted the opposite end of the bed. The room felt cold and damp, so she kept her coat on, but she took a towel and wiped it off before she sat down.

"Is Alex at rehearsal?"

"That's another long story. Boy, do we have a lot of catching up to do."

"Why? What happened?"

"Well, the play that she was in closed six months ago. That was the fourth play that she had been in that closed within three months of opening. One of them opened and closed on the same night. It was too bad that the Rockettes had to cut her; she was happy that first year. Oh, well, anyway, it really got to her, but that's show business, I tried to cheer her up, but she just couldn't find anything else. And, unfortunately, the reviews of those plays were so bad that it kept coming back to haunt her. Poor Alex, she really became discouraged. And then came the straw that broke the camel's back: we both auditioned for Joe Papp's, *A Chorus Line,* which is getting ready to open on Broadway, and I got called back, but she didn't. We both dreamed of that play. In fact, Alex wanted it even more than I did. I just wanted to be part of a Joe Papp production. The irony is that she's the dancer, not me. I want to act, but I got a dancer's role with a few lines of dialogue. Even though my part's a long way from a key part, I got in, and if I show Joe Papp that I've got talent, he'll help me along," Denise said, crossing her fingers.

"I'm really happy for you, Denise," Nealy said, leaning over and giving her a big hug. "Well, did she go home?"

"Two weeks ago. The day after my agent called to tell me that I'd been cast, she called her parents. Of course she bawled and squawled. I guess they suggested that she come home for a while because the next day she left."

"Didn't she talk to you about it?" Nealy asked.

"No, not really. That night, after she called home, we talked about the expenses. And evidently her parents had offered to help her out financially for as long as she needed them to, but she felt guilty about them having to support her. It had been a real struggle. And I'm certain that her parents didn't mind; God knows they could afford it. Everyone knew that they were the richest people in town. The grandmother left them a ton of money." But you know Alex. She's real stubborn...and this business with the play and all."

"So did she just leave?"

"Well, the next day I went to rehearsal for the play that I was in at the time, and when I got home at midnight, she was gone, clothes and all."

"You're kidding. She didn't even say good-bye?"

"No, but she left me a note. She said that she needed to leave before she changed her mind, and if she talked to me, it would be too hard to leave. But I got a letter from her yesterday, and if what I think you're going to tell me is true, it will create more irony in Alex's life," Denise said, looking down at the floor and releasing a heavy sigh.

"What do you mean?" Nealy asked confused.

"Remember Jeff? Jeff Wolfard? Tall, blonde, and totally delicious looking. Remember, we called him *Troy Donohue* because they could have passed for twins," Denise prodded in an effort to jolt her memory.

"That madman who threw the beer bottle at Alex and hit the wall behind us at that fraternity party?" Nealy cried.

"That's the one," Denise sneered. "Well, she's going to marry him. But, he's already been married and divorced and has a kid a year old."

"No," Nealy gasped. "Why is she doing that?"

"He's loaded, so it's a way out. He's from Houston, and his father owned some big oil company. Well, the father died and left him a bundle." Denise shook her head and frowned as if she were totally disgusted.

"I can't believe it. Did they stay in touch while he was married? How did this happen?"

"Well, he came up here a few times after you left. On about his third visit, I think, he told Alex to either marry him or he was going to marry this other girl. Well, when she told him "No," he got mad as hell and stormed out of here. Personally, I thought the guy was a maniac," Denise remarked profoundly.

"So he married the other girl, I take it."

"Well, he called Alex two weeks later and said, 'it's now or never.' Alex told him that she would think about it because her play had opened and closed; it really depressed her. She didn't really want to marry him I don't think, but he called at the right time. But, Nealy, here's the good part. Alex called him two weeks later and told him that she had decided to marry him. And guess what?" Denise said in total amazement.

"What?" Nealy asked, her eyes wide in anticipation.

"He had already married that girl." Alex cried, and then she laughed. "She couldn't believe it because just two weeks before he had cried like a baby, begging her to marry him. But the really good part," Denise chuckled, even though it really wasn't funny.

"There's more?" Nealy asked.

"Yes, and this will blow you away. He had the nerve to tell her, and I quote. 'You had your chance, baby, and you blew it. I married a wonderful *woman*, and we're in bed *doing it* at this very moment.' "
Can you believe that asshole?" she screamed.

"Oh my God! And Alex is going to marry this guy?"

"That's what she says. In fact, that's where the irony comes in. She said that you gave up acting to marry your old boyfriend, and it had worked out great. But from the look on your face when I first saw you, I'm not so sure that it's working out exactly great."

"Well, if you call screwing around with four or five nurses in a swimming pool not working out, I guess you're right," Nealy said coldly.

"Are we talking about *screwing,* as in *the act itself,* or just partying, as in drinking, etc.?"

"We're talking about 'fucking-their-brains-out," and that's from Jerrod's own mouth," Nealy said.

"Nealy, no," Denise cried.

"Yes, that bastard made a complete first-class-fool out of me in front of the entire medical school. Everyone knew but me."

"Oh, Nealy, I'm so sorry. When did you find out?"

"A few weeks ago. I caught him."

"Are you shittin' me?" Denise sat straight up in the bed. The very idea mortified her.

"Oh, Nealy I can't believe that bastard would do such a thing, but in a way, it doesn't surprise me. Nealy, I never saw him, but he had a real reputation in college for being a love 'em and leave 'em Romeo."

"He did? Why didn't anyone ever say anything to me," she cried, shocked, but not surprised.

"Well, I couldn't prove it. When I saw him, he seemed pure as the driven snow. Whenever we all went out together, he always acted as if you were the only girl on the face of the earth. So, I really had no proof, just gossip."

"I know, Denise, Jerrod's a real charmer. The worse thing is that he'd been doing it *before* and *after* we got married. That's what hurts. I'm so trusting, I'm stupid."

"Nealy, I'd have believed him, too. That guy could charm the horns off a billy goat. In fact—now this is strictly rumor—Jerrod got caught in Prissy Sissy Bedford's dorm room one night by the dorm mother."

"What?" Nealy screamed.

Nealy looked so horrified that Denise felt terrible, but Nealy needed to know the truth, the whole truth, and nothing but the truth about that bastard. Maybe, if she heard it all, it would keep her from forgiving him—that would be a big mistake. "Oh, Nealy, I'm sorry, but I want you to know him for what he really is, as if you don't already. So, please, just hear me out," Denise pleaded.

"I'm okay. Go ahead," Nealy softly said, tears rolling down her cheeks faster than she could wipe them away.

"From what I understand, he and Sissy were in the act, which we will refer to as the penis-vagina connection, and the ever-so-charming Jerrod actually convinced the dorm mother that they were studying. Now who else, besides Jerrod, could possibly get away with that!"

"Denise, how could I have been so gullible? I got at least three letters a week from him. And in every letter he told me how much he loved me and missed me and how lonely he was at school without me. He called me almost everyday. What a liar. And I trusted him completely," she cried out angrily.

"Well, what are you going to do now?" Denise questioned, reaching over and holding Nealy's hand.

"I don't know. I came to New York to recover from a tubal pregnancy and to pull myself together. I'm not sure yet, but I can't see me living with him for the rest of my life."

"You were pregnant?"

"Well, there's a lot more to it. I'll tell you the rest later. Why aren't you at rehearsal?"

"I have one more performance in *Grease* Saturday night. Then I start rehearsal for *A Chorus Line* on Thursday."

"Oh, Denise, that's great. I'm so proud of you. At least one of us will make it to stardom," Nealy praised, hugging her again.

"Thanks, Nealy. I guess I'll have to make it. I don't have any rich asshole from my past wanting to marry me," she said, and both of them laughed until they cried. Denise jumped up and ran for the bathroom because she laughed so hard that she wet her pants.

The girls visited for a while, and then made themselves a salad and some broccoli-cheese soup for lunch. It seemed like old times, but now things were so different. Nealy told her everything about her troubled marriage—every demeaning, deplorable, and disgusting detail. It felt good to tell someone. In a tell-all mood, Nealy told her about the her new friend, Dr. Phillip Pepper and his adorable sense of humor. When Nealy told her about the episode with the Dr. Pepper truck, which she found absolutely hilarious and very clever, they both died laughing. Denise brought her up to date on the city, the theater, the guys she had dated, and their old friends and neighbors. It was comforting to be in her home-away-from-home again. Denise and Nealy made plans to go out to dinner and go to Freddy's on Wednesday night, even though Nealy didn't really want Freddy to know why she had returned to New York. The time just wasn't right since she really didn't know what she planned on doing yet. Nealy also called Tony Rose, her former agent, and insisted that he join them. Of course, he agreed.

At three o'clock, Nealy left to catch the subway back to the apartment. The snow had slacked off somewhat, but there wasn't any sign of it stopping anytime soon. Nealy trudged down the snowed covered streets listening to the horns and the screams from angry drivers who were trying to make their way through the city. Nothing had changed; it's *insanity-at-large* on the streets of New York.

By the time she reached the apartment, at a quarter to five, she felt worn out. How she had managed during her one winter in New York baffled her; there had been many days and nights that she fought the bitter winter weather getting to and from Freddy's and the theater. Quickly, she got out of her wet clothes and headed for the shower in an effort to thaw her frozen fingers and toes.

As she stepped out of the shower, the telephone rang. So she grabbed her towel and attempted to dry off; she didn't want to track up the carpet.

"Hello," she said, wrapping the towel around her.

"Nealy, hi, it's Phillip."

"Oh, hi, Phillip."

"I've been calling you all afternoon. Have you been shopping again?"

"No, I went to visit Denise. My old roommate."

"Oh, good, I'm glad you got to see them. Wasn't the other one named Alex?"

"You have a great memory. Are you sure you didn't have a tape recorder at dinner?"

"I didn't. I promise," he chuckled.

"But anyway, she's gone. History."

"What do you mean, history?"

"She went home. It's a very long story, but an interesting one. I'll talk to you about it next time I see you. Maybe you can tell me what to do, if anything, to help her before it's too late."

"That sounds urgent. What are you doing tonight?"

"Nothing that I know of, why?"

"Well, since the weather is so bad, I thought we might go to this little pizza place not too far from your apartment. It has great pizza and a nice cozy atmosphere with a fireplace in the middle of the restaurant."

"That sounds nice. You can't find pizza anywhere else in the world that compares to the pizza in New York."

"It's all these wild and crazy cooking-Italians around here. Okay. Listen, I'll pick you up at seven," he replied excitedly.

"Okay. That sounds great." Nealy hung up the phone and finished getting ready.

As usual, Phillip picked her up at seven sharp. They decided to walk to the pizza place since it was only a couple blocks away. The snow had stopped, and it didn't seem real cold, but it was cold enough that Phillip had an excuse to snuggle up to Nealy in an effort to stay warm.

At the restaurant, they ate pizza and drank wine and beer in front of the fireplace. Nealy told him the story about Alex, and he made some suggestions. Nealy also confided in Phillip about her own problems because she trusted him. He listened mostly because he didn't want to push her into any decisions. Whatever she chose to do had to come from her, or it wouldn't work. Of course, he would like to hear her say that the marriage was over, but he had no intentions of putting words in her mouth.

While Nealy sat at the table, staring into the fire, Phillip got up and went to the bar to get himself another beer and Nealy another glass a wine. When she turned around, she noticed that he had gone behind the bar and helped himself. He returned to the table, acting silly and dancing a little jig as added entertainment for Nealy. Of course, she giggled and grinned at him.

"Do you come here often?" Nealy asked.

"Yes, why?"

"Everyone seems to know you, and you just helped yourself to the beer and wine," she smiled, resting her chin in the palm of her hand and watching him as he popped the top on the beer can.

The can exploded and beer spewed everywhere. Phillip jumped up, and Nealy screamed, giggling so hard she cried.

"Geezus," he shouted.

"See what happens when you act crazy," she said, giggling about the way he had inadvertently shook up the can of beer by dancing his way back to the table.

"This is your fault," he said, chuckling. "I just wanted to make you laugh." He wiped the beer off his face with his napkins, but he needed more napkins for the mess he made.

"My fault?" she screamed, questioning his reasoning. "Here, let me get some more napkins." Nealy went up to the bar and asked for something to clean up the beer, and Phillip followed her.

"Antonio, would you get a mop and some towels, please," Phillip said to the manager who handed him a clean towel.

"Sure, boss," he answered.

"Boss? Is that what he called you?" Nealy asked.

"I don't know. Is that what he called me?" Phillip answered a question with a question—*typical shrink behavior.* And without offering any further explanation, he took her arm and led her around to the other side of the fireplace. "Let's sit here so that they can clean up over there." He pulled out the chair for her to sit down, and then he went to their old table to retrieve her wine.

When he returned, he was still blotting his shirt with a napkin and chuckling to himself. Nealy loved his coarse laugh that rolled off his vocal chords in rapid succession; it matched his cheerful disposition perfectly. Smiling up at him, she took her wine and smiled graciously. "Thank you."

"You're very welcome. And I'm glad that you found my misfortune so amusing, but it's not polite to laugh at the misery of others?"

"I can't help it," she said, still giggling at him. "Okay, I'll make a deal with you—"

He chuckled softly. "Oh, no. I don't make deals with beautiful women, especially one as pretty as you."

"Why not?"

"Because I could never hold you to it," he admitted softly and sincerely as he stared directly into her emerald-green eyes.

The sweet grin and loving expression on his face made Nealy blush delightfully. "Okay, then, Doctor-don't-ask-me-no-questions-I'll-tell-you-no-lies-Pepper. No more mind games. I want to know why they called you boss?"

Phillip sat there thinking for a minute, and then he responded with a no-big-deal shrug of his shoulders. "Well, I guess it's because I own this restaurant."

With a big shit-eating-grin on his face, Antonio walked up beside the table and handed Phillip another beer, opened and ready to drink to prevent any further mishaps. "Try not to spill this one, Boss," he said, laughing out loud as he quickly walked away.

"You *actually* own this restaurant?" she asked.

"Yes, I *actually* own this restaurant," he repeated, taking a drink of his beer. "Is that a problem?"

"No, it's wonderful. But I'm shocked. I would never have guessed that you'd own a restaurant," she smiled at him. "So, what else can you pull out of your hat, Doctor, that might surprise me?"

"I'll never stop surprising you, Nealy," he said, looking very sure of himself. "That way, you'll never stop guessing."

"Oh, really." Nealy looked at him warmly, intrigued by his zealous nature. Phillip had many sides to his character, and, as far as Nealy could see, all of them were good. He had a boyish charm, which he used to keep others from being intimidated by his superior intelligence. If nothing else, it kept life very, very interesting. And from what Nealy had learned about him so far, she didn't doubt for a minute that his list of surprises were far from endless.

Back at the apartment, Nealy unlocked the door, and invited Phillip inside. In a gentlemanly fashion, he helped her with her coat, and then removed his. Carefully he hung them both on an antique coat rack next to the door.

"Come here and sit with me," he said sweetly, "I want to talk to you about something."

Nealy sat down beside him on the couch. "Am I in trouble because I laughed at you when that beer went up your nose?" she giggled. "I'm sorry, but I couldn't help it."

"No, it's not about that, although you should be ashamed for finding that so funny," he said placing his hand on hers. "What I want to talk to you about is much more serious."

"I'm sorry, but I've had too much wine to be serious," she giggled.

But when he took her hand and held it between his, she sensed that he had something on his mind. "Nealy, I've enjoyed getting to know you. You're the prettiest, sexiest, craziest, and brightest woman that I've ever known. I'd be a fool not to be attracted to you. But I'm also very aware of your situation, and I know how undecided you are right now. Therefore, I know better than to let my feelings go much beyond where they are now. We can be very good friends, even best friends, until you get your life in order. I just want you to know that I'm here for you."

"Phillip, I understand and I appreciate all you've done. We are friends, but I'm not sure if that's all. I feel strange because, as I've told you, I've never been involved romantically with anyone other than Jerrod. I can feel something happening between us, but I keep wondering if it's just feelings of insecurity."

"Nealy, you, of all people, need never be insecure about anything."

"But I wasn't enough for him. And he hurt me."

"I know, sweetheart, but that will pass," he said very sweetly, squeezing her hand. "If and when you divorce, you will have more men after you than you will ever need."

"Phillip, I've never had a lot of men after me, so why would I start now?"

"Trust me, there are plenty that want you, but they know how you feel about Jerrod. Up to now, you've always been taken, but when you're free, believe me, there will be a line competing for your affections," he said, smiling. "Me, for one."

"You're a sweet guy, Phillip Pepper." After she kissed him on the cheek, she stared at him for a moment before she said anything. "You know what I wish?"

"No, but your wish is my command," he smiled.

"I must warn you, it's a selfish wish."

"Nealy, you don't have a selfish bone in your body, so what is it?"

Shyly she said, "I wish that you could hold me because I'm so frightened."

"Why is that selfish?"

"Because I would be the only one to benefit from it. I feel so much anger bottled up inside, and if I let someone get involved with me, I might be doing it just to spite Jerrod. I don't know how I feel about anything or anyone, and I don't want you to get involved with someone who's so screwed up."

"I can protect myself pretty well, so why don't you let me make that decision," he said, pulling her into his arms.

"But Phillip—"

"Nealy, I'm a big boy," he interrupted, pulling her closer and kissing her. Each kiss became longer and harder, and then he pulled away, placing her head in the curve between his shoulder and neck while gently rubbing her back. Now he realized how right she had been about his getting too involved, but she needed him. If he let them go too far, he could lose her. Nealy wasn't ready for another man, even if she felt like she needed one. Phillip didn't want a one night stand with her; that was the last thing that he wanted. But stopping himself from making love to the woman of his dreams, the woman that he held in his arms at this very moment, would be a true test of his character and his fortitude.

Nealy raised her head up, and their eyes met. His heart raced and mentally he fought the urge to kiss her soft, pouty lips. Before he knew it, his lips were pressed hard against hers. Wanting her with all his heart, he didn't think that he could resist the urges to follow through with his natural instincts.

Nealy kissed him back, nurturing the strong needs that she had to be held and loved by a man. Her heart beat with excitement as her emotions ran wild. The only thing that mattered to her at that moment was unadulterated passion because it blocked out the rest of the world; her world stood still. The rules were fair and equal, which gave her the right to give and to take without asking or being asked.

Their bodies began to move together, becoming restless with the desire to go beyond the exchange of sweltering kisses. The passion grew to greater intensity moment by moment, nearing a point where it would be impossible to stop. Phillip felt her desire to be loved, and *God* knows, he wanted to love her from the very depths of his heart, but he sensed their bond of friendship and trust being destroyed by nothing more than their animal instincts. It couldn't go any further. He had to stop himself from making a terrible mistake, from alienating someone that could change his life. But how could he stop? He wanted her desperately.

Nealy felt good in his arms, and just as desperately as he wanted her, she wanted him. But was it really Phillip that she wanted, or did she just need to be loved by someone who cared? At this moment, she felt sure that she wanted *him*, but how could she be sure that she wasn't doing it to get even with Jerrod. If that turned out to be the case, then Phillip didn't deserve to be used. He deserved to be loved and cared for by someone with feelings that would extend beyond the heat of passion. Her conscience forced its way into her mind, shaking a finger at the fact that *two wrongs don't make a right*, but she forced it away by wrapping her arms tightly around him. Her conscience crept in again to express the image that she had created for herself, an image that she respected. Her conscience also pointed out the kindness bestowed upon her by Janey Randall in the use of her home, and the obligation to herself and everyone involved not to bring herself down to Jerrod's level. As they continued to smother each other with kisses of contentment, Phillip pulled the back of her blouse out of her skirt. He eased his hand up under her blouse and the minute he touched the soft skin of her back, they both broke away from each other simultaneously, "I can't."

Nealy giggled and Phillip chuckled softly. "Are we nuts or what?" she cried, covering her face with her hands and peeking through her fingers. "Oh, God, thank you for stopping."

Phillip released a heavy sigh, "No, thank you for stopping me."

"This would have been a mistake for both of us," Nealy said, pushing her eyebrows up with her fingertips.

"A year or two from now, I'd be in heaven," Phillip admitted touching her flushed cheek affectionately. "Actually tonight I'd be in heaven, but tomorrow would be hell. Nealy, you're the kind of girl that I'd like to take home to meet my mother, not have a brief affair with. So, when the times comes, I'd like to take this from the top again." Slowly, he traced a line from her ear, following the curve of her jawbone to her chin. "I may be doing a little wishful thinking here, but I feel something very special in our relationship. I really like you, and better than that, I think you're okay for a girl," he chuckled.

"I'll strike that last remark from your record," she teased.

"I'm teasing you, but I'm really very serious. I want to do whatever I can to maintain our friendship. I want to be the person that you call if you need someone to talk to while you're dealing with the ups and downs of the months ahead. It generally takes two years to resolve the anger, anxiety, and grief that comes with a separation, at least it does for most people. That seems like a long time, but divorce carries with it more emotional baggage than you realize. If, in fact, that's what you decide to do. Until you go through all the steps that it takes to fully recover, you should not make any major decisions. That's why I had to stop. Believe me, nothing would have brought me more pleasure, but *until you are ready*, I don't want to do anything that might cost me your friendship."

"I know what you're saying," she said, still lying across his lap. With anyone else, she would have jumped up immediately, but for some reason, she didn't feel uncomfortable, in fact, the conversation between them made her want to remain close to him. "Phillip, it's my fault for starting it, and I apologize. I shouldn't have let things go so far, but I thought I wanted it, or more so, I thought I needed it."

"Hey, I'm not complaining. Sampling your unleashed passion gave me something to look forward to," he said, his eyes dancing. He chuckled and smiled delightfully.

"Phillip," she said, "I'm embarrassed."

"Don't be. I'm not. In fact, it's obvious that I'm excited."

"Phillip," she cried, "maybe we both need a cold shower."

"Is that an invitation?"

"No," she said adamantly, but then she giggled. "At least not tonight."

"Well, I'll definitely take a rain check. But, for now, I need to go," he said, getting up from the couch. He had calmed his emotional needs to make love to her, but his physical needs had not quite gotten the message yet. "Excuse me," he said looking down, "Didn't you hear the lady? *Not tonight.*" Nealy got so tickled that she laughed out loud. Normally, a remark like that from someone that she'd only known for a week would have embarrassed her, but with Phillip it was funny.

Phillip pulled her up from the couch and led her to the door. Turning around, he leaned against the door and put his hands on her shoulders. "I wish I could close my eyes and turn time forward to at least a year from now. That would sure make things easier for *Big Jim and the twins*," he smiled wryly, lowering his head to acknowledge the bulge that remained manifested below his waist.

Nealy giggled loudly. "You're quite disturbed, Phillip Pepper. It's a good thing that I relate so well to crazy people," she said in jest. "Oh, and tell *Big Jim and the twins* not to worry, I'll invite them out to play again someday."

"And you think *I'm bad*," he replied, astonished at her sexual connotation. "I think I'd like to see the delightfully naughty side of you someday, pretty lady. So I'll hold you to that last remark." He kissed her on the cheek. "Good-night. In spite of the bad timing, I had a very memorable evening."

"Me, too," she said, smiling. "Tomorrow night some of my friends and I are going to Freddy's, the night club where I used to sing. Would you like to join us?" she asked.

"I'd love to." He smiled, happy to be included.

"Call me tomorrow, and I'll tell you where and when. Good-night, Phillip."

"Good-night, Nealy." Taking his coat from her, he backed across the hall, pushing the button behind him. His stare remained constant with hers; neither one wanted to deny themselves any second of shared admiration. After backing into the elevator, the door closed.

Nealy closed the door and closed her eyes in relief that she hadn't done anything that she would have regretted. Although, with all her heart, she wanted to be close to him, but it was too soon. Thank God for Phillip and his honorable attitude towards her. That showed definite signs of restraint on his part and hers, too. What a nice guy he had turned out to be, and a wonderful friend.

Nealy turned out the lights in the living room. It was after eleven o'clock, but she wasn't really sleepy. After she washed her face, she put on her gown, crawled into bed, and found her place in the new book. The first three pages that she read turned out to be a love scene between the two main characters, stirring the feelings that she had suppressed during her petting liaison with Phillip. For a minute, she wished that she hadn't stopped, that she had followed through to release the tension that she felt, but she knew that would have been a mistake. But she couldn't help imagining what it would be like with Phillip, which made her feel guilty. So, her mind took the moral path and wandered back into the bedroom that she had shared with Jerrod, thoughts which also aroused her. The harder she fought to erase those memories from her mind, the worse it became; she could almost feel him touching her sexually, which drove her crazy.

Finally, she jumped up and headed for the shower. Never had she actually taken a cold shower, but she had no other choice. She prayed that it really worked. This was the first time since leaving Galveston that she had felt anything for Jerrod other than contempt and anger. Letting go of that part of their ten year relationship would probably be the most difficult because it had been the strongest link, the link that kept them together all those years.

When the cold water hit her face, she drew a deep breath, and her entire body stiffened. For almost five minutes, she forced herself to remain under the cold water that sprayed out of the shower head, turning slowly until the cold water hit the small of her back and her buttocks. Suddenly, she decided that she couldn't take it any longer and she turned the water off, feeling nothing but cold. Sex was the last thing on her mind.

When she reached outside the shower for her towel, she heard the phone ringing. "Dammit, I think this place is bugged. The phone always rings when I get in the shower. Even in the middle of the night," she complained out loud to herself. "Who would be calling me at eleven-thirty?"

"Hello," she said, still shaking.

"Where have you been? I've called you all day and half the night," he snapped.

"Jerrod, I thought I asked you not to call me here."

"Nealy, regardless of what you think, I'm still your husband, and I'm concerned about you. New York is a big city and lots of things go on there. And clearly you're out and about. That concerns me."

"Jerrod, I'm fine. I don't owe you an explanation, but I went over to visit Denise today."

"And tonight? Where were you tonight?"

"That's none of your business?"

"I guess you were out with one of your old boyfriends. Is that it, Nealy?"

"Jerrod, I didn't have any old boyfriends,"she said very sarcastically. "Remember, I was this idiot saving myself for you, while you were down there copulating like the Creature From the Black Lagoon."

"Nealy, I'm sorry. I didn't call to fight with you."

"Well, then why did you call? Why can't you just leave me alone?" she asked, her voice weakening.

"I can't. Don't you understand, I can't. I know what I did was wrong, but I can't leave you alone, dammit! I need to know what you intend to do. Are you going to divorce me? I can't take the torture of waiting."

"Jerrod, please...I'll be home on Sunday. We can talk about this then. I've asked you not to push me. You won't like the decision I make if I'm forced to make it now. I told you, I'm still too angry to deal with this." Her face burned with so much anger that even a cold shower couldn' t cool the heat.

"Okay," he said remorsefully, "I'll see you Sunday night."

"Good—" The dial-tone interrupted her. Nealy rubbed her face, and she felt the tears that had escaped and rolled down her cheeks. Why did she let him upset her so much? Thank goodness she had taken a cold shower, because her frame of mind would have been much different if he had called earlier; her sexual needs might have weakened her anger and fogged her judgment. That had been a close call, literally, but fortunately she had maintained a strong position, even though a part of her wanted to forgive him just because she had made a promise before God. With that thought, she put her hands together to pray for help from a stronger power than her own. "Please *God*," she begged, "give me strength. I can't do this alone. I'm just too weak when it comes to this. I know that I made a promise to you, but I'm not in love with him. I pity him, but I can't let that tempt me into taking him back. I want to love and be loved, but not by someone that doesn't honor his vows and convictions. I don't want to live with someone that I can't trust or who will betray me. Please help me, *Lord,* please." Nealy fell down on the bed and cried as if she hadn't put any time or space between the past and the present. But suddenly, a peacefulness came over her and she stopped crying. Nealy reached over to turn off the light and pulled the covers over her body. As she lay there in the darkness, the sounds from the street faded, and the last words that floated through her mind were Longfellow's: "Drift gently down the tides of sleep."

CHAPTER TWENTY-NINE

WEDNESDAY MORNING she woke up feeling refreshed and happy. Thoughts of Phillip brought a smile to her face. But when she sat up on the side of the bed, she remembered being haunted during the night with that same dream where Michael Coupair stood above her, staring coldly with his brown-velvet eyes, his dark hair blowing in the wind. She could even smell the salty air from an ocean breeze. When he disappeared, she panicked, but she just kept standing there, waiting for him to reappear. It kept reeling over and over in her mind. She couldn't make it stop. "This is *too* weird. It's even a little creepy," she mumbled, getting out of bed. Would she ever shake that feeling she got when he held her hand so gently, looking deep into her eyes and tenderly kissing the back of her hand? It actually gave her goosebumps. That romantic demeanor must be inbred in European men, that innate ability to seduce the opposite sex with their eyes and their soft, sensual touch. Whatever that guy did, she felt sure that he did it well because he had that look: a man with the midas touch. This stranger had touched her heart and her mind and her soul and she couldn't make him go away. The feeling made her want to scream with fear, but then she felt almost pleasantly bewitched by him. What did all this mean?

After taking a shower, a nice hot one this time, she dressed and decided to make some telephone calls to catch up on life back in Texas. First, she called Francine to see how things were going at the studio, discovering that all was going very well. Miss Janik had pitched-in to help Francine in Nealy's absence which made her feel much better. Francine seemed exceptionally cheery and told her that things couldn't be better. Of course, when Nealy asked her if Randy had been by or called to check on things, she didn't answer the question exactly, but Nealy accepted "He's a wonderful guy" to mean that he had. Alicia wanted Francine to make sure and tell her that Chance had been a good dog, eating all of his dinner almost every night. Also, she wanted Nealy to know that he and Rags had been having a great time playing together and that he could stay as long as he wanted. Nealy's eyes watered, even though she smiled, as Francine relayed all the messages; she missed everyone so much. She told Francine, that if all went well, she would return to the studio on Tuesday because Rob Morris wanted to see her on Monday to make sure that things had done whatever it was that they were supposed to do.

Next, she called Janey just to say "thanks" for allowing her to use the apartment. They visited for at least twenty minutes, and Janey told her that she had spent more than an hour with Jerrod discussing the damage that he had obviously done to his marriage. Janey said that he felt terrible and that all he wanted to do was make everything up to Nealy when she returned home, but Janey knew it wouldn't be that simple. She had been there and knew all too well how hard it would be for Nealy to forgive and forget. Janey loved Jerrod, but she was not sympathetic to his position because he had brought it entirely up on himself. She stood firm in her convictions to accept Nealy's decision; Jerrod had made that bed. Nealy assured her that it took two to tango, and even though she didn't think that anything excused what he did, they shared equally the missing links in the marriage. Not knowing herself, Nealy couldn't tell Janey what she planned to do, but she assured her that she would talk to Jerrod on Sunday when she returned. For selfish reasons, Janey wanted her to take him back because the entire family loved Nealy and didn't want to lose her. Of course, Janey had not told anyone, and she felt sure that Jerrod hadn't either, and he wouldn't, unless he had to because his family his family would be too disappointed. The Catholic faith did not recognize divorce, so neither would his father. Time would tell. But for now, Nealy appreciated her kindness and her hospitality, and for giving her the opportunity to return to New York again, even if the circumstances surrounding her being there were not very pleasant.

When she hung up she wanted to cry, but she didn't. Determined not to let things get to her, she sang and rushed into the kitchen to prepare herself a light breakfast of cereal and bananas. Just as she put a big spoon full in her mouth, the phone rang, but she answered it anyway. "Hello," she said, trying to swallow her cereal without crunching into the telephone.

"Nealy, is that you?"

"Yes, it" s me...with a mouthful of cereal," 'Hi, Tony."

"Oh, you're eating," he replied, disappointed.

"Well, I made me a bowl of cereal, but I've only eaten three bites."

"Oh, good. Pour it out," he said emphatically. "I want to take you to lunch. I have reservations at *Tavern On the Green* for eleven-thirty. Aren't you just across the street from there?"

"Yes, but—"

"See you over there at eleven-thirty," he interrupted, hanging up quickly so that she couldn't decline.

"Well, if you insist," she said to a the dial-tone. "Am I missing something here? Where I'm from, people say good-bye." Nealy grumbled, tossing her cereal and retiring to the bedroom to dress. Tony sounded urgent, but since that's his general nature, she considered the source. *Tavern On the Green* had always been one of Nealy's favorite places even though she had only looked in from the park. When she lived in New York, she didn't have the time or the money to eat there; this would be a special treat.

At exactly eleven-thirty, Nealy walked into the foyer of the restaurant and searched the already crowded room for Tony, but she didn't see him. The snow, which always caused traffic problems, had probably made him late, so she decided to check her coat while she waited.

"Nealy!"

Hearing her name, she quickly turned around and smiled at Tony who made his way through the group that had gathered at the hostess station. "Tony, gosh it's good to see you again," she said, hugging him.

"You look wonderful," he exclaimed. "Thank goodness marriage was good to you. I worried about that, you know."

"What did you expect? Oh, let me guess. You thought I'd get fat, cut my hair, skip the make-up, and wear dark polyester pantsuits. Is that it?" she giggled wildly.

"No, but close," he smiled, taking her arm and pulling her through the crowd. "Let's see if our table's ready."

The hostess led them down a mirrored hallway that resembled a maze, zigging and zagging, until they reached the dining room. Then the waiter introduced himself and led them to their table. Nealy stood there in awe of this truly magnificent room with ten-foot high windows that formed a crooked semi-circle around at least two-hundred white wicker chairs and fifty tables to match, each adorned with colorful, fresh-cut flowers. The high, white ceilings were swirled with ornately textured designs which reflected the lights of ten enormous chandeliers in red and white, green, and blue. From inside, it looked like a winter wonderland outside. "Oh, Tony, this is a beautiful restaurant," she proclaimed ecstatically.

"I knew you'd like it. That's why I insisted that you scrap your cereal and come with me," he smiled, staring at her.

"I'm really glad. Thanks for being your typically pushy self," she giggled.

"God, Nealy, you look great! Welcome back to the *Big Apple*. Are you ready to go back to work?"

"Tony, no, I'm just here for a visit."

"Nealy, I know you well enough to have picked up on some *trouble in paradise*. So, what's the story?"

"Tony, it's really nothing," she softly said, taking a deep breath.

"Nealy, it's me, Tony. You know I'm going to badger you until you spill your guts." Tony reached across the table and took hold of her hand. "Now, come on, tell me what happened?"

"It's a very long story, Tony, and one that's not too pretty," she admitted sadly.

"Did he hurt you?" he asked eagerly.

"Yes, he hurt me alright...and in the worst way."

"Did he hit you?" he asked, getting angry.

"No, not that, Tony...oh, how can I say this delicately. I caught him in a swimming pool doing what most couples do in bed."

"That's unbelievable. Did you know the woman he was having an affair with?"

"Not woman, Tony. *Women.*"

"No shit!" he cried. "Oh, now, Nealy, don't cry," he begged. "That bastard's not worth it. In fact, the guy's a complete fool to do that to you."

Tears ran down her cheeks. "I was so naive. I never suspected anything. Tony, he made a complete idiot out of me." Nealy reached inside her purse and pulled out a tissue to blot her eyes.

"Well, you *are* divorcing him, aren't you?" Tony blurted out.

"I don't know. I came here to make some decisions about my life, but time's running out. I go home on Sunday, and I promised him that we'd talk then."

"Nealy, you've got to divorce this guy. He doesn't deserve you. You have to believe that," he stated flatly, lifting her chin.

"He claims he made a mistake. He wants to make it up to me."

"Is he harassing you here?"

"Well, he's called a couple of times. And every time he does, I get even more confused."

"Oh, Nealy, come on. You can't let someone do this to you. You're much too smart for that. He's that type. He'll do it again. I know that's harsh. But let's face it, that's reality."

"I know you're right, Tony, but I feel like such a failure. I didn't get married to get divorced three and a half years later."

"I know, but sometimes those things happen. And look, it's better that it happened now so you can go on with your life. Just think, you could have a little *rug rat*, and then things would really be tough. If you take him back, the next time—and trust me, there will be a next time—you may have two or three *rug rats* to take care of, and then where would you be?"

"Tony, you're terrible," she giggled, shaking her head. Of course, Tony made her laugh on purpose; he couldn't stand to see her cry. She blotted her eyes again for fear that her mascara had run down her face like the stripes on a zebra.

The waiter walked up to the table with their coffee. "Okay, let me see," Tony said, studying the menu. Selecting the same entree, they ordered the lunch special of baked white fish with a butter crust topping, green beans, and cottage fries. The restaurant smelled of fresh brewed coffee, light herbs, and chocolate, a clashing combination that smelled delectable. Stirring Nealy's appetite, she couldn't wait for the food to come.

While they waited, Tony brought up the subject of divorce forcing her to talk about it, and even though it upset her, she bounced back rather quickly when Tony changed the subject to crazy stories about his clients.

The waiter brought their lunch and sat it down in front of them, steam rising from the hot plate.

"Will there be anything else?"

"Yes, I have a friend coming for dinner, so I'd like two orders of this to go, please."

"To go?" he questioned in a puzzled voice.

"Don't look so worried, I'm just kidding," she replied. "What can I say, I have fast food mentality," she giggled infectiously.

Tony laughed, his eyes dancing between Nealy and the waiter. "Hey, Nealy, if you really want some to go, I've got connections."

"I'm kidding, guys. You people are too serious," she smiled, glancing up at the waiter. "'Amen, brother Ben, shot the goose and killed the hen. Dig in!'"

"What?" Tony crinkled his face.

"Didn't you say that when you were a kid?"

"I can't say that I did," Tony confessed.

"At family gatherings, the grown-ups put all the kids in another room to eat. My grandmother would say 'You kids take turns returning the blessing. Don't forget.' So, that's what we said," she admitted, studying the I-don't-get-it-look on his face. "Oh, for pity's sake. It's just a little Texas humor, but never mind. Let's eat before our food gets cold. Yum!" During the first week that she had spent in New York, she had barely eaten anything; the second week, that's all she had done. She felt fat, but everything had been so good that she couldn't help herself. After each meal, she vowed that she would walk an extra mile to make up for her indulgence.

When the waiter returned with the dessert tray displaying five heavenly desserts, she vowed to walk three extra miles. With that promise, she selected a marble cheesecake with raspberry sauce scalloped around the edge of a plate, not a saucer, a regular size plate. Now this is what she wanted to take home. She wondered if one slice cost six dollars, what would the whole thing cost?

Lunch with Tony had been wonderful. They had been such good friends over the past years, talking several times a year. Although over the years, she never told him any of the negative things that were taking place in her life, only the positive ones; he did the same. At one point he mentioned marriage to a stage actress. But, Denise told her later that the girl left to tour with a theatrical company and things went downhill from there. Tony didn't say much, but he did eventually tell Nealy that the marriage was off. He still looked the same with his reddish-hair and blue-green eyes. In fact, the hostess asked if he and Nealy were related, a suggestion which made all of them laugh when Tony said "Yes, and *incest is best*, but not for everybody of course."

While they visited, drinking a second cup of hot coffee, Tony became curious about a man that had been staring at Nealy during the entire meal. He sat about five tables away from them with two other gentlemen, but his mind certainly hadn't been on the conversation at his own table. Nealy sat with her side to him, so she hadn't seen him hanging on her every expression. At first, Tony didn't think too much about it. Nealy attracted attention. It amused him to watch the reaction of every man—and even many of the women—whenever she walked into a theater or a restaurant or almost any public place. It took him a long time to figure out exactly why that happened. In his line of work, he had entered rooms with many beautiful women and none of them had ever came as close to paralyzing an entire crowd the way Nealy did. But one day, when he sat in the back of Joe Allen's on Forty-sixth Street waiting for Nealy to join him for lunch, he finally realized what she had that so many other women didn't: Her warm smile and sweet face projected a wholesome quality that everyone loved, and her friendly, expressive and outgoing personality made her very approachable.

"Nealy, don't look now, but there is a man walking towards us that has been staring at you all through lunch. When he walks by, see if you know who he is," Tony said, trying to be inconspicuous. "I don't call too many men handsome, but this guy, by anyone's standards, would be considered very attractive. He's obviously got a few bucks, too. That's a Hugo Boss suit he's wearing. It cost at least fifteen hundred dollars. Maybe he's some big producer and remembers you from years ago."

"Oh, Tony, really," she giggled nervously.

"Okay, he's almost to us," he said through his teeth like a ventriloquist. "Look now."

Nealy casually turned around. Then her face turned bright red.

"Hello, Ms. James. How nice to see you again," Michael Coupair said in his very French accent.

Tony stood up. "Hi, I'm Tony Rose, her agent."

"Nice to meet you, Mr. Rose," Michael Coupair said politely, and then he turned all of his attention back to Nealy.

As usual, Nealy's eyes were glued to him.

"I'm surprised you recognized me without all of those packages."

"I would recognize you anywhere, Ms. James."

"Well, that's probably the one thing that we have in common. Not that I'd recognize *me*, but I'd recognize you," she said, giggling and talking with her hands in an effort to hide her nervousness, which failed miserably.

"Well, that's nice to know. I'll let you continue your lunch," he remarked, touching her shoulder very lightly and searching her face again as he had in the past. "Nice to have met you, Mr. Rose," he nodded to Tony. "Ms. James," he said, saying good-bye with his eyes only.

"Good-bye," she said shyly, mirroring his nod. "Ships that pass in the night," she whispered, watching him move gracefully through the dining room. But just before he walked out, he turned and gave her once last glance with his unbelievable brown-velvet eyes.

"Ships? Nealy, what are you talking about? Who is that guy?" Tony asked impatiently.

"I'm not sure," she said, fanning her face with her napkin.

"What's the matter with you? Your face is flushed. Are you feeling alright?"

"I'm fine, but that man gets me all shook up every time I run into him."

"You said something about ships. Did you meet him on a cruise?"

"No, I've never been on a cruise. He helped me with some packages last week in the elevator at the apartment. Since then, I've passed him several times in the building. It makes me think of ships passing in the night. I see him, and then he disappears for several days. Then out of the blue, he reappears, says hello, and then he's gone again. That's why I said that. I don't know what he does or where he does it, but he makes me nervous. Did you see me, I acted like a tongue-tied spastic, and I have no idea what I said to him."

"Well, he never took his eyes off you during lunch. I think he has the *hots* for you."

"Oh, Tony, he doesn't even know me. He's friendly, that's it. If he were interested, he would ask me questions or make more of an effort to get to know me. Maybe he *is* in show business and needs models or actresses. I don't know what to think about him. He speaks, so I speak," she said simply. "But his accent is still heavy, so if he lives here in New York, he hasn't been here for long."

"I'll check around and see if he's in the industry. If he is, somebody will know something about him," he said detectively.

"Well if he is, at least he knows I've got an agent," she gripped. "Tony, you just never stop."

"I am. Or I was, and I could be again. Who knows where you'll end up now that Jerrod is on the *Go Team*." Tony raised his eyebrows, cocked his thumb, and made a quick jerking gesture with his thumb pointing over his shoulder.

"Tony, I haven't said that Jerrod is going out of my life. I haven't made any decisions about that yet, and even if that happens, I can't come back to New York. I own a dance and theatrical studio now, remember?"

"Well, who's minding the store now? A good business can be run from anywhere as long as you have good help, which you must or you wouldn't be here. Or even better, it could be sold," he said smugly.

"Tony, I don't want to sell my business. And anyway, it's much too soon to even think beyond today. I'm taking things one day at a time, and each day when I exhaust myself with worry, anger and decisions, I forget about it, because...*there's always tomorrow*," she said in her best Southern accent as she rolled her head back, closed her eyes, and rested the back of her hand against her forehead.

Tony clapped. "See, Nealy, you still have it. Always an actress, always a woman," he said.

"Woman. Oh, Tony, that sounds so mature and obviously I'm not. Look at me, I fall apart when approached by a stranger. No, Tony, I think I'm definitely still a girl, a goofy girl at that," she giggled, putting her hand on top of his.

"Well, let's go, goofy girl."

"Outside the restaurant they hugged. I'll see you at Freddy's around nine."

"Okay," she said, kissing him on the cheek. "Thanks for lunch."

"You're welcome. See you tonight."

Nealy took a long walk through the park to get in a little exercise before she returned to the apartment. The skies still remained cloudy, but at least the snow had stopped for now. Everything seemed serene. The children were inside, so there wasn't any laughter. The birds weren't singing, so there was no music. Things were silent; she could think more clearly. In the distance, the inevitable honking of horns continued, but that had become subliminal and didn't interfere with her thoughts.

In only four days, she would be faced with one of the most important decisions of her life: to end her marriage or to accept what had happened. In her heart she knew what she wanted to do, but in her head she knew what she didn't want to do. So it became *the head vs. the heart,* the same conflict most people face in their lives and sometimes more than once. But as for her, she never wanted to make another decision like this one again. So she needed to make the right choice; one that she could live with and learn from. Bette Davis once said that the reason she had failed at marriage so many times was that she was "in love with falling in love." But didn't it make it less enjoyable each time she had to say good-bye and go through a bad divorce? Nealy didn't know much about divorce. But she did recall the bitter battle that Janey Randall went through when she divorced Roland and how publicized it had been. Nealy knew that she didn't want to go through that, but of course she wouldn't because Janey and Roland had been married a long time, they had well over five million dollars in community property and who knows how much money, and he had a very prominent position at the hospital. No one would really care about her problems, except for the families. If they divorced, she wanted to be civil about it, so she had to present her case to Jerrod where he would accept it as the only way. Avoiding a circus or a bitter confrontation would take a some planning on her part. If only she knew what to do, she could work out the rest, but it's hard to simple say it's over and end it. Breaking up *is* hard to do. How does one turn off love? But what good is love when there is no trust? And how does someone know when it's true love? The deep, forever kind. Or does that really exist? Nealy had so many questions and so many doubts. It had taken her years to realize that she loved Jerrod enough to marry him, and even when she finally made that decision, she still questioned her love at times. How did people know *love at first sight,* and how could someone say, "I knew I'd marry her from the first moment I laid eyes on her," or "I wanted him from the first minute I saw him." That seemed so storybook, like a scene from a movie or a romance novel.

Denise showed up at Janey's apartment building at six-o'clock so that she and Nealy could go out to dinner and visit some more before they went to Freddy's. Jigs called up to the apartment to verify her guest.

"Hello."

"Ms. Nealy, this is Jigs. Denise Pratt is here to see you."

"Thanks, Jigs. Could you send her up?"

"I sure will, Ms. Nealy." One minute later the door bell rang and Nealy rushed to answer it.

"Can you believe this place?" Nealy exclaimed. "It's a long way from Eighty-sixth Street isn't it?" Nealy pulled her inside.

"Holy shit! You aren't kidding. And the men around here aren't bad either," Denise profoundly stated.

"What?"

"I just saw an incredible gorgeous man on the elevator," Denise said, looking around the room.

"Six-feet tall, dark brown hair and *brown-velvet eyes* to die for," she said describing him.

"How did you know?"

"Denise, his name is Michael Coupair and he lives on the eleventh floor...well, I guess he does. I went shopping last week, and, being the *butter-fingered Betsy* that I am, I dropped packages all over the elevator. Out of nowhere, he appeared and helped me carry them to the apartment. Ever since then I've been running into him *everywhere.* I went to lunch with Tony today at *Tavern On the Green,* and Michael Coupair came over to our table and spoke to me. Tony's convinced that the guy's some big producer or director. Of course Tony had to tell him that he was my agent."

Denise laughed. "Tony has quite an imagination, but Nealy, who knows, he could be. You need to forget Jerrod Jones—that bastard—and hook that guy. If he lives in this building, he has tons of money."

"Denise, that guy is too damn good-looking. Plus he's French and he's too sophisticated for me. He's good for a marvelous fantasy, and besides, I couldn't *hook* him because I can't even talk to him," Nealy rambled on.

"I've never met anyone you couldn't talk to. No one's ever intimidated you," she said, unable to believe Nealy's admission of awkwardness.

"Well, you just met the first. I'm an idiot around him. I can't think, I can't speak, and when I do, I have no idea what I said. I guess he's just too gorgeous. And anyway, any man that looks like that has to be taken. He probably has ten children, married to his second—maybe third—wife who is outrageously beautiful, probably one of those fabulous French models."

"He wasn't wearing a wedding ring," Denise tattled.

"You looked for a wedding band?"

"I always do. Don't you?" she said indignantly.

"No, but I'm married. So what would it matter?"

"But not for long," Denise said, looking at Nealy for a response. "Nealy, you have to dump that two-timing Romeo."

"I should, but I'm still so confused, Denise. I can't be in love with him because I don't miss him. But I'm not sure what being in love is really like. I used to get goose bumps when I thought about him, but I don't anymore. We had some great sex, but that's about all."

"Nealy, this is not the love of your life. There are men out there that would die for you. Jerrod is the only jerk in America that would go to bed with someone else while being married to you. You are everything that any man would want. Jerrod is just a spoiled, selfish, self-centered sex maniac who only loves himself. Can't you see that?" Denise asked, wanting to shake some sense into her. "Nealy, if it's sex you want, I can line you up with two very qualified candidates who would do back flips across this city to do *it* with you. I know guys who would pay big bucks just to touch your big bosoms."

"Denise!'

"Well, it's true."

"I appreciate you trying to make me feel better, but evidently I don't know how to satisfy a man or he wouldn't have needed those sluttish mermaids. In fact, he said that and I quote. 'You are a naive bitch and if you weren't such a prude, you could join us.' "

"Oh, Nealy, I can't believe that you would let him destroy your faith in yourself like that. Pardon me, but he's as full-of-shit as a Christmas turkey. You're a nice person, and you have pride and morals. You would never stoop to screwing around in public with a group of perverts. That's not you, and it never will be. And Nealy, if you think you'll change or he'll change, you're wrong. You are what you are, and so is he. He's a bastard and you're a sweet, pretty, wonderful person who deserves so much more," Denise said defensively.

"Don't hold back, Denise, say what's on your mind."

"I'm sorry, but it just makes me angry to see you taking the blame for that...that jackass that let his libido turn your fairytale life into a poolside ménage à trois," she snapped.

"I know you're right about him, and I'm really glad you said all those things. I need to hear the truth. I'm just so tired of fighting that it'd be easier to accept full responsibility for everything that's happened. It's still hard for me to believe that my life has turned into such a mess," Nealy said sadly. "Let me show you around this *mansion in the sky,* and then let's go eat. But first, just who and how much are they willing to pay to touch my boobs?" They hugged and giggled wildly.

CHAPTER THIRTY

LATER THAT EVENING, Nealy and Denise walked down the stairs to the basement level that led into Freddy's nightclub. Nealy told Phillip Pepper to meet her there at nine-thirty so that she could have a chance to visit with Freddy, Frank, Jillie, and some of the others that still remained at the club. Denise had been to the club only three times since Nealy left, but she and Frank, the bartender and stand-up-comic-hopeful, had remained friends. They had even gone out a few times, and he kept Denise up-to-date on the club and the people. When they walked in, the lights went on, the crowd roared, cheering wildly, and Jillie belted out her rendition of "Back Where You Belong." Nealy laughed and cried at the same time. Everyone rushed over to hug her. It felt good to be back in her home-away-from-home with her friends that she had missed terribly during the last three years. But what made it even more special was the fact that Tony had planned the surprise.

Nealy hugged him tightly. "I can't believe you did this. This means so much to me. Thanks, Tony."

"Well, we missed you. And were glad you're back," he said, pleased that he had made her smile again, especially after knowing how unhappy she had been.

"Where's my girl?" a gruff voice called out in the crowd.

"Freddy!" Nealy screamed, pulling away from Tony's embrace and hugging Freddy, fat, cigar and all.

"How've you been, doll?" Freddy asked.

"Good, Freddy. How have you been?" she asked, grinning from ear to ear. "You're holding that shape pretty good, I see," she rubbed his extremely fat belly.

Yeah, doll, I take good care of my excess. This day and time you never know when you'll need it," he said, laughing and giving her another squeeze. "Boy, we sure miss you, doll. Are you back for good?"

"No, Freddy, I wish I were. This time it's just a visit."

"But I'm working on that, Freddy," Tony blurted out.

"Good boy. Don't give up," Freddy said to Tony and turned back to talk to Nealy. "We could use you around here, doll. It'd liven up the place again."

"Thanks, Freddy, it's nice to know I've been missed. I've really missed y'all too," Nealy said, her mood shifting from happy to sad and back to happy again.

"Well, you're as pretty as ever," Freddy said, taking a good look at her in the same up and down manner that he had the first time they met. Only this time she didn't mind.

"Now I know why I missed y'all so much. No one lies to me anymore," she teased, giggling loudly. Everyone laughed.

"Let's welcome Nealy back to Freddy's. Lights out and let's eat, drink, and be merry!" Freddy shouted.

"Come on, Nealy, I get the first dance," Tony said, dragging Nealy out onto the tiny dance floor. He held her close and enjoyed being near her again. It had been too long, and he planned on doing everything possible to keep her there permanently. It would take some work, but he made the mistake of letting her get away before without a fight, so this time he would give her a real fight to the finish. He had come a long way in the industry and developed a strong client base to some famous newcomers. And because of his accomplishments, he had more to offer Nealy than he had in the past. If she wanted security, he could give it to her now.

The song ended, and Tony led Nealy over to the table where their friends had gathered. Nealy, who had been watching for Phillip, saw him entering the club.

"Guys, excuse me for a minute. A friend of mine just walked in. I'll be right back."

"Denise, what friend?" Tony asked angrily.

"Some shrink-doctor friend of hers. They just met last week, but I know she likes him. It's a long story, but her doctor at home had this guy call her in case she became too depressed or something like that. I haven't met him, yet, but she told me all about him."

"Well, that's just great," Tony grumbled. "Just what she needs, another goddamn doctor to screw around on her." Tony watched them make their way through the crowd. Naturally, the guy would be stout as a bull and handsome, but he figured he'd be boring as hell. Most doctors have a personality equal to that of their stethoscope: they hear, but they just can't speak; and the talking ones are usually egomaniacs. Although, Tony had a couple of doctor friends that were terrific guys, but Nealy had a knack for picking the bad ones.

"Hi," Phillip said, smiling. "You must be Denise. And you must be Tony," he said, making eye contact and extending his hand as a polite gesture. "I've heard all about both of you." He smiled at Nealy, confirming his source.

"It's nice to meet you, Phillip," Denise said. "I've heard all about you, too," she said smiling at Nealy with a first-impression approval of her new friend.

"Yeah, nice to meet you," Tony said with much less enthusiasm. "Please, everyone sit. What can I get you to drink, Phillip?"

"Hmm, draft beer will do. Thanks."

A young woman walked up behind Phillip and ran her hands down his shoulders to his chest, and he wheeled around.

"Oh, hon, I like a man with quick reflexes."

"Phillip, this is Jillie Jahoda. Jillie meet Dr. Phillip Pepper," Nealy said, looking up at Jillie who still had her hands on his shoulders.

"Hi, Jillie, it's nice to meet you."

"Likewise, toots," she said seductively. "Nealy, where do you find these handsome doctors?"

"Well, I have a lot of physical and emotional problems these days," she said, smiling at Phillip. "So I find the ones who work cheap, work nights, and don't mind making house calls." Everyone laughed, except Tony, who had returned with their beers. He squeezed a chair in between Denise and Nealy in an effort to protect his territory.

"Would you like to sit down, Jillie?" Phillip asked politely, pulling up a chair.

"Ooh, Nealy, toots, he's handsome and polite, too. I like that in a man," she said, winking at him. "Phillip, I'd like to stay and chat, toots, but if you don't mind I'm going to drag Nealy up on stage with me for a little homecoming."

"By all means, take her away," he smiled back, standing up to pull out her chair.

"No, Jillie, I'm out of practice. I've barely hit a note since I left here."

"Good try, toots, but you don't lose your voice. It may need a little warming up, but it's like riding a bicycle. So come on, I promised the crowd," Jillie insisted, pulling Nealy up from the table. "Stay put, Doc, I may need a little mouth to mouth after this set," she teased, smiling at him again.

Phillip turned his chair around so that he had a better view of the stage. This was an unexpected treat and he didn't want to miss any of it. Nealy told him that she had worked at Freddy's doing a little singing, but she had been very modest about her talent.

Phillip settled back into his chair.

Tony felt threatened, even though Nealy had never given him any indication that she intended their relationship to be anything but platonic. But, when the time came, Tony planned on making his feelings known, and he didn't want another doctor—of all people—getting in his way.

Freddy announced the return of the duo of Jillie Jahoda and Nealy James who had performed together many times on his stage. The crowd roared in remembrance of the famous duo. The girls started out with some old favorites: "Deep In the Heart of Texas" and "The Battle of New Orleans." They sang together for almost an hour with the crowd singing along and dancing in the aisles, just like old times. Nealy felt good—like a star again.

Tony watched her with pride, and his theory that she lit up a room proved to be one-hundred percent accurate. Nealy was radiant, and every person in the room glowed. When they tried to stop, the crowd cheered them on with a standing ovation, forcing them to continue. Every so often, Tony turned to catch a glimpse of Phillip out of the corner of his eye and found him totally engrossed in the performance. His temperature rose with jealously because he could see *"That's my girl"* written all over the good doctor's face. But that would be over Tony's dead body. Not another doctor, no way.

Jillie left the stage, shouting, "Is there a doctor in the house? Quick! I need emergency medical attention! A little physical therapy—ooh, Doctor."

"Phillip, run!" Nealy warned over the microphone, giggling at Jillie running through the crowd. They roared at their comic performance.

Nealy pleased the crowd with *"When I Fall In Love, It Will Be Forever."* She wasn't quite sure what made her choose that song, but she sang it beautifully, as if it came straight from the heart.

"This next song seems very appropriate since this *is* my party and I'll cry if I want to," she said jokingly. The crowd laughed and cheered. "This song has been one of my favorites since Leslie Gore took it to the top of the charts in nineteen-sixty-three. Now you all know this song, so I expect a little help here."

When she finished, the audience cheered wildly. "Oh, thank you so much, guys, but I'm too tired to go on," she said, catching her breath. But the audience wouldn't take "no" for an answer. "Okay, one more," she consented. "Years ago, someone asked me what three things in this world made me the happiest. And I responded with sunshine, lollipops and rainbows. Today, if someone ask me that same question, my answer would be the same. And then, in nineteen-sixty-five, Leslie Gore came out with a song called just that, '*Sunshine, Lollipops and Rainbows.'* So you can guess what became my favorite song that year. And now I'd like to share three of my favorite things with some of my favorite people."

Nealy sang, giving all she had to give; she owed it to her to her audience. When she finished, they begged her to sing just one more, but she tried to refuse by screaming out. "Jillie...oh, Jillie, where are you?" she cried, putting her hand on her brow to buffer the bright lights.

"Toots, I'm doing just fine out here with the good doctor," Jillie said, sitting in Phillip's lap. "You go on. And don't mind us." Jillie wrapped her arms around him and gave him a big hug. Of course, Phillip, being such a good sport, hugged her back, playing along, which always made life more interesting.

Nealy could hear Phillip's distinctive chuckle, so she figured that he had accepted the things that he could not change: her crazy friends. "Okay, one more, but after this, Jillie, you need to tear yourself away from the *good doctor,* or I'll have you surgically removed," Nealy growled.

Jillie hollered back at her. "Damn, Nealy, you need to bring yourself back to New York. That Texas heat's making you meaner than *hell itself.*" The crowd roared with laughter again.

"Jillie hasn't changed a bit. She still has to have the last word. Have y'all noticed that?" Nealy said frankly, and then she laughed, infecting the crowd with her high-pitched giggle. "Okay, but now this is *it*. I'm going to do a medley that I arranged a long time ago, and I hope I remember all the words. But if I don't, I expect help from y'all or this *fool number one* will *rush in or out of love, go walkin' to New Orleans or Galveston*, and y'all will be nothing but *Memories*. And I'll never, as long as I live, *fall in love* with an audience *again*. So name these tunes," she challenged. As Nealy moved rhythmically into each new melody, the crowd yelled out the name of the song in unison, clapping for Nealy, the song and themselves.

As Tony watched her, he tried to figure out what he could do to get her back to New York. He couldn't let her throw away a life on the stage; she shined under the lights and gave new meaning to every word in an old song. But what could he do if she resisted? How could he make her realize that she belonged in show business?

Phillip had been completely stunned at Nealy's ability to perform, but he should have known how good she'd be. With her expressive personality and her sweet, beautiful face, she could steal the pulpit right out from under the Pope. In the meantime, Jillie had taken up permanent residency on Phillip's lap. And Tony had high hopes that Phillip would find her attractive and forget about Nealy. But that would probably never happen. Not that Phillip disliked Jillie but it was obvious that he had already fallen for the beautiful redhead on the stage.

Nealy ended with *"I'll Never Fall In Love Again,"* and she called Jillie back up to the stage to finish the set. The two of them did one last number together to appease the audience. They liked to do Southern numbers and had a particular interest in songs by the Southern boy, Johnny Horton, so they sang *"North To Alaska"* encouraging everyone to join in and really sing their hearts out.

The crowd gave them a standing ovation, and Nealy bowed three times before she left the stage and took her place back in the audience beside Phillip.

"Nealy, you were terrific," Phillip praised.

"Thanks, but I'm really out of touch with performing. I'm a dance teacher now, not a singer."

"Nealy," Tony snapped, "you're still a great singer and we've got to talk." He got up, took her arm, and pulled her up from the chair.

"Tony, where are we going?" she cried. "Phillip, I'm sorry, I'll be right back." Phillip watched her as Tony maneuvered her through the crowd. She looked back at him a couple of times, shrugging her shoulders so that he would understand that she didn't really want to go. He knew her relationship with Tony had been one of devoted friendship and respect because he had helped her find work when no one else would. Phillip and Nealy had talked at length about her friends, both male and female, and never once did she indicate that she felt more for Tony than friendship. From the looks of things, though, Tony wanted more from Nealy than friendship. Phillip didn't blame him because he felt the same way, so this could be a case of *may-the-best-man-win*.

Tony pushed open the door to Freddy's office and pulled her inside. "Freddy, help me convince Nealy that she needs to come back to New York. Tell her she can work here again."

"Well, sure, doll, you'll always have a job here. I told you that when you left," Freddy said, chewing harder on his cigar, his fat face jiggling.

"Thanks, Freddy, I really appreciate the offer. And I may need to take you up on it someday, but not now." Nealy smiled sweetly at Freddy and turned to address Tony. "Tony, you're one of my best friends, and so I know that you'll understand why I can't just pick up and move back here right now. Maybe someday I will, but for now, I'm obligated to my studio and my students. I have to end one life before I can begin a new one, she said very seriously." After hugging Tony and kissing him on the cheek, she walked behind the desk and leaned down to hug Freddy.

"Thanks, doll. And just remember, Freddy always has a place for you."

"Thanks, especially for the party and the opportunity to do what I love to do. For whatever it's worth, I feel like a new person with a healthier attitude after tonight. So, I'm grateful to both of you. And I love you both," she said smiling at them. "I'd better get back to the gang or they'll send a search party. Oh, great, another party!" she squealed, giggling and doing a little side step out of the office.

When she returned to the table, Denise had Phillip out on the dance floor. Nealy appreciated her keeping Phillip company while she returned to entertaining for an evening. Someday Phillip Pepper would make some lucky lady very happy. He had so much to offer, and he liked to give, instead of take. The thought of his being with someone else bothered her more than she wanted to admit, yet Nealy knew that she didn't have any rights at all to Phillip because she had a husband, at least for now. The thought of going home made her sad. If only she could stay in New York and start over. But Jerrod would show up, same as he had before, and screw up her life again. Jerrod was the last person that she wanted to think about, so she decided to take advantage of her freedom and avoid the reality of her life. Since the entire day had been perfect, Nealy didn't want to spoil it with the miseries of the past. For the rest of the night, she intended to pretend that this was the first day of the rest of her life.

The smoke in the room burned Nealy's eyes since she wasn't used to it anymore. Jillie had taken a break, and the jukebox played loudly throughout the club. Nealy sat down, took a deep breath, and then a drink of water. She could feel the perspiration running down her back; even her scalp felt sweaty.

"Tony seemed angry. Are you in trouble?" Phillip asked, sitting down beside

Nealy.

"No, that's just Tony's way," she replied.

"Did you guys have fun?" she asked Denise who sat down on the other side of her.

"Yes, but I had to drag him out on the dance floor. He says he doesn't really like to dance," Denise said, shaking her head.

Nealy looked at him strangely because she remembered the wonderful night that she and Phillip had spent at the Rainbow Room dancing almost non-stop for two hours. "Are you tired?" Nealy asked him. "It's eleven-thirty, and tomorrow *is* a work day for you."

"Well, I moved my appointments around again, so I don't have to be at the office tomorrow morning until ten."

"Oh, good, then I won't worry about you," she smiled.

"You would worry about me?" he asked, putting his hand over hers and squeezing it. "I like that," he said, winking at her.

"I'm burning up in here," Nealy complained. "I'm going out and get a little fresh air." She stood up and noticed a cute guy sitting at a table behind them who had Denise engaged in what appeared to be a very deep conversation. Nealy tapped her on the shoulder and smiled an approving smile when she cut her eyes over at the guy. When she turned around, she caught Phillip staring at her. "What's the matter?"

"Nothing," he smiled sweetly. "Do you mind if I join you?"

"I'd be hurt if you didn't," Nealy said, pulling him towards the bright orange *EXIT* sign over the door. "Oh, my goodness, it's so nice out here. I haven't been in a nightclub since I left here over three and a half years ago. And I'm not used to the noise or the smoky environment anymore."

"I'm not much of a nightclub person either, but I'd be here every night if you were singing."

"I'll take that as a compliment, Dr. Pepper," she shivered, wrapping her arms around her body.

"Oh, Nealy, you're cold. Here, wear my coat," he said, pulling off his jacket and putting it over her shoulders as they walked up the street in front of the club.

"Thanks. Phillip, why did you tell Denise that you don't like to dance? We danced for hours at The Rainbow Room. And I got the impression that you really liked it."

"Well, I do, but only with redheads," he said, putting his arm around her shoulders and pulling her close to him.

"Oh, I see." Nealy looked up at him and grinned. "Phillip, you're going to freeze. Maybe we should go back, even though I'd rather not. Don't get me wrong, I love Freddy and my friends, but I'm just not in the mood for all of this right now."

"I know, Nealy, things will be that way for awhile," he said, turning her back around towards Freddy's. "Why don't I give you a ride home. I think you've had enough excitement for one night."

"Uh-oh, the *doctor's* coming out in you."

"I know. It's a professional pitfall. I'm a little concerned about Tony. If we leave now it could upset him even more," Phillip said seriously.

"Why?" she asked, uncertain about his implications.

"He likes you, Nealy. And in my professional opinion, I'm pretty sure that he's in love with you."

"Tony Rose?"

"Yes, *Tony Rose,*" he mimicked her tone.

"Tony and I have been friends for a long time, and there's never been anything romantic between the two of us," Nealy defended.

"Remember what I told you the other night about there being a lot of guys out there who would come forward once you severed your relationship with Jerrod?"

"I remember. But not Tony."

"Yes, Nealy, it's obvious."

"Are you sure?"

"I'm real sure. The way he watches you and hangs on every word is pretty hard to miss. I know, because I do it too," he admitted rather timidly.

"Oh, Phillip, I've never noticed either of you doing that," she said, blushing.

He stopped near the railing at the top of the stairs that led to Freddy's and took Nealy's shoulders and gently turned her to face him. "Nealy, that's because you don't see yourself the way other people see you. You think you're just the average girl next door. And that unassuming nature is what makes you so desirable. The fact that you're just as beautiful on the inside as you are on the outside is rare in women today. All men want someone like you."

"But you don't really know me. I can be a bitch, just like anyone else," she said, trying to overturn his case.

"Nealy, I'm sure you get angry sometimes, everybody does, but a bitch, no," he shook his head side to side.

"Phillip, I can be," she said, shaking her up head and down. "I'm vain, snobbish—remember the Dr. Pepper truck?—opinionated, selfish, prejudiced, and even ego driven to the point of being pushy."

"Hmm, a real complex personality."

"I'm not the angel you think I am."

"Well, okay, answer this for me. And I want an honest answer."

"Okay. Ask me. You'll see," she smiled smugly.

"When you were growing up, did you treat the rich kids in your class any different from the poor ones?"

Nealy thought for a minute and she laughed. "What does that have to do with anything?" Her teeth chattered from being so cold.

"The answer is no, and we both know it. In fact, you probably went out of your way to be nice to the poor ones. Come on, admit it," he urged, smiling at her.

"Well, they needed someone to be nice to them."

"Nealy, this is what makes you so special. That's why people are attracted to you. You wouldn't treat the mechanic that works on your car any different than you would treat the President of the United States," he said, in an effort to make his point. "I'm sure you have your faults, but for the most part, you're an angel." Phillip hugged her, feeling the warmth generate by two bodies coming together. "Now that we're half frozen to death, maybe we should go inside, gather your belongings, and then I'll drive you home."

"I'm ready," she snapped.

They walked down the steps and entered the bar. Nealy spotted Tony and Denise and three of their friends sitting at the bar talking to Frank, the bartender. She and Phillip approached them, still trembling. "Hi, guys, what's happening?" she asked.

"Where did you go?" Tony asked her.

"We took a walk. I got so hot on stage that I needed a little fresh air," she answered, smiling at Tony.

"Well, did you cool off?" he asked in a miffed tone.

Ignoring his aloofness, she answered politely, "Yes, but now I'm cold." Nealy shivered.

"The doctor should be the one that's cold. You took his coat," Tony barked, unable to hide his discontentment.

"Oh, Phillip, I'm sorry, I forgot I had it," she apologized, pulling off the coat. "Tony, that's what I love about you, you're so observant." Nealy hugged him and ran off to gather up her things.

Phillip sat down on the barstool next to Tony in an attempt to change his attitude. "Tony, I'm a pretty direct guy, so I'll get right to the point. Nealy's a great lady, and I know that you like her a lot, which is perfectly understandable. She's crazy about you, and your friendship is very important to her, especially now. She's been through a lot, Tony, and she needs the support of her friends. There will be plenty of time for you to explore your feelings when she puts her life back together. But, Tony, if you're expecting more than friendship from her right now, you're going to be very disappointed. Nealy isn't ready. She's having a hard enough time loving herself because of what happened with Jerrod...and the miscarriage—"

"Nealy had a miscarriage?" Tony interrupted.

"Yes, and I'm sure she won't mind my telling you this since you two are close. It will also help you to help her through this. Anyway, that's how I came to know her. The doctor that suggested she get away and rest is a very close friend of mine. He called and asked me to see after her because she had just been through some very serious surgery."

"Oh, my God, she didn't tell me," he said sorrowfully.

"She would have, but it's still hard for her to talk about."

"Well, I guess so," Tony sighed.

"Tony, I read people for a living and I could tell that you were a little concerned about our relationship. Nealy's crazy about you, and I know that you want the best for her. When I met her, I really planned on touching base with her every few days in case she wanted to talk. But, after I got to know her, I genuinely liked her, and now I think we've become good friends. I only have her best interest at heart, and I want her to work through her problems. So, for now, try to love her a little less and help her a lot more. I think you'll be happy with the results," Phillip said, patting him on the back and getting up to go and find Nealy.

Tony turned around, "Hey, Phillip," he called out, "Thanks, buddy." Tony smiled at him, and Phillip smiled back.

Nealy ran into Denise in the ladies' room, and they talked for a while about her plans for the rest of the week. Denise had to start rehearsal and wouldn't have any free time to visit with her before she went home, but Nealy planned on catching her in her last performance in *"Grease"* on Saturday night. Denise promised to get her two tickets in case Phillip wanted to come with her. Even if he didn't know it yet, Denise could see that the guy had a serious case of the *likes* for Nealy.

"Phillip's giving me a ride home. Get your coat and we'll drop you off," Nealy suggested.

"Thanks, Nealy, but I'm going to stay for a while. Dan, the guy I've been talking to, is a lawyer at Bitner, Barneich, and Fluke. I met him last year on a blind date, but we didn't hit it off too well, so maybe I'll try again. He said he would take me home whenever I got ready."

"Oh, Denise, this could be love," she teased.

"Well, I don't know about love, but he's worth another try. I'll let you know. I'll call you tomorrow." Denise hugged her, and they vacated the restroom in search of their male companions.

Phillip waited for Nealy at the door while she told everyone good-bye. He watched as Tony put his arms around her and held her close for what he thought was much longer than necessary. Even though he didn't like it, he understood because he knew how much he cared about her.

As she wiggled through the crowd, she smiled at him and he smiled back. "Are you alright?"

"Yes, I'm fine," she answered, allowing him to help her with her coat. "I've really missed my friends here."

"They've missed you, too. Maybe you should come back more often, or maybe even permanently."

"I just might do that, Doctor. See that's another one of my faults: I'm whishy-washy and unpredictable," she said, cutting her eyes up at him and grinning.

CHAPTER THIRTY-ONE

PHILLIP DROVE NEALY to the apartment, but let her out at the door. He wanted to go in, but he had promised his restaurant manager at Peppee's Pizza that he would stop by after he dropped Nealy off; they had some details to go over about expanding the main dining room, and the contractors were due to start the next morning. He would have taken Nealy with him, but she seemed tired, and it was already after midnight. Nealy waved when she reached the door, and Phillip waved back.

At the door of the apartment, Nealy put the key in the lock, but before she could turn it, the door flew open, scaring her half to death. "Oh my *God!*" she cried, her hands clutched against her chest.

"Where have you been?" Jerrod snapped angrily, grabbing her arm just below her shoulder and yanking her inside.

"Jerrod, you're hurting my arm."

"I thought you came here to recuperate," he shouted. "It looks to me like you're out whoring around!"

"Jerrod, let go of me," she said, struggling with him.

"Not until you tell me where you were. It's almost twelve-thirty."

"I went to dinner with Denise, and then we went to Freddy's. Now, let go of me!" she yelled, finally freeing herself.

"Oh, I'm sure."

"I don't care if you believe me or not. And just what are *you* doing here?" she asked, glaring at him.

"I came to take you home."

"I want you to leave," she said, walking towards the bedroom.

He followed her. "I'm taking you back, Nealy. I have tickets for us to leave here at six-fifteen in the morning. And whether you like it or not, we're going to be on that plane."

Nealy took off her coat, laid it on the bed, and then turned to face him. "I'm not going anywhere with you, Jerrod. I'm sorry, but you wasted your time coming here."

"No, you're leaving with me in the morning, and that's that!" he shouted.

"You're leaving here in the morning. I'm leaving here on Sunday as I originally planned. You can sleep in your aunt's bedroom."

"I'm taking you home tomorrow if I have to drag you to the airport. I told you that I was sorry. We can work this out."

"No we can't! Does the name *Prissy Sissy* mean anything to you?" she asked, her face turning red with anger.

"Who told you about Sissy?"

"That's none of your business. You made a first-class fool out of me," she sneered. "But I can promise you one thing, I'll never let you do it to me again. You can sleep in your aunt's bedroom," Nealy brushed past him and walked into the bathroom, slamming the door behind her.

Jerrod stood there fuming with anger for a moment, and then he walked down the hall to the bathroom and opened the door. "In case you've forgotten, I'm still your husband. I'm not sleeping in my aunt's bedroom. Whether you like it or not, I'm sleeping with you. And *yes we are* going to work this out."

"No, not this time. I'm tired of solving all our problems with a *good roll in the hay*. That won't work anymore, Jerrod," she said facing the mirror and staring at him out of the corner of her eye.

Jerrod grabbed her arm, pulled her out of the bathroom, and attempted to drag her down the hallway as she fought against him. "Let go of my arm, dammit."

"Shut-up, Nealy," he said loudly, dragging her towards the bedroom. "I'm tired of this crap." He pushed her down on the bed and fell on top of her, trying to force her to kiss him.

"Get off of me!" she screamed, pushing him and turning her face from side to side to avoid his kisses.

"Nealy, stop fighting me. I know you want me."

"No...I...don't! Now get off me," she struggled furiously.

He held her arms above her head and tried to force his tongue in her mouth. When she turned away from him, he took both of her wrist with one hand and started to unbuckle his pants.

Taking the opportunity, she pulled her foot up and kicked him in the groin as hard as she could.

Immediately, he doubled up, "You bitch!" Then he dropped to the floor on his knees.

Nealy jumped up and ran out of the bedroom and down the hallway to the front door. She snatched her purse off the table and opened the door at the same time. When she reached the elevator, she proceeded to push the button over and over while she mumbled quietly to herself. "Oh, please, elevator, hurry," she begged, putting the strap to her purse over her shoulder.

Finally, the door opened and she got in, pushing the button several times to close the door. Her heart pounded as if it were about to jump out of her chest. "Please, close, please," she cried. Just as the doors started to close, Jerrod opened the apartment door. He quickly crossed the hall, grabbing for the elevator door, but it closed, almost catching his fingers. Nealy was trembling and when the door opened on the first floor, she cried out to the doorman who was sitting behind his desk and reading a book, "I'll be back." She ran by him, pushed the button to release the doors, and ran out into the night.

The doorman jumped up and ran over to the doors. "But, Ms. Nealy, you don't have on a coat. It's very cold outside," he called out, but she had already crossed the street. Without even thinking about where she was going, she ran to the corner of Seventy-second Street and made a right. Before she realized it, she was on Amsterdam Avenue running as fast as she could towards Peppee's Pizza. When she reached the restaurant, she flung open the door and ran inside. Panicked and out of breath, she called out to the bartender who was at the other end of the bar talking to two guys, "Is Phillip still here?"

"Uh, yeah, I'll get him," he said, aware of the urgency in her voice. Quickly, he ran to the back of the restaurant and returned seconds later with Phillip.

"Nealy," he said, rushing over to her. "What's wrong?"

Nealy, who appeared almost hysterical, tried to tell him. "Jerrod...he—"

"Come on," he said, guiding her back to his office. When they walked into his office, Phillip asked Antonio to excuse them for a minute, which he kindly did, closing the door behind him. Nealy sat down on the chair, shaking uncontrollably. Phillip took off his coat and wrapped it around her shoulders. He knelt down in front of her and held her hands. "Nealy, what happened? Was Jerrod at the apartment?"

"Yes," she cried. "When I got to the door, he opened it and pulled me inside. He started yelling at me, and we got into an argument. He said that he had come to take me home and that we were leaving in the morning. I told him that I wasn't going anywhere. Well, then one thing led to another, and he pushed me down on the bed and...he...he—"

"Nealy, he didn't—"

"No, but he was going to...but I kicked him. When he fell down, I ran out of the apartment. I don't know what made me run here. I just started running," she said, sobbing.

"Oh, sweetheart, I'm sorry. I should have gone up with you," he said, pulling her into his arms. "This guy is really sick. I need to talk to Antonio for a minute. Will you be alright?"

"Yes, I'm fine. I'm sorry I interrupted your meeting," she said, wiping her face with his handkerchief.

"You didn't interrupt. We were finished. I just need to tell him a couple of things, and then I'll take you to my place. I'll be right back," he said, slowly standing up. Phillip talked to Antonio for no more than two minutes, and then he returned for her. "Come on. My car's in the back," he said sweetly, taking her hand and leading her out the door.

Phillip drove them over to his apartment that was about twenty minutes away. Nealy didn't say too much, and he didn't encourage her to talk, in fact, he told her to relax and to take some very deep breaths.

By the time they reached his apartment, it was after one o'clock, and Nealy had calmed down dramatically. She even smiled at him when he opened the car door for her. "Thanks," she said, stepping out of the car.

"You're welcome," he said, winking affectionately.

Phillip put his key in the outside door that opened into a long hallway. They walked down the hall and took the elevator up to the fifth floor and got off. There were only five doors about twenty-five feet apart and Phillip had the one on the north end. When he opened the door and turned on the light, Nealy couldn't believe her eyes. The apartment had contemporary furnishings of black, white and chrome. The ceilings were two stories high, and he had a library in a loft above the living room. "Phillip, this is fabulous," she said, praising his good taste.

"Thank you," he smiled, glad that she approved. "You want something to drink?"

"Water, please."

Phillip went to the kitchen, and Nealy looked around the room, admiring all of his paintings. It was obvious that he liked contemporary art because he had four large, expensive pieces. Nealy liked them, but they looked as if someone had dribbled every imaginable color-concoction onto a large white canvas and then smeared them together. Of course, she had no idea who had painted them because she didn't know much about contemporary pieces or the artists. Who knows, maybe one of his crazy patients had painted them for him out of frustration or as some sort of therapy. Perhaps, if she decided to paint a picture it would look like that and she could call it *Fool's Brush*.

"You like Leroy Neiman?"

"Who?"

"The paintings," he said, pointing at the paintings on the walls. "They are part of Leroy Neiman's collection."

"If this Leroy person collects them, then why do you have his paintings hanging on your walls?" she asked seriously. Nealy held this dumb expression on her face; she couldn't wait to hear how he would delicately tell her that she was an idiot.

"Nealy...uh...a collection means—"

"Got cha!" she giggled wildly. "That's your payback for that incident with that damn Dr. Pepper truck."

"I guess I deserved that," he chuckled.

"You certainly did. Just so you won't think that I'm a real country bumpkin, I am familiar with Leroy Neiman. But, I'll admit, I didn't recognize these as his because, to be perfectly honest, I've never seen one up close and personal before," she giggled.

He walked over and kissed her on the cheek. "Sweetheart, I could never, not even for one moment, think that you are in any way a country bumpkin," he smiled. "Here's your water—except it's not water, it's wine. It'll help you sleep," he handed her the glass of white wine.

"Thanks." Nealy smiled at him and took a sip. "Phillip, don't let me keep you up. I know you have to go to work tomorrow. I feel terrible intruding on you like this."

"You're not intruding. In fact, I'm sending Jerrod a thank you note."

Nealy giggled. "Come on, *Peppee*, show me around. And then I want you to go to bed and get some sleep."

"I'll show you around. I'll consider your second request. And I'll even let you call me *Peppee*, but only because you're so cute and I happen to really like you," he said happily. "Follow me." He took her on a tour of his eight room apartment. From his dining room, which had a smoked glass table that easily seated ten people, the view of the city was awesome. His master bedroom had a split level plan where the bed was on one level, with two steps down to the sitting area, and then another level off to the side that went up three steps to his bathroom, closet, and exercise facility. For anyone that is unfamiliar with this layout, searching for the bathroom in the dark in the middle of the night could be hazardous to one's health. The kitchen and the service quarters were at the opposite end from Phillip's bedroom, and he had two guest bedrooms up the stairs next to the loft that opened up to the floor below. Also, he had a wine cellar, a separate study, and five bathrooms. Damn, this place must have cost a small fortune, she thought as she followed him around the house.

"Well, that's it. Just a little bachelor pad," he sighed.

"Right, Peppee," she said, giggling. "This place is big enough for you and three other bachelors. You must have some really neurotic patients with gobs of money or great insurance policies, Doctor."

Phillip shrugged his shoulders and looked around the enormous living room where three white leather couches formed a semi-circle in the center of the room. And then he studied the shiny-black baby-grand piano in the corner of the room before he turned to look at her again. "You're absolutely right, Mrs. Jones—no, I think I'll call you Ms. James, as your other friends do," he smiled.

"I'd prefer that you did, too," she agreed. "After tonight, that other name is short lived." Nealy looked away from him and stared out the solid wall of glass that exposed a sea of shimmering lights as far as she could see.

"Come on, let's get you to bed," Phillip said, taking her hand and leading her up the stairs and into the bedroom. "Oh, let me get you a shirt to sleep in, unless you prefer to sleep in the buff."

"No, a shirt, thanks." Nealy grinned at him and her face turned red as if she knew what he was thinking.

After staring at her very devilishly for a moment, Phillip took a deep breath, ran his hands through his dark-blonde curls, and exhaled. He turned and started down the stairs, but then he stopped and turned around looking very puzzled. "What was I going after?"

She giggled. "The shirt."

"Oh, yeah, the shirt. Are you sure you didn't say, *'in the buff?'* " he asked, chuckling to himself smugly. "I guess not," he said, heading down the steps.

Nealy sat down on the bed and rolled her neck around, trying to loosen the tension. Phillip was on his way back upstairs when the telephone rang. He walked into the room and answered it as he handed the shirt to her.

"Hello."

"Dr. Pepper, this is your service. I have an urgent message for you to call Denise Pratt at 662-3327."

"Thank you." He hung up.

"Nealy, that was a call from Denise. Do you want to call her?" he asked, handing the phone to Nealy.

"Thanks," she replied. "Now what has Jerrod done?" Nealy dialed Denise's number, and Phillip sat down on the bed beside her just in case there was another problem.

"Denise, this is—"

"You're alright, thank God," Denise said, cutting her off.

"I'm okay, a little shook up maybe. But I'm fine now, I'm with Phillip." Nealy reached over and held Phillip's hand.

"Nealy, Jerrod's nuts. He ranted and raved. He cursed me, cursed you, cursed God, and—"

"I'm so sorry, Denise. And you're right. He is nuts. He has some real problems. Last year, I had this self-defense instructor teach a few classes, and if it hadn't of been for that karate kick that I swore I could never do, I don't know what would have happened to me." The thought terrified her so much that her lip quivered and tears trickled down her cheeks.

Phillip moved closer to her and put his arm around her. "It's okay. You're safe now," he whispered, taking the phone from her.

"Denise, hi."

"Hi, Phillip. Thanks for rescuing her."

"I'm just glad that she knew where to find me. Oh, Lord, I shudder to think...well, I can't think about that.... Listen, maybe you should call him back and tell him that she went to a hotel. That way he won't come over to your place."

"Good idea."

"If you need me—you have a pen?"

"Okay. Go ahead."

"465-9995. Thanks, Denise. Call if you need anything. Nealy will call you tomorrow."

"Good-night," Denise said, relieved to know that she was safe.

"Yeah, good-night." He hung up the phone and took Nealy into his arms. "It's okay, sweetheart."

"My friends are going to hate me. They are either babysitting me, while I'm blubbering all over myself in some mass hysteria, or covering for me," she said sadly, putting her face in her hands and then sweeping back the long layers of reddish hair.

"No they won't. You'd do it for them," he smiled, giving her a sweet hug and a quick kiss on the forehead. "Now, put this shirt on and get in bed. You need some rest. I'm going to let you sleep in the morning, so make yourself at home when you wake up."

"He'll go home in the morning, hopefully. He said he had tickets, so I'm going to pray that uses them."

"Nealy, don't go over there by yourself. I'll be through at three o'clock and I'll take you."

"Thank goodness, I thought to grab my purse. At least, I have a toothbrush, a hairbrush, and a little make-up. Phillip, I'm so glad you were at your restaurant. I can't imagine what would have happened to me out there running around the streets of New York in the middle of the night."

"I'm glad I was there, too," he said, hugging her. "I really like your being here, even if it is in the guest bedroom. Good-night," he said softly, closing the door.

"Good-night." Nealy took a shower, put on his big shirt that hit her in the middle of the thigh, and climbed into the soft, comfortable bed. She felt strange being in his house and in his bed—well, not actually *his* bed. "Thank you *God* for Phillip Pepper and all my friends that have put up with me," she whispered and closed her eyes even though she knew that she couldn't go to sleep. Why did Jerrod have to show up? Nealy had just reached a point where she didn't cry every single time she thought about him and what he had done. What would happen if she went over there on Friday, and he was waiting for her again? Would he react the same way? Now she was afraid to face him for fear of what he might do to her.

Nealy dosed off at three o'clock, only to wake up screaming at four, sweating and crying. "No! Let go of me! Jerrod, don't do this!" she screamed.

Phillip came running up the stairs. "Nealy, it's only a dream," he said, pulling her up into his arms. He held her while she wept. "Sweetheart, you're safe now. Please don't cry. I promise, I'll never let anyone hurt you," he said. He leaned back against the pillows and pulled her up next to him, allowing her head to rest on his bare chest. Nealy fell asleep, and he held her tightly against his body for the rest of the night.

Phillip opened his eyes and looked at the clock, which read nine o'clock. He smiled when he looked at Nealy still fast asleep. This scene came straight out of his fantasy where he awoke and found her snuggling up to his warm body, her arms wrapped tightly around his neck. Of course in his fantasy, she didn't have on his shirt, but he could use his imagination for that part. But, if he didn't get up quick, he probably wouldn't need his imagination. He slipped out from underneath her, covered her back up and eased out of the room.

Thirty-five minutes later, after showering and dressing for work, he quietly walked back up the stairs to check on her before he left. He opened the door and found her still sleeping. He smiled at how pretty and peaceful she looked, just like an angel. How this creep could put her through so much was more than he could imagine. And he sure hoped that she wouldn't go back there until he could go with her. The minute he got to his office, he would call Rob Morris and have him check on Jerrod's schedule. At least that would give him an idea of whether or not Jerrod would remain in New York.

In talking to Rob, Phillip found out that Jerrod was not due back at the hospital until Saturday, which meant that he might still be in New York. So he called his house to make sure that Nealy had not gone back to the apartment. And much to his relief, on the third ring a very sleepy young lady answered.

"Hello," she whispered.

"I woke you. I'm sorry. I'll let you go back to sleep. Call me when you wake up," he said softly.

"No, Phillip, don't go."

"Are you okay?"

"I guess so. I...I'm so tired," she said, sounding exhausted.

"Sweetheart, go back to sleep. You're perfectly safe there. And I promise, I'll call you back in an hour."

"You promise?"

"I promise. Sweet dreams," he said. When he hung up the phone he felt guilty for having left her there alone because she had sounded so frightened.

Denise telephoned Phillip's office during a break from rehearsals to check on Nealy. When she reached him, she spent thirty minutes filling him in on some of the less than glamorous details that Nealy had not told him about Jerrod Jones. Denise didn't hold back; in fact, she told him every last ugly detail because she wanted him to keep Nealy away from that crazy bastard. With that information, Phillip planned to get Nealy out of town, if she would go, that is. But, he promised Denise that they would see her after the play on Saturday night.

After he hung up, he became even more concerned about her going back over to the apartment alone. He buzzed his secretary and asked her to cancel his afternoon appointments, making his apologies with a free session for his two o'clock, a CPA that he had been treating for several years.

On his way out the door, he stopped suddenly, "Oh, and one more thing. Could you call the Homestead Inn in Greenwich and make me a reservation for two rooms for tonight. If you don't have the number, I have it in my Rolodex. Thanks, Eve."

"Canceling your appointments. The Homestead Inn. She must be pretty special," she grinned.

"Very special," he smiled. "See you Monday." He closed the door and hurried to his car. He wanted to get home before she woke up. Knowing Nealy, she will feel like a burden and try to handle this herself. The traffic in New York City on Friday at straight-up noon was testing the patience of a trained psychiatrist who held clinics on stress management. But, on this particular day, he needed to get home, so therefore, he wasn't effectively dealing with the situation. The snow had started to fall again, and it was cold and damp. Horns honked more and more as drivers fought their way through the slow moving traffic; the easy-going Dr. Pepper found himself honking as well. Even though he lived only fifteen minutes away from his office, he drove his car most of the time because he often had meetings that required transportation. But today he wished he were walking; no doubt he could get home a lot sooner.

It took him forty long minutes to get home. He pulled into the parking garage and rushed upstairs, praying that she hadn't left. "Nealy," he called out, climbing the stairs two at a time. He knocked on her bedroom door, but he didn't get an answer. Carefully pushing it open, he called out again, "Nealy." Then he heard the shower in the bathroom, and he sighed with great relief. But he wanted to make sure, so he walked to the bathroom door and knocked, calling out to her again and pushing the door open just enough to talk. "Honey, I'm home!" he teased, chuckling out loud.

Nealy laughed her giggly, zany laugh, sounding as if the extra sleep had been just what the doctor ordered to put a smile back on her sweet face. "Well, if it isn't my favorite pizza man," she said, sticking her head out of the shower. "I'd ask you to join me, but I'm not decent."

"By my standards of decency, I'll bet your more than decent. So, does that mean I can join you?" he teased.

"No!" she squealed, "I'm kidding." Nealy giggled and Phillip left her to finish her shower in peace. "Oh, thank *God*," he sighed, feeling that a heavy burden had just been lifted off his chest. All the way home, he wished that he had called her back to tell her that Jerrod may still be in town, but he didn't want to wake her. She had been under such stress lately that he really wanted her to rest in the comforts of his own home.

While he waited on her to get out of the shower, he changed into more comfortable clothes for the trip to Connecticut and took out an extra change of clothes to wear back on Saturday. Taking Nealy to the Homestead Inn would be more enjoyable than the time he went alone, the day after his divorce; he needed to get away and wound up in there. He knew that the peacefulness of the country would be good therapy for her. The weather conditions were not good for driving, but the snow would make it look like a winter wonderland. It was only a light snowfall, and the Inn was only an hour away from the City. Even if they stopped at Macy's to pick up some clothes for Nealy, they could still be there before dark.

Phillip called Eve to confirm their reservations. Eve had even taken the liberty of reserving a suite with two bedrooms and a fireplace so that they could kick back and relax in front of the fire. Now, he couldn't wait to tell Nealy. He hoped that she wouldn't have a problem going away with him, just as friends of course.

Nealy stuck her head in his bedroom. Piled up on her head, she had wrapped a towel turban-style around her wet hair. "Hi," she said sweetly, "can I come in?"

"You're welcome in my bedroom anytime," he said, smiling at her as she stood in the doorway still wearing his shirt.

"I'm not very presentable, but my clothes had mud stuck to them from running in that slush last night. I need to go over to the apartment and get me some more clothes."

"Uh, speaking of the apartment," he said, taking her hand and guiding her toward the couch in his bedroom. "I called Rob Morris this morning, and Jerrod isn't due back at the hospital until Saturday evening at six. So, Nealy, it's probably not a good idea to go back there tonight. Besides, I have a better plan—"

"But, Phillip, I have no clothes. I can't go out in your shirt. I have no coat. I can't roll my hair," she interrupted, sounding desperate.

"Well, I thought about that, so I made plans to take you to an Inn in Connecticut where you can relax and we won't have to dress up. On our way out of town, we will stop at Macy's and pick you up some comfortable clothes and whatever else you might need, like lacy girl things. It's only one night in the country at a quaint little Inn. We'll come back tomorrow afternoon when the coast is clear so that we can make the play. Nealy, please do this for your favorite pizza man," he begged. "You'll love the Homestead Inn, I promise. It's strictly friend with friend enjoying a little *much needed* leisure time. You can trust me. I was a very trustworthy scout."

"You're impossible to refuse. Okay, but answer me just one question, Doctor. What do I wear to Macy's? The clothes I wore over here are wrinkled and wet."

"Your birthday suit, and my overcoat," he smiled.

"Very funny, *Peppee*, but I don't think so."

He got up from the couch and went into his closet, bringing out an old jogging suit that he claimed shrunk when he washed it. "How about this and my overcoat. You have your boots. And we'll get you some sneakers at Macy's."

"Phillip, are you adopting me?"

"Can I?" he asked dryly, but then he chuckled.

"I love your laugh. You sound like a toy machine gun. Sorry for that comparison, but I can't really describe it. Anyway, it's cute," she smiled.

"No, *you're* cute," he said, admiring her reflection in the mirror.

Taking a good look at herself, she sighed, "Oh, yeah, sure. If only you were a plastic surgeon, you could do something about these bags under my eyes and all this puffy skin. Are you sure you won't be too embarrassed to be seen with me?"

"I could never be embarrassed to be seen with you. Not even if you were covered in tar and feathered."

"In my present state, Doctor, that would be an improvement," she stated. "But right now, I need to dry my hair. And after I do, I may have to wear it in a ponytail because I'll look like a *bushman*. And, at that point, you may change your mind about dragging me through Macy's."

"If it's really that bad, I'll get two grocery sacks: one for you, and one for me in case yours falls off," he teased playfully.

"Now that's tacky," she said, giving him a injured look.

Gently, he took her hand and pulled her into his arms, giving her a hug. "I'm kidding you," he said, lifting her chin up. "Ms. James, you could never, in a million years, embarrass me. No matter what you look like, *I think you're the most beautiful woman on the face of God's green earth.*"

Moved by the sincerity in his voice and his face, she had tears in her eyes. "Phillip, that's so sweet."

"Connecticut's waiting," he said, in an effort to change the subject and stop himself from kissing her. "Go get ready...I'll get the grocery bags," he chuckled wildly.

"Phillip!" she screamed, sticking her tongue out at him on her way out of the bedroom.

CHAPTER-THIRTY-TWO

AT THREE-THIRTY, almost two hours after they left Phillip's apartment, they were en route for Connecticut. Nealy had picked up two jogging suits, at Phillip's insistence, some shoes, and those lacy girl things that he had even helped her select. That was the first time that any man had ever been with her when she bought lingerie. If it had been anyone else, she would have been embarrassed, but they actually had a great time. He did say on a couple of occasions that she had to model everything that she bought, and she surprised him with, "You never know. I'm very unpredictable, remember?"

Phillip picked out a white London Fog all-weather coat that he insisted on buying for her, and he refused to leave the store without it. Even though she did try to talk him out of it because it cost too much, she had to admit that she loved it. On her way out of the coat department, Nealy stopped to marvel at a long, winter-white two-piece suit with a fabulous white fur collar that was displayed on a red-headed manikin. "Oh, Phillip, isn't this gorgeous," she exclaimed, oohing and aahing.

"And it would be even more gorgeous on you instead of that ugly stiff."

Nealy laughed. "Poor thing could use a new wig. But this is a beautiful outfit," she said, barely touching the fur collar with the back of her hand.

"You want it?" he asked, as an offer to buy it.

"Now where would I wear that?"

"We'd find somewhere. Let's get it."

Nealy pulled him by the arm. "Come on. I need some curlers so that I can do something with this mop on my head or you'll find some pet name for me."

They made their way through the store over to the appliance department and purchased a travel curler set. Even shopping was fun with Phillip. But now Nealy wanted to get to the Inn and relax. She had never been to Connecticut, so she got excited as they drove out of Manhattan, traffic and all.

The snow drifted to the ground in small airish-looking flakes, but still, the countryside was covered with a blanket of white. The further they got away from the city, the vegetation became more dense and the housing communities became less congested. Nealy felt more relaxed than she had in months, and she made Phillip promise not to mention anything about the past, in fact, she wanted to pretend that it didn't exist. All she wanted to do was enjoy the present, one precious moment at a time. They had no real plans, except to get away and that's the way she wanted it to be. She just wanted to let things happen for a change without thinking about it first; she wanted them to do whatever made them happy as if today were the first and last day of their lives. Nealy had never done that because she didn't grow up that way. Everything had a time and a place and a reason why it should or should not be done one way or the other.

The traffic had thinned out quite a bit, and they were about a half hour away from the Inn. The low clouds made it seem later than five o'clock, therefore, it would be completely dark by the time they arrived. But it would be great to eat a nice dinner and relax by the fire in their suite or in the lobby at the Inn. At Phillip's request, Nealy sang songs from her nightclub act and he even sang the ones he knew with her, which reminded her of family trips when she was young; singing kept the children from fighting about whether or not they had crossed the invisible line into each other's space.

Phillip told Nealy about his parents, sister, and brother. His father had retired a year before from his medical practice where he had spent forty years catering to a farming community in Iowa. Since his mother and father had rarely left the state, they decided to travel and see the world. Phillip didn't see them too often because they were too busy flitting around the world by land, by air, and by sea. Emily, his sister, who was thirty-two, just two years younger than Phillip, lived in Iowa as well, and she had married Phillip's best friend, who became the neighboring veterinarian. Emily and Justin had two children, three dogs, two cats, four horses, three goats and two pet pigs. Phillip said they were a regular menagerie, but a fun family to be around. And last but not least, his younger brother, Ethan, who was twenty-nine, lived in Houston, Texas, where he would finish his residency in Cardiology in June. Ethan married his lab partner in their third year of medical school. When she finished her internship, she set up a general practice in a small town outside of Chicago where she grew up. Ethan and his wife, Mary Ellen, didn't see each other very often, and Phillip didn't put a lot of faith in the longevity of the marriage, especially since Ethan planned on staying in Houston where he could work with some of the best cardiologists in the country. Mary Ellen expected him to return to Chicago to practice after he completed his residency, but that didn't seem to be Ethan's plans. Phillip said that Ethan had come to New York the week before Nealy did to talk to him about his future. Phillip agreed that *some* marriages could work long distance, but he didn't see it working for Ethan.

Welcome to Greenwich, the road sign read, as they drove into town. And within minutes, they located Field Point Road, which took them to the Inn.

Phillip got out and opened the door for Nealy. He held her hand as they made their way through the snow in the parking lot up to the main entrance.

"Hello. And welcome to the Homestead Inn," the clerk said cheerfully from behind the half door to the right of the entrance.

"Hello. I'm Phillip Pepper, and I believe that my secretary made a reservation for us for this evening."

"Yes, she sure did, Dr. Pepper," the man said, giving Phillip and Nealy a funny smile as he said Phillip's name. Nealy smiled at Phillip reassuringly, as if to say, *It's okay if you have a funny name, I like you anyway.* "We have the suite that you requested waiting for you and your pretty wife, Doctor." He looked at Nealy and then quickly turned and smiled at Phillip.

Phillip winked at Nealy and hoped that she had not been offended by the man's assumption. She smiled and graciously said, "Thank you."

"It's up the stairs and to the right," the clerk said, pointing to a stairway to their left. "Would you like us to have someone get your luggage, Doctor?"

"No, that's alright. We're only here for the night, but thanks."

"Oh," the man cried out. "I almost forgot. Here is the itinerary regarding meals and entertainment in case you're interested."

"Thanks," Phillip said kindly, taking the packet from him. They had consolidated Nealy's purchases into his suitcase so that she didn't get embarrassed by walking into the inn with her sack full of clothes.

When they opened the door to their suite, the first thing that they noticed was the huge fireplace, which had a wonderful fire flickering in the dim light of the room. "Oh, Phillip, this is lovely," Nealy exclaimed. "It's so quaint and so homey."

"I'm glad you like it. Antiques aren't really my thing, but it's nice to go back in time every so often," he said, putting the luggage in the bedroom.

"They're not mine either, but like you, I really appreciate them if the setting is right...and this setting is perfect. I'd really fit in if I had on a long dress with long sleeves and a high neck, and a Bible under my arm," she giggled.

"Nealy, you're so cute," he said, smiling at her from across the room. He had trouble breaking his stare; she was breathtaking standing by the fireplace with the fire highlighting the gold in her hair. But he had to keep the mood very friendly so that he didn't torture himself for the next twenty-four hours. Phillip promised her that this would be a purely platonic relationship for the time being, and he had to keep that promise, even though he would love to hold her in his arms and make mad, passionate love to her all night long.

"This was so nice of you. I'm really happy," she said.

"I'm glad. Are you hungry?"

"Yes, I'm starved, but I need to do something with my hair and my clothes first," she said, pulling the scarf that allowed her hair to fall down below her shoulders.

"Well, why don't you take the bathroom first. I'll read about this place while I wait."

"Okay, I'll hurry."

"Take your time. Remember, 'We are here to relax and take it one precious moment at a time.' Those are your words, not mine," he said, quoting her.

"Yes, Doctor," she smiled at him and blew him a kiss across the room for being so sweet. In fact, he deserved a lot more, and Nealy really wanted to walk over and kiss his nice lips that came to two perfectly pouty points just below his nicely shaped nose, but she didn't dare tempt herself.

Nealy walked out of the bedroom in her green velour jogging pants and white t-shirt with bright green trim. She certainly didn't look like someone that intended to go jogging, but that had been the idea when she bought it. And of course, the outfit accentuated every curve, hugging her body like a glove. If she had tried the pants on in the store and noticed how tight they were, she probably would have gone up a size to enjoy the baggy comfort that most workout wear needs. But, Phillip, like most men, would most likely appreciate the fact that the suit didn't cover up what *God* gave her to show off.

"Nealy, I like that," he said admiringly, nodding his head in approval and getting up from the chair in front of the fire.

"I thought you would. It's a little tight," she complained, pulling at the back of the pants.

"I think it fits you just right." He walked over to the door where she stood, took the jacket to her suit out of her hand, and held it open for her to slip her arms into it. "I bet you're really hungry now."

"Yes, I'm famished. Oh, thanks," she said, pulling her jacket into place.

"Last year when I ate here, the food was delicious. I hope they have the same chef. I think he's French." They walked down the stairs to the lobby and into the main dining room where only a few guests had gathered for dinner. When they walked through the doors, the hostess greeted them cheerfully and then led them to a cozy table in the corner by a large fireplace that raged in a reddish-orange blaze above smoldering ashes.

"Your waiter will be right with you," the young lady said politely.

"Thank you," Phillip replied, taking the menu from her.

"Thanks," Nealy smiled, accepting her menu.

Nealy leaned over to Phillip and said quietly, "I think people see us as a couple, you know, the lovey-dovey kind who give each other dreamy gazes and sweet little kisses," she giggled softly.

He smiled. "I think you're right."

"Yeah, and every audience deserves a good performance." And without another word, Nealy slid her arm around Phillip's neck and pulled his lips to meet hers for a brief, but very convincing kiss. "Sorry, but the actress in me made me do that," she whispered, turning to smile cunningly at the people who were staring at them.

"Splendid performance, my dear," he whispered, kissing her tenderly on the cheek.

"Thank you, darling," she said, fanning herself with her napkin and cutting her eyes around the room.

"I like playing the leading man. I can hardly wait until the next scene."

"Good, because we have a long way to go before we take our bow this evening," Nealy giggled, and her expression grew almost devilish.

"Well, Scarlett, what are you going to eat this evening? From what I've witnessed so far, I think you're going to need your strength."

"Well, I do *de-clare*, there isn't one thing on this menu that I recognize. Oh, won't you help me, Rhett?" she whined.

Phillip couldn't help chuckling as he watched her fanning herself and batting her big green eyes. He picked up her hand and kissed her finger tips seductively, one at a time, before he responded. "Only for you, my *Angel lips*," he said, in an effort to impersonate, in voice and mannerisms, his hero, the late, great, Clark Gable.

"Oh, please, tell me you didn't call me Angel lips," she said in horror.

"Bad choice, huh?"

"Yeah. Clark Gable would never say that. And besides, Scarlett was anything but an angel," she replied, shaking her head. "I'm *so* glad that you had the good sense to become a doctor." For a moment, Nealy remained very serious, but then she cracked up, making him laugh, too. "Okay, now please tell me what to order off this menu chocked full of foreignism."

"Boeuf, poulet, or fruits de mer?"

"What?" she asked quizzically.

"Do you want to eat beef, chicken or seafood?"

"Oh," she giggled. "Seafood, please."

"Nealy, this place specializes in French cuisine. That's why the menu is in French. It creates the mood. See, look around you at the decor, it's like a bistro you'd find on the streets of Paris," Phillip explained.

"Oh, I see," she said, turning to observe the room. "I'll have to take your word for it since I've never been to France, but someday I'm going. Have you been there?"

"Yes, twice."

"Is Paris *really* the most romantic city in the world?"

"I don't know, I went with a bunch of guys the first time and alone the second time," Phillip confessed. "If I'd been there with you, I think it would have been different." He stared at her, making her blush.

"Okay, back to the menu. "I think I'll have Perch Court Bouillon. It sounds so French," she said, smiling.

"It does, and I'll have Terrine de Campagne. That's a dish with pork, beef and chicken livers. It's really good."

"If you say so," she grimaced.

The waitress took their order and brought them a cup of bouillabaisse made with sturgeon flown in from France. As dinner progressed, she served them their entrees with riz pilaf(rice pilaf) and zucchini maison. They enjoyed their food and the atmosphere and, especially, each other's company.

By the time they ordered dessert, almost everyone in the restaurant had finished eating and retired to the lounge or their rooms for the evening. Nealy commented on the piano music that escaped the lounge and entertained them as well.

The waiter set the French Custard down in front of Nealy and the Pears in Red Wine down in front of Phillip. It smelled like five pounds of sugar, which could only mean the dessert would be sweet and wonderful.

"I've learned one thing from this meal," Nealy commented.

"And what's that, Angel lips?" he smiled.

Nealy frowned at him. "French people couldn't cook if it weren't for sugar and wine."

"That's very true. Almost everything is cooked with wine. It gives their food that *burst of flavor* that they love."

"I thought French Cuisine was mussels and snails, or escargots, or whatever it is that they call those disgusting little creatures. Don't you remember that *I Love Lucy* show where they all went to Paris and Lucy ordered from that French menu, which she couldn't read any better than I did here tonight? And then, when the waiter brought her that plate full of slimy snails, she became irate. Those things are gross!" Nealy said, making a terrible face, much like one of Lucille Ball's famous faces.

"I do remember that, and Nealy, if you don't mind my saying so, I've noticed a lot of similarity between you and Lucy."

"Now wait a minute," Nealy quibbled. "I've gone from the Queen of Cutesy to the Queen of Cuckoo, not that I don't adore Lucille Ball, but really, I'm not *that* bizarre. I'd never work in a chocolate factory and cram my bosoms full of bonbons."

"Oh, but, Nealy, I think you would. You can be just that funny when you want to be. Remember, I saw you on stage the other night with Jillie, an even bigger nut than you."

"Well, yeah, but the sad thing is that I always wanted to be smart and sophisticated," she said sadly.

Phillip leaned towards her with a serious look on his face. "I like you just the way you are...cute and crazy."

"Phillip Pepper, I resent that!" she cried.

He motioned for the waiter. "L'addition, s'il vous plaît!"

"Oui, Monsieur."

"You speak French? Well, I'm impressed, Doctor," she said.

Moments later the waiter returned with their bill and started to hand it to Phillip. "Merci, no elle voudrait l'addition," Phillip said to the waiter, who smiled at him and handed the bill to Nealy, which she handed right back.

"What did he say?" she said annoyed.

"He said that you wanted the bill, madame."

"Oh, he did. How do you say 'Go to—' "

"I'm kidding. Give me the check," Phillip interrupted, smiling and taking the bill from the waiter. "Maybe you *should* work on becoming more sophisticated, Nealy."

"Excuse me," she responded, trying to keep a straight face.

"Let's go into the lounge and have some cognac. That ought to mellow you somewhat," he said, smiling and pulling her chair out so that she could get up.

The waiter, who had laughed at their fun-loving attitude, had gone up to the cash register by the door. He smiled and said, "Merci. Bonne nuit, Madame, Monsieur."

"Bonne nuit," Phillip said.

"Damn, you people are irritating. I got the 'thank you,' but you either said, good-bye, good-night or get lost," Nealy said, frustrated. Phillip and the waiter laughed out loud.

"You two," he pointed to each of them, "newlyweds?"

"Not exactly," Phillip said, taking Nealy by the arm. "Now say good-night to the waiter, *sweetheart*," Phillip said, guiding her out of the restaurant and into the lounge.

"Good-night," she smiled.

They selected a table by the piano so that they could enjoy the music being played by a very talented young man. He smiled at Nealy when they sat down. Phillip ordered some cognac for both of them, and they relaxed, listening intently to the soft melodies that he played by heart. At nine-fifty-five, he asked Nealy if she had a request for his last song, so evidently he stopped playing at ten o'clock. Since he had played mostly show tunes, she asked that he play the *"Theme From A Summer Place."* Phillip watched Nealy as her eyes danced with each note that he played. When he finished, all six people in the room applauded and the room grew very quiet when he left.

"I have an idea," Phillip said, smiling at her. "I'll be right back." He got up and walked over to the bar and talked quietly for a moment with the bartender. When he returned, he had that mischievous little grin on his face that he always had when he was up to something. "If you do one thing for me, I'll do whatever you want me to do, without any regrets or hesitation, for the rest of the trip."

"What's that?" Nealy asked reluctantly.

"Play one song for me."

"I can't just get up and take over the piano. We're guests here, Phillip."

"Yes, you can. I just asked, and the bartender would love for you to."

Nealy sat there staring at him, and then at the bartender that had granted his request. "Phillip, I don't have any music with me."

"Nealy, I watched you watching the pianist. You can play everything he just played. I'd bet money on it. So, come on, just one song and you'll own me until we leave tomorrow," he bargained.

"Alright, but only one song. Anything in particular, or do I get to pick the song?"

"You're choice. Listening will be mine. Oh, but one more thing."

"What's that?"

"You have to sing it, too."

"Sing, too."

"Please, you'll be the master of a very willing slave."

"One song," she said, getting up from her chair. Nealy took her place at the piano and played, *"Till There Was You,"* which she knew well enough to play confidently without the music. Several times she noticed Phillip poignantly watching as if he were daydreaming about some glorious place, a place as serene and beautiful as Heaven. Nealy sang the last few words with such emotion that it touched each person in the room. And when she finished, the applause sounded like a large crowd. "Thanks."

Nealy got up and graciously bowed, feeling somewhat self-conscious as well as a little light-headed from the food ladened with wine and two glasses of cognac and the anxiety of singing in a strange place.

"That was wonderful, Nealy. And thanks for doing it. I could spend the rest of my life sitting right here listening to you sing. I would be a very happy man."

"Thanks, Peppee," she giggled shyly. "At least I've found one dedicated fan who, I'm sure, is more than a little prejudiced, but I'll take whatever I can get."

"Okay, now that I'm indebted to you for the rest of the evening and most of tomorrow, what would you like to do? It's ten-fifteen."

"I'd really like to go relax in front of that wonderful fireplace in the suite."

"You got it, pretty lady." They got up from the table and started towards the door. "Go ahead, I'll be right with you," he said, walking towards the bar. An older man who sat at a nearby table with two ladies and another man called Nealy over to tell her how much they had enjoyed her singing. They asked her where she was from and if she sang professionally, which she responded with an emphatic "No." But Phillip returned to catch the end of the conversation, and he told them that she was just being modest. As they said good-bye, the gentleman, who had originally called Nealy over, winked at Phillip and said, "You got yourself a good one there, son. I'd keep her."

When they walked into their room, it was warm and cozy. Nealy immediately sat down on the fluffy rug in front of the fireplace. The heat from the fire felt so good; she became hypnotized by the flames. "I just love a big fireplace," she exclaimed. "They're always so comforting, but they can make you sad, too."

Phillip sat down on the rug about two feet away from her and gazed into the burning amber flashes that crackled every so often. "I know. A fire can easily influence a passion that burns within us."

"Hmmm, I like that word '*passion*.' 'A passion that burns within us.' I like that," she said, shifting her body back to rest against the couch.

The knock at the door spurred Phillip to get up quickly. He walked over and opened the door and invited the room service waiter in to place their bottle of wine, accompanied by two wine glasses, on the table. Phillip tipped him and closed the door. "A glass of wine?" he asked.

"Phillip, I'm feeling no pain as it is," she replied, looking up at him.

"Good, you're much too pretty for pain anyway," he teased, pouring each of them a glass of wine and then returning to his place on the floor next to her.

"What a pleasant evening," she smiled at him. "I haven't been this relaxed or this comfortable in a long, long time—if ever."

"Shall we," he held up his glass to toast. Nealy touched her glass together with his. "To us: a couple of best friends."

"Best friends," she blushed, smiling at him.

Phillip asked Nealy about her family since he had shared the facts of his life with her on the way up to the Inn. Gladly, she told him all about her family and even about her grandmother, from whom she had received her sense of humor. Phillip laughed so hard when she told him about her grandmother that her college friends referred to as *Granny Grunt*. She told him about the time that she and her grandmother were walking down the street in the small East Texas town where her grandmother lived, and the elastic garter that held her stocking up rolled down, freeing her nylon to flop around her ankle and over the toe of her shoe. When Nealy noticed it, she had cried out, but her grandmother "shushed" her, telling her that if she didn't bring attention to it, no one would even notice. Of course, like any other twelve year old, Nealy hid her face for fear that someone would recognize her.

The longer they talked, the more wine they drank. Soon they had become more relaxed; they laughed and teased each other as if they had known each other for years. Nealy placed her empty glass on the floor behind her, and Phillip got up and added three logs to the fire, stirring it to generate more flames. Then he returned to the soft rug and faced her again. He had been very careful not to touch her, except for a sweet pat on the hand here and there. He purely intended to keep his promise, which meant no hanky-panky, not even kissing, because that might allow the situation to get out of control.

Nealy studied Phillip's face as they talked, and she felt drawn to his incredible blue-gray eyes, which stood out against his tan skin. There is something so special about this person, something so sweet, so kind, and so genuine she thought to herself as she listened to him talk about his childhood. Nealy wanted to meet the people that produced this person and raised him to be so special. They were probably just like the parents on *The Donna Reed Show* where the father was a doctor and the mother spent all of her time rearing perfect children.

Nealy wanted to touch his smooth face, but more than that she had a terrible urge to kiss him. She thought it might be the wine making her feel a little amorous, but it could be that she wanted to be closer to him, to feel his heart beating against her own. He talked softly with his head cradled in the palm of his hand as he lay stretched out on his side. She tried to listen, but all she could think about was kissing him. Finally, unable to deny herself the pleasure any longer, she leaned over and kissed his lips lightly. But that wasn't enough, she wanted more. So she kissed him again, moving much closer to him.

At first, he didn't resist at all. He responded by wrapping his arm around her waist and pulling her even closer, but his promise to her rang out in his head. He forced himself to stop, tearing himself away from her.

"Nealy, I promised you I wouldn't do this."

"You're not. I am," she said seductively, kissing his smooth cheek and neck. Then she looked directly into his eyes and said adamantly, "You said if I sang, you'd do anything I wanted to do, that you would be my slave. Remember?"

"Yes, but—"

Nealy put her index finger over his mouth. "And you also said, 'with no regrets.' Therefore, you must do what I ask, and enjoy it, too," she said, smiling and giggling devilishly like the happy master of her very own slave. "Now that we have determined who's who, and without any further arguments, I want you to hold me and kiss me as if it were your idea." Nealy slid her arm around his neck and searched his face, waiting for him to follow her orders.

"But Nealy," he said, still keeping his distance just in case she was acting. He wanted her to have one last opportunity to change her mind. The fire had burned down until there were only a small flame and a dim light in the room, but the fire seemed hotter all of a sudden or their faces were just flushed from their emotions burning hotter inside of them. He wanted so much to kiss her and hold her and even make love to her, but he was afraid that he might lose her even though she seemed quite sure of herself. Gently pushing her hair away from her face, he kissed her forehead. Then desperately fighting his urges, he softly brushed his lips against her parted mouth several times, which gave him a feeling that he had never experience before with any woman. "Nealy, are you sure you want to do this?" he whispered.

"I'm sure. It's what I want, Phillip. This is the first day of my new life, and I want you to be part of it. Please kiss me," she begged softly, rolling slowly onto her back.

As he leaned across her body, her eyes closed, and she felt a wonderful calm as his lips pressed softly against hers. She wrapped her arms around his neck and twisted her fingers in the soft curls above his neck. His hands rested on each side of her face as he stroked her face with his thumbs, lifting her chin to deepen his kisses.

The room spun as Nealy became more and more intoxicated by the soft, but extremely passionate kisses that she exchanged with Phillip. Her needs for him grew even stronger than the first night that they had made-out on the couch at the apartment. She yearned to touch his bare skin, but her shyness kept her from taking the initiative, which was something that she had never had to do.

Nealy could feel his strong desires building, as he pressed his body against her thigh, but his kisses were still delicate and warm and sensitive and nourishing, not the grabbing, uncontrolled kind that usually came with twenty minutes of petting. It was the most gentle lovemaking that she had ever experienced, and even though she had become crazy with desire, she didn't make it known.

Finally, taking a deep breath, he broke the continuous string of kisses and rested his head back in the palm of his hand once again, smiling the sweetest smile that she had ever seen. He slowly slipped his right hand inside the neck of her shirt and softly massaged the nape of her neck and chest, while he watched her very curiously. "Well," he said quietly, "where do we go from here, Master?"

Surprised by his question, Nealy took a deep breath and pushed her hair off her face. Her heart felt as if it could beat right out of her chest. "I didn't know that the *Master* had to direct as well," she answered.

"I do only what my *Master* tells me to do," he responded very seriously, forcing her to accept responsibility for the turn of events.

"Oh, I see," she sighed, knowing that now she would have to find the nerve to pursue what she wanted because every cell in her body pulsated lustfully. She took a very deep breath, reached up and unbuttoned the first button on his shirt, staring squarely into his piercing blue-gray eyes. "From here on out, your *Master* wants you to do whatever it is that you do best."

"I only have two questions, that is, if slaves are allowed to ask questions."

"This is the seventies...slaves have equal rights."

"First, is this in conjunction with what my *Master* does best? Second, will I have my *Master's* full cooperation?" While he spoke, he eased her tee-shirt out of her pants, sliding his hand up under it, and resting his hand on her stomach, which made her draw another deep breath.

When she tried to speak, she felt her voice shaking, but she smiled and said, "Absolutely."

"Am I to assume that my *Master's* answer pertains to questions one and two?"

Nealy propped herself up on both elbows, with her chin almost resting on her chest, and rolled her large eyes upward to address him. "I think my slave is stalling."

"Maybe, but that doesn't mean he isn't eager. In fact, that may be part of the problem," he admitted, pushing her back down again and kissing her with slow, searching kisses, deep inside her mouth, which opened willingly, longing for him. If he set out to make her head spin, he had certainly succeeded.

Impetuously, she pulled his shirt out of his pants and pushed it off his shoulders, but it stopped at his wrists because of the buttons. He sat up, observing her closely as she slowly unbuttoned each sleeve, fumbling from nervousness. She even giggled softly, which made him smile. When he removed his shirt first, and then his undershirt, her heart skipped a beat. The thought of witnessing his bare body made her tingle all over, and especially, his chest, which revealed a golden tan by the light of the fire. His well defined chest was covered with curly, dark blonde hairs that made a narrowing trail down his firm abdomen. His neck and arms were well developed, and his forearms were covered with the same dark blonde hair that shined gold in the warm light. She couldn't take her eyes off him. Phillip affected her as no man ever had and she enjoyed the pleasure of feeling like a sexual creature who liked what she saw and wanted more.

Phillip pulled her up slowly, and with both hands he pulled her shirt up and over her head, tossing it towards the chair. "I'm just following my *Master's* lead," he said excusably as he caught her staring at him. Then he raised her chin up, looked deep into her eyes, and kissed her very lovingly on the lips, and then on the neck, which gave her goosebumps, so he rubbed her arms. As he kissed her neck, he slipped his arm behind her and carefully rested her back against the pillows. Slowly, he slipped her bra straps off her shoulders, softly kissed the tender red skin that had been marked and irritated. When he slid his hands underneath her, she arched her back, allowing him to unhook her bra. And, in almost slow motion, he pulled it towards him, exposing her full chest. "Nealy, you are so beautiful," he gasped, which made her reach up to cover herself. "Please," he said, pulling her arms down beside her and gently squeezing her hands, "let me look at you. You don't have to be embarrassed. Not when you've been blessed with such a beautiful body." He waited until she got comfortable before he touched her, and then he pulled her up and hugged her against his chest tightly, pulling her hair up and kissing her neck and shoulder. "Are you okay?" he whispered, pulling her away so that he could see her face when she answered.

"Yes," she said softly, smiling at him.

"Are you sure? I don't want to make you uncomfortable."

"I'm fine, really. I've never had an experience like this, but I like it. Phillip, don't stop...I need this. And I'm glad it's you," she whispered, wrapping her arms around his shoulders and kissing him deliberately. When she released him, she wanted him so much that she tugged at the elastic on his jogging suit. When she found the string that bound them so tightly, she untied it.

Quietly, he stood up, rolled the pants down and stepped out of them, while he steadied himself by placing his hand on her head. She glanced up at him, and he winked, making her smile shyly. When he dropped his pants to the floor, he reached down and pulled her up next to him.

First, he kissed her gently, and then he slipped her tight pants, along with her panties, down over her hips. She lifted each leg slowly and stepped out of her clothing. He was the perfect height for her to wrap her arms around his neck and be face to face with him.

With courage that came from some wild unknown source, she bent down, closed her eyes, and pulled his skivvies over his tight buttocks and down his firm thighs and protruding calves until he stepped out of them on the floor. When she looked up at him, he pulled her up into his arms and kissed her, pulling her body close to his. Slowly, he ran his strong hands down her back, pressing the small of her back in towards him tightly. Then, he cupped her buttocks and squeezed. In return, she kissed him madly.

"Nealy," he said, barely above a whisper. "I knew you were ravishing, but I never dreamed you'd look like this." He knelt down on the floor and pulled her back down beside him, kissing her stomach. Once again, he carefully eased her onto the rug. Both of them were panting with desire, but he wasn't ready to end such a beautiful moment. All he wanted to do was look at her and admire her beauty. As she lay on the white rug, her hair shined red and gold, and her eyes, which perused his face and his chest, twinkled in the dim light of the smoldering ashes and the small hurricane lamp on the table nearby.

Prolonging the climax, he sat with his arm across her body like a prop and kneaded the muscles in the nape of her neck until she seemed less excited. Needing to touch him, she reached up and ran her hands through the hairs on his chest and circled his pointed nipples that were surrounded by smooth, taut skin. And in turn, he circled her nipples that were erect above her swollen breasts. Her eyes closed, and her chest rose up and down as he circled slowly.

Driven by desire, she pulled him to her and slowly licked his nipples and pressed her tongue hard against them.

To control his lust, he raised up to return the pleasure. He placed his hands behind her back and lifted her chest towards him. And, to mimic the actions of his master, he flicked his tongue across her nipples in a catlike stroke as she dropped her head back, arching her body up towards the hot, moistness of his mouth. While he lowered her back onto the rug, with her back still arched, he kissed her stomach, and then massaged the mound of red, curly hair that covered her rigid center. He softly and slowly touched only the surface of her body, as he studied every inch of her. When she spread her legs and reached for him, he squeezed her hand softly and kissed her fingers. "I want to do my very best for you. Just relax, sweetheart," he said in a soft, hypnotic tone, easing her legs back together.

"I can't," she moaned.

"Yes, you can," he said, stroking her hair and kissing her softly on her forehead. "Take a deep breath." He breathed with her to calm her down and gently massaged her arms and her legs, sedating her with his touch. And when he felt her almost wilt, he straddled her and massaged her chest, touching everything but her nipples, which quickly came to attention again. He used his hands like a masseuse, working his way down her entire body. Skillfully, he parted her legs and massaged her inner thighs, without touching her hot spot that reached for him. Very slowly, he ran his middle finger up the inside of one leg and across to the other leg, and down. Each time he came closer and closer to the wet, moist-heat, until finally, his finger barely brushed it.

"Phillip," she cried out softly.

To pacify the urgency in her voice, he pulled her up and placed her hands around his hot penis as he held her close, cuddling her head in the nape of his shoulder. "Are you okay?" he whispered.

"Yes," she whimpered, her chest heaving. He gently scratched her back all the way down and under her bottom and back up. And when her breathing slowed once again, he slid his legs between her thighs and pulled her up and into his lap. He pressed his hard mass against her stomach and kissed her with force and wild passion, causing her to dig her fingers into his back, trying to pull him into her. "Phillip, I...can't...I need you."

"I know, sweetheart, I want you. Oh, God, I want you so much."

With her whole body pulsating, he raised her up with trembling arms and set her down on top of his erection. They pulled and thrust into and against one another like two wild animals until they both arched their bodies and cried out, as their chests heaved against each other. Finally, they grew rigid and drew their last deep breath, before falling forward into each other's arms. "Oh, my goodness," she cried, crumbling into his chest. He held her tightly, kissing her wet hair and shoulder.

"Are you okay, sweetheart?" he whispered, holding her very snugly in his lap.

"I'm not sure," she sighed, wrapping her arms, with what little strength she had left, around his shoulders and cuddling up as close as she could to his slippery body.

He chuckled, lifting her chin up. "What do you mean?"

"Never, in all my life, have I ever experienced anything like..." she glanced at the clock on the wall, "the last two hours," she said, still breathing as though she had just run a marathon. "Where did you learn such self-control?"

Phillip grinned at her. "It's easy when you want something this special to last."

"I'll sing for you anytime you want," she said, trying to gather up enough energy to smile at him.

"I'll hold you to that, *my pretty, pretty lady*," he said, kissing her several times on the lips before lifting her off him and cradling her in his arms as he stretched out on the rug. As she lay snuggled up on the floor next to him, he couldn't keep his hands off her, so he played with her hair, brushing it off her forehead and then, from time to time, he leaned down to kiss her lovingly.

"Phillip," she said softly, "thank you."

"Nealy, you don't have to thank me for the most wonderful night of my life. I should be thanking you."

Stroking his back, she smiled up at him. "Do you really mean that, Phillip?"

"Uh-huh," he grinned, kissing her and hugging her tightly.

"I've never felt this content after making love. You make me feel comfortable and special. Are you doing that on purpose or do you feel it, too?" she asked seriously.

"Nealy, the thought of letting go of you scares me to death. I'm afraid if I do, I'll never see you again." He wrapped his leg over hers and pulled her even closer, as if someone were trying to take her away from him.

"Phillip, trust me, after tonight I promise that you'll see me again. You may never see me in clothes again, but you'll see me."

He chuckled. "Nealy, clothes will always be optional and *only temporary* from this day forward."

Nealy tightened her arms around him. "Phillip, when I get myself and my life back in good shape, will you come to Texas to visit me?" she asked in search of a commitment that they would be together again.

"Nealy, since this is the first day of your new life, I think you're in pretty good shape, both emotionally and physically," he said, leaning back and quickly glancing up and down her body before he made eye contact again. "At least from what I see."

"Phillip!" she cried, burying her face in his chest. Suddenly, she had a flashback.

"Oh my God, I remember where I saw you."

"What?"

"That first night when you came to take me to dinner, I had this feeling that I'd seen you somewhere before. Well, I had. At Toot Shor's."

His face lit-up. "You know, I had that same feeling. That's why I kept staring at you. And you're right. You were that beautiful red-head that was going home to 'marry that asshole,' if I may quote your friend."

"Denise said that?" she questioned in disbelief.

"That's what she told the bartender."

"I can't believe it. I just saw that same look, the look you gave me when we first walked into the bar that night. That look in your eyes has haunted me for years."

"Yes, I'm guilty as charged. I lusted after you then, and I lust after you now...especially now," he said, slowly following the curves up and down her backside as he spoke very quietly about his feelings for her. "I remember you turned around just before you walked out the door and smiled at me. I wanted to run after you and beg you not to go. In fact, I said to the bartender, 'Now that's the girl of my dreams.' And he said, 'Then go after her, Doc. She wants you. I saw it in her face. It's obvious she doesn't love *that asshole* because she gave you that please-save-me look.' "

Nealy blushed..."He's right. I did. I couldn't believe it. I felt so guilty that I couldn't hardly sleep that night. I actually thought about going back to Toot Shor's to talk to the bartender. But, I figured that you were married—"

"I was," he said sadly. "But the marriage was over. That night, she had given me some ultimatums, which I turned down. So she told me about her affair and ask for a divorce. That's why I was there. I had a badly bruised ego, but that's about all. And, if I had not been in the middle of that three-ring fiasco, I would have gone after you. I didn't know how I would explain my situation and make you believe that my marriage was *really over*. I knew it would sound like a ploy to get you in bed—some kind of sick come on. You didn't look like the type of woman who'd be interested in getting involved with a married man, regardless of the situation."

"Isn't this ironic. Here we are, three or so years later, and it's the same scenario, but it's happening to me instead of you," she said, disgusted with *the hands of fate*.

"I know. I wish I had gone after you. I've never been a real impulsive person, but I swear to God, I would have gone after you if I'd thought for one minute that I could have convinced you to give up whatever it was that you were going after and wait for me. I came so close, Nealy. And by not following my instincts, I made the biggest mistake of my life. Just think...if I had, I could have saved you from an ill-fated marriage, and we could have spent the last few years curled up in front of a fire."

"Does that mean that you'll come to see me?"

"Nealy, there is nothing in this world that could ever keep me away from you if you want me, but I think you know that. So, whenever—day or night—you want to see me, all you have to do is call. And, sweetheart, I'll be there. I promise with all my heart." The clock struck two o'clock, and Phillip didn't want to separate himself from her long enough to rekindle the fire, so instead, he raised up, lifted her into his arms, and made his way into the bedroom where he threw back the covers on the bed. Gently, he placed Nealy down and crawled in beside her, wrapping the covers around them tightly like a cozy cocoon for two.

When she looked up at him, he lifted her chin and covered her mouth with his, kissing her deeply again and again. At this point, they both knew that this night would be a long one, filled with relentless passion, strong feelings, and whispered words about life and the happy times to come.

At almost ten the next morning, leaving Nealy to sleep a few minutes longer, Phillip slipped out of bed and called for room service to bring them some breakfast. He ordered two of everything. A night like the one he had just experienced had left him with a hearty appetite. While he waited for room service, he got back under the covers and watched Nealy sleep. He couldn't believe how pretty she was and that he was actually lying next to her. She looked so peaceful. He hated to wake her, but he wanted to make the most out of every minute that he had with her. When he kissed her perfect little button nose, she opened her eyes and smiled at him. "Good-morning," he whispered.

"Good-morning," she said, closing her eyes again.

"I ordered breakfast. Are you hungry?"

She opened her eyes and smiled, "Yes, for you."

And with that statement, he snuggled deeper under all the quilts on the bed and began to kiss her stomach, working his way up to her lips, the ones that he had come to crave in the strongest sense of the word.

And just at the most inopportune time, there was a knock on the door. "Oh, no," he said, "it's room service. Don't move, I'll be right back."

"I'll miss you," she said sweetly, holding on to his arm.

"Nealy, don't do this to me. I can't think straight as it is."

Nealy giggled. "Hmm, I'm glad I affect you that way," she raised up and kissed his back, while he slipped his jogging pants on.

The knock came again, but louder this time. "I'm coming," he yelled. He rushed away from the bed towards the living room, but stopped and looked back at her, and then down at the huge bulge in the front of his pants. "Well, there won't be any question as to what took me so long to answer the door." Nealy couldn't help giggling loudly, even though she felt responsible for his predicament. "Don't laugh," he scolded, "and don't move." Then, he pulled the bedroom door to. Nealy, still giggling snuggled down under the covers to wait for him.

When Phillip opened the door, the room service waiter took one look at him and knew exactly what had taken him so long to answer the door. From the time he walked inside to deliver the tray, until the time he left, he had a naughty smirk on his face, which should have embarrassed Phillip, but it didn't. All he could think about was returning to bed and to Nealy as soon as possible. The second the waiter left, Phillip closed the door and took less than five steps before he had climbed back into bed and snuggled up closely to her. "I'm sorry sweetheart, but breakfast will have to wait."

"I thought males were dominated by their instinct to eat as a measure of survival," she giggled quietly.

"That's the four legged kind, not the three legged ones. And that, *my dear Scarlett*, is the category I fall into at this very moment," he said, rolling over on top of her to make his point.

"You are *soooo* right, Rhett," she said, snuggling up to him.

Afterwards, they enjoyed a delightful breakfast in bed. Even though Nealy admitted that she had never eaten breakfast in the buff before, she found it interesting, to say the least; honey and jelly took on a whole new meaning. One thing that she would always remember about Phillip was his unique ability to be creative, in bed—or out—and there would be no such thing as bedroom boredom.

After a walk around the Inn later that afternoon, they had a snowball fight, chasing each other through the virgin snow on the lawn and around the trees that stood lifeless, waiting for the first signs of spring. They laughed and frolicked in the soft white powder like children; they even built a snowman. The smell of smoke in the air came from the many fireplaces nearby that had turned ordinary living rooms into toasty family havens. When the snow began to fall again, they retreated to shelter on the wraparound porch, which had been the perfect setting for many weddings in the past because of its home-spun ambiance.

It had gotten late, so they packed up their few things to return to the city. Neither of them wanted to go because the trip to the country had brought something special to their lives, and it seemed a shame to have it end so soon.

In the parking lot, Phillip opened the car door for Nealy and at the same time, both of them took one last look at the Homestead Inn. Nealy looked up at Phillip, and he held both of her hands together with his. "I don't know when, but I'm going to marry you on the porch of that elegant old house."

"Phillip—"

"I am," he whispered, kissing her softly to silence her. "Don't say anything or try to change my mind. It's made up. I promise, it *will* happen. You'll see. I missed my chance to be with you once. I won't miss it again." He waited while she slid into the seat, and then he closed the door.

Nealy stared out the car window at him as he made his way around the car to the driver's side. When he got in, he leaned over and kissed her again briefly in spite of the shocked and confused expression on her sweet face. "Sweetheart, don't look so skeptical. It's easy to make a statement like that when you're absolutely sure about something, or, in this case, someone," he said, his smile fading to establish credibility. "Nealy, I'm serious. And even though I don't know *when*, I do know *where*, and I do know to *whom*." Phillip pointed to the Inn and smiled, nodding his head up and down. "You and me—we're a couple."

CHAPTER THIRTY-THREE

ALMOST ALL THE WAY back to the City, they held hands and enjoyed the soft music that played on the radio. Every so often, Phillip would look at her and wink or smile a big toothy grin or bring her hand to his lips and kiss her fingers. Just as they reached the city limits, Phillip's electronic beeper sounded, alerting him that someone needed to reach him. So he pulled into the nearest convenience store and phoned his service, leaving Nealy to wait for him in the car.

When he returned a few minutes later, he had a solemn, almost worried, expression on his face. Not wanting to appear nosey, Nealy didn't plan on asking him any questions. But as soon as he got in the car, he began explaining. "I've got some good news and some bad news, so I think I'll start with the good news."

"What's the bad news?" she asked anxiously, knowing it had to be something that involved her.

"Nealy, calm down. Everything is fine," he said softly. "I'll get to that in a minute, but first, I want to give you the good news. I've been instructed by your physician and my friend, Rob Morris, to help you find a place to stay here in New York for the next two weeks. Of course, I won't have to look because I already know the perfect place," he said happily.

"But, Phillip, stay in New York. Why?"

"Nealy, it seems that Jerrod didn't take your disappearance too well. When he returned to Galveston, he went to the hospital and waited in the parking lot for a doctor named Randy—"

"Randy Richfield," she interrupted.

"Yes, that's the one Rob mentioned. Well, anyway, he waited for him in the parking lot and—"

"Oh, Phillip, no—"

"Now, sweetheart, don't get upset, he's alright," he said, gently pressing her hand between his. "Fortunately, a guard had spotted Jerrod, and even though he identified himself, the guard still kept an eye on him because he seemed a bit on edge or high on something. Later, when Randy came out of the hospital, Jerrod approached him, but the guard immediately intervened."

"So Randy wasn't hurt?"

"No, he's fine, but Randy contacted Rob. Then Rob contacted the hospital administrator who is a friend of his, and he called Jerrod on the carpet. When the administrator talked to him, he insisted that Jerrod spend time each day for the next two weeks with one of the psychiatrists on staff. He told me his name, but I can't recall it. Nealy, all of them feel that it would be better for you to remain here, at least for the next two weeks. By then, maybe he'll be able to handle all of this a little better. To be perfectly honest, sweetheart, they are afraid for you to confront him right now. Not that he's dangerous, but he is somewhat unpredictable. I mean, look what happened here the other night. None of us, me especially, want to see anything happen to you just because Jerrod is having some problems controlling his temper. Rob thinks that in time, and with some help, he'll accept whatever decisions you make. But right now, he's not up to handling rejection. The guy is having enough problems with the fact that you left. I can't even imagine what he would do if you told him you were divorcing him."

Trying hard not to expose her tears, she lowered her head and blotted the tears from the corner of her eyes. "Phillip, maybe I should just go back to him. I'm ruining his career and possibly his life."

"Nealy, you can't do that. And even if you did, it wouldn't help him. Past behavior, in most cases, predicts future performance. And the things he did that caused you to leave in the first place would only happen again, unless he gets help. And from what I've heard about Jerrod, he isn't the kind that readily admits that he has a problem."

"He says I'm the one with the problem," she said, still fighting back the tears.

"Nealy, sweetie, the only problem that you're guilty of is being too sweet and too soft-hearted. I know you want the best for him, but allowing him to take away your happiness will not help him. Jerrod needs to grow up and become responsible for his actions. It's time, Nealy, and the best thing that you can do for him is to allow that to happen. Now, if you're still in love with him and you think that you can live with him the way he is, then, by all means, you should go home and try it again."

"Phillip, *you*, better than anyone else, know that I'm not in love with him. I love him because we grew up together, and I feel sorry for him. But I'm not *in love* with him. If I were, I could never have spent the last twenty-four hours in your arms, loving you. I took my vows very seriously, and it had to be pretty special for me to break them. I didn't do it to spite Jerrod. I did it because I wanted to be with you more than anything else in the world. I know you know that because, even though you haven't known me very long, you know me very well."

"You're right, I do. I want you to stay with me for the next two weeks, and then you can go home and do what you have to do. Rob needs you to call him when we get back to my apartment. He doesn't want to interfere, but Nealy, he needs to know what you plan on doing. If you plan on divorcing Jerrod, then the psychiatrist would like to prepare him for that. He doesn't want you to give him false hopes because it will only make things harder in the long run."

Nealy leaned over, and Phillip put his arm around her. For a minute she quietly rested her head on his shoulder. "Okay, I'll call him, but why doesn't he want me to stay at Janey's? Surely Jerrod wouldn't come here again."

"He might, Nealy. As I said, he isn't taking this very well, so he might come back again. And, Nealy, I'm not willing to take any chances with your safety. When I think about you being out alone in this city in the middle of the night...well, I can't think about it. Sweetheart, that was really dangerous. Please, don't fight me on this. I'll get you a hotel room, but I'd really like to have you with me where I can look at your beautiful face and *lust* after God's most illustrious creation."

"Does that mean you like me?"

"I'm totally mad for you. You just *do it* for me in every possible way that a woman could affect a man, and I mean that, even in the purest sense of the word. I think that we should stop off and get your things and take them on over to my place."

"Phillip, I can't just take up housekeeping with you."

"Alright, I'll put your things in the guest room. Then at night, you can slip into my bed after midnight and slip back into the guest room before my alarm goes off."

Nealy raised up and smiled at him coyly. "You're pretty sure of yourself, Doctor."

"No, but I'll be waiting for you."

"Phillip Pepper," she squealed, "see what you're doing to me. I'm becoming too predictable...so in that case, I guess you'd better keep my side of the bed warm."

"It'll be steaming."

"Speaking of steaming. I think we need to go before we get arrested. People may think we're *steaming* now since the windows are all fogged up," he grinned.

"I think you're right. Let's go over to the apartment. I'm not going to insult you by asking if you mentioned my staying with you to Rob. I know you wouldn't do that, but where am I going to tell him I stayed?"

"You simply tell him that you stayed with a friend...and that's no lie because I really, really like you."

"*Peppee*, I got to hand it to you. You've got an answer for everything."

"When it comes to you, I have more than answers," he replied smugly, kissing her on the cheek.

It took them an hour to get across town and get her things together. Nealy cleaned up the apartment, which hadn't really gotten too messy, but she had a few dishes to put away. Later in the week, she planned to come back over and change the bed linens and collect anything that she might have forgotten.

When they arrived at his apartment, Nealy called Rob while Phillip returned to his study to call a couple of his patients. He never questioned her about their conversation, but after she unpacked, she sat him down and told him every word. Nealy didn't want to keep anything from Phillip; she wanted to share everything with him, even her life.

They had talked for an hour. When they realized how late it had become, they had to rush to get to the theater on time. Nealy couldn't disappoint Denise.

After picking up their tickets at the box office, they hurried up the winding stairs of the theater and took their seats just in time for the opening act. Nealy watched like a proud mother as Denise recited her few lines and danced her heart out with the chorus. It was her last performance, and she really put her heart into it. Phillip seemed very happy to be there, holding hands with Nealy and smiling.

After the play, Denise had to attend the cast party, but she and her new attorney-friend agreed to meet Nealy and Phillip at Phillip's restaurant at eleven-thirty for a private celebration of their own. The fact that they had two wonderful guys in their lives for a change deserved a party: a small intimate party for four. Denise was thrilled that Nealy and Phillip appeared to be falling in love because she thought they were a perfect match. Both of them were bright and funny and sweet and deserved the best. They made a beautiful couple: his boyish good looks, incredible eyes, and dark blonde curls, and her delicate features and *Miss America* head-to-toe beauty. Denise prayed that Nealy had finally gotten over the habit and out from under the influence of Jerrod Jones, that jackass, who could only—now or in the future—love himself, so in no way did he deserve someone like Nealy.

The following two weeks passed too fast for both Phillip and Nealy, but she needed to get home and take care of her personal matters and her business. Even though she had spoken with Francine on a daily basis, she still felt that she had abandoned her students and obligations. During the days, she walked, went to the theater to watch Denise rehearse for her new play, had lunch everyday with Phillip in a different place: the park, his office, restaurants, the Staten Island Ferry, and even on Liberty Island; if Nealy lived to be a hundred, she would never forget that lunch.

Things had started out like any other day. They discussed what sounded good and finally decided to take the ferry over to Liberty Island where they could grab a hot dog and some chips and enjoy the fresh air and the sunshine. At the refreshment stand, they ordered their hot dogs and walked over to the steps that led up to the Statue of Liberty to eat. After lunch, they walked to the edge of the wall surrounding the island and fed the seagulls, who were already so fat that they could barely fly. The view of the city was romantic, even in the daytime, and they exchanged sweet, innocent kisses to match the mood. The cold breeze off the water caused them to huddle together to stay warm, even though the sun shined brightly, and in turn their kisses became more and more passionate. The longer they stood there, the more involved they became. Finally, they agreed to stop before things got too carried away, and they returned to the ferry to go back over to the Manhattan. In order to enjoy the view of the city on the way back, they went up to the upper deck, which they had to themselves. Normally, the boat was filled up with people, but because of winter, there weren't a dozen people on board.

As they relaxed under the warm winter sun, one thing led to another, and before they knew it they were hugging and kissing like they were newlyweds. When they noticed that someone had joined them, they casually got up and walked downstairs to find a secluded spot to continue playing kissy-face or to cool off. Phillip smiled at Nealy very mischievously. She could tell that he had something very naughty in mind because; she knew that look. Across from the rail where they stood was the men's restroom. When the coast was clear, he grabbed Nealy's hand, opened the door, and pulled her inside. "Oh, Phillip, you can't be serious," she giggled, but he quickly closed the door and locked it.

"I'm very serious," he whispered. "This is an experiment for a new sex manual I'm writing." He lifted her up and sat her on the tiny cabinet that had a small sink in the center of it.

"Phillip," she whispered, "in five minutes we'll be back at the dock.

"Then I suggest we get busy and stop wasting precious time," he said, kissing her and pulling her close. And with the affect that his intoxicating kisses had on her, it didn't take long for her to forget that she was in the men's room of the Liberty Island Ferry. Phillip *did it* for her; whether they had five minutes or five hours, it really didn't matter. Every minute with him turned out to be better than the one before.

After the moment of passion fled, Nealy couldn't believe that they had actually made love in a public restroom in broad daylight like horny, love struck teenagers. She started giggling, and Phillip covered her mouth, trying hard not to chuckle himself. It just seemed so outrageous and so naughty, but it would be something to remember and laugh about for the rest of their lives. As she had said before, sex with Phillip would never be lacking in excitement.

Being quite the romantic, Phillip came home every night with flowers and wine and sweet little presents. They made love every night, Phillip's way, by maintaining control until they couldn't take another minute apart. Afterwards, they would hold each other and talk for hours about more things than Nealy could ever imagine. The closeness and the tenderness amazed her more and more. At times, she felt guilty about being with Phillip because legally she was still married to Jerrod, but he had destroyed their marriage and her feelings of loyalty to him. Of course, morally it wasn't right, but she needed Phillip so much, and he made her feel so special and so loved. Even though he had not actually said the words, she could feel it. His secretary, Eve, told her that she had never seen Phillip so happy in all the years that she had been working with him, and that she had never seen him take so much time for himself away from his practice. It was as if for the first time, he actually cared more about someone than he did his practice; she said that his face lit up at the mere mention of Nealy's name.

On the day that Nealy packed her things, she walked from room to room, collecting mental pictures of him in every place imaginable. It made her sad, but when she closed her eyes, she could feel him, and she wanted to take that feeling home with her. Although Nealy wasn't the type to play games, she left a few of her things there to remind him of their time together. During the week, she had bought a frame for the picture that they had taken in one of those little photo booths, and she left it on the nightstand by his bed where he had to see it each night before he went to sleep. On the frame was a little girl with red hair and a pouty face, and it said, *"Please don't forget me."*

As always, the *On-time-Phillip-Pepper* picked Nealy up at exactly two o'clock and drove her to Kennedy Airport. During the thirty-minute drive, he kept the conversation light and playful, trying to cover up how he felt about her leaving. Of course, Nealy knew because she felt the same way, but she had another life more than two-thousand miles away. Phillip had been adamant about not having a long distance relationship, at least not a lasting one that involved a dedicated commitment. He had hinted several times during the past two days, and in a round-about-way he encouraged her to give some thought to returning to New York to resume her singing career.

They had gone to Freddy's on Friday, and everyone insisted that she sing at least one song as a going away gift for her friends. At last, she agreed. When she chose *"Somewhere, My Love"* Phillip got the message loud and clear. He knew then that they had found something so special, even though timing had not been on their side. He knew that she didn't plan on returning to New York anytime soon, but he also knew that they would meet again *someday, somewhere, out of the long*—but hopefully not too long—*ago*. And he prayed that it wouldn't be too late for one, or both of them.

Phillip parked, and they carried her luggage into the airport to check her bags and get her ticket changed to reflect her new date of departure. Since they had forty-five minutes before her plane left, they grabbed a cup of coffee and spent their last moments together holding hands and discussing the fun times that neither of them could ever forget. "Phillip, I don't know how to say thank you for all you've done for me."

"You don't have to thank me, Nealy, and I think you know that. The last three weeks have been the best three weeks in my life," he said seriously.

"Mine, too," she said, smiling at him. "We found something very special, something that most people never find, and I hope that we can hold on to it. I don't want to lose you, Phillip, but I won't keep you from going on with your life either, and I would never interfere."

"But I want you to interfere. In fact, I want you to do more than interfere, Nealy," he said, his expression saying what he couldn't because he didn't want to pressure her.

"Phillip, I have nothing to offer you, but a little companionship here and there. I'm not free to give you what you need, and it would be too selfish to ask you to wait for me. I don't know what will happen over the next few months while I'm untangling this mess I've gotten myself into."

"I know, but good things are worth waiting for," he smiled, leaning across the table and kissing her cheek. "We better get you on that plane. The sooner you get there, the sooner you can go on with your life. And, Nealy, I told you that I'm going to be part of that life someday and I meant it. You make me happy, and I make you happy. We belong together." He walked her down towards the gate and pulled her into the first cutout along the corridor, kissing and hugging her tightly, not really caring who saw them. This wasn't public display of affection; it was love. "I'm going to miss you. Please come back, Nealy."

"I'm going to miss you, too, Phillip. And look at all the things that you have introduced me to. In my wildest dreams, I'd never have *made love* in the men's restroom on the Liberty Island Ferry. In fact, I still find that hard to believe. But I'll admit that it was exciting and terribly spontaneous and extremely crazy and maybe a tad bit immoral," she giggled, pulling away and looking into his sad, but beautiful blue-gray eyes.

"Well, sweetheart, that was a first for me, too, but I liked the hell out of it, immoral and all," he chuckled. "Come on before I find another cozy little place to drag you into."

"One last thing," she said, looking at him quizzically.

"What's that?"

"Are you really writing a sex manual?"

"No, I just said that. But it worked so well that maybe I should," he said, smiling smugly. "And, if I keep hanging out with this gorgeous redhead, the one that stimulates my sense of sexual adventure, I'll have a lot more material that could help my patients with their inadequate sex lives."

"You'd write about our sex life?"

Phillip pushed her hair off her shoulders and slowly moved his hands up her slender neck until her chin rested on the tips of his thumbs. "Something that beautiful and gratifying needs to be shared with the whole world. But, of course, the names would be changed to protect the pure and the innocent," he said quietly, and then he kissed her.

They walked hand-in-hand to the gate and kissed briefly, waving as she walked out of sight to board the plane. At that moment, his heart broke into a million pieces. Why couldn't things be simple? Why did the one person that he knew he could love more than life itself have to be so unavailable and so far away? Would he ever see her again or had he just said good-bye to the first woman that he had ever really loved? Nealy was the one for him; he could feel it in his heart. Now all he had to do was concentrate on the vow that he made to marry her on the porch of the Homestead Inn, no matter how long it took or what he had to go through to make that happen.

CHAPTER THIRTY-FOUR

NEALY FLEW HOME, feeling as if she had left a part of herself behind. The thought of facing Jerrod terrified her, but she wanted to get it over with because she had more important things to do with her life. She had barely thought about him during the last two weeks. Should she feel guilty? After all, this was the person that had been part of her life for ten years, and now he didn't seem to matter at all. Had Phillip done that, or did she finally see the missing link in their relationship? It seemed so strange because the one thing that had kept she and Jerrod together was their strong physical attraction to each other. All those years she had mistaken lust for love, not really knowing the difference, something that most young girls and boys have trouble distinguishing; that's why so many marriages fail. Jerrod touched her in all the right places, making sure that she climaxed over and over again, but it was just sex, no tenderness, no talking. That had been the reason that she felt so empty afterwards, but until Phillip came along, she really didn't know why she had felt that way. He wanted to hold her, to cuddle her, and he didn't have to be inside of her for her to feel loved. She could say, "Hold me," and simply be held. There were a few times, and only a few, when Jerrod had been tender and loving, but it only happened before the actual sex act and never afterwards unless, of course, he wanted more. And never once did they lie next to each other and simply talk. Never once did they lie next to each other with their bodies intertwined and read a book before going to sleep. Jerrod had never studied her body, touching her tenderly and telling her how much he loved to look at her and all of her beauty. Nealy had never even considered how important these things were in a relationship, but maybe Jerrod didn't know how to do that; maybe he had never been taught the tenderness of love making. Like most young boys, when they reach puberty they are interested only in special parts of the female anatomy. It's as if the rest doesn't exist because all they want to do is pull it out and plug it in to the nearest receptacle, preferably one that doesn't require too much attention. When boys get together, their vocabulary is limited to "*fondling boobs and humping cooters.*" And unfortunately, with the inhibitions carried over from the Victorian attitudes about intimacy, most of them never learn any different. As a result, they grow up doing just enough to *get it in* and *get off*. But fortunately, some men, Phillip in particular, had learned how to make love without rushing through foreplay and the satisfaction that comes from cuddling afterwards. Because of skillfulness in which he performed these tasks, he had either paid attention in medical school when it came to the study of women, read *show and tell* books, or been taught by some precocious young girl who didn't mind telling him what felt good and what didn't. Today, most women are much too timid when it comes to talking about sex with their partners, which has created most of the sexual tension in relationships. Society can be blamed for that because it rallies about the *fast girls* being the ones to freely discuss sex with a man. Therefore, until a woman finds a man that satisfies her sexually, as well as emotionally, she has a tendency to keep changing partners in search of Mr. Right.

The closer Nealy got to Houston, the more responsible she felt for the failure of her marriage. Maybe she should have talked to Jerrod more about what she needed from him and what he needed from her. Could that have made a difference. Probably, but now with all that has happened, she couldn't go back, not even out of guilt. She could never forget the looks on the faces of those girls in that pool and their naked silhouettes below the surface of the water. And the thought of Jerrod having sex with them made her sick. How could she ever erase such a terrible memory and be forgiving. Well she couldn't be. And besides, she couldn't deny her feelings for Phillip and ignore what had happened between them. Nealy could still feel his breath against her cheek and the touch of his lips on hers. This hadn't been some cheap, one-night-stand with a guy she'd picked up in a bar so that she could tell Jerrod how he did it to her all night long. She cared deeply about Phillip, a good person, someone who would take his vows to his grave. "Phillip, where are you?" she barely whispered, looking down at all the lights below, marking their approach into Houston. "I'm so scared, Phillip, I need you." Tears formed in her eyes, but she couldn't cry because Rob and his wife, Nancy, were picking her up, and she didn't want to be all emotional. She forced herself to think happy thoughts about the days and nights that she had spent with Phillip. She thought about making love on the Liberty Island Ferry and the beer spewing all over him at Peppee's. It worked, forcing her to laugh out loud, then she smiled like a smitten teenager in love for the first time with some silly boy who wrote her a goofy poem and had his friend give it to her because he was too shy.

The Morris family, both girls included, met her at the gate and helped her get her luggage to their car. They were surprised to see her with so much, but thrilled when they found out about her shopping spree. Although they didn't elaborate because of Rob's little girls who were much more interested in bringing her up to date on the latest happenings at the studio. In fact, they gave her a play by play accounting of Miss Francine and her new beau, Dr. Richfield. At first, Nealy couldn't believe it, but then she realized that they were a match made in heaven; she was extremely happy for them. In fact, she couldn't think of anyone more perfect for Randy than Francine. Francine is pretty, sweet and bright and she loves children, and Randy had a precious child and lots of love to give. Rob dropped the family off at home and drove Nealy home in order to fill her in on the outcome of Jerrod's visits with Dr. Zimmerman, the Psychiatrist.

"Nealy, how are you really?"

"I'm fine, Rob, thanks for asking. And thanks for picking me up and bringing the family. I've missed Nancy. I would like to see her more, so I think I'll make some time."

"She'd like that, Nealy. Call her next week. It'll be good for the two of you to get together and go to lunch or go shopping. You know, girl stuff."

"I will. Well, how is Jerrod? Have you seen him or talked to him?"

"I haven't, but Jim Zimmerman has met with him everyday during the last two weeks. Jim says that he's really remorseful and wants you back, but because you told me that you wanted out, I made sure that Jim prepared him for the worst. Have your feelings changed?"

"No. I want a divorce as soon as possible. I had a lot of time to think, Rob, and I came to the conclusion that I'm not *in love* with Jerrod. I hate to admit that, but I can't help it. There's just too much missing in our marriage and too much has happened," she said, looking down and playing with the button on her jacket.

"You mean with the so called *Swim Club set?*"

"Yes, that and other things," she said, smiling rather smugly, and letting the cat out of the bag just enough that Rob caught on.

"Phillip Pepper wouldn't have anything to do with this, would he?" Rob smiled.

Nealy took a deep breath. "Oh, Rob, I miss him already. We instantly hit it off, and we're great friends. Phillip's one of the nicest people that I've ever known. I hope you don't think I'm terrible, but I may even be falling in love with him."

"Nealy, Phillip is my best friend, and the two of you deserve each other, if you don't mind me saying so. I know what you're going through, but if and when the time comes, nothing would please me more to see you and Phillip together."

"Thanks for saying that, Rob. More than anything, I pray *that time* comes. But first, I have to straighten out my life. And, hopefully, Phillip will have the patience that he seems to think he has."

"Nealy, you're pretty special, so keep that in mind when you make your decision. Don't make a decision based on pity. No matter what happens, Jerrod will survive. I'm sure he loves you in the only way that he knows how, but Nealy be careful, Jerrod has a problem. In fact, Jim wants to see you sometime tomorrow, preferably before you talk to Jerrod. There are some things that he would like to talk to you about, so please don't be too hasty when he begs you to take him back."

"Rob, that sounds serious," she remarked, concerned.

"It is, Nealy, but I would rather Jim talk to you about it."

"Is he sick?"

"Not physically, but he has some emotional problems."

"Rob, I only know that too well, unfortunately."

"But, Nealy, there's more to it than just that. Let Jim discuss it with you. Now, how are you physically? You look great, if that's any indication."

"I'm fantastic. I walked all over the city. The cramps all went away, and I feel better than ever. I'm ready to go on with my life. I missed my studio and my students. I'm ready to go back to work."

"Great, I'm glad to hear it. If you need me, you have my number and that goes for Randy, too. He's very concerned about you and your well-being," he said, pulling into her driveway.

"I know. Randy's been a great friend to me. Is he and Francine really that serious, or did the girls get carried away?"

"Well, I'm not sure, but we had dinner with them last weekend, and, from what I observed, they seemed very sweet on each other."

"I'm thrilled. I love them both so much. I want them to be happy."

"That's exactly how I feel about you and Phillip, but I'll keep that to myself," he teased, getting out of the car. "I made sure that Jerrod was on call tonight so you could rest and have time to talk to Jim in the morning."

"Gosh, Rob, I really appreciate all that you've done. Y'all have been so nice to take care of everything," she said gratefully. "Oh, Chancey." Nealy dropped her bag and ran into the yard. Chance ran around the yard jumping and whining for her attention. She hugged him and squeezed him, and he cried as though she had been gone forever. While Nealy played with Chance, Rob brought her bags in and put them in the kitchen.

Nealy hugged Rob. "I can't thank you enough. It's nine-thirty, so I won't keep you. I'll call you tomorrow after I see Jim Zimmerman. Thanks again, Rob, for everything."

"You're welcome, Nealy. Don't be a stranger."

"I won't. I promise. Good-night," she said, waving to him as he walked out the gate. Nealy played and cuddled with Chance. Randy had been kind enough to bring him home for her arrival, knowing how much she wanted to see her faithful companion.

By ten, she was ready for bed. Being in her own bed again was wonderful, but she really missed having Phillip to snuggle up to. As she lay there, she thought about Phillip and closed her eyes to imagine him in his big bed all alone—at least he better be. Desperately wanting to talk to him, she picked up the phone and dialed his number, even though it was already eleven o'clock in New York. After the first ring, she almost hung up, but then she heard his voice.

"Hello," he said quietly.

"Hi."

"Nealy," he said excitedly.

"I'm sorry to call so late, but I—"

"God, I miss you, sweetheart."

"You do? Oh, Phillip, I'm so glad."

"I was just lying here staring at the picture you left for me and trying to figure out how to get you back here. I've never felt so alone in my life."

"I miss you, too," she said softly.

"I'm sorry, Nealy, I promised myself I wouldn't be *sappy* and say these things."

"I'm glad you did. At least I don't feel so foolish wishing that I were lying next to you."

"Oh, Nealy, I never expected this to be so hard."

"Me either. But it'll all work out. It has to," she said, trying to be positive. "Rob brought me home. When he asked me how we got along, I couldn't hide my feelings. I hope you don't mind. He knows that we're more than just friends."

"Nealy, he's already called me. I asked him to let me know if you got home alright. So, he called me about fifteen minutes before you did. I wanted to call you myself, but I wasn't sure what your situation would be. I didn't want to cause you any problems. I'm so glad you called. Hearing from Rob that you made it home alright helped, but it's not like hearing it from you. When he called, I couldn't hide my feelings either. We go way back. It would have been impossible to try and fool him. Anyway, since he instigated our meeting in the first place, he's delighted that it turned out so well."

"You mean he actually set this up in hopes that we would hit it off?"

"Not totally. I know that he was genuinely concerned about your health, but he had other motives as well."

"That little rascal. I actually felt guilty because he had conned you into babysitting me, and the whole time he was playing *Cupid*."

"Nealy, he knew the minute I saw you, I'd be hooked for life, and what can I say, other than *I'm hooked for life*. The irony of this is incredible. Rob and I talked a few nights after I saw you at Toot Shor's. And, believe it or not, I told him that I had seen the *girl of my dreams*. And do you know what he said?"

"No. What?'"

"He asked me why I let her get away?"

"So this time I won't let her get away. Mark my words. We haven't seen the last of the Homestead Inn."

Nealy giggled. "Will I get a hand written notice or a formal invitation, Doctor?"

"I've told you too much already. You'll just have to wait and see," he said, chuckling, even though he was serious as hell. "Oh, before I forget. Denise and Allen came by the restaurant tonight. She said she knew I'd be lonely because she missed you, too, so she thought that we could have a beer and cry on each other's shoulder. When one of the directors at the theater asked her personal questions about you, she told him that you weren't interested. I think she's looking out for me already."

"That's Denise. Oh, Phillip, I really miss you. I hope I can see you again soon."

"If you need me at any time of the day or night, I want you to call me. I'll be here for you, Nealy. I'll see you through this, and I'll also accept whatever decisions that you make. This isn't going to be easy because Rob told me that Jerrod isn't ready to let you go. But, no matter what happens, if you need me, I want you to call. Will you do that?" he asked, concerned about the silence. "Nealy, are you okay?" Nealy couldn't even answer. Her throat had become so tight, and she knew if she said anything else that she would cry.

Finally, she managed a weak, "Yes."

"Oh, sweetheart, I'm sorry. Please don't cry. I couldn't stand it if I made you sad."

"I'm okay, Phillip. I just miss you, and I'm tired, too. As I recall, we didn't get much sleep last night."

"If you say much more, I'll be on the next plane to Houston, Texas. I'll let you get some sleep. Call me if you need me. Nealy, I'm your biggest fan. Thanks for all the autographed notes you left scattered around my house. I'll never remove them," he said sweetly.

"I'm glad you liked them. Phillip..."

"What?" he asked in hopes that she would say she loved him, so he could say it, too.

"Uh...good-night." She wanted to say *I love you,* but she couldn't because it wouldn't be fair; she wasn't free.

"Good-night, sweetheart." He hung up the phone and stared at the picture until he fell asleep with it resting on his chest.

From exhaustion, Nealy had fallen fast asleep only to be awakened at twelve-thirty. Barely awake, she answered the telephone.

"Hello."

"Neal, oh, baby, I'm so glad you're back," Jerrod said. "I just ran into Rob Morris here at the hospital. When I told him I was going over to the house to wait for you, he said he'd just dropped you off at home."

"Yes, he and his entire family," she remarked sleepily.

"Oh, really. He brought Nancy and the kids. Well, I'm relieved to know that he doesn't have the *hots* for you, too."

"Oh, Jerrod, please. Nancy is one of my closest friends, as far as doctors' wives go," she said, disgusted at his ridiculous implications.

"I wanted to see you, but Rob said you were really tired."

"I'm exhausted."

"Yeah, I can tell. I'll let you go back to sleep. I guess you're going into the studio tomorrow?"

"Yes, I've got so much to catch up on."

"Then I guess we'll talk tomorrow night, huh?"

"Yes. I'll be home about seven-thirty or eight."

"That late, huh?"

"Jerrod, I have a class at six-thirty," she said, getting irritated.

"Okay, okay, I'll see you at home. And Neal, I've missed you. I'm glad you're home."

"We'll talk tomorrow night, Jerrod."

"Yeah," he said sadly and hung up the phone. From the tone of her voice, he knew that she hadn't forgiven him, but he could make up with her when he saw her. Nealy could never resist his charm.

Nealy went into the studio at six o'clock because her biological clock was still one hour earlier on New York time. Papers were piled high on her desk, and things were sort of unorganized. Francine had done the best that she could, not really being familiar with Nealy's books and records.

By eight o'clock the quiet had turned into chaos because Francine had arrived for class, joined by fifteen four-year-olds. The sound of little voices screaming "Ms. Nealy!" made her smile. Francine seemed relieved to have her back, and they hugged like long lost friends. Nealy didn't mention Randy; she really wanted to talk to her about it when they had more privacy, just in case Francine didn't want the entire studio of mothers knowing her private business.

At ten o'clock she slipped out leaving Francine to teach her class, while she went to talk to Dr. Zimmerman. Because of the misting rain, she grabbed her umbrella and made her way to the car, her feet sinking into the soft ground that covered her shoes in mud.

The hospital appeared quiet, but the noise level would certainly increase as the day progressed. "Hi, I'm Nealy Jones. I'm here to see Dr. Zimmerman," she told the receptionist in his office. Nealy took a seat. Anxiously she waited for him; he held the key to her future.

The door opened and a man walked into the reception area. "Hi, Nealy, I'm Jim Zimmerman," he smiled and shook her hand.

"Hi. Thanks for working me in."

"No problem. Come on in. I'm glad that you could make it before you saw Jerrod. Have a seat, Nealy, please. I'll get right to the point. Jerrod is a fine doctor, and that is why I want to do whatever I can to help him. I'm sure that you are aware of his problems because this is something that has been building for a long time. He has a problem with amphetamines, which he says he has been taking since college."

"He's hooked on speed?" Nealy couldn't believe it.

"Yes, but at times he can control it, Nealy, which is rather unusual. That's why over the years, you have seen erratic behavior, outbursts, and mood swings with periods of restlessness and irritability, alternating with extreme drowsiness. I've never really seen a case exactly like this. Jerrod is really not an addict because he may go for weeks and not take the pills, but then for some reason, he starts taking them again. To make it even worse, he mixes them with alcohol, which is why he has violent outbursts and loses control of his temper."

"Oh my God, I didn't realize that it was this serious."

"Well, now that we have uncovered the problem, I think that we can help him, that is, if he really wants the help. But sometimes when we're talking, I'm not sure if he really believes that he has a problem. He says he can quit, but that he will go through the treatment just to make sure. Truthfully, Nealy, I feel that the only reason he has agreed to treatment is strictly for your benefit. He thinks you'll stay with him if he gets help."

"Jerrod's very charming, and he wrote the book on lying, Dr. Zimmerman, which I'm sure you've noticed."

"Yes, I've noticed. But, he's also a good doctor and a pretty nice guy when he's not taking amphetamines and mixing them with alcohol. And Nealy, one other thing that we must consider here, too, is his sexual behavior. Jerrod produces very high levels of testosterone, which means that his libido, or sexual interest and capacity for arousal, is increased. So what we have here is a person who physically demands a very active sex life. So he takes amphetamines to help him meet those demands. And then as a means of coping with the war going on inside of him, he drinks and seeks sexual perversion to ensure arousal-worthy erections. When this happens, he can't face you because you won't understand. He says you are too nice to understand what he needs when things get him too stressed out. He says that's why he has other women. They will do whatever he wants and for as long as he wants it, regardless of how perverted it is without any demands, arguments, questions, or suspicions."

Nealy sat there, staring at the doctor, unable to really comprehend the whole scenario of Jerrod's problems. "Will he always be this way, or will it change if he gets off the amphetamines?"

"Well, he'll be better if he gets off the pills and the alcohol, but his sex drive is not likely to change. He's made that way, but, of course, as he ages, it will decrease somewhat. But even though Jerrod needs other women, he honestly *loves* you. So, if and when he gets off the drugs, you may be able to satisfy his needs. But, that's something I can't possibly determine. He's one of those men who likes perversion, Nealy, I can see it in his eyes when he talks about it. If you can deal with that, you can probably settle him down, but that's something that you and Jerrod will need to discuss. You need to find out just how far he needs to go—what it takes to satisfy him—in order to eliminate the other women. And then you need to decide if you can meet those demands."

"Oh, I don't know, Dr. Zimmerman."

"Nealy, please call me, Jim. I think we're going to become very good friends over the next month, and there will be no place for formality. You're going to need my friendship, as well as many others, if you decide to stay with Jerrod and see him through this."

"Thanks, Jim, but to be perfectly honest, I'm not in love with Jerrod. I love him and care about his well-being and his happiness, but that's about all. Physically, I'm very drawn to him, but we really don't communicate. We've always spent most of our time together in bed, but, at least, I know now why he wasn't capable of anything afterwards. Jim, I want to talk to him about a divorce, although I'm nervous about it. I'm afraid I'll allow him to talk me out of it, and if he does, I'll only be staying with him because I feel that it's the humanitarian thing to do."

"Nealy, I can certainly understand your feelings. And if you have made up your mind about divorcing him, then I'd like to ask you not to tell him anything definite until he has been in therapy for at least thirty days. During that time, I will do my best to prepare him for your decision. I hate to ask you to do that, but I really think that it will be better for everyone concerned if we postpone that reality."

"All right, Jim, I'll do whatever I can to make it easier for him. I want him to get well," she smiled.

"I know you do. And I do, too. If you need to talk to me, please call. I understand that you spent some time with Phillip Pepper while you were in New York."

"Do you know Phillip?" she asked excitedly.

"We went to med-school together at Columbia. He's a great guy."

Nealy smiled at him. She could feel herself blushing. "Yes, I agree. He's really a nice person. And he sure helped me, in spite of the fact that Rob forced him to babysit me."

The doctor walked her to the door, smiling kindly. "I know Phillip, and even though he's a doctor first, he's still a man. So I'm sure he enjoyed the company of a beautiful woman."

"You're very kind, thanks. Jim, I also want to thank you for being so patient with Jerrod," Nealy said, shaking his hand again. "I'll be in touch soon."

Nealy left the doctor's office and returned to the studio. She picked up some lunch for her and Francine so that they could eat and catch up on the past month. Francine told her all about her new found friendship with Randy, but Nealy could see that it was much more than a mere friendship. Francine had fallen in love, and she felt sure that the feelings were mutual. And that afternoon when Randy stopped by the studio to say "hello" and welcome her back, her suspicions were confirmed, especially with all the sweet exchanges between the two of them; without a doubt, things were definitely serious between Francine and Randy. Of course, Nealy pulled him into her office to give him a hug and express her happiness. Prior to meeting Phillip, a six-year age difference may have concerned her, but now she knew that age had very little to do with how one person feels about another. After taking over for Nealy, Francine had proven to be a very mature twenty-three-year-old, and like Nealy, she had been grown all her life and had a fairly good head on her shoulders. But, with the mess that Nealy had found herself in at the present time, it made her question her own good judgment.

After sitting behind her desk for twenty-minutes trying to convince herself that everything would be alright, she finally left a little before eight to go home and face Jerrod.

All the lights were on, so she knew he was there. After greeting Chance, she walked inside and found Jerrod sitting at the table.

"Hi," she said.

"Hi," he said, looking extremely remorseful. "I'm glad you're back. I missed you."

Nealy couldn't honestly say that she had missed him, so she just smiled. "It's good to be home."

Jerrod walked over and put his arms around her, and she froze, not wanting to hug him or be hugged by him. Nealy closed her eyes. Her heart sank. Could she get through with the long speech that she had prepared for him? "Jerrod, let me feed Chance. Then we can talk. Okay."

"I already fed him." He held her hands and stared at her.

"Oh, thanks. Okay then, we need to talk." Nealy led him into the living room where they rarely sat, so it seemed like mutual territory. She sat on the end of the couch, placing her arm across the back of it so that she could face him, and he sat down, facing her.

"Nealy, I know I've done so much, but I'm going to change. Will you give me a chance to prove that to you?"

"Jerrod, I've asked myself that a million times over the past month. I wanted to hate you for what you did. I called you every name in the book, and I'm not talking about the *Bible*. But I think I finally understand what went wrong."

"Please don't leave me, Nealy," he begged. "I promise I'll never talk to another woman again, except for my patients."

"Jerrod, we can't live our lives like that. It's that thing called trust. Without that, we don't have a marriage. But Jerrod, that's not really the problem. Don't you see, it wasn't all your fault?"

"What?" he said in disbelief.

"I should have thought about things more before I let us fall back into bed together at our reunion. It's a long story, but you'll understand in time. Before deciding to go to New York almost five years ago, I struggled with a decision: Did I want to be with you, or did I want a career? We grew up together and I'll always love you. You were the first boy that I ever kissed. You explained the facts of life to me. And you were the only boy that I ever slept with, even through college. We had sex, but we didn't communicate with each other, because I was much too shy and that wasn't important to you. I only knew one way, and that was your way. I couldn't teach you anything or be assertive enough to tell you what I needed or ask what you needed. And that's why you became bored with me and sought the affections of other females. Maybe if I had dated other people and had a few experiences of my own, I could have brought more to our sex life, a little variety—"

"You wanted to *get-it-on* with other guys?"

"No. Please, Jerrod, let me finish. What I'm trying to say is that...well, maybe I should have because something was missing, and I didn't have a clue what it was. I needed more, and you needed more."

"But Nealy, I can't stand the thought of another guy touching you. I'd kill both of you. You've always been mine. I knew you'd never let anyone else touch you."

Nealy flinched as the thoughts of she and Phillip making love in front of the fire flashed before her. "Jerrod, that's pretty strong language."

"I couldn't stand that, Nealy. Baby, Neal, I can't let you go. I love you. I have some problems, but with your help I can work them out."

"I know, I talked to Jim Zimmerman today."

Looking rather surprised, he asked, "You did? Did he tell you about the pills?"

"Yes, he told me everything, Jerrod, but there is still the thing about sex."

"Nealy, without the pills, you'll be more woman than I can handle. We've always had a *screw-each-other's-brains-out* kind of thing," he said without thinking. "I'm sorry, that sounded crude, but Nealy, we've never had a problem with sex."

Nealy looked away, and then looked back at him very serious. "Yes we have, Jerrod, but I didn't really know what the problems were. That is what I'm trying to tell you. I didn't want to spend hours humping—excuse the expression—I wanted to be held, and I wanted to talk and laugh afterwards."

"I can do that, Nealy. I swear I can, now that I know what you want from me. Baby, please give me a chance. Just help me get off the pills, and I'll show you. I'll never see any of those people again, and I'll be tender and considerate and loving and anything else that you want me to be. We don't even have to *do it* again until you're ready." Jerrod leaned over and kissed her cheek and took her hands in his. "Please, Nealy, just give me a chance. Please...please. And then if I screw up, which I won't, I'll let you go without any arguments." He begged her almost pathetically.

Nealy sat there, struggling desperately to find the courage to say no, but she couldn't find it in her heart to say what she really felt. This was her husband, the person that she had spent most of her young adult life with, and he was begging her. How could she say no? "Jerrod, I'd like us to try something."

"What?"

"I want us to separate at least for the next month while you're getting off the pills."

"No, Nealy," he cried. "I can't do this without you."

"No, it won't be like that. I want you to live at the fraternity house, but we'll see each other every night that you're not on duty. I need us to be sure. I can't go through another traumatic experience like what I just went through. That was just too hard on both of us. Jerrod, please, just until you get off the pills. And then we can start fresh." Nealy hugged him, trying to make him understand that she wasn't ending their marriage, at least not yet, but that she needed time, they both needed time.

"Will that make you happy?"

"Yes. We need to clear the slate, Jerrod, or it won't work. I need time to forgive you and forget all the terrible things that happened before I can be with you again. I really need this."

"Okay, I'll agree to that because I made so many mistakes. I want to prove to you that I can be faithful and free of the drugs. I want us to be together. I don't want a divorce."

"I know you don't," she said, her heart breaking at the thought of never seeing Phillip again. She could barely bring herself to speak, but she had to. "I'll help you, Jerrod."

Jerrod hugged her so tightly that she thought she couldn't breathe. It was as if he were holding on for dear life, which broke her heart and made her want to console him, even when she didn't want to. None of it made sense anymore, and she didn't know if she was strong enough to keep her distance from Jerrod and Phillip, too, at least until Jerrod got through with his therapy.

Jerrod pulled her onto his lap and stretched out on the couch, taking her with him. "Jerrod," she cried softly, "I don't want—"

"Nealy, I'm not going to do anything, I just want to hold you. Please, let me just hold you." She tried to relax and rest her head on his shoulder, but she felt so uncomfortable for fear that it was Jerrod's way of getting her into bed. After a few minutes, Jerrod began kissing her forehead, her face, and then he tried to bring her chin up so that he could kiss her lips, but she pulled away. "Can't we even kiss each other?"

"No, Jerrod, I just need some time. I won't see you if..."

"Okay. I'm sorry," he sighed.

"Would you like to go out and get something to eat?" she suggested as a way of getting him out of the house, which would prevent him from trying to pressure her into bed.

"I guess, if that's all we can do," he whined. He got up from the couch slowly, obviously disturbed by her cautious and distant attitude towards him.

But before they left, she helped him gather up some clothing to take back to the fraternity house.

After dinner, Nealy had Jerrod drop her off at the house, telling him that she was exhausted and wanted to go to bed early. She could tell that sending him away, not allowing him to spend more time with her, had made him slightly angry, but he didn't dare say anything. Nealy called Phillip and told him about everything that had happened. She was relieved that he understood why she had to stay with Jerrod for now, and he seemed extremely happy that Jerrod was moving into the fraternity house. Phillip cautioned her to be careful, not to provoke him. He warned her that, even though Jerrod said he wasn't really addicted, he would experience some withdrawals from the drugs, which would cause him to be edgy and irritable. Now, all she had to do was wait and be patient, and she would see Phillip again. But did it really matter? They were still two-thousand miles apart and both of them had worked hard to establish their careers.

CHAPTER THIRTY-FIVE

FOR THE NEXT MONTH Jerrod kept his promise to Nealy, but he did get a little angry when she pulled away from his attempts to kiss her or when she scolded him for putting his hand under her blouse and fondling her breasts or when he came up behind her and wrapped his arms tightly around her and massaged her crotch. It made her crazy, but she tried to be patient. At times, she even wanted to give in because it had been a long time since she had made love and it aroused her, but she didn't want Jerrod—she wanted Phillip.

Dr. Zimmerman called Nealy just before noon on Friday at the end of Jerrod's four week rehabilitation program. He asked her to drop by the office so that he could talk to her about Jerrod's progress. He seemed to think that Jerrod showed definite signs of improvement and he felt certain that he had given up the pills completely; they had tested him for four weeks on a weekly basis to see if the substance appeared in his system and there had not been even a trace. Dr. Zimmerman told her to pursue her plans regarding a divorce because in his professional opinion Jerrod could handle the truth and the rejection, if that were still her plan. And after weeks of separation, the timing would be right to make the break.

As soon as she got home from the psychologist's office, she called Jerrod at the hospital to tell him that she wanted him to come by the house that evening. Nealy wanted to tell him right away about her decision to file for a divorce so that she could go on with her life, the weeks away from Phillip had been torture.

"Jerrod, I need to see you. Can we get together tonight?"

The urgency in her voice excited him. Thank God, she had finally come around he thought. "Oh, baby I want to see you, too, but I'm on call until Sunday afternoon."

"You can't even get away for an hour?"

"Neal, baby, you're toying with me...but I like it," he said, enjoying the fact that she wanted him, finally. He could trade with someone, but she had put him through a nightmare of frustration for weeks so he wanted her to simmer for awhile. That way she would be out-of-control with desire by the time they get together.

Disappointed, she remained silent for a moment, and then she sighed heavily, "Okay, I guess I'll see you Sunday afternoon."

"I'm really sorry, Neal, but I'll make it up to you. I'll be just what you want, I promise."

Not really paying attention any longer she agreed, "Yeah, okay. Sunday's fine." Less than a minute after she hung up the phone, it rang. Because her mood had changed so drastically from a heavenly euphoria to a hellish deflation, she almost didn't answer it. But what if it were Phillip, she panicked, grabbing it on the fourth ring.

"Hello."

"Nealy, it's Tony."

"Oh, my God, how are you?"

"I couldn't be better. And you?"

"Good. I'm good," she struggled to sound up-beat.

"Hey, listen, I've got an offer you can't refuse," he blurted out too excited to pick up on her less-bubbly-than-usual voice. "Remember that girl I told you about a while back, you know, the dancer with the theatrical club?"

"Oh, sure, I remember."

"Well, I'm going to be her manager. And since I'll be going on the road for awhile, I thought you might want to use my spare office and find work for your actors, dancers, etcetera."

"Tony, are you sure?" The thought of being in New York brought life back into her voice.

"Sure, I'm sure. But, I need you to do me a favor in exchange for my generosity."

"I knew there'd be a catch. What is it?"

"Just help my clients, too, from time to time."

"You trust me to do that?" she asked, unsure of herself.

"You can do anything you set your mind to do, Nealy. I know you can do it. I've got everything arranged for you. My secretary will tell you how to get through the door, and you can do the rest. I need you, Nealy. Just think. You can hang out at Freddy's occasionally and get a little practice, if nothing else. And besides, you never know when you'll need the extra cash," he laughed.

"Well, ain't that the truth," she said, contemplating life as a single woman again.

"Good, I knew I could count you."

"Tony—"

"Oh, and one more thing," he intentionally interrupted. "You want to come to my wedding?"

"Wedding! Tony, when?"

"Tomorrow at five."

"What?"

"Are you deaf, or is that so hard to believe?"

"No, it's just that...uh, I'm speechless."

"You, speechless? Well, that's a first. No it's a second. That Frenchman left you speechless as I remember it," he snickered a little. "So, anyway, can you come? I know it's a short—real short—notice, and of course I'll understand if you can't make it."

"No, I'll be there," she blurted out, not even sure if she could get a flight.

"Great! Call me when you get to the city. I'll give you all details about the office, the wedding, and all."

"Okay, Tony. Hey, listen. I'm really happy for you."

That wasn't really what he wanted to hear, but, with that, he knew that he had made the right choice. Nealy didn't love him back and she never would. "Thanks, Nealy. I'm happy for me, too," he said, his voice drifting.

"You sound a little nervous, but I understand. Marriage is hard, but you'll do fine. I can't wait to meet the future Mrs.Rose."

"Why don't you bring the *good doctor* along in case I need one," he joked, trying not to sound sarcastic.

Nealy laughed. "Tony, you're so silly. But, maybe I will."

"What's happening with your marital situation?" he asked.

"Oh, I'm still married," she said, not wanting to tell him that another marriage was ending in divorce. That is not the sort of news that someone who is headed to the altar after avoiding it for years needs to hear. Of course when she walked into the chapel with Phillip, who she planned to take with her, Tony would know that she had made a decision. Nealy was not the type to be committed to one man and sleeping with another. Maybe Denise had talked to Tony and told him that she spent time with Phillip before returning to Texas. Maybe that's why he told her to bring him to the wedding. The timing for Tony's wedding had been almost perfect. *Perfect* would have given her one more week to tell Jerrod and file for divorce. More than anything she wanted to tell Phillip that they could look forward to a future together, that is, if he hadn't changed his mind. Changed his mind! Now that's a scary thought. Well, she would soon find out. Nealy wanted so much to see him and be with him again, and she prayed that he would be just as eager to see her. "Listen, Tony, I better go. I have a plane to catch. If we get a chance, we can talk about the office tomorrow. See you at the *'church on time'*," she sang, humming the familiar tune until Tony said good-bye and hung up.

Singing and dancing around the room, she got the phone book out and called the airlines, and then she called the hospital to tell Jerrod about Tony's wedding. Butterflies went spastic in her stomach as the phone at the nurses station rang over and over again before someone finally answered it.

"Fifth floor nurse's station."

"Dr. Jones, please."

"He's in surgery."

"This is Nealy Jones. Could I leave a message?"

"Sure."

"I'm leaving for New York. My friend is getting married—I just found out two minutes ago—and I will be home Sunday night. Tell him I'll call him the minute I get back."

"Okay, I'll give him the message."

"Thanks," she hung up in relief that she didn't have to talk to Jerrod. Next, she called the studio to talk to Francine who had taken over her afternoon classes. She prayed that she didn't have plans so that she could teach her classes on Saturday as well. Her prayers were answered because Francine seemed delighted. Nealy exclaimed, "I love you and I'll sing at your wedding." They both laughed. As she dialed the number to Phillip's office, her fingers shook and her heart pounded.

"Dr. Phillip Pepper's office," Eve said cheerfully.

"Excuse me, but in a case where there is obvious signs of extreme insanity would your shrink recommend a complete frontal lobotomy?"

"Nealy, is that you?" Eve laughed, recognizing her voice.

"Yes, it's me," she giggled happily.

"It's so good to hear your sweet, cheerful voice again. How are you, dear?" Eve asked, excited to hear from her.

"I'm wonderful, thank you. And you?"

"Oh, honey, I'm doing just fine. Hold on. Let me get the doctor for you," she said buzzing his office. "Phillip, Nealy's on line one."

He grabbed the phone for fear that something was wrong since she never called him in during the day. "Are you alright?"

"I will be if you can pick me up at ten-forty-five?"

He smiled and raised up in his chair. "Please tell me that you're talking about tonight."

"Yes! Tonight! I'll burst if I spend another night out of your arms," she cried ecstatically.

"Sweetheart, I'm on my way to the airport." Phillip jumped up out of his chair, grabbed his coat, and quickly walked out into his waiting room where he lifted Eve up into his arms and twirled her around.

"Doctor," she screamed, not sure what to make of his behavior.
He put her down and kissed her on the cheek. "Nealy's coming tonight. I'm out of here. Call me *only* if there is an emergency," he said, winking and smiling the biggest smile that she had ever gotten from him.

"That boy's in love," she stated out loud to herself, delighted that he had finally found the woman of his dreams.

From nine o'clock until ten-forty-five, Phillip paced the floor at the airport, eagerly awaiting Nealy's arrival. He felt like an expectant father waiting for the birth of his first child, and he appeared every bit as nervous. It had been a month since he had seen Nealy, and the anticipation of seeing her and being with her again excited him more than he ever thought possible. One big ball of nerves, he had worn a path between the gate and the monitors, checking to see if the flight had landed yet.

Finally, the monitor began to flash. The plane had landed. His heart raced, sending all of his blood to his face. Phillip watched as the airplane taxied into the gate. When the doors at the gate opened, he made sure that he had a clear view of the passengers as they came down the jetway.

When Nealy turned the corner she saw him. Her heart thumped so hard that it hurt. It seemed more like a year instead of a month since she'd seen him. Pushing her way past the other passengers, she dropped her two small carry-on's and threw her arms around his neck. "Oh my God, I've missed you," she said.

Phillip held her as if he never planned to let her go. "I've missed you, too. I never thought I could miss anyone this much." When he pulled back to look at her, he saw that she had tears in her eyes, which unnerved him. "Sweetheart, what's the matter?"

Wiping the tears away with her finger tips, trying not to ruin her make-up, she said, "Nothing, I'm just so happy to see you again. It's a girl-thing, you know, like bursting with joy," she giggled her zany giggle.

"That's not just a girl-thing, I feel like crying myself. Come here," he said, pulling her close and hugging her again tightly. "Oh, my pretty, pretty lady. I've missed you so much."

Nealy looked at him, and he really did have tears in his eyes. "Oh, Phillip, you really did miss me," she said softly, tears once again filling her big, emerald-colored eyes.

"Let's get out of here before we make a scene," he smiled. They retrieved the bags that she had dropped on the floor, which had been stepped on by several people, but she didn't care.

After stopping off at the baggage claim, Phillip led her outside to the curb. An attendant jumped out of a black stretch limousine and took her luggage from Phillip.

"What's this?" Nealy asked, surprised.

"I didn't want to waste one minute of the time I have to spend with you behind the wheel of a car, so I got us a limo for the week-end," he said, smiling and guiding her inside.

"This is wonderful," she exclaimed, "but Phillip, isn't this a little extravagant?"

"Not when I have only two days to spend with you. And during that time, I want to be touching some part of your incredible body at all times." Phillip pulled her close. "You get prettier every time I see you."

"Thanks. So do you," she smiled, kissing him softly and snuggling up to his chest. "I really missed you. Sometimes at night I would imagine that I was snuggled up to you, and I could feel your heart beating against my cheek. Phillip, that vision kept me going. When Tony called me about the wedding, all of my prayers were answered."

Looking down at her rather confused, he asked, "What wedding?"

"Tony's....Oh, that's right. I didn't tell you about that, did I? Tony's marrying some stage actress tomorrow at five o'clock. And we're both invited."

"Both of us?" he asked quizzically.

"Yes, both of us," she repeated. "In fact, he said, and I quote, 'Nealy, you can even bring *the good doctor* with you.' You'll go with me, won't you?"

"Nealy, I'd go to *hell* with you, if you wanted me to."

"Phillip," she cried. "Be serious."

"I am serious," he said, pulling her closer to him.

"But, there's more. He also wants me to sublet his extra office and help with some of his clients while he goes gallivanting around the country with his new wife and her repertoire group."

"You're kidding. Maybe I read Tony wrong. Hmm. I remember you telling me about that, but I thought it was his way of getting you back here for his own personal benefit."

"And you thought that Tony wanted more than friendship."

"He couldn't wait forever, Nealy. People have to go on with their lives even if they know in their heart that they'll *never* love anyone as much as they love you."

"Oh, Phillip, that's crazy," she giggled. "Tony sounded really excited about getting married."

"What's her name?"

"What?"

"What's the girl's name that he's marrying?"

"I don't know. He didn't say," she said innocently.

"Nealy, a man who is really crazy about a woman mentions her name over and over. There are two things that all people, including Tony, love to hear: their own name and the name of the person they love. Just ask Eve. I make her mention your name to me at least ten times a day." Phillip smiled and nodded his head up and down. "I do. I'm not kidding."

"Oh, you do not," she giggled, shaking her head back and forth to the side.

"Ask her the next time you talk to her. She'll tell you. In fact, she knew that I'd fallen in love with you before I did."

"You're in *love with me?*" she asked circumspectly in a whispered voice, getting teary-eyed again.

Phillip touched her face gently, "I'm desperately and hopelessly *in love* with you. I've never loved anyone as much as I love you, and I promise, as *God* is my witness, I *never* will." He kissed her sweetly and then held her close to him until they reached his apartment.

They made love all night long, not falling asleep until dawn appeared through the windows. Nealy's eyes opened around noon, and she lay very still, watching Phillip sleep for more than an hour. She enjoyed watching him sleep and listening to him quietly breathing in and out, obviously very contented.

Wanting to surprise him, she slipped out of bed, went downstairs to make breakfast, and then took it up to him in bed. When she softly called out to him, wearing only an apron that she had found in the drawer, he opened his eyes slowly. When he realized that all she had on was an apron, he sat up in bed. "Hmm, turn around," he ordered, smiling and raising his eyebrows. Slowly, she turned around, exposing her smooth backside. "That looks a lot better on you than it does on me."

Nealy giggled and sat his breakfast down. "I packed in such a hurry that I forgot to bring a robe or a nightgown. So, I borrowed your apron. I knew you wouldn't mind."

"No, I certainly don't. But knowing you as I do, I'm sure you wore more than that while you were cooking. If not, I'm sure my neighbors across the way enjoyed the scenery tremendously."

Nealy laughed. "No, this is just for your benefit. Downstairs, I wore your shirt, too."

After he sighed with relief, he took the tray and pulled back the covers for her to join him for breakfast in bed. "Would you do something for me?" he asked seriously.

"Anything," she snapped.

"Since I don't want to share one inch of your curvaceous body with even the eyes of another person, I'd like you to wear a nun's habit in public." Both of them laughed wildly, kissing and hugging like two gloriously happy people who were crazy about each other.

Since they had to cross the city, they had to leave for the wedding at four o'clock. When they walked into the chapel, Denise spotted them. When she got their attention she motioned for them to join her and Dan. Nealy asked if she had seen Tony, but he was no where to be found. Denise was afraid that he had gotten cold feet since he had decided to get married in less than a week. There were less than twenty people in the small chapel. Waiting patiently for the ceremony to start, and then, fifteen minutes late, the music started. Nealy and Denise look at each other and breathed a sigh of relief.

Tony appeared through a small door near the front of the church with two of his friends. When he saw Nealy, his face lit up, but then, when he saw *the good doctor* sitting next to her, his jaw tightened and he quickly looked away. Phillip saw the sadness in his face, and he looked at Nealy to see if she had interpreted his body language to mean what Phillip knew it meant. Still smiling, she obviously hadn't. The bride came down the aisle on her father's arm. A pretty brunette, tall and slender. Tony smiled slightly which displayed at least some reservations. But ten minutes later, the minister pronounced them man and wife.

At the reception, at a nearby restaurant, Phillip encouraged Nealy to speak to Tony about the office. Having an office in New York would ensure him spending some time with her until she finally settled her affairs in Texas. Unfortunately, it wasn't a good time to discuss business, so they agreed to talk more about it later. Phillip watched Tony. He could see how much Tony loved Nealy just by the way he stared at her when she talked; his eyes were sad. Tony's bride seemed sweet and bright, and he obviously cared for her, but clearly as a second choice. Not really knowing much about Nealy and the close friendship that she had shared with Tony, Marissa didn't notice the sadness in her new husband's face. And because Nealy was so sweet and genuinely elated about their marriage, Marissa immediately warmed up to her as most people did when they met Nealy Jones—soon to be James—and, if all went as planned, the future Mrs. Nealy Pepper.

Tony was cordial to Phillip, but it was easy to detect his jealousy when he introduced Phillip as *the good doctor*. But Tony had only himself to blame. During the year that Nealy lived in New York, she had spent most of her free time with him, but he never once told her how he felt.

After the reception, Nealy and Phillip went out to the Cafe Carlyle at the Carlyle Hotel for a steak dinner and to listen to Bobby Short sing romantic songs. It was the perfect way to set the mood for the long night of love making ahead of them, even though just being together seemed equally as intimate.

On Sunday, they stayed in bed most of the day, blaming it on the rain. By one o'clock, they had gotten pretty hungry, so Phillip called the restaurant and had two large pizzas delivered. In between napping, talking, and *fooling* around, they fed pizza to each other off and on for the rest of the day. With his arms tightly around Nealy's body, he whispered, "I can't let you go."

"I don't want to go," she whined, snuggling closer to him. "The fact that I'm here is like a dream come true. I thought up a thousand excuses to come back here during the last month, but I knew none of them would work. Whenever Jerrod came close to me, I wanted to scream out your name."

He pulled away to look into her eyes. "Oh, Nealy, I love you so much...although I know I have no right to say that to you."

Nealy folded her arms and placed them across his chest, resting her chin on her hands. "You have every right, just as I do. I love you, too, Phillip Pepper, with all my heart and soul."

"I'll probably tell you that I *love you* so much that you'll get tired of hearing it," he said softly, sweeping her hair up into a knot on top of her head.

"I'll never get tired of hearing it, not even if I lived to be a hundred," she said, smiling and rolling over onto her back. "Phillip, can we really be this much in love or is this just a wild case of lust? We just met two months ago."

Phillip raised up onto his side and looked into her eyes. "I never believed in love at first sight, but I honestly fell in love with you that first night. And that wasn't two months ago, it was three years, seven months, and nine days ago. My colleagues, as well as I, consider this sort of assumption contemptible, but when you smiled at me that very first time, I knew that we'd be together someday. And, Nealy, we will. I promise."

CHAPTER THIRTY-SIX

NEALY HAD BEEN SCHEDULED to leave on a one o'clock flight, but she couldn't stand the thought of leaving Phillip, so she called and changed her flight to late afternoon. Her meeting with Jerrod would just have to wait until the following night. The limousine picked Phillip and Nealy up at four o'clock and drove them to the airport. During the drive, the two of them mostly stared at each other and talked softly and slowly, nervously lacing their fingers together and then apart, over and over again.

"Excuse me, but could you give us a moment alone please," Phillip asked the limo driver.

"Certainly, sir," he said, opening the door and stepping outside.

Phillip took Nealy into his arms and held her close. The thought of returning to the loneliness that they had felt over the past month made it almost impossible for them to part. When they looked at each other, they both had tears in their eyes. "I won't cry if you won't," Phillip said, blotting her tears with his handkerchief.

"Okay," she said trying hard to hold back the tears. "I love you, *Peppee*."

"I love you, too...*Angel Lips*," he chuckled, wiping another tear off her cheek.

Nealy giggled out loud. "*Angel Lips*."

"Yeah, *Angel Lips*. If you can call me *Peppee*, I can call you *Angel Lips*." He grinned, and his clear blue-gray eyes, which were now streaked with tiny red lines, danced.

"If you insist on a nickname, I prefer *Scarlett*, but the only thing that worries me about that is the fact that you'll probably want to imitate Clark Gable again," she grinned.

"*Frankly, my dear, I don't—*" Abruptly, he stopped talking and pulled her into his arms. "Hold me," he whispered softly.

"Phillip, I love you. We'll be together again soon," she said, feeling his need for reassurance.

"I know we will." He kissed her and she desperately kissed him back, clinging to him for their final minutes of intimacy.

They held hands tightly as Phillip escorted her down to the gate. When their eyes met, he winked at her and smiled, and she smiled back shyly. Neither one of them could speak. Their teeth were clinched as massive lumps settled in their throats, making it hard to swallow, and the tightness that burned deep inside of their chests made breathing difficult. At the gate, he took her into his arms and held her until the last call was announced for her flight. For a brief, but intense moment, their eyes met. Phillip kissed away a tear from her face. "I love you."

"I love you, too." In slow motion, she backed away from him. They held hands until their fingertips no longer touched. Then she turned and walked numbly through the gate, glancing back only once to blow him a kiss.

For what seemed like hours on the airplane, Nealy starred down into the darkness, unable to ignore the pain that tugged at her heart. She prayed for a sign that things would be okay, that she and Phillip would be together someday. Then, from out of nowhere, came this multitude of lights that flickered brightly, sending her a coded message out of the black sky. A peace engulfed her, like some sort of divine intervention. And with that, she knew her prayers had been answered.

Afterwards she tried to read her book, but she found herself staring at the picture of her and Phillip like the one she had framed for him, which she used to mark her place. It would be safe there because her book went with her everywhere, and at night she kept it in her nightstand beside the bed.

At almost midnight, she walked inside her house and the phone rang out, making her jump. Quickly, she dropped her bags, turned on the kitchen light, and grabbed the phone, hoping that it would be Phillip on the other end. Before they left the airport, he told her that he would call just to make sure that she had gotten home alright. "Hello," she said cheerfully.

"Nealy, this is J.T. Is Jerrod home?" Nealy had been caught off guard because Jerrod's father rarely ever called their house, and he would never call at midnight.

"Uh, no, J.T., he isn't. He must be at the hospital. Is something wrong?" she asked, becoming alarmed.

"Well, they've paged him, but he didn't answer his page," he said nervously.

"You're at the hospital?"

"Yes. Nadine had a massive heart attack—"

"Oh my God," she cried out. "Are you in emergency?"

"Yes."

"J.T., I'll find him. We'll be right there," she said, hanging up the phone. "Sorry, Chancey, I have to go out again. Thank goodness for Francine. Chance's bowl had food in it, so Nealy knew that she had come by to feed him. Nealy thanked *God* for her friends on the way out the gate and prayed that he would take care of Jerrod's mother.

Nealy drove as fast as she could towards the fraternity house. When she got there, she hurried inside. Because it was late, no one lurked in the hallway, so Nealy ran upstairs to the room that Jerrod had moved into when they separated. She knocked on the door quietly, not wanting to disturb the whole place, but she had to get him up. When he didn't answer, she knocked a little harder. And finally, the voice of a female called out something that Nealy didn't understand. Then Jerrod yelled, "Go away."

Getting angry and determined to get his attention, she shouted, "Jerrod, open this fuckin' door! Your Mother has been taken to the hospital. Jerrod, please. Hurry!"

Immediately, the door swung open and Jerrod stood in the doorway without a stitch of clothes on. "What?" he said rubbing his eyes.

"Your father called the house. Your mother had a heart attack. Get dressed, and I'll meet you at the emergency room," she said rantingly.

Nealy rushed over to the hospital. She was out of breath and terrified at the seriousness of Nadine's condition.

"Nealy!" a voice called out to her.

She rushed towards her father-in-law, and gave him a hug. "Oh, J.T., I'm so sorry. How is she?"

"I don't know. Did you find Jerrod?"

"He'll be here in a minute. Are you okay?" she said, changing the subject.

"I'm fine," he said, running his fingers through his thick salt and pepper colored hair and sighing heavily.

"Where's Nadine?" she asked.

"The doctors rushed her somewhere. I'm not sure."

"Let me find out. Wait here." Nealy hurried over to the nurse's station and found out that they had taken her up to cardiology after the doctor had confirmed her diagnosis. "J.T., come on, let's go up to cardiology."

When they got upstairs, Randy was on call, and they had also called in the Head of Cardiology, who would be arriving any minute. "Randy, how is she?" Nealy asked.

"It doesn't look good. Surgery may save her. We just don't know yet. Nealy, I'm sorry," he said regretfully.

Nealy touched his arm. "Thanks, Randy. Can we see her?"

"Come with me," he said, leading them into the room where she was being attended to by nurses scurrying all around her.

Nealy took hold of J.T.'s hand and led him over to the bed. Nadine looked up and saw them. Her face was pale, and she had a very frightened expression on her face, which brought tears to Nealy's eyes. Nealy went around the bed so that J.T. could move closer and hold her hand. Nealy took Nadine's other hand and kissed her cheek. "You're going to be fine, Nadine," Nealy said softly and confidently. J.T. couldn't speak; he just stood there staring at her.

"Is Jerrod here?" she whispered. And about that time, the door opened, and Jerrod sailed into the room.

He affectionately touched his father on the back and leaned across the bed where he could talk to his mother. "Dr. Breckland will be here in a minute, Mom, so just relax. Everything's going to be fine," he said, smiling at her. Even though the oxygen mask covered her face, she managed to smile at her son. Jerrod looked at Nealy and saw the tears rolling down her cheeks. He walked around the bed and put his arm around her shoulders and squeezed her. "You okay?"

"I'm fine," she said, looking up at him compassionately.

"Nealy," Nadine whispered.

Nealy leaned down closer. "Yes," she whispered, straining to hear her.

Nadine tried to squeeze her hand around both Nealy and Jerrod's hands, linking them all together. "Nealy, take care of Jerrod. He needs you. I've always been there for J.T. I want you to promise me that you'll be there for Jerrod. Nobody's perfect, Nealy, but I know he loves you, so stand by him. I need you to promise me that so I won't worry. He's my only child. I...I want the best for him. Please...promise me, honey," she struggled with her words. Her eyes begged Nealy as her breath grew shallow.

Nealy put her other hand over both Jerrod and Nadine's hands, and desperately trying not to lose control, she answered softly, "I will, Nadine. I'll take care of him. I promise." Nealy looked up at Jerrod, and he actually had tears rolling down his cheeks. She could barely stand it. When she glanced up at J.T., he appeared calm, but his expression reflected the pain. His eyes were watering, but he didn't cry.

Finally, another doctor appeared and nodded for them to leave the room. Nealy led J.T. out of the room and left Jerrod to stay behind with the other doctors. On the way out, Randy smiled at her and touched her arm with a reassuring pat.

Within minutes, Jerrod came out and told his Dad that the doctors wanted to operate because they thought she'd have a better chance if they did. And of course his father gave his permission.

And for the next three days, Nealy waited with J.T. and Jerrod, who refused to leave the hospital. She would leave only long enough each day to go home, take a quick shower, feed the dog, and run by the fraternity house to gather up some clothes for Jerrod. Early on that Monday morning, before Nealy had a chance to leave, she had asked Rob to call Phillip because she knew he would be frantic with worry when she didn't answer the phone. And Francine, God bless her, took care of her business. Aunt Janey brought J.T. a change of clothes each day and stayed with him, along with her sisters, Ruth and Sarah Beth. Christine, J.T.'s secretary and lover of many years, called the hospital several times and asked for Nealy because Nealy had always been the nicest to her. Really, the family had always accepted the affair between J.T. and Christine because Nadine accepted it, which was something that Nealy had never really understood. But at least Christine hadn't come to the hospital, thank God she had some good sense and compassion.

Nealy made many phone calls during the day to the studio and to friends and to family, keeping everyone abreast of Nadine's condition. Her insides tore apart every time she picked up the phone because she wanted so much to hear the sound of Phillip's voice, but she just couldn't bring herself to call him under the circumstances. And every time Jerrod kissed her in front of the family, she tried hard not to pull away from him. He had not mentioned anything about her finding him in bed with someone else; in fact, he pretended that nothing had ever been anything but perfect. She played along with his little charade for the time being, but once his mother got well, it would all—now and forever—be over.

Before midnight on the third day after Nadine's surgery, the doctors called in the family. They tightly gathered around her bed. The Priest read the last rites over Nadine just before her spirit departed her earthly remains and descended into the Heavens to join her Heavenly Father. Most everyone wept, but Jerrod and his father stood there as if they couldn't believe it. Their eyes showed signs of deep sadness and sorrow with narrowing, slow blinks, but they didn't shed one tear because "real men" don't expose their emotions. To allow themselves to break down and weep wouldn't be manly; it would only prove the weakness in their character. Nealy wanted to cry for them as she watched their faces. They looked defeated by their loss; and Jerrod, a future cardiologist, couldn't save his own mother. How would he deal with that?

When they left the hospital, Nealy and Jerrod went home with J.T and Janey. They didn't want him to be alone, and it would be better for everyone to be there to discuss the arrangements for her funeral. Nealy slept in the same room with Jerrod because she promised his mother that she wouldn't leave him, and she said it right in front of his father. How could she have made such a promise? Because of it, she would be forced to live with a man that she didn't love, longing for another. How could she have done that? Why did Nadine have to put her on the spot like that? Maybe Nadine had accepted all of J.T.'s affairs over the years because his mother made her promise the same thing on *her* deathbed. But with Nadine gone, she would never know.

Nealy lay down on the bed because she was totally exhausted, and Jerrod did the same. She didn't even undress or get under the covers, but she held him because she knew he hurt. His mother had meant the world to him, and he had been her life. Now she was gone. He loved his father, but it wasn't the same. Boys, from birth, have this special bond with their mothers, just as girls do with their fathers.

At the funeral, Nealy sat between Jerrod and J.T., glancing up at them from time to time, out of concern. She ached for them because this had been so unexpected. Nadine always looked like the picture of health, but now she was gone. Jerrod's aunts sat on the other side of J.T., and Janey held his hand. The fact that her brother had been unfaithful to his wife for, most likely, all of his married life, didn't change her feelings for him at all. But it had certainly changed her feelings about her husband when she caught him. Nealy wondered why, but she figured that blood really is thicker than water. Most of them didn't acknowledge Christine, who slipped in and sat in the back of the funeral parlor, but Nealy smiled at her when they walked out. Nadine had called on Christine to take care of her personal things for years, knowing all along that her husband cohabited with her from time to time. J.T. and Christine often went off together for a week at a time, and Nadine knew full well that they didn't sleep in separate bedrooms. When he returned, he would sleep with Nadine as if she were the only one. Nadine liked Christine, so why shouldn't she be nice to her? After all, Christine would soon become Nealy's mother-in-law since she had promised Nadine that she would stay with Jerrod. Oh, dear Lord, what had she done?

Jerrod moved his things back home on Sunday after a long talk with Nealy about their future together. Nealy made sure that he understood that she promised not to leave him, but she didn't promise to sleep with him. And from that day on, she planned to sleep in the other bedroom because she didn't want a marriage like his father's. The fact that she had found Jerrod in bed on the night his mother took ill, had changed their agreement to talk about their marriage after his treatments. Of course, Jerrod thought, that Nealy couldn't resist his charm and that eventually she would give-in because he knew that she liked sex almost as much as he did. For the time being, though, he agreed to accept whatever arrangements she proposed to him, and he smiled at her constantly and showered her with compliments. Not one time during the few days that they had been back together had he tried to seduce her. Jerrod knew better, and he played it very cool.

Monday morning, before dawn, Nealy heard the back door close. Jerrod had left for the hospital. She got up and dressed so that she could get to the studio early and catch up, once again, on some paperwork. Just before she walked out the door, at six-forty-five, the phone rang and when she heard Phillip's voice, she burst into tears, blubbering all sorts of things.

"Nealy, sweetheart, what's the matter? I can't understand you," he said, begging her to talk to him. But she just held the phone to her ear and wept almost hysterical at times. "Nealy, please, get control of yourself. Sweetheart, just take one deep breath for me." He just kept talking to her in his never-failing, calming, psychiatrist-trained tone.

And finally, she drew a deep breath, "I'm sorry."

"Don't talk for a minute. Just relax and breathe deeply while I talk. I know about Jerrod's mother. I'm sorry, Nealy, and I'm sorry for Jerrod. That's really hard, especially with everything else that's going on. I got concerned when I couldn't reach you, but I know that you were a big help and that you had to be with him during this. Nealy, are you feeling better now?" he asked, wanting so much to hold her, to comfort her.

"Yes. But, Phillip, this has been such a mess. I feel sorry for him, but this has ruined my life. I'll never be able to be with you now," she cried, her voice cracking.

"Why? Nealy, what are you talking about?"

"His mother made me promise on her deathbed that I would stay with him. And Phillip, I told her I would. I didn't know what else to say. She made me promise," she cried out.

"But, Nealy, you can't be expected to do that. You were just trying to agree to her last wishes. Sweetheart, people do that all the time."

Nealy sat down on the chair and put her face in her lap, pressing the phone up against her ear. "But, Phillip, I promised. I can't break a promise that I made to someone who died," she cried. "Why did I do such a stupid thing? I'm an idiot. I guess this is what I deserve."

"Oh, come on, sweetheart, don't be so hard on yourself. This will pass, and things will get back to normal. I promised you that we would be together and I intend on keeping that promise," he said softly, trying desperately to console her.

"How can I expect you to keep yours, if I can't keep mine?"

"I made a huge mess of things, Phillip. And now Jerrod is back here."

"He moved back in?" he asked; a sharp pain ripped through his heart.

"Yes, he moved back here last night. He'll never let me out of that promise, Phillip. And he reminds me of it constantly. It's as though he planned it. I moved into the spare bedroom, but that's not going to last long. I know him, and I know how he works on my mind. He hasn't even mentioned the fact that I had to drag him out of bed with some girl that night when his father called looking for him. But I was doing the same thing, so what could I say. I'm not any better than he is," she said, her voice quivering as she talked.

"Nealy, I wish I could help you, but I can't. All I can do is love you more than life itself."

"You can't love me. Look what I did to us. I ruined every chance we had at being together. I screwed it all up. Don't love me, Phillip. I don't deserve someone like you. You would never do this to me," she screamed hysterically.

"Nealy, you're just emotional from all of this. Do me a favor, please. Are you listening to me?"

Nealy felt numb, hearing Nadine's words over and over again in her mind. "I...oh, God. I ruined it, Phillip. Please go on with your life. I've ruined everything for us. Good-bye, Phillip." Nealy hung the phone up and collapsed back into the chair, crying until she couldn't cry anymore. Then she washed her face and put on some more make-up and went to the studio. The spark had gone out of her smile. Nadine didn't die alone that night; Nealy died with her.

CHAPTER THIRTY-SEVEN

THE FOLLOWING SATURDAY, Nealy had just finished in the studio when the phone rang. Nancy Morris, Rob's wife, called and insisted that she come for dinner that evening at six o'clock. Nancy knew that Jerrod would be at the hospital until seven o'clock the next morning, so she wouldn't let Nealy turn down her invitation. Besides, the company would probably be good for her. It had been obvious to everyone around her all week that something had been terribly wrong with her, but they figured it to be the death of Jerrod's mother. Nealy had known Nadine Jones for most of her life, and the unexpected death of someone that close would be hard on anyone. Francine and the students had tried to keep things orderly in order to make work easier for her, but they really missed the old Ms. Nealy.

Jerrod had not given her any trouble. In fact, he tried to be very accommodating and friendly with no nonsense. Nealy didn't say too much to him, she couldn't because she felt dead inside. The loss of his mother had not really hit him yet, and Nealy wanted to save the only kind words that she had for him for when it did; he would need her then. And maybe by that time, some of the deep resentment that she felt would go away. Jim Zimmerman had asked that both of them continue to see him, at least for a while. Nealy seemed very glad, since she needed someone to talk to, and a psychiatrist would understand better than most people about her promise to Nadine. But she wasn't sure if she should tell him that she didn't intend to ever sleep with Jerrod again. If she did that, he would diagnose her to be extremely neurotic, a diagnosis which might be true, but she didn't want anyone telling her so. Nealy made her bed, and now she had to lie in it, regardless of how neurotic it seemed.

At three o'clock, she went home and rested for a while. The emptiness, the loneliness, and the depression that she felt made her tired. She took her book out of her nightstand and opened it to where she had the picture of her and Phillip, but she closed the book quickly. Why did she want to torture herself? That would only add masochism to her neurosis. How much longer could she go on like this? Each day she died a little more inside. Why didn't Jerrod realize that she didn't love him anymore? This was so unlike him to do without sex, so he had to snap soon. Surely he would leave her when he realized that she didn't care, and then he would divorce her. After all, Nadine had said, "Promise me that you won't leave him." She didn't say anything about his leaving her. All she could think about was Phillip, but she had to push him out of her mind because it hurt too much to think that she would never see him again. Nealy had to face the music—obviously ass-kickin' rock 'n' roll—that she had totally destroyed any chance for happiness.

Nealy rang Rob and Nancy's doorbell, and Nancy opened the door, giving her a big hug. When she walked into the family room, she immediately saw Phillip standing beside the bar. At first she just stood there staring at him, thinking that her very vivid imagination had played a dirty trick on her.

"Hi, Nealy," he said, staring back.

"Oh my God, it is you. I *haven't* lost my mind," she cried, running over to him, throwing her around his neck, and kissing him. Nancy and Rob left the room to give them a few minutes to be alone before dinner.

Not wanting to ever let her go, he held her tightly. "I had to come. I hope you're not angry with me, but you were so upset that I had to see for myself that you were alright."

She looked up at him and smiled. "I could never be angry with you. And I'm so glad you're here," she said, hugging him and releasing a very heavy sigh.

Gently, he held her shoulders and pushed her back so that he could see her face. "Nealy, are you alright?"

"No, Nadine took me to the grave with her. Phillip, I feel so dead inside," she whispered, tears forming in her eyes.

He pulled her close again. "Sweetheart, that will pass. These things take time. It's very traumatic when someone you are close to dies, and especially with her being your mother-in-law. You already felt guilty about leaving Jerrod, and now you feel even more guilty because you made a promise to his mother on her deathbed."

"It was guilt. And now it's bondage. Phillip, I could have said, 'I'll always love him' or 'Don't worry, he'll be just fine,' but I didn't. I said, 'I won't leave him.' I can't believe it," she cried. "Why did I say that unless subconsciously I wanted to stay with him?"

"Nealy, come over here and sit down," he said, leading her over to the couch and sitting down beside her. "Do you really think that you said that because you wanted to stay with him?"

"I must have, Phillip. I said it. I didn't have to, but I said it," she sobbed, putting her face into her hands.

"Don't you think, that by some small chance, you were just feeling very bad about her condition and the only thing that you could think about at the moment was her happiness?"

"I don't know what I was thinking. All I know is that I made a promise to a dying woman, and now I have to live with it, Phillip, even if that means sacrificing my own happiness. I wasn't brought up to break promises, and I already feel that I've failed *God* by breaking my wedding vows."

He put his arm around her and gently pulled her head down to rest on his shoulder. "Nealy, isn't it possible that you're dealing with a huge case of guilt? And maybe you're allowing yourself to think that this is *God's* way of punishing you. Could that be it?"

"Maybe he *is* punishing me. I slept with you. Then, to make it worse, I fell in love with you when I had no right to because I'm married to someone else. The fact that I don't love him, that I can't even let him touch me, doesn't matter. I married him for better or for worse."

Phillip stared off into space and kissed her forehead. "Nealy, you've got to see Jim Zimmerman. He can help you sort this out. You're carrying more guilt than one person can deal with. Sweetheart, this goes far beyond the promise. If it's Jerrod you're worried about, he won't expect you to keep that promise when he realizes that you don't love him anymore."

Nealy sat up and looked at him very seriously. "Phillip, what if you were dying and your sister was very ill with some rare disease and you knew that I was the only person that could help her live a relatively normal life. If you asked me to take care of her and I promised you that I would, wouldn't you expect me to keep that promise? Shouldn't I keep that promise?" Nealy stared at him.

"Nealy, what would give me the right to ask you to sacrifice your life?"

"Phillip, that is not the point. You asked me. And I promised. You weren't concerned with your rights or my rights. You were concerned about your sister. Good people only think about others, even when they're dying. Nadine was a good person. She was only thinking about her only child. I'm a good person, and I can't think about myself anymore. I have to think about Jerrod, regardless of how much I loathe the very idea."

"Don't you think that maybe instead of being a good person, Nadine acted more like a selfish person?"

"Please don't patronize me, Phillip. And please drop the psychoanalysis because all the psychology in the world can't change the fact that I made a promise to a dying woman. I have to keep that promise, Phillip, because I couldn't live with myself if I didn't."

"I'll drop it," he said sadly, "and I won't ask you to promise, but I would like to ask you to please see Jim."

Nealy stood up and looked down at him and held his hand, touching his fingers nervously. "Phillip, I will see Jim Zimmerman. I can promise you that much. And I'm *so sorry* that I let you get tangled up in my web...maybe I'm not such a good person after all. I've allowed the sweetest, kindest, and most caring person that I have ever known—my best friend—to become involved with someone that has turned out to be just as dangerous and devious as a black widow spider. Oh, *God,* I'm *so* sorry."

Nancy and Rob walked out of the bedroom together. "Are y'all hungry?" Rob asked. But he could tell by the seriousness of the conversation that food was the last thing on their minds.

She let go of Phillip's hand and walked towards them, giving each of them a hug, which they didn't really understand at the time. "I love you guys," she said, and then she turned to look at Phillip who had stood up. "I can't stay. I've hurt enough people—the people I love most. But, thank you, anyway. Phillip," she said, her voice trembling too much for her to talk anymore. Quickly, she turned and ran out the door. She got in her car and drove away, and didn't look back.

A few blocks away, Nealy stopped the car. Gripping the steering wheel, she screamed and sobbed: *"God, please forgive me. How could I do this to him? I love him so much. I wanted to spend the rest of my life with him. What did I do that was so wrong? Please forgive me, please."* She was hysterical, crying so hard that she felt sick. Then she heard Phillip talking to her.

"Nealy, sweetheart, calm down. Please...just take a deep breath."

Listening to him, she took several deep breaths, and finally she stopped sobbing. When she raised her head up from the steering wheel, she looked to see where he had gone. But he wasn't there. Her imagination had played a cruel trick on her. No matter how she felt about Phillip, she had to let him go. He had a right to a good life, not one that could only bring him pain and loneliness.

Over the next month, Nealy went twice a week to visit with Jim Zimmerman, both for herself and for Jerrod. He too practiced his psychological bullshit on her, but it didn't work. Her mind had been made up. Of course, she still wasn't sleeping with Jerrod, but she kept that to herself. Jerrod might have told Jim, but she doubted it because admitting that would bruise his ego more than Jerrod would ever admit. Women did not turn down the wealthy, god-like, Jerrod Timothy Jones, III; he had everything they wanted. Finding women to bow at his feet would never be a problem for him, and he knew it, but he also liked having Nealy as his wife, and now, his hostage.

Jerrod finally broke down and slipped into Nealy's bed one morning about two o'clock. As she slept soundly on her back, he began to massage her large breasts, which excited him because she seemed to like it, and her nipples grew stiffer as he gently flicked his finger back and forth across them. He didn't want to wake her until she wanted him just as much as he wanted her, and then she wouldn't fight him. He carefully unbuttoned her gown, exposing her breasts. Softly, he suckled each one, blowing his warm breath on them as his tongue made its way around the taut peaks. Nealy moaned. Her mouth opened. Her legs opened. So Jerrod decided that she was ready. He pulled the covers off of her and very quietly straddled her, slowly sliding his finger under the crotch of her panties to feel the wetness. Subconsciously, she cooed and moved her pelvis upward, driving his finger deeper into the soft flesh, which really excited him. Oh, he wanted her desperately. Then she mumbled something that sounded like, "Oh, I want you to feel it," so he reached further inside and he could feel how ready she had become. So with a strong erection, he leaned over her, but the minute his penis touched her, she woke up screaming. "Stop it! Get off of me!"

"Come on, Nealy, you want me. You told me to feel it. So I did. And you were ready. Please don't stop. This will bring us closer again. I've missed you. Dammit, I've got to have it," he said loudly, trying to hold her down.

"No! I don't want you. In fact, I hate you! And I'd never tell you to *feel it*. I've never said that in my life. Now, get the hell off me, or we're through for good!" She pushed and shoved at him, but her strength was no match for his. And when he tried to kiss her, she refused, fighting him.

Finally, when he realized that she had no intentions of willfully making love to him, he got off and stood in the darkness, watching as she pulled her clothes back together. The street lights offered just enough light that he could see the anger and the fear in her face. "I'll leave you alone, but in time you'll want to go all the way again. You wanted to tonight, but something stopped you. So, it won't be long, and you'll want to *screw me* as much as I want to screw you. Until that time comes, I'm not going to do without, and, Nealy, there isn't a damn thing that you can do about it because you promised my mother. I know you, Nealy, you'll go to your grave with that promise. You're fucked, baby, you know that. I could even bring some slut home and fuck her right in front of you, and there wouldn't be one goddamn thing that you could do. Maybe you'd even get excited enough to join us!" he yelled, obviously frustrated.

"You're a sick bastard, Jerrod. Now get out of my room," she ordered wearily, almost sadly, realizing what had happened. Because she missed Phillip so much and wanted to be with him, her subconscious led her to believe that Phillip was on top of her and that is why she called out "Phillip," which Jerrod mistook for *"feel it."* Nealy rolled over and put her face in her pillow and wept until she fell back asleep hours later, exhausted.

Her alarm went off at six o'clock. She put on her robe and ambled into the kitchen to make coffee. Just as she finished, the back door opened and Jerrod walked in, glaring hatefully at her.

He walked over to her and gently put his arms around her as though he wanted to apologize. "Well, you don't have to worry about me slipping into your room anymore until you ask me to."

"Jerrod, it's too early for this. I'm tired," she said, trying to loosen his arms from around her waist.

"Ask me 'Why?' Nealy," he said, tightening his grip.

"Jerrod, stop it!"

"Go ahead. Ask me'Why?'" he held her tightly.

Too weak to challenge him, she rolled her eyes up to look at him and said, "Why?"

"Remember that girl that you saw me with at the airport after our honeymoon?"

"I remember," she replied, getting irritated.

"Well, she's back. And she fucks like a mink."

"Jerrod, let go of me! I don't want to hear this," she cried, struggling to get away from him.

"No, you're going to hear it," he said, holding her hands behind her with his hand and holding her face with the other to force her to look at him. "Because from now on, every time you tell me to get out of your room, I'm going over to her place and let her bring me more pleasure than you ever could. I'll stay in her mouth and between her legs until she can barely talk or walk without excruciating pain." He ran his tongue over her lips. "We *did it* all night long. Can you taste it, Nealy?"

Losing her temper, she yanked her arm out of his grip and pushed him away from her. "Stop it! Just stop it! And you can spare me anymore of the fucking details because I don't care!" she yelled. "I don't love you. And I don't care what you do or who you *do it* with! Can't you see that?" Jerrod stormed out of the house and left, which suited her just fine. Sliding down the front of the slick enameled cabinet, she sat down on the floor, rested her head on top of her knees, and cried out, "Oh, *God*, please help me. Make him leave me, please, God...*please.*"

CHAPTER THIRTY-EIGHT

THE ENGAGEMENT and upcoming wedding plans for Jerrod Timothy Jones, Jr. and Christine Criswell circulated throughout the family in early May. When Christine called Nealy and asked her to be her Matron of Honor, she reluctantly accepted. Nadine had barely gotten cold in the ground in three months, but it didn't come as a shock: actually, she was surprised that they had waited that long. Nealy avoided helping with the wedding plans by making excuses about having to work. And she really had missed quite a bit of work during the last four months because of everything that she had been through, so it seemed like a good excuse. In all honesty, the thought of those two getting married made her want to throw-up. Why didn't Nadine make the elder Jones bastard promise to keep his penis in his pants and grieve for her for the rest of his life? That seemed like a more reasonable request than asking Nealy to stay with her son while he flaunted his infidelities in her face.

Nealy thought about Phillip everyday, but she didn't dare call him. He deserved much better, and she knew it. And of course, he hadn't called her because she specifically asked him not to. Nealy recalled what Phillip had said to her when she told him that Tony was getting married. He said, "People can't wait forever, they have to go on with their lives." So even though she still loved him desperately, she had to let him go on with his life, she could never interfere. Whenever she saw Rob, she knew that he knew how she felt because she couldn't hide the pain. With the mere mention of Phillip's name her eyes would tear, turning the whites to pale shades of red around her green eyeballs, which made them look like pathetic Christmas ornaments. Nancy and Nealy had lunch every couple of weeks, and Nealy didn't try to hide how much she loved Phillip, but she told her that is was over. And when Nancy asked her about Jerrod, she led her to believe that things were coming along. Of course, she really wanted to tell her that he was a sick bastard and that she hated his guts, but she didn't. Maybe Nancy knew the truth, but because she was a good friend, she let Nealy continue her charade.

Jerrod came only into her bedroom one more time, but she woke up immediately and threw him out, even though he said that he just wanted to talk. Then one Friday night, he came home drunk about ten o'clock and caught Nealy in the bathtub, trying to relax from her exhausting week at the studio. Realizing his condition, she tried to reason with him, but it didn't do much good. He held her in the bathtub, while he took off his clothes and climbed in with her. She was terrified that he might try to drown her, but she fought him anyway. The small bathtub made it impossible for him to rape her, especially with her fighting him, so finally he climbed out, got dressed, and left the house, and didn't return for several days. Fortunately, Nealy had resigned herself to the miserable life that had been appointed to her by her dear, late mother-in-law, so it didn't upset her quite as much anymore. Whatever Jerrod did really didn't matter anymore and nothing surprised her.

On the night of June first, Nealy stood next to Christine in the living room of the house that J.T. Jones had shared with his late wife for more than thirty years. It nearly made her ill physically to be participating, but she had to attend. Of course, Jerrod stood next to his father as his *Best Man!* They were two peas in a pod, and they certainly deserved to stand up for each other. Jerrod was without a doubt his father's son. His father had even brought home some floozy for Jerrod to screw for his sixteenth birthday present. This woman had been instructed to teach Jerrod all about the birds and the bees for several hours under his own roof, and Nadine didn't do one thing about it. Whatever J.T. wanted, J.T. got. Nealy had only found out about this little experience during the last three months because Betty Lou had finally broken down and told her. They all knew everything, and Nealy had never even suspected a thing. Over the years, she saw or heard only what Jerrod wanted her to, but the truth had finally come out!

After all the I do's were said, Nealy mingled, making every attempt to look like the happy, devoted wife of the charming Prince Jerrod. By ten o'clock, she wanted to leave, but she couldn't find Jerrod. He had been drinking heavily all night long, and the thought of going home with him made her more than uncomfortable. Maybe he had passed out on one of the upstairs beds, and she could leave him there to sober up. Just as she started up the stairs to look for him, she got a message from one of the servants that Jerrod was in his father's study and that he needed to show her something. On her way up, she wondered how she would get in because the study door remained locked at all times, but when she got there she found the door ajar so she pushed it open, and then closed it behind her. The lights were out, making the spacious office dark. "Jerrod, are you in here?"

"Back here," he yelled, calling from the large vaulted storage room where a dim light shined. His father liked the privacy of that room, and he spent a lot of time back there with Christine, alleging that they were digging through his personal and private documents; it was something private alright, but it had nothing to do with documents.

Nealy entered and stopped dead in her tracks. "Oh...my...God," she said under her breath. Jerrod stood in front of Christine who sat on the desk without a stitch of clothes on and her hands bound behind her back with a necktie.

Jerrod's pants and his underwear were on the floor around his ankles. Both of them looked straight at Nealy with flushed faces.

"Sorry, Neal, we had to start without you. Christine couldn't wait," he said smugly, thrusting his hips forward.

"I see," Nealy managed to say. She wanted to close her eyes, but she couldn't, she had to make a point.

"Christine, tell her how good it feels," Jerrod demanded. When she didn't respond he stopped penetrating her.

"No, Jerrod...please," she cried.

"Then tell her. Or it's over."

"It feels good," she whined, panting.

"Don't whine! Tell her what you tell me," he roared.

"It feels *so* good," she moaned, her chest heaving.

"What do you love, Christine?" he asked, teasing her.

"I can't stand it...please, put it back in!"

"Then tell her what you love!"

"Your dick in my pussy!" she cried out loudly.

"Nealy loves it, too, don't you, Neal?" he asked, grabbing Christine's buttocks and driving himself deeply between her legs. When she cried out, he looked at Nealy and smirked.

Nealy looked away in total disgust, but she wasn't about to walk off, allowing him to think that it upset her to see him with another woman. In fact, it really didn't. Although the idea of watching two animalistic people fornicate right before her eyes did. But she intended to stand right there and watch the climax, even if she had to clamp her hand across her mouth to prevent her from vomiting. This had been a first for her, and it left her feeling cold and full of hate and contempt for him. When both of them exploded into each other, she clapped her hands together slowly. "Bravo," she said apathetically, glaring at them. "Are you quite done, or should I hang around for the multi-orgasmic performance?"

Christine wiggled her hands free from the tie, and grabbed her dress to cover her large breasts when she realized that Nealy didn't approve and had not come there as a willful observer.

"Nealy, Jerrod said that you knew about us. That you wanted to watch."

"You know, Christine, you're even more brain-dead than I thought. I guess I gave you too much credit. And on your wedding day, no less, with your step-son just three months after his mother's death. You people are revolting and ill. Asking you how your conscience allows you to do such a thing would be a ridiculous question. Obviously, neither of you have one. I pity both of you. But, I must say, it's truly a match made in *hell,*" she said, staring hatefully at both of them for a long moment. "Now that I think about it, you and Jerrod disappeared during our reception. I guess this is where you ended up that time, too. Huh, Christine?"

"But, Nealy, you asked me to take care of him. Don't you remember? The photographer—"

"You son-of-a-bitch," Nealy interrupted in amazement. "You screwed her on *our* wedding night?"

"I thought you didn't care," he yelled sarcastically.

Nealy drew a deep breath and exhaled in an effort to regain her composure. "That should make you feel better, Christine. I'm just as brain-dead as you are," she said, shaking her head. "Well, I hate to be a party-pooper, but if you'll excuse me, I hear someone calling me." Nealy smiled at both of them, giving them a thorough once-over. Then she nodded briefly, like royalty, as she turned, threw her head up in the air, and made a very dramatic exit. Once she got out of sight, she ran down the hall and into one of the extra bedrooms. She barely made it to the bathroom before she violently regurgitated. "Oh, *God*, please get me out of this," she quietly whimpered. Even though she felt as if she were about to die, she couldn't help being proud of her performance. Under the circumstances, it had been an oscar winner; on stage, she would have gotten at least two curtain calls. And if, by the grace of God, she could just hang in there, the consolation would come: Jerrod would eventually leave her, which would be the only way out of her promise.

A couple of weeks later, Nealy came home from the studio one night and Jerrod was waiting for her when she walked inside. It shocked her because they hadn't spoken a word since the wedding. His face had an expression of anger that she had never seen before, and she noticed an empty bottle of scotch sitting on the table. "Who the hell is this?" he shouted.

Nealy glared at him and then looked at the picture that he had in his hand. "That's me and a friend," she said calmly, wanting to grab the picture of her and Phillip away from him.

"Did you fuck him?"

"Don't use that filthy language with me," she said angrily.

"Grow up, Nealy, you're not that innocent. Now answer my fuckin' question. Did you *fuck* this guy?" he yelled.

Nealy walked past him and into the bedroom. "Get out, Jerrod!"

He followed her and grabbed her arm, jerking her around to face him. "I'm going to ask you this one more time—"

"Yes," she screamed, interrupting him. "Are you happy now?"

He started shaking her madly. "Who is he?"

"That's none of your business. Let go of me!" she cried.

"Oh, it's none of my business, huh? I'm just your goddamn husband. So I think it is my business when my wife's screwin' some guy that I don't even know."

"Would it be better if you knew him? I guess you'd like to make a threesome!

Or maybe we could make it a foursome and invite Christine or Kris. Or better yet, have an orgy and invite all of your whores that you've been fucking for the last ten years."

Jerrod slapped her so hard across the face that she fell back onto the bed. She could taste the blood in her mouth and she knew that her nose was bleeding because drops of blood fell onto her blouse when she sat up, but she didn't dare move. She just held her head back and covered her nose with her hand. "And everybody thinks you're *soooo* nice. I should kill both of you," he said, glaring down at her. "You're nothing but a tramp, just like the rest of them. No wonder you didn't want me touching you. You were too busy being balled by this son-of-a-bitch! Isn't that right, Miss Prim and Proper? Ha!" He just stood there shouting at her, and then he held the picture up and looked at it again. "You are really something, Nealy. You know that? You're a fuckin' whore who's too good to fuck her own husband. Imagine that." Then he got right in her face and softly said, "If I ever catch you with this guy again, I won't be responsible for what I do." And then he tore the picture in half, separating them right down the middle, and threw her half at her.

At that point, Nealy started to cry and grabbed for the picture, which he jerked away from her. "No," she cried softly, upset that he had destroyed her only picture of Phillip. "You're my wife until the day you die, do you understand me, baby?" Then he turned and left the house, peeling out of the driveway.

Nealy got up and made her way into the bathroom with blood dripping from her face. She took several washcloths out of the cabinet, and wet them. Then she got some ice and made an icepack to stop the bleeding. Even though she cried, she felt cold inside, all except for the part of her that grieved over her picture.

An hour later the phone rang, but she didn't want to answer it because she still had a nosebleed and she didn't feel like talking. After ten rings, she picked it up.   "Hello," she said softly, the icepack still pressed against her nose, making her sound nasal.

"Are you alright?" a male voice asked.

"Who is this?"

"It's Rob, Nealy. I just saw Jerrod in the hospital parking lot and he told me that I might want to call you and get my name on the list to—well, the rest isn't worth repeating. When I smelled liquor on his breath, I reported him. Then I decided that I had better call to see if you were okay."

Nealy burst out crying.

"I'll see you in a minute." He hung up and drove as fast as he could over to Nealy's house. When he got there, he walked inside, not knowing what to expect. For all he knew, she could be shot or mangled or God knows what else. When he saw the blood all over the kitchen floor, he held his breath and walked into the bedroom, drawing a sigh of relief when he saw her lying on the bed in one piece. "What happened?"

"He found a picture of me and Phillip," she said sadly.

"Oh, Nealy, I'm sorry," he said, taking the ice pack from her and pressing it against her face. "We need to get you over to the hospital."

"No, Rob, I'm fine. It's just a nosebleed."

"Nealy, it's more than that. I'll feel much better if we check you out."

"No, really, I'm okay. Actually, I'm getting used to being slapped around," she mused.

"Nealy, why are you staying with this bastard?"

"Rob, please—"

"Okay, I'm sorry," he said, not wanting to upset her anymore. He sat down beside her and she rested her head on his shoulder while he held the icepack. Before he left, he made sure that her nose and the lacerations on her face and inside her mouth had stopped bleeding and that she seemed alright emotionally. The sight of her beautiful face all bruised and bleeding made him want to go after Jerrod himself, but that wouldn't accomplish anything.

Nealy went into the kitchen and added more ice to her icepack to prevent her cheek and her eye and her lip from swelling even more than they already had. Then she curled-up on the bed and pressed the icepack against her face again. Why were her friends always having to rescue her? It had become a nightmare. But she still felt bound by her promise, regardless of what her friends said, or what Jerrod did to her. Nealy had to stand on her promise.

When Rob returned home, he told Nancy all about Nealy's latest confrontation with Jerrod. Then he called Phillip to keep a promise that he had made to him. Back when Phillip had come to town to visit them in order to see Nealy, he made Rob promise to call if anything ever happened to her or if he could help. All of them understood her position, but, on the other hand, it seemed like such a waste to live with Jerrod after all that he had done, regardless of her promise. Phillip loved her because of her convictions, and, therefore, he couldn't try to talk her out of them. So, he prayed for her safety and well-being and her happiness, which at this point didn't exist. It became obvious to everyone that Jerrod had certainly not stopped the pills or the booze or the womanizing, but there didn't seem to be anything that anyone could do. Rob told Phillip the whole ugly story, and Phillip fumed with anger because he felt so helpless. When he hung up, he cried because he loved her so much and he couldn't help her. No one knew what to do, except be her friend.

Phillip called Nealy because he *had* to even though he told himself not to. He was afraid that it would only upset her even more, but he just couldn't help it.

Nealy had fallen asleep on the bed with the icepack still pressed against the side of her face. By this time, the area around her eye had started discoloring, which would become a full blown black eye by morning. She jumped when the telephone rang.

"Hello."

"Nealy, I'm sorry to call you so late, but I just talked to Rob. I had to call."

She sat up on the side of the bed. "Phillip," she muttered, surprised to hear his voice.

"Nealy, Rob told me what happened. He said you were fine, but I needed to hear that from you."

"I'm okay. I'm sorry you had to be bothered with this. But I'm glad to hear from you," she said, her heart aching for him.

"Are you still seeing Jim Zimmerman? Do you tell him these things? Nealy, I know how you feel, but please don't let that bastard...hurt you." The words *kill you* almost came out, which brought tears to his eyes. "Please, sweetheart, do something. Nealy, you didn't answer me. Are you still seeing Jim?"

"I see him sometimes. But I can't tell him this. I'm...I don't know what I am," she admitted sadly. "It wouldn't matter anyway."

"Please go, Nealy. It *will* help, I promise."

"I will, Phillip. So, how are you?"

"Professionally things are real good. Personally, I'm okay," he said gloomily, avoiding what he didn't want to say.

"Phillip, I owe you an apology for running out on you when you were here. But I couldn't be near you any longer. I'm sorry. That was the worst day of my life."

"I understood, Nealy. You don't have to apologize."

"But just think, *Peppee*. I've been with you on the best days of my life—I mean, the very best!—and I've been with you on the worst day of my life," she giggle coquettishly as she thought about the times that she had spent with Phillip.

He felt a hundred pounds lighter in his chest when she giggled, even if it wasn't her happiest giggle. He absolutely loved to listen to her laugh, which he had missed terribly. "Well, *Miss Scarlett*, I'd be most interested in hearing about your very best day, my dear."

"Oh, no, please don't make me laugh," she said, holding her bruised face.

"Oh, I'm sorry," he said, gritting his teeth to stop him from telling her how he felt and how it hurt him to think about her being abused. He had to change the subject. "Well, how's your studio doing? Are you still thinking about that deal with Tony Rose and the offer he made to you about his office?"

"My studio's doing great. The deal with Tony...well, I'm not sure. He's called me several times about it, but I knew I couldn't be in New York and not see you. I'm not that strong yet. Phillip, I won't stand in the way of your happiness. That's a promise I made to myself. You deserve much more than that. It wouldn't be fair."

"Nealy, I'm a big boy. Haven't you heard that it's 'better to have loved and lost, than never to have loved at all.' "

"You're so philosophical, *Peppee,* which makes you perfect for your profession," she said, giggling again. "That's just a line that *Tennyson* made up to mislead his readers. He wanted them to think that he had all the answers; all they had to do was read his poetry. In some cases I'll agree with him, but in others, I'm not too sure."

"Well, in this case, pretty lady, I wouldn't have it any other way. And I don't think you would either."

"I think we're leading into the '*I'm okay, You're okay*' therapy, Doctor. But you're okay, and I'm totally screwed up. At this very moment, though, I'm happy because you make me happy. Phillip...I'm glad you called, but we have to face what we're dealing with here. Jerrod found out about us tonight and he called me a tramp and a whore and two weeks ago he *got it on* with his step mother on the *very* night that she married his father. He even tricked me into watching, but I still can't leave him because of my promise. He told me that I would always be his wife, and if he caught me with you or anyone else that he couldn't be responsible for his actions. Phillip, I'll never be free...please go on with your life. It's because of you that I know I'll be all right. Even during the worst moments of my life, I smile when I think about you. I'm going to be fine, but I won't be if I'm ruining your life, too. Please...forget about me and go on. I love you with all my heart and forever, but I'm not good for you. So, for me, please find someone special to love that can give you the kind of love you deserve. Good-bye, Phillip."

"But Nealy—"

"Phillip, please...just say good-bye and mean it."

There was a long silence, and then he cleared his throat. Only a whisper escaped, "Good-bye, Nealy."

"Good-bye, Phillip." And when she heard him hang up, she whispered, "*God knows,* I'll always love you." And then she wept.

After that night, Jerrod rarely came around whenever she was home. On July the Third, exactly four years after their reunion, Jerrod called and wanted to talk to her about a divorce. Nealy hated him, but yet she still had some feelings for him. At times, as more and more of his personal belongings disappeared from their home, she thought about not loving him anymore after all they had been through over the years, and it made her sad.

Jerrod walked up to the back door and knocked, which surprised her. When she opened the door, he walked in and smiled briefly before he sat down at the table. He petted the dog and pulled out a treat for him. "Chancey stays," she snapped.

He raised his head up and looked surprised. "I know, Nealy. He's your dog. I wouldn't take him back."

"I can't be sure. You've taken everything else," she said, sitting down at the table across from him.

"I know, and that's why I'm here. I know you want out of this marriage and out of the promise that you made to my mother. I've done so many terrible things. I don't deserve you. And I don't even blame you for having an affair. I know you hate my guts, and you should. I'm a bastard. You've said it a thousand times and you're right. I know that. And I also know that you can never forgive me for the things I've done to you. So, I'm ready to let you go, Neal."

Nealy couldn't believe her ears. Was this just another remorseful moment? Would he twist off in a minute and throw her down on the floor to rape her like a madman? "I can't forgive you, Jerrod, you're right. But amazingly, I don't hate you. But even more amazing is the fact that in some ways I still love you. I guess it's because you were my first love, and a part of me will always love you, just like a part of you will always love me. Things will happen, and you'll smile because it will take you back to the times when we were happy. We're just not good for each other anymore. Jerrod, we're not *in love*. I didn't know the difference, but I do now. And not because of anyone else, but because I knew something was missing between us. I told you, I'm equally, well maybe not equally," she grimaced, and he smiled at her, "as responsible for the break-up of this marriage as you are. I made a choice when I moved to New York five years ago. Jerrod, I wanted a career more than I wanted to be with you. Why did we allow ourselves to forget that? We had this strong physical attraction to each other, which we still do, at least, I do, I can't speak for you."

"Nealy, I have too much physical attraction to you. I can't get beyond that. When I look at you, I just want to make love to you. I don't want to talk to you, I don't want to go eat with you, I don't want to do anything but touch you all over and get inside of you. That's a sickness. It's the same thing as being an alcoholic, but with sexual desires. Jim and I have discussed this for the past two weeks. I've really got a problem. Not having you is killing me, but I can *never* be faithful to you, even though, more than anything, I want to be," he reached over and took her hand in his.

When Nealy looked up at him, he had tears in his eyes. "I know, Jerrod. But you *can* get well, though it's going to take a long time. You're a wonderful doctor. I think you need to concentrate on that entirely for a while."

"That's what he says. I have to quit the pills and the booze. I have to give up all my vices because if I don't, I'll lose everything," he said, expressing his worst fears.

She still felt her insides stir a little when he looked at her, but she knew she could never be with him again. It was his undeniable good looks, but over the past few years, she had finally come to realize that looks really were *only skin deep*.

They talked for two hours, and it was probably the best two hours that she and Jerrod had ever spent together. For once, they talked and even laughed occasionally. Not one time did Jerrod mention a *good roll in the hay* or try to touch her sexually, as he had always done in the past. Why couldn't they have built a marriage based on good communication instead of good sex? Maybe the marriage could have survived. Next time, Nealy wanted both—that is, if she could ever find it in her heart again to trust another man enough to actually marry him. Jerrod had done so much that she couldn't shake the coldness out of her system. She gave up everything for him and he nearly destroyed her vibrant spirit and her love for life.

The following Monday, Nealy filed for divorce and swore her lawyer to silence. Jerrod even pulled strings to keep their names out of the legal section of the newspaper. Nealy didn't want anyone to know until the divorce was final. Even though Jerrod seemed to be handling the divorce well, she never knew when he might call the whole thing off. His family had power and they could get almost anything taken care of if they wanted to.

With the idea of being finally free, her life had almost returned to normal. Not one day went by that she didn't pick up the phone to call Phillip, but she always hung up before someone answered. Until the day came that she could call him and say her marriage had ended morally, emotionally, and legally, she couldn't call. Anyway, he lived and worked in New York, and she had a business that she loved in Texas; so it couldn't possibly work out. It would be best to leave him alone and let him find some New York beauty-queen, even though the thought of him with another woman tore her apart. So she tried not to think about it.

On September twenty-third, Mr. and Mrs. Jerrod Timothy Jones, III, brought an end to their marriage on their fourth anniversary. They had spent ten years of their lives together, and four of those years as husband and wife. It took only three minutes for the judge to grant their divorce and give Nealy her name back. Nealy James got the dog, the house, the car, the studio, and plenty of money; after what she had been through, she stood firm on the acceptable amount.

After leaving the courthouse, she and Jerrod decided to celebrate with dinner. After all, people celebrate the marriage, so why not celebrate the divorce. They drove down the boulevard and ate at the Seawall Restaurant, curb side, like they had always done in the good old days. They ordered greasy hamburgers and fries and rootbeers that came in big, frosty mugs. They were like teenagers again who had gone out on date-night, which had always been on Saturday; but Tuesday worked just as well.

After dinner, Jerrod brought Nealy home and came inside to get some more of his things. He had found himself a house only three blocks away, which made her uncomfortable, but at least he no longer shared her home. He had already taken most of his clothes and personal items, but he had a few things stored up in the attic that he wanted. As Nealy and Jerrod rummaged through the attic, they would stop to reminisce whenever they came across something that brought back fond memories. It made them both sad that things had turned out so badly, but it proved that even the worst marriages had some redeeming moments.

Right before Jerrod walked out the door for the last time, he and Nealy hugged desperately, but they knew that their life together as husband and wife had ended. Maybe in time they could forget the hurt and the anger and the pain and be friends, something that they had never been in all the years that they had known each other.

Jerrod had to make himself let go of her, and for the last time he stroked away the bangs from her brow. "I'm really sorry, Neal, for my behavior. I acted very childish and obnoxious, and whether you believe it or not, I'm ashamed of the things that I've done to you. You have every right to hate me, and if you do and you never want to see or talk to me again, I'll understand."

"Jerrod, I can never hate you. It takes two people to make a marriage and two people to break one. I want us to be friends. People don't spend this many years together and not have some feelings for each other. We had good times, and as the years go by, those are the ones that we will remember, not the bad times."

He hugged her again and softly said, "You really are a nice girl, Nealy. I want you to be happy. I die inside when I think of you with someone else, but I know you deserve the love of a wonderful, caring man. And I want that for you, baby, I do."

"I want that for you, too," she said, and then she giggled. "Not the love of another man—you haven't done that, have you?"

He gave her a now-what-do-you-think look.

"Oh, thank goodness. I'd hate to be replaced by a man. You talk about humiliation. Wow!" she giggled.

"Could we see each other, as friends I mean, like we did tonight?" he asked, his eyes almost begging.

Nealy looked up at him with tears in her eyes. "Jerrod, I think we need to let go. It will only make things harder if we still see each other right now. Someday, after we have really gotten over all of this, maybe then we could." Of course, she knew that in time, Jerrod would find someone else that would enjoy his perverted ways and he would forget about her, but it didn't hurt to give him a little hope until that person came along. Letting go of love, good or bad, had to be one of the most difficult moments in a person's life. Nealy knew that all too well, and not one day went by that she didn't think about the day that she walked out of Rob and Nancy Morris' home and out of Phillip Pepper's life.

Nealy got ready for bed and rested against three pillows, just thinking and listening to the radio. She had pulled out her book and tried to read, but her mind kept wandering through her life. It was two o'clock, but she still wasn't sleepy. Too much had happened. When Nealy recognized an old song on the radio, she reached over and turned up the volume, listening intently to the song, *"Popsicles and Icicles,"* sung by the Murmaids. That song had such special meaning to her. On her birthday in the summer of Sixty-three, she and Jerrod had parked on the beach in his new Chevrolet convertible, and as that song played in the background, he gave her a beautiful birthstone ring. When he slid it on the third finger of her left hand, she remembered him saying, "This will be replaced by a wedding ring someday. You'll be mine forever and ever. With all my heart, I love you Nealy James." And at the time, she knew he meant it. But life is full of good intentions, filled with words of love and eternal commitment that often end up as broken promises. Nealy kept thinking about Phillip. "I will marry you someday on the porch of the *Homestead Inn.*" Of course, those were just words spoken from the heart during a sweet and tender moment, just more promises never meant to be broken.

By Halloween, Nealy had almost returned to her normal self, which thrilled her family and friends. Her friends had always known that their divorce was inevitable. Jerrod had turned out to be a monster in their eyes, and they all wanted a better life for Nealy. Jerrod had called Nealy almost every day for the first few weeks after their divorce, but, as time passed, he called less frequently. He had obviously made a new life for himself, which suited her just fine. Nealy had finally gotten over him, and she fully intended to put her life back together again. She looked and felt better than ever. The studio had become her refuge and her life. The only thing that could make it more perfect would be to see an old friend again, the one that drifted in and out of her thoughts throughout each and every day. Even though her divorce had been finalized, she still had not called him. By now, he was over her, and she didn't want to interfere in his life. Nealy started drinking Dr. Pepper, stocking her refrigerator with cartons of the prunish-tasting soft drink. And every time she popped the top, she smiled at the memories of her own Dr. Pepper.

Joy and happiness came in November when Randy Richfield married Francine, although Nealy feared that she would lose Francine. Good news came for all when he joined a practice with several other highly respected cardiologists in Clear Lake City, just a half hour away from Galveston. They planned to live halfway between Galveston and Clear Lake because Randy knew how much Francine enjoyed working at the studio with Nealy. With that settled, Nealy took Tony up on his offer to sublet the office from him in New York. Nealy James had now entered into another new and exciting field: theatrical placement of her upcoming stars.

CHAPTER THIRTY-NINE

TWO WEEKS BEFORE THANKSGIVING, Nealy left for New York to move into her new apartment and organize her office. She had trained another student to assist Francine with the studio in Galveston, which would allow her to spend two weeks a month in New York getting the agency up and running. To help her out, a friend of Denise's had found Nealy a small apartment in the same building where she would be close to work. As fate would have it, Phillip's office was equally as close. Now that concerned her. Could she be that close to him and resist the temptation of going to see him? She had not heard from him in three months, so she felt sure that he had gone on with his life. Nealy had been too busy to see much of Rob or Nancy, which she used as an excuse. But, if the truth be known, she feared that they would tell her that Phillip had married someone else, which she wasn't prepared to deal with, at least, not yet.

By Wednesday, Nealy had furnished her office with rental furniture, ordered supplies, and already started making calls to get acquainted with some of the directors. It was twelve o'clock and a beautiful day in Manhattan, so she put on her walking shoes and left the office. It would be fun to grab a bite to eat at one of her favorite sidewalk cafes, and then take a long walk. With Phillip's office only a few blocks away, she decided to walk in that direction, even though she had no intentions of going to see him. But it would do her heart good just to get a glimpse of him on his way out to lunch, although her chances of seeing him were slim since he usually took a later lunch. Anyway, it would be worth a try.

When she arrived at the corner of Park Avenue and Fifty-third, she hung around and looked up at the tall building, wanting so badly to find the courage to go inside, but she just couldn't. Why had she gone there in the first place after promising herself not to interfere in his life again? If she went up to see him, what could she say? "Oh, Phillip, surely you didn't take me seriously when I told you to forget me," or "I didn't call because I wanted to surprise you." No, she couldn't. She didn't have the nerve. She had said "Go on with your life. I won't interfere." This wasn't an immature school boy; Phillip didn't need to be told twice, especially when she had been so adamant. And he was definitely smart enough to see that he had no future with her, and after what she had put them through, why would he want one?

Nealy walked around the block and decided that she had probably missed him, so she conjured up enough nerve to go up and say hello to his secretary, Eve. Nealy really liked Eve, and she knew that she would be glad to see her, at least she thought she would. But what if Eve didn't like her anymore because she hurt Phillip, or what if Eve didn't work there anymore? Well, she'd cross that bridge when she came to it. And if all else failed, she could fall back on her acting ability.

Her palms were sweating and she felt weak in the knees as she got off of the elevator. Quickly, she darted into the restroom to check her hair and face— a little vanity at large, but she wanted to look good, not wind blown, just in case Phillip happened to be there.

Slowly, she opened the door and saw Eve sitting behind her typewriter, her fingers typing away. When she opened her mouth to say hello, no words came out. So she tried it again. "Eve," she said softly.

Eve quickly turned towards the door and within seconds she had jumped out of her chair and crossed the room, giving Nealy a big hug. "Oh, honey, it's so good to see you," she said, smiling and hugging her again. "How *are* you?"

"I'm great," she said enthusiastically, hugging her back. "I just opened an office over on Forty-fifth Street."

"Oh, Nealy, that's wonderful. What are you going to do?"

"I'm going to act as an agent for my students who need help getting started in New York. My former agent is on the road with a play. So, I'm going to work with some of his clients as well." Eve hadn't mentioned Phillip. So Nealy figured he'd gone to lunch, which made her heart feel like exploding inside her chest.

"Are you here permanently?" Eve asked, still smiling.

"Well, sort of. I still have my studio in Galveston, but my assistant is going to keep things going down there so that I can spend enough time here to get this office up and running. I'll be here ten days to two weeks each month."

"That's wonderful, Nealy. Phillip told me what happened, dear. I'm sorry."

"Oh, thanks, Eve, that's sweet—"

They were interrupted when Phillip's office door opened and a woman walked out in front of him. When he saw Nealy, he froze in place. Nealy immediately smiled at him. She had to think of something clever to say to break the silence felt by everyone in the room. The expression on the woman's face grew colder, as if she didn't care for Nealy. Did Nealy know her? No...definitely no. But she had a familiar face. Nealy panicked. Think. Think fast. Should she just ramble? Oh, why not. "Sorry to drop by, but a police officer dropped me off. He told me to see the shrink on the eighth floor. When he pulled me off that ledge on the eighty-sixth floor of the Empire State Building I tried to explain to him about my audition for the part of Tinkerbell that's coming up next week. I'm an actress for goodness sake! Geezus, can't a girl even rehearse in this town anymore?"

Of course Eve and Phillip cracked up. But the woman, much older than

Phillip, with an upsweep hairdo and wearing a very expensive dress, didn't smile at all. In fact, she only glared at Nealy. Phillip pushed passed her and hugged Nealy. "How are you?" he asked politely.

"I'm great, thanks," Nealy said, feeling a little awkward and out-of-place.

With an air of arrogance, the woman walked over to Nealy and stuck out her hand. "I'm Victoria Dorimarr."

"Hi, I'm Nealy J—"

"I know who you are," she said, cutting Nealy off abruptly. "I've seen your picture. I'm Phillip's fiancée." The woman grabbed Phillip's arm, making sure that Nealy got the message.

Nealy froze. The blood drained from Phillip's perfectly tanned face. Eve didn't move, but her eyes shifted from Phillip to the woman and back to Nealy. It would be an understatement to call the moment tense or uncomfortable. Nealy couldn't stand it any longer. Desperately, she wanted to get out of that office before she fell apart. Her alter-ego came to her rescue, transforming her into a charming actress.

First, she smiled at Eve, giving her a quick hug, and then she looked at Phillip, but only in passing. "Well, I hate to run, but I think I'll try to rehearse again while that damn cop's taking a nap in Battery Park," she said sharply, flashing a slight smile and a little wave as she walked out the door. Her heart raced as if she really *had* tried to jump off a building. She practically sprinted down the hall towards the elevator. Nervously she punched the button four or five times as if that would bring the elevator faster. When she heard footsteps coming down the hall, she didn't move, nor did she consider turning around. Closing her eyes, she prayed that it wasn't Phillip. Nealy wanted to get the hell out of that building before she lost it and made a fool out of herself.

Phillip walked up behind her and turned her around. "Let me explain," he said, praying that she would listen.

"Phillip, you don't owe me any explanations. You did just what I asked you to do. I'm happy for you, honest," she said, lying through her teeth.

"But Nealy, I...I don't—"

Nealy touched his hand, which sent a sharp pain through her whole body like an electric shock, so she jerked her hand away. "Phillip, it's alright. You had to go on with your life. You had no idea—and neither did I for that matter—that I'd get a passport from hell."

"You did? When?"

"Late September."

"Why didn't you call me?"

"I didn't want to disrupt your life. Now isn't that ironic? Here I am disrupting your life," she smacked her forehead with the palm of her hand. "Phillip, I shouldn't have come. I'm sorry." The elevator door opened, and Nealy rushed inside. Phillip reached for her arm, but she lifted it slightly to resist his touch again; she couldn't bear it. It would only make things harder for both of them.

He held the elevator door open against its will. The buzzer sounded. He pleaded, "Nealy, please tell me where I can I call you?"

"No, Phillip, please. I've become a 'real pro' at making beds that I have to lie in. So please go on with your life," she said. Phillip slipped into the elevator to stop the buzzing, allowing the doors to close behind him.

Nealy looked up at him seriously. "The only thing that bothers me about this is that I never thought of you as one who could be bought. I couldn't place her until now. That is *the* Victoria Dorimarr of Dorimarr Pictures, isn't it?"

"Yes," he answered, hating the admission. He held Nealy's arms so that she would be forced to face him. "Nealy, I've only been *truly in love* with one woman in my life. And when I couldn't have *you*, I allowed myself to become involved with someone who could accept what little I am capable of giving. Victoria knows the score."

"The score? Oh, Phillip," she muttered. "This isn't you talking. I feel as though I just lost my best friend. Good-bye, Phillip." In the lobby, Nealy brushed passed him, but he followed, calling out to her. Refusing to turn around, she couldn't let him see the hurt in her face and the tears in her eyes. Why did she go there? Why didn't she just let it be?

Nealy ran out into the street to hail a cab. The tears in her eyes had blurred her vision and she didn't see the cab that came speeding around the corner. "Nealy!" Phillip screamed out. Thankfully, the cab driver was able to stop before he hit her.

When Nealy realized that the cab had stopped behind her, she rushed around and got in. "Public Theater, please."

"Nealy, please wait," Phillip screamed.

Forcing herself to look straight ahead, she mumbled to herself over and over, "*Scarlett* wouldn't cry. *Scarlett* wouldn't cry. When Rhett Butler went away, *Scarlett* didn't cry." When the cab driver dropped her off in front of the theater, she went inside to find Denise.

The director, who was sitting mid-way in the dark theater, glanced up. "Can I help you?" he called out.

Nealy stopped and turned around. "I'm looking for Denise Pratt."

"I remember you. You came to a rehearsal a few months back. You're her friend from Texas."

"Yes, that's right." Nealy extended her hand. "I'm Nealy James. Is Denise here?" her voice still trembling.

"I don't know, Ms. James, but we can sure find out," he said, smiling at her. "Come with me. Oh, by the way, I'm Robbie."

"Nice to meet you...Uh..." Nealy couldn't think. Her brain searched for the name.

"Robbie," he repeated.

"I'm sorry....of course. Robbie. Robbie. Robbie," she whispered, trying to unscramble her mind. "Oh, I'm Nealy."

"Okay, Nealy," he said. Walking down to the front of the stage. "Where's Denise," he called up to a young lady rehearsing her line.

"Hadn't seen her," she answered without looking up from her script.

"Well, go find her," he snapped. "Please," he said kindly, turning to smile at Nealy again. "Tell her that her friend from Texas is here. She'll be out here with me," he shouted back. "Nealy, please, have a seat."

"Thanks." Nealy sat down across from him at a table just below center stage.

"What brings you back to New York?" he asked.

"I've opened an office here."

"Oh, really. What kind of office?" he asked curiously.

"A theatrical placement agency," she said, forcing a smile. Her stifled tears brought pain to her eyes.

"Nealy!" Denise screamed, squinting to see over the bright lights.

Nealy jumped up and ran up to hug her. "Denise!" she shrieked softly, trying not to disturb the people who were rehearsing their lines.

"What's up? Why are you here?"

"I sublet Tony's office."

"You're kidding! Oh, Nealy, you're back. That's great!"

"Well sort of," Nealy said, trying to sound happy.

"Nealy, uh-oh, something's wrong. What's wrong? Come on, let's go back to my dressing room." Denise took her hand and led her backstage, which really wasn't allowed. But this particular director had been a little sweet on Nealy, so he wouldn't say anything.

Nealy burst into tears. "I'm such and idiot. Why did I go there?"

"Go where?" Denise asked, trying to calm her down.

"Phillip's office."

"Nealy, you love the guy, that's why," she rubbed her back gently.

"I go from one disaster to the next," she cried. "But of all people—Victoria Dorimarr."

"I wanted to tell you—"

"You knew about her? Denise, why didn't you tell me?"

"You wouldn't discuss Phillip, remember?"

"I'm so stupid."

"No you're not. You're brighter than anyone I know. You're just going through a difficult period right now."

"That's what you call this? I call it rotten timing, but that's the story of my life: Too many *fucking* promises and *fucking* bad timing."

"Nealy," Denise squealed.

Nealy's eyes widened. "Hey, that language always made Jerrod—See, I knew it. I've become him—anyway, it made him feel better. So, I'm waiting," she pulled the corners of her mouth into a smile.

"Okay, see it's coming...coming. Okay," she removed her hands.

Denise hugged her, laughing loudly, "Nealy, you're a funny girl."

Nealy giggled, hugging her back. "Yeah, well just call me *Lucy*."

Denise couldn't understand why two people who loved each other and deserved each other had such a tough time getting together. It didn't seem fair. She had talked to Phillip over the months in regards to Nealy's dilemma. Denise felt so sorry for him because she could tell how much he loved Nealy and how frightened he was for her. Denise wanted to help him, but she knew how stubborn Nealy could be when it came to breaking a promise or sacrificing a principle.

When Nealy got ready to leave the theater, the director asked her if she wanted to go to dinner with him that evening after the play. No, she thought. No, not tonight. But she seemed so unhappy that Denise insisted. Since Nealy wouldn't go without Denise, Denise told Robbie that he had to take her and Dan along with them as chaperons. That didn't fit into his plans, but he didn't have a choice, so he agreed. Robbie had been decent to Denise, and if Nealy went out with him, he might be even nicer in the future. Not that she was trying to use Nealy for the benefit of her career, but show business is definitely a business where it's not what you know, but who you know.

As usual, they wound up at Freddy's after going to eat at Sardi's with Robbie, who by the way, wasn't too thrilled with Freddy's until he heard Nealy sing. Then, he relaxed and had a great time.

Phillip had taken Victoria to lunch as scheduled, but it had been very strained. He couldn't get Nealy out of his mind, and Victoria knew it, but it didn't matter. They had agreed to get married, and she expected him to honor that agreement. Victoria, a tall, skinny woman in her mid-forties—ten years Phillip's senior—had been classified as attractive in an odd sort of way by the gossip columnist. Her brother went to Phillip for therapy after the break-up of his marriage, and following Dorman's divorce, they had become friends. About a month after Phillip had returned from Texas, Dorman invited him to join him for dinner at his parents' mansion in Connecticut. That night Victoria set her mind to marry Phillip, and she made that perfectly clear in the coming weeks. He told her all about Nealy, and he kept the picture of him and Nealy next to his side of the bed on the nightstand, where he vowed it would remain forever. So Victoria knew from the beginning that Phillip would never love her the way he loved Nealy who would remain the sole owner of his heart for the rest of his life. But he also told her that Nealy would never be free to marry him, so he had to let go. Therefore, if she still wanted to marry him under those conditions, he would agree. Victoria thought that in time he would forget Nealy, but months had passed and he still pined for her. And now, with Nealy back in New York, Victoria felt threatened, but she had no intentions of letting him go.

Still upset over seeing Nealy in his office, Phillip went home early and called Rob to see if he knew where to find her, but he didn't. Then he called Denise's flat, but no one answered. He tried to sleep, but he couldn't. Victoria called him every hour making all kinds of threats since he had refused to see her that evening. Each time the telephone rang, he prayed that Nealy would be at the other end, but she wasn't. At mid-night, he decided to go to Freddy's just in case she had gone out with her friends.

When he walked in, he saw Denise sitting at the bar, so he felt sure that Nealy was there somewhere. Then he saw her on the dance floor with some guy. His face turned red with jealousy. His instincts told him to go and tear her away from the guy, but his brain told him to sit down and watch. The song ended, but the guy kept her out on the floor chattering until the jukebox selected the next song, a slow and romantic tune. The guy seemed to be enjoying himself, pulling her closer and closer as they danced. Phillip couldn't stand it, so he got up and went outside until the song ended. When he returned, another song had started, so obviously the guy had no intentions of letting her get away. Phillip had never seen this guy before, so he went searching for Denise. He walked up behind her at the bar and Freddy recognized him.

"Well, if it isn't the *good doctor*," he said, imitating Tony and chewing on his cigar.

Denise wheeled around, worried that Jerrod had shown up again. Momentarily, her heart stopped beating. "Oh, thank God it's you, Phillip. I thought it might be Jerrod the way Freddy said that," she said, hugging him.

"Who's the guy that thinks he owns Nealy?" he asked enviously, staring out at the dance floor.

"That's Robbie Roberts, one of the directors of my play."

"The one that took a fancy to her before?"

"Yeah, I'm afraid so," Denise said, smiling at him sadly. "After she left your office today, she came to the theater. Naturally, Robbie jumped at the chance to take her out."

"I bet he did. Did Nealy tell you about seeing Victoria?"

"Oh, yeah. Yes she definitely did that. It almost killed her, Phillip, but she won't talk to you. She swore after today that she would never interfere in your life again. And you know Nealy, she's more stubborn than a mule."

"That's for sure. What can I do, Denise?" he said, still watching her.

"Go on with your life, Phillip. Nealy's really down on men, as well as herself. I had to *make* her come tonight. I'm sorry, I just didn't want her to be alone. She's been through enough. I know she loves you, Phillip, but she won't change her mind. So I'd go on with my plans, that is, if you're really in love with *that woman*."

"I don't love *that woman*, Denise," he said, reflecting her same tone. "I'm in love with Nealy, and Victoria knows that. But she's willing to accept me that way. She's also very powerful and does not intend to let me out of this arrangement. She said that she could never allow me to humiliate her in front of her friends. She invited half of New York to the wedding in January. First, Nealy can't get out. And now I'm stuck. I guess it isn't meant to be, huh?"

"I guess not, Phillip." She hugged him and she could see the devastation in his face, but she knew that Nealy had made up her mind not to interfere in his life. "Phillip, Nealy said that it wouldn't be fair to come back into your life and disrupt your plans. She told me that you wouldn't be marrying this woman if you didn't love her. Since you are *engaged* to *that woman*, you will have a difficult time convincing her that you are not in love with her. I wish I could do something, dammit. The two of you belong together. I've said that from the beginning. If it makes you feel any better, you are, without a doubt, the love of her life. I can see it in her face when she talks about you. That night when the two of you came back from the Homestead Inn, I knew that you were the one. Nealy took on a different look: A woman of contentment. A woman truly in love for the first time. Jerrod didn't do that for her. It's just been bad timing all the way around. Let it go for now, Phillip. Think positive. Maybe Victoria will have a change of heart and break things off with you. None of us thought that Jerrod would ever leave Nealy, but he did. Just don't give up hope. I'll do whatever I can to convince her to see you. If this is any consolation at all, Phillip, I know that she will always love you regardless of what happens."

"Denise, do me a favor. Don't tell her that I was here. You said it, 'She's been through enough.' I can't bear the thought of causing her anymore pain. Nealy is the most wonderful person in the world. She deserves to be happy for a change," he said, giving her a hug. "I just love her so much."

"I know you do, Phillip. I'm so sorry things didn't work out," she said, choking up.

"Thanks. Please take care of my girl," he said sadly. He walked slowly towards the exit sign. Before he closed the door, he took one long last look at Nealy on the dance floor. As the door closed, he whispered, "So long, *Scarlett.*"

Seconds later, Nealy came running over to Denise at the bar. "Denise, I thought I saw Phillip walking out the door. Was he here?" she asked, her voice shaking.

"Nealy, Phillip's engaged to *that woman*. Now do think for one minute that she would even consider letting him out of her sight as long as she knows you're in town? Not on your life. Now go dance with Robbie. He's a nice guy." Denise couldn't look at Nealy, and she winked at Freddy. They had to protect Nealy. Enough already. Let her get a life.

A few minutes later, Nealy professed to being tired and asked Robbie to take her home. At the door, she gave him a quick peck on the cheek and said,

"Good-night."

Every day Nealy and Denise talked, but Nealy made Denise promise not to interfere with Phillip's plans. Denise promised only that she wouldn't interfere as long as Phillip remained engaged to *that woman*. Nothing more. Should something just happen to come between Victoria and Phillip, then it would be up to her to help bring them together where they belonged!

Nealy left early Friday afternoon. She had to spend the following two weeks in Galveston at the studio so that Francine could take two weeks off for her honeymoon that had been postponed because of her and Randy's busy schedules at the time of the wedding. When she drove in the driveway around eight o'clock, Francine's car was there, and the lights were on inside. She figured that Francine got out of the studio late and brought Chance home, who had practically taken up residence at Randy and Alicia's house. When she walked inside, Randy and Francine were sitting at the table. Both of them looked distraught.

"Hi, guys, what's up?" she asked cheerfully.

They looked at each other and then at Nealy. "Nealy, Chance got hit by a car today," Francine said sadly.

The color left her face. "Is he alright?"

Francine got up out of the chair. "Yes, he's going to be fine. He's got a broken leg and a fractured hip."

"Where is he?"

"We took him to Dr. Cross' Clinic on Broadway. I'm really sorry, Nealy, but it was just one of those freak things. Randy brought Alicia and the dogs down to the studio tonight to wait for me to get off. They were playing out front. Chance never goes out in the street, but he chased the ball. Lindsey Martin's mother pulled in the parking lot, she didn't see him. It all happened so quickly. Oh she felt horrible."

"Oh, my poor little guy. Don't worry," Nealy said, hugging Francine who had tears in her eyes. "Hey, it's alright. These things happen. Randy, don't let her cry."

"I've tried to tell her, Nealy, but she feels responsible."

"It's my fault. I had them bring him to the studio," Francine cried.

"Francine, he'll be fine. He's tough. Can I go see him?"

"Yes, Dr. Cross said to call him as soon as you got home."

"Oh, good. He'll feel much better when he sees me. Well at least I'll feel better."

They all drove down to the clinic. And that night Nealy met the next man in her life: The sweet, sensitive, kind, and very nice, Dr. Kendall Cross. But Nealy met him on the rebound; bad timing once again. Of course Kendall thought that the distance between them and her inability to commit came from the break-up of her marriage, but that had only been a small part of the problem. What really stood in her way was her inability to forget a Freudian-type who locked up her heart and threw away the key. No one knew about him, except for Rob and Nancy, so she never really said much to Kendall about her brief affair with Phillip. She wanted so much to love Kendall, and in the beginning she thought she did. But, once the new wore off, so did her feelings even though she knew he would be good for her. Unfortunately, there seemed to be a bone of contention when it came to what her head wanted and what her heart wanted. Nealy cared about Kendall and she didn't want to hurt him, mainly because he deserved better. He treated her with respect and kindness and loyalty. And unlike Jerrod, he didn't have one womanizing bone in his body, and Nealy knew that he loved her. But she didn't feel that strong physical attraction to him, which bothered her. She didn't want to make any more mistakes when it came to love. Nealy had been hurt twice, so she put up a self-protecting barrier to guard against future emotional disasters. It would take a pretty charming guy to break through her defenses.

Many nights Nealy lay awake wondering whether or not Phillip had married *that woman* yet; she could hardly bring herself to say her name because she envied her so. Nealy had never been a jealous or insecure person, but Phillip had a way of tapping into all of her emotions. If he didn't love Victoria, how could he marry her? Well, the money may have a big influence on him. The woman's worth millions, if not billions. But Phillip never seemed like the type who could be bought. He had plenty of money, and a bright future as a super-shrink. The more she thought about it, the angrier she became, but she still couldn't forget him. Since their last weekend together, time had stood still. The soft scent of Brut after shave lingered with her. With each deep breath, she smelled him. When she made love with Kendall, which wasn't very often, she would sometimes pretend to be with Phillip, sensing his soft sensitive touch against her skin. That's why she couldn't marry Kendall, but she kept hoping that something would happen between them, that she would change her mind. Kendall would be perfect for her. He would be a great husband and a great father; he lived and worked in the same city; he loved animals; her family loved him; her friends loved him. But a marriage of convenience would never work for her because it would be the same as living a lie, and honest, caring people would never cheat themselves out of their own happiness. Nealy needed that special blushing, rushing kind of love that made her feel like a *woman in love with the right man*, or she just couldn't do it again.

CHAPTER FORTY

French Riviera, October, 1976

"*LADIES AND GENTLEMEN*, we will soon be landing in Nice, France," the captain said over the intercom. "It has been our pleasure to serve you and we hope that you have enjoyed your flight with us. Please enjoy your stay in France. On behalf of Air France, we would like to invite you to travel with us again soon. Thank you."

Nealy sat up and stretched after spending ten hours cooped up on an airplane. The long night had been exhausting because she didn't sleep well sitting up in a chair, especially with two children climbing all over her. So, needless to say, she felt like hell and more than likely she looked worse. Slowly, Nealy got up and made her way to the restroom to freshen up. When she saw herself in the mirror she didn't see much hope for her hair or her face, at least not until she got to the ship and took a good hot shower.

Returning to her seat, she slid over next to the window and raised the window shade. It took a minute for her eyes to focus because of the bright, glaring daylight and the reflection off the silver wing of the airplane. Far below, she saw nothing but water, the blue waters of the Mediterranean that sparkled beneath the beams of sunlight. How exciting. For so long she had dreamed about going to Europe, and now her dream had come true. Soon she would be landing in Nice, where she would be transported by a chartered bus down to Monte Carlo. And for the next two glorious weeks she would do nothing except rest and relax while sailing the blue seas of the French Riviera.

Nealy turned around to speak to her new friend that she had talked to most of the way. Nealy had been amazed at how well the young woman had handled her four little ones on an overseas flight, but, of course, Nealy had helped her. Kimber and the children were all going to join her husband, who had been stationed for the last six months in the military in Marseilles, France. The entire family would be there for at least two more years, and then they would return to the United States. "Good-morning," Nealy said to Kimber.

"Good-morning," she responded, smiling. "I hope my children didn't drive you crazy last night."

"No, they were great," Nealy smiled back, hiding the real truth. Actually, the children had almost worn her out because she wasn't accustomed to lifting and chasing children. But, she had to admit that it'd been fun, in spite of her fatigue. Plus, it brought out her maternal instincts. As soon as the beautiful little blonde headed girl heard Nealy's voice, she immediately made her way up the aisle to Nealy and climbed up into her lap.

"Can you brush my hair?" she asked in her sweet, *Chatty-Cathy* voice.

"I'd love to, sweetie." Nealy took her brush from her. "Now tell me if I pull your hair, okay?"

"I will," she said, smiling like a chubby-cheeked cherub.

"Do you have any kids like us?"

"No, but I wish I had a little girl that looked just like you. You are so *pretty*." She had dark-blonde hair, striking blue-gray eyes and light-olive skin; in Phillip's arms they would be mistaken for father and daughter. Nealy's eyes watered. Why did she still do that every time something reminded her of Phillip? If things had worked out between them, they might have a precious little girl like Becky or a cute little boy or at least working on one. Until that very moment, Nealy had never envisioned herself with a child. Why didn't she think about having a child with Kendall instead of Phillip? That made more sense because Kendall wanted to marry her and have children and Phillip had married someone else.

Getting a little jealous of the attention that Becky got from Nealy, one of the twin guys, who had spent most of the night in Nealy's lap, held on to the seats and made his way back up the aisle. "Hi, Mikey," Nealy said sweetly to him. His great big brown eyes sparkled when he flashed a big grin at her. Pretty soon, Nealy had both of them back up in her lap.

Their mother looked around the chair and grimaced. "Nealy, I'm sorry. Are they bothering you?"

"Oh, no, they're alright, Kimber. You've had your hands full trying to dress all of these guys. I'll watch these two for a while," she said, smiling at the kids. Nealy took one of their books and read to them until the captain came back on the loud speaker and told the passengers to prepare for arrival. Nealy got up and moved across the aisle with them to a row of empty seats. Then, she strapped each child into a vacant seat on each side of her and they all sang kiddy songs until the plane landed.

When the airplane stopped at the gate, Nealy helped Kimber collect all of the children's things that had gotten scattered in every direction. Then she deplaned carrying her two small travel bags, her briefcase full of books, her purse, and two kids in tow.

"James," over here, Kimber called out to her husband, who pushed his way through the crowd. "This is Nealy James. You owe her a debt of gratitude for helping me with *your kids.*"

Nealy shook his hand and smiled. "Nice to meet you, James. Your wife and children are wonderful."

"Thanks. And thanks for helping. I know they're a hand full."

"Busy," Nealy laughed, "but adorable. In fact, it made me want one or two someday."

"Well, take these," Kimber said handing her their bags. They all laughed, teasing each other.

After collecting their luggage, they exchanged addresses and telephone numbers just in case Nealy got back to France or they ended up in New York or Texas. Even though they had just met, they became friends but it wasn't surprising. Wherever Nealy went, she attracted people with her warmth and her friendliness. And if she promised to stay in touch, she meant it; she loved people and cared about their lives. They all hugged and waved good-bye as Nealy boarded her bus for the harbor in Monte Carlo.

The driver stored the passengers' bags in compartments under the bus, and then counted heads before departing for the cruise ship. The tour guide, who answered the questions being ask of him, worked for the cruise lines. His name badge read, Louie LaFitte, *obviously French*. And he wore a white nautical suit. He resembled the older French men that Nealy had often seen in the movies: Five-ten, dark hair, dark olive skin, and a firm pot belly. When he spoke, his chubby face creased, creating slight dimples in his cheeks. Even though he spoke English fairly well, the passengers still had to pay close attention to what he said. Nealy had taken the front seat directly behind the driver and the tour guide so that she could enjoy all the scenery along the way and ask questions regarding the sights. When she noticed the driver smiling at her in his rearview mirror, she smiled back.

Then suddenly the bus driver stopped, and, without a word he jumped down and scurried away.

Nealy turned around to talk to the couple behind her. "What's that all about? Did we forget someone?"

"Foreigners. Who knows about them," the woman said.

Nealy giggled. "True, but I think *we're* the foreigners now," she said wryly.

"Oh that's right," the woman said, opening her eyes wide to look at Nealy over the top of her bifocals.

"I'm Nealy James. Where are y'all from?"

"Jersey," a man with a sweet, smiling face spoke up.

"*New* Jersey, honey. She's obviously from the South. She may not know what you're talking about."

"I'm from the South alright, Galveston, Texas, but I lived in New York City for a while."

"Oh, I'm Charlotte, and this is my husband, Bob," they smiled.

"Nice to meet you both," Nealy said, demonstrating good Southern hospitality.

"Is this your first cruise, Nealy?" Charlotte asked.

"Yes. How about y'all?"

They nodded. "Yep, first time. Are you alone?"

"Yes. *All alone am I,*" she said in a fainting voice.

"Brave woman," Charlotte added.

"Your husband let you come to France all by yourself?" Bob questioned,.

"I'm not married." Nealy responded.

"Well, you better look out. I hear those Frenchman are really *hot* for American woman."

"Oh, honey, mind your tongue," Charlotte said, elbowing him in the side.

Nealy giggled loudly. "That's okay, Charlotte, I've heard that already. And besides, I'm not interested in men right now."

"Oh, poor dear, did you have a bad experience?" Charlotte sighed empathetically, yet somewhat intrusive.

"*Now* look who's getting in her business," Bob dropped his jaw and nodded at his wife.

"That's okay, too, Bob. I don't mind," Nealy said, smiling at him. "And yes, Charlotte, I had a *few* years of bad experiences."

"Did your husband beat you, dear?" the woman next to her chimed in officiously, dying to hear the gory details.

Nealy's eyes opened wide. "Well, not exactly," she smiled.

"Some man had the nerve to beat-up a pretty little thing like you? Well, I sure hope you dumped him," Bob remarked, appalled that a man could do such a thing.

Nealy couldn't believe this conversation. "It wasn't quite as bad as all that. But yes, I definitely dumped him—well, we divorced."

"Good girl," Charlotte said. "We've been married thirty-five years and I double-dog dared him to ever touch *me*," she said, flashing her husband a look as if he were responsible for all the "sorry" men in the world.

When the driver boarded with two older, but very spry people, he said something into some sort of radio and then headed the bus out of the airport.

As they entered Nice, Louie LaFitte picked up a microphone. "Welcome everyone," he said, smiling at the passengers. "I'm Louie LaFitte with Southern France Tourist Lines. I will be giving you some information about the area and your cruise destinations during our half hour trip." Noticing how Nealy hung on every word, he found himself directing much of his conversation to her. He told them that many of the structures which he would point out along the way had been standing since the Romans had established the Provence in 125 B.C. As they drove through Nice, he directed their attention to the spot where General Bonaparte launched his Italian campaign in the year seventeen-ninety-six. Louie had an enthusiastic way of holding the interest of his audience as he pointed out historical sights. Everyone witnessed the spot where Napoleon marched through Cannes and Grasse en route to Paris and Napoleon's Hundred Days.

As they curved around the side of a high cliff overlooking the

Mediterranean, the guide directed their attention to their ship that awaited them in the harbor in Monte Carlo.

"Oh y'all look," Nealy cried. "That's incredible." Nealy smiled at Louie and then turned to the lady sitting next to her. "This is going to be fabulous. I'm fixin' to sit back and do nothing but soak up plenty of rays."

"What's a *fixin'* mean, madame?" Louie asked and everyone laughed out loud.

Her face turned red and she giggled. "Sorry. When I get excited my Texas accent comes out. We say *fixin'* instead of going. I could have said, 'I am *going* to sit back and soak up some sun.' Same thing."

"Oh, I see," he smiled kindly.

"I'm surprised that you weren't already familiar with that word, Louie," Nealy said, smiling back. "After all, it had to be some of your ancestors that invaded Galveston, Texas, in the early Eighteen Hundreds. Remember? That notorious pirate, Jean LaFitte?"

"Ahhh, yes," he replied joyfully, impressed that she had made the connection. "I guess I must be a direct descendent, but it's very far removed." Louie gave her a great big grin and then turned his attention back to the bus full of passengers. "Ladies and gentlemen, shortly we will be pulling up to the dock at the harbor where we will transfer your luggage onto the ship. If all of you will be kind enough to wait by the bus and identify your luggage for the attendants, it will help us to put the right bags in the right rooms aboard the ship.

"Now, let me give you just a brief itinerary, but do not worry if you miss something because each of you will have a copy of it in your room. Tonight, we shall sail over to the Island of Corsica and dock in the harbor at Calvi for the next two days. It will be restful, but there are many sights as well. For those of you who are history buffs, this town is the birthplace of Columbus," he said, looking directly at Nealy.

"Then, we will go further west until we reach Marseille for one day of shopping for good prices on perfumes or leather goods. In France, we know that Americans love 'blue-light-specials,' " he snickered and his belly jiggled like a bowl of jelly. The passengers laughed, surprised that he actually knew about Kmart.

"From there, the ship will head back east along the Riviera to St. Tropez for three days of relaxing on the beaches, if the weather permits, or shopping in the chic shops or sightseeing in the village. Many original painting are displayed on the wharf.

After departing St. Tropez, the ship will port in Cannes for the following three days for glamorous shopping on Rue d'Antibes—many rich and famous people shop here. Cannes is known as the liveliest pleasure port on the Riviera, so you will enjoy the nightlife.

As your final destination, the ship will return to the harbor in Monte Carlo for the remaining three days for more gambling and more nightlife or whatever you wish to do. Welcome to Monte Carlo and the *Southern Queen*," he said happily. "Please remember to claim your baggage. If you have any questions, I will be aboard the ship in the evenings." The passengers cheered, clapping gratefully.

Taking two steps down to the ground, Nealy glanced up at Louie, "Merci beaucoup, y'all." Louie and the driver roared with laughter. But then she realized how stupid she must have sounded by adding a very southern "y'all" to "Thank you very much." But she didn't know how to say "y'all" in French.

Even though Nealy felt as if she had made a complete fool of herself, Louie, being a gentleman, answered her with a sweet, "My pleasure, madame." Louie observed her as she chatted with the other passengers who listened intently to her accent and her angelically engaging voice. But, he thought, there is something more that attracts them to her. This woman had a rare quality that brought happiness to those around her. And when she smiled, she could mellow *God's* most crotchety creature. Louie had never met anyone quite like her.

The *Southern Queen* stood in the harbor as beautiful and as picturesque as a large white swan. Nealy breathed deeply, enjoying the smell provided by the masses of blossoms that fragrantly permeated the air like an exotic potpourri. The flowers covered the hillsides in shades of red, pink, blue, yellow, white, and purple. In awe of this wonderful place, she gazed in all directions, lingering over the palace which sat high up in the hills, surrounded by the beauty that nature so graciously provided. The pink palace, the Grimaldi fortress, overlooked the Côte d'Azur—the Riviera—from the City of Monaco. When Grace Kelly married Prince Rainier in that royal palace, she changed a fairy-tale into a reality.

As Nealy studied the incredible castle, she thought about her daydreams as a child, about being a beautiful princess who marries a handsome prince. The details had remained vivid in her mind over the years: The gown that she wore over a large hoop had been sewn out of the finest satin, making a swishing noise as she danced to a lovely waltz with her handsome prince. Drawn to her loviness, he couldn't take his piercing blue eyes off of her. Her ladies in waiting twisted her long hair up into a pile of curls held in place by an ornately jeweled tiara. The prince's touch was soft and gentle, making her blush, but she couldn't live without it, and she longed to be near him. The prince lived only for her happiness. Now, all these years later, Nealy knows that fairy tales *don't* really come true. And that Prince Charming was more than likely a completely selfish bastard. In fact, the whole *thing* is a crock!

Returning to the real world, Nealy sensed someone watching her. Her eyes were drawn upward toward the bow of the overwhelming structure in the harbor next to her. Nealy saw Louie LaFitte standing beside a dark haired man who wore a white sailor-looking outfit, much like Louie's, but much more elegant. Louie did all the talking while the man watched her intently. When she tried to turn away, she couldn't; she felt spellbound. Doing a little wishful thinking, she thought it might be nice if he worked on the ship. If so, she could get to know him instead of making goo-goo eyes from a distance. But she had really planned to relax and try to sort out her feelings about Kendall. And romantic entanglements certainly were not high on her list of priorities. But...dinner may be okay. It doesn't get any better than a handsome man speaking the *language of love* over baked red snapper in wine sauce. Why was he staring at her? Feeling strange, she finally broke the spell and turned to look up at the lush green hills above Monte Carlo. Of course she knew that any minute the laughter would come. It had to. Louie had an audience. By now everyone had heard about the ditz from Texas who created her own version of the *language of love*.

When she looked down, the shadow of the two men darkened the sunlit sidewalk in front of her. Staring at the shadow of the taller man, she had a feeling come over her: an overpowering intuition. Nealy racked her brain, trying to place him. Dressed in a uniform, he obviously worked for the shipping lines. Can he be the captain? Curiosity finally got the best of her, and she turned to look up at him again. This time she felt a strange magnetism which embraced her emotionally. Even though she knew that she couldn't possibly know him, she still felt drawn to him. It didn't make sense. Why did this always happen to her? And only with men? Did she have some sort of Male Extrasensory Perception—MESP? Maybe she was a black cat with big, scary yellow eyes in a former life; a witch.

The fact that he had been staring at her for the last five minutes didn't seem to bother him. And, from the distance, she detected an aloofness exuding an air of confidence which she had never seen before in any man. Finally, he slowly turned and disappeared.

CHAPTER FORTY-ONE

ONCE NEALY had identified her luggage, the crew tagged each piece and gave her the claim check. Then she had to check in at a table that had been set up beside the gang plank that led up to the ship. The beauty and the massive size of the *Southern Queen* gave Nealy goosebumps. Nealy had always had a passion for ships, sailing, and the open seas, which she came by naturally since her father and her grandfather had been Navy men. The entire James family were native Galvestonians who had always been involved in the shipping business except, of course, Nealy's great-great grandfather who spent most of his time in jail. From what she had been told, he had promoted unethical boxing matches above a saloon off Market St., bootlegged, and organized cockfighting in Oleander Park. Even worse, he left the family with a *Past*. As a member of the *Downtown Gang*, he was allegedly shot to death as a direct order from some man named *"Dutch"* of the Beach Gang. Thank goodness Papa Joe's off-spring inherited Mama Josephine's Christian ways, her redeeming qualities, and became more responsible citizens.

When Nealy's Grandpa James passed away, he passed down his import/export business, which specialized in break bulk cargo such as pipe, coffee, and cotton, to his only son, Neal. Neal had worked in his father's business from the time he was a young lad, and after receiving his degree in Industrial Engineering from Texas A & M University and serving two years in the Navy, he returned to the business full-time. Within five years, Neal had taken an already successful business and made it even more successful by changing the company's image. Then he bought two large ships and took on such clients as *Dole* and *Farmarco Grain*. Nealy inherited her father's business sense, the desire to make money, and his ambition. So during summer vacations she worked in her father's office and on the docks in shipping and receiving, but, by no means did this experience play a part in her plans for the future. Even though Nealy seemed determined to become an entertainer, her father kept hoping that she would change her mind, encouraging her to spend time on his ships.

Waiting patiently in line next to *Southern Queen*, Nealy realized that even her father's best ship couldn't compare to this awesome structure. And although Nealy had never been on a cruise ship, she knew it wouldn't have that overpowering smell of freshly harvested wheat, the aroma of ground coffee beans, or the sweet smell of ripe pineapples.

On deck two, Nealy opened the door to her cabin. "Oh, my god, it smells like a florist in here," she exclaimed, dropping her carry-on bag inside the doorway. On the table by the bed, sat a crystal vase with at least three dozen red roses in it. Nealy bent over and stuck her nose down to the petals of one of the roses and took a good whiff. They smelled sweet and fragrant like the fresh morning dew. It impressed her that the cruise line had gone to such lengths to welcome their guests. What a special treat, but a very expensive one; but they probably got a huge discount because France has worlds of beautiful flowers, that in some areas, bloomed all year. Nealy opened the card that had been pinned to the large red bow on the front of the vase and it read:

Ms. James, *welcome aboard the Southern Queen.*
M.A.C. *Ship Lines of Southern France*

Nealy smiled and set the card down on the table. When she opened the door to her tiny bathroom, it had a beautifully marbled, but very compact shower. "Jack Sprat could fit in here, but his wife... I don't think so," she said out loud, giggling at her warped sense of humor. It's amazing the things that stick in ones mind from childhood, she thought. Why didn't she remember things like the capital of Ecuador? She knew the country imported coffee and bananas because she had seen crates marked, *Republic of Ecuador,* but that's where her knowledge ended. But, "Jack Sprat who could eat no fat, and his wife who could eat no lean," well, she knew all about them.

Nealy unpacked and put her things away in the dresser and the closet with mirrored doors, and then she took a quick shower and curled her hair. "Hmm, what can I wear?" she said, perusing her wardrobe and finally deciding on a lime-green sunsuit.

After dressing, she set out to explore and ended up looking for her friends who said they would be out wandering around. From the Veranda, she heard someone calling out to her.

"Hey, Nealy, up here," Charlotte screamed from the observation deck. Nealy took the steps up to join them.

"Hi, y'all," she yelled to be heard over the roaring breeze.

"You Texans slaughter the English language," Bob teased, yelling back.

"No, we're just lazy, so we use a lot of contractions," she smiled, the wind blowing so hard it felt as though her lips were being wrapped around the sides of her face and pinned to her ears.

The women anticipated getting plenty of sun, but they agreed to spend the entire day together in Marseille shopping until each of them had "maxed" all of their credit cards. When their husband's threatened to take away their cards and cut them up, they laughed. Charlotte jumped up, electing herself spokeperson for the group.

"Yeah, and you guys have a better chance of getting struck by lightning in the Astrodome than taking our credit cards!"

Nealy applauded Charlotte's uncanny analogy which she used to make a Texan feel at home in a group of Yankees who teased her constantly. If this was any indication as to how the rest of the trip was going to be, she was in for the time of her life!

At five-thirty the ship pulled away from the dock and belted out three near-deafening fog-horned sounds: two long and one short. As the *Southern Queen* made her passage out of the harbor, the people on the shore shouted and waved ecstatically, bidding a fun farewell to the passengers.

"This is even more exciting than I thought it'd be," Nealy said to Fern Rogers who stood next to her waving and blowing kisses as if she knew everyone personally.

"Oh, it's marvelous!" Fern exclaimed.

The wind blew fiercely once they left the protection of the harbor, and the ship raised up and down with the swells as she moved into much deeper waters. "This water is incredible. Look at the color. It's deep blue, but yet it's green," Nealy remarked, giggling because the wind blew so hard that it jiggled her checks and impaired her speech. Moving slowly out to sea, they left behind the high cliffs along the Riviera and the Pink Palace in Monaco that seemed to grow smaller and smaller in the distance. "Well, I'm going down and dress for dinner. I'll see y'all in the dining room." Nealy yelled to be heard.

"Okay, we'll save you a seat." Charlotte said.

When Nealy returned to her cabin, she took on the task of selecting what to wear to dinner on her first night; she wanted to look perfect. After shopping for weeks and buying some fabulous clothes, she couldn't decide. Avoiding a quick choice, she kept going over to the table to smell the rose petals, trying not to bruise them. They were so beautiful and they made her smile. It seemed odd that no one mentioned getting roses; maybe she's just more easily impressed. She had received plenty of roses from Jerrod during their relationship, but the beauty had been diminished because they reminded her of his guilty acts of infidelity. Although, during the two weeks that she had spent in New York with Phillip, flowers took on a special meaning again because he brought different ones home to her each day. With that thought, Nealy sat down on the bed. She remembered his sweet, gentle ways and the fun they had together. If he were on this cruise with her, things would be perfect. *God*, how she missed him and, because she couldn't stop thinking about him, she probably always would.

Nealy left her cabin and followed the magnificent aroma down the hall, up the stairs, and into the dining room on the third deck. At the door, she searched the room for a familiar face. In the far corner of the room, she saw

Fern and the others. Wearing a royal blue sequined dress that fit like a glove, she made her way through the room as heads turned. Nealy simply smiled and said "Hi" to each person that she made eye contact with along the way.

"Can I join y'all?" she asked, smiling at the sixteen or so people sitting at the table.

"Sure," cried Fern.

"Hey, Nealy, come sit by me," cried Bob.

"Bob, I should have known. You're a real sucker for a pretty face," his wife Charlotte said, smiling and winking at Nealy. So Nealy sat down next to Charlotte instead, which really made her feel more comfortable.

"Why did you sit down next to her?" Bob asked, making a sad face.

Nealy thought for a second. "Well, Bob, my dress and that bright, flowery Hawaiian shirt would clash—my gosh, now those *are* some very large hibiscus! But Bob, trust me, I'm not being critical. They are definitely you—you're just a bright and colorful kind of guy," she giggled sweetly.

"Oh, okay, but next time you'll sit by me. I promise I'll wear something plain," he allowed.

"It's a deal, Bob." Nealy agreed, smiling at him.

Charlotte looked at her husband and then at Nealy. "You made the right choice, babe. He's got terrible table manners," she said seriously, and then roared with laughter.

Nealy couldn't help laughing at Charlotte because she looked and sounded so much like her crazy friend Jillie from Freddy's. Nealy was amazed at how much a New Jersey accent and a South Louisiana accent sounded alike. As she looked at the people around the table who were laughing and cutting up with a drink in one hand and a cigarette in the other, she knew she was in for a wild and crazy night.

Nealy looked up and down the table, speaking to each person or at least making eye contact. "I'm really impressed. Look at all of this food, and all those beautiful roses...well, this is really first class," Nealy said, her eyes large and innocent.

Puzzled, Charlotte spoke up. "Roses? What roses are you talking about, dear?" she asked.

"The ones in our cabins. The ones welcoming us aboard," Nealy said sincerely.

"We didn't get any roses," Fern said disappointed.

"Nobody got roses?" Nealy asked addressing each puzzled face.

"No, not one single, solitary bud," Fern complained.

"Hmmm, now that's odd. Oh, well, I'll be happy to share," Nealy said cheerfully. "Drop by cabin two-twenty-two later and I'll give you each a couple," she smiled, wondering why she had been the only one to get roses. How strange.

Along one wall, enormous tables were covered with food: hors d'oeuvre by the thousands, colorful fruits, salads and vegetables, both raw and steamed; beef, pork, seafood and poultry that had been fried, sauted or baked, and that came complete with white, yellow and brown sauces; breads in every color, shape, form and fashion; and desserts that were the out of this world. Unable to decide, Nealy just took a little bit of everything, except for the desserts. With the size of her shower, she had better wait until the second week to indulge.

The chatter in the dining room made it very noisy, but no one seemed to mind. They simply ate, drank and laughed merrily while the ship glided through the water with almost no detectable motion. Nealy expected to chase her plate all over the table the way she had in her family's boat on a day long picnic at sea in the Gulf of Mexico.

Nealy sat across from Fern with her back to the door of the dining room. When Fern lifted her fork to take a bite of food, she looked up from her plate and her face froze in place with her mouth hanging open in a position prone to excessive drooling.

"Are you okay, Fern?" Nealy asked. Then she noticed that everybody facing her had gotten very quiet and seemed to be staring with a blank expressions on their faces.

Fern cleared her throat, but she didn't get the chance to speak.

"Good-evening, Ms. James."

Nealy knew that voice. Slowly, she followed the eyes around the table. As her head turned upward over her shoulder, her eyes locked with the *brown-velvet eyes* of Michael Coupair. "I don't believe it," she exclaimed softly. "Well, I should have known. You always appear out of nowhere. That was you, right? The man talking to Louie?"

"Yes," he replied. "It's wonderful to see you again."

No one at the table said a word, they just kept staring at him. "It's nice to see you, too," she replied nervously, staring into those luscious dark eyes. Finally, she giggled softly. "Uh, I must have left my manners back in Texas...sorry...uh, everybody this is Michael Coupair. And that's Fern, Joe, Charlotte, Bob, and— oh, there's too many of us. Y'all take it from here," she smiled, pointing to the person next to Bob, allowing each person to introduce themselves.

"It's nice to meet you all. And welcome to the *Southern Queen*. Are you enjoying yourselves so far?" he asked politely. Everyone nodded and politely responded. "And you, Ms. James?"

"Uh, yes. Everything's perfect, thanks." Nealy smiled at him, experiencing that same awkward nervousness that she had always felt in his presence.

"Very well, Ms. James, I will let you finish your dinner, but I must say that having you aboard will bring an even greater beauty to the *Southern Queen*."

Nealy blushed from head to toe. "Uh...that's sweet...uh, thanks," she fumbled for her words. He kept staring at her. What else could she say?

"Umm…I'm really looking forward to the next two weeks," she blurted out finally.

"Me, too," he said, reaching his hand out to her. When she placed her hand in his, he looked directly into her eyes and kissed the back of her hand. "I will see you later, Ms. James." Michael Coupair smiled, glancing at each individual at the table briefly before politely excusing himself.

All eyes were on Nealy. "I guess you want details. Is that it?" she asked, still in shock.

"It's none of our business, but tell us anyway," Charlotte insisted.

"You're just like Jillie. She, too, loved all the juicy details. But actually, there isn't much to tell. I met him a year ago in New York in an elevator. I'd been shopping and I had so many packages that I tried to do a balancing act. When I dropped them, he helped me pick them up and take them to my apartment. After that, I only saw him two or three more times in passing, just long enough to say 'Hello.' That's it. Honest Indian," she grinned making the peace sign.

"That's it," Fern cried.

"Sorry, but *that's it*, guys. Nothing happened. I swear. I barely know him…but, who knows," she smiled cunningly, "I may *get* to know him. Ask me again at the end of this cruise. Maybe, I'll have a juicier story to tell," Nealy giggled.

In spite of the wonderful food and the crazy company, Nealy couldn't forget about seeing Michael Coupair again after all this time. Why was he here? Could he be the captain? Not in a million years would she have envisioned him behind the wheel of a cruise ship. No, he couldn't be. Or could he be? Louie! There's her answer. Louie would know all there is to know about the suave and debonair Mr. Coupair.

After dinner, everyone went down to the lounge to relax for a drink and to enjoy the entertainment. Nealy had one glass of wine, and then politely excused herself. Curiosity was about to get the best of her. She had to find Louie who said he'd be on the ship at night if anyone had any questions. Well, she had a question or two, and she intended to find him. One thing for sure, it was highly unlikely that he was a producer or director as Tony had originally thought; the fact that he had turned up aboard the *Southern Queen* all dressed in white eliminated that theory.

Nealy checked out the other lounge and even asked the bartender. Then she looked in the door of the dining room, thinking that maybe the crew ate late, but she didn't see him. Then she circled through the casino, but she didn't see him anywhere. Finally, she decided to brave the wind and check each deck. But the wind had come up and getting the door open was the first obstacle that she had to overcome, but she finally managed. What seemed like hurricane winds made it difficult to walk up towards the bow of the ship. "Damn," she cried, grabbing the rail to keep from losing her balance. Now she knew why no one bothered to go outside under the moonlight. When she saw the lights in the wheelhouse, she wondered if he might be inside steering or pushing the buttons or whatever the hell they do on fancy ships today.

Peering through the window, she pulled her hair out of her eyes so she could see. Three men were talking, but unfortunately none of them were Louie. Well, she had exhausted every place that she knew to look, she decided that he must have turned-in early. But, as most stubborn people, she was determined to find him, so she decided to check one more place: the veranda on the stern of the ship.

Nealy walked down the stairs and took the promenade all the way back to the veranda. When she got there, she became so overwhelmed by the silver-streaked reflection following the ship that she forgot all about Louie. As she walked over to the rail, she marveled at the moon rays that fell from the sky, leaving a trail that appeared to go on forever on top of the blue-black mass of water.

"Aren't you cold?"

Nealy nearly jumped out of her skin. Reflexively she whirled around to find Michael Coupair standing behind her. "You scared me half to death," she cried, clutching her chest.

"I'm sorry, I didn't mean to frighten you," he apologized.

"That's alright. I guess I got so caught up in the moon's glow that I wasn't paying attention," she smiled. "It's so beautiful out here."

He smiled at her and his dark eyes glistened as the light from above highlighted them. "There's nothing more beautiful than the sea," he said, searching Nealy's face for a reaction. "She has grace and style and power. She is a creator of magic and miracles by day, and a dark, drawing mystique by night. And she expects fortitude from those who challenge her. Much like a beautiful woman, Ms. James."

Nealy gazed at him in awe. "That's a wonderful interpretation. Did you just make that up or did you hear it somewhere?" she asked curiously, smiling at him.

"I heard most of it from my father and my grandfather when I was a boy growing up on these waters," he said, smiling at her. Nealy appeared even prettier than he remembered.

Nealy smiled and trembled as the cold wind cut through to her bones. "My Grandpa James used to say things like that to me when I was a little girl. Sometimes, when I would be afraid to get in the water, he would say, 'Now, Nealy, there's nothing to be afraid of as long as you show respect for the ocean and her creatures.' I didn't understand it, but it always gave me courage."

"You are trembling," he said. "Would you prefer to go inside?"

"No, I'm okay. I like it out here."

"So, Ms. James, you know the ocean, do you?"

"I grew up on the Gulf of Mexico. Galveston."

"Ah, yes, that is right," he remembered.

"My family owns a shipping business," she said.

"Is that why you were in New York? For your family?"

"No. I'm a dance teacher. I just helped out in the summers when I was in school. When I was very young, I used to ride from the Port of Galveston to the Port of Houston with my grandpa on his tankers and cargo barges. He carried mostly cotton in the old days. Then when my father took over the business, I used to load and unload the ships. Well, not physically, but I worked on the docks. You know, shipping stuff."

He chuckled softly, smiling at her. "I knew we had many things in common from the moment I laid eyes on you, Ms. James."

"Why is that, Mr. Coupair?" she asked, smiling at the way she must sound when she pronounced his name. She tried to remember how he had said it and mimic him with the long *o*, like Coo-pear, but she knew it still came out too twangy to sound French because he smiled when she said it.

"My father, like my grandfather, was a fisherman. And when I was only a young boy of eight, my father moved the family to Toulon where he built a boat to fish for sardines," he grinned at the face she made.

"Sardines. Those smelly little *things* in the cans?" she grimaced.

"Yes, those smelly little *things* in the cans," he repeated, and then laughed out loud.

Nealy couldn't believe it. Not only did this man look like a first-class-act, he even laughed with class: soft and smooth and controlled. "I'm sorry, I'm not being condescending, but I've just never cared much for sardines. My father loves them, so they must be good," she said, trying to get her foot out of her mouth as usual.

"That's perfectly all right, Ms. James. I don't eat those smelly little *things* either."

"Since this boat doesn't fish for sardines, this must be a pleasure trip for you, right?" she asked, trying not too sound too intruding.

He smiled, but his eyes narrowed and his brow creased, "No, not really, but since you are aboard, Ms. James, I think it will turn out to be very pleasurable."

Of course, Nealy noticed that he didn't answer her question, but she let it go. "Are you this charming to all the girls?" she asked, running out of ways to say "thank you."

"Only the beautiful ones."

"Thanks. And that's really flattering. But before I can accept anymore compliments, I think that you should call me Nealy. Unless, of course, it's a French custom, you know, addressing women by their proper names," she said nervously.

He smiled. "No, it's not a custom. So if you will call me Michael, I will call you 'Nealy.' It's an unusual name, but a beautiful one."

"I'm named after my Daddy. His name is Neal, and they—my mother and father—added a y. So it's Neal-y. I wonder why they didn't add an *e*? Oh, well," she shrugged, rambling again; he brought that out in the her.

"Well, I feel closer to you already now that we have this name thing straightened out," she giggled, making him laugh.

He put his arm around her waist. "I think that we should go in now, Nealy. I don't want you getting sick from the cold, damp air." He guided her towards the stairs.

"You're probably right, Michael." Although she had to be freezing, she didn't feel a thing. His staring had brought her body temperature up to a high fever of at least a hundred and five or six.

"Where would you like to go?" he asked. "There is a show starting in the Cabaret Room on the Lido Deck. Since you are a dance teacher, I think you might enjoy it. Would you like to go?"

"I'd love to," she said, allowing him to hold her arm as they made their way down the stairs.

He led her inside and over to a table right next to the stage. "I'll be right back," he whispered.

A couple of minutes later, he returned and the show began. Every once in a while he would look at her and smile only with his eyes, which made her feel nervous all over again. During the intermission, a young lady walked over and handed her a dozen long-stemmed red roses. "These are for you, Ms. James," she said, smiling at Nealy, and then at Michael Coupair.

"Oh, they're beautiful," she cried, "but, who are they—" But before she finished asking, she knew. Michael Coupair had sent them. "Thank you, Michael, they're lovely. The roses in my cabin, I guess you did that, too?" she nodded, certain that he had. He smiled, confirming her suspicion, which made her blush.

If he kept this up, her face would be a permanent shade of red. "Thank you, again. They're lovely."

"But you are much lovelier, Nealy."

"I think I'm going to like it here, Michael. You can keep the flowers and the compliments coming," she giggled, though she felt a little uncomfortable with all the attention.

After the show, Michael walked her down to her cabin door. "I owe you lunch, you know."

"What?" she asked.

"In New York," he said, staring at her again.

"Oh, that's right. You do. In the elevator. Yes, I remember now. But I never saw you again after that," she smiled.

"I will explain all of that tomorrow at brunch. That is, if you will join me?"

"I'd like that," she smiled, even though her jaws were aching from constantly smiling at him.

Sweetly, he took her hand and kissed the back of it very softly. Then he took her key and unlocked the cabin door, holding it open for her to enter. "Good-night, *Nealy James*."

"Good-night, *Michael Coupair*."

CHAPTER FORTY-TWO

THE NEXT MORNING Nealy woke up bright and early, put on her jogging clothes, and made five laps around each promenade deck. Afterwards she returned to her cabin to do some floor work before she had to get ready to go to breakfast with Michael Coupair. Could this be fate? Kendall canceling and the *brown-velvet eyes* emerging above the deep blue sea. But how could she believe in fate anymore? Phillip was suppose to be her destiny, and as it turned out she had only been brutally tempted by the cruel hands of misfortune. So maybe Michael had been sent to help her get over Phillip once and for all; any man that gorgeous had to be a gift.

The note left on her door said that Mr. Coupair would pick her up at ten o'clock and that she should dress comfortably; they would be doing some sightseeing. Nealy put on a white sailor outfit that had a short-sleeve double-breasted jacket trimmed with blue and gold cording. The fitted jacket tapered at the waist and wrapped snugly around her hips over a short, split skirt. Since he sounded as if they would be doing some walking, she wore her navy Keds instead of her sandals. A nervous wreck, she walked into the bathroom to check out her hair and make-up at least ten times and her stomach had enough knots in it to hang from a six story building. And when the knock finally came at the door, she panicked. Her heart pounded so hard that she considered hiding in the closet, but that seemed utterly ridiculous, so she took a deep breath and opened the door.

"Bonjour," she said, trying not to laugh. Even in France she felt like a *complete* moron trying to speak French.

"Bonjour," he said softly, taking her hand and kissing the back of it again. "Are you ready?"

"I'm ready," she said, grabbing her tote bag and hanging it over her shoulder.

Michael had a shiny black Mercedes limousine waiting for them at the dock and Nealy noticed that the license plate had M.A.C. on it. When the chauffeur addressed Michael as "Mr. Coupair, sir," Nealy knew for sure that he wasn't the captain of the ship.

"Michael, I'm not trying to be nosy, but what exactly is your relationship with this ship?"

With his *brown-velvet eyes*, he stared at her rather seriously, as if he were trying to come up with the right answer before he said anything. "I own it."

As they pulled away from the dock, she looked back at the *Southern Queen*. "You actually *own* that ship?" Nealy couldn't believe it. The men in her life were always full of surprises, and they always *owned* things and places; this one probably *owned* a few people, too.

"Yes," he said, nodding confidently.

"Well, no wonder you own an apartment on Central Park West. But, if you own a ship in France, what were you doing in New York?"

Michael proceeded to tell her that he owned not only this ship but that he owned three others as well, and a shipping lines that imported sardines to American and to other countries around the world. Because of his business and his cruise line affiliations in America, he had to spend time in New York City. No wonder the man looked like a millionaire, he was!

They had brunch at a quaint restaurant in the small town of Calvi. Michael ordered for them in French and told her not to even ask what he had ordered. He wanted her just to taste it, and he would tell her what it was at a later time. She made him promise that it wasn't prepared with sardines, dogs or horses, which made him laugh, but he promised. Some of it was smoked ham because she could taste the salt and because she could also taste the smoke flavor, but the pates were rather disguised, so she just ate them, not really wanting to know what they were. French food came from many unusual sources and being prepared with wine, it became hard to identify. In this particular area there was an abundance of wildlife and seafood, and from what Nealy understood, they even ate different birds, like blackbird and thrush. All of the wines that she had been served so far were excellent, and Michael insisted that she do a little tasting of several others to explore her preference.

Following lunch, they drove through the mountainous areas and ended up at Golfe de Porto for a view of one of the most beautiful panoramas of sea and landscape that Nealy had ever seen in her life. As far as she could see, the blue water extended from a point of craggy red granite cliffs and boulders. They got out of the limo and walked along the top of the cliffs as Michael explained the scenery and its fascinating origin from the eruption of volcanos and the natural destruction from the wind and water over the years. The terrains changed constantly going from beaches to mountains with trees to mountains without trees exposing rocks and boulders and back to beaches again. The tour fascinated her and her personal tour guide entranced her. By the end of the day, he had completely seduced her with his charm and his polite, quiet ways; it surprised her that he had been a perfect gentlemen for six hours.

That evening at dinner, he had invited Nealy and her friends from the bus to join him at his table. Her off-the-wall group of American friends were probably a little on the wild side for his sophisticated demeanor, but he tolerated them well enough, smiling at their jokes and even laughing out loud a time or two.

They left the dining room at nine o'clock to attend the show. By then, he had obviously had enough, inviting Nealy to join him in a more secluded place: his cabin. The thought of going to his private quarters alone with him made her uncomfortable, but she was dying to see what a floating penthouse on the *Southern Queen* looked like.

And as she expected, ten of her cabins would fit inside of his enormous suite. Nealy sat down on the circular, brown leather sofa in the living room, and Michael poured her a glass of wine that just happened to be the one that she had liked most at the restaurant where they ate lunch. Jerrod had always been charming, but he couldn't even be compared to Michael Coupair; this man knew how to charm the pants off of any woman, and that's probably not a figure of speech; resisting him would be the real challenge.

Their eyes were like magnets, therefore Nealy's complexion maintained a reddish-glow until she finally got used to it. He insisted that she tell him about her visit to New York, but as it turned out, he already knew most of the story. A person in his position can find out almost anything they want to know about someone, though he didn't have the facts exactly right. The information that he received said that Nealy James Jones lived in Galveston, Texas, with her husband, Jerrod, and that she had three brothers and one sister. He assumed that Tony was her brother because they favored, and he mistook Phillip for Jerrod. The last report he received was that she had returned to Texas with her husband. As she tried to sort out the facts for him, she couldn't believe that even in the presence of the most attractive man that she had ever seen in her life, she still felt that hard twinge of pain when she spoke about Phillip. But maybe after Michael kissed her, which she felt intrigued to do for a lot of reasons—his good looks, his power, his money, his prestige—all of which made it seem more exciting. And maybe if he kissed as good as he romanced, she would forget all about Phillip. After all, Phillip had been the one to take her mind off the *brown-velvet eyes*, so perhaps it would work in reverse.

Finally, that moment came when he slowly removed her wine glass from her hand and sat it down on the table.

"Would you mind if I kissed you, Nealy?" he asked her sweetly. "I have dreamed about holding you and kissing you for such a long time."

Never being asked before, she really didn't know how to respond, so she nodded delicately and closed her eyes. In slow motion, he eased his hand up under her hair, grasping the soft nape of her neck and pulling her face to his. Then he kissed her softly and gently on the lips. Nealy felt like *Jean Harlow* in *When the Lion Roars* when the handsome Clark Gable took her into his arms and smothered her with a long, lingeringly kiss. Michael eased away from her, staring deeply into her eyes, and then he stood up, took her hand and pulled her up to kiss her again. The kisses were nice, but she wasn't prepared to hop into bed with a man that she had just met. And from what she had always heard about European men being the *World's Greatest Lovers*, she figured this had to be some sort of foreplay: slow sensual kisses, first on the mouth, then the neck, and downward from there. Oh, Lordy, she could be in trouble.

Michael distanced himself from her and took her hand in his. Slowly he led her towards the door in silence. After opening the door, he smiled at her and then stepped back, allowing her to walk out ahead of him.

Nealy smiled at him on her way out, and weakly said, "Thank you." It was more than just a gentlemanly gesture, much more mysterious and somewhat intriguing. Where were they going? Was he walking her to her room again? And if so, did he plan on coming in? She couldn't figure it all out. Maybe he didn't like the way she kissed, and therefore he wanted to walk her back to her room and say, "Don't call me, I'll call you" in his polite French way. All she could do was smile or chatter a bit.

At the door to her cabin, he stopped and took her hands in his. "I had a wonderful day with you, Nealy," he said, kissing her lightly on each cheek.

"Me, too. Thanks for the day and the tour," she smiled. Being a very perceptive person, she had become confused by his charming nobility. "Michael, is everything alright?"

"It's perfect. Why do you ask?"

"Well, you're so quiet. I guess I'm just not used to someone being so mysterious. Remember, I'm a Texan. And by nature we're pretty rowdy folks."

He looked at her very puzzled. "Rowdy?"

"Oh, I can tell that I've lost you," she giggled. "I'm sorry. Rowdy means loud and boisterous."

"Oh, I see," he said.

"And since I grew up with five siblings, it was always noisy. Talking. Laughing. We were only quiet if we were unhappy about something."

"So you think I'm unhappy?"

"Well, you *are* very quiet. And when you kissed me, you didn't say anything. Didn't you like it?"

Michael laughed and hugged her. "Oh, my beautiful, Nealy. Of course I liked it. I told you. I dreamed of kissing you ever since the first time I saw you. It's even better than I imagined—"

"Wait a minute," she interrupted. "You dreamed about kissing me?"

"Yes, many times. After I saw you in New York, I wanted you. And I thought about you often," he said, glancing down and sliding his hands gently across her breasts, to move her hair around her shoulders and onto her back. Flinching slightly, he took his focus off her chest and back into her eyes. "But, my darling, I adore you. I don't want to rush things. For the rest of my life, I will cherish the first time that we make love. Anyone can see that you have a beautiful body. Everything about you is ravishing, but I also know that you are very bright. I want to explore your mind first, and then I'll explore your body," he said seductively, making her blush far beyond any other time; even brighter than a vine-ripe tomato in mid-July.

"Will I see you tomorrow?" he asked.

"Uh, sure...but don't you have work to do or something?"

"I am working. Are you not a passenger aboard this ship?"

"Well, yeah, but—"

"I'll pick you up at nine tomorrow morning. I'll take you into the village for breakfast. And then I'll show you some more of the countryside. Goodnight, Nealy," he said, kissing her hand as he examined her face with his eyes.

"Uh...good-night," she said barely above a whisper.

Nealy dressed for bed. She couldn't get over the mystery of this man. His looks, his mannerism, his touch, his voice, and his words were all so alluring, so enticing, so seductive, and so romantic. *"Explore your mind first. And then I'll explore your body."* Geezus, that's pretty direct. She couldn't help wondering how long he intended on exploring her mind before he started *exploring* her body. And when he's ready to explore her body, would she be able to say no if she needed more time? The whole thing made butterflies in the pit of her stomach; actually, it scared her to death. But Jillie and Claudia, her friends in New York, would really flip out over this man. They would tell her to relax and enjoy every glorious minute with this dreamboat. And Denise, well, she would be beside herself. Nealy could still hear her: "Forget Jerrod. Hook that Frenchman." This guy had probably picked up plenty of women in and out of elevators. At least Nealy had gotten to know him well enough that she didn't become deaf, dumb and ignorant whenever he spoke to her, thank goodness, except of course when he said things about exploring her mind and her body. Now that made her feel weak in the knees. And she melted when he said "he adored her" and then called her, *"my darling."* Holy shit! This guy truly personifies romance. Phillip had been romantic, too, but he didn't scare her. God, she missed him. Maybe Michael was *God's* way of telling her to turn Kendall loose, let go of Phillip's memory, and move on to a new romance, but she still missed Phillip, which made it hard to even think about making a new life with someone else. If only— "Oh, Phillip, where are you?" she whispered, sitting down on the side of the bed. Within seconds, tears rolled down her cheeks.

As promised, Michael picked her up at nine, and the limo carried them into the village for breakfast. He held her hand, kissing it frequently and talking softly about his life and how he came to own his shipping lines. Nealy loved listening to his accent, and she tried desperately to pick-up the language whenever he spoke in French. He took her down by the shore where he used to play as a small boy while his father and his uncle made their way around the island, dropping their nets in the coves where the fish fed. Then he drove her through the Chestnut Groves. In the late afternoon, they picnicked on a secluded beach underneath a giant cliff, which extended out over the water. The day had been so pleasant and relaxing. Michael attended to her every wish, making sure that she had everything she needed to satisfy her comfort, her hunger, her thirst, and her happiness. They talked non-stop, but Nealy spent most of her time trying to give meaning to what she was saying and the expressions that she used.

When he walked her back to her cabin following dinner, which he had insisted that they enjoy alone, he had already planned for them to spend the next day together as well. "We will be sailing on to Marseille tonight. I want to take you shopping tomorrow," he said, taking her key to unlocked the door as he always did. She walked inside and suddenly remembered that she had told Fern and the others that she would shop with them in Marseille. "Oh, Michael, I can't tomorrow. I promised to shop with my friends. Remember, the *rowdy* ones from dinner?"

"Can't you cancel?"

"No, I promised," she said sadly.

"Then, I will see you for dinner tomorrow night, yes?" he asked, obviously disappointed.

"Oui," she smile, kissing him on each cheek. "When in France, you do as the French do." Nealy laughed at herself.

"Au revoir, my beautiful Nealy." He smiled, kissed his index and middle fingers, and then blew her a kiss as he walked away.

CHAPTER FORTY-THREE

THE NEXT DAY Nealy, Fern, Charlotte, and three other woman hit the stores in Marseille. All day, they questioned Nealy about her new beaux and practically drooled on themselves as she told them about the past two days. Of course they were happy for her, but they were also a little concerned about her getting involved with a wealthy foreigner. Nealy's a big girl and she can take care of herself, but it didn't take a rocket scientist to recognize his keen ability to manipulate. And what young American woman could resist a gorgeous Frenchman showering her with compliments and gifts and promises to show her that money can buy happiness? It worried them, but they were also green with envy.

The born-to-shop group of woman walked for six hours and bought all kinds of things. Nealy wanted a dark-green, knee-length leather jacket, which she fell in love with immediately. It fit her perfectly, and the others said it made her eyes even more green, encouraging her to get it. So she did. Nealy bought French perfume for Betty Lou and Kati Sue since both of them had gotten divorced during the last year and needed some cheering up. Also, she bought her mother a Lladro—fine porcelain figurine—of a young girl playing a violin; it was so sweet that she had to buy it for her.

On the way back to the ship, Nealy stopped in the post office to buy some stamps and mail some post cards back home to her family and friends, which turned into a real fiasco. No one could understand her, even when she spoke in her limited French. The whole thing became very frustrating so she flipped through her French book to find the words that she needed. Finally, she went outside and stopped people on the street to see if she could find someone who could speak English. "Parlez-vous anglais?" she asked frantically, but those that acknowledged her shook their heads no. "Well, shit!" she cried, aggravated at the language barrier. And to her surprise, that disgusting little word turned out to be the universal link that brought two young men to her rescue. Finally, she got her cards in the mail, but quite doubtful that they would ever reach the U.S.A.

There wasn't a cloud in the sky by high noon. So they ate lunch at a dirty little sidewalk cafe to enjoy the sunshine and the lovely climate. Each of them had a fruit cup, a wonderful croissant—bad girls, but they couldn't resist—and a cup of the strongest coffee that any of them had ever tasted; New Orleans didn't have a thing on the real French people. This stuff could walk right out of the cup.

Nealy had told her friends that she and Michael would join them that evening for dinner even though Michael had expressed that he preferred an intimate dinner for two. But, after a little friendly persuasion on her part, he finally agreed to join them. "You look very beautiful tonight, Nealy," he whispered in her ear. "Green is your color."

"Thank you, I mean, Merci," she said graciously, but she couldn't hold back her laughter. "Why do I sound so silly when I speak French?"

Fern laughed and commented. "Nealy, it's that Southern drawl of yours."

"No, Nealy, I think it's that nasal twang. And let's face it, anything that comes out the nose, can't be too romantic," Charlotte said, cracking herself up. The others joined her with their own silly comments. Everyone had become hysterical, except for Michael. Unfortunately, he didn't find them humorous at all.

Finally, he spoke up, bringing the laughter to a halt. "I find Nealy's voice sweet and lovely. It adds to her beauty." He put his arm around her to reassure her. Michael had obviously been offended by their lack of sensitivity for her feelings.

"Michael, they're just teasing me," she said. "It's called kidding. It's only in fun. Texans talk through their noses. That's just how it is. I had to have speech therapy in New York before I could get a speaking part in the theater. What can I say? I'm from the South. So I don't mind if they tease me. Really, it's harmless. And they wouldn't tease me if they didn't like me."

Charlotte could see the anger in his face and realized that French people didn't have much of a sense of humor, at least this one didn't. She could also see how possessive he had become with Nealy, which she could see as a potential problem; somehow she didn't see Nealy as the type to appreciate or tolerate a possessive man.

Michael relaxed and even smiled a time or two after that, but he still didn't care for their fun. After dinner, he pulled Nealy away, and they took a walk on the promenade deck. He held her close to him and asked her questions about her marriage, which she didn't really care to talk about, but she did. Of course Jerrod's infidelities didn't seem unreasonable to him, but some French people have a higher level of tolerance for affairs and do not find that reason enough to divorce, which disturbed her somewhat. Nealy asked him questions about his childhood, and he became terribly sentimental when he talked about his father who had died two years earlier. He seemed content to stare at her in the dark and lift her hair up and kiss the soft area on her neck, sending chillbumps up and down her entire body.

"Come with me. I have something for you," he said eagerly.

"What is it?"

"I can't tell you. It will ruin the surprise," he said, pulling her by the arm towards the door. He took her down to his cabin. When they got inside, he handed her a box.

"What is it?"

"Go on. Open it. See for yourself."

Nealy unwrapped the box. "Oh, Michael, it's beautiful. Thank you...but I can't let you spend this much money on someone that you just met," she said, taking the bracelet out of the box.

"I've known you for more than a year, remember?"

"I know...but—Why do men do that? They calculate different from women—you see, you've only *really* gotten to know me in the last few days."

"It doesn't matter. I fell in love with you the moment I saw you, Nealy," he said, kissing her lightly on the lips. Then he took the bracelet from her and fastened it around her small wrist.

"Michael, you don't know me well enough to be in love with me. Do you? You can't...I think I'm being swept off my feet," she said, shaking her head.

"Par-don?"

"Nothing. It's just a figure of speech," she looked down at the bracelet. "It's so beautiful. Thank you, Michael." Nealy put her arms around his neck and kissed him, which she had been too nervous to do until now. In the few times that he had kissed her, she just froze when he touched her, making it impossible for her to respond with anything other than her mouth.

"It's not half as beautiful as you, my darling."

"Thank you," she said shyly. Nealy blushed.

"Come and lie by me," he said, taking her hand and turning her towards the large bedroom.

She hesitated for a moment, but when he looked at her with the *brown-velvet eyes* and tugged at her arm, she followed him. He turned down the lights and slowly pushed her back on the bed. Gently rubbing her ankles he removed her shoes and massaged her feet for a couple of minutes before he lay down beside her. "Relax, my darling," he whispered. "I just want to talk to you and be near you."

"I'm a little nervous, Michael," she said, taking a deep breath. But that wasn't exactly the truth; she was terrified.

"Darling, there is nothing to be nervous about. I'm not going to make love to you yet. I just want to be near you." He gently touched her face, staring at her for more than an hour before she fell asleep.

At midnight, he woke her up and escorted her down to her cabin and only lightly kissed her before he said good-night. Nealy didn't know what to make of this relationship. Michael seemed to be the perfect gentleman and genuinely concerned about her feelings.

The next morning Nealy woke up as the sunshine came through her small porthole beside her bed. She looked out at the glassy-smooth surface of the water that led up to the beach in the distance. It was almost seven o'clock and she had promised to meet Michael at eight-thirty for breakfast. Nealy enjoyed being with him, but she missed her new friends, too. Nealy thought about how much more fun she and her friends would be having with Phillip, but of course Phillip was the perfect, all-American male that all parents wished for their daughters. Phillip had a very outgoing personality, much like Nealy's, and he liked being with people. He could fit into almost any crowd, but Michael was more like Jerrod, and he didn't really want to be with anyone other than Nealy. Also, Nealy didn't see him as one to share her with anyone, including family and friends. Michael talked as if it would be all right for him to look at other women, but not for her to look at another man; she got the feeling that he and Jerrod shared the same set of double standards. Phillip had been the easiest to be with, and he could hold his own in a crowd; he didn't need to be pampered. But Phillip had married someone else. When would she let go? Suddenly, Nealy realized that she had never asked Michael about marriage. Of course she assumed that he had been married because he had three children who were practically grown, although he appeared too young to have grown children. That was another thing, his age. She guessed thirty-five or so, but with Michael it was very hard to tell. His perfect face had very few wrinkles, even with his being in the sun most of his life, and he had only a few strands of grey among his very dark-brown hair. Maybe the time had come for her to ask him some personal questions. Miss Janik had practically destroyed her life with a man that she knew nothing about, assuming that she knew everything.

Nealy dressed, taking time out every few minutes to examine her new bracelet: six carats—three each—of diamonds and rubies that's separated by bars of gold. Although she felt guilty about accepting a gift of this magnitude at this point in their relationship, she couldn't return it. Michael's ego would not allow it.

When she opened the door, she discovered a note attached to it with her name on the front. She stepped back inside to read it:

My darling Nealy,

Please forgive me, but I had to take care of some business this morning. I will be back later today and I will pick you up at your cabin for a late lunch. I will miss you my darling, so please be waiting for me and forgive my broken promise. I will make it up to you.

Love, Michael

Nealy left the note on her dresser and went up to meet her friends for breakfast. Since Michael had to work, she was free to go to the beach with them afterwards, which she looked forward to. She stuffed herself on fresh fruit, however she preferred four or five eclairs. Boy, did they look good, but she knew that they would go right to her butt or her stomach or to her boobs where she did not need it or want it. So, if she planned to hang out at the beach in a skimpy two-piece, she didn't want her stomach pouching out, her butt drooping, or her boobs sagging.

The tender took them ashore at Tahiti Beach because there wasn't a harbor in this particular area of St. Tropez. As they walked along the beach, Nealy's eyes got bigger and bigger. Most of the woman had no bathing suit tops, and some of them were even playing ping-pong on the shore with their breasts flopping from "here to yonder," as her Grandma Gobel would say. "Hey, Fern, Charlotte," Nealy whispered, "they know we're Americans."

"Who?" Fern said.

"These French people," Nealy whispered.

"How?" Charlotte asked.

"Because we're staring. Our mouths are hanging open. And we are definitely overdressed," Nealy said jokingly.

Fern and Charlotte cracked up laughing, but it was so true. The first part of the beach had yellow umbrellas which signified the area where mostly Americans and other tourists sunbathed in fairly conservative two-piece suits or tanks. On further down the beach under the green umbrellas, the Europeans or other less inhibited people, had only bottoms. But then, under the blue umbrellas, were the total nudes with the exception of maybe a hair ribbon.

Nealy and the other nine people in her group found a good front row spot under the yellow umbrellas, but even there Nealy caught her breath every time someone walked by topless; this type of sunbathing would require an adjustment period. Of course the men delighted in the scenery. Bob smiled at Nealy a few times as some "babe," as he called her, casually strolled down the beach.

"Hey, Nealy," he said, "in Rome, you do as the Romans do, so in France, the least we could do is go nude on their beach. I will, if you will." He smiled devilishly, and Charlotte punched him.

"Not on your life, Bob, but Charlotte might," she giggled.

"I'd die first," she snapped, cutting her eyes at Bob. "And you won't either if you know what's good for you, buster."

They spent the day laughing, talking, staring, gawking, and poking one another when something or someone of interest appeared on the scene. They spotted Princess Caroline and her entourage sitting not too far from them. At first, they thought it was Stephanie, but then they decided that she was too young and that it had to be Caroline. She and some man, who had to be much older than she, talked to each other only on occasion. They didn't pay much attention to the crowd, and surprisingly no one approached them, however, there were five muscle-bound men that made a nice tight circle around them.

Bob took a walk. When he returned, he wanted Nealy and Charlotte to take a walk down the beach with him. He had discovered a guy with an "enormous set of family jewels," he said, but both Nealy and Charlotte refused to go with him. They had already taken one walk too many down that beach to witness dark, leathered people lying side by side in their *birthday* suits; it reminded her of the Holocaust.

They had lunch in the cafe next to the beach, and afterwards they relaxed again under the sun. Nealy's skin felt slightly burned, and she could already see freckles popping out all over her pale body. An hour later, Charlotte nudged her, and she woke up. Michael sat down beside her. "Hi," she said. "I didn't expect you back so soon."

"I asked you to wait for me in your cabin. You will only burn your beautiful porcelain skin out here in this sun, Nealy."

"Oh, Michael, I always burn, but it goes away just as fast," she smiled. "And besides, this has been a real experience for me."

"What do you mean?"

"People are either naked or almost naked," she grimaced.

"Nealy, in our country the naked body is a work of art, a beautiful creation. It's nothing to be ashamed of. That's why we don't wish to hide it," he said seriously.

"Maybe so. But where I'm from you'll get thrown in jail. It's called 'Indecent Exposure.'" Eavesdropping, Charlotte and Fern burst out laughing, and then Nealy giggled out loud.

But Michael glared at her with a look of disapproval on his face, and then he glanced at the others. "Nealy, darling, you are getting too much sun out here. Come on. Gather up your things. We'll go for a boat ride."

"I'm fine, Michael. Stop worrying about me."

"Darling, I will always worry about you. Please don't take that pleasure away from me," he said, handing her a t-shirt to put on. He helped her gather up her things and carried them out to his private, sleekly designed power boat that he had left tied to the end of the dock; the same place that the tender had dropped them.

Nealy looked at her friends, shrugged her shoulders, and made a funny face as she walked away. They were starting to dislike this smooth talking, dominating, possessive, casanova-type Frenchman, and it worried them that he had taken such control over her. In less than a week, he acted as if he owned her already.

He started the loud engines on his boat and took them for a spin along the Riviera for an hour, insisting quite often that Nealy cover her fair skin to protect it from the wind and sun. As they pulled up next to the ship, the crew met them and pulled them aboard. On the way to her cabin, Michael looked at her rather puzzling. "Nealy, where is your bracelet?"

"I left it in my cabin. I didn't want to get sand in it," she replied innocently.

"I gave it to you to wear. You can't hurt it. Nealy, it's good jewels and eighteen-carat gold."

"I know, but I didn't want to take a chance. I don't normally wear my good jewelry on the beach, Michael."

"Don't you treasure it?"

"Oh, yes, I love it. It's the most beautiful bracelet that I've ever seen," she cried, afraid that she had hurt his feelings by not wearing it. Nealy took his hand and kissed the back of it. "I'll wear it to dinner. I promise."

He unlocked the door for her, and this time he walked in behind her and closed the door. Then he backed her up against the wall and kissed her deep, long and hard. "Nealy, I missed you today. I don't want you out of my sight again."

"If this is how you act when you miss me, maybe you should stay away more often," she said, kissing him again.

"I want to have dinner in my cabin. I will come for you at seven," he whispered, pulling her arms from around his neck and moving backwards towards the door. As he left, he blew her a kiss.

"My god," she said, touching her burning lips. "Now I know where they got the term *hot-blooded*." But it wasn't just his kiss that made her lips hot, she discovered a major sunburn over most of her body. After she showered, she covered herself in lotion, but she couldn't reach her back. And because of that, she actually thought about Kendall for the first time. At the beach he would put the sunscreen on her back, and then later that night, after she had cooked herself, he would rub on the Solarcain. Nealy felt bad about not missing him, but she couldn't help it; she just didn't. Even at home when she wasn't traveling, they both went their separate ways most of the time anyway. They didn't do the same things, and both of them stayed so busy with their careers. When they first met, they spent a lot of time together, but over time it dwindled to once a week. They would go out for dinner and then spend the night together to satisfy their physical needs, which sounded cold, but that was usually the extent of it. That seemed to make Kendall happy, and for the time being, it worked for her, too. Now, after being away for five days and not missing him at all, she knew that she couldn't marry him regardless of how good a husband and father he would make. The simple truth was that she didn't love him in the right way, and she had to tell him as soon as she got home. It had nothing to do with Michael, except when he kissed her she knew that Kendall didn't spark the same kind of emotions in her. Nealy had promised herself that she wouldn't marry again unless she found someone who could make her feel as alive, both physically and emotionally, as Phillip had made her feel. He had unleashed a passion in her that she couldn't explain; it made her crazy with desire, and not just the sexual kind.

That evening in Michael's cabin, the waiters brought in their dinner, a fish dish, but Nealy didn't understand what the waiter called it. Anyway, she ate it and said she liked it, even though she really didn't. But the more wine she drank, the better it tasted. During her brief association with Michael, she had learned how much the French enjoyed wine and lingering, two-hour dinners. Personally, she had been drinking too much wine, and now she remained in a state of dizziness. Her face felt flush which she attributed to the wine and the terrible sunburn. Michael smiled at her and poured her another glass of wine.

"I don't think I can drink anymore wine, Michael. I'm feeling hot," she said, trying to focus on him. He smiled at her. "Maybe I should clarify that. It's not sexy hot, it's sort of *sick hot.*"

"Are you not feeling well?" he asked, seemingly concerned.

"No, I'm really not. I think I got too much sun today."

"I warned you about this sun on your fair skin. It doesn't take long to burn on our beaches. Come," he said, getting up and taking her hand. "Come. Rest for a few minutes." He walked her into the bedroom, directing her toward the bed.

"I'm sorry. I should have listened to you."

"You will next time. I'll make sure of it because from now on you will always be with me. Now close your eyes, my darling. I'll go get you something for your sunburn. It will make you feel much better." He touched her face adoringly, and then left the cabin.

CHAPTER FORTY-FOUR

NEALY WOKE UP the next morning still in Michael's bed, and she felt very groggy, almost too groggy to care where she had spent the night. The longer she lay there, the more awake she became and the more uncomfortable she felt. Once she got awake enough, she pulled the covers back to get up, only to discover that she didn't have on one stitch of clothing. "Where the hell are my clothes?" she cried, grabbing the sheet to cover herself. "And just *who* took them off me?"

The door opened and Michael spoke to her cheerfully as he walked towards the bed. "Bonjour."

"Don't say good-morning until you tell me what I did last night that I don't remember doing."

"Darling, you didn't do anything," he smiled, sitting down on the bed beside her. "Don't you remember? You weren't feeling well because of your sunburn. So, I got some ointment from the ship's physician to put on your burned skin."

"Yes, but how did I get out of my clothes?" Nealy's face turned pale.

"It was *I* who took them off. I had to put ointment on your sunburn. It would have ruined your clothes so I left them off."

"Wait a minute. Let me get this straight. First, you took my clothes off and then you rubbed some kind of ointment all over my body?" Nealy said, pulling the covers up to her neck.

"Yes, I did that. Don't you feel much better today?"

"I'm not sure how I feel yet. While I had my clothes off, did we do anything else?" she asked, holding her breath.

Michael laughed and looked at her very curiously. "If you are asking me if we made love, the answer is no."

"But you took my clothes off?"

"Oh, Nealy, you are so American," he said, smiling at her.

"Well, what would you think if a woman took your clothes off in the middle of the night? Wouldn't you wonder whether of not you made love to her?"

He shook his head, "Nealy, darling, we didn't make love. I already told you that. You had a sunburn, which made you sick. I wouldn't undress a woman who had passed out on my bed from a very bad sunburn and make love to her. It would be like making love to a dead person. Regardless of what you think of me, I do not make love to live men or dead women."

Nealy giggled at his honest attempt to convince her that nothing happened. "But you undressed me."

"Nealy, I'm thirty-seven years old, and I *have* undressed a few women over the years. Granted, I made love to most of them, but not all of them. And in this case, I did not."

"You just *simply* undressed me? That's it?"

"Yes, darling, that's it," he smiled.

"But, Michael, you saw me naked," she said, embarrassed by the mere thought of him taking her panties and bra off and rubbing stuff all over her body while she lay unconscious.

"Nealy, I have also seen many naked women. This is not such a big deal to me, I assure you." She held the sheet so tightly up to her neck, that he had to pry her hands away to kiss them.

"Oh, God, I'm too embarrassed," she said, closing her eyes.

"Nealy, I don't want you to be embarrassed. I saw you with only your bathing suit on yesterday, right?"

"Yes, but—"

"Nealy, you are acting so silly," he smiled. "There is not much left uncovered in a modest—much like you—bathing suit. Do you agree, yes?"

"No there isn't much more to see. But certain parts are still covered," she argued.

"Nealy, I grew up on these waters and these beaches. Most European women wear no swimsuit at all on the beach or out boating. Therefore, I don't think of—oh, how do I say this—I don't think of sex every time I see a naked woman. Making love is an emotional thing, not just a physical thing. Making love starts in the mind, and you had no mind. You were passed out. I'll admit, I did like touching your soft skin, but it did not turn me on because you could not respond to my touches—"

"Oh, God, I knew it. You did touch me," she cried, pulling the covers over her head.

Michael laughed at her American madness, which he called it, over something so natural to him. He just couldn't believe how totally inhibited she was at her age. "Oh, Nealy, you are so...so *American*, my darling. Maybe that is why you intrigue me so. That and, of course, your beautiful breasts," he teased, making matters even worse.

"Stop it." She screamed from under the covers which made him laugh even louder.

"Now come on, Nealy, get up and take a shower. I'll get you a robe to wear back up to your cabin so you can dress."

"Are you crazy?" she cried. "I'm not going to walk back to my cabin in your bathrobe."

"Nealy, I think you are overreacting."

"Michael, if I can't buy this story, do you think for one minute that I could sell it to any of my friends. I might as well spend the day *doing it* with you because I'm going to be accused of it anyway."

"Well, we can, if you prefer," he said, smiling.

"No," she snapped. "I'll just put my clothes back on and shower in my own cabin, thank you."

He leaned across her, staring boldly into her eyes as he bent down and kissed her sensuously. "After we make love, Nealy, you will not have any more anxiety of this nature, I promise. I will make sure that you become comfortable with your body."

"Michael, I'm comfortable with it. I'm just not comfortable with you with '*eet*,' " she said, mimicking his French accent.

"You will be, I promise." He got up and walked over to the door. "I'll pick you up at noon."

Nealy rolled over and smothered her face in the pillow so she could scream without anyone hearing her. She couldn't believe this had happened. Of course, it was no big deal to him at all. "Lots of women," he said. How smug. Well, he had seen it all—that's for sure—so there wasn't anything left to his imagination now. But she had to admit, her sunburn didn't hurt at all anymore. It looked sunburned, but it didn't feel it. What was this stuff he slowly and meticulously rubbed all over her body? The thought of his doing that made her cringe with embarrassment; she wanted to crawl under the bed and stay there for life. Now if this had happened with Jerrod, he would have gotten turned on and spent the night *doing it* over and over again to this mound of motionless flesh. It wouldn't have mattered to him and she knew that to be a fact because it happened once when they were in college.

It was their freshman year and at a party one night he very persuasively talked her into drinking a shot of tequila with him, followed by a shot of schnapps, and then another tequila, and so on, until she passed out. The next day, she found herself in a hotel room with a dreadful hangover and as naked as the day she was born. She felt as though she had been hit by a truck because every conceivable part of her body ached so much that she could hardly move. Clearly, she knew that Jerrod had taken advantage of her even though he swore that she had been awake and had enjoyed it just as much as he had. She got angry and went back to school, refusing to speak to him for more than two weeks. He too argued that she had made too big a deal out of the whole thing. However, that ended her experimenting with tequila and schnapps or shots, and she has not passed out since, at least until now. And, like the last time, she ended up in her *birthday suit*. So why should she believe Michael either, except for the fact that the only thing bruised this time was her pride?

That afternoon Michael escorted Nealy off the ship to take her to lunch.

Instead of the limousine taking them this time, Michael wanted to drive her around and show her the sights himself.

When they approached his car, Nealy looked at it and then looked at him rather confused. "Michael, is this your car? It's just a plain silver Ferrari sedan," she teased. "I expected a wealthy entrepreneur to be driving a bright red convertible."

"Nealy, this isn't just a Ferrari," he rebutted sharply. "This is a 365 GT 2+2 with a V-12 engine. On the open road this car will exceed a hundred and fifty miles an hour."

"Michael, I was kidding," she said, giggling. "This car is *really fine*...but, if you plan on going a hundred and fifty miles an hour with me in there, we need to talk."

Michael kissed her on the lips, which totally changed her attitude, and then he lowered her into the car. "Nealy, I'd never put your life in jeopardy. It's much too precious to me." He kissed her again lightly on the lips, and she blushed.

They drove through the hills of Massif des Maures and ate lunch in a charming village where he bought Nealy a box of marrons glaces, delicious sugary chestnut candies. Further up into the hills, he drove past beautiful waterfalls and through forests of carefully cultivated cork-oak and chestnut trees. Every so often, Nealy got a glimpse of the sea far below and oohed and aahed like an awestruck tourist.

Later in the day, he stopped at a designer boutique and insisted on buying her a couple of evening dresses to wear out to the casinos when they arrived in Cannes. Of course, the owner knew him well and brought out several dresses which she thought would be perfect for Nealy and very much in Michael's taste. Nealy had very little to say about trying the dresses on. When she modeled them for Michael, he made it clear which ones he wanted her to have.

"Oh, yes, darling, that is perfect for you. Oui, Marie," he said to the owner, nodding, which meant that he would take the dress.

"Michael," Nealy said softly, "this is a gorgeous dress, but I feel uncomfortable. It's rather low-cut, don't you think?"

"Darling, there you go again being *very American*."

"That's 'cause I *am* very American, *darling*," she said in a bittersweet tone, smiling at him.

Michael got up and walked over to her, and Marie left the room for a moment. "Nealy, I love this dress on you. It makes you even more beautiful. I want you to wear it out with me. Please, darling, do not argue."

"But, Michael, my breasts are barely covered. I'll feel so self-conscious."

"Darling, you have beautiful breasts. I think you should be proud of them and not so embarrassed by them. They are a gift," he smiled and softly kissed the exposed flesh of her breasts.

Nealy felt a little faint, but her mouth opened and the words came out. "Okay, if you like it that much."

"I do. I want you to have it." Nealy ended up with two of the most gorgeous dresses she had ever seen: a gold beaded dress that stopped just slightly—and when we say slightly, we are talking just *slightly* above her nipples—and a green sequined dress that had a slit cut up the side to the top of her thigh. Getting Nealy to wear these dresses out in public would be a real test for Michael's persuasive powers over her, and the fact that he had paid a small fortune for them made her even more uncomfortable.

That evening after dinner, Michael and Nealy walked the promenade under the moon and then retired to his cabin. Still very red from her sunburn, he insisted that she change into his robe and allow him to anoint her burns with the lotion to prevent her from peeling. Of course, she argued, but, of course, he won. She lay perfectly still as he rubbed the greasy lotion from head to toe, very much as he had the evening before most likely. He laughed and teased her when she insisted on doing her own front, but in the end he did that area, too, as she tightly squeezed her eyes shut and covered her breasts below the red lines with her hands.

Afterwards he held her and kissed her softly which stirred lots of feelings, but she wouldn't allow it to go beyond heavy petting. He took it well and seemed to enjoy just kissing and caressing her body even though this time, she had definitely aroused him.

The following day he took her to Frejus, a Roman city with a Fifth-Century baptistery and cloisters dating to the Twelfth Century. Michael knew all about his country and its history and its archaeology. She was very impressed by his knowledge and the love that he expressed as he talked about his ancestry. He followed the promontories and the long, deep indentions of the coast that linked beach resorts and isolated panoramic points until he arrived at pic du Cap Roux, a high peak with a circular view of the sea. Nealy gasped as she stared out at the deep blue water that sparkled like crystal beneath the radiant rays of the sun. "Oh, Michael, this is magnificent! It's just breathtaking," she exclaimed, stepping out of the car to get a better view.

"You like?" he asked, smiling at her.

"Oh, Michael, your country is so incredibly beautiful," she cried, captivated by a vision of grandeur. Nealy turned and hugged him tightly. In awe of everything, she got so excited that she kissed him with such force that he kissed her back equally as excited.

He whispered, gazing strongly into her eyes, "I want you to love it so much that you will not want to leave." Then he kissed her deeply again and again until Nealy insisted that they go.

CHAPTER FORTY-FIVE

SHORTLY AFTER DAYBREAK, the *Southern Queen* anchored off shore in Cannes. The water splashing against the ship awakened Nealy out of a deep sleep. Still groggy, she raised up to look out of her cabin window at the most magnificent view of the Croisette, a row of hotels, both modern and nostalgic, lined up along the Riviera waterfront. Nealy had drifted into dreamland where she lived with Michael in one of those gorgeous, romantic hotels when a knock at the door, startling her back to reality. Still in her nighty, she walked over to the door.

"Yes?" she asked.

"Your breakfast, madame," a female voice said.

"My breakfast?" she asked, confused. Nealy grabbed her robe and opened the door.

"Yes, madame," the young woman said, walking across the room and placing the tray on the table. "Enjoy your breakfast."

"Merci," Nealy smiled, proud that her French had improved; she actually knew two words right off the top of her head, a thought that made her giggle. She took the card off the tray and read it:

Nealy, my darling,
  I want to spend the rest of my life having your breakfast served to you in bed. Remain in your cabin and I will come for you at ten o'clock. Dress comfortably.
  Oh, how I adore you.

  Love, Michael.

Nealy smiled and held the card up to her lips. "God, he's so wonderful," she whispered. The past ten days had been too good to be true. Here she was in a land where fairytale lives really do exist, and she had found the perfect prince who made her life *Princess Perfect*. He lived to show her the good life, to watch over her, to take care of her, and to buy her all that money can buy. Was this a happy destiny? Or doom?

That afternoon the limousine drove them up to a small village called St-Paul-de-Vence, which had been built in the Sixteenth Century by Francois I. The village had spade-shaped walls that surrounded it as it rose high into the sky. These walls were built very steep so that they protected the residents from the enemy during times of unrest. There were terraces covered with vineyards and bright reddish-purple bougainvillea bushes that emitted a sweetness into the air that even roses couldn't fragrantly match.

As they strolled up and down the cobblestone streets that were only four to five feet wide, they stopped to look at some of the paintings by local artists as well as some of France's more renowned artists. They had lunch at *The White Dove* that had become famous for displaying the works of artists who showed signs of greatness. Michael always insisted on ordering for Nealy because he wanted her to try the more aristocratic dishes prepared by his favorite chefs. A marvelous garden aroma of herbs, fresh spices, olive oil and garlic filtered from the kitchen into the dining room. This time he ordered Chicken Roti(spit-roasted);a disturbing choice. Did someone actually spit on it before roasting the poor little bird? Yuck! Also, he ordered rataouille which had tomatoes, onion, aubergine(yucky, mushy, gagging eggplant), courgette(oh, that must be zucchini because she found some green peeling) or was it green peppers? Well, she ate it somewhat reluctantly, but Michael kept encouraging her. "Darling, it's just a different taste to you. The more you taste it, the better you will like it," he coaxed, assuring her that a fabulous dessert would follow.

As promised, he had them bring her a piece of tarte tropezienne which was simply yellow cake filled with custard and dusted with powdered sugar.

"Michael, this is by far the best part of the meal, but if I keep this up I'm going to get very fat," she giggled.

He took the fork out of her hand and squeezed her fingers together. "Nealy, you must never get fat. I could not accept it," he said seriously.

"Michael, you need to lighten up. I'm teasing you. I'm much too health conscious and much too vain to ever get fat."

"Will you promise me?"

"Yes, of course I'll promise you. I cross my heart and hope to die," she said, smiling and using her finger to make an *x* across her chest.

"I love you just the way you are with your perfect breasts and your perfect derriere." He smiled, gently touching her respective body parts as he leaned close to her face and spoke softly.

"Michael, please." Nealy took his hand and held it. "You people are a lot more comfortable with touching than Americans."

"But that is good. Touching brings pleasure," he said, rubbing his finger slowly back and forth over the nipple of her left breast. "See there, you like my touch. And in your face I can see that you feel it between your legs, too." He smiled alluringly.

"Michael, don't do that!" she ordered softly.

"Nealy, I must teach you to touch more. It's very healthy."

"We'll see," she smiled.

They walked out of the restaurant and across the way where some men were gathered under large trees that enclosed a cleared area. They were throwing a large silver ball across the dirt.

"What are they doing?" she asked.

"That's the Place de Gaulle. They are playing a game of bowls; it's very popular in this village."

A man dressed in a white short sleeved shirt and white slacks threw the ball and yelled something in French. Nealy thought for a second and then remarked out loud, "That man sounds like Yves Montand. And he looks like him, too."

Nealy had barely gotten the words out of her mouth when the man turned around and caught them staring at him. After a moment, he cried out, "Coupair, bonjour."

"Bonjour, Montand, my friend," Michael replied, waving. The man stood there staring at Nealy much the same as Michael had when he first saw her in the elevator in New York.

"That's really Yves Montand? I can't believe it. He made that movie *On A Clear Day You Can See Forever* a few years ago with Barbara Streisand."

"Yes, I saw that film in Cannes at the film festival in nineteen-seventy, I believe."

"I love that man," she gasped.

Michael looked at her disapprovingly. "Well, there he is. Go to him."

"Michael, I don't mean I *love him* like that. I just mean I love him in the movies. I love his acting and his singing and his very French accent. I don't love him as I love you," she said, shocked to hear those words come out of her mouth. So how did she feel? Infatuated for sure. But, *in love*, probably *not*. She had come to love his generosity and the way he cared for her and treated her so special, like a queen, but she didn't love him as in true love, not yet. At least she didn't think so.

"Nealy, I only want you to love *me*. I get jealous when you look at other men."

"Michael, that's silly. Anyway, I'm surprised. You, of all people should not be so insecure. And, besides, I'm here with you. I don't want to be with anyone else." Her assumption about his jealous nature had proved to be true.

He led her in between two brick buildings and smothered her with kisses until she had to come up for air. "I want you to make love with me tonight, Nealy."

Dizzy and feeling very vulnerable, she whispered, "Maybe we can. I'm just not sure yet."

As he gazed into her eyes, he could see her own desire to make love with him growing stronger. He knew that the longer he waited, the more exciting it would be for both of them because she would be less inhibited with her own sexuality and her body and touching. "I want you, but I'll be patient, my darling."

That evening he came by her cabin to escort her into Cannes' Palm Beach Casino. The ship had planned for everyone on board to go for a night of entertainment and gambling. When he knocked, Nealy opened the door. She smiled at him as he stood in front of her in a black tuxedo. What a beautiful man, she thought; he looked more like a movie star than a ship builder. "Hi. Come in. I'm almost ready."

"Where is the gold dress?" he asked sharply.

"Michael, I put it on...but I took it off again. I just can't go out in that dress. Not when everyone on this ship is going to be there."

"Nealy, you look gorgeous in that dress. If they stare, they will only be jealous. Nealy, I want to walk into that casino with you on my arm in that dress. Now, please, change. And wear the corset that I bought you to hold up your stockings. I will go crazy when I see you in that," he said, smiling lustfully at her.

"But Michael—"

"Put on the dress," he said, kissing her. "I'll be back in five minutes. Oh, and pack an overnight bag."

"For what?"

"We are not coming back to the ship tonight. I want to take you up to my chalet above Cannes." He patted her on the bottom and left.

Nealy dressed, but she felt terribly self-conscious, so she opened the bar and pulled out a small bottle of wine. After pouring herself a glass—guzzling it down without taking a breath—she poured herself two more. Normally, Nealy would never deliberately get herself tipsy, but she needed some liquid courage to get her through the evening in a dress cut down to her belly button and up to her ying-yang.

When Michael returned, he studied her carefully. "I've never seen anyone so beautiful, Nealy."

"I feel like a real exhibitionist," she whined.

"Darling, that is not bad. Why do want to hide such a magnificent body? Your modesty is causing you such anxiety. I'll never understand American women," he held her face and very lovingly touched her cheek and lips with his middle finger before attempting to kiss away her fears.

Afterwards, she had to touch up her make-up, but his tender kisses and the wine had made her feel less uncomfortable. "I'm as ready as I'll ever be."

"You look fan-tas-tic, *ma chérie.*"

"I'm *your darling* alright because no one else could talk me into wearing this dress out in public," she smiled, trying to make the best of her situation to please him. "Oh, and thanks for the *'fan-tas-tic!'*" she giggled, covering her shoulders with the gold-colored wrap that matched the dress.

"You can put that on outside. For now, I want to admire your beauty," he said, removing the wrap and placing it across her arm.

As they walked through the main lobby of the ship, flies could have made a permanent home in the mouth of everyone who passed them. Nealy returned their stares and smiled. But when she saw Fern, Charlotte, and the others, she wanted to crawl in a hole and not come out. Uncomfortable, she held the wrap up in front of her and spoke to them, smiling as she always did.

At the Casino, everyone proceeded back to the veranda to watch the cabaret show of singers and dancers. It was a perfectly clear night with just a hint of coolness in the air, which left Nealy with goosebumps covering most of her exposed flesh. When the live entertainment ceased, Michael held her close and danced with her, which helped to warm her.

"Come. Let's go inside. I want to play a few hands of baccarat. You can watch," he said, leading her off the dance floor.

Michael took his place at the table and told Nealy to stand behind him for good-luck. He had to be aware of all the men that were staring at her, but he made sure that everyone knew *with whom* she had arrived.

After a half hour of standing behind him like a mannequin, she bent down and whispered, putting her hand over her chest to prevent her breasts from falling out of her dress, "Michael, I'm going back out to the veranda to watch the show. I want to sit down because my feet are killing me." She left quickly before he had a chance to argue.

As she sat under the stars on the bank of the Riviera, she lulled over the moonstruck water with the stars glistening above. The air was fresh smelling, but cold. Nothing could be more perfect for her, except maybe, more clothing. She placed her wrap around her shoulders as she listened to the singer stretch his vocal chords to reach the higher octaves of his seductively written love songs.

"Hi, would you like to dance?" A man asked kindly.

Nealy looked up at him. "You're American!"

"Yes. And you *looked* American. So far everyone I've asked to dance rejected me for lack of understanding—or, at least that's how I preferred to interpret their decline," he said, smiling at her. "So, would care to dance with another fellow American?"

"I'd love to," she smiled at his attempt to humor her. Unfortunately, she had to leave her wrap on the chair because it would only fall off as she danced. While dancing for almost thirty minutes, they talked about their home towns and their reasons for being in France.

Abruptly, they were interrupted. "Excuse me, but the lady's with me," Michael said, grabbing Nealy by the arm.

"Sure, no problem. Thanks, Nealy. It's been nice talking to you."

"You, too, Tom."

"Lets go," Michael said, pulling her by the arm towards the door.

"Michael, I need to get my purse and my wrap." Nealy pulled away from him and ran back to collect her things from the chair.

When she returned, Michael stared at her angrily. "Who was that man?"

"Just a nice American guy that asked me to dance, Michael."

"I thought your feet hurt," he sneered.

"They did," she said, "but when I'm around music I get happy feet." Nealy giggled softly.

"I never want to see you in the arms of another man, Nealy."

"Michael, I was only dancing. Are you jealous?"

"Yes. I don't like that. And I'm not amused. So, please, do not laugh."

"Michael, there is nothing to be angry about. Please, don't be mad."

In the car he was very quiet and Nealy tried to humor him, but they were nearly to his house in the hills before he spoke to her again. They drove into a densely-wooded hide-a-way that seemed to hang vertically upon the mountainside. It had a wall that ensured privacy with an enormous gate at the entrance.

Inside Nealy couldn't believe what she saw. It had large rooms with ornately carved wood on the massive stairwell. "Michael, this is beautiful." Nealy took in as much as she could as he held her arm and escorted her up to the bedroom to put her things away. He shut the door to the bedroom. Then forcefully, he led her over to the bed and pushed her down. "I thought you loved me," he said, obviously still miffed.

"I do. What's wrong with you?"

"When a man loves a woman, she belongs only to him. I can not and I will not have you with other men. Do you understand me?" he shouted.

"Michael, I told you. I was just dancing with that guy. It didn't mean anything," she explained.

"I do not care what you were doing. To be seen with another man is the same thing as fucking with him," he shouted very close to her face.

Nealy got up and walked angrily past him towards the door. "This is ridiculous. I refuse to let this go any further. Good-bye, Michael," she yelled.

He ran after her. Then he grabbed her arm and turned her around towards him. He hugged her close to him. "No, Nealy, please don't leave me. I'm sorry."

"Let me go!" she shouted.

"No," he cried, holding her tightly. "Please, darling, I'm sorry. I just got so angry when I saw you with that man."

"Michael, you have to trust me, or this can't work."

He held her face and kissed her. "I do, but you are just so beautiful that it frightens me. I know any man would want you."

"Well, in this dress probably," she giggled. "I look like a high-classed hooker. Any guy on the *make* would want me."

"You are even more beautiful in this dress," he said, kissing her almost-bare chest, which sent chills up her spine. Slowly, he stepped her backwards toward the bed, pushed her down easily, and then lowered his body down on top of hers. As he studied her face with his luscious eyes and kissed her madly, her anger dissipated. Unable to resist him, she responded to his desires by returning his hot kisses. Michael took the pins out of her hair and ran his hands through it, massaging her scalp gently. Then he brought her to her feet and unzipped the back of her dress, allowing it to fall to the floor. "My God, darling, that corset is so sexy on you. Model it for me. Go ahead, turn around. Let me look at you.

"Michael, I feel silly."

"Then, my darling, take it off."

"I can't," she whined, her heart beating rapidly, as if she been frightened by a monster.

"Why are you so shy with your body? I've seen it all. So, I beg you. Take off the stockings...slowly."

"Okay, I will, if you'll turn off the lights."

"No. But I will dim them. I want to see you."

"But, Michael, I can't do this with the lights on," she whined.

He stood up, pulled her into his arms and kissed her. When he let go of her, he sat back down on the bed and tilted his head to stare at her. "Now darling, please, take off the stockings...slowly...one at a time." He watched as she unhooked the first garter and nervously rolled the stocking down her long, shapely leg.

"Good, darling. Now, the other one," he motioned.

"Nealy, look at me. I adore you. You don't need to be ashamed or nervous. Come closer," he whispered, taking her hands and pulling her towards him. He kissed her stomach. When he unhooked the corset, she held it in place. "Please, my darling...let it drop—"

"I can't," she cried softly.

Noticing the fear in her face, he pulled her into his lap and pressed his face against her bare bosoms which spilled over the sweetheart neckline of the corset.

"I'm sorry, Michael, I'm not real good at this sort of thing. It's silly, I know, especially since I've been married and had...well...enough said on that subject," She shrugged.

"With many lovers, you are still so shy that you can't undress in front of me?"

Nealy raised up. "Many lovers? Three men in twenty-seven years does not classify me as a reckless floozy," she said offensively.

He laughed. "Darling, three men are not so many, but surely one of them taught you about your body, no?"

"We didn't play school—although when I was about twelve, Rayford Morris and I played doctor once, but it was just the basic stuff like checking the heart with the stethoscope and giving shots, not touching and junk—but back to your question, no, nobody talked about, well, you know," she gestured, rolling her eyes and her hands nervously to avoid getting personal.

Sounding more serious, he said, "Nealy, you are so uncomfortable with your body, even talking about this is difficult. I am disturbed by this. When you were a child, didn't your mother talk to you and teach you about your body, about men?"

"My mother? Are you kidding. Sex was *never* discussed in the James household."

"Why not? It's so natural."

"Then why doesn't it come *naturally?*" she asked sweetly, but bordering on sarcasm.

"Nealy, my darling, it must be taught."

"Please don't tell me your *mama* taught you," she said frowning.

Michael laughed loudly. "No, of course not. My papa did."

"Oh my God. Like show and tell?" she exclaimed.

"Nealy you are so amusing. We had a father-and-son talk about women and men and how they fall in love. Then I would listen outside their bedroom door."

"You eaves-dropped on your parents?" she asked.

He obviously didn't know that word. "I did not join them, Nealy, I just wanted to learn from them."

"Not join them, Michael. Listened to them," she corrected.

"They were very much in love, so who better to learn from. Also, I learned from my father and his friends. While they fished, I pretended to sleep. They would talk about their women. They were very explicit about making women feel good with touching and kissing—"

"You were a promiscuous little fellow—but, wait a minute," she interrupted herself, "your father was married. He had women?"

"Many women, I'm sure. Nealy, my father also taught me that women sometimes do not need as much as men. When my mother said no, out of respect, he would go to other women. That was another lesson from my father: *No* meant *no*. So, until I reached the age to know more about the women who did not need a commitment, he told me to masturbate—"

"Your father told you to *master*—well...that word?" she said, her eyes as wide open as a walnut.

"Nealy, my darling, masturbation is also natural. It teaches you about your sexuality, the human anatomy. The body is an art form, and a science to explore and understand. You are making too much of this. You need to relax."

"That's what my ex-husband said, but he wanted me to undress and make love in public. I don't care *how damn natural* it is, I just couldn't do it," she said, her face full of doubt and apprehension.

"I would never want you to do that. Only with me. And in private. Then it is beautiful. I've noticed that you only relax when you are aroused. This is no good, my darling. Come." Michael took her hand and led her into his massive bathroom where there was a huge bathtub. He sat her down on the stairs that led up into the tub while he filled it with very warm water and a few bubbles. While he took off his clothes, Nealy kept her eyes on the bubbles that were forming over the surface of the water. He stepped in the tub and pulled her up. "Come. Join me." He took her hand and she stepped into the tub, staring away from him and holding her top in place, which she didn't drop until she turned around. Michael slipped her underwear over her hips and then sat down, pulling her down into his lap.

"I'm sorry, Michael," she trembled.

"It's alright. I want to help you get over your fears. Will you let me, please?" he begged, holding her snugly in the warm bath, feeling her body as she relaxed against him.

"Yes," she answered weakly.

He eased her away from him and tilted her head back into the warm water. "Have you ever let a man wash your hair?"

"No."

"Then I want you to lie back and close your eyes. This will feel wonderful to you." He gently massaged her head, turning the shampoo into a rich lather and then washing it out. He pulled her back into his lap and wrapped his arms snugly around her waist. "You like?"

"Yes, but I still feel a little uncomfortable. But I'm getting used to whatever this is that we're doing here."

Michael whispered to her softly. "Do you trust me, Nealy?"

"Yes, of course I do."

"Then I want you to do just what I ask, alright?"

"Like what?"

"No questions, ma chérie," he whispered. "This will help you, but you must listen to me. Promise me."

"Alright, I promise," she whispered reluctantly.

Michael took her hands and placed them on her breasts. When she started to raise up, he quietly whispered in her ear. "You promised. Just do as I ask. Now, close your eyes and just relax." As he continued to talk softly, allowing his warm breath to blow into her ear, he kneaded her breasts with his hands covering hers. "These beautiful breasts belong to you, Nealy, and they will respond to your touch. He removed his hands. "Now you must massage them until you feel comfortable. Circle your nipples. *That's ma chérie.* Now, gently brush your fingers over your nipples. See how they respond to you. Now open your eyes and look at them. There is nothing to be afraid of. Don't stop. Do you feel it here?" he said, running his hand down between her legs.

"Uh-huh," she said softly.

"Don't stop. Roll your nipples between your fingers. Is that good?"

"Yes," she sighed, starting to enjoy her own touch.

Gradually, he eased her legs over his, parting her thighs. Then he put his hands over hers and guided them between her legs. When she stiffened, holding her breath, he spoke softly again. "I know you liked touching your breasts, and you will enjoy this even more if you just relax." He forced her to massage and explore and caress herself as he kissed her face and her neck. Finally, he removed his hands and held her thighs firmly apart. "See how good that feels. It's okay. It's your body and you have every right to touch it and feel good when it responds to you."

"Michael," she whined.

"No, my darling, my turn will come. I want you to open your eyes and watch as your fingers explore your body. Open," he encouraged, gently pushing the bubbles aside. "It so natural to touch yourself if it feels good. And it feels good, doesn't it, Nealy?"

"Yes," she said, her breathing becoming shallow.

"Now, just do what feels natural," he whispered softly."

"Oh, Michael—"

"I know, my darling," he said, putting his tongue inside her ear. "Now, I want you to remove your fingers and slowly bring your fingers across your stomach up to your breasts. Massage them, darling, give them the tenderness that they deserve. Do you feel them swell under your touch?"

"Uh-huh," she said breathlessly, biting her bottom lip.

"Good. Very good, darling. Don't close your eyes. Now slowly move your hands down between your legs and let your body respond to your touch as you watch."

"Michael...Michael," she whimpered.

"Nealy, darling, it's alright," he said softly, kissing the side of her face. "Relax, my love, and do what your body wants—explore, touch, feel, move." He could feel her body shaking. "Now, let it go," he whispered, still holding her thighs firmly as she wiggled to free them. "Don't close your eyes, Nealy. Look at your body as it responds."

"Touch me, Michael—"

"No, darling, not this time. You must satisfy yourself with your own touch. That's it. Now *come...come hard*, Nealy."

When she cried out, her chest heaved as she gasped for air, and then he held her tightly and pressed his erect penis against the small of her back until he came, whispering, "Yes, yes, yes, my darling."

Nealy let her body relax back against him, placing her head against his shoulder. "Oh my," she sighed, as her chest rose and slowly lowered back into the water.

"Oh, my darling, that was wonderful. How do you feel?" he asked, kissing her bare shoulder.

"Shaky, but good, I think," she uttered quietly, still breathing hard.

"Nealy, you must feel more than good."

"Relaxed. Peaceful. Happy. Hell, I don't know," she said out of breath.

"Well, that's a start," he said, kissing the side of her face. "But we are not through yet. We have a much more training left to do. I want you to feel wonderful and free."

Michael got out and helped her out of the tub. First, he slowly dried her off, and then he had her dry him off with explicit instructions for certain areas. He took her to bed and made her watch as he took her step by step through foreplay that led to a hard climax. When his turn came and he asked Nealy to arouse him provocatively, she began to cry because it made her feel afraid and ashamed. She had never had to arouse or stroke or fondle a man's body while they both watched. Michael held her and talked to her about the importance of feeling free of guilt about her sexuality, and when she reached for cover, he refused to let her hide her body. Finally, he talked her into arousing him by showing and telling her where and how to touch him; a way that would make any man burn with desire. But when he wanted to make love to her in the true sense of the word, she refused.

"No, I can't go *all the way* with you until I know something about you. I've told you all about my life, but I know nothing about yours, except the little bit about your childhood on the sea," she complained.

"What do you want to know?" he ask, raising up on his elbow.

"Well, I know that you have three children, but I have no idea what their names are or where they live or what they do. I don't know about your marriage to their mother and what went wrong and why you haven't remarried. I refuse to get anymore involved with you until I know these things."

"What does all that matter, Nealy? My life only began when I met you."

"Bullshit, Michael," she said. "I want to know. I don't want another failed relationship. I don't want to be hurt again," she said, tears forming in her eyes.

"Come," he said, pulling her close to him to snuggle her. "We will fly to Paris when we get back to Monte Carlo day after tomorrow. I will introduce you to my son, Aury, and my twin daughters, Michelle and Breille. Will that make you happy?"

"Yes," she said, relaxing her head on his shoulder. "Michael, thank you."

"For what?"

"For being so patient with me. For the first time in my life, I actually feel comfortable with myself and my sexuality. Before, I always needed to be seduced into a state of extreme passion or drink several glasses of wine. I don't want to feel so tense and ashamed. I want to give back love when I'm given it."

"I will teach you how to take love and to make love. And, after I'm done, you will be a *great lover*."

"Whew, I'd be careful if I were you, Michael. With you as my teacher, I might become this erotic fantasy. I could become too much for you to handle," she giggled. But, of course, she knew that this man had tried and mastered it all when it came to sexual experiences, and life, too, for that matter. And he made a great sex therapist for an inhibited American female who wanted to learn more about the birds and the bees; to become more sexually aggressive. Even though she and Phillip had a very fulfilling sexual relationship, she couldn't seduce *him* or act provocative or take her own clothes off in a sexy, sensual way to arouse him or talk openly about what had happened between them or what she wanted or what he wanted; she could act playful, but if things grew serious, it made her feel uncomfortable. He had opened her up to express her feelings, but only after she had been overcome with passion. And even though she felt deeply loved after making love with Phillip, she still felt the need to cover herself. Now that she felt more free, she wished that she could be with him and return some of the joy of giving, emotionally as well as physically, that he had brought to her. When it came to bringing feelings to the surface, he wrote the book, a very special edition about love and communication and sharing. But with great sadness, Nealy had been forced to close his book before she got to the *happily-ever-after* ending. And with that thought, she fell sound asleep.

CHAPTER FORTY-SIX

EARLY THE NEXT MORNING, Michael quietly got up and got ready to go back to the ship for a while. Nealy slept so peacefully that he planned to let her catch up on her rest, but when he bent down to kiss her, she opened her eyes. "Good-morning, darling," he said sweetly.

She rubbed her eyes and stretched. "Good-morning."

"I've got to take care of some business back at the ship. I'll be back later to join you for lunch. Marie, my cook, will bring your breakfast in to you shortly. Make yourself at home. I'll be back as soon as I can."

"Okay." She smiled sleepily as he left the room. Nealy got up and put on her swimsuit so that she could rest by the pool and read a book after breakfast. Michael's black-bottom, laguna-style pool was nestled among perfectly sheared shrubs and surrounded by huge trees on all sides except for the side that faced the sea, offering an incredible view. There were flower beds that splashed pink, red and yellow colors throughout the area and a waterfall that trickled over huge rocks; it spelled *big bucks*. This guy had to be more than just rich. But how? His father was a fisherman. Nealy grew up around fishing and she had never seen anyone reach this level by peddling fish to the local markets. How did he do it? How did he ever get enough money to build ships like the *Southern Queen*? Well, hopefully, her questions would be answered when she went to Paris to meet his family, if not before. She had to find out before she let herself get too comfortable with being spoiled and living like a queen in the midst of wealth: big boats, fancy sports cars, expensive clothes, limousines, and houses that look more like world-famous castles.

Later that afternoon, Nealy was suddenly awakened. "I'm back, my darling," Michael whispered, kissing her lips softly as she slept in the chaise lounge.

Nealy smiled at him. "I'm glad. I missed you."

"Me, too," he said, lying down on top of her. His chest was covered by thick black hair that covered his tanned skin. He had changed into a skimpy latex swimsuit which exposed his thin, but well-toned body. It embarrassed Nealy because she had never been too comfortable with men in those tight-bikini suits, but every man that she had seen on this trip, except for the Americans, wore them. But at least he had on a suit, which surprised her. Michael didn't have one single, itty-bitty inhibition when it came to nudity. He called it "Naturalistic". Nealy called it *just plain naked*. He constantly worked on her attitude, and he didn't intend on giving up until she enjoyed the freedom that he thought she deserved; All women should love their bodies.

"How was your morning?" he asked.

"Wonderful and relaxing. This view is awesome. I could barely read for staring out at the haze and watching it rise slowly above the blue waters. How do you ever leave this place?"

"I have to work. That's how I got all of this."

"Now that you mentioned it. How *did* you get all of this?" she asked, looking around at the house and its picturesque setting.

"Well, I had a dream for one thing."

"But, Michael, lots of people have dreams, but they don't end up with all of this and become zillionaires to boot."

"A what?"

"A zillionaire. That means more than billions, which from what I see, you have to have, Michael."

He laughed. "Nealy, I don't have billions, but I'm very close."

"You have millions of dollars? How? Your father taught you to fish. I guess fishing in France pays a lot better than fishing in America."

"It's a long story."

"I have five days left to listen," she said, staring at him intently.

"Don't talk about leaving me," he said sharply.

"Michael, that is just an expression of sorts. It means that I have time to hear your story. So tell me? How did you get millions of dollars?"

"My father and I were fishing one day when I was about ten years old and this huge cruise liner sailed by us. I told my father that I would build ships someday. Of course, he laughed, but I meant it. And by the time I was fifteen, we had worked long and hard and added four more boats to our fishing fleet. My father's boyhood friend owned a freight company and shipped goods to England and other neighboring countries and even to America. So, he and my father decided to go into business together as partners even though he had much more money than my father. It worked very well, and then they added ten more fishing boats, growing more and more prosperous. I put away all of the money that I earned. I never spent it. I was always determined to build me a big ship like the one I saw that day. Of course, going to school, I could only work after school and on week-ends, but my father paid me well. He promised to always make me feel like a partner if I worked hard and did right by him and Michael Modiano, his boyhood-friend and business partner. My father had no sisters or brothers, so I was named after Michael, who is also my godfather and who later became my father-in-law. The rest is, as they say in America, history. I now build big ships for tourism."

"You married the daughter of your father's best friend and partner?"

"Yes, but I don't want to talk about that now. That was over a long time ago. All I want to do now is caress your beautiful body and kiss your luscious lips." He kissed her, rubbing his body against hers as she lay beneath him.

Nealy whispered, trying to avoid his kisses. "Michael, someone's coming."

"It's only Marie bringing our lunch," he mumbled, still trying to kiss her.

"But shouldn't we get up or something?"

"Darling, this is all part of your training. Marie is a woman, and it will not matter to her if I seduce the woman I love in my own home."

"We're not inside your house. We're outside."

"Nealy, we are just kissing. We are not making love. Have you never kissed a man in front of your friends before?"

"Well I've kissed them, but I've never *necked* in front of them."

"Necked? I don't know necked."

"Well, it's like making-out. Petting—oh, you probably don't know that either—it's when two people are doing everything in the heat of passion but without actually *doing it,* you know, the act itself."

"Oh, I see. It's like when we are burning hot with desire, kissing and slobbering wildly all over each other's bodies, and I finger your wet puss and suck madly on your tits and my—"

"Yes, that's it," she said, putting her hand over his mouth. "That's definitely necking." Nealy dropped her head back and rolled her eyes up at the heavens. "Dear *Lord,* I don't believe I'm having this conversation." Then she giggled, shaking her head. "Michael, I can't believe your choice of words. Is that *naturalistic,* too?"

"Yes, darling, it's only pet names. It makes things more exciting instead of so puritanical. I guess in the throes of passion you scream out things like, I want your penis in my vagina. Or...it feels good when you plunge my breasts with your mouth?"

"I don't scream out anything," she replied, laughing at his blunt condescension.

"Oh, but you will. That's in my next lesson, my little sex kitten."

"Oh, this ought to be interesting," she giggled nervously at more thought of his implications. Nealy just couldn't imagine herself ever, in her wildest dreams, screaming out during sex.

"It will be very interesting," he said seductively, kissing her softly. Marie had finally finished setting the table for their lunch.

"Is that all, Mr. Coupair," Marie asked from the table at the other end of the pool.

"Yes, thanks, Marie...oh, Marie, wait," he called out. He pulled Nealy up to a sitting position on the chaise. And when he hugged her, he unhooked the top of her swimsuit and quickly got up and walked over and handed it to Marie. "Please take this inside. Put it in my room. Ms. James would like to take advantage of the sun."

"Bring that back," she cried, but it was too late. Marie had already headed inside to do as she had been instructed. "Damn you, Michael." Nealy held her arms across her chest.

"Nealy, you are still much too modest. Have I made no progress with you at all? There is no one here but my servants, who are only women. A bare chest is—"

"I know, nat-u-ris-tic."

"Yes, that's it," he smiled. "Now, come...let's eat lunch." He pulled her up from the lounger and led her over to the table without allowing her to cover her bare chest.

"I'm very uncomfortable. Michael, I'm feeling faint. I'm warning you—oh God—I'm going to faint," she whined dramatically.

"Oh, Nealy, darling, you are not relaxing. In a while you will be happy, I promise. I have no shirt on, and I feel *very good*. Nealy," he said, turning her to face him, "you must understand one thing. A bare chest is not sexual. It looks sexy, especially when it is as beautiful as yours, but I'm not going to attack you just because you have no top on. Okay?"

"Okay," she said, getting very flushed in the face, "but I *promise you* that I'm not only feeling faint but sick, too."

"Darling, you are so dramatic," he laughed.

By the time they finished lunch, which thankfully had included two glasses of wine, Nealy had relaxed a little, but she still had problems adjusting. And for the rest of the afternoon, she spent much of the time in the pool or lying on her stomach on the lounger. Every so often Michael would insist that she turn so that he could reapply sunscreen to prevent her from burning again as she had in St. Tropez. She had to admit that being topless actually had some advantages; she wouldn't have a white strip across her back; she didn't have to worry about jumping up and forgetting that she had unhooked her bathing suit while she was tanning; and she didn't have to strain awkwardly to hook it without exposing herself when she tried to hook it back. Maybe, eventually, she would get used to it. Of course, Michael assured her that she would under his expert conditioning.

Later that evening, they went out to dinner, but only because Nealy insisted. Michael preferred staying home for more lessons on the joys of sex and eating by the pool in his birthday suit. Nealy wanted to dig further into his life, and he always loosened up during their meals together, even though he refused to talk about his failed marriage.

When they returned, he poured each of them a glass of wine, and they sat in the jacuzzi under the millions of stars that loomed in the sky overhead. After the third glass, they were definitely necking, but Nealy wouldn't let him go back on his word to wait; heavy foreplay would just have to do for now. Nealy was surprised at how much self-control she had with him because she remembered with Phillip, after that first night, she lost all control. He could have been *Jack the Ripper,* and for some reason, it wouldn't have mattered. Instantly, she had trusted Phillip, and she would have done whatever he wanted her to do without any argument, and she would have liked it. But the fact that Phillip was Rob Morris' best friend probably had a lot to do with it. It was different with Michael. He was from another country, and she knew very little about him. He could be married, but she doubted that because there were no signs of a woman living in his house. Of course the grin on Marie's face when he handed her the bathing suit top had said plenty. Nealy knew that she had not been the first woman that Marie had seen in the arms of the dashing Mr. Coupair. In fact, Marie could probably write a very interesting book, although she would need to embellish the facts somewhat when it came to the nitty-gritty-sex-parts because Michael respected his women enough to keep most things behind closed doors. He had been very good to Nealy and, for the most part, he had worked very hard at making her comfortable; in less than two weeks she actually felt less inhibited, which she attributed to his gentle ways and his power of persuasion. The man had definitely brought her out of her hiding place. In her opinion, Michael Coupair had definitely missed his calling: Sex Therapist Extraordinaire.

But, if what people say about *European* men and their strong desires for American women are true, it amazed Nealy that he had been a perfect gentleman. And whenever she said, "Stop," he stopped. His father evidently taught him well, in spite of his own infidelities. But, of course, Michael claimed his mother encouraged such behavior; Jerrod would love this country.

On Monday morning, Michael left to go into his office in Cannes, and Nealy decided to see if she had the nerve to go out by the pool without the top of her bathing suit. Michael has always pushed her, and without his prodding, she doubted that she could actually go outside, even if it is the natural thing to do; this would be a true test of courage since she had come to depend on Michael in the same way that she had depended on Miss Janik to help her overcome her stage fright; and she overcame that beautifully. With that thought, Nealy stepped into the bottom of her suit, put her hat on her head, placed her towel over her arm and counted to three before she walked through the kitchen past Marie. "Bonjour, Marie," she said confidently in her best French accent.

"Good-morning, madame," she returned graciously, not even blinking an eye. But she snickered once Nealy stepped out of sight. Marie couldn't help but notice her misgivings and discomfort with the European ways.

Nealy ate breakfast, but she kept her hair hanging directly over her breasts for emotional support. After breakfast, she fell asleep in the chaise lounge under the warm sun while staring out at the sea.

When Nealy heard voices, she stirred, but not enough to actually wake up until her nostrils filled with the strong smell of Polo aftershave.

"Hello, madame, I'm Pierre Simone," he said, standing over her.

Nealy jumped up and grabbed her towel. "Hi. You startled me," she said, shaking his extended hand.

"I'm so sorry," he begged forgiveness. "I stopped by to leave some papers for Michael. Marie told me to wait out here."

"Oh, certainly. Please, sit down," she said, pointing at the chaise next to hers. Nealy fumbled with her towel, horrified that she had been found almost naked by a strange man. His presence made her extremely uncomfortable, but the longer they visited, the more at ease she became, although she kept her towel stretched tightly acrossed her chest and tucked firmly under her arms. Pierre, a stylish European-looking man in his mid to late thirties, had dark hair and eyes and bushy eyebrows. Also he had polite mannerisms and spoke softly. But Nealy had him laughing almost hysterically by the time Michael came home and found them out by the pool. Obviously incensed, he immediately invited Pierre to return inside with him. Nealy and Pierre barely had time to make their polite good-byes before Michael, glaring at her intensely, nodded to Pierre and turned toward the house. Nealy could sense his anger even though she really didn't understand it; her conversation with Pierre had been far from intimate.

Five minutes later, Michael returned poolside and he angrily pushed Nealy's leg over on the chase lounge and sat down. "What was all of that about? I can't even leave you alone in my own home without you flirting with my employees."

"Michael, I can't believe that you're jealous. Pierre seemed like a nice guy. We were *just* talking about some of the funny things that I've been through trying to talk your language."

"I don't like you talking to my employees. And where the hell is your top? Did he turn you on, so you took it off? Well, something happened. I've had to beg you to loosen up."

"You're being ridiculous. I merely came out here like this today to see if I had the nerve. I would not deliberately expose myself to a stranger. And besides, you're the one that said, and I quote, 'Frenchmen do not pay attention to topless woman. It's nat-u-ris-tic.' Your words, Michael, not mine," she said sarcastically, in an angry tone.

Michael held her arm tightly. "Don't ever let me catch you, dressed or undressed, talking to my employees. Do you understand me?"

"Does that include Marie?"

"Don't patronize me, Nealy. I do not wish my employees to get close to you. They might think you want to sleep with them. I will not have that," he shouted, right in her face in a whispered voice.

"You think I would sleep with Pierre? Come on, Michael. Give me a little credit here. I don't sleep around. And I certainly wouldn't sleep around with your employees or your friends. This is a terribly absurd conversation. So why don't you just go to hell," she said, glaring at him coldly. Nealy went to get up and Michael pulled her back down.

"Sit down and stop this," he shouted. "And don't you ever curse me again."

"Let go of my arm," she snapped.

"I will when you come to your senses."

"*Oh, please.* Now let go of my arm," she ordered, struggling to free her wrist from his clutches.

"Nealy, you are making me more angry with this attitude of yours."

"And I guess you think I'm *just* thrilled with yours."

"No, but we must discuss this calmly. You belong to me. I must make you understand."

"Michael, I don't belong to anybody. That's not what love is all about. Loving someone is trusting that person. If you don't trust me, then we can't go on. I can't. And I won't live like that. My ex-husband almost destroyed my ability to trust because he cheated on me. So I would never do that to you or anyone else. It hurts too much. And it's wrong."

"Nealy, please calm down and let me talk to you."

"Why? So you can accuse me of something even more ridiculous."

"No...because I love you."

"Accusing me of seducing your employees is not love, Michael."

"Okay, I'm sorry for that. I just got angry because I found you out here with Pierre. Darling, I'm jealous. I'll admit it. It's as I told you the other night. You are this American beauty that any Frenchman, or any man for that matter, would love to have for their own. I want you for *my* own. I can't share you, darling. I can never share you. I want you for my eyes only. And I want to be the only man who touches your soft skin," he said, softly rubbing his flat hand back and forth across her bare chest which was exposed above the towel. His touch, his soft kisses on her pouted lips, and his never-failing stare with his magnificent *brown-velvet eyes* slowly turned her angered frown into a sweet smile. They made up, and after lunch they retired to his bedroom for a nap and private lessons in *Sex Education: 101*.

CHAPTER FORTY-SEVEN

MICHAEL AND NEALY had returned to the ship shortly before midnight since the ship was scheduled to set sail for Monte Carlo at twenty-four hundred hours. Of course, Michael had not been concerned because, even if they had run a little late, the *Southern Queen* would not have left without them.

The morning sun had barely broken through when they were taken to the Nice airport to fly into Paris on Michael's private jet. Looking out the window of the airplane, Nealy could see the landscape in Paris wrapped in a trailing blue mist, which Michael referred to as the city's *"stylish veil."* At times the sun would highlight a golden rooftop here and a patch of green there. How exciting. Nealy James in Paris; she couldn't believe it! She thought about the night that she and Phillip were lying in bed snuggling and talking about things that they had done. He told her all about Paris and how he wanted to take her there someday. If only he were with her, they could visit the *City of Love* together. How could she even think about that when she had Michael sitting next to her. Nealy couldn't explain it, and she had to stop thinking about Phillip.

On the ground, that beautiful *stylish veil* became a chilly, damp mist. Nealy stopped to pull a sweater out of her bag before proceeding towards the limousine. They were staying at the Hotel de Crillon on George the Fifth Avenue right in the heart of Paris so that Michael could show Nealy as much of Paris as possible before taking her to meet his family. Nealy didn't know what to expect, so she admitted to being uptight, but Michael assured her that the evening would be perfect. But even so, Nealy couldn't push the thought of a ready-made family out of her mind. During her marriage, the thought of having a child terrified her, so how would she do with grown children?

They strolled the streets of Paris after breakfast, hand in hand, as Michael pointed out places of interest that had been homes and refuges to kings, emperors, philosophers, ambassadors, and celebrities alike. They stopped in a small hat shop on the Champs-Elysees Avenue where Michael bought Nealy a hat to keep the sun off her face. Of course Nealy had a great time trying on every hat in the store. But finally, she decided on the caramel-colored one with a brim that flipped up in the back and had a yellow ribbon around it to match her outfit. They walked further down the street to the famed promenade crowned by the Arc de Triomphe in the center of Place Charles de Gaulle

Etoile. Eager to get over the arch, Nealy took off across the street and found herself in the middle of the circle dodging traffic. Michael had to run out into the traffic jam to prevent her from getting run down by angry motorists. Even though she felt like an idiot, and especially after he led her to the underground passageway further around the circle, she giggled wildly; Although Michael did not find any humor in her actions. The arch had been completed in eighteen-thirty-six and commemorated the victories of the Napoleonic Empire. An unknown soldier had been buried beneath the arch in nineteen-twenty and an eternal flame marked his grave. From the top of the tower, Nealy marveled at all the people below wandering up and down the street. With binoculars, she spotted an adorable little bistro where she begged Michael to take her for lunch, and though he had a much more elegant place in mind, he relented. Nealy actually recognized her food for the first time in over a week. All she wanted was a turkey sandwich on a fresh baked roll; *and it was good.* To further indulge herself, she had a horn-stuffed pastry filled with whipped cream and was covered in powdered sugar, much to Michael's chagrin.

After lunch, they casually walked through the parks and along the sidestreets. Everything was so green, and there were so many little garden groves and silent little courtyards scattered about the city. They took a walk along the Seine River's edge. Nealy fell in love with Paris, and at the same time, she felt like she might even be falling in love with Michael. Paris seemed to have that effect on everyone; people were lying in the parks on the grass staring into one another's eyes. The birds serenaded the mind, while their lovers stirred their emotions. Love was in the air.

Michael wanted to take a helicopter out to Versailles since it was thirty minutes away from Paris, but Nealy wanted to do as the French people do, so they took the underground metro over to the train station, which Michael loathed. People crammed into the metro, and Nealy tried to catch a word or two of what they were saying, but they talked too fast. The passengers on the train stared at her, and she smiled at them, which didn't please Michael. He held her close to him at all times, which bothered her because she wasn't used to anyone smothering her. Nealy was very independent, but when she looked into Michael's *brown-velvet eyes,* she was drawn even closer to him.

Nealy stood outside the gate at Versailles with her mouth open so wide that she could easily catch a june bug, which had actually happened to her once, so she quickly closed her mouth at the horror of that ever happening again. But, the palace had to be the most incredible place that she had ever seen. The gate itself had real gold adorning the ornate iron poles, and a cobblestone foyer paved up to the palace doors. This domain encompassed more area than most Texas towns. There were gardens, parks, stables, an orange grove, and fountains in every direction that were filled with different statues of wild horses and other animals, fish, and people. There were queen's rooms, king's rooms, the Hall of Mirrors, the Hall of Battles, drawing rooms for everything imaginable, and a cottage that King Louis the Fourteenth built for Queen Marie-Antoinette, complete with a multi-acre rowing pond. Now Nealy knew just exactly how good ol' King Louie got away with having mistresses living under the same roof without them finding out about one another. If he were in the king's bedroom, and sent one of them to fetch his slippers from the bath apartment, she wouldn't return for two weeks! And no wonder the people of Paris revolted when they were literally starving to death and *these* people built a *little house in the country* larger than Galveston Island. And the nerve of that queen bitch who screamed, "Let them eat cake!" Well, when the people of Paris formed a revolution, hunted her down, and chopped off her head, the ugly bitch definitely stopped screaming. So guess who got the last laugh? Rest assured, it was not the headless heroine!

After what had seemed like a day's journey at Versailles, Michael and Nealy hopped on the train enroute for the Louvre, the historic palace built in the thirteenth century during the reign of Louis XIV. As one of the world's largest and most famous museums, it houses treasures from artist such as Rembrandt, Rubens and Titian, and statues created by many famous sculptures. Even though Michael did not enjoy the lifestyle of the typical Parisian and most of the tourist who used public transportation system, he tried to be a good sport. More than anything, he wanted Nealy to love his country. Beneath the glass pyramid inside the Louvre, Michael directed Nealy towards the hall where the famous armless statue of the Venus de Milo stood alone in all her greatness. Nealy no sooner flashed her camera when an attendant rushed towards her.

"Sorry, madame, no flashes allowed in the museum."

"Oh, I'm sorry," Nealy said smiling sheepishly. "Please don't take my camera. I'll die if you do. You see, I'm from America and I can't understand you people and I can't read your language—"

"Madame—"

Nealy cut her off again. "Oh, please," she pleaded, tears forming in her eyes. "Are you going to take my camera?"

"No, madame, but do not use your flash again or I will have to take your camera," she scolded, shaking her finger. "Remember, pictures okay. No flash."

Nealy turned to talk to Michael, but he had walked over by the window, leaving her to accept her punishment like a woman who purposely ignored the signs. "Hey, why didn't you help me out? All you had to do was bat those *brown-velvets* of yours and she would have melted. Then I wouldn't have gotten in trouble."

Michael smiled, accepting her flattery, but he didn't approve.

"Oh, but my darling, you deserved that lecture."

"I just wanted a souvenir snapshot. Is that so wrong? Damn, did you see her? She looked mean as hell. I guess to her, I'm the ugly *American*," she said making a face.

"No, darling, you could never be the ugly American, but you were a very naughty girl."

"Well, sue me," she giggled.

To avoid any further confrontations, Michael led her down some stairs and up some stairs and through a long hallway lined with famous, but mostly grotesque paintings. A crowd of people bunched up in the middle of the wood-floored hall, obviously admiring something very interesting. "Come, darling," Michael said, pulling her through the tourist to get a closer look at the *Mona Lisa*. "Isn't she magnificent?"

Nealy studied the portrait enclosed in a glass case. "Well, yes because Leonardo da Vinci put her in the history books. But I swear that's a man dressed up in drag," she rubbed her chin, and then giggled loudly.

"Shush," he scolded. "This is a serious masterpiece."

"Sorry, but why? If that's a woman, then she desperately needs a new *do*. Poor thing. Now that's a bad hair day," Nealy teased Michael, even though she felt a deep sense of appreciation for the world famous piece; in fact, she had goosebumps. So why had Nealy become so mischievously defiant? This was totally out-of character for her. Suddenly, without any reservations, Nealy focused her camera and flashed her very own picture of the Mona Lisa. Then she grabbed Michael's hand. "Come on let's get the hell out of her before that mean woman comes after me." Walking at a very fast pace, they weaved their way through hundreds of tourists.

Running out of time, Michael insisted on getting a cab to visit one of his favorite museums, Musee Rodin, on Rue de Varenne in the Hotel Biron where the famous sculptor, Auguste Rodin, lived and worked. Behind a row of gorgeous dark red rose bushes and hidden in a charming garden, Nealy fell in love with the sculpture of *The Thinker*; he reminded her of Hercules in repose. His features were brutish, and his physique masculine, which showed signs of great strength, beneath a bull-neck. The intricate lines in his face gave him character, and his serious expression suggested meditation. Although he was cast in bronze, he was verdigris in color, which accented the intricate carving. Nealy knew exactly why Michael favored this museum over the others. There were dozens of erotic looking sculptures of naked men and women and children in compromising positions. On one, the face of the man was buried so deep in the bosom of the woman that it looked as though he had grown out of her chest. Rodin was either an incurable romantic or a demonically depraved madman. Or just another sick bastard!

A man in a long black cloak strolled through the garden ringing his bell. Nealy had found the land of enchantment. "Oh, Michael," she sighed. I want to savor these memories. This museum is sacred, like a chapel. I can feel the presence of Rodin all around me.

"Yes, he is here, Nealy. If this moves you so much just wait until you see the Eiffel Tower. Come...let's go on because we are running out of time. Remember, we are having dinner at nine."

As they approached *"Eiffie,"* Michael touched Nealy's arm to get her attention and he felt chillbumps. And then he noticed that she had tears in her eyes. "I can't believe it. I'm looking at the *La Tour Eiffel,"* she said, rolling her tongue to sound remotely French with romantic over-tones. "I just never thought that I'd see this."

"Darling, you will be perfect for my country," he said, smiling at her. "You have a greater appreciation for France than many of its own people."

"I do love France, Michael," she said, resting her head on his shoulder.

"Come...let's go up and see Paris. We can either take the elevator up two-hundred-seventy-six meters or walk the sixteen-hundred and forty-seven steps. Which do you prefer?"

"Definitely the elevator," she giggled.

"Thank goodness, I'm going to need my strength," he smiled. Michael held her snugly around the shoulders and guided her into the oversized elevator.

When they reached the third landing, he pointed out the sights as they looked down at the many vistas of the city. As the night slightly began to fall on the city, the skies turned a champagne-color above the palisade of rich northern lights that twinkled, turning the ground below into a gigantic sparkler.

"Michael, I swear to God, this is more moving than sex," she stated emphatically.

"Nealy, *nothing* is more moving than sex with me, especially in the City of Love. I become a bold Latin lover," he bragged seductively. "And after tonight, I'm sure that you will agree."

"Mr. Coupair," she said, turning to face him and putting her arms tightly around his neck. "I am so enchanted and inflamed with love for this city that my head is spinning. I can barely breathe. And since you're so confident about having a stronger effect on me than this, I'd say you've got some pretty good tricks up your sleeve that I haven't seen yet."

"Ms. James, I don't need tricks. My thirst for your soul is immortal...and my thirst for your body is immoral."

"Yep, that'll do it," she snapped, the blood rushing to her face. After kissing him above all of Paris from the most notable tower in the world, they strolled back to the hotel in the damp night air like two lovebirds.

At eight-thirty, Michael led a very nervous Nealy down to the limousine and they proceeded to the western edge of Paris for dinner with his family. Since it was still dusk out, even though it was almost nine o'clock, Michael pointed out more sights as they crossed the city. They passed a huge park, Bois de Boulogne, which Michael said had attracted him to that area. When his children were small, he said that he took them to the park on weekends. That gave him a chance to spend some quality time with them, but regretfully, he worked so much that the trips to the park had been much fewer than he would have liked. In all honesty, he said that he had neglected both his children and his wife, but because of his generosity towards them during the past ten years, all had been forgiven.

Nealy got out of the limousine, ringing her hands together. "Do I look alright?"

"You look incredibly beautiful, my darling. So stop worrying. My children will love you," he said, kissing her lightly on the lips as they walked through the huge gate.

Michael opened the door and allowed Nealy to walk inside in front of him. One of the servants met them. "Good-evening, Mr. Coupair. They are waiting for you in the parlor off the main dining room."

"Thank you, Millicent."

"Michael, I forgot to ask you. Do your children speak English?"

"Of course, darling. Now relax, please." He smiled at her.

"Oh, good." Michael led Nealy through some huge doors and passed two other large rooms before she heard the chatter of voices. It sounded as if there were more people than she had expected.

Michael continued to lead her into a big room that had four tapestry couches in groups with two chairs and coffee tables. The tapestry on the couches matched the wallpaper on the twenty-five foot walls, and the chairs were different solid colors coordinating with the couch in each setting. Gaudy was the word that came to Nealy's mind; much too busy for her taste. But of course she knew that they had paid a lot of money to make it look that *gaud awful*. Old mansions in Europe always had the old Mediterranean decor.

"Hello, Pop," a young man said, walking over to greet them.

"Good-evening, Aury," Michael said, embracing his son and then kissing each cheek. "I would like for you to say hello to Ms. James."

Nealy held out her hand and he placed his hand in hers. "It's nice to meet you, Ms. James."

"It's nice to meet you, Aury. Please call me Nealy," she said, smiling at the very handsome young man who favored his father, especially in his eyes, which were the same cocoa brown.

"Good-evening, my sweet," Michael said to the young lady who had walked over and kissed him.

"Good-evening, Papa," the young lady replied, glaring at Nealy.

"Michelle, I'd like for you to meet Nealy James."

"Hello," she replied coldly.

Before Nealy could reply, they were interrupted by a shrill scream. "Papa!" A beautiful girl ran across the room into Michael's arms.

"Oh, my pretty pet, how I've missed you. How was London?"

"Wonderful, Papa, but I'm glad to be home."

"Breille, I'd like you to meet Nealy James."

"Hello, it's very nice meeting you," she said, smiling from ear to ear. "Oh, Papa, she is very pret-ty."

"Yes, she is, Breille," he replied, smiling at Nealy, and then at Breille.

"Mama," Breille cried out. Come...meet Papa's friend."

"Hello, Nealy, I'm Victoria. Michael has told me all about you. It's nice to meet you. Welcome to our home."

"Thank you. It's nice to meet you, too." But of course Nealy had heard nothing about her. Nealy was caught off-guard because she never expected to meet the former wife, but she seemed very nice and she was somewhat attractive, although not anything like what Nealy had expected. When Michael told Nealy that he would introduce her to the *whole* family, he had meant the whole family, former spouse an all. But *why* did her name have to be Victoria? That name reminded her of *that woman*, Victoria Dorimarr, who introduced herself to Nealy as Phillip's fiancée, and, even though a year had passed, the thought of that moment still hurt.

"Nealy, I'd like you to meet Claude Charbrom," Victoria said, smiling up at him adoringly, which led Nealy to believe that he was Victoria's husband.

"Hi, it's nice to meet you, Claude," Nealy said, smiling as he kissed the back of her hand and held it so gently.

"My pleasure, Nealy."

"Nealy," Breille said, "would you sit by me at dinner?"

"How sweet. I'd love to."

"Great! I like your accent," she said, smiling girlishly.

"Thanks, Breille. I like yours, too," Nealy smiled.

"Come, everyone, dinner is served," Victoria announced.

The servants served the salad of fresh fluffy greens and plump tomatoes on some ornately painted china that resembled the loud wallpaper. Like every other fancy dish in France, Nealy didn't recognize the main course. When she looked at Michael, he could see the questions in her expression.

"That's *Sole Normandy*. The sauce is shellfish, truffles, and champagne. It's rich, but very delicious."

"Oh, it smells wonderful," Nealy said, smiling at Victoria who had obviously selected the menu. Or perhaps she had cooked it herself, although she didn't look like the cooking type. Actually, she didn't appear domestic at all, but why should she; so far Nealy had seen as many as four servants.

"Thank you, Nealy. I hope you like it. I wanted to serve something very special for Michael's guest," she smiled.

During dinner everyone made polite conversation. Aury talked about his plans to go to America after he graduated from the University de Paris in May.

"And what will you do in America, Aury," Nealy asked.

"I'm going to medical school," he answered proudly.

Of all things, she thought. "Oh, that's wonderful. You want to be a doctor?" she nodded, trying to hide the hurt that she felt. It never failed. No matter how hard she tried to push Phillip out of her life, he always came back to haunt her.

"Yes. An obstetrician," he responded. "I love children. Someday I want to have many of my own."

His father held his head up and smiled with pride at his only son's plans for a bright future. Aury had his father's drive and the good sense to go after what he wanted. "My son is a good boy, but he never liked me calling him that. He always wanted to be a man," Michael laughed softly, smiling at his son, and then at Nealy.

"Where will you go to school, Aury?" Nealy asked, praying that he wouldn't say Columbia.

"Columbia. I understand that it is one of the best in America."

"Yes...it...uh," she choked on her words as Phillip's sweet face flashed in her mind like a bright yellow caution light.

"Are you alright, darling?" Michael asked, searching her face.

Nealy covered her mouth to cough delicately. "Yes, thanks, my food went down the wrong pipe. Please, excuse me," she said, clearing her throat gracefully. Still struggling with the vision in her head, she continued. "I know some very good doctors that went to Columbia. You made an excellent choice."

Michael patted her back gently. "Better?"

"Yes, much. Thanks," Nealy smiled as Michelle glared at her from across the table.

Not pleased with her twin sister's attitude and obvious animosity towards her father's new friend, Brielle changed the subject to something less conservative. "Papa, did you know that I learned to milk a cow?"

"What?" Michael asked, seemingly appalled.

"Yes," she laughed, "I did. But I didn't like it," she shook her head and grimaced. "When I went to London to work on my project, you know— comparing French cultures and English cultures—well, I had to live on a dairy farm since that is a major part of both economies. Papa, have you ever squeezed big tits like those?"

Everyone burst out laughing. Michael blushed, which Nealy couldn't believe; she didn't think that anything or anyone could ever embarrass Michael Coupair. This is a man who relieved himself while Nealy stared into the bathroom mirror—horrified, to say the least—trying to concentrate on applying her make-up.

"Oh, Papa, I didn't mean...oh, I meant like *milking a cow?*" she said, trying to explain, although the damage had been done. Michael took it well and laughed with the others, but his face remained red for a few minutes; he had certainly fondled some *big tits* in his day, but the very idea of him grabbing hold of a cow's udder seemed grossly absurd. He had produced many things, but milk wasn't one of them. But, Nealy had to commend him, he had produced some very bright and attractive children. The only one of them that had not shown approval of Nealy arriving on the arm of their father was Michelle, who actually favored him the most, and who apparently had also inherited his jealous nature. Nealy could tell that Michelle hadn't particularly liked it when Michael spoke softly to her or smiled affectionately at her during dinner. Throughout most of the meal, Michelle had her hand resting on Michael's arm, making sure that Nealy understood her position. Michael directed several questions to her that he felt would draw her out, but she refused to open up. So, he left her alone to come around on her own.

After dinner, they retreated back to the parlor for brandy and Claude talked to Nealy about her days on the stage in New York. He had known an American woman back in the mid-sixties who had been in several plays on Broadway, but he had lost contact with her after he met Victoria. From his admission, Nealy knew that Michael and Victoria must have divorced many years before. Nealy had become quite comfortable, and she had actually enjoyed the evening very much. And now that she had met the family, she felt that she could let go and give Michael the go ahead to woo her affections. Michael didn't seemed so mysterious anymore; he turned out to be just a nice man with nice children and a very amiable relationship with his former wife. Nealy realized that Michelle would need more time to accept her, but eventually she would. Nealy had a lot of patience, and she would make sure that Michael gave Michelle plenty of attention so that she wouldn't feel threatened. The thought of a former wife where children were involved had always concerned Nealy, but in this case, it didn't seem to bother her because Victoria had a husband. When she looked at Michael, she couldn't imagine him ever being married to Victoria; she didn't seem like his type. Michael had an obvious attraction to beautiful bodies, which she realized immediately when they met for the first time in New York. When he looked at her his eyes had lingered slowly all the way down her body, and during the past two weeks, he spent hours almost obsessed with just admiring her. Even though Victoria had a sweet, kind face, she had a very round body, which she knew Michael would not tolerate; he made that perfectly clear to Nealy when she teased him about getting fat.

Nealy mingled with the family, which had grown in number since dinner. Two of Victoria's cousins had joined them, along with their respective spouses and their children. It made a large group, which intimidated Nealy because they all spoke to one another in French. Rarely did she understand a word of what they were saying, except when they arrived and said, "Bonjour," or when someone passed them something during dinner, and they said, "Merci." Michael had stayed by Nealy's side for most of the evening, but he would be pulled away from time to time to visit a relative. When someone approached her chattering away, she became so frustrated trying to figure out what they were saying that she would finally smile and give them a polite wave as she walked away.

Michelle had avoided her most of the evening, but finally she walked up to Nealy and displayed her dislike for her with a cocky little smirk on her face. "So, Nealy, how long have you been seeing my father?"

"Well, as we said at dinner, we met in New York a year ago, but we actually started seeing each other almost two weeks ago when we met again on the ship."

"Oh, really. Why did it take you so long to start seeing him?" she asked rather smugly.

Nealy stopped smiling and almost told her that it was really none of her business, but she had to remember that she was talking to a child who obviously felt insecure about Nealy's place in her father's life. "Well, to be honest, Michelle, I had just separated from my husband. I wasn't ready to get involved with anyone at that time." Except for Phillip, she thought, sending a sharp pain through her heart.

"Oh, yes, the doctor, right?"

Deep in thought about her early days with Phillip, she didn't answer right away... "Uh...Yes, that's right."

"Was he rich?"

"Excuse me?" Nealy asked, shocked that she would get so personal.

"Was...the...doctor...rich?" she repeated, hanging on each word.

"Well, Michelle, this is really none of your business. But since you seem so interested, yes, I guess you could call him rich. His family has money, and he inherited a bundle."

"Did you take *all* of his money when you divorced him?"

"Now that, young lady, *is not* your concern," Nealy replied as politely as she could. "But, Michelle, I *do* have my own business. I didn't really need any of *his* money although that's not to say that I didn't take my fair share. In some divorces there are extenuating circumstances which entitle one or both parties to receive certain things. And in this case I deserved my fair share. I'm sure that Michael was very generous with your mother and with the three of you."

"What do you mean?" she snapped bitterly.

"When your father divorced—"

"My father didn't divorce my mother," she interrupted, raising her voice.

"I'm sorry. When your mother divorced—"

"And my mother did not divorce my father. They will always be married. So if it's money you're after, you can forget it!" she screamed.

Nealy felt all of the blood leave her face. The room grew quiet and everyone turned to stare at the two of them. "Excuse me," Nealy said softly. Without making eye contact with anyone, she turned towards the hallway and left the room very hurriedly. When she reached the door, she opened it, not having a clue as to where she planned on going. Nealy's first reaction had always been to escape as quickly as possible from any confrontation and think about it later. That was not the right way to handle things, but she couldn't help it. She ran down the long driveway to where the limousine was parked and jerked the door open. "I'm not feeling very well. Could you please drive me back to the hotel?"

"Yes, of course, madame." But instead of leaving the house, he pulled up in front and stopped. Then he got out and opened the door for Michael.

"Nealy, what happened between you and Michelle?"

"Just leave me alone?" she snapped.

He moved closer to her and she moved further towards the door. "Nealy, what did she say to you, dammit? I can't talk to you about this if I don't know what is going on."

"That you're still married. That you would always be married to her mother," she said curtly. Nealy always cried when she became very angry, but she tried desperately to control it.

Michael didn't respond immediately; he just stared. "Nealy, I'm sorry that you had to find out this way."

"You bastard," she screamed, glaring at him. "Get the hell away from me." She moved across to the other seat and stared out the window. When he started to follow her, she screamed at him. "Stay away from me. I hate men. And I especially hate you at this moment...so, just stay the hell away from me. This is why Miss Janik told me to find out about strange men before I slept with them. What's with you Central Park millionaires? You like having your cake and eating it, too? Is that it? Or have Texas women lived such sheltered, naive lives that it's easy to take advantage of us? Tell me, Michael? Do I appear that gullible? Or desperate maybe? Perhaps a little dim witted? What is it?"

"Nealy, I intended to tell you, but I just hadn't found the right moment yet. It's a long story. It's a very delicate situation. My life with Victoria has been over for more than ten years. In fact, Claude has been living with her for the last ten years. They are in love."

"Then why haven't you divorced so that she could marry him? Or do people just prefer living *in sin* in France?"

He stared at her and she glared back angrily. "Nealy, darling, it's not that simple. When we get back to the hotel, I'll tell you everything. But you need to calm down so that we can talk about this rationally."

"When we get back to the hotel, you'll never see me again. I promised myself that no man would ever make a fool out of me again. Now, here I am again—*Fool number two*. So do me a favor, Michael, and just shut-up!"

And with that, Michael sat back in the seat and glared at her until they reached the hotel. She had gotten so angry by then that she couldn't even cry. And when the driver opened the door for her, she jumped out and raced inside the hotel towards the elevator. The doors opened, and she got on and pushed the button, allowing the door to close in his face. When she got to the top floor, she realized that she didn't have a key to their suite. So she just stood outside the door with her arms folded tightly across her chest, staring into space. Nealy had never been so furious with anyone in her life. This, for some reason, had seemed like an even bigger betrayal than when she caught Jerrod in that swimming pool. This was a deliberate lie as far as she was concerned. And what was all that bullshit about how much he loved and adored her and wanted to spend the rest of his life with her? What nerve. Finally, at the ripe old age of twenty-seven, she had come to the conclusion that all men graduated from the U of A (University of Assholes), and that some of them had mastered in one of several subjects: Adultery; Becoming Perfect Assholes; The Unique Art of Playing the Field; Marrying for Money; and How to Make a Complete Fool Out of the Women In Your Life.

Michael walked off the elevator and opened the door without a word. When they got inside the room, Nealy got her suitcase and started putting her things back inside. She raced madly from room to room, without even looking at him, gathering up her belongings. He glared at her angrily as he pulled off his clothes.

Then, as she approached the bed to pick up her tennis shoes, he grabbed her and pulled up her dress. "Take off your clothes. You need to get laid all-the-way! That ridiculous fooling around has left you horny and moody," he shouted, holding her as she tried to get away from him. "A good fucking and you'll be happy to listen."

"You think I'm angry because I'm frustrated? Now *that's* ridiculous. Let go of me, you fuckin' jerk." And when he wouldn't let go of her, she bit his shoulder.

He screamed out and violently pushed her to the floor. "You mad bitch. I'm bleeding," he said, racing off to the bathroom to check his wound.

"Good! I hope you get rabies," she screamed, grabbing her small suitcase. But before she left, she walked over to the bathroom door and glared at him in the mirror.

Michael was holding a washcloth up to his shoulder. "Don't you ever do that again," he growled.

"Didn't your mother ever call you aside and tell you not to mess around with mad bitches?" she said sarcastically. "They're very unpredictable. And they viciously bite their enemies." Nealy turned and stormed out of the suite, getting to the elevator just in time. In the lobby, she hurried over to the front desk. "How can I get to Monte Carlo tonight?" she asked the desk clerk.

"Tonight?" the desk clerk asked, shaking his head side to side.

"Yes, right now," she said anxiously.

"You can't tonight, madame. It's after midnight. There is no public transportation leaving the city at this hour."

"Oh, that's just great," she cried.

"But, Madame Coupair—"

"Don't call me that," she snapped. "It's *Ms. James*." If looks could kill, the poor clerk would have died instantly. Nealy turned and hurried out the door of the hotel. She wasn't sure where she was going, but she knew for sure that she wasn't spending one more night with Michael Coupair. "That goddamn smooth-talkin', lyin'-ass creep," she whispered, tears spilling from her eyes as she walked down the lighted street.

When she reached the marquise above the Hotel George V, she decided to go inside and get a room for the night. Once she had calmed down, she realized how vulnerable she looked walking the streets of Paris in the middle of the night with her suitcase in her hand. And besides the fear of being mugged, she trembled from the cold, damp night air and her feet were killing her from walking on the hard pavement in heels. The last time she fled out in the middle of the night, she had run to Phillip and he made everything seem so much better. But there was no Phillip to run to this time, and things were not going to get any better. Not now, and probably not ever.

The first thing the next morning, Nealy got up and sat by the window in her room. Sadly, she looked out over Paris. If things had worked out differently, she might have seen much more of this beautiful city, but now she just wanted to get the hell out on the next train or plane or whatever she could find to take her back to Monte Carlo where she could get her clothes and go home to Texas.

At the front desk, she did her best to communicate, but even when these people spoke English, she could barely understand them. Maybe it was her accent that got them so flustered or their accent that got her so flustered. Who knows? "Ms. James, your bill comes to two-thousand-one-hundred-ten French francs."

"Geezus, I don't want to buy the hotel. How much is that?"

"Two —"

"I heard you," Nealy said, interrupting her. "That was simply a shock reflex. I wanted to know how much real money—not goddamn funny money. But screw it. Who cares." Nealy grimaced and pulled out her travelers checks.

The woman seemed totally confused by Nealy's outburst, and she hadn't understood most of what she said, "Is there some-problem that I can help you with?" she asked, aware that Nealy was upset.

Nealy gave the clerk her traveler's checks and enough francs to cover her bill, and then she smiled sweetly. "No, I'm sorry. And please forgive my attitude. It sucks, I know. But there's a damn good reason. You see," she said leaning closer to the clerk, "I'm horny," she smirked and walked over to the concierge's desk. "Hi, I need to get back to Monte Carlo. What's the most economical way to get there?"

"Are you in a hurry?"

"To get out of France, yes. But to get back to Monte Carlo, no." Nealy hadn't planned on flying around France, and she didn't want to run out of money before she returned home.

The woman smiled because Nealy smiled, but she didn't act as though she really understood what Nealy meant. "Would you like to take the scenic route on the T.G.V...the train, madame?"

"Is it cheaper than flying?" Nealy asked.

"Oh, yes," the concierge, the clerk assisting hotel guests, said with confidence.

"Then that'll be good."

The woman had a pleasant smile and Nealy wished that she felt more like smiling back, but actually, she wanted to scream. "The rail station has a train leaving at ten-forty-one to Nice. In Nice, you will take the train on to Monte Carlo at five-thirty-eight. If you hurry madame, you can make it."

"Merci...thanks," Nealy said, smiling like the happy little Miss Congeniality, but through her teeth, she mumbled, "Oh, I'll hurry alright if it'll get me the fuck out of here." Then she scolded herself for allowing her anger and her frustrations to control her mouth and her mood. Thank God she knew what was causing her frustration: She was *fuckin'* horny!

Nealy caught a cab in front of the hotel. "Train station, please." The cab driver drove for the next ten minutes and pulled into a big station-looking building.

When he stopped, he turned and looked at her and mumbled something about francs. "Five-hundred-ten-francs, madame."

"Is this the train station, too? All I see are buses?"

"Par-don?" he asked, looking confused.

"Is this the train station? Like, toot-toot," she said, moving her arms like a locomotive and pretending to pull the cord down to toot the whistle.

He smiled, looking even more confused. "Par-don?"

"Shit!" she screamed, throwing herself back on the seat. "I'm sitting in the middle of Paris playing fucking charades with a taxi driver. Trains, dammit! Like, choo-choo," she cried, pretending to pull the whistle on a train again."

"Choo-choo?" he mirrored her singing sound.

"You people are really starting to piss me off. I had a perfectly miserable night, and now I'm having a perfectly miserable day. I don't want to go to Monte Carlo on the *bus*. I want to go on the goddamn *train*! Choo-choo, choo-choo," she acted out one more time. Finally, she started giggling. "Oh, God, I can't take this. I'm taking the *Lord's* name in vain. I'm cursing every time I open my mouth. I'm losing it. And I'm making an absolute fool of myself. Okay...One more time," she said to the poor guy who was laughing, even though he still didn't understand. "Trains. Railroad station. The rail service. The

T.G.V!"

"Oh, yes, oui, the T.G.V.," he smiled, nodding that he finally understood her.

"Yes! Oui! That's it! The T.G.V. Oh, thank you, *God*." Nealy got so excited that she reached up in the front seat and actually hugged the guy.

"Par-don, madame," he grimaced. Then he held up one finger and twisted the steering wheel. "Un taxi."

Nealy studied him carefully trying to figure out what he was trying to tell her. "I don't get it. Par-don is excuse me. But it means sorry, too. Wait! I got it. Sorry...un...is one...you're sorry and it's your first day to drive a taxi? Par-don, un taxi!"

"Oui, yes," he said, smiling.

Nealy looked up and started laughing. "Why me, *Lord?*"

"Par-don?"

"Nothing," she snapped, waving her hands and shaking her head from side to side. "Just take me to the T.G.V."

"T.G.V., Oui?"

"Oui, s'il vous plaît," she said, shocked that she had said yes, please without even thinking about it. "Damn, I'm getting pretty good at this French stuff. I know at least ten words now," she giggled. "But it doesn't matter at this point because I'm getting the hell out of Paris if I have to sprout wings and fly. Now, hurry...please," she cried. What was it with her and men and cab drivers? Every time she got mixed up with the wrong man, she had a dreadful experience in a taxi—remember that horrid night in New York? It must be an omen: stay away from men or stay out of taxi cabs. Definitely, stay away from *men!*

"Yes, madame," he said, smiling at her in his mirror and driving fast towards the train station.

Nealy arrived exactly five minutes before the train left. If they didn't let her on that train, she planned to make a huge scene; "Hell hath no fury like that of a woman scorned." At this point, she had every intention of getting back on that ship in time for dinner so that she could see her friends. And hopefully, Michael Coupair would remain in Paris. In fact, she prayed most of the way that he would be so angry that he would just stay the hell away from her forever.

CHAPTER FORTY-EIGHT

AT EXACTLY seven-twenty-one that evening, Nealy arrived back on the *Southern Queen*. There were not too many people wandering around the lobby since it was the dinner hour, so she slipped down to her room unnoticed. When she opened the door, it was like déjà vu; roses by the dozen. But this time, she didn't feel as moved as she had on the day that she had arrived. Too much had happened since that day, and she was tired of men sending her flowers just to get back in her good graces. Forget it; that had happened one time too many. And just how could a man think that he could get away with not telling the person that he said he loved that he was married? Why would he want to make her appear *foolish* in front of the whole world—okay, twenty people or so? What if her friends on the ship find out? They'd think that this guy had only wined and dined her with less than honorable intentions. Well, Nealy Samantha James had come to the end of her rope; to hell with charm, good looks, and flowers.

Oh, no. Did the flowers mean that Michael had returned to the ship? Or did he have them sent? Well, she had come to terms with her anger, but she wasn't ready to talk to him, not yet anyway. And besides, talking wouldn't change the fact that Michael Coupair was married, although she had mellowed out enough to wonder what was going on because Victoria seemed madly in love with Claude, the man that she had lived with for *ten years*. It just didn't make any sense. Why didn't Victoria divorce Michael and marry him? Maybe Claude was after her money? But after ten years, surely he could find someone else with money that was free to marry and share more than her bed. There had to be more to this than met the eye, and Nealy was curious enough to put her anger aside just long enough to find out the truth.

When she walked into the dining room, she spotted Charlotte and Bob at a table across the room with the rest of their group. She maneuvered her way around the tables in the dining room, not looking in any direction except straight ahead. If Michael were there, she didn't want to see his *brown-velvet eyes*. She wasn't prepared to deal with that before dinner. "Hi, guys."

"Where's you-know-who?" Charlotte asked.

"Who knows where you-know-who is? And who cares?"

"Uh-oh. Lovers spat," Fern said.

"More like the French-American Revolution. After I bit the enemy,

I escaped by train. So if you see Mr. Coupair and he's foaming at the mouth, don't be alarmed," Nealy grinned smugly.

"Well, let's hear it." Charlotte said. "What happened?"

"It's a long story. And it didn't have a very good ending," Nealy said wearily. "The French outnumbered the Americans, five to one. Four too many for me."

"Oh, Nealy, we're really sorry," Fern said.

"Thanks, Fern, but it's all for the best. He's too foreign, and I'm *so* American," Nealy said, rolling her eyes. "Anyway, I'm glad to be back with you guys. I've missed y'all."

"Well, we missed you, too," Bob said. "But I have to ask. Is that guy as loaded as he looks?"

Nealy giggled before she answered. "Bob, let me put it this way. If I'd been playing *only* for money, I could honestly say that I'd hit the biggest jackpot of all times and I'd still be in Paris. I sure wouldn't have spent the last ten hours trekking across France on a noisy train. But, not all was lost. The scenery between the North of France and the Riviera is incredible. There were massive lakes and running rivers, miles of vineyards—Did you know that there is at least forty varieties of grapes? And in case anyone ever ask, Vitis vinifera is the viticultural term for grapes. Hmm, I'm impressed that I actually remembered that. But, from the looks on your faces, I seriously doubt that any of you give a *hoot-in-hell*. So, where was I," she thought for a second, giggling at herself.

"Stuff you saw from the train," Fern reminded.

"Oh, I know, the sunflower farms. There were acres of those huge yellow sunflowers. Did you know they came from France? Now that was a breathtaking sight, not to mention educational. It was like a field trip—Remember in elementary school when the teachers loaded the kids up on a big yellow bus and drove them out to Podunkville to look for butterflies, beetles and different witch hazel trees, like the sweetgum that's used in perfume and chewing gum. And don't forget those cotton patches with rows that stretched from here to yonder. Now, not a one of you *damn* Yankees better not tell me I ain't smart. Why I'm just a little ol' Southern walkin' encyclopedia," she said, mocking Scarlett O'Hara as she blinked her eyes and fanned herself with her napkin.

Everyone laughed and clapped. Nealy stood up and took a bow, but the smile on her face disappeared when she thought about Phillip and his horrible Rhett Butler impersonation. They were so good together because they made each other laugh. Now Nealy only felt like laughing when she pretended to be someone else for the amusement of others. Would she ever be that happy again, could she be? For some reason her happiness and unhappiness came from the men in her life. Finding them seemed to be easy, because, for some strange reason that she really didn't really understand, men found her desirable, but her relationships never seemed to work.

Sensing that all of her friends were waiting for the second act, she managed to find her smile. Who knows. Maybe one day she could return to Paris in the springtime with the real *Mr. Right,* if there is such a male-counterpart for her. Nealy glanced around the table at the sunburned faces who appeared to be waiting in anticipation, and she smiled a big toothy grin. "Well, I wish I had more knowledge to share with you colorful fellow sponges, but I'm all rung out. My only regret during the past twenty-four hours is that I had to leave—'I love Paris in the fall,' " she sang softly.

"You went to Paris?" Fern asked surprised.

"Yes, we flew up there yesterday on Michael's private jet."

"You're shittin' me? You dumped this guy, and he's got his own jet?" one of the other men snapped.

"As I said, money isn't everything. But I'll have to admit, I could have become accustomed to the lifestyle of the rich and famous," she smiled sadly. "Doesn't it really blow your mind when you let little things like broken promises and principles come between you and millions of dollars? I must be nuts! Oh, well, it's that old saying: 'Win a few, lose a few.' And since I'm three to zip, I'm out on men." Since Nealy knew that she wasn't hiding her anger and sadness very well, she got up and went to get herself some food from the buffet tables.

After dinner, they all went in to the casinos in Monte Carlo to try their luck at the blackjack tables. Nealy had never been very good at cards, but she wanted to play so that she could tell people back home that she gambled with people who laid down a grand on one hand. Unfortunately, and even with three nice men trying to help her, she got kicked off the table when she screamed *"Blackjack"* and pulled in all the chips, when actually her cards had added up to twenty-two. Oh, well, maybe Monte Carlo wasn't the place to learn. Or maybe, because of her bad mouth and behavior this was truly poetic justice.

When she returned to the ship that night, she bid farewell to everyone and turned in. It had been a very long day and she could barely keep her eyes open. When she opened the door to her cabin, she had an uninvited guest. "I think this is breaking and entering," she said sarcastically.

"It's my ship," he said, his *brown-velvet eyes* staring at her intently.

"I paid for this room regardless of who owns this ship. Therefore, you're trespassing and I'd like you to leave this minute." Nealy stood in the doorway firmly holding her own.

He got up and walked over towards the door. "I need to talk to you, please...and when I'm finished, if you still want me to leave, I will." He pulled her inside and closed the door. Then he led her over to the bed, and she sat down on the edge of it. Michael pulled up a chair to face her and took her hands in his.

"Michael, you're married. There isn't much else to say."

"But, Nealy, I'm only married because Victoria and I promised my father and her father that we would never divorce."

"Oh, no, not more deathbed promises."

"Par-don?"

"Nothing. I'm sorry. Go on."

"Victoria and I grew up together on the fishing boats. I didn't have much time for girls because I wanted to work hard and save my money. All I cared about was building big ships someday. However, when I turned sixteen, I could no longer ignore those urges, as most young boys can't, to have sex. Since Victoria and I knew each other so well, we started to experiment when our fathers left us with the boats at night to clean up. We were not in love, but we quickly became madly in lust because it was exciting and it gave us such pleasure. We didn't think about the consequences. We were kids. Then Victoria got pregnant. We knew our fathers would kill us if they found out. We didn't know what to do. So finally we went to them and told them that we were in love and that we wanted desperately to get married. We even told them that we would run away if they didn't give us their blessing. So finally, after our mothers cried and begged them, they gave us their blessings, but we had to sign a *Letter of Promise* to both them and to *God* that we would never divorce; with their strong Catholic beliefs they were certain that divorce would be a sin too great for us to bear. Victoria and I didn't even think about what we were promising. We just knew that we had to get married. We could not tell them that she was pregnant until we were married, and it had to happen soon. So, we signed the paper."

"Oh, Michael, I'm sorry," Nealy empathized, clearly understanding the meaning of such a promise.

"Please, Nealy, let me finish. There is so much more."

"Okay, I'm listening."

"Well, we were happy for a while. I finished school, but she didn't. Her father would not allow her to go to school after we told them about the baby. He just felt that she had moved into womanhood, and it did not look right to be in school when she was in the family way. Then we had Aury, who, thank goodness, came almost a month late, and then one year later, we had the twins. Then we matured, and we realized that we were not in love with each other, but that didn't matter. The only thing that mattered to me was building ships. I stayed gone most of the time, and Victoria took care of the children. That helped us to live with our promise. I worked all day, and I went to college at night. I wanted to be smart enough to build the ships of my dreams. We even lived with her family so that we could save money for my business. After seven years of marriage, I obtained my degree in Design Engineering. Our fathers offered to give me whatever money, over what I had saved, so that I could go to Glasgow, Scotland, to design and build my first ship. I was gone for six months. When I returned I had designed the most incredible cruise liner in the world, or so I thought; but then we had some production problems, so I had to go back to Scotland. I remained there for almost a year. During that time, both Victoria and I had met other people. We talked about a divorce, but when we approached our fathers, they wouldn't hear of it. They pulled out the paper that we had signed. They said that if we did not live up to our promise to *God* and to them, they would cut off the funds that I needed to finish building my ship. So, Victoria and I knew that we could never divorce because we had worked so hard and we wanted so much for ourselves and for our children."

"Oh, Michael, I'm really sorry. And I do understand, with all my heart," she said, clutching his hands.

"Then you will stay with me? We could be together for always. I will be faithful and love you more than anyone could ever love you. You are what I've wanted all my life. It would be the same as marriage but without the ceremony, which is, in fact, just an old Swedish peasant custom; we don't need that to be happy. The revolutionary St. Just said, "Those who love each other are man and wife." See, we could have our own vows to each other. That is what Claude and Victoria have done. It works for them. Oh, Nealy, please, darling...."

"Michael, I don't know. I don't think I can do that. If I ever consider another relationship, I want a husband and a family."

"I can give you a family. In fact, I'd want to make babies with you. I'm still young, Nealy. I could even be a better father now. I have more money than I need. And I could spend time with you and the children. I didn't do that with Victoria."

Nealy hugged him. She didn't know what to do or even how she felt. Too much had happened. "Michael, I need to think about this. I care about you a great deal, but I'm not sure that I'm really *in love* with you. Because you know what, if I were this probably wouldn't matter. I would want whatever I could have with you. I'm just not sure. This whole thing has confused me so much."

"If I go, will you sleep on it, please?"

"Yes. I'm just so tired after being on the train all day."

"You took the T.G.V.?"

"Yes. And that's another long story."

"No wonder I could not find you at the airport. I stayed there all night. I had people looking for you."

"I'm sorry, Michael, but I had to get away from you. I got so angry."

"Yes, I know. I fear you now, that's for sure."

Nealy giggled. "I'm sorry I bit you. I was a biter as a child. So it brought back fond memories of when I used to bite my brothers." She giggled, and Michael laughed slightly.

He pulled her up and hugged her tightly. "I hope you will not leave me, Nealy."

"Michael—"

"Not now. Sleep on it, my darling," he said softly, and then he left.

Nealy didn't sleep too well even though she felt exhausted. Her life had just started to take on a whole new light when all of this happened. She had even thought that she could live in France and start a new life, but now that all seemed impossible. How could she accept living with a man who had a wife and children, regardless of the circumstances? That was certainly not the way fairytales worked out. Of course with Michael, she would never want for anything. He could give her everything that she had ever dreamed about, the lifestyle of a princess, but she would always be his "girlfriend," "his lover," "his live-in," "his roomy," but never his wife. And how could she even consider having children with a married man? Well she couldn't. That was simply out of the question because for one thing, her children would be illegitimate in the eyes of God. No. Nealy James wasn't brought up that. Even as wonderful as most of her life would be, it would never work. Nealy decided that she would tell him tomorrow. Stringing him along would be useless and too hard for both of them. Also, she had made a decision to tell Kendall that they needed to go their separate ways. It had become obvious to her during this trip that she wasn't *in love* with him either. He was a terrific guy, and she loved and respected him, but she could never be *in love* with him. So, as soon as she got home, she would tell him. Nealy decided to be alone for a while. So much had happened to her. Maybe she just wasn't ready to commit to anyone again. And making a commitment to someone for the rest of her life was something that she couldn't possibly make on the spur of the moment.

The next morning Nealy met her friends in the dining room and ate breakfast. All of them wanted to go up the hill on Monaco Rock to tour the Jacques Cousteau Museum and the pink palace of Princess Grace. They made a date to meet in the lobby at nine o'clock.

Nealy wanted to run back to her cabin, brush her teeth, and grab a sweater because the day had turned out rather dreary and cold and damp. When she opened the door, she had another enormous arrangement of roses on the table. It had, at least, three dozen roses with lots of greenery. She smelled them, which is a natural thing to do, but she didn't open the card. And besides, she was in a hurry and she didn't want to get bogged down with guilty feelings over Michael. The flowers were beautiful, but it didn't change her mind. Their relationship had ended and she wanted to forget about *all* men. Nealy brushed her teeth while she dug her sweater out of her suitcase. Trying to do two things at once, she dripped toothpaste on her clothes. "Dammit," she cried, but she had to hurry before Michael came by and she had to break the bad news; just thinking about it made her nervous and all knotted up inside.

Upon the rock, Nealy and her friends wandered through the oceanographic museum and viewed giant—enormous—skeletons of various sea creatures from all over the world. In the basement, the sealife of the Mediterranean was on display with species of every shape, color and size. What a terrific education!

But even more than the sealife, Nealy had become fascinated by all the tourists from different countries that had gathered inside one museum. Hardly anyone spoke English. There were people wrapped from head to toe in garbs of clothing that covered every inch of their bodies except for their eyes and their jeweled foreheads. Like Michael Coupair they smiled at her with only their eyes.

On the streets, there were storefronts with clusters of the biggest grapes that she had ever seen in her life—each grape was the size of a half dollar. Nealy watched a man purchase a loaf of bread that was not wrapped, and when he turned to leave the store he stuck the loaf of bread under his armpit. Nealy almost gagged because she knew that he fully intended to take that bread home to his family for dinner. The French people had some strange customs, and they were not particularly friendly. Some of them were, of course, but for the most part they were not. Evidently, they still held it against all of the other countries that had "kicked their butts" during war times. Well, she smiled a lot anyway, and if they didn't smile back, too bad, it's their loss. But of course France is accustomed to losing, although they didn't like to admit it.

They hurried up to the palace to catch the changing of the guards, complete with fife and drums. It turned out to be very entertaining and quite moving. These guys really put on a show even though their expressions never changed. Charlotte and Fern dared Nealy to flirt with one of the guards who was really cute. So when he got right in front of her, she did her best *Marilyn Monroe* impersonation: Sweet eyes, puckered lips and sexy kisses, and seductive winks. Charlotte grabbed her chest and said, "Oh, my heart."

Inside the palace, there were rooms filled with more of that traditional gaudy furnishings and ornately painted ceilings. But, just the thought that real life princes and princess had lived there and that the walls contained history dating back to the Thirteenth century gave Nealy a warm-all-over feeling. They toured the salons, like the Louis Fifteenth, a marvel in gold and blue, and the Mazarin, which was panelled in wood with arabesque motifs, and the Throne Room, which contained a huge Renaissance fireplace where historic festivals and ceremonies had been held since the Sixteenth century. The Main Quadrangle was paved with three million white and colored pebbles forming immense geometrical patterns and the staircase was Carrara marble. The palace had traces of history scattered throughout, and even with all its gaudiness, it had a certain appeal to modern day Americans.

When Nealy arrived back in her room, she had a note on the door from Michael inviting her to join him for the evening. She sat down on the corner of the bed to think about whether or not she should go. It didn't make sense that she would even consider going. Was she a glutton for punishment or just plain stupid? But, it was her last night in France, and then she would go home and never see Michael Coupair again. So, it couldn't hurt anything, and besides, she honestly understood his situation. If only he'd told her the truth, instead of living a lie, which made her look like a fool in front of his family. And it didn't help when his damn daughter rubbed Nealy's face in the fact that she would never be anything other than her father's mistress. How could she forget that and go out with him again? Well, that's easy, her mother told her to. Gracie James always said, "Nealy, honey, you must forget to forgive, and you must forgive those who hurt you. You can't bottle up your anger. You must let it out, and then move on. You're a sweet girl. And I'd rather that you be too nice, than not nice enough. Always remember that no one is perfect; everyone makes mistakes. Now, dry those pretty green —"

Green! she interrupted her thoughts. What about green? The ballet. That's tonight. Michael had bought her that green evening gown for her to wear to the ballet at the Salle Garnier—the auditorium of the opera. Now she had to go with him; she couldn't miss the ballet.

At four-forty-five there was a knock at the door, which caught her in her underwear since Michael was not due to pick her up until five o'clock. "Just a minute," she called out, slipping into her dress and tugging at the zipper. "Come on zipper. If this damn dress wasn't so tight...I swear to god I'm poured into this baby," she complained. When she opened the door she turned pale as a ghost. "Kendall," she said breathlessly.

"Hi. I was in town so I thought I'd drop by and say hello," he said happily.

Nealy stood there speechless, staring at him. "I...I can't believe you're here."

He stepped inside and closed the door. "Didn't you get my note with the flowers?"

"Flowers?"

"Yes, these," he said, pointing to the roses in the vase. "I know these are the flowers that I sent because I had them mix red and yellow roses. I know you love them both."

"You sent those flowers?"

"Didn't you read the card?" he said, taking the card out of the roses and handing it to her.

She opened it and read the note:

> *I love you and I miss you. Maybe if I join you,*
> *you'll marry me. Love, Kendall.*

Her face turned even more pale. Even in her bright green dress she didn't have any color left. "I'm sorry, but I didn't read the note. I left in such a hurry this morning to go sightseeing that I didn't even see it."

"Well, it doesn't matter," he said, taking her into his arms and hugging her. "I'm here now. Nealy, I missed you so much. I knew that I'd made a mistake by letting you go without me. And the longer you were gone, the more I missed you." He pulled away and looked into her eyes. "I love you and I want you to marry me. Right here. Tonight. Although, you're not exactly dressed like a bride. You know, I've never seen you look quite this gorgeous, and certainly never this sexy. Damn, that's some dress. And I've never seen you show *any* cleavage, or any leg for that matter. Is that how they dress on this ship?"

"Some people do," she said softly, still trying to figure out what she was going to do. "Kendall, we need to talk."

"I know I've surprised you, but I love you. I had to come. I know now that I took you for granted. I let my practice keep me away from you. I'll never let that happen again. I promise I'll pay more attention to you and take you on vacations and spend time with you."

"Kendall, you didn't take me for granted. I worked as much as you did. That worked for us...or it seemed that it did. But the real problem is—"

A knock at the door interrupted her sentence and she froze, terrified at the thought of opening the door.

When she didn't answer it, and the knock came again, Kendall looked at her quizzically. "Aren't you going to answer the door?"

"Nealy." Michael called out.

She took a deep breath. "Coming." When she opened it, Michael walked inside. For a brief moment, he stared curiously at Kendall. Nealy could see his anger because his nostrils were beginning to flare and his face grew stern. "Michael, this is Dr. Kendall Cross, a friend of mine from Galveston."

"Hello," Kendall said, reaching out to shake Michael's hand as he glared at Nealy.

"Hello," Michael said coldly.

"Oh, dear," Nealy sighed, running her hand through her hair.

"What's going on here, Nealy?" Kendall asked bitterly.

"Ms. James and I are going to the ballet, so if you will excuse us," Michael said, walking over and taking her arm.

"Wait just a goddamn minute, pal. Ms. *James* isn't going anywhere with you. I flew all day and half the night to get here, and I just asked her to marry me!" he shouted, grabbing her waist and pulling her close to him.

Michael's eyes were fixed on Nealy. "And what did she tell you, Dr. Kendall?"

"It's Dr. Cross. And that's none of your business."

Michael maintained eye contact with her waiting for her to answer. "Nealy, do you intend to marry this Dr. Cross?"

Nealy looked up and moved her hands away from her mouth. She could barely bring herself to speak as she looked into Michael's eyes, just as she had the first time they met. "Uh...I—"

"I think I get the message, Nealy. It certainly didn't take you long to find someone else," Kendall shouted.

"Kendall, this wasn't planned. I met Michael in New York before I ever met you."

His expression teetered between hurt and anger. "You've been seeing this guy in New York and stringing me along?"

"No," she cried. "I met him in New York a year ago. And when I got on the ship, I ran into him again. This is his ship."

Kendall turned red in the face. "He owns this ship?"

"I own more than just this ship, Dr. Cross," Michael spoke up. "And I, too, want to be with Nealy forever."

"I get it, Nealy. I never could give you as much as your fuckin' rich ex-husband and so you found someone else who could."

"Kendall, it's not like that," she cried.

"The hell it isn't. I'm not blind. And it's obvious what's going on here. I guess that's why you didn't bother to read the note with the flowers. You were too busy being wined and dined and God knows what else by your rich Latin loverboy here. Don't try to deny it, Nealy. That dress cut down to your belly button and up to your ass speaks for itself."

"I will not have you insulting her," Michael said angrily.

"And you can kiss my ass!" he yelled, walking towards the door. Angrily, he stared at Nealy. "I guess you had this planned all along since he owns this ship—"

"I swear I didn't know—"

"Save it, Nealy. It really doesn't matter anymore. But it's funny how you know me better than I know myself. You knew I wouldn't go. This worked out perfect for you, didn't it? What a idiot I've been! I thought you'd miss me. I came here to marry you, and I find you with another man. But that's the problem. I'm just not exciting enough for you, isn't that right? Well, don't worry about it. I knew the answer would be no, but I just thought I'd ask anyway. You can't blame a guy for trying. I'll see myself out. Good-bye, Nealy." He walked out and slammed the door.

Nealy shut her eyes, but she could feel the tears forcing their way out. Michael walked over and put his arms around her, and she placed her head on his shoulder. "I'm sorry, Nealy. I'm glad that you told me about him, or I would have punched the guy. But I understand his pain. I'm in the same boat, literally," he smiled, making her smile back at him.

"I had no idea he would come here. I feel so bad."

"Nealy, you can't feel bad. He chose not to come with you, and even if he had, I would have taken you away from him. I had to have you."

"Isn't this ironic? I have two men who say they love me, but I can't be with either one because I don't love Kendall and you're married."

"Nealy, I talked to Victoria about a divorce. I explained to her that since our parents are gone now that maybe we should go on with our lives. We are going to talk to our children and our Priest. She wants to marry Claude as much as I want to marry you."

"Oh, Michael, I don't know if I can let you do that. You made *too many promises*, and the problem with the world today is that too many of those promises are broken."

"But you will leave me if I can't marry you."

"Michael, I have to go home, at least for now. I have a business and a life back there. And I need to be completely sure of my feelings because if I married you, I would have to live your life, not mine."

"Nealy, darling, that would not be so bad. I could give you a better life. You wouldn't need a business. You would have everything that you ever wanted."

"I know that, Michael. Don't you see, I would feel dependent on you. Owned."

"But you would own me, too."

"I don't want to own you. And besides, that's different for a man. By nature men feel independent. Women have to fight for their independence. And, Michael, I've seen how possessive you are with me."

"Nealy, that's only because I feel insecure about your love. Once we're married, I will know that you love me. I won't have to be jealous of other men. Anyway, you will always be with me."

"Michael, I'm very friendly, and I can't change that. Even though I'm very loyal, I'm still who I am. And I know from experience how difficult that would be for you."

"If you are saying that I would still be jealous, you are right. But I'm that way because you are so beautiful. When you become my wife I can still be jealous. A little jealousy is good for men. It keeps them on their toes, keeps them good lovers."

"Michael, you just don't understand."

"I only understand that I love you and that I want you. Now I want to take you out to dinner and show you off in that dress. It makes you look like a movie star, but even more beautiful."

"Thank you," she blushed. "And thanks to you I don't even feel self-conscious. In fact, I feel sexy for the first time in my life. This will be my coming-out-of-the-closet night on the town. My friends always said 'If you got it, flaunt it.' So, I guess that's what I'm doing," she said, smiling at him.

Michael pulled her into his arms and kissed her until she could feel both of them wanting more, so she pulled away and took a deep breath. This was not the time for sex, especially since she could see Kendall's hurt face whenever she closed her eyes. Why did he have to come to France? Nealy never wanted to hurt him like that, but, because of this, she didn't have to tell him that it was over between them. Now he could find a nice person to settle down with and have babies and chickens and ducks and horses and cows and a life filled with rodeos and horse shows.

Michael took her to dinner at the Folie Russe in the Hotel Loews which had to be terribly expensive. After they ate, they danced slowly so Michael could snuggle up to her. He reminded her of the life he could give her and talked about children and how much he wanted to start over. Of course he knew that was exactly what she wanted to hear. And since she would be leaving the following day, this would be his last chance to persuade her to come back.

They left the restaurant and the limousine dropped them off at the atrium in front of the auditorium, which was paved in marble and surrounded by twenty-eight Ionic columns in onyx. The red and gold interior depicted the grandeur of past centuries with a profusion of bas-reliefs, frescoes, and sculptures; Nealy craved culture. Michael knew that the ballet would capture her heart. More than anything, he admired her deep sensitivity and her kindred spirit. He even loved her feistiness, which, in time, would make her a great lover, wild with passion.

When they returned to the ship, Michael held her close. "Please stay with me tonight," he begged.

"I can't, Michael. Part of me wants to, but then another part of me says no. I've hurt Kendall, and I'm confused about us and France and your wife and children. The list just goes on and on."

"I just want to hold you for the last time. I promise to be good, even though I got so turned on every time I looked at you in that dress. I noticed others looking at you, too. I think you turned on many men tonight. Their wives should be thanking you for the *romp* that is being bestowed upon them at this very moment."

"Michael," she said, blushing. "I didn't see anyone staring at me."

"Yes, but that's because I helped you appreciate your beauty instead of being so inhibited by it."

"Well, you certainly did that. I'm happy to give you all the credit. I always played down what I had so others wouldn't feel threatened by me. But thanks to you, I'm really proud of my looks and my body now. I like the new me."

"Then why don't you show me? I'd like to see a very erotic strip tease with a sexy corset and silky black stockings. It makes me crazy for you just thinking about it," he said, his *brown-velvet eyes* seducing her.

"Michael, I'm saving that for my wedding night, that is, if I ever get married again. And if I do, that night will be more than just sexy; it will be *downright erotic*," she smiled seductively. Then, unable to keep a straight face, she giggled.

"Then I had better be present on your wedding night. I don't want to miss that performance."

Nealy kissed him good-night and hugged him tightly. She owed Michael so much, after all, he had been responsible for giving her a new lease on life; a freedom to do or say what comes naturally; a taste for experimenting and touching; the nerve to let go; and a desire for being naughty and liking it and not feeling guilty before, during, or after she did it. Yes, she had really grown in two weeks, allowing herself to be transformed into a woman with so much more to offer. Nealy had always liked herself, that wasn't the problem. But now she loved herself, and she had a new appreciation for being a woman.

Early the next morning, Michael served Nealy breakfast in bed, but this time he actually brought it himself. After trying for two hours to talk her into to staying, he helped her pack, but he didn't give up. "Please, Nealy, stay with me. I'll settle this matter with Victoria. We can get married. Just don't go."

"Michael, I have to go. I have a business, remember?"

"Can I see you in New York?"

"It's possible."

"Nealy, everything is possible if you want it bad enough."

"Michael, that's just it. I have to want it bad enough. I'm not sure what I want. I'm nervous about leaving my home and my family. You said yourself many times that I'm *very American*. And you're right, I am. I can't speak this language. I need to think about this. I don't make instant decisions anymore. I was always the kind of person who thought things out before I acted, that is, until I said 'Yes' to Jerrod. And that was a terrible mistake that caused us more pain than I could ever imagine. So, until I can say yes beyond any shadow of a doubt, I can't say it."

"I'll come after you. You know I can't let you go."

"Oh, Michael, that's what you think now. But after I'm gone, you'll forget all about me. You have a passion for beautiful women. And, trust me, there are a lot of woman looking for to-die-for millionaires. But I don't have to tell you that. Remember? *'You've had many women.'* I'll just be one more to add to the *'many'* pretty-play-things that you entertained. In a month, I'll be history," she said using his own words.

"Nealy, you are so wrong. I will show you. I will come for you in New York or Texas or wherever. We lost each other once, and then we met again. I think this is destiny, darling."

"Maybe you're right. Oh, I don't know, Michael, I've had an incredible time with you. You're the most gorgeous man that I've ever seen in my life. I used to lie awake at night and imagine your *brown-velvet eyes* watching me. I'll never forget the first time I saw you in that elevator. I couldn't even speak. You had this tremendous power over me."

"I could see that, my darling. And I must admit, I played with your mind because of it."

"You did? Michael, that's mean and terrible!"

"I loved doing it because I wanted you to think about me. Nealy, darling, I always want you to think about me. I want you to imagine our making love and making babies together. They would be so beautiful. Please make love to me so you can lie in bed at night and imagine our lovemaking and imagine how our children will look. You won't be able to resist their sweet, beautiful little faces as you nurture them with the milk from your perfect breasts," he said, pushing her up against the wall and caressing her breasts as he kissed her softly.

"Michael, you're making me crazy."

"With desire, I pray."

"Yes. No...I don't know. It's just making this more difficult."

"I must have you before you leave," he insisted, picking her up and carrying her over to the bed.

"Michael, we are *not* making love. I've explained all of this to you. And I'm glad that we didn't actually make love. God knows we came close, but we didn't. I've never made love to a married man, and even though you and Victoria are separated, you're still married to her. If and when you ever get divorced, call me. Then we can talk about this, but until then I'm not making love with you."

"I have feelings, too, Nealy. Doesn't that matter to you?"

"Yes, your feelings matter to me, but I have principles. Getting involved with a married man only leads to heartbreak. And believe me, I've had all the heartbreak that I need for one lifetime, thank you."

"This is different. I haven't lived with my wife for more than ten years. You just don't want me."

"Michael, I refuse to argue with you. The answer is still 'No.' Remember what your father said. 'No, means No!' So, stop it. Let me up, please."

Slowly, he got up, glaring at her for a minute before leaving the cabin.

Nealy packed the rest of her things as she thought about how men say and think the same things. Universally, they must all subscribe to a newsletter with helpful tips on dealing with women: If she says, "No," make her feel guilty; If she says, "It's over," try hard—literally—for one last sex scene in the sack; How to make her believe with every fiber of your being that you can't live without her; *Never* allow her to have her own life; and *always* tell her to think about making love with you and making babies with you (This one really works, fellas!) Nealy couldn't wait to get off that ship and on that airplane and back to America. Under her breath, she began to sing:

"My country tis of thee, keep these bas-tards away from me. Let freedom ring."

Then she fell down on the bed giggling hysterically to keep from crying.

As Nealy stood outside the bus talking to her new friends, she noticed that suddenly everyone stopped talking. Intuitively, she turned to see what they saw, but this time she wasn't the least bit surprised. So, in her best Mae West impression, she said, *"Now, listen, sugar, we simply must stop meeting like this. I'm a nice girl, and, hey, I got a reputation to protect!"* For the first time, Nealy didn't experience that awkwardness that she normally felt when she looked into those magnificent eyes *brown-velvet eyes* surrounded by a perfect face.

"Nealy, may I talk with you, please?" he asked politely.

"I can't, Michael, I'm fixin' to leave."

"It will only take a minute. And don't worry, the bus will not leave you. I own that, too," he said arrogantly.

"Well, in that case, I guess I have time. Excuse me, folks," she said, her voice reflecting his pompous attitude.

They walked down the dock along the harbor. "I don't want you to leave angry with me," he said.

"Michael, you're pushing me to do something that I don't feel right about."

"I'm sorry," he said, stopping and turning her to face him. "I don't want you to go. I was grasping for anything to make our relationship more binding."

"Why do men feel like that?"

"Like what?"

"Like they need something to force you to stay with them. Men are much more insecure than women. They can't relax and just let things happen naturally. You have to trust me, Michael. If this is meant to be, it will happen. We don't have to consummate our relationship for it to work out. Love doesn't mean *making love,* it means trusting and sharing something very special. And when love is real, it doesn't disappear. It stays in your heart."

"I'm coming to New York in two weeks. Can I see you?" he asked.

"I'm not sure if I'll be in New York in two weeks, Michael. I have an apartment there, but I also have a home and a business in Galveston."

"I know exactly where you live in New York and in Texas."

"How do you know that?"

"I know everything about you, Nealy. That's what love is."

"That's spying."

"I prefer to call it caring. Nealy, I will find you," he said, kissing the back of each hand.

"You make it sound as if I'm running away from you, Michael. I'm not. You said that you didn't want to share me with another man. Well, I don't want to share you with another woman. I prefer to sleep with my own husband, not the husband of another woman. Is that too much too ask?"

"This would not be sharing."

"Michael, it all boils down to the fact that I don't want to shack up. If I share your bed, I want to share your name. And I want children—legitimate children. I don't want my grandmother rolling over in her grave," she said, crossing her eyes and making a silly face so that he would laugh, or at least smile.

Finally, he smiled and hugged her. "Okay, you win. I'll be in New York or Texas in two weeks. I want to see you unless you marry someone else who is more available before I get there."

"Michael, that's the most ridiculous thing that I've ever heard in my life.

Getting married is the last thing on my mind right now. I need to concentrate on getting through one day at a time...but I'll admit one last thing: I'm going to miss you. This has been the most interesting two weeks of my life, not counting the most educational."

"My darling, you were one of my best students. Still a little modest, but you are on the way to freedom I think," he shrugged.

"Michael, thanks for showing me your country. It's very beautiful and fascinating. I'll never forget this trip. Just call me, Nealy James, Travel Ambassador to France."

He laughed. Then, after a long seducing look with those eyes that had paralyzed her from the first moment she saw them, he kissed her. With the pink palace sitting high upon the hill behind them and the blue waters of the Mediterranean sprawled out in front of them, this scene came right out of *Love In the Afternoon*.

On the airplane, Nealy felt numb. The last two weeks didn't seem real. In fact, she kept pinching herself to make sure that she hadn't fallen asleep on the plane on her way to France and dreamed up the entire story. She had never expected to see the *brown-velvet eyes* again, much less spend two weeks with him. And the fact that he said he loved her and wanted to spend the rest of his life with her seemed outrageous. Nealy reflected upon her entire life, and the more she thought about it, the more colorful it became. The past five years had been without a doubt the most interesting and exciting and wonderful, and, at times, the most depressing, period in her life. Most people could live an entire lifetime without going through some of the crazy and somewhat trying things that she had been through. Geezus, why didn't she read the card on those flowers? If she had, maybe she could have talked Kendall out of flying all the way to France. Now he hated her because he thought that she went there to be with another man. What a mess, she thought. How could things get more screwed up? The more she hurt others, the more she came to understand what her mother had meant. How could she hate, when she didn't want to be hated? That is why she had forgiven Jerrod. Life takes turns: people hurt, and they get hurt. Life is funny that way, but hopefully it won't come around too many more times for Nealy James. She just wanted to love and be loved by a man that she would believe to be the most fabulous man in the world. When Nealy got back home she planned to talk to Kendall, that is, if he would talk to her. Even though the relationship had ended, she didn't want him to hate her. Nealy still valued his friendship, and she didn't want him to think that she would deliberately hurt or betray him. The thing with Michael had just happened...and her trip of a lifetime, well, that had definitely turned out to be the ultimate challenge.

CHAPTER FORTY-NINE

NEALY HAD TELEPHONED Betty Lou from New York and asked her to pick her up at the airport. Under the circumstances, she knew that Kendall would not be there as planned. After leaving the airport, they stopped at the Steak and Ale on the Gulf freeway to eat dinner and catch up on things. Nealy told her all about France and Michael Coupair, starting with their original meeting in New York, which made Betty Lou green with envy. Why couldn't she find someone like that? Betty Lou would gladly shack-up with some rich, good-looking guy and let him spoil her rotten. But, when Nealy told her that Kendall had come to France and found her with him, her face turned almost as white as Nealy's had that day in France. Betty Lou's only comment was "Oh, shit!" They talked about France and men and the fact that Betty Lou was considering getting married again. As she talked about meeting this wonderful doctor named Ethan from Iowa whom she had met at Methodist Hospital, Nealy drifted in and out of the conversation. Betty Lou just chatted away about how she had met this doctor when she went to the hospital to do some research for a paper that she was writing on *Physical Therapy Programs for Convalescing Heart Patients* for her masters degree. Ethan was the doctor that had been asked to spend a little time with her for a question and answer period about the disease. As it turned out, they spent more than a *little* time together talking about a lot more than heart disease. Their time together quickly became a *matter of the heart* alright, and Ethan had all the right answers. But, there was only one problem: three of her friends had married doctors, Nealy to name one, and their marriages had ended in divorce.

While Betty Lou discussed all the wonderful qualities of the new man in her life and her fears about marriage, Nealy had been so lost in thought that she failed to hear all of the details. Not that she didn't care about Betty Lou, she loved her dearly, but the thought of ever being married to Jerrod and never being married to Phillip made her crazy with frustration. Why had she allowed herself to be so foolish? If only she had known then what she knows now; But doesn't everyone use that as an excuse? Hopefully Betty Lou had learned from Nealy's mistakes and this guy would be the right one; God knows she deserved to find happiness. Nealy had been afraid that Betty Lou's problems with Beaux and her experience with divorce had left her too bitter to ever love another

man again. Nealy would never forget that day in the courtroom. That awful
Judge Dick—perfect name for a male chauvinist—made her out to be some
whiny woman who had refused to be submissive to her husband's sexual needs.
Of course Beaux had denied ever forcing Betty Lou to have sex with him against
her will, and the judge actually smirked when he discounted the accusations,
even though he did grant her a divorce. That bastard! His insults caused Betty
Lou to cry for days, but at least she was out of that marriage. Betty Lou was not
a fighter, so Nealy had feared for her life until she finally left Beaux and held
him at bay with a restraining order. But Nealy had never thought of herself as
a fighter either until five years before when Jerrod tried to stop her from buying
her studio; she found out real quick that beneath her angelic exterior lived a
fiery temper just ready and waiting to strike back if and when the time came.

Betty Lou had dropped Nealy off around eight o'clock, and she crawled
into bed about ten, but her days and nights were so mixed up because of the six
hour time difference between the United States and France that she couldn't
get to sleep. After growing tired of tossing and turning and thinking about
things that she didn't want to think about, she got up and made herself a cup of
hot chocolate. A cold front had come in early, just in time for the padded
pumpkins, ghosts and goblins who planned to hit the streets the following
evening to trick-or-treat. Already, she missed the moderate climate on the
Riviera. Just as she turned the kitchen light off, she thought that she heard a
car pull up in her driveway, and then moments later she heard scratches on her
back door which she knew belonged to Chance. She put on her heavier robe
and rushed back into the kitchen to let him in. He was so happy to see her that
he raced through the house jumping and whining, and after their happy reunion,
Nealy looked up at Kendall. "Thanks for bringing him home."

"Well, I had to meet some people at the clinic, so I took Chance with me.
He's been a little restless, so I decided to bring him on home. He missed you.
We both did."

"I'm glad you did. I couldn't sleep, so I had some hot chocolate. Want
some?"

"No, thanks."

"Kendall, we need to talk if you can stay a minute."

"Nealy, I don't think there is anything left to say."

"Please, Kendall, just hear me out."

He sat down at the kitchen table, but he appeared distant and sad. "Okay,
what?"

"I didn't know that Michael Coupair would be in France. I barely knew
the man. Remember when I had surgery and went to New York for that month?"

"You told me that you went to New York, but you never mentioned the
French guy," he said, staring at her coldly.

"I didn't mention him because there wasn't anything to mention—my gosh,

I'm sick of telling this story—I dropped my packages in the elevator. He helped me pick them up. I assumed that he had an apartment in the building because I saw him a few times after that and we spoke, but that's all. I had no idea who he was or what he did. And then, when I got on that ship in Monte Carlo, there he was. He showed me around in each port. Kendall, he's married. He has three almost grown children who live in Paris. I'll admit his marriage is not traditional. Some Europeans see things differently than we do. He dressed me up. He took me out. He wined and dined me. Let me tell you, it was an adventure, but I came home. I don't want you to think that I went there to see him. I wanted you to go with me, remember? In fact, I begged you to go. And when you didn't, well, this thing with him just happened. It was a *timing* thing. He was alone. I was alone. But I'm sorry that you came there and got the wrong impression. I never meant to hurt you. I value your friendship. You're a very special person, and you have so much to offer."

"Are you trying to tell me that you want to be friends?"

Nealy looked at him sadly because she knew how this was going to hurt him. "Yes, but please don't hate me, Kendall."

"You don't love me, do you?"

"I love you...but I don't think I'm *in love* with you. I need to be honest."

"You don't know? How is that being honest? Either you are or you're not," he said impatiently.

Nealy stared out the window. "Then I'm not, I guess. Kendall, I thought about you, but I didn't miss you. That must mean that I'm not in love with you."

"Why would you miss me? You had that millionaire French guy showering you with gifts and flowers and shit."

"How did you know he gave me flowers?"

"Nealy, that's why you didn't bother to read the card I sent. You assumed they were from him. Your room looked like a florist. It didn't take a genius to figure that out."

Nealy couldn't look at his hurt face. She wanted to cry, but that wouldn't help the situation. "I'm really sorry, Kendall."

He reached across the table and took her hand in his. "Let's not call it quits just yet. Just give it a little time. Let me do things a little differently. If it's romance you want, I can try to be a little more romantic. At one time, we had something special, Nealy, I know we did. I felt comfortable with you. But maybe because of that, I took you for granted. I should have gone with you and held you under the moonlight. I know that now. Please give me another chance."

"But, Kendall, I really don't think that things would have been different because..." Oh, God how she wanted to tell him the truth. After dreaming about Michael Coupair, she had to find out what it all meant, and what kissing him and staring intimately into those *brown-velvet eyes* would be like. If Kendall had gone, he would have gotten hurt anyway because she could not have resisted Michael Coupair's advances. And Kendall's presence would not have stopped Michael from pursuing her affections. What Michael wants, Michael gets. The scene would have been much worse. And Nealy, even as much as she would not have wanted to hurt Kendall, she would have because she needed a sexual adventure; she had lived a terribly sheltered life and she had all the inhibitions to prove it. It would have been different if she and Phillip would have stayed together because he satisfied her, but Kendall didn't. But she just couldn't tell him. "I needed—"

"Nealy," he interrupted softly, "I know what you needed. Please, I deserve another chance. I love you. I just want to show you how much." He pulled her up into his arms and held her tightly for several minutes.

Nealy didn't have the heart to tell him no. Maybe he could win her over. Even though she didn't think so, she had to let him try. Why was she so soft hearted? Why couldn't she just say "No," and kick these men out of her life? "Kendall, I'm glad you're not still angry with me. I never want you to hate me."

"I could never hate you. I love you, silly," he smiled at her. "Get some sleep. Want to go on a picnic tomorrow?"

She smiled at the very idea of Kendall on a picnic. "Okay. That'll be fun."

As he drove out of the driveway, she wondered if she could ever love him enough to marry him. Kendall was so good, but something was missing in their relationship. But people can come out of their shell, just as she had in France. Change isn't impossible, so maybe he will.

The next day he picked her up at eleven o'clock, and they drove up to League City Park to enjoy the sunshine and picnic on the steep bank of Dickenson Bayou. They spread out their blanket and ate a nice, snacky-type lunch filled with sandwiches, fruit and assorted cookies that Kendall had his housekeeper prepare for them. Afterwards, they lay next to each other and talked about her trip, with the exception of Michael Coupair, of course. Then in the afternoon, they played baseball with some children who needed a couple of extra players. The day had been sunny and happy, but Nealy didn't feel moved by his presence. And when he kissed her at the door, it didn't turn her on. Living a lie made her feel guilty. But maybe she just needed more time, after all she wasn't in any hurry to make decisions about her future.

On Monday, the studio turned into a madhouse, which spilled over into the entire week. Poor Francine had pushed herself to the limit, and, at seven months pregnant, the heavy schedule exhausted her. Kay, the assistant that Nealy hired the year before had been great for the studio, but Nealy needed to hire one more person, since Francine would be taking maternity leave soon, and she needed to go back East. Nealy had hired a young man named Fred to work in her New York agency. He had several years experience, and for the most part, he had adapted to Nealy's practices very quickly. They had developed a great working relationship, and she trusted him with her business whenever she had to return to Texas.

Nealy never dreamed that her studio could get any busier, but it seemed to grow larger every month, which made her feel that she hadn't let Miss Janik down. Of course, Miss Janik, who had just recently become Mrs. Marshall Hibbard, hadn't had much time to worry about the studio; she was busy traveling back and forth between homes in Switzerland and Hawaii with her new husband. It seemed strange that after all those years alone, Miss Janik had finally married. The whole thing was ironic because she married her lawyer who had taken care of her business for twenty years, who just happened to be her high school sweetheart. It's funny how things work out.

After two weeks of fourteen and fifteen hour days, Nealy felt as though she needed another vacation. It had been very hectic, but between Nealy and Kay and Francine, they had managed. Nealy had also hired a new teacher named Matthew, but she and the others called him Matty, a nickname that his parents had given to him at an early age. Matty had taken lessons from Miss Janik since childhood, and amazingly he had survived all the teasing over the years. Nealy thought that his drive might help other young boys who wanted to dance but who didn't want to be called a *sissy*. Also, Nealy thought that it would be good to add some male influence to her staff, and besides, Matty was a very serious student with aspirations of dancing on Broadway someday. Nealy's goal was to help him once he graduated from college, which was still three years away. By that time, she should have established herself in New York as an agency that represented talented performers with impressive credits to their names. Even though she had higher expectations, Nealy wasn't complaining because her first year had been much better than she had ever expected. Of course Tony's clients and contacts had given her a jump-start, and Fred's know how and his connections had helped as well. Nealy had been fortunate when it came to employees; she treated them as equals and paid them well, which pays off in the long run.

If all went well, Nealy would be back in New York within the next two weeks. Being in New York always made her sad because she couldn't help thinking about Phillip from the time she got there until the time she left again. Almost everyday she would pick up the phone to call and say 'hi,' but she always hung up before she finished dialing. It became a ritual every afternoon right before she left for lunch. And even though she didn't go through with it, it made her think about the times when she called him each day at that time to plan their lunch together. Although it seemed as if it had been forever since Nealy had seen Phillip, it had only been one year, one month, and eleven days; it had been too long. But regardless of how long it had been, it didn't make him any less married, or her any less miserable.

Nealy left the studio at five o'clock on Friday since she had accepted an invitation to go to dinner with Kendall. She really wanted to go home and crash, but she hadn't spent much time with him since she got home, so she really couldn't refuse. He told her that he would be there around seven which gave her plenty of time to take a nice hot bath in order to relax before they went out.

At six-fifteen, Nealy was resting peacefully, submerged under mounds of bubbles, when she heard a knock at the front door. She couldn't imagine who it could be unless she and Kendall had gotten their wires crossed about the time. But, even if they had, he wouldn't go to her front door. As she stepped out of the tub, she grabbed her towel and wrapped it around her bubble-covered body. As she made her way through the house towards the front door, she left wet foot prints on the hardwood floors. When she opened it, she only cracked it enough to see who it was without exposing the fact that she had been to in the tub. As she stuck her head around the door, she couldn't believe her eyes. "Jerrod!" she cried, shocked to see him standing on her front porch. What are you doing here?"

"I saw your car in the garage, so I thought I'd stop by. Can I come in?"

"Well, I'm not very presentable."

"You must have been in the tub. You have bubbles on your face and in your hair," he said, smiling.

Nealy giggled. "Yeah, I still love bubble baths."

"I've seen you covered in bubbles before, so I don't mind."

"Oh, okay. Come on in," she said, opening the door. "I need to put some clothes on, so make yourself at home." As she started to the bedroom he whistled and she turned to make a face at him.

He smiled, watching her closely. "You still look great in a towel, Neal."

"Thanks," she called out as she closed the bedroom door. Quickly, she put on a sweat suit and took down her hair which she had piled on top of her head before she got into the tub. "Well, I haven't heard from you in quite a while. How are you?" she said, walking back into the living room and sitting down on the opposite end of the couch.

"I'm doing great. My residency is going great. And I just finished almost a years worth of counseling with Zimmerman."

"I didn't know that you were still seeing Jim."

"I never stopped. I told you that I would get help, and I did. Nealy," he said, scooting over much closer to her on the couch, "I finally have control over my life. I'm drug free, and I rarely even have a beer. Also, I quit that nonsense at the fraternity house, and I've tried to stay away from women. You would be proud of me, at least, I think you would."

"Oh, Jerrod, I'm very proud of you. You know, you do seem much calmer. You're more like that handsome guy that I fell in love with thirteen years ago."

"Neal," he said, taking her hands in his, "do you think that we could try again?"

"What?"

"Neal, now wait. Please, just hear me out. I told Jim that I would wait until I had been completely free of my addiction problems for at least six months before I even talked to you about trying to put our marriage back together again. Well, it's been almost a year. I'm not asking to move back in. I'm just asking if we could start over and take it one day at a time. I'd really like to try again, to make a fresh start. Baby, we had a great relationship once. I really think it's worth starting over. Neal, is that possible?"

"Jerrod, you're serious aren't you?"

"I went to see the priest last week. He said that I should talk to you. In the eyes of the church, we're still husband and wife, and in my heart, we are, too. I've never stopped loving you. And, with what I've been through, I know I can be everything that you want me to be. I know that I can be a faithful, loving husband to you and a good father to our children."

Nealy stared at him. She could hardly believe her ears. "Jerrod...I don't know what to say. I never expected this to happen." Nealy got up and walked into the kitchen.

Jerrod followed her. "I stayed away from you until I could honestly say that I'm well. Jim Zimmerman said that he would be happy to talk to you. I've tried really hard to pull myself together, Neal, and it's only because of you that I was able to do it. When I heard that you were about to marry that duck doctor, I almost threw in the towel, but Jim convinced me to keep going. He told me not to give up because you hadn't married the guy yet."

Nealy almost lost it when he called Kendall a *duck doctor*, but she couldn't dare laugh because that would only encourage him. And besides, it would be mean. So she tried to concentrate on the crazy things that he was saying. "Jerrod, this has really caught me off-guard. When you stopped calling me, I assumed that you had gone on with your life, so I did, too."

"Neal, is there someone else? You can't be *in love* with that duck doctor."

"Quit calling him a duck doctor," she said, not finding the humor in it anymore and becoming annoyed at his lack of respect. "How would you like someone calling you a pump doctor? Kendall's a veterinarian."

"I don't care what he is. I asked you if you were in love with him?"

"Yeah, I love him."

"But you're not *in love* with him, are you?"

Nealy locked eyes with him, and she couldn't lie. "No," she sighed. Nealy could feel her strong physical attraction for him stirring inside. Why were physical attractions so strong? Even when a person stops loving someone that physical *thing* still exists. And the crazy thing was that she didn't want him, it was just there pulling at her. She wanted to break and run, but something held her in place.

"Then why can't we at least see each other. I'll go slow. I won't push you, Neal, I promise. We'll start with dinner and let things happen from there. I think we can make it this time. I want my wife back. I'll do anything," he pleaded, moving closer and closer to her.

The closer Jerrod got to her, the more she eased away from him, until she backed into the wall beside the sink. Out of nervousness, Nealy put her fingernail in her mouth and bit down on it. "But, Jerrod, I just don't think—"

"Neal, I know you loved me. And I think that you still do," he said softly. He pulled her finger out of her mouth and placed her arms around his waist. Then he placed his hands on each side of her face and guided her lips up to meet his. Deeply, he kissed her, and then he put his arms around her, pulling her closer to his body.

"Jerrod," she said, trying to pull away from him. Then there came a knock at the kitchen door and seconds later it swung open.

Jerrod loosened his embrace, but he didn't let go of her. "Are you in a habit of coming inside without an invitation?"

"Jerrod, I'll handle this," Nealy snapped. "Kendall, I'm sorry," she said, pulling Jerrod's arms from around her.

"Nealy, this is the second time in two weeks. Is this intentional? Why don't you just tell me to get lost?"

"Kendall, wait," she said, walking towards the back door. Jerrod caught her by the arm and she stopped mid-way between the two of them.

"I think I've seen enough. But tell me, Nealy, is this someone that you've just met, too?"

"This is my ex-husband, Jerrod Jones. This is Kendall Cross," she said, turning back to look up at Jerrod. "Maybe you should go."

"I'm not going anywhere. I told you. I want my wife back. I love you, Neal."

"Nealy, I can't believe that you'd do that after everything he did to you."

"I haven't done anything. Jerrod just stopped by to talk."

"No, I came by to get you back. She still loves me, Cross, and she just admitted that she didn't love you."

"Jerrod, stop it! I didn't tell you that," she said, glaring at him.

"Well, why don't *you* tell *me that*, Nealy," Kendall yelled. "Go ahead. Tell me! Then I'll leave."

"No, tell him how you felt when you kissed me, Neal. I felt it. And you *had* to."

"Stop it! Both of you. I can't handle this. I want both of you to leave. Now!" she shouted, motioning for Jerrod to leave through the front door and Kendall to leave through the back door. She felt like an airline hostess directing her passengers towards the exits. But neither of them moved; it was more like a Mexican standoff. "I don't love either of you. There, I said it. Now, get out!"

Both of them looked at her in complete surprise, but then they turned, and like opponents retreating to their corners, they left angrily, slamming the doors behind them. Nealy sat down at the kitchen table because her legs were shaking so much that she could barely stand. "Dear *God*, I can't believe this." Two weeks ago she came home from France thinking that she would be free of men forever, and now she had more than she wanted or needed. Why was it always feast or famine with men? The time had come for her to go to New York. At least there she could find a little peace and quiet, that is, if Michael didn't show up. Well, the way she felt about men at this moment, she could easily tell him to *get lost,* too.

Nealy had moved half of her things to New York so that she wouldn't need to pack every time she went. Now all she had to do was get dressed and lock up the house. Instead of dropping Chance off at Randy and Francine's—Kendall certainly wouldn't be taking care of him anymore she decided—to take him with her. After all, Chance had never been to New York, so it was high time that he went to the Big Apple; this would be his trip of a lifetime.

On her way out of town, she stopped by the studio and called Francine to tell her that she needed to get back to New York. She had left written instructions for her, just in case she had forgotten to tell her something. Thank *God* for Francine.

CHAPTER FIFTY

AT THE AIRPORT, Nealy gave Chance to the baggage people who put him in a big cage. Although he seemed confused, he liked going so much that he licked them and wagged his tail. Nealy boarded the plane and finally, for the first time in the past three hours, she drew a deep breath and exhaled a huge sigh of relief. Her life had momentarily gotten way out of control and all men were starting to get on her nerves. If she ever heard another one say, '*I love you*,' it would be too soon.

When she arrived at the apartment, it was almost two o'clock in the morning because she had caught the last plane out of Houston. Nealy let Chance sniff out the new territory for a few minutes before they turned-in, but she promised to show him around the next day. Only one other tenant had a dog, that she knew of. The other dog belonged to a dancer that performed in *A Chorus Line* with Denise, which is how Nealy found the apartment in the first place. Nealy knew that Chance would love Angie's dog, a big black lab named Sadie, and maybe even a bit too much. In order to play it safe, Nealy planned to call Angie the next day to make sure that Sadie wasn't in the mood for love; she wasn't ready to become a grandmother anytime soon.

Before eight o'clock, Angie was knocking on Nealy's door for what turned out to be a proper canine introduction between their dogs. And of course it was love at first sight; Chancey wooed her affections with lots of kisses and romping around. Angie told Nealy that Denise had some really big news and she wanted to be the first one to tell her. Angie wanted to spill the beans, but she didn't dare, so instead she took the dogs down to the small yard while Nealy called Denise.

When Denise answered, Nealy didn't even give her time to say hello. "What's the big news?"

"Nealy!" Denise cried out with excitement.

"Well, what is it? I'm dying to know. Wait! I know...the lead broke her leg. You got the part."

"Better than that. I'm getting married."

Nealy squealed. "Big Dan?"

"Yes! He broke down and asked me last night during the intermission. I never expected it. I was in my dressing room and he came back stage to see me.

He said that he was sitting in the audience watching me do my number and all of a sudden he realized how much he loved me. Later, at intermission, he came back stage and proposed before he chickened out. Is that some romantic shit or what?"

"I think that's wonderful *'shit,'* " Nealy repeated. "I'm so happy for you, Denise."

"And just think, I almost made the biggest mistake of my life. Nealy, if you hadn't talked me into giving him another chance, this wouldn't be happening to me. I owe you. It's been so perfect ever since that night when you brought Phillip to Freddy's, and then we all went to Peppee's for pizza." Denise caught herself, and a dead silence fell between them. Denise forgot how sensitive Nealy was about Phillip. "I'm sorry, Nealy. I didn't think."

Nealy's heart felt as if had stopped, but she should be getting used to that by now because it happened every time she thought about him. "It's okay, Denise. I need to get over it. Do you ever see him or talk to him?"

"No, I've been so busy with the play and with Dan that I haven't had time to call. I ran into him once with that *bitch Victoria,* and since I hated her immediately, I never went by his pizza place after that."

"Don't feel bad. I hated her, too. Isn't that awful? She's probably nice. And she's real *fuckin'* rich," Nealy said, and then she giggled.

"Nealy, I can't believe you said that. But it's true." Both of them laughed. "Come to the play tonight. You can sit with Dan. Meet him in front of the theater at seven o'clock. He'll have the tickets. Afterwards, we can all go over to Freddy's. The gang would love to see you."

"Okay, it's a date. Denise, I'm real happy for you and Dan. At least things worked out for y'all. See you tonight."

"Hey, Nealy, wear something fabulous. My crystal ball tells me that you will meet a tall, handsome stranger tonight."

"Oh, please, Denise, if you're trying to fix me up with some guy, don't. I can't even begin to tell you how much I hate men right now."

"All men?"

There was a long pause before Nealy answered. "Yes, well, all except for one...but he's taken. I'll see you tonight," she said, fighting back the tears.

When Nealy stepped out of the cab at the theater, Dan waved wildly to get her attention. "Nealy!" he shouted. "Over here!"

Nealy pushed through the crowd that had gathered on the sidewalk. "Hi, Dan. Congratulations," she said, giving him a big hug.

"Thanks. It's good to see you. You look great."

"Thanks. So do you," she smiled.

Dan shivered. "It's getting colder than hell out here. I guess a cold front's moving in tonight. Come on. Let's get inside." They made their way through the crowd and up into the balcony where they found their seats.

Nealy took off her coat and looked around the theater. "This is so strange. I came to this theater exactly one year ago to watch Denise rehearse. I can't believe a year has passed already."

"Yes, and a lot has happened. I owe so much to you, Nealy. Denise told me that you encouraged her to see me again. I'm not sure I would have if I'd have been her. The first time we went out, I was a real jerk. I remember how arrogant and obnoxious I was. I had her on trial all night, but that's the lawyer in me. Thanks for telling her that even the worst jerk in the world deserves a second chance. I really love her."

"Oh, Dan, that's so sweet. She loves you, too."

"Nealy, she wants you to be happy, too."

"I know. And for the most part I am."

"Denise told me all about that mess with Jerrod and his mother. That was really a bummer. I was sorry to hear that because you and Phillip seemed so happy."

"We really were, Dan. I had never met anyone like Phillip and I probably never will again. He was the perfect man for me, but I really screwed that up."

"Nealy, you did what you thought was right. That was a real judgment call. But I'll agree with you, Phillip is a great guy. I really enjoy being around him."

Nealy dabbed her eyes with a kleenex. "Have you seen him lately?" she asked, since Dan sounded as if he had.

Dan thought for a second. "Uh...well, no, not too recently. Did you ever see him again after you got divorced?" he asked.

"Yeah, once. It was one year, one month, and twelve days ago, but who's counting," she smiled, sniffling and drying her eyes again with the kleenex. "You remember. It was that time when you and Denise and Robbie and I went to Freddy's?"

"Oh, yeah, I remember. I talked to Phillip that night at Freddy's. He hung around for the longest time and watched you dance with that director—"

"Phillip came to Freddy's that night?" she interrupted sharply.

"Yes. Didn't Denise tell you?"

"No! You know, I thought I saw him, but Denise said he hadn't been there," Nealy said, getting upset.

"Well, I asked her if she wanted me to break-in while you were dancing so I could tell you that he was there, but she said 'No.' She said that you made her promise not to interfere in his life, and she said that you definitely didn't want to see him."

"I did do that, Dan. After all, he had gotten engaged and I couldn't interfere in his life again," she said sadly, realizing why Denise had told her that he hadn't been there. She knew how much it would have upset her again.

"Maybe you should have interfered, Nealy. Phillip really loved you. He would have dumped that ugly bitch in a heartbeat."

"Dan, how rude," she giggled, but she loved hearing it.

"It's not rude if it's the truth," he smiled. "Nealy, maybe you should have given him a second chance. What would you do if he walked up to you right now and asked you to marry him?"

Nealy smiled and looked up at him. "You mean if he gave *me* a second chance?"

"Yeah," he grinned.

"I'd do just what you're doing. I'd marry the person of my dreams. But that can't happen," she said remorsefully, "because he's married to *that woman*."

Dan put his arm around her shoulders, and she rested her head, drying her eyes with her tissue. "I'm really sorry, Nealy, but I have a feeling that things will somehow work out. Friends have a way of helping each other." The lights went down in the theater. And after the second announcement, the curtain rose above the stage. Nealy became so involved in the play that she started to smile again and clapped loudly at the end of each act.

Dan and Nealy went backstage afterwards to congratulate the actors and the dancers. They had been incredible. She couldn't believe how well it had all come together. Without a doubt, this would be a very long running play, but, of course, with Joe Papp in charge, how could it fail; the man had the midas touch when it came to the theater. Denise rounded everyone up who planned to go to Freddy's with them. "Hey, Ang, you going with us?"

"No, I'm beat. I'm going home and going to bed."

"Are you sure, Angie? It's really fun," Nealy encouraged.

"I'm sure. Can Chance sleep over with Sadie?" Angie asked, winking at Denise.

"Sure, that would be great. I hated to leave him since we just got here. Poor little guy, I'm always going off and leaving him. Here's my extra key. I really appreciate this, Angie. I'll do the same with Sadie next time you go out."

"Okay. Have fun guys," she said, winking at Denise again.

"What's she winking at you for, Denise?"

"Oh, she's not winking. She has this twitch."

"Huh? I've never noticed that before."

"It only happens when she's really tired. Thank God she's going home to rest. Come on. We need to get going."

Nealy followed Denise and Dan out to the curb where a white limousine was waiting for them. "Who got this?" Nealy asked.

"I did," Dan spoke up. "Tonight's special."

"Oh, right," Nealy said, "you're celebrating."

"Right," he said. Six people piled into the limousine and they drove through the fierce Saturday night traffic in downtown Manhattan. Horns honked, people shouted, and lights flashed all around them. It was a crazy place, but Nealy loved being back. All of her memories of New York were fond ones, and they made her forget about her problems. Jillie would want her to join her for a few songs, which she looked forward to doing. They had a great time together, and Nealy welcomed the excitement and the cheering crowds; her ego could certainly use a little boosting right about now. To pass the time, Nealy told them all about her trip to France since none of them had ever been. She even shared a few stories about her rendezvous with the shipping magnate just in case he showed up at Freddy's. Denise and Dan looked at each strangely when she mentioned it. "Do you really think this guy would come to Freddy's?" Denise asked.

"Denise, this guy could show up anywhere. He told me that he knew everything about me. He knows where I live, both here and in Texas, he knows where my parents live and even my friends. Money can find out just about anything; it knows no boundaries, even when it involves spying. In fact, does anyone know this driver?" Nealy asked, making an effort to be funny, even though she was serious as hell.

"No, he just came with the car," Dan said, laughing.

"Well, before the nights over, trust me, he could be owned by Michael Coupair."

"Nealy, are you serious?" Denise asked, looking rather concerned.

"Oh, Denise, I'm kidding. At least I think I'm kidding," she giggled. "But with the way my luck's been going lately, he'll probably show up. So everybody be on the look out for this gorgeous French guy who looks like a million bucks."

"How will we know if he shows up? None of us have ever seen him," Dan asked.

"Denise has seen him," Nealy said frankly.

"Nealy's right. He looks like *more* than a million."

"This guy will stand out like a sore thumb in Freddy's. He's not your average looking guy." Once again, Denise and Dan mirrored each other grimly. "Relax guys. He's not mafia or part of any terrorist group. He's just this powerful, rich guy who likes to own things, and I think that includes me. But that's *not* going to happen. Remember? I hate men. All men."

"Now, Nealy, you admitted to me on the phone that there was *one man* that you didn't hate," Denise said sweetly.

Nealy's expression changed dramatically and softened with a slight smile. "Well, maybe that *one*, but it really doesn't matter because he's taken."

"Yes, Nealy, I'm afraid you're right about that, and he's been taken for a long time," Denise said, giving Nealy a hug.

When they finally arrived at Freddy's, they filed out of the limousine one by one—like people coming out of a bus with heads down and bobbing up as they hit the curb. Dan smiled at the driver and said, "Later, dude."

The driver smiled and nodded, "I'll be waiting, sir."

Inside, Nealy made the rounds to hug all of her friends that she hadn't seen in a while. For some strange reason, she felt at home in Freddy's, even with all the smoke and the neon lights and the loud music and the heavy duty camaraderie among its regulars who lived to party. And some of them were real party animals who liked to guzzle two beers at once and then burp real loud. Gross bastards. They ranged from being just plain uncouth to being deeply disgusting, but Nealy was one of those who didn't judge; she liked variety, even in people. In fact, she felt that it was good to deviate from the norm from time to time and migrate from one's safe little cocoon out into the real world.

Getting ready for the midnight show, Dan pulled several tables together to make room for twenty people or more. Then Frank the bartender brought two big buckets filled with cold beer over to the table. Jillie walked up to the table where everyone was busy gabbing to one another and broke in rather abruptly. "Hey, Nealy. Come on, toots, we got work to do."

"Oh, Jillie, why don't you start. I'll join you in a few minutes," she cried, stalling for a little more time to visit with her friends.

"Not on your life. I'm not ready to face this wild bunch by myself. Too many crazies in here tonight. So get your tight little prissy ass moving."

"She's such a lady...and she has such a way with words that can only to compare to that of a drunken sailor," Nealy said, shaking her head and rolling her eyes.

On stage, Nealy sat down at one piano and Jillie sat down at the other. Facing each other across the small stage, they started their New Orleans—Pat O'brien-style—show, which incidentally, is where Jillie got her start in the entertainment business. They always started with the favored "Great Balls of Fire," which got the crowd fired up and put Jillie's piano playing to the test. During the first hour they took requests from the audience who wanted to hear songs like, "Hang On Snoopy," "Stop! In the Name of Love," "Battle of New Orleans," "Elvira," "The Candy Man," "Ahab, The Arab," and "One Tin Soldier," one of Nealy's favorites, probably because she got a standing ovation every time she sang it. Then Denise sent a request for Nealy to sing "My Man." Nealy thought this song would be too melodramatic for this crowd, but she did it anyway, even though the lump in her throat got bigger and bigger. By the end of the song she practically whispered the last few words.

"No matter where my man...is...I am his...forever...more."

When she finished, she reached up and blotted the tears that trickled down her cheeks. Afterwards, Jillie got a tissue and blew her nose into the microphone which sounded like a fog horn in the middle of a sleeping forest. The audience roared with laughter and Jillie growled back at them, "Oh, shut-up. Y'all ain't got no heart if that didn't move ya. That's a damn sad song, folks. You're worse than that bunch of Bohunk relatives of mine. They wouldn't cry for nothin' over a sad song like that, but yet they've been known to crack up during the eulogy of one of their dearly departed."

"Jillie!" Nealy cried, "that's pathetic."

"Pathetic, but true as the big bosomed blonde who said men loved her for what she had up top," she joked, taking a piece of paper being passed to her from a guy sitting next to the stage.

"Forgive her y'all," Nealy giggled. "She's either in-bred and doesn't know any better, or she's just in a real tacky mood tonight."

Jillie squinted because the bright lights at the edge of the stage were reflecting in her face. Then she slowly looked up from the piece of paper. "Hey, Nealy, toots, this is different. This note's from some guy who wants you to sit back and shut-up—well, actually, he says 'listen.' But listen, shut-up...what's the difference. Damn, his writing's the pits. I can barely read this. Must be a damn doctor. Hmm, speaking of that. You know, that's probably why there are so many sick people in the world today. Doctors prescribe medicine, but when the pharmacist can't read the writing, hell, they just give us something to shut us up. Now ain't that a damn shame. We get a head cold and end up with these bullet-looking suppositories that hurt like hell when you try to shove them up your nose." The audience got hysterical. "Hey, this is serious, people. You're laughing your asses off and that's really where it goes." Nealy covered her face, but she was laughing so hard that tears were leaking out of the corners of her eyes.

"Jillie, you're totally demented," Nealy said, once again shaking her head and giggling wildly.

"Okay, okay, that's enough. Now, this *is* serious. I gotta sing. I just hope I don't lose my job over this one."

"One of these days they're going to haul you away in a straight jacket. Maybe there's a good *shrink* in the club," Nealy said, smiling.

"What do you mean by that? Do you know something I don't?" she asked, snapping at Nealy for asking.

"I know a lot more than you, Jillie, but I was just being cute. Got cha!" Nealy giggled.

"Oh, you're cute alright, toots, according to this note. Now, dammit, hush, 'cause I gotta sing. Time's ticking away here. And this guy's probably running out of patience."

"What?" Nealy asked.

"Never mind, it's a sick—as in a patient-doctor sort of thing. Never mind, I'll let him explain it to you later—"

"Him, who? Why are you rambling on like a crazy person tonight? Are you nervous about something?" Nealy asked.

"Yeah. And it's you. You're making me nervous. Now, hush, I said!"

"I'm hushin', okay. So go ahead. Sing. Play. Do whatever." Nealy rolled her eyes and twiddled her thumbs in her lap.

"Well, thank you," she remarked sarcastically. Jillie started to play and the melody immediately got Nealy's attention. But when she started to sing the words:

"*Goin' to the chapel and I'm…gonna get ma-a-ar-ried. Gee, I really love you and I'm gonna get ma-a-ar-ried—*"

"Wait a minute! Hold everything. What kind of joke is this?" Nealy interrupted.

"Toots, I don't think this *is* a joke. It says:

'*I'd like to request a song to be played for Ms. Nealy James.*
The song is'—*well, you heard the song*—'*I promised to marry her someday on the porch of the Homestead Inn.*

Scarlett, will you marry me?' It's signed, Rhett."

"Phillip," Nealy whispered. Slowly, she pushed the piano bench back and stood up. Desperately, she searched through the audience, but she couldn't see very well because of the blinding lights.

"Wait!" Jillie said, "there's more. He says 'I never make a promise that I can't keep. I'm here to tell you that I love you and I won't take no for an answer.' " The audience oohed and ahhed and sniffled. "Wait, now! There's one more thing. 'I made reservations for tomorrow afternoon at five o'clock.' " Jillie rolled her eyes up from the paper. "Well, don't just stand there, toots, dripping like a broken faucet. Go find him. Hey, Phillip, get your butt up here before we all start bawling."

Jumping upon the stage, Phillip smiled at her and asked, "Well, Scarlett, do we have a date?"

"Oh, Phillip," she cried, throwing her arms around his neck and holding on for dear life.

"Geezus," Freddy cried, storming out of his office. "What the hell's goin' on here?" When he saw Nealy in Phillip's arms and heard Jillie continuing to play the chapel song, he shook his head and chewed harder on his cigar, mumbling, "Oh, no, not another goddamn doctor."

Denise hugged Dan and cried, "Thank *God*, it worked…it actually worked!"

CHAPTER FIFTY-ONE

November 15, 1976

A CARAVAN OF THREE WHITE LIMOUSINES pulled into the inn in Greenwich, Connecticut, at three o'clock on Sunday morning after making two stops on the way out of New York for blood tests and a marriage license. So, without any further delays, Phillip Pepper planned on marrying Nealy Samantha James on the front porch of one of the most romantic inns in America. Nealy had snuggled in his arms all the way to the inn, exchanging soft words and kisses. Phillip told her that Victoria had broken up with him a few weeks after Nealy had seen them in his office; she couldn't live with Nealy's picture on the nightstand beside his bed for the rest of her life. Nealy questioned why he hadn't called her, but he had done much more. He had actually gone to Texas to tell her in person, but when he arrived at her house, she and Kendall were just leaving. Then he had Rob Morris make some phone calls to find out if the relationship between them was serious. Much to his chagrin, Phillip had been told that they seemed very much in love and that Kendall had already proposed. But, as irony would have it, Nealy had refused his proposal. Why didn't he call her and find out for himself? He wanted to, but he couldn't interfere with her life, just as she had refused to see or talk to him after finding out about his engagement. That's what love is all about: the unselfish act of denying one's own needs for those of another.

The fact that Phillip had made all of the plans in such a short period of time amazed her. How did he do it? As they snuggled together on the couch in front of the fire in their same suite, Nealy quizzed him. "Phillip, how did you find out that I was here? No one knew I was coming. I didn't even know myself until late Friday."

Phillip smiled smugly. "I have my sources."

"Oh, I see. May I ask who these sources are?"

"Since we will never have any secrets between us, yes you may," he said, lifting up her chin to kiss her sweetly.

"Well, who are they?"

"Denise "

"Well, I should have known. Nealy cut him off. When I called her this morning she insisted that I wear my best dress. But I thought she was trying to fix me up with that director again. Did she call you?"

"Yes, but, Nealy, there's a lot more to this. When I came back from Texas, I ran into Dan and Denise in my restaurant one night. Unfortunately, it was the night that Victoria came by to see if I had changed my mind and wanted to try again. Of course I hadn't. So she was extremely rude to them. A month later I called Denise to tell her that my engagement to *that woman*—"

"Oh, God, she told you that?" Nealy buried her face in his chest.

Phillip laughed. "That's why I couldn't marry her, sweetheart, don't you see. I knew you loved me because you were jealous enough to be catty. Nealy, that's not your nature unless you feel threatened by someone who has something that you want."

"But why didn't Denise call me? She knew how much I loved you. And she knew how miserable I was without you," she said closing her eyes and kissing him. "So, why didn't she call me?" she whispered.

"I made her promise not to interfere in your life. All that has ever mattered to me was your happiness. Nealy this guy seemed perfect for you because you both lived and worked in Galveston, he had a good practice, and he had a reputation for being a nice guy. Denise promised not to say anything to you, but she didn't think that it would work out. Did she ever meet him?" he asked, stroking her hair gently.

"Yes, once when he came to New York."

"Well, that makes sense," he said nodding his head. "Denise said he hated New York and seemed a bit on the boring side but nice. That gave me hope right there, because I couldn't imagine you with anyone boring. Anyway, she assured me that you'd never marry him. And to give her a lot of credit, which she deserves, she did tell me that she felt certain that you were hopelessly in love with me. Nealy, sweetheart, that kept me going, even if it were only her own intuitions and wishful thinking. Denise kept telling me that we belonged together. She wanted to tell you, but I didn't want to flatter myself by thinking that you'd drop him and come running back to me."

"Phillip, you know I would have. I missed you everyday. And I thought about you constantly."

"Remember that day you came by the office, well, that night I went to Freddy's."

"I know. I just found that out last night. I sensed you in the room. That sounds crazy, but, Phillip, I did. This feeling came over me. Then I thought I saw you going out the door. I asked Denise, but she made light of it."

"Nealy, I asked her not to tell you. I knew how hurt you were. I could see it in your face that day. It almost killed me, sweetheart. And then when I saw you dancing with that guy, I just couldn't stand it. But, like you, I had made my bed, and I also had to lie in it. That's why I've waited. That wasn't going to happen again. Oh, Nealy, I missed you everyday. I prayed that things wouldn't work out, even though I wanted you to be happy. I couldn't help it. I asked God everyday to take care of you and watch over you, but then I always threw in a little prayer to keep me in your thoughts."

"So it was you all the time." Nealy sat up to look at him.

"What?"

"You were haunting me. Something kept me from committing to that relationship. I decided that I had some sort of MESP. You know, Male Extrasensory Perception or something weird like that," she said, being serious.

Phillip chuckled loudly. "You're so hilarious!"

"Phillip, don't laugh. I did. You were making me crazy. You were in my head day and night. I fought it. I tried to convince myself to let go, to move on, but I couldn't. This feeling that I had wouldn't let me. And all the time it was you. Oh, Phillip, I'm so glad. I could never be happy without you. I wanted you so much," she said, throwing her arms around his neck and hugging him.

After kissing her several times, he sighed deeply. "Now don't let this go to your head—You are *so* pretty " he blurted out.

"Thanks. But don't let what go to my head?"

"See what you do to me. Just looking at you causes me to lose my train of thought. Anyway, I had made up my mind to wait for you. In my heart I knew that you were the one for me, and if I couldn't have you, then I had decided to go it alone," he finished.

"Oh, Phillip, I felt the same way. But how did you make these arrangements? I only talked to Denise this morning."

"Word travels fast. When you called Francine last night to tell her that you were leaving for New York, she told Randy, who in turn called Rob, who called me."

"You're kidding?" she giggled softly.

"No. They were all pulling for us. They called us 'a couple' and said that we belonged together. Nancy Morris was another one that wouldn't let me give up. She said over and over again that you were in love with me and not that other guy. She said that they invited the two of you to dinner and she didn't see that spark that she saw between the two of us."

"Oh, I wish they could be here with us. If it weren't for them this wouldn't be happening," Nealy said shyly.

"Oh, sweetheart, I wish they could too," he said regretfully.

"Okay, so go on," she said, touching his face sweetly to prove to herself that Phillip was really sitting next to her, that it wasn't a dream. "So how did you and Denise and Dan get this all put together?"

"When I found out that you were coming, I called Denise, but she didn't answer. So I called the theater. They gave her a message and she had Angie, the girl that lives in your apartment complex, on the look out for you."

"I called Angie first thing this morning to talk about our dogs. You mean she already knew about all of this?" she asked.

He nodded his head and smiled. "Yes, she knew everything. When she found out that you had brought your dog—and by the way, she said I'd love

Chance—she volunteered to take care of him while we go on our honeymoon."

"He'll love you as much as I...wait a minute. We're going on a honeymoon?" she asked, interrupting herself.

"Well, I was going to surprise you, but since I started this I'll go ahead and tell you. Monday morning we are leaving for Hawaii for two weeks, that is unless you would prefer to go somewhere else."

"Oh, Phillip, Hawaii. We're going to Hawaii?"

"Maui. I thought that two weeks of total togetherness in a place where neither one of us has ever been would be a perfect way to make up for lost time."

"We do have a lot of lost time to make up for. And I can assure you that I'm going to do my part," she smiled seductively.

"I like the sound of that, *Miss Scarlett*. Maybe we should skip the wedding and leave now."

"No way. You promised to marry at the Homestead Inn and you're going to keep that promise, even if it's the last thing you ever do."

"That is far from the last thing that I'll ever do with you. In fact, it's a new beginning with much more to come. I promise to hold you in my arms and make mad passionate love to you for at least twelve out of every twenty-four hours for the next two weeks. I promise to have at least two children with you in the next six years, that is, if you agree. I promise to build you a big house wherever you want it built. I promise to spend time with you and our family and give you everything that you've ever wanted. And I promise to take a two week vacation with you, alone, without our offsprings, every year for the next fifty years."

"Now that's a lot of promises, even for Rhett Butler," she giggled happily.

"Well, *Scarlett*, as *God* is my witness, I promise to keep every one of them," he said, smiling at her and hugging her tightly, as if he never wanted to let her go.

Resting in his arms, she kept digging for details. "Now Phillip, I know that you and Denise got everyone involved at Freddy's, but this inn?"

"After that last weekend that we spent together, I knew that I wanted to marry you—correction—I was going to marry you. We had talked about it, and you were going home to start divorce proceedings. The next weekend I came back up here and made arrangements with them to handle everything whenever the time came. Of course, I didn't expect it to be almost two years, but that doesn't matter anymore. We're here now. Then last month, when you were in New York and you saw Denise, she called me and told me that it looked as if things were ending between you and that veterinarian. Then she talked to you the night before you left for France, and you told her that you were going alone. She also said that you were coming back to New York in a month."

"I've changed. I've become the most predictable person on the face of the earth."

"No, sweetheart, this is the answer to a lot of prayers and wishful thinking. In fact, you were the only thing that I have thought about since I first saw you in Toot Shor's almost five years ago."

"I never stopped thinking about you either. It's that *MESP*. I'm telling you I've got it. For the longest time after that night, I thought about you and I tried to put a name with your adorable face. But...Doctor, I'll have to admit, Pepper wasn't on my list," she giggled, kissing his perfect nose.

"Nealy, I could kick myself. Why didn't I run off with you that night?" he said seriously, searching her face.

"Why didn't you? If anyone could make me behave irrationally, you could. Phillip, not being with you was the hardest thing that I've ever been through— and trust me, that's saying a lot. The mention of your name sent awful pains through my heart," she smiled at him and placed her hand over her heart. "Okay, I don't want to think about not being with you. We're forever, Dr. Pepper, so go on. You called the Homestead Inn."

He held her close as he continued. "Yes, I took a chance."

"That's why we belong together," she giggled softly. "You're in my head and my heart. You know what makes me tick."

"Umm, I sure do. Tonight's going to be a night neither one of us will ever forget."

"Ah-em, Dr. Pepper, could this be a night filled with erotic fantasies?"

"I hope so. I've had this same fantasy for the last twenty months about this red headed madonna that seduces me into her bedroom after this brief encounter at the altar."

Nealy giggled softly again and kissed him. "Well, my goal in life is to fulfill all of your fantasies, Doctor."

"I wish you hadn't said that. Come here," he said, pulling her into his lap.

"Now, Phillip, control yourself. I don't know about *you* but I'm saving myself for marriage." They laughed and snuggled, cooing like little doves settling into a nest.

Phillip sent Nealy off with Denise to get a few hours sleep before she had to meet with the alterations person. He planned to surprise her with the suit that she had seen in Macy's on their brief shopping spree before their first trip to the Homestead Inn. He knew how beautiful she would look in that suit, so he had gone back and bought it for her. Phillip kept it in the bag in his closet, and from time to time, he would take it out and imagine her in it. Eve, Phillip's secretary, had also been recruited to help him with the wedding, and she had rushed out to pick up all of the accessories to match the suit. Angie had packed Nealy's suitcase, and Phillip stopped by and picked it up before he went to Freddy's. An hour after Phillip left the apartment, the *brown-velvet eyes* showed-up looking for Nealy. Angie recognized him immediately from Denise's description; she had called Angie from Freddy's to put her on the alert since

Nealy said that he might show up. Angie kept going to the window all night long to see if the long, black limousine remained parked across the street. And at seven-thirty, she finally called Denise in Connecticut which made her a nervous wreck. No one, especially a fast-talking Frechman was going to butt in on her labor of love; five o'clock couldn't get there soon enough. Nealy certainly had this guy pegged right: He went after what he wanted. But Nealy didn't want him, she wanted Phillip. And everyone who knew them wanted to get these two people to the altar before anymore promises or bad timing could interfere with their happiness.

Nealy had been too excited to sleep, but she relaxed happily for a couple hours. When the alterations lady took the suit out of the bag, Nealy cried. "I can't believe he bought that suit," she said, wiping the tears off her cheeks.

After the alterations lady finished fitting the suit, Denise took Nealy into the quaint little town of Greenwich to do some shopping at Phillip's insistence; he wanted to get Nealy away from the inn for a while. Denise had been given carte blanche to buy Nealy whatever she thought she might need on their honeymoon. Even though he had made most of the arrangements ahead of time, he had to take care of a few last minute details for the reception, which would take place following the wedding. Thank goodness, the weather had cooperated. It turned out to be a beautiful sunshiny day and just cold enough for a nice fire during dinner, as well as in their suite for their honeymoon night. Phillip couldn't wait to make love in front the fireplace as they had the first time, but this time would be even more special because Nealy would be his wife.

Nealy dressed in Denise's room, putting on the suit that brought smiles and tears every time she looked in the mirror. A knock came at the door. It was Eve checking to see if she could help with anything else. Nealy kept saying, "I can't believe he remembered this outfit. How did he know?"

Eve said, "Nealy, he knew this day would come. We all did. This is destiny for two people who love and deserve each other."

"Eve, thanks for being here," Nealy said hugging her again.

"Honey, I wouldn't have missed this for the world. Phillip Pepper is one special man. We had many conversations about you. Nealy, he's crazy about you. He loves you more than life itself."

"Oh, Eve, I love him, too, but you more than anyone knows that."

"Yes, I do know that, honey. My heart broke that day when you came by the office. If only Victoria hadn't been there, things would have happened much sooner. Nealy, he never loved her, not even for a minute. He's never really loved anyone but you. Thank God, you're together now. And that's all that matters."

"We'll make up for lost time, I promise," Nealy said, looking naughty, but then she giggled. "But, you, Denise, I never knew how undermining you could be," she teased.

"Like Eve said, you and Phillip belonged together and I wasn't going to let you waste not even one more precious day. We went right to work."

"Life can't get any better than this," she grinned at them.

They talked until they heard a knock at the door. Nealy opened it and screamed with joy, "Daddy! Oh, my God. What are you doing here?"

"I came to give my little girl away. So come on, let's not keep the groom waiting." The four of them walked down the hall towards the front porch. Nealy wiped away the tears as they rolled down her cheeks and she held tightly to her father's arm. That Saturday morning Phillip had wired Nealy's parents tickets to come for the wedding, although at the time, she hadn't accepted. Phillip had taken so much for granted, but he knew that they loved each other; he had always known that in his heart.

When Nealy got to the front door, her mother waited with open arms. Then she saw Rob and Nancy Morris, who had also been wired tickets by Phillip. Nealy couldn't believe it! No wonder they didn't answer when she tried to call them with the great news. "I just can't believe it," she kept saying.

"Come on, let's find the groom so that you two can say your 'I do's,'" Nancy said, hugging Nealy. Leaving her behind with her father, Nancy, acting as the bridesmaid led Denise, the maid of honor, Eve and Nealy's mother out to their places on the porch in front of Nealy's entire family, her friends and Phillip's family. Just another surprise for Phillip's bride.

Nealy's father smiled at her and said, "I think you found the right one this time, honey. Phillip's a good man. And he loves you. Your mother and I liked him from the minute he walked into our house. We're just real happy for you both."

"Phillip came to see you?"

"Yes, last year sometime. He came by our house and introduced himself as the guy who really loved our daughter. That took a lot of guts, Nealy. He's a mighty good man."

"Thanks, Daddy, for telling me that. I'm very lucky to be marrying him. I've never been this happy in my life," she said, hugging her precious father.

To the melody of soft music, Nealy's father walked her slowly towards the gazebo. When she saw her family, Betty Lou and Kati Sue, and Francine and Randy all gathered around, she exclaimed, "What a marvelous conspiracy!" Everyone grinned and softly laughed at her bright, surprised expression. Nealy smiled, and her green eyes sparkled. When she looked up at Phillip, their eyes locked tighter than ever. He stepped forward and took her hand from her father who kissed her sweetly on the cheek, and then patted Phillip lightly on the shoulder. As Nealy stepped up beside Rob, she hugged him and whispered as she kissed him on the cheek, "Thank you very much."

Rob smiled back, and in a hushed voice he said, "You're very welcome." As

Phillip's groomsman, he proudly stood next to Phillip's brother, Ethan, who acted as Phillip's best man. Phillip looked so handsome in his dark navy pin-stripped suit and a light blue shirt that made his eyes appear even more blue-gray than the winter sky above. Before the minister began the ceremony, Nealy looked up at Phillip and smiled.

"You're beautiful," he whispered, grinning at her. Nealy looked like a pure vision of loveliness in her ivory velvet, floor-length suit. The plush-velvet jacket had a scooped neckline with a row of fluffy ivory fox fur that followed the neck line from front to back. The front buttoned with large decorative loops that were covered in spun-silk. The bodice hugged her body, tapering to the waist and then flaring slightly at the hips. From under the jacket came a slim fitting skirt that followed the shape of her long, slender legs. To set off her beautiful face, she had a halo-style hat of matching ivory fox that rested gracefully on the top of her head, bringing attention to her huge green eyes. Nealy had twisted her reddish hair into a tight knot at the nape of her neck. Her hands were buried snugly in a matching fur muff, which she passed to Nancy to hold.

The minister spoke softly, but quickly. The sunset made the sky radiant with shades of pink and fiery golds, and even though the air had turned colder, no one seemed to notice. The love that this group shared kept them warm and cozy.

"Will you, Nealy Samantha James, take Phillip for your lawfully wedded husband, to love, to honor, to cherish, to have and to hold, in sickness and in health, from this moment on and until death do you part?"

"I will," she said, smiling up at him.

"Will you, Phillip Aaron Pepper, take Nealy for your lawfully wedded wife, to love, to honor, to cherish, to have and to hold, in sickness and in health, from this moment on and until death do you part?"

"I will," he replied, fighting back tears.

"The rings please," the minister directed to Denise. The skies to the West turned red with joy, or so it seemed, as they placed the rings on each other's fingers. When Phillip placed the simple gold wedding band on her finger, she smiled sweetly and softly whispered the words "I love you." Then he reached into his pocket and pulled out a large emerald-cut diamond solitaire that he placed in front of the band. And even though it was exquisite, Nealy would have been just as happy with the never-ending circle of gold.

After she placed a matching gold band on his finger, she looked up into Phillip's face and he had tears in his eyes.

With that, the minister quickly pronounced them husband and wife. "And from what I understand, this is truly a match made in Heaven. May the Lord bless this union. You may kiss your bride." Phillip pulled her into his arms, and they kissed, almost to the point of embarrassment.

"Hey, kids, it's a done deal now," Rob said jokingly. "You'll have plenty of time for this later."

Nealy giggled, and when Phillip stepped back away from her, she turned to hug her mother and father, and then Phillip's mother and father. Then she made her rounds among the families and friends that were gathered on the cold, but romantic porch.

Inside, the group of twenty-eight gathered in the dining room for dinner and a quiet celebration. Phillip had selected the food which included different dishes of the classic French cuisine prepared by the Inn's Parisian chef. Phillip kept the wine flowing around the table for those who wanted to partake and toast to the bride and groom. Everyone made a warm, wonderful toast to the happiness of these two special people. Nealy and Phillip held on to each other, and they kept pinching themselves just to make sure that it wasn't a dream. Phillip had ordered a beautiful wedding cake; it had five tiers and on the top he had them put an angel with reddish-blonde hair and a harp in her hand with a note that read, *"For my Angel."*

Of course, Nealy had tears running down her cheeks when Phillip stood up to thank his guests. "This is the most important day of my life. Nealy means more to me than anyone else in the whole world. She is everything that I have ever wanted, everything I've dreamed about, and I honestly can never thank you enough for all that you have done to make my dreams come true. But I promise that I'll do everything earthly possible to see that she has a happy life. More than anyone I know, she deserves it. So from the bottom of my heart, I want to thank you for taking time out of your busy lives on such short notice to be here with us. It has meant more than I can ever say." Then he looked down at Nealy and smiled. "I love you, Mrs. Pepper."

Nealy blushed, and then she looked up at him and smiled back. "I love you, too." Rob handed her his handkerchief.

After dinner everyone chatted for a while and shared stories about the bride and the groom for fun and a few laughs. Phillip asked Nealy's family and her friends what she had been like as a child. He wanted to get an idea of what to expect from the *"little red Peppers"* that they planned to bring into this world someday. Also, he was curious to know if she had always loved to sing and dance and clown around. All of them agreed, maintaining that they had always expected her to become an entertainer because she had always loved to entertain. "Nealy had to have an audience," her mother remarked, smiling. They told him about how she put on shows for the family and how she imitated Lucille Ball and Harpo Marx and dressed up in big clothes and pretended to do a strip tease. Phillip laughed and said, "Oh, really. Now I'd pay big bucks for a ticket to that performance."

Nealy smiled at him amorously and said, "Since you married me, Doctor, I'll do it for you for free," she giggled, smiled and blushed, all at the same time.

"Ooh," came a soft, sexy sound from Ethan, Phillip's brother who sat next to Betty Lou with his arm around her chair and his hand resting on her shoulder for closeness; it truly is a small world. In Nealy's wildest dreams, she wouldn't have considered Phillip's brother to be the "Ethan" that Betty Lou told her about when she returned from France. Why didn't it register with her? Well, for one thing, she was still in a state of shock because of her own problems. If she had been thinking more clearly, surely she would have caught the "I met a doctor named Ethan from Iowa." Now, if all went well, she and Betty Lou would not only be best friends, but forever sisters-in-law.

Phillip's parents were everything that Nealy envisioned them to be and she loved them already. In fact, the entire Pepper family was just another special gift from Phillip who had made her the happiest woman on the face of the earth.

Curious as to where Nealy and Phillip would live, everyone asked, even though they expected them to live in New York. Since Phillip had an extremely successful practice, he would remain in New York, but what did Nealy plan to do? Would she commute or move or what? Nealy had so much to think about, but more than anything else in the world she knew that she wanted to be with Phillip. And for the first time in years, she didn't need anything more from life. Phillip would let her be as much of her own person as she wanted to be and support her in anything that she wanted to do. His love was and always would be totally unconditional. As long as she was happy, she could stay home, work, sew, sing, dance, or act; he didn't care, as long as they were *"a couple"* forever." But Nealy just wanted to be near him and love him and rear their children in a happy home just like the ones that she and Phillip had known.

As much as Nealy and Phillip were enjoying being with their family and friends, they were ready to be alone. They began to make their good-byes, promising to visit everyone as soon as they could.

At the door to their suite, Phillip picked Nealy up and carried her over the threshold, kicking the door shut behind them. He carefully placed her on the same rug where they had made love the very first time. "Nealy, I've imagined you lying here beside me a thousand times. I could feel your soft skin. I smelled your sweet perfume. Sweetheart, I thought I would lose my mind."

"Me, too," she said, putting her arms around his neck and pulling him closer. "Isn't it funny how we went through so much and now it doesn't matter at all."

"I know, it's strange. Now that we're together, it's as though we were never apart. I guess that's because I thought about you every single day. This is my dream come true," he smiled.

"Mine, too."

Phillip kissed her softly and then more and more deeply. Then he stopped to remove her fury hat and take the pins out of her hair. For a minute, he looked at her warmly, and then at the same time, they lost control. They kissed harder and harder with a passion that burned wild and strong. They squirmed in each other's arms, tugging desperately at their clothes. Their kisses grew deeper and wetter and longer. And without ever knowing the moment when they finally came together, they let their minds and their bodies take them far beyond any lovemaking that they had ever known. Phillip held Nealy tightly as his body moved over her body and his mouth lingered over her mouth. "Yes..." he said again and again. "Nealy, I love you so much...yes, oh, yesss..." It couldn't end. Oh, no, not yet...no. But it had to end, or his mind would explode.

Nealy swirled beneath him, her body rising up and down with a rhythm that matched his. Her mouth opened, yearning for his wet kisses. She made soft cooing sounds "Ooh...ooohh..." that grew louder and louder. She whispered, "I love you...I love you," over and over. "No," she cried out softly, "ooohhh..." She didn't want to let go. She wanted the moment to last forever.

But finally, when they could not longer wait, she cried out, and then he cried out and pushed for the last time, unleashing massive explosions throughout his body and his mind and his soul before he collapsed on top of her, showering her with wet, gentle kisses. "I love you so much," he said.

"I love you, too," she said, softly raking her fingernails up and down his backside as her lower body still clung to him.

He raised up and gazed into her eyes. "I'm sorry, Nealy, it's just been so long that I—"

"Phillip, don't apologize. I couldn't have waited another second. I wanted you so much I couldn't stand it."

"Say that again."

"I wanted you so much I couldn't stand it!" she cried out, kissing him as she talked. "I got so carried away that my mind went completely numb. You have that affect on me, you know."

"I'd embarrass us both if I said what kind of affect you have on me," he chuckled, then he sighed softly, touching her face and rubbing her cheek ever so slightly with the back of his hand. "Oh, sweetheart, I still can't believe that we're married and that we never have to be apart again."

"I'll never be apart from you. We will always, always be together. I'm going to sell my business in Galveston."

"Nealy, you don't have to do that. You know I'll understand if you want to commute."

"No, I'm your wife now, Phillip. I don't want that responsibility anymore. I'm going to have enough just taking care of you and my agency and our *little red Peppers*," she giggled. "And just where did you come up with that?"

"It fits," he smiled. "I visualize our children to have your reddish hair and they will make funny faces just like you do. The name, of course, came from me. I can already see our son telling us to sit down and watch his show, just as you used to do when you were young. Can't you see him? See how his little eyes twinkle when he sings?"

"We just got married three hours ago and already we have a son. What a creatively persuasive mind you have, Dr. Pepper."

"That's my strong-suit. After all, I got you to marry me just sixteen hours after I asked you, didn't I?"

"You really are pretty amazing," she said, snuggling against him and kissing the golden hairs on his tanned chest. "Phillip, the moment I became your wife my life started over. It's as if nothing else ever existed. I'm so happy and I love you so much."

"I love you, too, Nealy, " he said, easing away from her. "Do I say that too much?"

"You can never say that too much."

Phillip kissed her softly several times. Her clothes were still half on and half off, much the same as his. He sat up and began to take off the rest of his clothes in order to get more comfortable.

Nealy raised up and took off her jacket. Then devilishly, she smiled at him. "Don't move. I'll be right back." Nealy went into the bedroom, dug through her new clothes, and pulled out one of the outfits that Denise insisted she get for their honeymoon. After she put on the black bustier, she put on a pair of black nylons and hooked them to the garter belt. Then she put on her black heels and a very short, black sheer robe that tied at the waist. She turned on the radio to provide a very soft background of music, and then she paraded into the living room where Phillip sat naked, relaxing in front of the fire.

The minute she pranced up in front of him, she got his undivided attention. "I'm going to die a happy man," he said, raising up to take a better look.

Nealy knelt down in front of him to fluff the pillows that he leaned against, and then she kissed him, allowing her tongue to teasingly touch and wet his lips. "Now sit back and enjoy the show," she whispered, smiling at him.

"I think this could definitely be a 'Kodak moment.' Should I get the camera?"

"No cameras allowed in any of my performances," she said in a very sensuous tone, but then she giggled. "Well, next time we may sneak in a polaroid or two, just to prove to our children that we were really young once." Then she smiled, and slowly rose to her feet, allowing her breasts to barely touch his face. Nealy had never acted so seductively, but Phillip was enjoying every minute of it. As she sang her rendition of "Gypsy Rose Lee," she took off the robe, allowing it to drop between his legs, and then she teased him as she brushed it against his chest and then hung it around his neck. After kicking off her shoes, she placed one foot upon the end table next to him, unhooked her stocking, and slowly rolled it down her leg. Then she repeated that move with her other leg. When the time came to remove her bustier, she unhooked it slowly, one hook at a time, and then tossed it across the room. Phillip had to fold his arms in front of his chest to keep him from grabbing her. For the finale, she inched her bikini panties down her body, shifting her hips dramatically from side to side. After stepping out of one leg, she raised her other foot in the air and kicked her panties in his direction for him to catch. And then for almost a minute, she stood motionless, posing naked like a sculpture with pristine poise and a shameless style that seduces her sculptor to reach inside himself and find the face, that one perfect expression that will breathe life into his piece of work... At the precise moment, she broke the spell and summoned him to follow her into the bedroom by provocatively curling her index finger as she slowly backed away.

In the bedroom, Phillip watched as she threw back the covers and stretched out across the bed on her back in a totally uninhibited position. "I'm lonely," she purred.

"Well, we can't have that," he said, crawling into bed next to her. Intrigued by her amorous behavior, he gazed into her eyes in anticipation of what would follow such an act. And she didn't let him down. Nealy knew just what to do to make him feel loved and wanted. Skillfully, she touched and massaged his body, making him dizzy with desire, causing invisible currents to push him closer and closer to the jolt that would bring them together as one and take them over the edge of excitement. Not only had he found the perfect wife, he had found the perfect lover.

Afterwards, Nealy snuggled up to him feeling all warm and cozy, making sweet sounds of joy. Phillip pressed his chest up against her back and held her tightly in the lap of his body. His strong arm draped across her body to gently cup her right breast in his hand. He kissed her cheek and her ear and her neck. "Nealy Pepper, my beautiful, beautiful wife," he repeated happily. "What a *truly incredible act*. And just where did you learn that?" he asked, contented, and in love for life.

Giggling shyly, she said, "Oh...let's just say that *for you my love*, I studied in France."

The End

...until we meet again

Coming this fall

from

ccpost

Sweet Hearts
Of Steel

PROLOGUE

"Get a grip on yourself, Ashlee," she whispered to herself, her face an inch from the mirror. Her hand shook as she squeezed the eyelash curler around the eyelashes of her left eye, catching part of her eyelid. "Ouch! Why don't you just poke your finger in your eye? It'd probably hurt less," she cried, sarcastically scolding herself.

Ashlee dropped the deadly gadget and squinted while she reached for a tissue to prevent the tears from streaking the rest of her carefully applied make-up. It seemed crazy to be so nervous, but today is one of the most important days of her life. The fact that she received the assignment to interview the three most successful women car dealers in the United States had been what she termed as "a miracle from above," the fourth floor being the "above."

During Ashlee McCoy's senior year in college, recruiters from *Automotive World* visited the campus at the University of Michigan and interviewed hundreds of Journalism students for possible employment with the magazine. When she received a call a month later from the recruiter, she could hardly believe that they wanted her to come for a second interview. Although she had made decent grades, she certainly wasn't at the top of her class.

And now, after only five years as a reporter, Ashlee has been assigned a new beat: New Car Dealers. And, needless to say, she is thrilled, but also a little apprehensive, which is understandable for a young, relatively inexperienced reporter. In her assignment, she will be going *one on one* with the most successful people in the industry to talk about top achievements, family succession, strikes and unions and how they affect the Big Three, as well as the industry as a whole, white collar crime, and anything else that gets thrown her way. This promotion was a dream come true for Ashlee because she had grown up in the car business. Her father, Ashworth McCoy, has been a new car dealer in Fort Worth, Texas, for more than twenty years, and he put her to work on the washracks before she started to school. Ashlee was the boy he never had, but in spite of her gender, he fully expected her to follow in his footsteps...but she didn't, she had other aspirations.

Her first assignment to interview three very powerful women with rather unusual backgrounds had turned her dream into a terrible nightmare. But when she became fascinated with the details of the story, it changed her entire attitude. Interestingly enough, all three of them had become car dealers, all three of them were about to receive the Master's Achievement award from General Motors, and all three of them had graduated the same year from Chippewa

Valley High School in Mt. Clemens, Michigan, a small town in the suburbs of Detroit, the automotive capital of the world. A coincidence or what? The editor, Delton Wart, had sensed Ashlee's apprehensions in the beginning, even though she tried to cover up her fears with an even greater enthusiasm than normal. In talking with Ashlee, he seemed to think that a female would relate better to the problems that these women have had to overcome in a field dominated by men, and also, he felt that Ashlee could talk "car-talk" with them since she knew the business better than most car dealers.

All three women had been invited to stay at the St. Claire Inn at the expense of *Automotive World,* of course. The quaint little Inn has a lovely location in the heart of St. Claire, Michigan, on the St. Claire River that separates Michigan and Canada. People of all ages, primarily couples, both young and old, who are seeking peace and quiet and great food, vacation there year around because of its romantic ambiance. And even though it's still quite cold in early Spring, the guests delight in watching the icebergs break apart in the thawing waters and drift down river towards Detroit. The fact that all three women had grown up in the area and visited the inn on many occasions, they gladly accepted.

Ashlee went up to the St. Claire Inn a few days early to prepare for the arrival of her guests. And, at her request, the innkeeper reserved her a table riverside where she could entertain her guests with a view of the indelible blue-green water of the St. Clair River. Ashlee, a dreamer in her own right, knew how entrancing a divine setting of purely picturesque serenity could be, moving even the coldest of hearts. So, for either of the three, this should be the perfect backdrop for telling all. With her somewhat limited, but natural reporter savvy, and gifted charm, thanks to her father, the car dealer, she knew that a warm smile and a certain degree of tranquility would help her get all the answers to the many personal questions that she planned to ask. During the past three days, she had sat alone at the dining table, rehearsing over and over again, her line of questioning, and even though the people at the tables close by stared oddly, she had to practice. This assignment had to be a success. If she screwed this up, her life would be over. Well, not really, but it could be extremely detrimental to her career as a reporter who planned to join the ranks on the "fourth floor." She spent an enormous amount of time talking to people, both in the business and out, who knew these women, then and now, and, as far as she knew, Ashlee had read every article that had ever been written about them, so she had plenty of questions. To say that she had been astounded and intrigued with what she had uncovered, would be more than just an understatement. So, it would be very interesting to see how much they would tell her because she had dug up some pretty juicy information about one in particular.

Constance Devereaux had been suspected of killing her wealthy husband only two years after they married, a story that made headlines in newspapers all across the country. Ashlee recalled the scandalous tale of Goodson "Goodie" Devereaux who had divorced his wife of twenty-nine years to marry a thirty-six-year-old, thrice divorced woman who had worked for him at his local dealership for seven years prior to their marriage. And, according to the papers, the new Mrs. Devereaux had inherited more than twenty dealerships nationwide, not to mention, millions of dollars, thanks to the generous provisions set out in her late husband's will. It smelled *fishy*, so that's all it took for the police to go after her hook, line, and...well, anyway, they arrested her and she ended up behind bars. And even though the pieces of the puzzle seemed to fit because, after all, Constance Devereaux became a wealthy woman, literally overnight, Dr. Fritz Kearn, a forensic pathologist, turned lawyer, and his brother, Barnum Kearn, a police detective for the City of Detroit, did not believe in her guilt. For one thing, she didn't seem like the type, and, for another, she obviously loved the guy, and even though he had the same insecurities that any man would have being married to someone as beautiful as Constance, he loved her, too. And, from past experiences and their understanding of the law, a case built on purely circumstantial evidence is hard to win.

Darcy O'Donnell, a less colorful individual, but not without skeletons in her closet: a shotgun wedding, a still-birth, a nasty divorce, and a trip abroad for *daddy's little girl* to recover from the perils that had left his nineteen-year-old daughter emotionally devastated. The days in the life of Darcy O'Donnell had definitely sparked a great deal of curiosity for Ashlee. Darcy had inherited ten dealerships that were scattered throughout Michigan after her father passed away from a massive coronary. Being bright, talented, and, to quote the media, "quite ruthless and rather conniving," she had expanded her chain to sixteen dealerships with the help of her substantial inheritance. And from what Ashlee had concluded from her research, Darcy's older brother, Derrick, should have been the one to follow in his father's footstep, but instead, he had spent time in prison for possession of cocaine and drug trafficking, although he claimed that, because of sibling rivalry, he had been set up. Derrick had not been the model child, in fact, he would get high and show up at the dealership in a rage, shouting obscenities at his father across the showroom floor. And, even though he adamantly denied all charges, the evidence against him resulted in an eighteen month prison sentence. Unfortunately, the automobile industry has very strict policies with issues involving felony conviction and a history of *doing time*, so therefore, it had ruined his chances of ever taking over the family business that both he and Darcy had been involved in since they were kids. A reporter from the Detroit Free Press said that Derrick shouted profanities at Darcy as the bailiff lead him out of the courtroom. He swore that he'd make her pay for what she had done to him. At that point Darcy actually smirked, which broke the stone-faced expression that she had maintained throughout the trial.

The *only* one that really earned her way was Barbara Gail Bulaski, who had been nicknamed Babs. And, at thirty-six, her family still calls her *little Babsy*. She could die. Especially when her mother comes to see her at work and calls out, "Where can I find my *little Babsy?*" Even Ann Landers had no advice. And even though Babs went to the same high school as Darcy and Constance, she didn't really know either of them very well. Well, actually, she didn't know Darcy at all, other than on sight, but she really didn't care to because it was clear to everyone that Darcy selected her friends, they did not select her. But Constance treated everyone like a friend; she had invited Babs to sit beside her for lunch a time or two when she saw her scouring the room for a familiar face. Of course, they didn't hang out together because in reality they each had their own crowd. (Both Darcy and Constance had been cheerleaders and appeared to be very close, but from what Ashlee had determined, they had always been highly competitive with one another, or at least Darcy had when it became necessary to win.) Although Babs had been considered a nerd, she had still been popular, but in a different way: Student Council President, which was unheard of for a girl at that time, and class valedictorian. But, with the guys, as in men, and the *in-crowd*, she had basically been shunned because she came from a poor family, unlike Darcy, and she certainly wasn't pretty like Constance, but not too many people were; since junior high, she had been loved and adored by all of her classmates because she was the epitome of that age old adage that makes girls "Sugar and spice and everything nice." Of course, Babs quickly found out that looks and popularity can be bought, not that Connie had bought hers because she was real and her beauty was more than skin deep. But, for the right price, anyone can be *Ms. Superficial*, and the friends will come. So, as her bank account and her career flourished, so did her face and her figure. Some say the changes were incredible, but, with the advances in cosmetic surgery on the rise, no wonder. And, if all it takes for a woman to feel good about herself is some red-hair dye, a button nose, and a size *36D*, hey, go for it. But still, looks weren't nearly as important to Babs as succeeding in business, and she had never lost sight of her goals. In fact, she kept a quote by Henry Wadsworth Longfellow on her desk that read, "Perseverance is a great element of success. If you only knock long enough and loud enough at the gate, you are sure to wake up somebody." And that she did until her knuckles bled.

The local Pontiac dealer hired Babs as a part-time cashier when she turned sixteen and she continued to work there in her spare time throughout high school and even after graduating. As much as she dreamed of going to college, she couldn't because her family needed her income to keep a roof over their heads. So, as the years passed, she moved from position to position until she had learned just about everything there was to know about a dealership. When the dealer became ill, he left his longest employee, Babs Bulaski, in charge of the store while he regained his health. By this time, Babs had spent ten years with Mr. Stompoli and they had formed a mutual respect for each other's knowledge and abilities. So, when Mr. Stompoli had an opportunity to purchase an additional dealership, he did, and he made Babs Bulaski the General Manager, and eventually she took total control of both of his dealerships because of his faltering health. Two years later, he made her an offer to buy him out, backing her at the bank so that he could retire. With her commendable success and commitment to the automobile industry, she went on to purchase ten more stores. Babs dedicated her life to her work, never marrying, but, as the story goes, she had several explosive affairs over the years. But, considering the latest rumors to be true, Babs had finally met the man of her dreams, even though no one had ever seen him. Not talking, Babs refused to share any intimate details about her personal life with anyone. At this point, he is a real mystery.

ccpost